THE
CAMBRIDGE EDITION OF
THE LETTERS AND WORKS OF
D. H. LAWRENCE

THE WORKS OF D. H. LAWRENCE

EDITORIAL BOARD

WOMEN IN LOVE

D. H. LAWRENCE

EDITED BY
DAVID FARMER
LINDETH VASEY
AND
JOHN WORTHEN

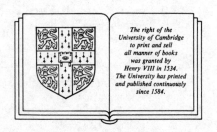

The right of the
University of Cambridge
to print and sell
all manner of books
was granted by
Henry VIII in 1534.
The University has printed
and published continuously
since 1584.

CAMBRIDGE UNIVERSITY PRESS

CAMBRIDGE
LONDON   NEW YORK   NEW ROCHELLE
MELBOURNE   SYDNEY

Published by the Press Syndicate of the University of Cambridge
The Pitt Building, Trumpington Street, Cambridge CB2 1RP
32 East 57th Street, New York, NY 10022, USA
10 Stamford Road, Oakleigh, Melbourne 3166, Australia

Printed in Great Britain at the University Press, Cambridge

British Library cataloguing in publication data
Lawrence, D. H.
Women in Love.—(The Cambridge edition of
letters and works of D. H. Lawrence)
I. Title II. Farmer, David III. Vasey, Lindeth
IV. Worthen, John V. Series
823'.912F PR6023.A93

Library of Congress cataloguing in publication data
Lawrence, D. H. (David Herbert), 1885–1930.
Women in love.
(The Cambridge edition of the letters and works
of D. H. Lawrence)
I. Farmer, David R. II. Vasey, Lindeth.
III. Worthen, John. IV. Title. V. Series:
Lawrence, D. H. (David Herbert), 1885–1930. Works. 1979.
PR6023.A93W63 1986 823'.912 87-31367

ISBN 0 521 23565 0 hard covers
ISBN 0 521 28041 9 paperback
CE

CONTENTS

GENERAL EDITORS' PREFACE

D. H. Lawrence is one of the great writers of the twentieth century – yet the texts of his writings, whether published during his lifetime or since, are, for the most part, textually corrupt. The extent of the corruption is remarkable; it can derive from every stage of composition and publication. We know from study of his MSS that Lawrence was a careful writer, though not rigidly consistent in matters of minor convention. We know also that he revised at every possible stage. Yet he rarely if ever compared one stage with the previous one, and overlooked the errors of typists or copyists. He was forced to accept, as most authors are, the often stringent house-styling of his printers, which overrode his punctuation and even his sentence-structure and paragraphing. He sometimes overlooked plausible printing errors. More important, as a professional author living by his pen, he had to accept, with more or less good will, stringent editing by a publisher's reader in his early days, and at all times the results of his publishers' timidity. So the fear of Grundyish disapproval, or actual legal action, led to bowdlerisation or censorship from the very beginning of his career. Threats of libel suits produced other changes. Sometimes a publisher made more changes than he admitted to Lawrence. On a number of occasions in dealing with American and British publishers Lawrence produced texts for both which were not identical. Then there were extraordinary lapses like the occasion when a compositor turned over two pages of MS at once, and the result happened to make sense. This whole story can be reconstructed from the introductions to the volumes in this edition; cumulatively they will form a history of Lawrence's writing career.

The Cambridge edition aims to provide texts which are as close as can now be determined to those he would have wished to see printed. They have been established by a rigorous collation of extant manuscripts and typescripts, proofs and early printed versions; they restore the words, sentences, even whole pages omitted or falsified by editors or compositors; they are freed from printing-house conventions which were imposed on Lawrence's style; and interference on the part of frightened publishers has been eliminated. Far from doing violence to the texts Lawrence would have wished to see published, editorial intervention is essential to recover them. Though we have to accept that some cannot now be recovered in their entirety because early states have not survived, we must be glad that so much evidence remains. Paradoxical as it may seem, the outcome of this recension will be texts which differ, often radically and certainly frequently, from those seen by the author himself.

Editors have adopted the principle that the most authoritative form of the text is to be followed, even if this leads sometimes to a 'spoken' or a 'manuscript' rather than a 'printed' style. We have not wanted to strip off one house-styling in order to impose another. Editorial discretion has been allowed in order to regularise Lawrence's sometimes wayward spelling and punctuation in accordance with his most frequent practice in a particular text. A detailed record of these and other decisions on textual matters, together with the evidence on which they are based, will be found in the textual apparatus or an occasional explanatory note. These give significant deleted readings in manuscripts, typescripts and proofs; and printed variants in forms of the text published in Lawrence's lifetime. We do not record posthumous corruptions, except where first publication was posthumous.

In each volume, the editor's introduction relates the contents to Lawrence's life and to his other writings; it gives the history of composition of the text in some detail, for its intrinsic interest, and because this history is essential to the statement of editorial principles followed. It provides an account of publication and reception which will be found to contain a good deal of hitherto unknown information. Where appropriate, appendixes make available extended draft manuscript readings of significance, or important material, sometimes unpublished, associated with a particular work.

Though Lawrence is a twentieth-century writer and in many respects remains our contemporary, the idiom of his day is not invariably intelligible now, especially to the many readers who are not native speakers of British English. His use of dialect is another difficulty, and further barriers to full understanding are created by now obscure literary, historical, political or other references and allusions. On these occasions explanatory notes are supplied by the editor; it is assumed that the reader has access to a good general dictionary and that the editor need not gloss words or expressions that may be found in it. Where Lawrence's letters are quoted in editorial matter, the reader should assume that his manuscript is alone the source of eccentricities of phase or spelling. An edition of the letters is still in course of publication: for this reason only the date and recipient of a letter will be given if it has not so far been printed in the Cambridge edition.

ACKNOWLEDGEMENTS

We are very grateful to the following for all their encouragement, advice and support; without them, our work on this volume could not have been carried through: Michael Black, James T. Boulton, Carol A. Farmer, Warren Roberts, Cornelia Rumpf-Worthen, Ronald Vasey. The preparation of the volume was also made possible (in part) by a grant to David Farmer from the Program for Editions of the National Endowment for the Humanities, an independent federal agency.

We are also grateful to the staff of Cambridge University Press; to Charlotte Carl-Mitchell, Ken Craven, Cathy Henderson, John Kirkpatrick and the staff of the Harry Ransom Humanities Research Center; to Richard Landon and the staff of the Thomas Fisher Rare Book Library, University of Toronto.

We would like to thank the following for their generosity in making available manuscript materials: the Harry Ransom Humanities Research Center, University of Texas at Austin, for all their manuscripts, typescripts and corrected proofs of *Women in Love*; to the University of Toronto, for their typescript of *Women in Love*; to George Lazarus and to W. Forster.

We would like to thank the following for their particular contributions: Harold Acton, Lynn Alexander, Frank Bacon, the late John Baker, Jr., Michael Balfour, Helen Baron, Marshall Best, Andrew Brown, Brian Cainen, Chris Calladine, L. D. Clark, Christopher Collard, Malcolm Cowley, Philip Crumpton, Keith Cushman, Tom Davis, Eric Domville, Priscilla Dorr, Ellen Dunlap, John Dunlop, George Evans, Marie Flagg, Susan Gagg, Franklin Gilliam, Andor Gomme, Mary Grant, Rachel Grover, Charles W. Hagelman, Jr., Nora Haseldine, Alice and Paul Heapy, Jane Hodgart, Terry Holmes, Otto Holzapfel and the Deutsches Volksliedarchiv, Alistair Horne, J. M. Irvine, Dennis Johnson, Lisa Jones, Rüdiger Joppien, Mara Kalnins, Charles Kemnitz, Denise Kidd, Mark Kinkead-Weekes, Gerald Lacy, Richard Landon, Guy Logsdon, C. H. C. Lyal and the Natural History Museum, Mary McMonagle, M. D. McLeod and the Museum of Mankind, Sue Martin, John Merritt, the late Harry T. Moore, D. B. Nash and the Imperial War Museum, A. J.

Nicholls, Ann Parr, Hans Popper, Peter Preston, Charles Ross, Charles Rossman, Anthony Rota, Wilfried Rumpf, David Rundle and the British Institute, Florence, Linda Secord, Rosemarie Spaulding, Norman Stone, Rennard Strickland, Lola Szladits, William B. Todd, John Turner, F. B. Vasey, Giles Waterfield and Dulwich Picture Gallery, the Wehrgeschichtes Museum, Schloss Rastatt, F. M. and D. G. Worthen, Marjorie Wynne.

March 1985   D.F.
                                                        L.V.
                                                        J.W.

CHRONOLOGY

11 September 1885	Born in Eastwood, Nottinghamshire
September 1898–July 1901	Pupil at Nottingham High School
1902–1908	Pupil teacher; student at University College, Nottingham
7 December 1907	First publication: 'A Prelude', in *Nottinghamshire Guardian*
October 1908	Appointed as teacher at Davidson Road School, Croydon
November 1909	Publishes five poems in *English Review*
3 December 1910	Engagement to Louie Burrows; broken off on 4 February 1912
9 December 1910	Death of his mother, Lydia Lawrence
19 January 1911	*The White Peacock* published in New York (20 January in London)
19 November 1911	Ill with pneumonia; resigns his teaching post on 28 February 1912
March 1912	Meets Frieda Weekley; they elope to Germany on 3 May
23 May 1912	*The Trespasser*
September 1912–March 1913	At Gargnano, Lago di Garda, Italy
February 1913	*Love Poems and Others*
mid-March 1913	Begins 'The Sisters'
22 March 1913	'The Sisters' – 46 pages
5 April 1913	'The Sisters' – 110 pages
23 April 1913	'The Sisters' – 145 pages
c. 2 May 1913	'The Sisters' – 180 pages
17 May 1913	'The Sisters' – 256 pages
29 May 1913	*Sons and Lovers*
1 June 1913	'The Sisters' – 283 pages: 'nearly finished'
c. 4 June 1913	Finishes 'The Sisters'
June–August 1913	In England
August 1913–June 1914	In Germany, Switzerland and Italy
24 August 1913	'The Sisters II' – 'two false starts already'
4 September 1913	'The Sisters II' – 'has quite a new beginning'
15 September 1913	'The Sisters II' – 100 pages
18–30 September 1913	Travels from Germany through Switzerland to Lerici, Gulf of Spezia
2 December 1913	'The Sisters II' – 'writing . . . slowly'

12 October 1916	*Women in Love* – 'still typing'
13 October 1916	*Women in Love* – 'about two-thirds ' done; abandons typing
25 October 1916	Sends untyped MS to Pinker; 'nearly finished'
31 October 1916	Sends conclusion to Pinker for typing
6 November 1916	Pinker returns first batch of typescript
by 13 November 1916	Pinker returns second batch of typescript
20 November 1916	Sends revised and assembled TSIa to Pinker, revised and assembled TSIb to Catherine Carswell
by 20 December 1916	Methuen reject novel (rejected mid-January 1917 by Secker, Duckworth and Constable)
c. 29 January 1917	Sends TSIb to Pinker for retyping as TSII
23 March 1917	Copies of TSII sent to DHL, Pinker and Koteliansky
after 9 July 1917	Sends TSII to Cecil Palmer (returned in August)
11 July 1917	Little, Brown & Co. reject novel
15 October 1917	After twenty-one months' residence in Cornwall, ordered to leave by military authorities
October 1917–November 1919	In London, Berkshire and Derbyshire
November 1917	Plans private publication of novel backed by Bennett and Galsworthy; revises TSII
December 1917	*Look! We Have Come Through!*; Hone and Fisher Unwin reject novel
19 February 1918	Sends TSII to Beaumont for private publication backed by Bibesco and Beaumont; TSII returned in April 1918
October 1918	*New Poems*
Late August–September 1919	Seltzer cables for *Women in Love*; Secker reads it, probably in September
by 7 September 1919	Revises TSII and sends it to Seltzer
12 September 1919	Writes 'Foreword' to the novel
2 November 1919	Requests Seltzer to return TSII for Secker; repeats request until June 1920
November 1919	To Italy, then Capri and Sicily
20 November 1919	*Bay*
17–27 December 1919	Negotiating with Secker
January 1920	Secker offers to purchase rights of novel; DHL rejects Secker's offer; offers novel to Duckworth. Asks Seltzer to give up novel to Huebsch; Seltzer refuses
9–11 February 1920	Seltzer sends contract for novel
c. 3 March 1920	Moves to Taormina, Sicily
22 March 1920	Renews offer to Secker; Secker offers terms on 28 March

August 1924	*The Boy in the Bush* (with Mollie Skinner)
10 September 1924	Death of his father, John Arthur Lawrence
February 1925	Secker's fourth printing of *Women in Love*
14 May 1925	*St. Mawr together with The Princess*
September 1925–June 1928	In England and, mainly, in Italy
7 December 1925	*Reflections on the Death of a Porcupine* (Philadelphia)
January 1926	*The Plumed Serpent*
June 1927	*Mornings in Mexico*
24 May 1928	*The Woman Who Rode Away and Other Stories*
June 1928–March 1930	In Switzerland and, principally, in France
July 1928	*Lady Chatterley's Lover* privately published (Florence)
September 1928	*Collected Poems*
July 1929	Exhibition of paintings in London raided by police; *Pansies* (manuscript earlier seized in the mail)
September 1929	*The Escaped Cock* (Paris)
2 March 1930	Dies at Vence, Alpes Maritimes, France

CUE-TITLES

A. Manuscript locations

BL	British Library
LC	Library of Congress
NWU	Northwestern University
NYPL	New York Public Library
UIll	University of Illinois at Urbana-Champaign
UT	University of Texas at Austin
UTor	University of Toronto

B. Printed works

(The place of publication, here and throughout, is London unless otherwise stated.)

Draper R. P. Draper, ed. *D. H. Lawrence: The Critical Heritage.* Routledge & Kegan Paul, 1970.

Garsington Robert Gathorne-Hardy, ed. *Ottoline at Garsington: Memoirs of Lady Ottoline Morrell 1915–1918.* Faber & Faber, 1974.

Letters, i. James T. Boulton, ed. *The Letters of D. H. Lawrence.* Volume I. Cambridge: Cambridge University Press, 1979.

Letters, ii. George J. Zytaruk and James T. Boulton, eds. *The Letters of D. H. Lawrence.* Volume II. Cambridge: Cambridge University Press, 1982.

Letters, iii. James T. Boulton and Andrew Robertson, eds. *The Letters of D. H. Lawrence.* Volume III. Cambridge: Cambridge University Press, 1984.

Nehls Edward Nehls, ed. *D. H. Lawrence: A Composite Biography.* 3 volumes. Madison: University of Wisconsin Press, 1957–9.

OED Sir James A. H. Murray and others, eds. *A New English Dictionary on Historical Principles.* 10 volumes. Oxford University Press, 1884–1928.

Ottoline	Robert Gathorne-Hardy, ed. *Ottoline: The Early Memoirs of Lady Ottoline Morrell*. Faber & Faber, 1963.
Phoenix	Edward D. McDonald, ed. *Phoenix: The Posthumous Papers of D. H. Lawrence*. New York: Viking, 1936.
Phoenix II	Warren Roberts and Harry T. Moore, eds. *Phoenix II: Uncollected, Unpublished and Other Prose Works by D. H. Lawrence*. Heinemann, 1968.
Roberts	Warren Roberts. *A Bibliography of D. H. Lawrence*. 2nd edn. Cambridge: Cambridge University Press, 1982.
Twilight	D. H. Lawrence. *Twilight in Italy*. Duckworth, 1916.
Whitelock	G. C. H. Whitelock. *250 Years in Coal: The History of Barber Walker and Company Limited*. N.p., n.d. [1957].

INTRODUCTION

Bibliographical Notes		Version	Date
Pp. 291–6 in Warren Roberts's *Bibliography of D. H. Lawrence*, MS Catalogue no. E441a	MS ?296pp. 'The Sisters'	One	March–June 1913
Unfinished; pp. 373–80 in Roberts E441a	MS ?380pp. 'The Sisters II'	Two	August 1913–January 1914
Not extant	MS ?600pp. 'The Wedding Ring'		
Typed by Dunlop; TCC pp. 219–75, 279–84 in Roberts E331a	TS ?500pp. 'The Wedding Ring' TCC ?500pp. 'The Wedding Ring'	Three	February–May 1914
Roberts E331a	MS & TCC 811pp. *The Rainbow*		November 1914–March 1915
Unfinished first draft; Roberts E441b	MS 55pp. 'The Sisters III'	Four	April 1916
Pp. 650–863 in Roberts E441c	*MS* 863pp. 'The Sisters III'		April–June 1916
Pp. 1–368 typed by DHL, pp. 369–666 typed by Pinker: Roberts E441d & e	*TSIa* 666pp. *Women in Love* *TSIb* 666pp. *Women in Love*	Five	July 1916–January 1917
TCCs not extant; *TSII* = Roberts E441f	*TSII* 766pp. *Women in Love* TCC ?766pp. TCC ?766pp.	Six	March 1917–September 1919

INTRODUCTION

D. H. Lawrence began the composition of his two greatest novels as a single work named 'The Sisters', the first stages of which he wrote in the spring of 1913. As the writing progressed, the novel grew so dramatically in scope (coming to include a great deal not only about the sisters Ursula and Gudrun Brangwen and their relationships, but about their parents and grandparents) that Lawrence decided eventually to split the book into two volumes. He finished one novel – *The Rainbow* – for publication in 1915, and in 1916 returned to the other, which he rewrote as *Women in Love*; he was, however, unable to find a publisher for it until 1920.

'The Sisters' (first version, March–June 1913)

In the middle of March 1913, while living at Gargnano on the Lago di Garda, Lawrence began to write a novel[1] which on 5 April he could cheerfully refer to as a 'pot-boiler' (i. 536) then 110 pages long. He badly needed to write a new book; *Sons and Lovers*, finished five months earlier, was accepted but as yet unpublished and he had little other prospect of income. He had also spent a good deal of time that spring writing a novel ('The Insurrection of Miss Houghton') which seemed at that stage to be unpublishable.[2] By 23 April he had moved to Germany and was up to page 145 of the new book, but complained to his friend Arthur McLeod[3] that it was 'a novel which I have never grasped ... and I've no notion what it's about. I hate it. F[rieda] says it is good. But it's like a novel in a foreign language I don't know very well – I can only just make out what it is about' (i. 544). Around 2 May he told Edward Garnett,[4] his literary adviser and reader for Duckworth (about to publish *Sons and Lovers*), that he had written 180 pages of a projected 300-page work titled 'The Sisters':

[1] See *Letters*, i. 530; on 22 March it was 46 pages long. (Subsequent references to *Letters*, i., ii. and iii. are given in the text with volume and page number.)
[2] Totally rewritten in 1920 as *The Lost Girl*; see the Cambridge edition, ed. John Worthen (Cambridge, 1981), pp. xix–xxiv.
[3] McLeod had been a fellow-teacher of DHL's at Davidson Road, Croydon (*Letters*, i. 136 n. 3).
[4] See ibid. 297 n. 2.

It was meant to be for the 'jeunes filles', but already it has fallen from grace. I can only write what I feel pretty strongly about: and that, at present, is the relations between men and women. After all, it is *the* problem of today, the establishment of a new relation, or the re-adjustment of the old one, between men and women.

(i. 546)

At this point Lawrence estimated a month to completion. He was at page 256 by 17 May 'but still can't see the end very clear' (i. 550). A fortnight later he told Garnett that he was 'nearly finished', having reached page 283, and around 4–5 June 'The Sisters' must have been complete for on 10 June he asked Garnett if he had received its second half (ii. 20).

A few pages, numbered 291–6, are the only surviving fragment of an early version which was probably chronologically (and perhaps textually) close to the first draft; they are not, however, written in the first person which Lawrence twice indicated was the format of the novel's first draft, and so probably derive from a slightly later revision.[5] The fragment tells of Gudrun Brangwen back in England, pregnant with Gerald Crich's child. There is an altercation between Gerald and the sculptor Loerke, who both wish to marry her. Loerke departs in a rage, and although Gudrun believes Gerald only wants to marry her because of the baby, she accepts his offer. As the fragment ends, she admits that she would not have cared for any other man's child. The two sit quietly: 'There was a good deal that hurt still, between them.' Since Lawrence had estimated that the first draft would be 300 pages long, this early fragment is most likely the ending itself.

'The Sisters II' (second version, August 1913–January 1914)

After spending the first part of the summer in England, Lawrence and Frieda returned to Germany in August 1913, when Lawrence again began work on the novel. By 24 August, he had 'made two false starts already' (ii. 66); a week later, complaining that he was writing things 'about which I know nothing – like a somnambulist', he seems to have begun yet again: 'I've begun a novel on the same principle: it's like working in a dream, rather uncomfortable – as if you can't get solid hold of yourself. "Hello my

---

[5] Roberts E441a, UT. For a description of the manuscript, see David Farmer, 'A Descriptive and Analytical Catalogue of the D. H. Lawrence Collection at The University of Texas at Austin' (unpublished Ph.D. thesis, UT, 1970), A57. The fragment will be printed in the Cambridge edition of *The Rainbow*, ed. Mark Kinkead-Weekes. If Birkin or Ella (the name of the Ursula figure in 'The Sisters') had been the first person narrator, it is possible that no 'I' narration would appear in the surviving pages.

lad, are you there!" I say to myself, when I see the sentences stalking by.'[6]
This second sustained writing of the novel he would eventually (provision-
ally) retitle 'The Wedding Ring'; he wrote on 4 September that 'The
Sisters has quite a new beginning – a new basis altogether. I hope I can get
on with it. It is much more interesting in its new form – not so damned
flippant' (ii. 67–8). By 15 September Lawrence was planning a walking
trip across Switzerland, having finished the first hundred pages; he hoped
to complete the draft in another month (ii. 74–5). The walk, however,
followed by a move to Italy, prevented much consecutive writing; although
he remarked that he was working on the novel at the beginning and at the
end of October (ii. 82, 93), it was probably not until early in December
that he was able to concentrate on it. This time it went 'slowly' (ii. 118). At
the end of the year we find him telling Edward Garnett that, in a few days,
he would send

the first half of the Sisters – which I should rather call The Wedding Ring – to
Duckworths. It is *very* different from *Sons and Lovers*: written in another language
almost. I shall be sorry if you don't like it, but am prepared. – I shan't write in the
same manner as *Sons and Lovers* again, I think: in that hard, violent style full of
sensation and presentation. You must see what you think of the new style.   (ii. 132)

He sent Garnett the first half of 'The Sisters II' on 6 January 1914
(ii. 134). Garnett must have read it and sent his observations to Lawrence
immediately, for on 29 January Lawrence wrote to him that 'I am not very
much surprised, nor even very much hurt by your letter – and I agree with
you': but he stood his ground on one point: 'I *must* have Ella [later to be
called Ursula] get some experience before she meets her Mr Birkin ...
tell me whether you think Ella would be possible, as she now stands,
unless she had some experience of love and of men ... I feel that this
second half of the Sisters is very beautiful, but it may not be sufficiently
incorporated to please you' (ii. 142–3).

In this letter Lawrence gave some indication of how 'The Sisters II' was
moving closer to *The Rainbow*, which in its later sections would deal with
Ursula's (Ella's) 'experience of love and of men'. But he also voiced
satisfaction with the second half of the novel, that portion which apparently
began to deal at length with Ella and Birkin, and would finally be
transformed into *Women in Love*: 'I prefer the permeating beauty. It is my
transition stage – but I must write to live, and it must produce its flowers,

---

[6] Letter to John Middleton Murry, 30 August 1913; quoted in Sotheby's Sale Catalogue,
  'English Literature and History', 22–23 July 1985, item 269. Murry (1889–1957),
  journalist and critic, and his companion Katherine Mansfield (1888–1923), New Zealand
  short-story writer, had met the Lawrences in July 1913 (*Letters*, i. 507 n. 3, ii. 31 and n. 3).

and if they be frail or shadowy, they will be all right if they are true to their hour.' He again explained that 'I have no longer the joy in creating vivid scenes, that I had in *Sons and Lovers*', and described his new method as 'exhaustive': he was no longer writing 'pure object and story' (ii. 142–3). He had reached p. 340 by 19 January (ii. 137). And he was going to send on 150 pages of this second half on 30 January (ii. 142).

Only one fragment, probably from the last part to be written of 'The Sisters II', has survived in a brief set of pages numbered 373–80. It reveals that the relationship between Ella and Birkin has begun, but also describes the continuing power over Ella of an earlier relationship with Ben Templeman, apparently a new development (ii. 142), and strong evidence that this draft succeeded the fragment numbered 291–6:

Ella felt the blood rush from her heart. For a second she seemed to lose consciousness. A wave of terror, deep, annihilating went over her. She knew him without looking; his peculiar, straying walk, the odd, separate look about him which filled her with dread. He had still power over her: he was still Man to her . . .[7]

However, shortly after responding to Garnett's criticism Lawrence left off writing 'The Sisters II', and embarked upon the next sustained composition.

'The Wedding Ring' (third version, February–May 1914)

By 7 February 1914, Lawrence had 'begun it again'; two days later he wrote to McLeod that it was for 'about the seventh time', and a month later claimed to be starting for 'about the eleventh time' (ii. 144, 146, 153). But after the initial difficulties he seems to have grown in confidence as this third sustained version developed. In the same March letter, the novel was 'on its legs and . . . going strong' (ii. 153); as proof of what he saw as its publishable quality, he began to have a ribbon and a carbon copy typescript made of it as he wrote.[8] On 22 April, with only 80 pages remaining to be written, he sent the available typescript to Garnett: 'I am sure of this now, this novel. It is a big and beautiful work. Before, I could not get my soul into it. That was because of the struggle and the resistance between Frieda and me. Now you will find her and me in the novel, I think, and the work is of both of us' (ii. 164). Early in May, Frieda suggested the new title *The Rainbow* (not adopted at this stage); by the 16th Lawrence had finished the novel and checked the typescript (ii. 173, 174). Sixty-two pages of carbon

---

[7] Roberts E441a, UT, p. 380. See Farmer, 'A Descriptive and Analytical Catalogue', A57. The fragment will be included in the Cambridge edition of *The Rainbow*.

[8] His typist was Thomas Dunlop, British Consul in Spezia; see *Letters*, ii. 152 n. 1.

copy incorporated in the final manuscript of *The Rainbow* survive from this third major version,[9] and it is possible to learn still more about it from a contemporary reader's report. Submitted on 10 November 1914 in the form of a letter from Alfred Kuttner to Mitchell Kennerley, who had published four of Lawrence's first five books in the USA, the report reads in part:

The real story is concentrated in the lives of Ella and Gudrun and the novel does not strike its best pace until we deal with them. But that does not become clear until we are almost half way through the novel so that the first part of the plot has a rambling quality which greatly contributes to the feeling of over-lengthiness. Mr. Lawrence takes us through practically three generations but our real interest lies only in the third.[10]

Kuttner clearly responded most readily to the stories of Ella and Gudrun, who had been the central characters – the sisters of the title – since the very first version. He generally liked what he read, but argued strongly for it to be 'condensed and foreshortened', as well as 'expurgated, not for moral reasons but for artistic effect. Mr. Lawrence sees sex too obsessively.' Kuttner also reported that this version of the novel contained a scene of 'Gerald Crich raping Gudrun in a boathouse'; he criticised Lawrence's lack of restraint in phrases like 'With what an agony of relief he poured himself into her'. It seems probable that the 'rape' was Kuttner's way of describing a preliminary version of the encounter which takes place in Gudrun's bedroom in chapter XXIV of *Women in Love*.

From Kuttner's report we can also gain a sense of the structure of 'The Wedding Ring': 'the whole story of Tom Brangwen's courtship of the Polish woman as well as Anna's marriage could be told in retrospect in much less space if the novel began with Ella's childhood.' After a year of writing and many drafts, the novel had come to contain a great deal of what became *The Rainbow* as well as much that would become *Women in Love*.

'The Wedding Ring' also provoked from Lawrence the famous defence of his fictional method in a letter to Edward Garnett of 5 June 1914. Garnett had been critical both of the second version of the novel and of the third, but Lawrence was now prepared to resist his criticism.

I don't agree with you about the Wedding Ring. You will find that in a while you will like the book as a whole. I don't think the psychology is wrong: it is only that I have a different attitude to my characters, and that necessitates a different attitude in you,

---

[9] In Roberts E331a, UT. The surviving typed pages were originally numbered 219–75, 279–84, are re-numbered 548–604 and 608–13. See Farmer, 'A Descriptive and Analytical Catalogue', A40.

[10] Located at LC; the report will be printed in the Cambridge edition of *The Rainbow*.

which you are not as yet prepared to give ... somehow – that which is physic – non-human, in humanity, is more interesting to me than the old-fashioned human element – which causes one to conceive a character in a certain moral scheme and make him consistent. The certain moral scheme is what I object to ... You mustn't look in my novel for the old stable ego of the character. There is another ego, according to whose action the individual is unrecognisable, and passes through, as it were, allotropic states which it needs a deeper sense than any we've been used to exercise, to discover are states of the same single radically-unchanged element. (Like as diamond and coal are the same pure single element of carbon. The ordinary novel would trace the history of the diamond – but I say 'diamond, what! This is carbon.' And my diamond might be coal or soot, and my theme is carbon.)

You must not say my novel is shaky – It is not perfect, because I am not expert in what I want to do. But it is the real thing, say what you like.   (ii. 182–3)

Garnett's criticism also mattered less because the novel was not now going to Duckworth;[11] by the middle of May 1914, the firm of Methuen had offered an advance of £300 (in two payments) for the new novel. The news had come to Lawrence through the literary agent J. B. Pinker, whom Lawrence would take as his own agent in July,[12] and the money (as Lawrence told Garnett) was 'a pretty figure that my heart aches after' (ii. 174). He signed Methuen's contract and received £150 in late June, but his happiness was short-lived; early in August, while on a walking tour in the Lake District, he learned of the outbreak of the First World War, and by 10 August Methuen had returned his typescript.[13]

The Rainbow and 'The Sisters III' (fourth version, two novels, November 1914–March 1915 and April–June 1916)

Lawrence must have begun his next sustained version of the novel late in November 1914; on 3 December he wrote that he was 'working *frightfully* hard – rewriting my novel' (ii. 239). On 5 December he sent the first 100 pages to Pinker, followed by another instalment on the 18th (ii. 240, 245). By 5 January 1915 he had done 300 pages, and on the 7th sent Pinker a further 100 pages (ii. 255, 256).

But the single most important development in the writing of *The*

---

[11] Duckworth accepted a book of short stories in lieu of the novel; see *The Prussian Officer and Other Stories*, ed. John Worthen (Cambridge, 1983), p. xxvii.

[12] See *Letters*, ii. 31 n. 1.

[13] Ibid. 206–7, 240–1. Methuen would claim at the *Rainbow* prosecution in November 1915 that they had asked for the novel to be rewritten, but a great many literary manuscripts were returned to their authors simply because of uncertainty following the outbreak of war. Methuen probably did no more than return the novel in a routine way, with a suggestion that some changes would be in order.

Rainbow and *Women in Love* now occurred. In that letter of 7 January to Pinker, Lawrence announced that he had decided 'to split the book into two volumes: it was so unwieldy. It needs to be in two volumes' (ii. 256). It may have been Kuttner's suggestion that the Brangwen saga was really separate from the story of Ella and Gudrun that prompted Lawrence to consider dividing and expanding his work rather than shortening it; there is evidence that he read Kuttner's report.[14]

From January to March work on what was now simply *The Rainbow* progressed rapidly, while the *Women in Love* material was put aside. The manuscript of *The Rainbow* was finished on 2 March 1915, and the novel itself was published on 30 September 1915, only to be suppressed in November;[15] Lawrence turned to revision of his travel essays for their collection in *Twilight in Italy*, to philosophical work and to some short stories and poems.

However, in March 1916, when he and Frieda had been living for two and a half months in Cornwall, he began to consider writing another novel: novels had always been his major source of income. His first plan was to resume work on the unfinished 'Insurrection of Miss Houghton', which he had given up in 1913, but the manuscript was in Bavaria and he could not get it back (ii. 580, 595). After a month's wait – and just after Middleton Murry and Katherine Mansfield had come to live in the next cottage at Higher Tregerthen (ii. 596–7) – he went back instead to the *Women in Love* material. His income was tiny, his health had been bad in the winter, his attitude to the war and to British society in general had grown wholly antagonistic. As he told Barbara Low in May 1916:

I would write to you oftener, but this life of today so disgusts one, it leaves nothing to say. The war, the approaching conscription, the sense of complete paltriness and chaotic nastiness in life, really robs one of speech . . . I have begun the second half of the *Rainbow*. But already it is beyond all hope of ever being published, because of the things it says. And more than that, it is beyond all possibility even to offer it to a world, a putrescent mankind like ours. I feel I cannot *touch* humanity, even in thought, it is abhorrent to me.[16]

Nevertheless, by 26 April he had begun writing, with that combination of optimism and bewilderment which so often attended the start of a major piece of work. That day, he told the artist Mark Gertler and Lady Cynthia

[14] Letter from Kuttner to Kennerley, n.d.: 'Of course I should not have written my criticism in just that way if I had intended it for Mr. Lawrence's ears but . . . I don't mind your sending it on to him' (LC).
[15] See Explanatory note on 485:11.
[16] *Letters*, ii. 602. Barbara Low was a pioneer in psychoanalysis, and an aunt of Catherine Carswell (see below); see ibid. 279 n. 6.

Asquith how 'this last week' he had begun a novel 'that really occupies me'.[17] Ten days later, Lady Ottoline Morrell was told about 'a new novel: a thing that is a stranger to me even as I write it. I don't know what the end will be.'[18] He was not, then, going to end the novel where 'The Sisters' had ended, with Gerald and Gudrun together; nor, presumably, where 'The Wedding Ring' had ended. April was most likely the time when Lawrence wrote the opening two chapters (later abandoned) entitled 'Prologue' and 'The Wedding'.[19] While the former explores the deteriorating relationship between Rupert Birkin and Hermione Roddice, it concentrates upon Birkin's feelings for men and his attraction to Gerald Crich. Such writing would perhaps be one reason why Lawrence felt that his new novel was already 'beyond all hope of ever being published'.

On 19 May Lawrence wrote to Pinker that he was 'half way through a novel, which is a sequel to the *Rainbow*, though quite unlike it' (ii. 606). On the 24th he told Lady Ottoline: 'I have got a long way with my novel. It comes rapidly, and is very good. When one is shaken to the very depths, one finds reality in the unreal world. At present my real world is the world of my inner soul, which reflects on to the novel I write' (ii. 610). Six days later his sense of accomplishment was still strong as he wrote to Barbara Low that Ursula was now married, and the novel 'two thirds' written: 'It goes on pretty fast, and very easy. I have not travailed over it. It is the book of my free soul'.[20] By 19 June he was 'nearly done'; he probably finished before 28 June, when he had to go to Bodmin for medical examination: on 30 June he told Pinker that 'in effect' the novel was finished (ii. 617, 619). What he meant is clarified in a letter to S. S. Koteliansky ('Kot') of 4 July: 'I have finished my novel – except for a bit that can be done any time' – and his friend the Scottish writer and critic Catherine Carswell was told about 'a last chapter to write, some time, when one's heart is not so contracted'.[21] The novel as it now stood consisted of an autograph manuscript (no longer

---

[17] Ibid. 599, 601. Lady Cynthia had been a friend of the Lawrences since 1913 (ibid. 41 n. 4), Gertler since 1914 (ibid. 214 n. 1).

[18] Ibid. 604. The Lawrences had stayed with Lady Ottoline at Garsington Manor in 1915 (ibid. 253 n. 3).

[19] Roberts E441b, UT (see Farmer, 'A Descriptive and Analytical Catalogue', A58); first edited by George Ford and published in *Texas Quarterly*, vi (Spring 1963), 98–111 and *Texas Studies in Literature and Language*, vi (Summer 1964), 137–47 respectively. They are printed as Appendix II below.

[20] *Letters*, ii. 614. Having written half the novel in almost exactly four weeks, and two-thirds in less than six weeks, DHL seems to have taken three to four weeks over the last third.

[21] Ibid. 621, 627. For Koteliansky, see ibid. 205 n. 4; for Catherine Carswell, see ibid. 187 n. 5. Pinker must immediately have asked Methuen if they wanted the book; they replied cautiously on 10 July that they 'should prefer to see the MS. of his new book before deciding if we would care to cancel the agreement or not' (NYPL).

extant), probably in notebooks, up to page 649, and five further notebooks paginated 650–863 which do survive; the last of them almost completely empty, leaving space for that 'last chapter . . . some time'.[22]

Women in Love (fifth version, July 1916–January 1917)

Lawrence decided to type his novel himself; he could not afford to pay anyone else, he probably foresaw that he would want to revise it (and could do so while typing) and it was a book to which he felt so close that he was reluctant, at this stage, to let anyone else see it. He had probably begun by 12 July (ii. 529, 630); when complete, in ribbon and carbon copies, this typescript would constitute the novel's fifth version. But he typed fewer than fifteen pages in July; 'it got on my nerves and knocked me up' (ii. 637), and he also needed a new typewriter ribbon.[23] But having done some pencil rewriting around 21 July to what he was now confident was 'the fourth and the final draft', now '$\frac{2}{3}$ done',[24] and having also been on the point of sending the untyped manuscript to Pinker to be typed (ii. 637), he settled down in earnest in August to the typing, and probably typed for most of the month, telling Amy Lowell on the 23rd that the typewriter she had given him 'runs so glibly, and has at last become a true confrère. I take

[22] Notebooks 3 and 7–10 of the surviving ten (the other five dating wholly from October 1916), Roberts E441c, UT (see Farmer, 'A Descriptive and Analytical Catalogue', A59): see also footnote 28. A calculation (almost certainly by DHL) on the inside cover of notebook 7, opposite original page 650, shows 700 multiplied by 135 to calculate word length: i.e. the number of pages written and the number of words per page (between 130 and 150 in notebook 7). If the first 649 pages had contained the same number of words as pp. 650–700, they would have been pages of the same size; the whole of the April–June draft was probably, therefore, written in similar notebooks.

[23] His typewriter (an L. G. Smith & Bros. No. 2 model) had been given him by Amy Lowell (*Letters*, ii. 222–3), and he had typed the first seven pages of *The Rainbow* on it (in Roberts E331a, UT). Between 4 July and ?1 August he had had trouble securing a new ribbon from London for it; it took five letters (and two wrong ribbons) before he got what he needed (*Letters*, ii. 621–38). The ribbon copy p. 15 (in Roberts E441d, UT) shows the impression of a much blacker typewriter ribbon, two-thirds the way down the page, and must mark the new ribbon's arrival.

[24] *Letters*, ii. 637. DHL's 'fourth and the final draft' can be explained in one of two ways. If he started counting from the original 'Sisters' of 1913, the second complete draft (not counting the false starts, and the 'Sisters II' incomplete draft) would have been the 'Wedding Ring' of February–May 1914, the third complete draft (again, not counting the *Rainbow* version of November 1914–March 1915) would have been 'The Sisters III' of April–June 1916, and the 'fourth and the final draft' the typescript and revised notebook *Women in Love* of July–October 1916. If, however, he had started the count of drafts from the division of the novel into two volumes in January 1915, then the unused typescript left over from *The Rainbow* would have constituted the first draft, the April 1916 false start evidenced by the two abandoned opening chapters the second, the 'Sisters III' version the third, and the July–October 1916 *Women in Love* the fourth.

so unkindly to any sort of machinery. But now I and the type writer have sworn a Blutbruderschaft' (ii. 645). Earlier in the month he had given Catherine Carswell – who was also writing a novel – his reasons for abandoning 'The Sisters' as a title: it was too close to May Sinclair's *The Three Sisters*, published in 1914.[25] On 9 September, he told Pinker that the novel was 'half done' (ii. 653), meaning (presumably) half typed; on 26 September, Lady Ottoline heard that only a week or two more would be needed. But the ease of his writing between April and June had been replaced by the old sense of struggle: 'I only want to finish this novel, which is like a malady or a madness while it lasts' (ii. 656). He was not a skilled typist,[26] remarking in 1921 that 'I *hate* doing it' (iii. 677), and he was actually revising as he went: 'I recomposed all the first part on the typewriter'.[27] He was also ill from early September onwards, and was depressed by the continuously wet weather of the late summer. Although he told Amy Lowell on 12 October that he was still typing (ii. 665), that remark was probably designed to please the typewriter's provider; the very next day he asked the mother of Douglas Clayton (who had typed for him 1913–15) if she would type the remaining third of the novel (ii. 666), as he could take no more of the strain. Altogether, he typed 368 pp., but had only managed to type about a sixth of it between 9 September and 12 October. Katherine Clayton agreed to finish the typing, but instead Lawrence took Pinker up on an offer to have the rest of the manuscript typed without charge (ii. 668) in his office; Pinker would, of course, go on making both a ribbon and a carbon copy.

From 13 October, then, Lawrence began preparing the end of the novel for Pinker's typing; he did this by writing out the penultimate part in notebooks 1–6 of the ten which still survive, and then revising notebooks 7–10 to create the very end of the novel. It is at this stage that we find him confidently naming it *Women in Love*; the title appears with no alternative

---

[25] *Letters*, ii. 639. See ibid. 640 for other suggestions – some facetious – about titles. DHL first mentioned the final title to Pinker on 13 July 1916 (ibid. 631). He later considered using 'Dies Irae' (see below); in November 1917, thinking about the book as 'more or less a sequel to *The Rainbow* . . . I think I'll call it "Noah's Ark"'' (ibid., iii. 183). As well as May Sinclair's novel, a novel called *Sisters* (1904) had been published by Ada Cambridge (1844–1926). *Women in Love: eight studies in sentiment* had been published by Alfred Sutro (1863–1933) in 1902, but DHL did not learn that until 1921: see Sutro, *Celebrities and Simple Souls* (1933), p. 100.

[26] He had to type a page twice on six occasions (pp. 57, 144, 228, 275, 305 and 338) because he failed to insert carbon paper, or inserted it reversed.

[27] *Letters*, iii. 79. The process is visible when he had to retype the pages described in the previous footnote; he would incorporate autograph revisions made to the first typing, and make still further changes as he typed.

in notebooks 2 and 4–6.[28] The inside cover of notebook 1 shows the title 'Dies Irae' written under *Women in Love*; on 30 October, Lawrence told Pinker that Frieda was in favour of that title (ii. 669). He used this stage of the novel's composition to incorporate an incident based on a very recent event: he had learned early in September about Katherine Mansfield walking out of the Café Royal with a copy of his poetry collection *Amores* (1916), which she had taken out of the hands of mocking critics.[29] This was the source of new material incorporated in chapter XXVIII. When he had completed the sixth (new) notebook, he started revising the ending of the novel as it had appeared in notebooks 7–10 in the April–June draft; as he was to tell Catherine Carswell in November, 'there was a lot of the original draft that I *couldn't* have bettered' (iii. 25). The first batch of notebooks went to Pinker for typing on 25 October (ii. 669); on 31 October Lawrence sent his agent 'the conclusion of the novel . . . all but the last chapter, which, being a sort of epilogue, I want to write later – when I get the typescript back from you. You got the preceding MS. which I sent last week, didn't you?' (ii. 669). Exactly what he had in mind as the 'sort of epilogue' is not clear. One direction he might have taken is suggested by a deleted fragment on the pages inserted at the end of the tenth notebook, which must (from its pagination number) have been written late in October:

A year afterwards, Ursula in Italy received a letter from Gudrun in Frankfurt am Main. Since the death of Gerald in the Tyrol, when Gudrun had gone away, ostensibly to England, Ursula had had no news of her sister.

"I met a German artist who knew you," Gudrun said, "and he gave me your address. I was silent for so long because there was nothing I could say.

I have got a son—he is six months old now. His hair is like the sun shining on the sea, and he has his father's limbs and body. I am still Frau Crich—what actually happened is so much better, to account for one's position, than a lie would be. The boy is called Ferdinand Gerald Crich.

As for the past—I lived for some months with Loerke, as a friend. Now I am staying   [p. 427]

The incomplete sentence suggests that, at one time, the passage continued further. But whether or not Gudrun's future was to have been the subject of the epilogue, it was never written in the form of the 'small last chapter'

---

[28] Notebook 3, like notebooks 7–10 (see footnote 22), shows the title 'Sisters' deleted and 'Women in Love' inserted; it was at one time the last notebook of the April–June 1916 'Sisters III', containing pages 861–3 (the number '861' is also deleted on its cover). In October, DHL tore out the used pages, inserted them at the back of notebook 10 (where they still are), and then re-used the almost empty notebook.

[29] See Explanatory note on 384:34.

(iii. 29) Lawrence was still planning in November. The last scenes of the novel would, however, be completely altered (and extended) in revision between 1917 and 1919.

After Lawrence had sent the last manuscript notebooks of *Women in Love* to his agent, the history of the novel moves into a new phase marked by continuing revision, by numerous unsuccessful attempts to find a publisher, by fears of suppression after publication and by readings of the typescript by friends and potential publishers. By 13 November Lawrence had already received in two batches (the first on the 6th) the part which Pinker had had typed in his office, for he told Pinker that he would be returning the complete assembled novel in a week's time (iii. 22, 28–9); he confirmed this schedule when on 17 November he wrote to say that he would be posting it 'on Monday [the 20th], or thereabouts' (iii. 34).

Close examination of the two typescripts (hereafter TSIa and TSIb, both containing a mixture of carbon and ribbon pages) reveals much about Lawrence's procedure at this stage. He had a great desire to revise them,[30] and must have started doing this during his own typing in the summer and autumn (his own section of the typescript is far more heavily revised than the section typed in Pinker's office[31]). After entering almost all of the initial revision (distributed between the two copies) in his own hand, he had allowed Frieda to help by copying the new readings into one copy or the other. Usually she had followed him accurately, but sometimes she had been either careless or had deliberately inserted her own reading. As the published texts were to derive ultimately from TSIb, such alterations do not affect the transmission of the text when they appear in TSIa, or in the portions of TSIb which Lawrence later rewrote. However, some of her mistranscriptions (and failures to transcribe) in TSIb were carried over into the fresh typescript (TSII) made January–March 1917; see 'Text' below.

On 20 November Lawrence sent TSIa to Pinker (ii. 35), to be offered to

---

[30] A photograph of Gertler's painting *The Merry-Go-Round* which he had seen early in October (*Letters*, ii. 660–1) provoked revisions in chapter XXIX, for example: see Explanatory note on 423:14.

[31] It is clear in the two copies (Roberts E441d at UT, and E441e at UTor) where DHL's typing ends. Although the typefaces are similar, DHL indented only a few spaces for paragraphs, left a blank space between opening inverted commas and the first word following, and left very narrow margins on all sides. There is also, to p. 368, an average of 3.5 incidents per page of strike-overs or run-on words; from p. 369 onwards, the average drops to 0.1 per page, and the text follows notebooks 1–10. See Explanatory note on 302:2.

his contracted publisher Methuen; probably on the same day he sent TSIb (eventually intended to be sent to publishers in the USA) to the Carswells. At first he had no intention of using TSIb for anything except corrections, comments on 'discrepancy' from them (iii. 36) and advice from Catherine's husband Donald, a barrister, about possible libel: he told Carswell that 'Halliday is Heseltine, The Pussum is a model called the Puma, and they are taken from life – nobody else at all lifelike' (iii. 36). (Heseltine did indeed think the character libellous when the book was published in England in 1921; see below.) But Carswell also made some further suggestions,[32] and Lawrence was already thinking of allowing someone else to read TSIb: Esther Andrews, a friend of Robert Mountsier (later Lawrence's American agent[33]). However strong Lawrence's initial reservations about people reading the new novel, others would hear about it and begin asking to see it. Word quickly reached Lady Ottoline, for example, that Lawrence had used her as a model for Hermione; Lawrence told Catherine Carswell on 27 November that 'I heard from Ottoline Morrell this morning, saying she hears she is the villainess of the new book. It is very strange, how rumours go round. – So I have offered to send her the MS. – So don't send it to Pinker till I let you know' (iii. 41). As other friends sought to read the novel Lawrence generally made some attempt to prevent them, but then gave in. At first he did not want Barbara Low to see the book, but by 11 December he agreed to let her finish it since she had read the beginning on a visit to Cornwall (iii. 41). The list of those who saw it grew to include the American poet Hilda Doolittle (iii. 56), who was to send TSIb to Lady Ottoline; the latter had read it by 20 January 1917.[34]

By 20 December Methuen & Co. had seen TSIa, and immediately cancelled their contract for the rights to Lawrence's next three novels after *The Rainbow* (iii. 58). This left Pinker free to offer the novel to other, potentially more likely publishers. But Lawrence was no longer simply relying on the prospect of publication through the usual channels. Two

---

[32] See footnote 74 and Explanatory notes on 60:33, 63:20 and 449:1.

[33] 1920–3; see *Letters*, iii. 24 n. 4.

[34] Hilda Doolittle ('H.D.'; ibid., ii. 203n), in her autobiographical novel *Bid Me To Live* (1960), 'hadn't the strength nor the equipment to dredge the ore out of the manuscript you sent me' (p. 183); 'it seemed very long, very confused' (p. 66). Lady Ottoline noted 'Frieda's handwriting' in TSIb, gave it to Aldous Huxley (*Garsington* 128), and probably Clive Bell and Philip Morrell (letters from Bell to Ottoline, n.d. [Jan.–Feb. 1917], UT, and to Vanessa Bell, 20 Jan. 1917, King's College, Cambridge). Dorothy Brett knew it by 14 Jan. (*Collected Letters of K. Mansfield*, ed. V. O'Sullivan & M. Scott, Oxford, i. 292); Edward Marsh (*Letters*, i. 459n) may have seen it in January (iii. 76).

days earlier, Koteliansky had suggested publication in Russia if a translation could be made;[35] Lawrence was also turning to Lady Cynthia
Asquith and to Catherine Carswell (iii. 55, 58) with questions about the
protection he might gain by dedicating his work to a patron or patroness.

By mid-January 1917, Lawrence's old publisher Duckworth had also
refused the novel (iii. 80). During January, too, Martin Secker (who would
publish the novel's first English edition in 1921) turned the book down,
explaining to Pinker a few days later that 'the difficulties with which we are
contending just now . . . compel us to adopt the policy of not increasing our
present commitments until there is an end to the War and a return to
normal working conditions'.[36] Then, on 23 January, Constable & Co.
wrote to Pinker that they were rejecting the novel upon the recommen-
dation of two readers:

One of our readers wondered whether Mr Lawrence really meant the first part of
the book to be published as it stands, because it has been very much altered, and in
some cases the alterations do not fit into what follows. Also we feel that the present
would be a most unfavourable time for the publication of the book in its present
form. In the first place, there are the writer's expressions of antipathy to England
and the forms of English civilisation. At the present time, when people are
sacrificing all that is dearest to them for their country, such expressions are we
think bound to rouse the resentment both of the reviewers and the public. In the
second place, the destructive philosophy as it is expressed in this book would we
think be particularly unwelcome at the present time, and the same might
perhaps be said of the author's 'detached' attitudes toward the events of the present
day.[37]

Constable then said that they would reconsider the novel if Lawrence
would alter, compress or modify it. The report is the only surviving
pre-publication account of *Women in Love* from a publisher's point of view,
and sheds considerable light on the attitudes which made publication so
difficult to arrange. For Lawrence to question the 'forms of English
civilisation' while the First World War raged was unforgivable. For his
part, given such a reaction, Lawrence would have liked not to offer the
novel to the English public at all (iii. 67, 72, 76, 78), but because he was so
short of money he stopped short of asking Pinker to withdraw the book
completely.

---

[35] Ibid. 54. Catherine Carswell believed that the scheme for publication in Russia was mostly
'an excuse' for Koteliansky to send DHL £10 'on account from Russia' (*The Savage
Pilgrimage*, 1st edn., 1932, p. 80 n. 1).

[36] Letter from Secker to Pinker, 6 February 1917, UIll.

[37] Located at NWU.

Women in Love (sixth version, March 1917–September 1919)

Just before the end of January 1917 Lawrence recovered TSIb from his friends and sent it to Pinker for retyping; Constable's remarks about the heavy revision in TSIa may have encouraged him to do so, Donald and Catherine Carswell's suggestions needed to be incorporated, and Lawrence wanted an extra copy to send to Russia for possible publication there (iii. 79).

Meanwhile, he had heard that Lady Ottoline Morrell was considering legal action against him, in the event of publication. In February he reassured Pinker: 'There *is* a hint of [Ottoline] in the character of Hermione: but so there is a hint of a million women . . . Anyway, they could make libel cases for ever, they haven't half a leg to stand on' (iii. 95). He went on to say, however, that it hardly mattered; there was no point in trying to publish the novel in England until the war ended. As the new copies of TSII[38] were nearing completion in March, his thoughts were still running on Lady Ottoline's reaction; he told Pinker '*I wish I could have a copy*' of the new typescript so that he could look at her 'imaginary portrait again'.[39] When the copies were done, 'the one for Koteliansky and the one for me' (iii. 104), he told Koteliansky to lend his copy to Gertler or to Gordon Campbell should they wish to read it;[40] on the same day he wrote to Gertler (a frequent guest of Lady Ottoline's): 'tell me how much likeness you can see between Hermione and the Ott. The Ott. is really too disgusting, with her threats of legal proceedings . . . We have flattered her above all bounds' (iii. 109). He told Lady Cynthia Asquith, as she recorded in her diary for 19 April, that he

had not made a portrait of Ottoline in his new novel. His woman was infinitely superior, but the Morrells were so furious at the supposed lampoon that Morrell wrote – inconceivable as it sounds – to the publisher, asking him to come down and identify the character as his wife, and Ottoline asked Lawrence to return an opal pin she had given him. Fancy calling in that worm of a publisher as detective![41]

[38] Roberts E441f, UT (see Farmer, 'A Descriptive and Analytical Catalogue', A61): a mixture of ribbon and carbon pages. There were probably two additional copies (*Letters*, iii. 79), present location unknown, one for Koteliansky and one for Pinker: that would explain DHL's reference in 1920 to Pinker having had '*3* copies' (ibid. 466) – i.e. TSIa, TSIb and the third copy of TSII.

[39] Ibid. 104. The copies were ready on 23 March, the date when Pinker sent Koteliansky his copy (letter in BL); DHL thanked Pinker for his on 28 March (*Letters*, iii. 105).

[40] Campbell had been a friend of the Lawrences since 1913 (see ibid., ii. 51 n. 1).

[41] *Diaries: 1915–1918* (1968), p. 294. Lady Cynthia must have meant that Lawrence's agent Pinker was contacted, as no publisher had yet accepted the book; Lady Ottoline confirms

During 1917, Lawrence worked intensively on his own copy of the new typescript (TSII); it contains heavy interlinear revision. It is mostly impossible to date the revisions, except in such cases where a revised passage corresponds so closely to a remark in a letter that it seems that both belong to the same period.[42] As well as general revision throughout the year, Lawrence probably did some particular work on the typescript in July 1917, before it went to Cecil Palmer to be considered for publication (iii. 137). In all, he added whole pages of autograph revision to supplement the interlinear revision; he also retyped a number of pages. As he sold his typewriter to Catherine Carswell's brother in the summer of 1919 (iii. 365 and n.3, 393–4), the pages he retyped on his own machine must therefore have been done earlier (see 'Text' below for details). He made alterations in November 1917 (iii. 185); still further revision was done in September 1919, some of it in what is now a reddish brown ink,[43] before TSII was despatched to America (iii. 390).

But although he went on revising it minutely, and with loving care – 'I consider this the best of my books' (iii. 390) – from early 1917 the problems the book caused must also have been intensely depressing to him. In March 1917 he told Ernest Collings that 'I have done a novel, which nobody will print, after the *Rainbow* experience. It has been the round of publishers by now, and rejected by all. I don't care. One might as well make roses bloom in January, as bring out living work into this present world of man'.[44] Yet, in April, he suggested Eveleigh Nash to Pinker as a possible publisher (iii. 111); only to inform his friend Murry in May that there was 'no writing and publishing news. Philosophy interests me most now – not novels or stories. I find people ultimately boring: and you can't have fiction without people. So fiction does not . . . interest me any more' (iii. 127).[45] In April, he had reached the point where he did not want any more of his acquaintance, especially the 'Ott. crowd', to read the novel; he told Kotelianksy that he felt bad about 'that novel, and I will not publish it now', though 'I *know* it is a good book' (iii. 112).

that 'As it was obviously libellous, Philip went to . . . Lawrence's agent, and told them that if it was published as it stood he should bring an action against the Publishers for libel' (*Garsington* 129).

42 See, e.g., Explanatory notes on 127:27 and 427:2.

43 See Charles Ross, *The Composition of 'The Rainbow' and 'Women in Love': A History* (Charlottesville, 1979), pp. 118–19 and n. 11. At least some of the reddish brown ink revision was, however, done at an earlier date; two stages of revision in that ink colour can for example be seen in TSII p. 155.

44 *Letters*, iii. 100. Collings was an artist and illustrator with whom DHL had corresponded since late 1912 (see ibid., i. 468 n. 1).

45 He was engaged on the (lost) book 'At the Gates' (see ibid., iii. 143 n. 3 and 152).

However, in June 1917 he had to tell his agent that 'I am afraid I am coming to the end of my resources' (iii. 135); he wondered whether Pinker would feel able to make an advance, while (naturally) continuing his efforts to place the book. Lawrence suggested that Cecil Palmer, who owned and operated a small press and publishing house, might be worth approaching, but Pinker apparently did not send him a typescript; Lawrence sent his own copy of TSII instead, only to have it rejected in August (iii. 137, 151). The relationship between author and agent was starting to come under strain, partly because of the difficulties in placing *Women in Love*, and Lawrence's inability to earn his living. Pinker did send a copy to Little, Brown & Co. in America, but the book was rejected in July: 'we feel that it is not as good as SONS AND LOVERS, and that Mr. Lawrence has not made as good a presentation of his theme as we expected. Under the circumstances we feel compelled to return the manuscript.'[46] At the suggestion of Gordon Campbell, Lawrence himself contacted Joseph Hone at Maunsel's in Dublin, but Hone replied that Maunsel did not want to publish any English books during the war (iii. 187). Fisher Unwin saw the novel in December 1917 (iii. 191), but did not take it. In fact, from the publisher's standpoint (as Lawrence himself recognised), the book was too dangerous to handle; its author's last novel had been suppressed, and the new one questioned English attitudes in time of war. As Lawrence wrote in August 1917, 'it would be folly, I think, to publish it in the ordinary way, so exposed' (iii. 147). And yet he desperately needed income; and he knew the book was a good one. The whole problem was, of course, further exacerbated by the decline in British publishing between 1914 and 1917.[47]

Another scheme, in November 1917, quickly foundered: to publish the novel privately under the auspices of Arnold Bennett and John Galsworthy. Lawrence lunched with Galsworthy in November to help promote this idea (iii. 183); Galsworthy read the novel, but his reaction cannot have been encouraging, for nothing further happened.[48]

A further abortive scheme followed in 1918. Once again Lawrence contemplated publication with a private press: at the suggestion of Michael Sadleir he contacted Cyril Beaumont in February.[49] His letters betray a

---

[46] 11 July 1917, NWU.

[47] The total number of new books published fell from 12,379 before the war to 8,131 in 1917; labour and paper costs were normally blamed.

[48] *Letters*, iii. 185, 187. Although it is uncertain whether Bennett ever read the novel, George Moore did – and, according to DHL, praised it highly (ibid. 191 and n. 1).

[49] Ibid. 212; Beaumont, bookseller and publisher (see ibid. 212 n. 1), published DHL's book of poems *Bay* in November 1919 (see Roberts 34–6). For a short time, it appeared that Prince Antoine Bibesco (1878–1951) might give the novel financial support (see *Letters*, iii. 220 and n. 3).

mixture of concern and indifference as, yet again, he contemplated the possibility of the novel being published. He told Koteliansky that he was bored with the matter, but he also approached Lady Cynthia several times about raising money by subscription (iii. 219–20); he even suggested approaching Lady Ottoline to see if she would contribute: 'I know she would like the thing to appear, for self-advertisement – and her sheep-faced fool of a husband would like to denounce it, for further self-advertisement' (iii. 220). But Beaumont's response was exceptionally cautious: he did not want to be identified with the publication, if he did proceed it must be done 'delicately', and perhaps £150 towards the printing bill of £365 would have to be paid in advance (iii. 219–20). Assistance from Lady Cynthia and other friends was not forthcoming and the cost was, anyway, prohibitive: the novel was returned to Lawrence (iii. 237).

Lawrence's irritation at his failure to engage the interest of a publisher, coupled with his utter disenchantment with England in the midst of war, was made still worse by his deteriorating relationship with Pinker. He had frequently been critical of what he saw as Pinker's ineffectualness, and in November 1918 wrote suggesting a break:

I have an idea that you would rather not be bothered any longer with my work: which certainly must be no joy, nor profit, to you. Will you let me know if this is so. I remember you said when we made the agreement that it might be broken if either was dissatisfied. If you have any desire to break it just let me know.   (iii. 296)

The formal break with Pinker came thirteen months later. While Pinker had not been the active agent Lawrence thought he should have been – he apparently never sent a copy of *Women in Love* to Lawrence's American publisher of *The Rainbow*, B. W. Huebsch, the most likely man in America to have taken it – it must be admitted that Lawrence had not been a model client either. He was not above working behind Pinker's back, in an attempt to earn a little money without his agent's intervention (or percentage).[50]

However, before the final break with Pinker, Lawrence's life and prospects had gradually been transformed. First came the ending of the war, and with it the symbolic end of an agonised and embittering period, during which *The Rainbow* had been suppressed, his other writing frequently censored or rejected, he and Frieda had been prevented from leaving the country, suspected of spying and finally expelled from Cornwall. They had been frequently impoverished, sometimes homeless, and had more than

[50] E.g., DHL arranged the American publication of *New Poems* directly with Huebsch: 'if Pinker has to come in, he can come in after' (*Letters*, iii. 388); and cf. his dealings with Secker over *Women in Love* in September 1919: 'don't speak yet to Pinker . . .' (ibid. 391).

once been reduced to living on charity. Although in 1918 and 1919 Lawrence had tried to promote his work, only two, slight volumes resulted: *New Poems* published by Martin Secker, and *Bay* by Cyril Beaumont. Lawrence had also often been ill; indeed, it is arguable that the poverty and illness of the war years in England accelerated his early death. There is a profound bitterness and anger evident in his letters and other writings of this period. Yet, one by one, the restrictions and irritations of the war years fell away; and in November 1919 Lawrence was able to leave the 'grey, dreary-grey coffin of England'[51] on his way to Italy and, as it turned out, almost permanent exile. Before he left, however, he was at last approached by the two publishers who would eventually bring out *Women in Love*.

Publication

Late in August or early in September 1919 Lawrence received a cable from Thomas Seltzer in New York asking to see the novel. Douglas Goldring, also a writer and a friend of Lawrence, had been acting as a kind of London representative for Seltzer, and he had written numerous letters in 1919 promoting Lawrence; his efforts had finally borne fruit.[52] On 7 September Lawrence replied:

I had your cablegram – at least as enclosed. I was away, so there is some delay. I wanted moreover to go through the MS. [i.e. TSII] of the novel once more. – I consider this the best of my books. – Please be careful with the MS., as it is the most complete one: – I am forwarding it to you by the next mail.

Meanwhile Martin Secker writes that he would like to publish the book next spring, under its old title 'The Sisters'. He has another copy [see footnote 38]. – I would like the book to come first in America. I shall never forgive England *The Rainbow*. – If you wished to publish this novel, would you like me to write a short Fore-word?[53] – And which title do you prefer, *Women in Love*, or 'The Sisters'.

(iii. 390–1)

Secker was at this stage probably by no means as committed as Lawrence suggested 'to publish the book next spring', though he had read it and was certainly interested. Lawrence's attempts to secure a contract in both the

---

[51] *Kangaroo* (1923), chap. XII.

[52] See *Odd Man Out: The Autobiography of a Propaganda Novelist* (1935), p. 247. Thomas Seltzer, in brief partnership with Temple Scott, had just founded a publishing firm that in its six years of life published DHL, Henry James, Stefan Zweig and E. E. Cummings, among others. See *Letters*, iii. 390 n. 2, and G. Thomas Tanselle, 'The Thomas Seltzer Imprint', *PBSA*, lviii (1964), 380–488.

[53] DHL's Foreword, written 12 September 1919 and published as an advertising leaflet for the novel by Seltzer (see Roberts 39 for a discussion of its two printed states), is printed as Appendix I.

'The Publication of *Women in Love*'

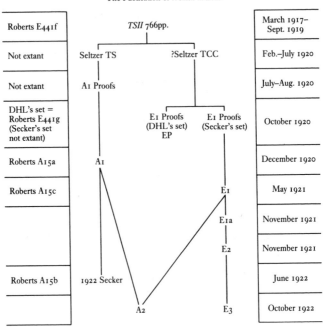

Roberts E441f	*TSII* 766pp.	March 1917–Sept. 1919
Not extant	Seltzer TS	?Seltzer TCC	Feb.–July 1920
Not extant	A1 Proofs	July–Aug. 1920
DHL's set = Roberts E441g (Secker's set not extant)	E1 Proofs (DHL's set) EP	E1 Proofs (Secker's set)	October 1920
Roberts A15a	A1	December 1920
Roberts A15c	E1	May 1921
	E1a	November 1921
	E2	November 1921
Roberts A15b	1922 Secker	June 1922
	A2	E3	October 1922

USA and England become clearer in a letter he wrote to Secker the following day:

About *Women in Love* – I am just corresponding with America about it. If it actually comes off, and is published there this late autumn, would you like to have sheets? I'll tell you in about 3 weeks time. – 'The Sisters' was one of the original titles – but somebody – some woman – has used it.[54] To me the title is a matter of indifference. I would like you to publish the book – I know it is my best – but don't speak yet to Pinker, wait a bit till I let you hear about America. (iii. 391)

Lawrence knew from experience that near-simultaneous publication in the two countries could be advantageous to publishers and himself, especially if one of the publishers could be offered the incentive of buying printed sheets from the other, rather than bearing the more substantial cost of typesetting and printing. But he was also encouraging each publisher by emphasising the interest of the other.

Writing to Secker again late in October and in November, Lawrence stressed that he must print from TSII or from American proofs (iii. 408, 410–11); and on 2 November Lawrence wrote to Seltzer that he needed TSII returned at once, 'as Secker urgently wants it to print from. He is including the novel in his Spring list – title The Sisters. If you are printing, send sheets, proofs, as soon as you get them from the printer' (iii. 408). But Seltzer neither returned TSII nor began to have it printed, and left Lawrence with the impression that he was unlikely to proceed with publication (see below).

Lawrence, however – now without an agent, and in Italy – had to continue to work on his potential publishers, in an effort to get them to commit themselves. On 17 December he wrote to Secker to be '*sure* and tell me when you have the MS. of *Women in Love* – The Sisters if you like – and tell me what you are doing with it' (iii. 434). Then, ten days later, presumably now accepting that English publication couldn't be as early as he had hoped in September, he wrote to Secker with a new proposal:

Mackenzie said you thought of printing the *Rainbow*. Do that, and you have my eternal allegiance. He suggested it be called 'Women in Love Vol I.', with a foreword by himself. I think 'Women in Love, Vol I and Vol II' is a very good idea. I am anxious to hear from you. If you do this, *The Rainbow* as a Vol I of *Women in Love*, then I must make a sort of permanent agreement with you. (iii. 439)

Compton Mackenzie had met Lawrence through a mutual friend in 1914, and as one of Secker's most popular authors he was in a good position to promote Lawrence's books. His influence with Secker was further

---

[54] May Sinclair: see p. xxx.

enhanced in 1920 by his purchase of a one-third silent partnership in
Secker's publishing firm: a matter which had been under discussion for
almost two years.[55] Mackenzie and Lawrence had met again in Capri at the
end of December 1919, and must have discussed Lawrence's commercial
prospects, and the best way of approaching Secker. The latter meanwhile
replied to the suggestion of the two-volume publication proposed by
Lawrence; the letter went to Mackenzie.

> Yes, the economic problem of the novelist without popular sales is very difficult. I
> could make him an offer to purchase the rights of *Women in Love* for £300 . . . &
> *Rainbow* for £200. £500 in all. On this he could live comfortably in Italy for a year
> during which time he would finish another book & we might come to an
> agreement.[56]

But in mid-January 1920 Lawrence turned down such an offer flat. 'I
should never sell the *Rainbow* for £200. I'd rather go back to my old
arrangement with Duckworth, of royalty and £50. advance: or even no
advance. The fact that I have no money would never make me jump at a
lump sum.' He then made a counter-offer which grew out of discussions
with Mackenzie (iii. 458–9): he would lease the copyrights in *The Rainbow*,
Women in Love and his proposed new novel (which would become *The Lost
Girl*[57]) until they came into profit; the copyrights would then revert to
Lawrence, and he would receive a royalty. In the same letter, Lawrence
continued to press for a two-volume edition of *Women in Love* and *The
Rainbow* together. It had been clear from September 1919 that Secker
preferred the title 'The Sisters' – it must have struck him as less
provocative – but, in contrast with his attitude the previous autumn,
Lawrence was now unyielding in his insistence upon *Women in Love* as his
title. He did agree to make 'some few alterations' (iii. 459) to *The Rainbow*
for its new publication, but he also stressed his belief that a new edition
would not automatically be suppressed; and Mackenzie appears to have
supported him.[58]

   However, with Secker's terms currently unacceptable, at the end of
January Lawrence turned back to his old publisher Duckworth in an
attempt to arrange dual publication with him instead. They do not appear
to have got as far as discussing terms, because Duckworth insisted as a

---

55 Letter from Secker to Mackenzie, 12 February 1920, UT. For Mackenzie, see *Letters*,
    iii. 398 n. 2.
56 4 January 1920, UT.
57 Secker published *The Lost Girl* on 25 November 1920; see Introduction, ed. Worthen,
    pp. xxvi–vii. Secker re-issued *The Rainbow* in 1926.
58 See letter from Secker to Mackenzie, 27 January 1920, UT.

pre-condition that a chapter of *The Rainbow* (probably 'Shame') would have to be removed. This was even worse than Secker's attempt to buy Lawrence's copyrights outright, and in March Lawrence turned back to Secker:

> You snapped off our last negotiations. Don't know if you feel like returning to them. – I wish you didn't ask me to sell my books outright. I don't like their going clean away from me.
>
> Nevertheless, because you dont ask me to make alterations in the books, if you still offer me the same terms I'll take them, and thank you, and be damned to the rest. (iii. 490)

And so, on 28 March 1920, Secker sent Lawrence the proposal he was to accept for the publication in England of *Women in Love*,[59] almost exactly seven years after the novel had been first begun. Secker also withdrew his demand to buy the copyrights outright, but still baulked at the idea of 'Women in Love, Vol I and Vol II'. Instead, as he told Mackenzie, he

> made him an offer to publish both books, with an option on his next five . . . I feel most strongly that I must reserve my decision to publish *The Rainbow* until after *Women in Love* has appeared . . . & done something to rehabilitate the author – in fact, to be guided to a great extent by its reception. Also I must take legal advice to make sure that I am not automatically committing a contempt of court by re-issuing the book *de novo*. I am not prepared to invest £1500 in a *cause célèbre* to entertain the world of letters . . .
>
> Why I want D.H.L. to change the provocative title of *Women in Love* to the quiet, even dull one of *The Sisters* is just for the very reason that it is important from D.H.L.'s point of view to be as unprovocative as possible in order to get the book taken anywhere. To give it that title is to tie a red rag onto it. By the way, the copy he wishes me to set up from is the typescript now in America, considerably altered he tells me, which may differ from mine by having all the best bits taken out & a lot of Lesbianism written in. So obviously I must see this American typescript first, although I do not imagine of course that what I have suggested above is really the case.
>
> I feel instinctively that anything to do with D.H. is rather dangerous, but I am prepared to take risks fortified by what I know to be your wishes that I should give him another chance. I agree that he may go mad if he does not have something in print soon.[60]

Lawrence's negotiations with Seltzer had been almost as prolonged. He had attempted to speed up American publication by conveying what he hoped was Secker's commitment; but in spite of receiving an advance of

[59] *Letters*, iii. 499; the contract between DHL and Secker for *Women in Love* is dated 14 April 1920, UT.
[60] 14 April 1920, UT.

£50 from Seltzer late in 1919, Lawrence was still profoundly unsure of him. 'I heard from Scott and Seltzer – they sent me £50 for the novel – but I doubt if they'll publish it' (iii. 441). His uncertainty about Seltzer was aggravated by a complication which arose with his previous American publisher Huebsch. Although the latter had published *The Rainbow* in 1915, he had distributed the book very cautiously to avoid suppression. He had cabled Lawrence in November 1919 (iii. 409 n. 1) that there had been some misunderstanding about the new novel *Women in Love*: he had never seen it. He confirmed his interest in the book by cabling Lawrence twice at the end of December, warning him against Seltzer (iii. 456 n. 1). When Lawrence received the cables, he wrote to Seltzer asking him to relinquish *Women in Love*:

I hear from Huebsch that he is anxious to secure the publishing of *Women in Love*. I understood that my agent Pinker had sent him the MS. long ago. Apparently it was not so. Since Huebsch has done *The Rainbow* it is most fair that he should have the offer of *Women in Love*. If you can see your way to do so, I wish you would relinquish to me again the MS of the novel, and I will at once return the £50 advance . . .
   If you cannot see your way to relinquishing the MS., then first and foremost will you let Martin Secker have the copy you promised. He writes insistently about it, and I am concerned that he has not received it.   (iii. 457)

Lawrence concluded with a request for Seltzer to draw up an agreement, stating his terms for the book. At this stage, he gave Seltzer an alternative to relinquishing the novel; but after another angry letter from Huebsch, on 29 January he wrote again to Seltzer giving him no alternative (iii. 466, 467). This, as it was perhaps meant to, provoked Seltzer into action. On 9 and 11 February 1920 he sent Lawrence contracts for a privately printed edition of *Women in Love* and for other books (iii. 484–5). All Huebsch could be offered was an explanation of Pinker's failure:

Simply, it never occurred to me that Pinker could have had that MS. for almost two years, all the while assuring me that he was doing everything possible, without ever even mentioning it to you. It just didn't occur to me. I thought you'd seen it and turned it down months and months before . . . If I'd thought Pinker hadn't shown you the MS. – he had *3* copies – wouldn't I have sent it you a year ago? (iii. 466)

But although Lawrence was 'sorry about Huebsch', the latter also came in for his share of Lawrence's criticism: 'Huebsch was always *so* vague and friendly . . . Huebsch should have been more to the point with me, and not have acted behind the publisher's veil'.[61] What cannot have escaped

---

[61] *Letters*, iii. 484. Further information about the split between DHL and Huebsch appears in 'The Reminiscences of B. W. Huebsch' (1965), Columbia University Oral History Research Office.

Lawrence was the irony of the book's three-year-long failure to find a publisher being ended by two publishers quarrelling over it.

Despite securing contracts with Seltzer and Secker, Lawrence was still obviously concerned over Seltzer's failure to send either TSII or a copy of it to Secker; on 1 June 1920 he threatened, indeed, not to send Seltzer the typescript of his new novel *The Lost Girl* until Secker received *Women in Love* (iii. 540). Lawrence obviously expected Seltzer's typesetting to move more quickly than it did, but in June and July Seltzer sent off, in at least two batches, a typescript made from TSII.[62] In August, he began sending proofs to Lawrence; one set to be corrected and returned, and the other to be passed on to Secker after correction (iii. 586). Because of delays in the Italian post that year, and his own summer travels, however, Lawrence did not receive all Seltzer's proofs until 18 October (too late for his own proof-correction, or to be much use to Secker); but he noted 'only very slight incorrections. I am looking forward to your volume: it comes out immediately, Mountsier says' (iii. 613, 618). (Mountsier was now acting as Lawrence's agent in the USA.) *Women in Love* was finally published in America on 9 November 1920. Lawrence wrote to Seltzer on 11 December:

Today have come ten copies of *Women in Love*. I am very pleased indeed with it: feel it has made us friends for life: and sincerely hope so. It's a real book. Now I pray it will bring you your money quickly, and be a success in that way. It is my best book. I was glad you said you began to like it. It needs a bit of getting used to.   (iii. 635)

Textual evidence demonstrates that in England Secker chose not to wait for the duplicate corrected proofs; he began setting from the copy of TSII he had been sent,[63] and though he may in the end have acquired a full set of corrected American proofs, it seems most likely that the copy of TSII he received from America incorporated most of the changes from TSII also found in Seltzer's text.

On 14 October 1920, Secker sent Lawrence English proofs up to p. 128; he also made the first in a series of requests for textual adjustments. Another thing which worried him was the lack of chapter titles in a novel which would run to over 500 pages.[64] By 12 November the Dunedin Press in Edinburgh had finished setting type for the English edition; on

[62] *Letters*, iii. 559, 573. Secker had the complete typescript by 21 July (letters to Seltzer, UIll). Seltzer made at least one and probably two typescript copies of TSII (DHL had heard this by February 1920, *Letters*, iii. 472), one for Secker and one for his own printer: see 'Seltzer TS' and '?Seltzer TCC' in the diagram above. He himself retained possession of TSII, and still had it in February 1921 (ibid. 674).

[63] See, e.g., Textual apparatus for 10:4 and Explanatory note on 59:14.

[64] Letter from Secker to DHL, 14 October 1920, UIll (*Letters from a Publisher*, 1970, p. 6).

10 and 22 November Lawrence returned batches of corrected proofs, having added chapter titles (his duplicate proofs, hereafter EP, survive), and having also divided chapter XXIX into two, making thirty-two chapters in all.[65] But Secker now began to insist upon more textual changes, and must have returned the proofs of chapter VII:

In reading through the book again, I am more than ever pleased with it and think it contains some splendid scenes ... I wonder whether you would mind making the very few verbal alterations in chapter [VII] for England removing the references to the unconventional manner in which the occupants of the flat used to sit about in the morning. I do not expect that you attach any particular importance to the scene or think that it is in any way vital to the book. It is just the sort of thing that enemies are likely to concentrate on.[66]

Lawrence sent back a revised proof of this chapter on 30 November, remarking 'If enemies want to fasten, they'll fasten anywhere', but had 'altered it a bit: enough, I think' (iii. 628). Eight alterations of wording in this chapter, four of them removing references to casual dress and nakedness, appeared in the English edition.[67]

But, during October and November, Secker had been sending batches of proofs to New York, and on three occasions offered to sell Seltzer sets of sheets.[68] This was particularly strange, as he knew all about Seltzer's edition; Lawrence had begun to send him its proofs back in August (iii. 586). We subsequently find Secker explaining to Seltzer – presumably after protests from the latter – that 'I do not think there was intimation in your previous letters that "Women in Love" had already been set up and published in America, and why I sent you proofs and quoted you terms for an edition in sheets was because I gathered from your letter of July 6th that you contemplated issuing the book in the ordinary way.'[69] Seltzer's was an expensive, private edition; Secker probably thought that he would want sheets for an ordinary trade edition. But Secker may also have been trying to ascertain Seltzer's progress with his edition; at all events, he only succeeded in creating hard feelings between the two of them, with Seltzer suspicious of what seemed to him like an English publisher's attempt to get into the American market.

[65] Letter from Secker to Seltzer, 12 November 1920, UIll; *Letters*, iii. 621, 625. EP, the duplicate proof copy (Roberts E441g), is at UT; DHL wrote (with slight variations) the titles on the contents page as well as at the head of each chapter.

[66] Letter from Secker to DHL, 25 November, UIll. Most of this was omitted 'Owing to illegibility' in *Letters from a Publisher*, p. 8.

[67] See Textual apparatus for 77:10, 77:34, 78:26, 78:36, 79:2, 79:4, 79:5 and 79:31.

[68] Letters to Seltzer, 21 July, 12 October and 12 November 1920, UIll.

[69] Letter from Secker to Seltzer, 7 December 1920, UIll.

As it was, details of publication in England were still not settled. In mid-October, Secker had forecast publication in February (iii. 606), but late in November he wrote that he hoped to bring it out 'next April or so'.[70] On 22 and 30 November, and again on 12 December, Lawrence suggested to Secker that review copies should not be sent out; *Women in Love* was the books he had 'most at heart', and he preferred it to be published simply for sale in bookshops, without either reviews or library sales. 'I do so hate the critics, they are such poisonous worms, especially for a book like this' (iii. 625, 628, 638).

On 12 December, Lawrence also told Secker that he did not want the English edition published before 1 May 1921 (iii. 638). Lawrence, Mountsier and Seltzer were concerned over copies of the English edition of *The Lost Girl* filtering into New York – copies which they thought Secker had sold directly to America, in advance of Seltzer's own edition;[71] and Lawrence wanted to allow Seltzer time to market his expensive private edition of *Women in Love*, costing $15.00 as compared with Secker's English selling price of 9s,[72] before any copies of the English edition of the novel interfered with American sales. And, of course, back in September 1919 Lawrence had told Seltzer that he wanted *Women in Love* to come out first in the USA, because he was still angry over the banning of *The Rainbow* in England.

Secker did not reply until 31 December, by which time he had information for re-negotiating his terms for *Women in Love*. *The Lost Girl*, which he had issued on 25 November 1920, had sold approximately 2,000 copies, 1,000 of which had been taken by the lending libraries such as Mudies and Boots. But the libraries had only taken *The Lost Girl* on condition that changes were made to some objectionable passages;[73] without the libraries, sales would have been halved. Secker concluded that a profitable circulation of *Women in Love* would necessitate a further 'two or three excisions or paraphrases in the text'; in its present state it would not be taken by the libraries. If the libraries were thus to be ignored, he would print only 1,500 copies instead of 2,000, and Lawrence's advance on the novel would have to be cut from £100 to £50 (iii. 647n).

When Lawrence got this letter in mid-January 1921, he wrote asking to see the 'excisions or paraphrases' required (iii. 647); he also told Mountsier that 'Secker wants me to cut *W. in Love*. I won't' (ii. 651). However,

---

[70] 25 November 1920, UIll.
[71] See 'Introduction', *The Lost Girl*, ed. Worthen, pp. li–lii.
[72] Equivalent to $1.68 in late 1920 (conversion rate of $3.73 to the £).
[73] See 'Introduction', *The Lost Girl*, ed. Worthen, pp. xxix–xl.

Secker wrote again on 28 January to say that, after re-reading the proofs, he had decided that the book should after all only be sold through bookshops – it was impossible to expurgate the text to the 'Mudie–Boots level'. He also softened a little concerning the advance, reducing it only to £75; but he also specified changes he felt to be necessary even if the book were not intended for the libraries, 'in order to remove any possible chance of misconstruction' (iii. 660n). These were in addition to the changes in chapter VII; four of the new changes requested, however, involved sexual meanings, while the other was a possibly actionable reference to Eleonora Duse. Lawrence offered emendations for all five in his reply of 4 February (iii. 660), and Secker incorporated four of them. Secker also, however, made an extra cut on one of the pages in question without consulting Lawrence; and, furthermore, two paragraphs in chapter XXV in which Birkin and Gerald discuss Birkin's special concern for a 'creative' relationship between two men, intact and unaltered in the page proofs, were omitted from Secker's first edition.[74] There is no evidence that Lawrence authorised this deletion either; Secker was almost certainly responsible. Later in 1921 he would express himself willing to make changes or excisions in the text 'without further reference to Mr Lawrence', and he had made changes in *The Lost Girl* without consulting Lawrence.[75] These additional alterations to *Women in Love* probably delayed its appearance; and there was a further delay in May, when transport difficulties meant publication being postponed again (iii. 722n). *Women in Love* was finally published in England on 10 June 1921, in an edition of 1,500 copies, more than eight years after Lawrence began to write it.

Lawrence was not happy with the appearance of the English edition (the American one had been particularly handsome): 'Secker's are so scrubby! I got a copy of his *Women in Love* the other day, and fairly spat' (iii. 732). But the sales must have pleased him better: within a month, 1,123 copies had been sold, even though no libraries took it except the Times Library.[76] By the end of the summer of 1921 Seltzer, too, was telling Mountsier that *Women in Love* was doing well in America, and predicting that most of the

---

[74] See Textual apparatus for 108:21, 353:16, 422:24 and 449:1; DHL also inserted the three last in EP. Donald Carswell had advised altering the name of Duse in 1916; see Explanatory note on 449:1. Secker's extra cut was at 107:40 and the deleted paragraphs at 352:30.

[75] Letter from Secker to Messrs. Clifford, Webster, Emmet & Coote, 4 November 1921, UIll; 'Introduction', *The Lost Girl*, ed. Worthen, p. xxxix.

[76] Letters from Secker to DHL, 8 June and 12 July 1921, UIll.

1,250 copies of his limited edition would be sold out by the end of the year.[77]

But the issue of censorship continued to recur. On 17 June 1921 Seltzer admitted to Mountsier that there were two omissions in his limited edition:

One omission occurs on p. 384, line 7 from bottom, after the sentence: 'Like a child at the breast, he cleaved intensely to her, and she could not put him away.' The sentence omitted is: 'And his seared, ruined membrane relaxed, softened; that which was seared and stiff and blasted yielded again, became soft and flexible, palpitating with new life.'
I cannot for the life of me remember the second omission. I know it is slight, quite slight. I will get it soon by application and will let you have it. I think both are in Secker's edition.[78]

In England, meanwhile, Philip Heseltine was threatening a libel suit over Lawrence's alleged description of him and Minnie Channing. A letter from Heseltine's solicitors reached Secker's office on 5 September, and Secker undertook to ensure that the novel 'shall not be further circulated until the matter is settled'. But as the first edition had been 'almost exhausted' on 16 August, this probably only meant that he delayed reprinting the book.[79] After a meeting between Secker and the solicitors on 12 September, marked pages from the novel were sent to Lawrence in Italy for him to consider. He got them at the end of the month, together with 'a solicitors information . . . that a libel action is impending. – Sweets to the sweet'.[80] On 8 October, under protest – 'I think it all perfect nonsense' – he provided Secker with the following changes: the Pussum, originally dark-eyed with dark fluffy hair, acquired blue eyes and fair hair; Halliday, pale and fully built, was changed to black, swarthy and slender; the title of chapter VII was changed; and descriptions of manservant, flat

[77] Letter from Seltzer to Mountsier, 20 August 1921, UT (*D. H. Lawrence: Letters to Thomas and Adele Seltzer*, ed. Gerald Lacy, Santa Barbara, 1976, pp. 214–15).

[78] UT (*D. H. Lawrence: Letters to Thomas and Adele Seltzer*, ed. Lacy, pp. 209–10). The quoted omission is recorded in the Textual apparatus for 345:13; the 'second omission' is probably the adjacent pair recorded at 384:16 and 17. A pencil question mark appears in TSII at that point, and Seltzer printed the original, deleted reading of TSII. DHL wrote to Seltzer about one change made (probably in proof) by his editor Harold Matson (b. 1898): 'Tell Matson there's no substitute for the right word' (*New York Times*, 1 May 1986, p. 25).

[79] Letter from Secker to the *Spectator*, 16 August; to Messrs Clifford, Webster, Emmet & Coote, 7 September: UIll. Secker wrote to DHL on 15 November that he was just going to press 'with a new edition, so that it will once more be on sale after a lapse of three months', UIll. He later denied, however, that the first English edition had been 'withdrawn from circulation' (Edward D. McDonald, *A Bibliography of the Writings of D. H. Lawrence*, Philadelphia, 1925, p. 52).

[80] Letter to Earl and Achsah Brewster, ?28 September 1921.

and sculpture were altered.[81] Lawrence asked Secker to 'go through it all carefully, to see there are no discrepancies'.[82] For his part, Secker wrote two letters on 18 October to Heseltine's solicitors stating that Lawrence was

prepared to make the verbal changes shown on the marked pages which I send herewith, not . . . that he considers the matter important, but in deference to my wish that no reasonable effort should be spared to remove any possible objections which your client may have. If your client agrees to the text as modified in this manner, I will undertake to carry out the alterations and to see that no further copies are issued in the original state.

Secker naturally refused to admit that Heseltine had 'been grossly libelled'.[83] After pointing out that he had suspended circulation of the book at a financial loss, Secker noted that if Heseltine were not satisfied with what had been offered he would have to take whatever steps he found necessary.[84] But 'Heseltine refuses in any way to accept these modifications, and says – or his lawyer says – he is now going to bring an action against the book for libel.'[85] Heseltine and his solicitors only accepted the alterations (with the additional substitution, apparently demanded by Heseltine towards the end of negotiations, of 'Minette for Pussum') when Secker also offered £50 payment for damages, and ten guineas costs. Lawrence referred to this as 'hush-money'.[86] On 15 November Secker told Lawrence of the settlement, which made the latter 'sick with rage . . . *Really*, one should never give in to such filth'. But Secker also announced that he had 'now gone to press with a new edition, so that it will once more be on sale after a lapse of three months. I hope there will be no further bother.'[87] This much damaged and altered text remained in print in England for the next sixty years.

[81] See entries marked *E1a* and *E2* in Textual apparatus between 62:18 and 81:13, at 95:13 and 96:29, and between 381:4 and 382:40.

[82] Letter to Martin Secker, 8 October 1921; but see footnote 103 below.

[83] Letters from Secker to Messrs. Clifford, Webster et al., UIll. For Heseltine's point of view, see Nehls, ii. 92–4.

[84] Secker and his counsel were probably aware that, as Heseltine told his solicitors, 'I can't afford to fight them' (Nehls, ii. 93). This fact suggests the unreliability of Compton Mackenzie's allegation that 'Philip Morrell . . . offered to finance Peter Warlock [Philip Heseltine], the composer, in a libel action. He was furious with an alleged portrait of his wife, Lady Ottoline, in the book, but did not want her to sue' (*My Life and Times: Octave Five*, 1966, pp. 172–3).

[85] DHL to Donald Carswell, 15 November 1921.

[86] Letters from Secker to Messrs. Clifford, Webster et al., 4 and 8 November 1921, UIll; DHL to Mountsier, 26 November 1921.

[87] DHL to Secker, 23 November 1921; Secker to DHL, 15 November 1921, UIll (*Letters from a Publisher*, p. 14). The second impression (E2) of November 1921 was reprinted in

As 1922 began, Lawrence and Frieda were making travel plans which would take them from Sicily across the ocean to Ceylon, thence to Australia, finally to San Francisco on 3 September. When they arrived in the USA, Seltzer had just defended *Women in Love* successfully against action taken by John Sumner and the New York Society for the Suppression of Vice. By winning against Sumner's attack, Seltzer stimulated a huge demand for the novel, and published a trade edition of 3,000 copies on 18 October 1922. A second printing was necessary by 3 November,[88] and a third printing the following month; as Lawrence wrote on 17 December to Catherine Carswell from New Mexico: 'I seem to have a fair sale over here – *Women in Love* going now into 15,000. Why do they read me? But anyhow, they *do* read me – which is more than England does.' 1923 brought a fourth American reprint in March, and a fifth in August.[89] Paradoxically, after nearly a decade of struggle through all the stages of composition and all the obstacles to publication, the success of *Women in Love* marked a decisive change in Lawrence's fortunes as a writer.

Reception

There were few reviews of *Women in Love*. In the USA the book was privately printed; however, John Macy gave particular and intelligent attention to it in the *New York Evening Post Literary Review* on 19 March 1921. He wrote of the new novel as a sequel to *The Rainbow*, but thought the first story of the Brangwen family richer than the second because of its greater breadth and scope. He described Lawrence as a tragic poet, and as dangerous to public morals as Hardy and Meredith; Lawrence, like Meredith, was 'almost too lyric and his phrases threaten to overflow the rigid dykes of prose' (p. 3).[90] He nevertheless believed that Lawrence controlled the 'ecstatic flights' and the 'bitterness of ecstasy' of his

December, and a third impression (E3) issued in October 1922 (1,000 copies printed on each occasion; information from ledgers held by Secker & Warburg Ltd., which contradict the details on the verso of the title pages of E2 and E3). A fire at Secker's stock warehouse, Messrs. James Burn and Co., on 12 September 1924 destroyed 16 unbound copies, presumably of E3 (Secker Memorandum, UIll); the fourth impression, issued in February 1925, may have been brought out because those unbound copies were all that remained of E3. See footnote 103. In June 1922, Secker also issued a limited autographed edition (Roberts A15b) of 50 copies, made up from sets of sheets imported from Thomas Seltzer; this sold at 63s.

88 Letters from Seltzer to Mountsier, 3 and 22 November 1922, UT (*D. H. Lawrence: Letters to Thomas and Adele Seltzer*, ed. Lacy, pp. 244–5). See 'Text' below for an account of the text of the trade edition.
89 For a complete account of publication, see Roberts 42.
90 Draper 157–60.

characters because he was a philosopher as well as a poet. It was noticeable that the American reviewers of the book were much more open to it, much less willing to characterise it as absurd or its author a madman, than their English counterparts.

Lawrence had been in correspondence with Evelyn Scott, a young American novelist and poet, before her review appeared in April 1921, and he subsequently told her that 'I didn't think your *Women in Love* review in *The Dial* very sensible. But there, we have different sets of values' (iii. 734; 693–4). She did not find the book especially successful; it 'falls, as if outside itself, into the category of confessions. Having written it, Lawrence might turn philosopher or priest. It is the last word of his living truth . . . the last word of an age in revolt against the intellectualism to which it has been betrayed' (p. 435). She recognised the 'polarised relations' of Ursula and Birkin, and linked them with the poems in *Look! We Have Come Through!*, but thought them 'less convincing than anything in the book'; and while Thomas Crich and Hermione struck her as 'subtly authentic', she felt that the novel as a whole 'lacks that quality of the arrested ephemeral which is in the pure art form'.[91]

In England, Lawrence had originally asked that no review copies be distributed (see above), and Secker at first sent out only one review copy, to the *Times Literary Supplement*; when no immediate review appeared he wrote to say that he was disappointed no reference had been made to the book.[92] A week later, on 9 June, *Women in Love* was the first novel reviewed in the 'New Novels' column of the *TLS*. The reviewer – the young poet Edmund Blunden, a regular visitor to the Morrells at Garsington Manor – found Lawrence's 'conception of love . . . defined with jubilant brutality again and again'. The scene with the rabbit in chapter XVIII was quoted at length (more than a quarter of the review consisted of quotation) to demonstrate Lawrence's fascination with 'curious' subjects, his 'unconvincing pencraft' and his preoccupation with sex. The only positive note in the whole review was that Hermione Roddice seemed a character of 'immense dignity', the 'one thing in the whole work which was worth Mr. Lawrence's powers and time or the reader's' (p. 371). Blunden's loyalty to Lady Ottoline was probably responsible for this remarkable judgment, and the *TLS* had ensured a hostile reaction to the book by choosing him for its reviewer; he declared it a 'dull, disappointing piece of work'.

Secker, however, must have been reassured by the review, and by the

[91] Draper 161–4.
[92] 2 June 1921, UIll.

initial reaction to the book; 'No prosecution papers', as he told Lawrence in July (Lawrence having 'dreamed of huge blue prosecution papers: so it is quite safe' in June). And even before the *TLS* appeared, he had assumed (he told Lawrence) that he could use his discretion 'in sending copies to a few papers, such as The [Manchester] Guardian and the Westminster Gazette, where at any rate, it will be certain of receiving proper consideration'.[93] Accordingly, other reviews began to appear in England (though Secker continued to exert discretion, refusing a review copy – for example – to the *Daily Herald*).[94] The existing reviews can be divided into those which showed some understanding of what Lawrence had accomplished and those which did not. The most extravagant of the latter was by W. Charles Pilley, assistant editor of *John Bull* (to which Secker would certainly not have sent a copy). On 17 September, he called for the suppression of the novel: 'This is the sort of book which in the hands of a boy in his teens might pave the way to unspeakable moral disaster . . . If *The Rainbow* was an indecent book this later production is an obscene abomination. The police must act' (p. 4). Pilley knew what he was doing in mentioning *The Rainbow*, which had been suppressed shortly after some reviews had called for it to be banned. According to Lawrence, Secker was 'very sick' over the *John Bull* review, but Secker recognised Philip Heseltine's threatened libel action as 'more serious'.[95] No police action was taken against the book.

In spite of Secker's belief in the paper's integrity, however, the *Westminster Gazette*'s review (written by Rose Macaulay) poked fun at the novel. It made much of the number of characters who take their clothes off; it jeered at the brightly coloured clothes of Ursula and Gudrun. Miss Macaulay also found 'Ursula and Gudrun . . . as indistinguishable in character and conversation as they are in their amours and their clothing'. Her review in *Time and Tide* was equally damning, stressing Lawrence's 'literary incompetence, silliness and imbecile-like unpleasantness'.[96] She was not alone in feeling unable to distinguish between the characters. Even John Middleton Murry in the *Nation & Athenæum* of 13 August declared that they were 'all the same', and that the relationship of Ursula and Birkin appeared no different from that of Gerald and Gudrun. But Murry at least

[93] Letters to DHL, 8 June and 12 July, UIll; DHL to Secker, 12 June 1921.
[94] 14 June 1921, UIll.
[95] DHL to Catherine Carswell, 25 October 1921; Secker to DHL, 14 September 1921. Curtis Brown, however, thought that there was 'the likelihood of police suppression, of "Women in Love"' (Curtis Brown to Mountsier, 17 September 1921, UT).
[96] *Westminster Gazette*, 2 July 1921, p. 15 (Draper 165–7); *Time and Tide*, 1 July 1921, ii. 628–9. See Explanatory note on 59:14.

responded to what he termed the 'vehemence' of Lawrence's passion. He did not find *Women in Love*, like Lawrence's earlier works, notable for its 'sensitive and impassioned apprehension of natural beauty ... or an understanding of the strange blood bonds that unite human beings, or an exquisite discrimination in the use of language, based on a power of natural vision'. Nevertheless Murry saw Lawrence not only as the 'outlaw of modern literature' but also as 'the most interesting figure in it'.[97]

The *Observer*'s unsigned review of 26 June concentrated on Lawrence's abandonment of the traditional mode of fiction. The reviewer saw how *Women in Love* 'bears all the signs of having been written before *The Lost Girl*', for in the new novel 'logical sequence, either in conversation or description, is deliberately abandoned' (p. 4). But the reviewer felt that this resulted in 'page after page' reading 'like the ravings of some unfortunate being subjected to the third degree'; the book was filled with 'nauseating rubbish about the sexes, the anger of love', where 'Mr Lawrence really comes very near quite ordinary nonsense'. The *Observer* too identified Hermione as a real and pitiful character standing 'out from the confused welter of talk and eroticism'. She and Thomas Crich were the two most memorable characters in the novel, the death scene of the latter being written with 'power and imaginative sympathy' by the Lawrence who had written *Sons and Lovers*. Even serious reviews like this were more concerned to dismiss the novel as absurd than to see what it might be saying about contemporary society.

To the *Manchester Guardian* on 15 July Frank Swinnerton contributed the novel's most positive review. He felt that at its best *Women in Love* was 'in a class apart from other novels. No writer of today has such an electrically vivid power to imagine a scene as Mr. Lawrence' (p. 5). He called attention to chapters VI, XIII and XIV as the most vivid, with such 'warm and lovely intimacies that one reads absorbed'. Swinnerton criticised Lawrence as obsessed, his language as 'goaded and extravagant', the book as 'static' and 'difficult to read'. 'It is full of absurdities', he insisted, but saw it as the writing of a man who if he got rid of 'his metaphysics and his verbiage ... will produce a masterpiece'. 'The words obey the imagination ... the best of "Women in Love" stands by itself in modern fiction.' It is indicative of the general contempt of reviewers for the book that such a critical review should also have been its most positive.

H. C. Harwood, in the *Outlook* on 13 August, also sensed Lawrence's development as a novelist; *The White Peacock* and *Sons and Lovers* were 'heavily insipid' in comparison with the new book, which was filled with

[97] P. 713; Draper 168–72.

'the passion for truth and the passion for beauty' (p. 135). But Harwood criticised the book's obscurity, the fact that its subject was 'love alone', and the way that it 'attempted a realistic setting', thus creating a 'dissonance between the characters and the background'. This suggested that 'Lawrence is a realist who has gone mad about sex, while in fact, as the whole course of his development shows, he is a romanticist and philosopher who has with difficulty disengaged himself from the realistic conventions overshadowing literature at the beginning of his career.'

Rebecca West, writing in the *New Statesman* of 9 July, found *Women in Love* 'a work of genius. It contains characters which are masterpieces of pure creation' (p. 388). This was not true of Birkin, who was seen as a 'mouthpiece', always 'patronising and knowing, like "Our London Correspondent" writing his weekly letter in a provincial newspaper'. However, Hermione was so well drawn that Lawrence 'makes visible [her] unhappy physical presence', and Thomas Crich and his wife were also 'great figures'. But Rebecca West found Lawrence 'so much a poet that it is difficult for him to express himself in prose, and in particular the prose required of a novel'. So he turned to 'desperately devised symbols' such as the bright clothes the women wear, or the 'very dark scene' of Hermione and the paperweight. Rebecca West thought Lawrence successful in conveying 'the spiritual truth with which he is concerned at the moment', though at the cost of 'a distortion of life's physical appearances'; he was 'an El Greco of literature'.

Apart from the purely hostile reviews in *John Bull*, *Time and Tide* and the *Saturday Westminster Gazette*, and the stand taken in the *TLS*, the early notice of *Women in Love*[98] was characterised by a sense that Lawrence was more a poet than a novelist, more interested in philosophy and sex than in writing convincing fiction. The extraordinariness of the book was seen as an effort (and as a failure) to enliven psychological drama; most reviews, describing the novel as feverish and its characters as unreal, contrasted it with conventional fiction in a most unhelpful way. The fact that Thomas Crich and Hermione were so frequently found the 'best drawn characters' also demonstrates the prevailing conventionality of judgement. The novel was exceptionally difficult for reviewers to come to terms with, but they showed a widespread impatience with what Lawrence might even be trying to do; a tone varying between cheerful mockery and open contempt characterised their relegation of the book to the category of the bizarre,

[98] Other reviews appeared in the *Nation* (New York) by Carl Van Doren, 26 January 1921, pp. 121–2; *London Mercury* by Edward Shanks, August 1921, p. 433; *English Review*, September 1921, p. 247; *Nation* (New York) by B. L. Burman, 17 January 1923, p. 89.

the obsessive, the muddled and the absurd. Only a handful of its reviewers – Rebecca West, Frank Swinnerton, John Macy – managed to escape the stock reaction of patronising dismissal.

Text

The earliest complete text of the novel survives in the fifth version, comprising 368 pp. of typescript in each of TSIa and TSIb making up the first three-fifths of the book, typed and revised by Lawrence between July and October 1916, together with the surviving ten-notebook draft (MS) of the remainder, either freshly written or revised during October 1916. The punctuation, styling and words of this version, however, are frequently superseded by Lawrence's revision of the typescript subsequently made of the last two-fifths of the novel, and in particular by his revision of the second typescript (TSII) typed from TSIb early in 1917. He kept TSII beside him to work on between March 1917 and September 1919 (when he sent it to Seltzer in the USA). His revision affected over 90 per cent of the pages of TSII; he also rewrote 10 per cent of it. He inserted nine pages in his own handwriting; he typed and inserted a further eight replacement or additional pages; he inserted interlinear revision on thirty-five pages so extensive that at most only a few words of the original typescript remained, and often not even those; on a further twenty-four pages his revision was so heavy that only a few phrases of the original typescript survived.[99] In this way, 76 pages out of 766 were effectively rewritten. The novel's conclusion, for example, was completely altered; the original typescript pages were removed, and four handwritten pages inserted. TSII also originally possessed thirteen chapter divisions, but in revision Lawrence divided it into thirty-one (and into thirty-two in proofs of the English edition). Because of the way in which TSII was, over an extended period of time, subjected to extensive alteration, and because it was revised after Lawrence had discovered that the novel was unlikely to be published while the war continued (and could therefore afford to revise it to accord with his own feelings of social and cultural desperation), it has been adopted as base-text. The procedure for its emendation is described below.

Because of the extreme interest of the developing text of the novel, and the difficulty of making all its successive stages of revision accessible to readers through the medium of a Textual apparatus, a supplementary volume (to be entitled *The Sisters*) will be issued at a later date, which will

[99] The handwritten pages in TSII are pp. 58–60, 331, 402, 773–6; the retyped pages are pp. 37–40, 42, 44–5, 190. See Explanatory notes on 28:13 and 124:34.

provide both the text of the novel as it stood at the end of November 1916 (when it might conceivably have been accepted by a publisher), and the variant and deleted readings of MS, TSIa and TSIb.

Lawrence posted TSII to Seltzer in September 1919; the latter retyped it, and used one of the new typescripts as his own setting-copy, while posting the other to Martin Secker in England. Neither of these typescripts is now extant, but numerous errors common to the American and English first editions (hereafter A1 and E1) must have derived from them.

Seltzer's privately printed edition of November 1920 was issued in two distinct states; in the second of these, four small errors were corrected.[100] The text of A1 is the closest of all published texts to TSII because, apart from the two omissions admitted by Seltzer, it escaped non-authorial alterations; a great many errors of transcription (particularly of punctuation), however, found their way into A1.

The surviving corrected proof copy (EP) of Secker's first English edition is a duplicate of that returned to Secker in November 1920, which does not survive; in it, Lawrence recorded (sometimes in variant form) the corrections he made for Secker. He also added to EP, in February 1921, three of the four additional alterations which Secker persuaded him to make that month.[101] EP allows us to distinguish in most cases between changes made under pressure from Secker, specific changes which Lawrence made of his own volition and those which Secker adopted in E1 without Lawrence's permission. Most of the other differences between EP and E1 are very small, and are either the result of compositor's (or publisher's) intervention, or the result of Lawrence making different alterations in his two sets of English proofs. In cases where the reading of E1 differs from the autograph corrections in EP, and cannot confidently be ascribed to compositor's (or publisher's) intervention, it has been adopted (with an Explanatory note in many cases) as almost certainly the result of Lawrence making extra or other corrections in the set of proofs he chose to return to Secker.

The textual problems in E1, published in June 1921, are considerable. There are, first, the changes Lawrence made under pressure in the page proofs and in response to Secker's subsequent requests. There is, secondly, the problem of unauthorised changes made by Secker. Thirdly, in mid-July 1921 Secker had only 377 copies unsold of the first edition of

[100] 'Im' (70:18), 'yong' (70:23), 'hinself' (218:8), 'curacoa' (282:9). It is not clear from *Letters*, iii. 618 whether DHL returned the proofs in which he noted 'slight incorrections' in time for correction of the first state of A1, or indeed whether he returned a proof to Seltzer at all.

[101] See footnote 74.

1,500 copies, and presumably only a handful of sets of unbound sheets. Sometime after October 1921, such sheets were in a few cases bound in combination with newly printed sheets containing some of the alterations demanded by Heseltine and made by Lawrence in September–October 1921; one copy of mixed gatherings (hereafter E1a) has been located.[102] Nearly all of the required changes were incorporated in the second English printing (E2), issued in November 1921, but references to 'Pussum' in chapters XVII and XXVIII remained in print for the duration of the edition.[103]

In preparing the American trade edition of October 1922 (hereafter A2), Seltzer checked A1 against E1 and incorporated some of E1's punctuation, but only selectively included E1's changes of wording.[104] It is most unlikely that Lawrence asked for or saw proofs of the composite text of A2; it bears no authority, and although it has been collated with A1 and E1, its readings have not been included in the Textual apparatus.

Emendation of the base-text TSII must take into account the sources of error and difference. Pinker's typist made errors when typing the last two-fifths of TSIa and TSIb, and also in TSII (probably typed by the same person, to judge by the similarities of layout and style.) Lawrence's revision of the two typescripts TSIa and TSIb began when he was still typing; this can be seen when he had to retype a page after failing to insert carbon paper. He incorporated revisions already made to the first ribbon copy, showing that those revisions had been made immediately after the page was first typed.[105] His normal practice was to correct one of the two copies of a particular page or section, and then transfer the corrections to the other copy; or leave that responsibility to Frieda Lawrence. However, there is no evidence of his having designated one copy the primary copy;[106]

---

[102] At UT; see Roberts 43. Eighteen signatures of E1 never appear to have been re-set (A-B, H-K, P-S, Z-2A, 2C-2I), though signature 2C had a number of changes stripped into pp. 403–6 when it appeared in E2. E1a contained signatures C-D, G, L-O, T-Y in the re-set form in which they appeared in E2 (signatures D and G also being revised following Heseltine's demands), but it retained signatures E-F and 2B (which were re-set for E2, E-F revised) in their original state.

[103] At 233:8 and 380:31. It seems possible, too, that E2 utilised some of the unaltered and unused signatures printed for E1. E3 was a reprint of E2, with the exception of two minor typographical changes (at 44:14 and 330:30); the fourth impression of February 1925 reprinted E3.

[104] The three changes of wording in A2 which originate neither in A1 nor in E1 are most unlikely to derive from proof-correction by DHL (see footnote 100). See Explanatory notes on 181:5, 455:7 and 463:20.

[105] E.g. p. 338, where TSIb represents the second (and revised) typing.

[106] DHL appears to have made one copy of his two typescripts of *Mr Noon* primary (although he did not treat them in this way: both were sent out for publication): TCCI contains

it can be seen that he revised both TSIa and TSIb on several different occasions, sometimes working first in one and sometimes first in the other; he included some carbon pages in the ribbon copy, and vice versa, according to no observable pattern. He does not, therefore, appear to have been constructing one primary text and one subsidiary, but to have been preparing two typescripts, each including early and later revisions, first and second thoughts, which now occur at random. As he also made most of his corrections with the same pen, in the same ink, it is normally impossible to be certain in what order they were made, or – if they differ – which were made first. Nor can we always be sure whether his variant revisions in the two typescripts resulted from second thoughts, or from error.[107]

The extent of Frieda's contribution to the novel, too, is questionable. She was responsible for helping to transcribe Lawrence's revisions from TSIa into TSIb (on over 145 pages), and vice versa (on over 75); her work ranged from correction of typing errors, to copying single words, to transcribing nearly a complete page of dialogue. However, she also mis-transcribed (or failed to transcribe) on numerous occasions; her errors ranged from altering punctuation to the addition of a word or words (or their omission); she also mistakenly deleted and left in lines. In several instances, she made changes on both copies of the typescript. Although her handwriting is markedly different from Lawrence's, because she used the same ink (and possibly the same pen) it is often impossible to decide which of them was responsible for a deletion appearing in only one copy, or for deletions in both copies, or for punctuation variants between the two copies. Again, we cannot always tell whether the non-transference of a revision from one copy to the other was due to her error, or to the fact that Lawrence continued to make revisions in the copy she had transcribed from, after her work was over.[108] The problem is compounded by the fact that, as stated above, we often cannot be certain of the sequence of Lawrence's revisions, or of transcriptions by either of them, in the same pair of pages.

Because Lawrence sent TSIb to Pinker in January 1917, in the full knowledge that it would be used to create TSII, his own revisions in TSIb

most of his latest revisions, TSI was usually revised first (see *Mr Noon*, ed. Lindeth Vasey, Cambridge University Press, 1984, pp. xxxviii–xxxix).

[107] E.g. p. 363, where DHL created punctuation variants ('yourself,' and 'womanhood—' in TSIa, 'yourself' and 'womanhood,' in TSIb); see too footnote 115.

[108] E.g. p. 118, where 'then' is deleted in TSIa but not in TSIb, and p. 186, where 'since' is replaced by 'when' in TSIa but not in TSIb. Transcriptions by DHL and Frieda appear on both pages in TSIb; it is impossible to decide whose responsibility it might have been to transfer the revisions. See Explanatory note on 203:10 for an example of Frieda's failure to transfer a revision from TSIa (p. 249).

should take priority over those he made in TSIa. But great care needs to be exercised in ruling whether a revision present in TSIa should have been transferred to TSIb, either by Lawrence or by Frieda, or in ruling whether it was error, or choice, that prevented its transcription. The procedure adopted, therefore, needs to be described.

1. When Frieda introduced mistranscriptions into TSIa, they have been ignored.

2. When Frieda introduced mistranscriptions into TSIb, Lawrence's reading in TSIa has normally been given priority;[109] exceptions have been discussed in the Explanatory notes.

3. Where subsequent revision by Lawrence in TSII is so extensive as to prevent any return to his original reading or revision in MS or TSIa, then the reading of TSII (which in some cases must incorporate Frieda's influence upon the text) has normally been accepted;[110] exceptions have been discussed in the Explanatory notes.

4. Where Frieda was responsible for the reading of both TSIa and TSIb, it has been judged that her influence has acquired the status of collaboration, and her contributions have been accepted unless there are additional reasons for rejecting them.[111] In the latter case, Lawrence's original readings have been restored, and an Explanatory note provided.[112]

5. Where apparently authorial revisions of punctuation and underlining were made in TSIa but were not transferred by Frieda (or by Lawrence) to TSIb, they have normally been adopted, on the grounds that such revisions would have been exceptionally easy to overlook.[113]

6. Where it is impossible to be certain whether revisions in TSIa should have been transferred to TSIb by Frieda – either because the revisions may have been added after her job of transcription was over, or because both Lawrence's and Frieda's handwriting appears on the page in question in TSIb, proving them both at different times responsible for transcribing revisions on to the same page – then editorial policy has

[109] See Textual apparatus entries for 86:25, 86:26, 90:40 etc. Entries showing TSIa preferred to TSIb normally represent such cases. Frieda's influence on the text was, however, minimal in the two-fifths of TSI typed in Pinker's office and corrected by DHL and Frieda in November 1916; see e.g. Explanatory notes on 405:16 and 406:37.

[110] See Explanatory notes on 86:23, 97:2, 212:34 and 268:16 for instances where Frieda's influence on the text remains. Entries at 136:31 and 267:18 show where DHL's revision (provoked by Frieda's effect on the text) has been rejected in favour of his earlier reading.

[111] See Explanatory notes on 142:9, 184:31, 187:39, 189:4, 198:6, 230:10, 237:27, 269:32, 280:14 and 294:14.

[112] See Explanatory notes on 88:16, 155:28, 159:9, 239:7 and 261:11.

[113] See e.g. Textual apparatus entries for 188:14 and 192:1.

been conservative. We have accepted that Frieda failed to transcribe only where there is evidence – or a strong probability – that she failed to do so.[114]

7. Where it is probable that the failure to transcribe revisions was Lawrence's own responsibility, to judge by the presence of his hand-writing alone on the equivalent pages of both TSIa and TSIb, then the readings of TSIb have been adopted.[115]

Punctuation alterations made in pencil in TSII[116] have been assumed not to be by Lawrence, except in short sections where substantives were also revised in pencil.[117]

The base-text has been emended from EP and E1 only where they offer clear evidence of Lawrence making changes without external pressure; such cases are, of course, listed in the Textual apparatus, and a number are also discussed in the Explanatory notes.

The punctuation and wording of base-text have, therefore, been emended where earlier states of the text can be used to correct errors in transcription, or where later states of the text include revisions which must take priority. This edition thus strips off layers of error and mistranscription which affected both first editions produced in the author's lifetime, and which have been enshrined in all subsequent printings. It also restores passages which were censored or changed in E1 through threat of legal action. For the first time, Lawrence's 'terrible and horrible and wonderful novel' (ii. 669) appears in a text in which his own expectations may be said to have been realised: 'The book frightens me: it is so end-of-the-world. But it is, it must be, the beginning of a new world too' (iii. 25–6).

---

[114] See e.g. Explanatory notes on 95:8 and 256:37.

[115] E.g. in TSIa (p. 103), but not in TSIb, DHL revised 'looked at' to 'apprehend'; in TSIa (p. 117), but not in TSIb, he revised 'flowerlike' to 'Bacchic' and 'in tiers' to 'in three levels'. His hand alone appears in the revisions on both pages.

[116] E.g. commas or full stops revised to question marks (TSII p. 133), an accent added (TSII p. 92), a ligature added (TSII p. 202). TSI also shows pencil corrections, not by DHL, where a reader altered 'rowed' to 'paddled' (TSIa, pp. 198 and 218) and underlined 'disquality' three times (TSIb, p. 276). See too Explanatory note on 132:8.

[117] E.g. TSII pp. 212–26, 577.

WOMEN IN LOVE

Note on the text

The base-text for this edition is the corrected final typescript (TSII) which was typed early in 1917 and which DHL finally revised for publication in September 1919; it was the copy from which a clean typescript was made for Thomas Seltzer's first American edition (A1) and for Martin Secker's first English edition (E1). TSII is in the Harry Ransom Humanities Research Center, University of Texas at Austin.

Emendations have been adopted from DHL's own typescript (TSIa and TSIb) up to the end of chapter XXII and from his manuscript (MS) and from revisions to the second part of the typescript, prepared by Pinker; from DHL's revisions in the duplicate surviving page proofs (EP) for E1; and from the revisions which must have been in the set of page proofs returned to Secker for E1. In addition, the apparatus records the changes and omissions required by both Seltzer and Secker for censorship purposes (some made without consulting DHL), and the changes, some made by DHL, which were forced on Secker and DHL by Philip Heseltine's threat of a libel suit (see Introduction, pp. xlix–l). Also, Frieda Lawrence assisted DHL by copying revisions into TSIa and TSIb: in doing so, she made errors or introduced changes of her own, and these are recorded (see Introduction, pp. xxxii, lix–lxi and also Explanatory notes).

1. Clearly inadvertent spelling and typesetting errors have been corrected. DHL occasionally closed conversation with a comma, changed the punctuation but failed to delete the superfluous comma, e.g. 'now?," ' (240:15); the comma has been silently deleted.

2. Inadvertent omissions, i.e. incomplete quotations marks and full stops omitted at the end of sentences where no other punctuation exists, have been supplied. Omitted or misplaced apostrophes in possessive case, colloquial contractions and the apostrophe in 'o'clock' have been supplied or corrected.

3. DHL often wrote and sometimes typed colloquial contractions without joining them up, e.g. 'does n't', and typed them without the apostrophe, 'dont', while Frieda sometimes misplaced the apostrophe, 'does'nt'; these have been normalised, 'doesn't'.

4. The typists of the second part of TSI and of TSII, and A1 and E1 consistently presented 'to-day', 'to-morrow', 'to-night' and 'good-bye', 'good-night' (DHL wrote and typed these as one unhyphenated word); TSII and A1 gave 'Mr.' and 'Mrs.' (DHL usually wrote and typed them without the full stop); A1 sometimes house-styled '-is-' to '-iz-' (DHL wrote 'realise' and 'civilised'). In all these instances, DHL's practice has been preserved.

5. DHL often followed a full stop, question mark or exclamation mark with a dash before beginning the next sentence with a capital letter, e.g. 'consideration.—One' (21:6). His typists and the typesetter of E1 frequently omitted the dash, which has been restored in this edition. A1 and E1 printed punctuation following an italicised word in italics, e.g. '*Really!*' (8:1), whereas DHL usually did not italicise punctuation; italic punctuation is only recorded when it is part of another variant.

6. Many pencil corrections were made to TSII while it was being prepared for the typist or the printer, including the marking of foreign words and phrases to be italicised and the alteration of DHL's punctuation to the more usual question mark (e.g. 45:7; 50:9). As most such pencil changes are non-authorial, DHL's original punctuation has been reinstated.

7. A1 does not have the chapter titles which were inserted in EP by DHL at Secker's request. DHL wrote the titles in upper and lower case and sometimes put a full stop after them in EP, but E1 printed the word 'Chapter' and the titles in capitals with no stop; emendation to lower-case type and deletion of the full stops have not been recorded.

8. Because of Heseltine's threatened lawsuit Secker agreed to change the name 'Pussum' and 'the Pussum' to 'Minette', and references to 'Pussums' to 'Minettes'. This was done in E1a (on signatures D and G) and on more than sixty occasions in E2. The original name has been restored.

9. Inconsistencies in DHL's hyphenation have been regularised according to majority usage in this text. Inconsistencies in paragraphing have also been regularised.

Contents

Chapter I

Sisters*

Ursula and Gudrun Brangwen* sat one morning in the window-bay of their father's house in Beldover,* working and talking. Ursula was stitching a piece of brightly-coloured embroidery, and Gudrun was drawing upon a board which she held on her knee. They were mostly silent, talking as their thoughts strayed through their minds.

"Ursula," said Gudrun, "don't you *really want* to get married?"

Ursula laid her embroidery in her lap and looked up. Her face was calm and considerate.

"I don't know," she replied. "It depends how you mean."

Gudrun was slightly taken aback. She watched her sister for some moments.

"Well," she said, ironically, "it usually means one thing!—But don't you think, anyhow, you'd be—" she darkened slightly—"in a better position than you are in now?"

A shadow came over Ursula's face.

"I might," she said. "But I'm not sure."

Again Gudrun paused, slightly irritated. She wanted to be quite definite.

"You don't think one needs the *experience* of having been married?" she asked.

"Do you think it need *be* an experience?" replied Ursula.

"Bound to be, in some way or other," said Gudrun, coolly. "Possibly undesirable, but bound to be an experience of some sort."

"Not really," said Ursula. "More likely to be the end of experience."

Gudrun sat very still, to attend to this.

"Of course," she said, "there's *that* to consider."

This brought the conversation to a close. Gudrun, almost angrily, took up her rubber and began to rub out part of her drawing. Ursula stitched absorbedly.

"You wouldn't consider a good offer?" asked Gudrun.

"I think I've rejected several," said Ursula.

7

"*Really!*" Gudrun flushed dark.—"But anything really worth while? Have you *really?*"

"A thousand a year, and an awfully nice man. I liked him awfully," said Ursula.

"Really! But weren't you fearfully tempted?"

"In the abstract—but not in the concrete," said Ursula. "When it comes to the point, one isn't even tempted.—Oh, if I were tempted, I'd marry like a shot.—I'm only tempted *not* to." The faces of both sisters suddenly lit up with amusement.

"Isn't it an amazing thing," cried Gudrun, "how strong the temptation is, not to!"

They both laughed, looking at each other. In their hearts they were frightened.

There was a long pause, whilst Ursula stitched and Gudrun went on with her sketch. The sisters were women, Ursula twenty-six and Gudrun twenty-five. But both had the remote, virgin look of modern girls, sisters of Artemis rather than of Hebe.* Gudrun was very beautiful, passive, soft-skinned, soft-limbed. She wore a dress of dark-blue silky stuff, with ruches of blue and green linen lace in the neck and sleeves; and she had emerald-green stockings.* Her look of confidence and diffidence contrasted with Ursula's sensitive expectancy. The provincial people, intimidated by Gudrun's perfect sang froid and exclusive bareness of manner, said of her: "She is a smart woman." She had just come back from London, where she had spent several years, working at an art-school, as a student, and living a studio life.

"I was hoping now for a man to come along," Gudrun said, suddenly catching her underlip between her teeth, and making a strange grimace, half sly smiling, half anguish.

Ursula was afraid.

"So you have come home, expecting him here?" she laughed.

"Oh my dear," cried Gudrun, strident, "I wouldn't go out of my way to look for him. But if there did happen to come along a highly attractive individual of sufficient means—well——" she tailed off ironically. Then she looked searchingly at Ursula, as if to probe her. "Don't you find yourself getting bored?" she asked of her sister. "Don't you find, that things fail to materialise? *Nothing materialises!* Everything withers in the bud."

"What withers in the bud?" asked Ursula.

"Oh, everything—oneself—things in general."

There* was a pause, whilst each sister vaguely considered her fate.

"It does frighten one," said Ursula, and again there was a pause. "But do you hope to get anywhere by just marrying?"

"It seems to be the inevitable next step," said Gudrun.

Ursula pondered this, with a little bitterness. She was a class mistress herself, in Willey Green Grammar School, as she had been for some years.

"I know," she said, "it seems like that when one thinks in the abstract. But really imagine it: imagine any man one knows, imagine him coming home to one every evening, and saying 'Hello,' and giving one a kiss—"

There was a blank pause.

"Yes," said Gudrun, in a narrowed voice. "It's just impossible. The man makes it impossible."

"Of course there's children—" said Ursula, doubtfully.

Gudrun's face hardened.

"Do you *really* want children, Ursula?" she asked coldly.

A dazzled, baffled look came on Ursula's face.

"One feels it is still beyond one," she said.

"*Do* you feel like that?" asked Gudrun. "I get no feeling whatever from the thought of bearing children."

Gudrun looked at Ursula with a mask-like, expressionless face. Ursula knitted her brows.

"Perhaps it isn't genuine," she faltered. "Perhaps one doesn't really want them, in one's soul—only superficially."

A hardness came over Gudrun's face. She did not want to be too definite.

"When one thinks of other people's children—" said Ursula.

Again Gudrun looked at her sister, almost hostile.

"Exactly," she said, to close the conversation.

The two sisters worked on in silence, Ursula having always that strange brightness of an essential flame that is caught, meshed, contravened. She lived a good deal by herself, to herself, working, passing on from day to day, and always thinking, trying to lay hold on life, to grasp it in her own understanding. Her active living was suspended, but underneath, in the darkness, something was coming to pass. If only she could break through the last integuments! She seemed to try to put her hands out, like an infant in the womb, and she could not, not yet. Still she had a strange prescience, an intimation of something yet to come.

She laid down her work and looked at her sister. She thought Gudrun so *charming*, so infinitely charming, in her softness and her fine, exquisite richness of texture and delicacy of line. There was a certain playfulness about her too, such a piquancy of ironic sugges-
5 tion, such an untouched reserve. Ursula admired her with all her soul.

"Why did you come home, Prune?"* she asked.

Gudrun knew she was being admired. She sat back from her drawing and looked at Ursula, from under her finely-curved lashes.

10 "Why did I come back, Ursula?" she repeated. "I have asked myself, a thousand times."

"And don't you know?"

"Yes, I think I do. I think my coming back home was just *reculer pour mieux sauter*."*

15 And she looked with a long, slow look of knowledge at Ursula.

"I know!" cried Ursula, looking slightly dazzled and falsified, and as if she did *not* know. "But where can one jump *to*?"

"Oh, it doesn't matter," said Gudrun, somewhat superbly. "If one jumps over the edge, one is bound to land somewhere."

20 "But isn't it very risky?" asked Ursula.

A slow, mocking smile dawned on Gudrun's face.

"Ah!" she said, laughing. "What is it all but words!"

And so again she closed the conversation. But Ursula was still brooding.

25 "And how do you find home, now you have come back to it?" she asked.

Gudrun paused for some moments, coldly, before answering. Then, in a cold, truthful voice, she said:

"I find myself completely out of it."

30 "And father?"

Gudrun looked at Ursula, almost with resentment, as if brought to bay.

"I haven't thought about him: I've refrained," she said coldly.

"Yes," wavered Ursula; and the conversation was really at an end.
35 The sisters found themselves confronted by a void, a terrifying chasm, as if they had looked over the edge.

They worked on in silence for some time. Gudrun's cheek was flushed with repressed emotion. She resented its having been called into being.

40 "Shall we go out and look at that wedding?" she asked at length, in a voice that was too casual.

"Yes!" cried Ursula, too eagerly, throwing aside her sewing and leaping up, as if to escape something, thus betraying the tension of the situation, and causing a friction of dislike to go over Gudrun's nerves.

As she went upstairs, Ursula was aware of the house, of her home round about her. And she loathed it, the sordid, too-familiar place! She was afraid at the depth of her feeling against the home, the milieu, the whole atmosphere and condition of this obsolete life. Her feeling frightened her.

The two girls were soon walking swiftly down the main road of Beldover, a wide street, part shops, part dwelling houses, utterly formless and sordid, without poverty. Gudrun, new from her life in Chelsea and Sussex, shrank cruelly from this amorphous ugliness of a small colliery town in the midlands. Yet forward she went, through the whole sordid gamut of pettiness, the long, amorphous, gritty street. She was exposed to every stare, she passed on through a stretch of torment. It was strange that she should have chosen to come back and test the full effect of this shapeless, barren ugliness upon herself. Why had she wanted to submit herself to it, did she still want to submit herself to it, the insufferable torture of these ugly, meaningless people, this defaced countryside? She felt like a beetle toiling* in the dust. She was filled with repulsion.

They turned off the main road, past a black patch of common-garden, where sooty cabbage stumps stood shameless. No one thought to be ashamed. No one was ashamed of it all.

"It is like a country in an underworld," said Gudrun. "The colliers bring it above-ground with them, shovel it up. Ursula, it's marvellous, it's really marvellous—it's really wonderful, another world. The people are all ghouls, and everything is ghostly. Everything is a ghoulish replica of the real world, a replica, a ghoul, all soiled, everything sordid. It's like being mad, Ursula."

The sisters were crossing a black path through a dark, soiled field. On the left was a large landscape, a valley with collieries, and opposite hills with cornfields and woods, all blackened with distance, as if seen through a veil of crape. White and black smoke rose up in steady columns, magic within the dark air. Near at hand came the long rows of dwellings, approaching curved up the hill-slope, in straight lines along the brow of the hill. They were of darkened red brick, brittle, with dark slate roofs.

The path on which the sisters walked was black, trodden-in by the feet of the recurrent colliers, and bounded from the field by iron fences; the stile that led again into the road was rubbed shiny by the moleskins* of the passing miners. Now the two girls were going between some rows of dwellings, of the poorer sort. Women, their arms folded over their coarse aprons, standing gossiping at the end

5 of their block, stared after the Brangwen sisters with that long, unwearying stare of aborigines; children called out names.

Gudrun went on her way half dazed. If this were human life, if these were human beings, living in a complete world, then what was her own world, outside? She was aware of her grass-green stockings,

10 her large, grass-green velour hat, her full, soft coat, of a strong blue colour. And she felt as if she were treading in the air, quite unstable, her heart was contracted, as if at any minute she might be precipitated to the ground. She was afraid.

She clung to Ursula, who, through long usage was inured to this

15 violation of a dark, uncreated, hostile world. But all the time her heart was crying, as if in the midst of some ordeal: "I want to go back, I want to go away, I want not to know it, not to know that this exists." Yet she must go forward.

Ursula could feel her suffering.

20 "You hate this, don't you?" she asked.

"It bewilders me," stammered Gudrun.

"You won't stay long," replied Ursula.

And Gudrun went along, grasping at release.

They drew away from the colliery region, over the curve of the hill,

25 into the purer country of the other side, towards Willey Green. Still the faint glamour of blackness persisted over the fields and the wooded hills, and seemed darkly to gleam in the air. It was a spring day, chill, with snatches of sunshine. Yellow celandines showed out from the hedge-bottoms, and in the cottage gardens of Willey

30 Green, currant-bushes were breaking into leaf, and little flowers were coming white on the grey alyssum* that hung over the stone walls.

Turning, they passed down the high-road, that went between high banks,* towards the church. There, in the lowest bend of the road,

35 low under the trees and the wall of the churchyard, which was above their heads, stood a little group of expectant people, waiting to see the wedding. The daughter of the chief mine-owner of the district, Thomas Crich,* was getting married to a naval officer.

"Let us go back," said Gudrun, swerving away. "There are all

40 those people."

And she hung wavering in the road.

"Never mind them," said Ursula, "they're all right. They all know me, they don't matter."

"But must we go through them?" asked Gudrun.

"They're quite all right, really," said Ursula, going forward.   5

And together the two sisters approached the group of uneasy, watchful common people. They were chiefly women, colliers' wives of the more shiftless sort. They had watchful, underworld faces.

The two sisters held themselves tense, and went straight towards the gate. The women made way for them, but barely sufficient, as if   10
grudging to yield ground. The sisters passed in silence through the stone gateway and up the steps, on the red carpet, a policeman estimating their progress.

"What price* the stockings!" said a voice at the back of Gudrun. A sudden fierce anger swept over the girl, violent and murderous. She   15
would have liked them all to be annihilated, cleared away, so that the world was left clear for her. How she hated walking up the churchyard path, along the red carpet, continuing in motion, in their sight.

"I won't go into the church," she said suddenly, with such final   20
decision that Ursula immediately halted, turned round, and branched off up a small side path which led to the little private gate of the Grammar School, whose grounds adjoined those of the church.

Just inside the gate of the school shrubbery, outside the church-yard, Ursula sat down for a moment on the low stone wall under the   25
laurel bushes, to rest. Behind her, the large red building of the school rose up peacefully, the windows all open for the holiday. Over the shrubs, before her, were the pale roofs and tower of the old church. The sisters were hidden by the foliage.

Gudrun sat down in silence. Her mouth was shut close, her face   30
averted. She was regretting bitterly that she had ever come back. Ursula looked at her, and thought how amazingly beautiful she was, flushed with discomfiture. But she caused a constraint over Ursula's nature, a certain weariness. Ursula wished to be alone, freed from the tightness, the enclosure of Gudrun's presence.   35

"Are we going to stay here?" asked Gudrun.

"I was only resting a minute," said Ursula, getting up as if rebuked. "We will stand in the corner by the fives-court, we shall see everything from there."

For the moment, the sunshine fell brightly into the churchyard,   40 there was a vague scent of sap and of spring, perhaps of violets from off the graves. Some white daisies were out, bright as angels. In the air, the unfolding leaves of a copper-beech were blood-red.

Punctually at eleven o'clock, the carriages began to arrive. There
5 was a stir in the crowd at the gate, a concentration as a carriage drove up, wedding guests were mounting up the steps and passing along the red carpet to the church. They were all gay and excited because the sun was shining.

Gudrun watched them closely, with objective curiosity. She saw
10 each one as a complete figure, like a character in a book, or a subject in a picture, or a marionette in a theatre, a finished creation. She loved to recognise their various characteristics, to place them in their true light, give them their own surroundings, settle them for ever as they passed before her along the path to the church. She knew them,
15 they were finished, sealed and stamped and finished with, for her. There were none that had anything unknown, unresolved, until the Criches themselves began to appear. Then her interest was piqued. Here was something not quite so preconcluded.

There came the mother, Mrs Crich, with her eldest son Gerald.
20 She was a queer unkempt figure, in spite of the attempts that had obviously been made to bring her into line for the day. Her face was pale, yellowish, with a clear, transparent skin, she leaned forward rather, her features were strongly marked, handsome, with a tense, unseeing, predative look. Her colourless hair was untidy, wisps
25 floating down on to her sac coat* of dark blue silk, from under her blue silk hat. She looked like a woman with a monomania, furtive almost, but heavily proud.

Her son was of a fair, sun-tanned type, rather above middle height, well-made, and almost exaggeratedly well-dressed. But
30 about him also was the strange, guarded look, the unconscious glisten, as if he did not belong to the same creation as the people about him.

Gudrun lighted on him at once. There was something northern* about him that magnetised her. In his clear northern flesh and his
35 fair hair was a glisten like cold* sunshine refracted through crystals of ice. And he looked so new, unbroached, pure as an arctic thing. Perhaps he was thirty years old, perhaps more. His gleaming beauty, maleness, like a young, good-humoured, smiling wolf did not blind her to the significant, sinister stillness in his bearing, the lurking
40 danger of his unsubdued temper. "His totem is the wolf," she

repeated* to herself. "His mother is an old, unbroken wolf." And then she experienced a keen paroxysm, a transport, as if she had made some incredible discovery, known to nobody else on earth. A strange transport took possession of her, all her veins were in a paroxysm of violent sensation. "Good God!" she exclaimed to herself, "what is this?" And then, a moment after, she was saying assuredly, "I shall know more of that man." She was tortured with desire to see him again, a nostalgia, a necessity to see him again, to make sure it was not all a mistake, that she was not deluding herself, that she really felt this strange and overwhelming sensation on his account, this knowledge of him in her essence, this powerful apprehension of him. "Am I *really* singled out for him in some way, is there really some pale gold, arctic light that envelopes only us two?" she asked herself. And she could not believe it, she remained in a muse, scarcely conscious of what was going on around.

The bridesmaids were here, and yet the bridegroom had not come. Ursula wondered if something was amiss, and if the wedding would yet all go wrong. She felt troubled, as if it rested upon her. The chief bridesmaids had arrived. Ursula watched them come up the steps. One of them she knew, a tall, slow, reluctant woman with a weight of fair hair and a pale, long face. This was Hermione Roddice,* a friend of the Criches. Now she came along, with her head held up, balancing an enormous flat hat of pale yellow velvet, on which were streaks of ostrich feathers, natural and grey. She drifted forward as if scarcely conscious, her long, blenched face lifted up, not to see the world. She was rich. She wore a dress of silky, frail velvet, of pale yellow colour, and she carried a lot of small rose-coloured cyclamens. Her shoes and stockings were of brownish grey, like the feathers on her hat, her hair was heavy, she drifted along with a peculiar fixity of the hips, a strange unwilling motion. She was impressive, in her lovely pale-yellow and brownish-rose, yet macabre, something repulsive. People were silent when she passed, impressed, roused, wanting to jeer, yet for some reason silenced. Her long, pale face, that she carried lifted up, somewhat in the Rossetti fashion,* seemed almost drugged, as if a strange mass of thoughts coiled in the darkness within her, and she was never allowed to escape.

Ursula watched her with fascination. She knew her a little. She was the most remarkable woman in the midlands. Her father was a Derbyshire Baronet of the old school,* she was a woman of the new

school, full of intellectuality, and heavy, nerve-worn with consciousness. She was passionately interested in reform, her soul was given
up to the public cause. But she was a man's woman, it was the manly
world that held her.

5   She had various intimacies of mind and soul, with various men of
capacity. Ursula knew, among these men, only Rupert Birkin,* who
was one of the school-inspectors for the county. But Gudrun had
met others, in London. Moving with her artist friends in different
kinds of society, Gudrun had already come to know a good many
10   people of repute and standing. She had met Hermione twice, but
they did not take to each other. It would be queer to meet again down
here in the midlands, where their social standing was so diverse,
after they had known each other on terms of equality in the houses of
sundry acquaintances in town. For Gudrun had been a social
15   success, and had her friends among the slack aristocracy that keeps
touch with the arts.

Hermione knew herself to be well-dressed; she knew herself to be
the social equal, if not far the superior, of anyone she was likely to
meet in Willey Green. She knew she was accepted in the world of
20   culture and of intellect. She was a *Kulturträger,** a medium for the
culture of ideas. With all that was highest, whether in society or in
thought or in public action, or even in art, she was at one, she moved
among the foremost, at home with them. No one could put her
down, no one could make mock of her, because she stood among the
25   first, and those that were against her were below her, either in rank,
or in wealth, or in high association of thought and progress and
understanding. So, she was invulnerable. All her life, she had sought
to make herself invulnerable, unassailable, beyond reach of the
world's judgment.

30   And yet her soul was tortured, exposed. Even walking up the path
to the church, confident as she was that in every respect she stood
beyond all vulgar judgment, knowing perfectly that her appearance
was complete and perfect, according to the first standards, yet she
suffered a torture, under her confidence and her pride, feeling
35   herself exposed to wounds and to mockery and to despite. She
always felt vulnerable, vulnerable, there was always a secret chink in
her armour. She did not know herself what it was. It was a lack of
robust self, she had no natural sufficiency, there was a terrible void, a
lack, a deficiency of being within her.

40   And she wanted someone to close up this deficiency, to close it up

for ever. She craved for Rupert Birkin. When he was there, she felt complete, she was sufficient, whole. For the rest of time she was established on the sand,* built over a chasm, and, in spite of all her vanity and securities, any common maid-servant of positive, robust temper could fling her down this bottomless pit of insufficiency, by the slightest movement of jeering or contempt. And all the while the pensive, tortured woman piled up her own defences of aesthetic knowledge, and culture, and world-visions, and disinterestedness. Yet she could never stop up the terrible gap of insufficiency.

If only Birkin would form a close and abiding connection with her, she would be safe during this fretful voyage of life. He could make her sound and triumphant, triumphant over the very angels of heaven. If only he would do it! But she was tortured with fear, with misgiving. She made herself beautiful, she strove so hard to come to that degree of beauty and advantage, when he should be convinced. But always there was a deficiency.

He was perverse too. He fought her off, he always fought her off. The more she strove to bring him to her, the more he battled her back. And they had been lovers now, for years. Oh, it was so wearying, so aching; she was so tired. But still she believed in herself. She knew he was trying to leave her. She knew he was trying to break away from her finally, to be free. But still she believed in her strength to keep him, she believed in her own higher knowledge. Her own knowledge was higher, she was the first* touchstone of truth. She only needed his conjunction with her.

And this, this conjunction with her, which was his highest fulfilment also, with the perverseness of a wilful child he wanted to deny. With the wilfulness of an obstinate child, he wanted to break the holy connection that was between them.

He would be at this wedding; he was to be groom's man. He would be in the church, waiting. He would know when she came. She shuddered with nervous apprehension and desire as she went through the church door. He would be there, surely he would see how beautiful her dress was, surely he would see how she had made herself beautiful for him. He would understand, surely he would understand, he would be able to see how she was made for him, the first, how she was, for him, the highest. Surely at last he would be able to accept his highest fate, he would not deny her.

In a little convulsion of too-tired yearning, she entered the church and looked slowly along her cheeks for him, her slender body convulsed with agitation. As best man, he would be standing beside the altar. She looked slowly, deferring in her certainty.

And then, he was not there. A terrible storm came over her, as if she were drowning. She was possessed by a devastating hopeless-
5 ness. And she approached mechanically to the altar. Never had she known such a pang of utter and final hopelessness. It was beyond death, so utterly null, desert.

The bridegroom and the groom's man had not yet come. There was a growing consternation outside. Ursula felt almost responsible.
10 She could not bear it that the bride should arrive, and no groom. The wedding must not be a fiasco, it must not.

But here was the bride's carriage, adorned with ribbons and cockades. Gaily the grey horses curvetted to their destination at the church-gate, a laughter in the whole movement. Here was the quick
15 of all laughter and pleasure. The door of the carriage was thrown open, to let out the very blossom of the day. The people on the roadway murmured faintly with the discontented murmuring of a crowd.

The father stepped out first into the air of the morning, like a
20 shadow. He was a tall, thin, careworn man, with a thin black beard that was touched with grey. He waited at the door of the carriage patiently, self-obliterated.

In the opening of the doorway was a shower of fine foliage and flowers, a whiteness of satin and lace, and a sound of a gay voice
25 saying:

"How do I get out?"

A ripple of satisfaction ran through the expectant people. They pressed near to receive her, looking with zest at the stooping blond head with its flower buds, and at the delicate, white, tentative foot
30 that was reaching down to the step of the carriage. There was a sudden foaming rush, and the bride like a sudden surf-rush, floating all white beside her father in the morning shadow of trees, her veil flowing with laughter.

"That's done it!" she said.

35 She put her hand on the arm of her careworn, sallow father, and frothing her light draperies, proceeded over the eternal red carpet. Her father, mute and yellowish, his black beard making him look more careworn, mounted the steps stiffly, as if his spirit were absent; but the laughing mist of the bride went along with him un-
40 diminished.

And no bridegroom had arrived! It was intolerable for her. Ursula, her heart strained with anxiety, was watching the hill beyond; the white, descending road, that should give sight of him. There was a carriage. It was running. It had just come into sight. Yes, it was he. Ursula turned towards the bride and the people, and, from her place of vantage, gave an inarticulate cry. She wanted to warn them that he was coming. But her cry was inarticulate and inaudible, and she flushed deeply, between her desire and her wincing confusion.

The carriage rattled down the hill, and drew near. There was a shout from the people. The bride, who had just reached the top of the steps, turned round gaily to see what was the commotion. She saw a confusion among the people, a cab pulling up, and her lover dropping out of the carriage, and dodging among the horses and into the crowd.

"Tibs!* Tibs!" she cried in her sudden, mocking excitement, standing high on the path in the sunlight and waving her bouquet. He, dodging with his hat in his hand, had not heard.

"Tibs!" she cried again, looking down to him.

He glanced up, unaware, and saw the bride and her father standing on the path above him. A queer, startled look went over his face. He hesitated for a moment. Then he gathered himself together for the leap, to overtake her.

"Ah-h-h!" came her strange, intaken cry, as, on the reflex, she started, turned, and fled, scudding with an unthinkable swift beating of her white feet and a fraying of her white garments, towards the church. Like a hound the young man was after her, leaping the steps and swinging past her father, his supple haunches working like those of a hound that bears down on the quarry.

"Ay, after her!", cried the vulgar women below, carried suddenly into the sport.

She, her flowers shaken from her like froth, was steadying herself to turn the angle of the church. She glanced behind, and with a wild cry of laughter and challenge, veered, poised, and was gone beyond the grey stone buttress. In another instant the bridegroom, bent forward as he ran, had caught the angle of the silent stone with his hand, and had swung himself out of sight, his supple, strong loins vanishing in pursuit.

Instantly cries and exclamations of excitement burst from the crowd at the gate. And then Ursula noticed again the dark, rather stooping figure of Mr Crich, waiting suspended on the path, watching with expressionless face the flight to the church. It was over, and he turned round to look behind him, at the figure of Rupert Birkin, who at once came forward and joined him.

"We'll bring up the rear," said Birkin, a faint smile on his face.

5   "Ay!" replied the father laconically.

And the two men turned together up the path.

Birkin was as thin as Mr Crich, pale and ill-looking. His figure was narrow but nicely made. He went with a slight trail of one foot, which came only from self-consciousness. Although he was dressed

10   correctly for his part, yet there was an innate incongruity which caused a slight ridiculousness in his appearance. His nature was clever and separate, he did not fit at all in the conventional occasion. Yet he subordinated himself to the common idea, travestied himself.

He affected to be quite ordinary, perfectly and marvellously

15   commonplace. And he did it so well, taking the tone of his surroundings, adjusting himself quickly to his interlocutor and his circumstance, that he achieved a verisimilitude of ordinary commonplaceness that usually propitiated his onlookers for the moment, disarmed them from attacking his singleness.

20   Now he spoke quite easily and pleasantly to Mr Crich, as they walked along the path; he played with situations like a man on a tight-rope: but always on a tight-rope, pretending nothing but ease.

"I'm sorry we are so late," he was saying. "We couldn't find a button-hook, so it took us a long time to button our boots. But you

25   were to the moment."

"We are usually to time," said Mr Crich.

"And I'm always late," said Birkin. "But today I was *really* punctual, only accidentally not so. I'm sorry."

The two men were gone, there was nothing more to see, for the

30   time. Ursula was left thinking about Birkin. He piqued her, attracted her, and annoyed her.

She wanted to know him more. She had spoken with him once or twice, but only in his official capacity as inspector. She thought he seemed to acknowledge some kinship between her and him, a

35   natural, tacit understanding, a using of the same language. But there had been no time for the understanding to develop. And something kept her from him, as well as attracted her to him. There was a certain hostility, a hidden ultimate reserve in him, cold and inaccessible.

40   Yet she wanted to know him.

"What do you think of Rupert Birkin?" she asked, a little reluctantly, of Gudrun. She did not want to discuss him.

"What do I think of Rupert Birkin?" repeated Gudrun. "I think he's attractive—decidedly attractive.—What I can't stand about him is his way with other people—his way of treating any little fool as if she were his greatest consideration.—One feels so awfully sold, oneself."

"Why does he do it?" said Ursula.

"Because he has no real critical faculty—of people, at all events," said Gudrun. "I tell you, he treats any little fool as he treats me or you—and it's such an insult."

"Oh, it is," said Ursula. "One must discriminate."

"One *must* discriminate," repeated Gudrun.—"But he's a wonderful chap, in other respects—a marvellous personality.* But you can't trust him."

"Yes," said Ursula vaguely. She was always forced to assent to Gudrun's pronouncements, even when she was not in accord altogether.

The sisters sat silent, waiting for the wedding-party to come out. Gudrun was impatient of talk. She wanted to think about Gerald Crich. She wanted to see if the strong feeling she had got from him was real. She wanted to have herself ready.

Inside the church, the wedding was going on. Hermione Roddice was thinking only of Birkin. He stood near her. She seemed to gravitate physically towards him. She wanted to stand touching him. She could hardly be sure he was near her, if she did not touch him. Yet she stood subjected through the wedding service.

She had suffered so bitterly when he did not come, that still she was dazed. Still she was gnawed as by a neuralgia, tormented by his potential absence from her. She had awaited him in a faint delirium of nervous torture. As she stood bearing herself pensively, the rapt look on her face, that seemed spiritual, like the angels, but which came from torture, gave her a certain poignancy that tore his heart with pity. He saw her bowed head, her rapt face, the face of an almost demoniacal ecstatic. Feeling him looking, she lifted her face and sought his eyes, her own beautiful grey eyes flaring him a great signal. But he avoided her look, she sank her head in torment and shame, the gnawing at her heart going on. And he too was tortured with shame, and ultimate dislike, and with acute pity for her, because he did not want to meet her eyes, he did not want to receive her flare of recognition.

The bride and bridegroom were married, the party went into the vestry. Hermione crowded involuntarily up against Birkin, to touch

5 him. And he endured it.

Outside, Gudrun and Ursula listened for their father's playing on the organ.* He would enjoy playing a wedding march.—Now the married pair were coming! The bells were ringing, making the air shake. Ursula wondered if the trees and the flowers could feel the

10 vibration, and what they thought of it, this strange motion in the air. The bride was quite demure on the arm of the bridegroom, who stared up into the sky before him, shutting and opening his eyes unconsciously, as if he were neither here nor there. He looked rather comical, blinking and trying to be in the scene, when emotionally he

15 was violated by his exposure to a crowd. He looked a typical naval officer, manly, and up to his duty.

Birkin came with Hermione. She had a rapt, triumphant look, like the fallen angels restored, yet still subtly demoniacal, now she held Birkin by the arm. And he was expressionless, neutralised, possessed

20 by her as if it were his fate, without question.

Gerald Crich came, fair, good-looking, healthy, with a great reserve of energy. He was erect and complete, there was a strange stealth glistening through his amiable, almost happy appearance. Gudrun rose sharply and went away. She could not bear it. She

25 wanted to be alone, to know this strange, sharp inoculation that had changed the whole temper of her blood.

Chapter II

Shortlands

The Brangwens went home to Beldover, the wedding-party gathered at Shortlands, the Criches' home. It was a long, low old house, a sort of manor farm, that spread along the top of a slope just beyond the narrow little lake of Willey Water. Shortlands looked across a sloping meadow that might be a park, because of the large, solitary trees that stood here and there, across the water of the narrow lake, at the wooded hill that successfully hid the colliery valley beyond, but did not quite hide the rising smoke. Nevertheless, the scene was rural and picturesque, very peaceful, and the house had a charm of its own.

It was crowded now with the family and the wedding guests. The father, who was not well, withdrew to rest. Gerald was host. He stood in the homely entrance hall, friendly and easy, attending to the men. He seemed to take pleasure in his social functions, he smiled, and was abundant in hospitality.

The women wandered about in a little confusion, chased hither and thither by the three married daughters of the house. All the while there could be heard the characteristic, imperious voice of one Crich woman or another calling, "Helen, come here a minute," "Marjory, I want you—here!" "Oh I say, Mrs Witham—." There was a great rustling of skirts, swift glimpses of smartly-dressed women, a child danced through the hall and back again, a maidservant came and went hurriedly.

Meanwhile the men stood in calm little groups, chatting, smoking, pretending to pay no heed to the rustling animation of the women's world. But they could not really talk, because of the glassy ravel of women's excited, cold laughter and running voices. They waited, uneasy, suspended, rather bored. But Gerald remained as if genial and happy, unaware that he was waiting or unoccupied, knowing himself the very pivot of the occasion.

Suddenly Mrs Crich came noiselessly into the room, peering about with her strong, clear face. She was still wearing her hat, and her sac coat of blue silk.

23

"What is it, mother?" said Gerald.

"Nothing, nothing!" she answered vaguely.

And she went straight towards Birkin, who was talking to a Crich brother-in-law.

5 "How do you do, Mr Birkin," she said, in her low voice, that seemed to take no count of her guests. She held out her hand to him.

"Oh Mrs Crich," replied Birkin, in his readily-changing voice, "I couldn't come to you before."

10 "I don't know half the people here," she said, in her low voice. Her son-in-law moved uneasily away.

"And you don't like strangers?" laughed Birkin. "I myself can never see why one should take account of people, just because they happen to be in the room with one. Why *should* I know they are
15 there?"

"Why indeed, why indeed!" said Mrs Crich, in her low, tense voice. "Except that they *are* there.—*I* don't know people whom I find in the house. The children introduce them to me—'Mother, this is Mr So-and-so.' I am no further. What has Mr So-and-so to
20 do with his own name?—and what have I to do with either him or his name?"

She looked up at Birkin. She startled him. He was flattered too that she came to talk to him, for she took hardly any notice of anybody. He looked down at her tense clear face, with its heavy
25 features, but he was afraid to look into her heavy-seeing blue eyes. He noticed instead how her hair looped in slack, slovenly strands over her rather beautiful ears, which were not quite clean. Neither was her neck perfectly clean. Even in that he seemed to belong to her, rather than to the rest of the company; though, he thought to
30 himself, he was always well washed, at any rate at the neck and ears.

He smiled faintly, thinking these things. Yet he was tense, feeling that he and the elderly, estranged woman were conferring together like traitors, like enemies within the camp of the other people. He resembled a deer, that throws one ear back upon the trail behind,
35 and one ear forward, to know what is ahead.

"People don't really matter," he said, rather unwilling to continue.

The mother looked up at him with sudden, dark interrogation, as if doubting his sincerity.

40 "How do you mean, *matter*?" she asked sharply.

"Not many people are anything at all,"* he answered, forced to go deeper than he wanted to. "They jingle and giggle. It would be much better if they were just wiped out. Essentially, they don't exist, they aren't there."

She watched him steadily while he spoke.

"But we don't imagine them," she said sharply.

"There's nothing to imagine, that's why they don't exist."

"Well," she said, "I would hardly go as far as that. There they are, whether they exist or no. It doesn't rest with me to decide on their existence. I only know that I can't be expected to take count of them all. You can't expect me to know them, just because they happen to be there. As far as *I* go they might as well not be there."

"Exactly," he replied.

"Mightn't they?" she asked again.

"Just as well," he repeated.

And there was a little pause.

"Except that they *are* there, and that's a nuisance," she said.

"There are my sons-in-law," she went on, in a sort of monologue. "Now Laura's got married, there's another. And I really don't know John from James* yet. They come up to me, and call me mother. I know what they will say—'How are you, mother?' I ought to say, 'I am not your mother, in any sense.' But what is the use? There they are. I have had children of my own. I suppose I know them from another woman's children."

"One would suppose so," he said.

She looked at him, somewhat surprised, forgetting perhaps that she was talking to him. And she lost her thread.

She looked round the room, vaguely. Birkin could not guess what she was looking for, nor what she was thinking. Evidently she noticed her sons.

"Are my children all there?" she asked him, abruptly.

He laughed, startled, afraid perhaps.

"I scarcely know them, except Gerald," he replied.

"Gerald!" she exclaimed. "He's the most wanting of them all. You'd never think it, to look at him now, would you?"

"No," said Birkin.

The mother looked across at her eldest son, stared at him heavily for some time.

"Ay," she said, in an incomprehensible monosyllable, that sounded profoundly cynical. Birkin felt afraid, as if he dared not realise. And Mrs Crich moved away, forgetting him. But she returned on her traces.

"I should like him to have a friend," she said. "He has never had a friend."

5　　Birkin looked down into her eyes, which were blue, and watching heavily. He could not understand them. "Am I my brother's keeper?" he said to himself, almost flippantly.

Then he remembered, with a slight shock, that that was Cain's cry. And Gerald was Cain, if anybody. Not that he was Cain, either,
10　although he had slain his brother.* There was such a thing as pure accident, and the consequences did not attach to one, even though one had killed one's brother in such wise. Gerald as a boy had accidentally killed his brother. What then? Why seek to draw a brand and a curse across the life that had caused the accident? A man can
15　live by accident, and die by accident. Or can he not? Is every man's life subject to pure accident, is it only the race, the genus, the species, that has a universal reference? Or is this not true, is there no such thing as pure accident? Has *everything* that happens a universal significance? Has it? Birkin, pondering as he stood there, had
20　forgotten Mrs Crich, as she had forgotten him.

He did not believe that there was any such thing as accident. It all hung together, in the deepest sense.

Just as he had decided this, one of the Crich daughters came up, saying:
25　"Won't you come and take your hat off, mother dear? We shall be sitting down to eat in a minute, and it's a formal occasion, darling, isn't it?"—She drew her arm through her mother's, and they went away. Birkin immediately went to talk with the nearest man.

The gong sounded for the luncheon. The men looked up, but no
30　move was made to the dining-room. The women of the house seemed not to feel that the sound had meaning for them. Five minutes passed by. The elderly man-servant, Crowther,* appeared in the doorway exasperatedly. He looked with appeal at Gerald. The latter took up a large, curved conch shell, that lay on a shelf, and
35　without reference to anybody, blew a shattering blast. It was a strange, rousing noise, that made the heart beat. The summons was almost magical. Everybody came running, as if at a signal. And then the crowd in one impulse moved to the dining-room.

Gerald waited a moment, for his sister to play hostess. He knew
40　his mother would pay no attention to her duties. But his sister merely

crowded to her seat. Therefore the young man, slightly too dicta-
torial, directed the guests to their places.

There was a moment's lull, as everybody looked at the *hors
d'oeuvres* that were being handed round. And out of this lull, a girl of
thirteen or fourteen, with her long hair down her back, said in a calm,
self-possessed voice:

"Gerald, you forget father, when you make that unearthly noise."

"Do I?" he answered. And then, to the company, "Father is lying
down, he is not quite well."

"How is he, really?" called one of the married daughters, peeping
round the immense wedding cake that towered up in the middle of
the table shedding its artificial flowers.

"He has no pain, but he feels tired," replied Winifred, the girl
with the hair down her back.

The wine was filled, and everybody was talking boisterously. At
the far end of the table sat the mother, with her loosely-looped hair.
She had Birkin for a neighbour. Sometimes she glanced fiercely
down the rows of faces, bending forwards, and staring unceremo-
niously. And she would say, in a low voice, to Birkin:

"Who is that young man?"

"I don't know," Birkin answered discreetly.

"Have I seen him before?" she asked.

"I don't think so. *I* haven't," he replied.

And she was satisfied. Her eyes closed wearily, a peace came over
her face, she looked like a queen in repose. Then she started, a little,
social smile came on her face, for a moment she looked the pleasant
hostess. For a moment she bent graciously, as if everyone were
welcome and delightful. And then immediately the shadow came
back, a sullen, eagle look was on her face, she glanced from under
her brows like a sinister creature at bay, hating them all.

"Mother," called Diana, a handsome girl a little older than
Winifred, "I may have wine, mayn't I?"

"Yes, you may have wine," replied the mother automatically, for
she was perfectly indifferent to the question.

And Diana beckoned to the footman to fill her glass.

"Gerald shouldn't forbid me," she said calmly, to the company at
large.

"All right Di," said her brother amiably.

And she glanced challenge at him as she drank from her glass.

There was a strange freedom, that almost amounted to anarchy, in

Women in Love

the house. It was rather a resistance to authority, than liberty. Gerald had some command, by mere force of personality, not because of any granted position. There was a quality in his voice, amiable but dominant, that cowed the others, who were all younger than he.

5 Hermione was having a discussion with the bridegroom about nationality.

"No," she said, "I think that the appeal to patriotism is a mistake. It is like one house of business rivalling another house of business."

"Well you can hardly say that, can you?" exlaimed Gerald, who
10 had a real *passion* for discussion. "You couldn't call a race a business concern, could you?—and nationality roughly corresponds to race, I think.—I think it is *meant* to."

There was* a moment's pause. Gerald and Hermione were always strangely but politely and evenly inimical.

15 "*Do* you think race corresponds with nationality?" she asked musingly, with expressionless indecision.

Birkin knew she was waiting for him to participate. And dutifully he spoke up.

"I think Gerald is right—race is the essential element in nation-
20 ality, in Europe at least,"* he said.

Again Hermione paused, as if to allow this statement to cool. Then she said, with strange assumption of authority:

"Yes, but even so, is the patriotic appeal an appeal to the racial instinct? Is it not rather an appeal to the proprietory instinct, the
25 *commercial* instinct? And isn't this what we mean by nationality?"

"Probably," said Birkin, who felt that such a discussion was out of place and out of time.

But Gerald was now on the scent of argument.

"A race may have its commercial aspect," he said. "In fact it must.
30 It is like a family. You *must* make provision. And to make provision you have got to strive against other families, other nations. I don't see why you shouldn't."

Again Hermione made a pause, domineering and cold, before she replied: "Yes, I think it is always wrong to provoke a spirit of rivalry.
35 It makes bad blood. And bad blood accumulates."

"But you can't do away with the spirit of emulation altogether," said Gerald. "It is one of the necessary incentives to production and improvement."

"Yes," came Hermione's sauntering response. "I think you can do
40 away with it."

"I must say," said Birkin, "I detest the spirit of emulation."

Hermione was biting a piece of bread, pulling it from between her teeth with her fingers, in a slow, slightly derisive movement. She turned to Birkin.

"You do hate it, yes," she said, intimate and gratified.

"Detest it," he repeated.

"Yes," she murmured, assured and satisfied.

"But," Gerald insisted, "you don't allow one man to take away his neighbour's living, so why should you allow one nation to take away the living from another nation?"

There was a long slow murmur from Hermione before she broke into speech, saying with a laconic indifference:

"It is not always a question of possessions, is it? It is not all a question of goods?"

Gerald was nettled by this implication of vulgar materialism.

"Yes, more or less," he retorted. "If I go and take a man's hat from off his head, that hat becomes a symbol of that man's liberty. When he fights me for his hat, he is fighting me for his liberty."

Hermione was nonplussed.

"Yes," she said, irritated. "But that way of arguing by imaginary instances is not supposed to be genuine, is it? A man does *not* come and take my hat from off my head, does he?"

"Only because the law prevents him," said Gerald.

"Not only," said Birkin. "Ninety-nine men out of a hundred don't want my hat."

"That's a matter of opinion," said Gerald.

"Or the hat," laughed the bridegroom.

"And if he does want my hat, such as it is," said Birkin, "why, surely it is open to me to decide, which is a greater loss to me, my hat, or my liberty as a free and indifferent man.* If I am compelled to offer fight, I lose the latter. It is a question which is worth more to me, my pleasant liberty of conduct, or my hat."

"Yes," said Hermione, watching Birkin strangely. "Yes."

"But would you let somebody come and snatch your hat off your head?" the bride asked of Hermione.

The face of the tall straight woman turned slowly and as if drugged to this new speaker.

"No," she replied, in a low inhuman tone, that seemed to contain a chuckle. "No, I shouldn't let anybody take my hat off my head."

"How would you prevent it?" asked Gerald.

"I don't know," replied Hermione slowly. "Probably I should kill him."

There was a strange chuckle in her tone, a dangerous and convincing humour in her bearing.

5 "Of course," said Gerald, "I can see Rupert's point. It is a question to him whether his hat or his peace of mind is more important."

"Peace of body," said Birkin.

"Well, as you like there," replied Gerald. "But how are you going 10 to decide this for a nation?"

"Heaven preserve me," laughed Birkin.

"Yes, but suppose you have to?" Gerald persisted.

"Then it is the same. If the national crown-piece is an old hat,* then the thieving gent may have it."

15 "But *can* the national or racial hat be an old hat?" insisted Gerald.

"Pretty well bound to be, I believe," said Birkin.

"I'm not so sure," said Gerald.

"I don't agree, Rupert," said Hermione.

"All right," said Birkin.

20 "I'm all for the old national hat," laughed Gerald.

"And a fool you look in it," cried Diana, his pert sister who was just in her teens.

"Oh, we're quite out of our depths with these old hats," cried Laura Crich. "Dry up now, Gerald. We're going to drink toasts. Let 25 us drink toasts. Toasts—glasses, glasses,—now then, toasts! Speech! Speech!"

Birkin, thinking about race or national death, watched his glass being filled with champagne. The bubbles broke at the rim, the man withdrew, and feeling a sudden thirst at the sight of the fresh wine, 30 Birkin drank up his glass. A queer little tension in the room roused him. He felt a sharp constraint.

"Did I do it by accident, or on purpose?" he asked himself. And he decided that, according to the vulgar phrase, he had done it "accidentally on purpose."* He looked round at the hired footman. 35 And the hired footman came, with a silent step of cold servantlike disapprobation. Birkin decided that he detested toasts, and footmen, and assemblies, and mankind altogether, in most of its aspects. Then he rose to make a speech. But he was somehow disgusted.

At length it was over, the meal. Several men strolled out into the 40 garden. There was a lawn, and flower-beds, and at the boundary an iron fence shutting off the little field or park. The view was pleasant: a high-road curving round the edge of a low lake, under the trees. In the spring air, the water gleamed and the opposite woods were purplish with new life. Charming Jersey cattle came to the fence, breathing hoarsely from their velvet muzzles at the human beings, expecting perhaps a crust.

Birkin leaned on the fence. A cow was breathing wet hotness on his hand.

"Pretty cattle, very pretty," said Marshall, one of the brothers-in-law. "They give the best milk you can have."

"Yes," said Birkin.

"Eh, my little beauty, eh, my beauty!" said Marshall, in a queer high falsetto voice, that caused the other man to have convulsions of laughter in his stomach.

"Who won the race, Lupton?"* he called to the bridegroom, to hide the fact that he was laughing.

The bridegroom took his cigar from his mouth.

"The race?" he exclaimed. Then a rather thin smile came over his face. He did not want to say anything about the flight to the church door. "We got there together. At least she touched first, but I had my hand on her shoulder."

"What's this?" asked Gerald.

Birkin told him about the race of the bride and the bridegroom.

"Hm!" said Gerald, in disapproval. "What made you late then?"

"Lupton would talk about the immortality of the soul," said Birkin, "and then we hadn't got a button-hook."

"Oh God!" cried Marshall. "The immortality of the soul on your wedding day! Hadn't you got anything better to occupy your mind?"

"What's wrong with it?" asked the bridegroom, a clean-shaven naval man, flushing sensitively.

"Sounds as if you were going to be executed instead of married. The *immortality of the soul!*" repeated the brother-in-law, with most killing emphasis.

But he fell quite flat.

"And what did you decide?" asked Gerald, at once pricking up his ears at the thought of a metaphysical discussion.

"You don't want a soul, today, my boy," said Marshall. "It'd be in your road."*

"Christ!, Marshall, go and talk to somebody else," cried Gerald, with sudden impatience.

"By God, I'm willing," said Marshall, in a temper. "Too much bloody* soul, and talk altogether—"

He withdrew in a dudgeon, Gerald staring after him with angry eyes, that grew gradually calm and amiable as the stoutly-built form
5   of the other man passed into the distance.

"There's one thing, Lupton," said Gerald, turning suddenly to the bridegroom. "Laura won't have brought such a fool into the family as Lottie did."

"Comfort yourself with that," laughed Birkin.

10   "I take no notice of them," laughed the bridegroom.

"What about this race then—who began it?" Gerald asked.

"We were late. Laura was at the top of the churchyard steps when our cab came up. She saw Lupton bolting towards her. And she fled.—But why do you look so cross? Does it hurt your sense of the
15   family dignity?"

"It does rather," said Gerald. "If you're doing a thing, do it properly, and if you're not going to do it properly, leave it alone."

"Very nice aphorism," said Birkin.

"Don't you agree?" asked Gerald.

20   "Quite," said Birkin. "Only it bores me rather, when you become aphoristic."

"Damn you, Rupert, you want all the aphorisms your own way," said Gerald.

"No, I want them out of the way, and you're always shoving them
25   in it."

Gerald smiled grimly at this humorism. Then he made a little gesture of dismissal, with his eyebrows.

"You don't believe in having any standard of behaviour at all, do you?" he challenged Birkin, censoriously.

30   "Standard—no. I hate standards. But they're necessary for the common ruck.—Anybody who is anything can just be himself and do as he likes."

"But what do you mean by being himself?" said Gerald. "Is that an aphorism or a cliché?"

35   "I mean just doing what you want to do. I think it was perfect good form in Laura to bolt from Lupton to the church door. It was almost a masterpiece in good form. It's the hardest thing in the world to act spontaneously on one's impulses—and it's the only really gentlemanly thing to do—provided you're fit to do it."

40   "You don't expect me to take you seriously, do you?" asked Gerald.

"Yes Gerald, you're one of the very few people I do expect that of."

"Then I'm afraid I can't come up to your expectations here, at any rate.—You think people should just do as they like?"

"I think they always do. But I should like them to like the purely individual thing in themselves, which makes them act in singleness. And they only like to do the collective thing."

"And I," said Gerald grimly, "shouldn't like to be in a world of people who acted individually and spontaneously, as you call it.—We should have everybody cutting everybody else's throat in five minutes."

"That means *you* would like to be cutting everybody's throat," said Birkin.

"How does that follow?" asked Gerald crossly.

"No man," said Birkin, "cuts another man's throat unless he wants to cut it, and unless the other man wants it cutting. This is a complete truth. It takes two people to make a murder: a murderer and a murderee. And a murderee is a man who is murderable. And a man who is murderable is a man who in a profound if hidden lust desires to be murdered."

"Sometimes you talk pure nonsense," said Gerald to Birkin. "As a matter of fact, none of us wants our throat cut, and most other people would like to cut it for us—some time or other—"

"It's a nasty view of things, Gerald," said Birkin, "and no wonder you are afraid of yourself and your own unhappiness."

"How am I afraid of myself?" said Gerald; "and I don't think I am unhappy."

"You seem to have a lurking desire to have your gizzard slit, and imagine every man has his knife up his sleeve for you," Birkin said.

"How do you make that out?" said Gerald.

"From you," said Birkin.

There was a pause of strange enmity between the two men, that was very near to love. It was always the same between them; always their talk brought them into a deadly nearness of contact, a strange, perilous intimacy which was either hate or love, or both. They parted with apparent inconcern,* as if their going apart were a trivial occurrence. And they really kept it to the level of trivial occurrence. Yet the heart of each burned from the other. They burned with each other, inwardly. This they would never admit. They intended to keep their relationship a casual free-and-easy friendship, they were not going to be so unmanly and unnatural as to allow any heart-burning between them. They had not the faintest belief in deep relationship between man and man, and their disbelief prevented any development of their powerful but suppressed friendliness.

Chapter III

Class-room

A school-day was drawing to a close. In the class-room the last lesson was in progress, peaceful and still. It was elementary botany. The desks were littered with catkins, hazel and willow, which the children had been sketching. But the sky had come over dark,* as the end of the afternoon approached, there was scarcely light to draw any more. Ursula stood in front of the class, leading the children by questions to understand the structure and the meaning of the catkins.

A heavy, copper-coloured beam of light came in at the west window, gilding the outlines of the children's heads with red gold, and falling on the wall opposite in a rich, ruddy illumination. Ursula, however, was scarcely conscious of it. She was busy, the end of the day was here, the work went on as a peaceful tide that is at flood, hushed to retire.

This day had gone by like so many more, in an activity that was like a trance. At the end there was a little haste, to finish what was in hand. She was pressing the children with questions, so that they should know all they were to know, by the time the gong went. She stood in shadow in front of the class, with catkins in her hand, and she leaned towards the children, absorbed in the passion of instruction.

She heard, but did not notice the click of the door. Suddenly she started. She saw, in the shaft of ruddy, copper-coloured light near her, the face of a man. It was gleaming like fire, watching her, waiting for her to be aware. It startled her terribly. She thought she was going to faint. All her suppressed, subconscious fear sprang into being, with anguish.

"Did I startle you?" said Birkin, shaking hands with her. "I thought you had heard me come in."

"No," she faltered, scarcely able to speak.

He laughed, saying he was sorry. She wondered why it amused him.

"It is so dark," he said. "Shall we have the light?"

35

And moving aside, he switched on the strong electric lights. The class-room was distinct and hard, a strange place after the soft dim magic that filled it before he came. Birkin turned curiously to look at Ursula. Her eyes were round and wondering, bewildered, her mouth
5 quivered slightly. She looked like one who is suddenly wakened. There was a living, tender beauty, like a tender light of dawn shining from her face. He looked at her with a new pleasure, feeling gay in his heart, irresponsible.

"You are doing catkins?" he asked, picking up a piece of hazel
10 from a scholar's desk in front of him. "Are they as far out as this? I hadn't noticed them this year."

He looked absorbedly at the tassel of hazel in his hand.

"The red ones too!" he said, looking at the flickers of crimson that came from the female bud.

15   Then he went in among the desks, to see the scholars' books. Ursula watched his intent progress. There was a stillness in his motion that hushed the activities of her heart. She seemed to be standing aside in arrested silence, watching him move in another, concentrated world. His presence was so quiet, almost like a vacancy
20 in the corporate* air.

Suddenly he lifted his face to her, and her heart quickened at the flicker of his voice.

"Give them some crayons, won't you?" he said, "so that they can make the gynaecious flowers red, and the androgynous* yellow. I'd
25 chalk them in plain, chalk in nothing else, merely the red and the yellow. Outline scarcely matters in this case. There is just the one fact to emphasise."

"I haven't any crayons," said Ursula.

"There will be some somewhere—red and yellow, that's all you
30 want."

Ursula sent out a boy on a quest.

"It will make the books untidy," she said to Birkin, flushing deeply.

"Not very," he said. "You must mark in these things obviously.
35 It's the fact you want to emphasise, not a subjective impression to record. What's the fact?—red little spiky stigmas of the female flower, dangling yellow male catkin, yellow pollen flying from one to the other. Make a pictorial record of the fact, as a child does when drawing a face—two eyes, one nose, mouth with teeth—so—
40 ."* And he drew a figure on the blackboard.

At that moment another vision was seen through the glass panels of the door. It was Hermione Roddice. Birkin went and opened to her.

"I saw your car," she said to him. "Do you mind my coming to find you? I wanted to see you when you were on duty."

She looked at him for a long time, intimate and playful, then she gave a short little laugh. And then only she turned to Ursula, who, with all the class, had been watching the little scene between the lovers.

"How do you do, Miss Brangwen," sang Hermione, in her slow, odd, singing fashion, that sounded almost as if she were poking fun. "Do you mind my coming in?"

Her grey, almost sardonic eyes rested all the while on Ursula, as if summing her up.

"Oh no," said Ursula.

"Are you *sure?*" repeated Hermione, with complete sang froid, and an odd, half-bullying effrontery.

"Oh no, I like it awfully," laughed Ursula, a little bit excited and bewildered, because Hermione seemed to be compelling her, coming very close to her, as if intimate with her; and yet, how could she be intimate?

This was the answer Hermione wanted. She turned satisfied to Birkin.

"What are you doing?" she sang, in her casual, inquisitive fashion.

"Catkins," he replied.

"Really!" she said. "And what do they learn about them?"

She spoke all the while in a mocking, half teasing fashion, as if making game of the whole business. She picked up a twig of the catkin, piqued by Birkin's attention to it.

She was a strange figure in the class-room, wearing a large, old cloak of greenish cloth, on which was a raised pattern of dull gold. The high collar, and the inside of the cloak, was lined with dark fur. Beneath she had a dress of fine lavender-coloured cloth, trimmed with fur, and her hat was close-fitting, made of fur and of the dull, green-and-gold figured stuff. She was tall and strange, she looked as if she had come out of some new, bizarre picture.*

"Do you know the little red ovary flowers, that produce the nuts? Have you ever noticed them?" he asked her. And he came close and pointed them out to her, on the sprig she held.

"No," she replied. "What are they?"

"Those are the little seed-producing flowers, and the long catkins, they only produce pollen, to fertilise them."

"Do they, do they!" repeated Hermione, looking closely.

"From those little red bits, the nuts come; if they receive pollen from the long danglers."

"Little red flames,* little red flames," murmured Hermione to herself. And she remained for some moments looking only at the small buds out of which the red flickers of the stigma issued.

"Aren't they beautiful? I think they're so beautiful," she said, moving close to Birkin, and pointing to the red filaments with her long, white finger.

"Had you never noticed them before?" he asked.

"No, never before," she replied.

"And now you will always see them," he said.

"Now I shall always see them," she repeated. "Thank you so much for showing me. I think they're so beautiful—little red flames—"

Her absorption was strange, almost rhapsodic. Both Birkin and Ursula were suspended. The little red pistillate flowers had some strange, almost mystic-passionate attraction for her.

The lesson was finished, the books were put away, at last the class was dismissed. And still Hermione sat at the table, with her chin in her hand, her elbow on the table, her long white face pushed up, not attending to anything. Birkin had gone to the window, and was looking from the brilliantly-lighted room on to the grey, colourless outside, where rain was noiselessly falling. Ursula put away her things in the cupboard.

At length Hermione rose and came near to her.

"Your sister has come home?" she said.

"Yes," said Ursula.

"And does she like being back in Beldover?"

"No," said Ursula.

"No. I wonder she can bear it. It takes all my strength, to bear the ugliness of this district, when I stay here.—Won't you come and see me? Won't you come with your sister to stay at Breadalby for a few days?—do—"

"Thank you very much," said Ursula.

"Then I will write to you," said Hermione. "You think your sister will come? I should be so glad. I think she is wonderful. I think some of her work is really wonderful. I have two water-wagtails, carved in wood, and painted—perhaps you have seen it?"

"No," said Ursula.

"I think it is perfectly wonderful—like a flash of instinct—"

"Her little carvings *are* strange," said Ursula.

"Perfectly beautiful—full of primitive passion—"

"Isn't it queer that she always likes little things?—she must always work small things, that one can put between one's hands, birds, and tiny animals. She likes to look through the wrong end of the opera glasses, and see the world that way.—Why is it, do you think?"

Hermione looked down at Ursula with that long, detached, scrutinising gaze that excited the younger woman.

"Yes," said Hermione at length. "It is curious. The little things seem to be more subtle to her—"

"But they aren't, are they? A mouse isn't any more subtle than a lion, is it?"

Again Hermione looked down at Ursula with that long scrutiny, as if she were following some train of thought of her own, and barely attending to the other's speech.

"I don't know," she replied.

"Rupert, Rupert," she sang mildly, calling him to her.

He approached in silence.

"Are little things more subtle than big things?" she asked, with the odd grunt of laughter in her voice, as if she were making game of him in the question.

"Dunno," he said.

"I hate subtleties," said Ursula.

Hermione looked at her slowly.

"Do you," she said.

"I always think they are a sign of weakness," said Ursula, up in arms, as if her prestige were threatened.

Hermione took no notice. Suddenly her face puckered, her brow was knit with thought, she seemed twisted in troublesome effort for utterance.

"Do you really think, Rupert," she asked, as if Ursula were not present, "do you really think it is worth while? Do you really think the children are better for being roused to consciousness?"

A dark flash went over his face, a silent fury. He was hollow-cheeked and pale, almost unearthly. And the woman, with her serious, conscience-harrowing question tortured him on the quick.

"They are not roused to consciousness," he said. "Consciousness comes to them, willy-nilly."

"But do you think they are better for having it quickened, stimulated? Isn't it better that they should remain unconscious of the hazel, isn't it better that they should see as a whole, without all this pulling to pieces, all this knowledge?"

"Would you rather, for yourself, know or not know, that the little red flowers are there, putting out for the pollen?" he asked harshly. His voice was brutal, scornful, cruel.

Hermione remained with her face lifted up, abstracted. He hung silent in irritation.

"I don't know," she replied, balancing mildly. "I don't know."

"But knowing is everything to you, it is all your life," he broke out. She slowly looked at him.

"Is it," she said.

"To know, that is your all, that is your life—you have only this, this knowledge," he cried. "There is only one tree, there is only one fruit, in your mouth."

Again she was some time silent.

"Is there," she said at last, with the same untouched calm. And then in a tone of whimsical inquisitiveness: "What fruit, Rupert?"

"The eternal apple,"* he replied in exasperation, hating his own metaphors.

"Yes," she said. There was a look of exhaustion about her. For some moments there was silence. Then, pulling herself together with a convulsed movement, Hermione resumed, in a sing-song, casual voice:

"But leaving me apart, Rupert; *do* you think the children are better, richer, happier, for all this knowledge, do you really think they are? Or is it better to leave them untouched, spontaneous. Hadn't they better be *animals*, simple animals, crude, violent, *anything*, rather than this self-consciousness, this incapacity to be spontaneous."

They thought she had finished. But with a queer rumbling in her throat she resumed, "Hadn't they better be anything than grow up crippled, crippled in their souls, crippled in their feelings—so thrown back—so turned back on themselves— —incapable—" Hermione clenched her fist like one in a trance—"of any spontaneous action, always deliberate, always burdened with choice, never carried away."

Again they thought she had finished. But just as he was going to reply, she resumed her queer rhapsody—"never carried away, out of themselves, always conscious, always self-conscious, always aware of themselves.——Isn't *anything* better than this? Better be animals, mere animals with no mind at all, than this, this *nothingness*—." 5

"But do you think it is knowledge that makes us unliving and self-conscious?" he asked irritably.

She opened her eyes and looked at him slowly.

"Yes," she said. She paused, watching him all the while, her eyes vague. Then she wiped her fingers across her brow, with a vague 10 weariness. It irritated him bitterly. "It is the mind," she said, "and that is death." She raised her eyes slowly to him: "Isn't the mind—" she said, with the convulsed movement of her body, "isn't it our death? Doesn't it destroy all our spontaneity, all our instincts? Are not the young people growing up today, really dead before they have 15 a chance to live?"

"Not because they have too much mind, but too little," he said brutally.

"Are you *sure*?" she cried. "It seems to me the reverse. They are over-conscious, burdened to death with consciousness." 20

"Imprisoned within a limited, false set of concepts," he cried.

But she took no notice of this, only went on with her own rhapsodic interrogation.

"When we have knowledge, don't we lose everything but knowledge?" she asked pathetically. "If I know about the flower, don't I 25 lose the flower and have only the knowledge? Aren't we exchanging the substance for the shadow, aren't we forfeiting life for this dead quantity of knowledge? And what does it mean to me, after all? What does all this knowing mean to me? It means nothing."

"You are merely making words," he said; "knowledge means 30 everything to you. Even your animalism, you want it in your head. You don't want to *be* an animal, you want to observe your own animal functions, to get a mental thrill out of them. It is all purely secondary—and more decadent than the most hide-bound intellectualism. What is it but the worst and last form of intellectualism, 35 this love of yours for passion and the animal instincts? Passion and the instincts—you want them hard enough, but through your head, in your consciousness. It all takes place in your head, under that skull of yours.—Only you won't be conscious of what *actually* is: you want the lie that will match the rest of your furniture." 40

Hermione set hard and poisonous against this attack. Ursula stood covered with wonder and shame. It frightened her, to see how they hated each other.

"It's all that Lady of Shalott business,"* he said, in his strong, abstract voice. He seemed to be charging her before the unseeing air. "You've got that mirror, your own fixed will, your immortal understanding, your own tight conscious world, and there is nothing beyond it. There, in the mirror, you must have everything. But now you have come to all your conclusions, you want to go back and be like a savage, without knowledge. You want a life of pure sensation and 'passion.'"

He quoted the last word satirically against her. She sat convulsed with fury and violation, speechless, like a stricken pythoness of the Greek oracle.*

"But your passion is a lie," he went on violently. "It isn't passion at all, it is your *will*. It's your bullying will. You want to clutch things and have them in your power. You want to have things in your power. And why? Because you haven't got any real body, any dark sensual body of life. You have no sensuality. You have only your will and your conceit of consciousness, and your lust for power, to *know*."

He looked at her in mingled hate and contempt, also in pain because she suffered, and in shame because he knew he tortured her. He had an impulse to kneel and plead for forgiveness. But a bitterer red anger burned up to fury in him. He became unconscious of her, he was only a passionate voice speaking.

"Spontaneous!" he cried. "You and spontaneity! You, the most deliberate thing that ever walked or crawled! You'd be verily deliberately spontaneous—that's you.—Because you want to have everything in your own volition, your deliberate voluntary consciousness.—You want it all in that loathsome little skull of yours, that ought to be cracked like a nut. For you'll be the same till it *is* cracked, like an insect in its skin.—If one cracked your skull perhaps one might get a spontaneous, passionate woman out of you, with real sensuality.—As it is, what you want is pornography—looking at yourself in mirrors, watching your naked animal actions in mirrors, so that you can have it all in your consciousness, make it all mental."

There was a sense of violation in the air, as if too much was said, the unforgivable. Yet Ursula was concerned now only with solving her own problems, in the light of his words. She was pale and abstracted.

"But do you really *want* sensuality?" she asked, puzzled.

Birkin looked at her, and became intent in his explanation.

"Yes," he said, "that, and nothing else, at this point. It is a fulfilment—the great dark knowledge you can't have in your head—the dark involuntary being. It is death to one self*—but it is the coming into being of another."

"But how? How can you have knowledge not in your head?" she asked, quite unable to interpret his phrases.

"In the blood," he answered; "when the mind and the known world is drowned in darkness.—Everything must go—there must be the deluge. Then you find yourself a palpable body of darkness, a demon—"

"But why should I be a demon—?" she asked.

"*Woman wailing for her demon lover*—"* he quoted—"Why, I don't know."

Hermione roused herself as from a death-annihilation.

"He is such a *dreadful* satanist, isn't he?" she drawled to Ursula, in a queer resonant voice, that ended in a shrill little laugh of pure ridicule. The two women were jeering at him, jeering him into nothingness. The laugh of the shrill, triumphant female sounded from Hermione, jeering him as if he were a neuter.

"No," he said. "You are the real devil who won't let life exist."

She looked at him with a long, slow look, malevolent, supercilious.

"You know all about it, don't you?" she said, with slow, cold, cunning mockery.

"Enough," he replied, his face fixing fine and clear like steel.

A horrible despair, and at the same time a sense of release, liberation, came over Hermione. She turned with a pleasant intimacy to Ursula.

"You are sure you will come to Breadalby?" she said, urging.

"Yes, I should like to very much," replied Ursula.

Hermione looked down at her, gratified, reflecting, and strangely absent, as if possessed, as if not quite there.

"I'm so glad," she said, pulling herself together.—"Some time in about a fortnight? Yes?—I will write to you here, at the school, shall I?—Yes.—And you'll be sure to come?—Yes.—I shall be so glad. Goodbye!—Goo-oodbye—."

Hermione held out her hand and looked into the eyes of the other

woman. She knew Ursula as an immediate rival, and the knowledge strangely exhilarated her. Also she was taking leave. It always gave her a sense of strength, advantage, to be departing and leaving the other behind. Moreover she was taking the man with her, if only in
5 hate.

Birkin stood aside, fixed and unreal. But now, when it was his turn to bid goodbye, he began to speak again.

"There's the whole difference in the world," he said, "between the actual sensual being, and the vicious mental-deliberate profli-
10 gacy our lot goes in for. In our night-time, there's always the electricity switched on, we watch ourselves, we get it all in the head, really.—You've got to lapse out before you can know what sensual reality is, lapse into unknowingness, and give up your volition. You've got to do it. You've got to learn not-to-be, before you can
15 come into being.*

"But we have got such a conceit of ourselves—that's where it is. We are so conceited, and so unproud. We've got no pride, we're all conceit, so conceited in our own papier-mâché realised selves. We'd rather die than give up our little self-righteous self-opinionated
20 self-will."

There was silence in the room. Both women were hostile and resentful. He sounded as if he were addressing a meeting. Hermione merely paid no attention, stood with her shoulders tight in a shrug of dislike.

25 Ursula was watching him as if furtively, not really aware of what she was seeing. There was a great physical attractiveness in him—a curious hidden richness, that came through his thinness and his pallor like another voice, conveying another knowledge of him. It was in the curves of his brows and his chin, rich, fine, exquisite curves,
30 the powerful beauty of life itself.* She could not say what it was. But there was a sense of richness and of liberty.

"But we are sensual enough, without making ourselves so, aren't we?" she asked, turning to him with a certain golden laughter flickering under her greenish eyes, like a challenge. And immedi-
35 ately the queer, careless, terribly attractive smile came over his eyes and brows, though his mouth did not relax.

"No," he said, "we aren't. We're too full of ourselves."

"Surely it isn't a matter of conceit," she cried.

"That and nothing else."

40 She was frankly puzzled.

"Don't you think that people are most conceited of all about their sensual powers?" she asked.

"That's why they aren't sensual—only sensuous—which is another matter. They're *always* aware of themselves—and they're so conceited, that rather than release themselves, and live in another world, from another centre, they'd—."

"You want your tea, don't you," said Hermione, turning to Ursula with a gracious kindliness. "You've worked all day—"

Birkin stopped short. A spasm of anger and chagrin went over Ursula. His face set. And he bade goodbye, as if he had ceased to notice her.

They were gone. Ursula stood looking at the door for some moments. Then she put out the lights. And having done so, she sat down again in her chair, absorbed and lost. And then she began to cry, bitterly, bitterly weeping: but whether for misery or joy, she never knew.

Chapter IV

Diver

The week passed away. On the Saturday it rained, a soft, drizzling rain that held off at times. In one of the intervals Gudrun and Ursula set out for a walk, going towards Willey Water. The atmosphere was grey and translucent, the birds sang sharply on the young twigs, the earth would be quickening and hastening in growth. The two girls walked swiftly, gladly, because of the soft, subtle rush of morning that filled the wet haze. By the road the blackthorn was in blossom, white and wet, its tiny amber grains burning faintly in the white smoke of blossom. Purple twigs were darkly luminous in the grey air, high hedges glowed like living shadows, hovering nearer, coming into creation. The morning was full of a new creation.

When the sisters came to Willey Water, the lake lay all grey and visionary, stretching into the moist, translucent vista of trees and meadow. Fine electric activity in sound came from the dumbles* below the road, the birds piping one against the other, and water mysteriously plashing, issuing from the lake.

The two girls drifted swiftly along. In front of them, at the corner of the lake, near the road, was a mossy boat-house* under a walnut tree, and a little landing-stage where a boat was moored, wavering like a shadow on the still grey water, below the green, decayed poles. All was shadowy with coming summer.

Suddenly, from the boat-house, a white figure ran out, frightening in its swift sharp transit, across the old landing-stage. It launched in a white arc through the air, there was a bursting of the water, and among the smooth ripples a swimmer was making out to space, in a centre of faintly heaving motion. The whole otherworld, wet and remote, he had to himself. He could move into the pure translucency of the grey, uncreated water.

Gudrun stood by the stone wall, watching.

"How I envy him," she said, in low, desirous tones.

"Ugh!" shivered Ursula. "So cold!"

"Yes, but how good, how really fine, to swim out there!"

The sisters stood watching the swimmer move further into the grey, moist, full space of the water, pulsing with his own small, invading motion, and arched over with mist and dim woods.

"Don't you wish it were you?" asked Gudrun, looking at Ursula.

"I do," said Ursula. "—But I'm not sure—it's *so* wet."

"No," said Gudrun, reluctantly.

She stood watching the motion on the bosom of the water, as if fascinated. He, having swum a certain distance, turned round and was swimming on his back, looking along the water at the two girls by the wall. In the faint wash of motion, they could see his ruddy face, and could feel him watching them.

"It is Gerald Crich," said Ursula.

"I know," replied Gudrun.

And she stood motionless gazing over the water at the face which washed up and down on the flood, as he swam steadily. From his separate element he saw them, and he exulted to himself because of his own advantage, his possession of a world to himself. He was immune and perfect. He loved his own vigorous, thrusting motion, and the violent impulse of the very cold water against his limbs, buoying him up. He could see the girls watching him a way off, outside, and that pleased him. He lifted his arm from the water, in a sign to them.

"He is waving," said Ursula.

"Yes," replied Gudrun.

They watched him. He waved again, with a strange movement of recognition across the difference.

"Like a Nibelung,"* laughed Ursula.

Gudrun said nothing, only stood still looking over the water.

Gerald suddenly turned, and was swimming away swiftly, with a side stroke. He was alone now, alone and immune in the middle of the waters, which he had all to himself. He exulted in his isolation in the new element, unquestioned and unconditioned. He was happy, thrusting with his legs and all his body, without bond or connection anywhere, just himself in the watery world.

Gudrun envied him almost painfully. Even this momentary possession of pure isolation and fluidity seemed to her so terribly desirable, that she felt herself as if damned, out there on the high-road.

"God, what it is to be a man!" she cried.

"What?" exclaimed Ursula, in surprise.

"The freedom, the liberty, the mobility!" cried Gudrun, strangely flushed and brilliant. "You're a man, you want to do a thing, you do it. You haven't the *thousand* obstacles a woman has in front of her."

Ursula wondered what was in Gudrun's mind, to occasion this
5 outburst. She could not understand.

"What do you want to do?" she asked.

"Nothing," cried Gudrun, in swift refutation. "But supposing I did. Supposing I want to swim up that water. It is impossible, it is one of the impossibilities of life, for me to take my clothes off now and
10 jump in. But isn't it *ridiculous*, doesn't it simply prevent our living!"

She was so hot, so flushed, so furious, that Ursula was puzzled.

The two sisters went on, up the road. They were passing between the trees just below Shortlands. They looked up at the long, low house, dim and glamorous in the wet morning, its cedar tree slanting
15 before the windows. Gudrun seemed to be studying it closely.

"Don't you think it's attractive, Ursula?" asked Gudrun.

"Very," said Ursula. "Very peaceful and charming."

"It has form, too—it has a period."

"What period?"
20 "Oh, eighteenth century, for certain; Dorothy Wordsworth, and Jane Austen,* don't you think?"

Ursula laughed.

"Don't you think so?" repeated Gudrun.

"Perhaps. But I don't think the Criches fit the period. I know
25 Gerald is putting in a private electric plant, for lighting the house, and is making all kinds of latest improvements."

Gudrun shrugged her shoulders swiftly.

"Of course," she said, "that's quite inevitable."

"Quite," laughed Ursula. "He is several generations of youngness
30 at one go. They hate him for it. He takes them all by the scruff of the neck, and fairly flings them along. He'll have to die soon, when he's made every possible improvement, and there will be nothing more to improve.—He's got *go*, anyhow."

"Certainly he's got go," said Gudrun. "In fact I've never seen a
35 man that showed signs of so much. The unfortunate thing is, where does his *go* go to, what becomes of it?"

"Oh I know," said Ursula. "It goes in applying the latest appliances."

"Exactly," said Gudrun.
40 "You know he shot his brother?" said Ursula.

"Shot his brother!" cried Gudrun, frowning as if in disapprobation.

"Didn't you know? Oh yes!—I thought you knew. He and his
brother were playing together with a gun. He told his brother to look
down the gun, and it was loaded, and blew the top of his head   5
off.—Isn't it a horrible story?"

"How fearful!" cried Gudrun. "But it is long ago?"

"Oh yes, they were quite boys," said Ursula. "I think it is one of
the most horrible stories I know."

"And he of course did not know that the gun was loaded?"   10

"Yes. You see it was an old thing that had been lying in the stable
for years. Nobody dreamed it would ever go off, and of course,
no-one imagined it was loaded. But isn't it dreadful, that it should
happen?"

"Frightful!" cried Gudrun. "And isn't it horrible too to think of   15
such a thing happening to one, when one was a child, and having to
carry the responsibility of it all through one's life. Imagine it, two
boys playing together—then this comes upon them, for no reason
whatever—out of the air. Ursula, it's very frightening! Oh, it's one of
the things I can't bear. Murder, that is thinkable, because there's a   20
will behind it. But a thing like that to *happen* to one—"

"Perhaps there *was* an unconscious will behind it," said Ursula.
"This playing at killing has some primitive *desire* for killing in it,
don't you think?"

"Desire!" said Gudrun, coldly, stiffening a little. "I can't see that   25
they were even playing at killing. I suppose one boy said to the other,
'You look down the barrel while I pull the trigger, and see what
happens.' It seems to me the purest form of accident."

"No," said Ursula. "I couldn't pull the trigger of the emptiest gun
in the world, not if someone were looking down the barrel. One   30
instinctively doesn't do it—one can't."

Gudrun was silent for some moments, in sharp disagreement.

"Of course," she said coldly, "if one is a woman, and grown up,
one's instinct prevents one. But I cannot see how that applies to a
couple of boys playing together."   35

Her voice was cold and angry.

"Yes," persisted Ursula.

At that moment they heard a woman's voice a few yards off say
loudly:

"Oh damn the thing!"   40

They went forward and saw Laura Crich and Hermione Roddice in the field on the other side of the hedge, and Laura Crich struggling with the gate, to get out. Ursula at once hurried up and helped to lift the gate.

5 "Thanks so much," said Laura, looking up flushed and amazon-like, yet rather confused. "It isn't right on the hinges."

"No," said Ursula. "And they're so heavy."

"Surprising!" cried Laura.

"How do you do," sang Hermione, from out of the field, the

10 moment she could make her voice heard. "It's nice now. Are you going for a walk? Yes. Isn't the young green beautiful? So beautiful—quite burning. Good morning—good morning—you'll come and see me?—thank you so much—next week—yes—goodbye, go-o-o-dby-y-e."

15 Gudrun and Ursula stood and watched her slowly waving her head up and down, and waving her hand slowly in dismissal, smiling a strange affected smile, making a tall, queer, frightening figure, with her heavy fair hair slipping to her eyes. Then they moved off, as if they had been dismissed like inferiors. The four women parted.

20 As soon as they had gone far enough, Ursula said, her cheeks burning,

"I do think she's impudent."

"Who, Hermione Roddice?" asked Gudrun. "Why?"

"The way she treats one—impudence!"

25 "Why Ursula, what did you notice that was so impudent?" asked Gudrun, rather coldly.

"Her whole manner—Oh, it's impossible, the way she tries to bully one. Pure bullying. She's an impudent woman. 'You'll come and see me,' as if we should be falling over ourselves for the privilege."

30 "I can't understand, Ursula, what you are so much put out about," said Gudrun, in some exasperation. "One knows those women are impudent—these free women who have emancipated themselves from the aristocracy."*

"But it is so *unnecessary*—so vulgar," cried Ursula.

35 "No, I don't see it.—And if I did—pour moi, elle n'existe pas.* I don't grant her the power to be impudent to me."

"Do you think she likes you?" asked Ursula.

"Well, no, I shouldn't think she did."

"Then why does she ask you to go to Breadalby and stay with

40 her?"

Gudrun lifted her shoulders in a slow shrug.

"After all, she's got the sense to know we're not just the ordinary run," said Gudrun. "Whatever she is, she's not a fool. And I'd rather have somebody I detested, than the ordinary woman who keeps to her own set. Hermione Roddice does risk herself in some respects."

Ursula pondered this for a time.

"I doubt it," she replied. "Really, she risks nothing.—I suppose we ought to admire her for knowing she *can* invite us—school-teachers—and risk nothing."

"Precisely!" said Gudrun. "Think of the myriads of women that daren't do it. She makes the most of her privileges—that's something. I suppose, really, we should do the same, in her place."

"No," said Ursula, "no. It would bore me. I couldn't spend my time playing her games. It's infra dig."

The two sisters were like a pair of scissors, snipping off everything that came athwart them; or like a knife and a whetstone, the one sharpened against the other.

"Of course," cried Ursula suddenly, "she ought to thank her stars if we will go and see her. You are perfectly beautiful, a thousand times more beautiful than ever she is or was, and to my thinking, a thousand times more beautifully dressed, for she never looks fresh and natural, like a flower, always old, thought-out; and we *are* more intelligent than most people."

"Undoubtedly!" said Gudrun.

"And it ought to be admitted, simply," said Ursula.

"Certainly it ought," said Gudrun. "But you'll find that the really chic thing is to be so absolutely ordinary, so perfectly commonplace and like the person in the street, that you really are a masterpiece of humanity, not the person in the street actually, but the artistic creation of her—"

"How awful!" cried Ursula.

"Yes Ursula, it *is* awful, in most respects. You daren't be anything that isn't amazingly *à terre*,* so much *à terre* that it is the artistic creation of ordinariness."

"It's very dull to create oneself into nothing better," laughed Ursula.

"Very dull!" retorted Gudrun. "Really Ursula, it *is* dull, that's just the word. One longs to be high-flown, and make speeches like Corneille,* after it."

Gudrun was becoming flushed and excited over her own cleverness.

"Strut," said Ursula, "one wants to strut, to be a swan among geese."

5   "Exactly," cried Gudrun, "a swan among geese."

"They are all so busy playing the ugly duckling," cried Ursula, with mocking laughter. "And I don't feel a bit like a humble and pathetic ugly duckling. I do feel like a swan among geese—I can't help it. They make one feel so. And I don't care what *they* think of

10   me.—*Je m'en fiche*."*

Gudrun looked up at Ursula with a queer, uncertain envy and dislike.

"Of course, the only thing to do is to despise them all—just all," she said.

15   The sisters went home again, to read and talk and work, and wait for Monday, for school. Ursula often wondered what else she waited for, besides the beginning and end of the school-week, and the beginning and end of the holidays. This was a whole life! Sometimes she had periods of tight horror, when it seemed to her that her life

20   would pass away, and be gone, without having been more than this. But she never really accepted it. Her spirit was active, her life* like a shoot that is growing steadily, but which has not yet come above ground.

Chapter V

In the Train

One day at this time Birkin was called to London. He was not very fixed in his abode. He had rooms in Nottingham, because his work* lay chiefly in that town. But often he was in London, or in Oxford. He moved about a great deal, his life seemed uncertain, without any definite rhythm, any organic meaning.

On the platform of the railway station he saw Gerald Crich, reading a newspaper, and evidently waiting for the train. Birkin stood some distance off, among the people. It was against his instinct to approach anybody.

From time to time, in a manner characteristic of him, Gerald lifted his head and looked round. Even though he was reading the newspaper closely, he must keep a watchful eye on his external surroundings. There seemed to be a dual consciousness running in him. He was thinking vigorously of something he read in the newspaper, and at the same time his eye ran over the surface of the life round him, and he missed nothing. Birkin, who was watching him, was irritated by this duality. He noticed, too, that Gerald seemed always to be at bay against everybody, in spite of his queer, genial, social manner when roused.

Now Birkin started violently at seeing this genial look flash on to Gerald's face, at seeing Gerald approaching with hand out-stretched.

"Hallo Rupert, where are you going?"

"London. So are you I suppose."

"Yes—"

Gerald's eyes went over Birkin's face in curiosity.

"We'll travel together if you like," he said.

"Don't you usually go first?" asked Birkin.

"I can't stand the crowd," replied Gerald. "But third'll be all right.* There's a restaurant car, we can have some tea."

The two men looked at the station clock, having nothing further to say.

"What were you reading in the paper?" Birkin asked.

53

Gerald looked at him quickly.

"Isn't it funny, what they *do* put in newspapers," he said. "Here are two leaders—" he held out his *Daily Telegraph*,* "full of the ordinary newspaper cant—" he scanned the columns down—"and

5 then there's this little—I dunno what you'd call it, essay, almost— appearing with the leaders, and saying there must arise a man who will give new values to things, give us new truths, a new attitude to life, or else we shall be a crumbling nothingness in a few years, a country in ruin—"

10 "I suppose that's a bit of newspaper cant, as well," said Birkin.

"It sounds as if the man meant it, and quite genuinely," said Gerald.

"Give it me," said Birkin, holding out his hand for the paper.

The train came, and they went on board, sitting on either side a

15 little table, by the window, in the restaurant car. Birkin glanced over his paper, then looked up at Gerald, who was waiting for him.

"I believe the man means it," he said, "as far as he means anything."

"And do you think it's true? Do you think we really want a new

20 gospel?" asked Gerald.

Birkin shrugged his shoulders.

"I think the people who say they want a new religion are the last to accept anything new. They want novelty right enough. But to stare straight at this life that we've brought upon ourselves, and reject it,

25 absolutely smash up the old idols of ourselves, that we s'll* never do. You've got very badly to want to get rid of the old, before anything new will appear—even in the self."

Gerald watched him closely.

"You think we ought to break up this life, just start and let fly?" he

30 asked.

"This life—yes I do. We've got to bust it completely, or shrivel inside it, as in a tight skin. For it won't expand any more."

There was a queer little smile in Gerald's eyes, a look of amusement, calm and curious.

35 "And how do you propose to begin? I suppose you mean, reform the whole order of society?" he asked.

Birkin had a slight, tense frown between the brows. He too was impatient of the conversation.

"I don't propose at all," he replied. "When we really want to go for

40 something better, we shall smash the old. Until then, any sort of

proposal, or making proposals, is no more than a tiresome game for self-important people."

The little smile began to die out of Gerald's eyes, and he said, looking with a cool stare at Birkin:

"So you really think things are very bad?"

"Completely bad."

The smile appeared again.

"In what way?"

"Every way," said Birkin. "We are such dreary liars. Our one idea is to lie to ourselves. We have an ideal of a perfect world, clean and straight and sufficient. So we cover the earth with foulness, life is a blotch of labour, like insects scurrying in filth, so that your collier can have a pianoforte in his parlour, and you can have a butler and a motor-car in your up-to-date house, and as a nation we can sport the Ritz, or the Empire, Gaby Deslys* and the Sunday newspapers. It is very dreary."

Gerald took a little time to readjust himself after this tirade.

"Would you have us live without houses—return to nature?" he asked.

"I would have nothing at all. People only do what they want to do—and what they are capable of doing. If they were capable of anything else, there would be something else."

Again Gerald pondered. He was not going to take offence at Birkin.

"Don't you think the collier's *pianoforte*, as you call it, is a symbol for something very real, a real desire for something higher, in the collier's life?"

"Higher!" cried Birkin. "Yes. Amazing heights of upright grandeur. It makes him so much higher in his neighbouring colliers' eyes. He sees himself reflected in the neighbouring opinion, like in a Brocken mist,* several feet taller on the strength of the pianoforte, and he is satisfied. He lives for the sake of that Brocken spectre, the reflection of himself in the human opinion.—You do the same. If you are of high importance to humanity you are of high importance to yourself. That is why you work so hard at the mines. If you can produce coal to cook five thousand dinners a day, you are five thousand times more important than if you cooked only your own dinner."

"I suppose I am," laughed Gerald.

"Can't you see," said Birkin, "that to help my neighbour* to eat is no more than eating myself. 'I eat, thou eatest, he eats, we eat, you eat, they eat'—and what then? Why should every man decline the whole verb. First person singular is enough for me."

"You've got to start with material things," said Gerald.

5 Which statement Birkin ignored.

"And we've got to live for *something*, we're not just cattle that can graze and have done with it," said Gerald.

"Tell me," said Birkin. "What do you live for?"

Gerald's face went baffled.

10 "What do I live for?" he repeated. "I suppose I live to work, to produce something, in so far as I am a purposive being. Apart from that, I live because I am living."

"And what's your work? Getting so many *more* thousands of tons of coal out of the earth every day. And when we've got all the coal we 15 want, and all the plush furniture, and pianofortes, and the rabbits are all stewed and eaten, and we're all warm and our bellies are filled and we're listening to the young lady performing on the pianoforte— what then? What then, when you've made a real fair start with your material things?"

20 Gerald sat laughing at the words and the mocking humour of the other man. But he was cogitating too.

"We haven't got there yet," he replied. "A good many people are still waiting for the rabbit and the fire to cook it."

"So while you get the coal I must chase the rabbit?" said Birkin, 25 mocking at Gerald.

"Something like that," said Gerald.

Birkin watched him narrowly. He saw the perfect good-humoured callousness, even strange, glistening malice, in Gerald, glistening through the plausible ethics of productivity.

30 "Gerald," he said, "I rather hate you."

"I know you do," said Gerald. "Why do you?"

Birkin mused inscrutably for some minutes.

"I should like to know if you are conscious of hating me," he said at last. "Do you ever consciously detest me—hate me with mystic 35 hate?—There are odd moments when I hate you starrily."

Gerald was rather taken aback, even a little disconcerted. He did not quite know what to say.

"I may, of course, hate you sometimes," he said. "But I'm not aware of it—never acutely aware of it, that is."

40 "So much the worse," said Birkin.

Gerald watched him with curious eyes. He could not quite make him out.

"So much the worse, is it?" he repeated.

There was a silence between the two men for some time, as the train ran on. In Birkin's face was a little irritable tension, a sharp knitting of the brows, keen and difficult. Gerald watched him warily, carefully, rather calculatingly, for he could not decide what he was after.

Suddenly Birkin's eyes looked straight and overpowering into those of the other man.

"What do you think is the aim and object of your life, Gerald?" he asked.

Again Gerald was taken aback. He could not think what his friend was getting at. Was he poking fun, or not?

"At this moment, I couldn't say off-hand," he replied, with faintly ironic humour.

"Do you think love is the be-all and the end-all* of life?" Birkin asked, with direct, attentive seriousness.

"Of my own life?" said Gerald.

"Yes."

There was a really puzzled pause.

"I can't say," said Gerald. "It hasn't been, so far."

"What has your life been, so far?"

"Oh—finding out things for myself—and getting experiences—and making things *go*."

Birkin knitted his brows like sharply moulded steel.

"I find," he said, "that one needs some one *really* pure single activity—I should call love a single pure activity. But I *don't* really love anybody—not now."

"Have you ever really loved anybody?" asked Gerald.

"Yes and no," replied Birkin.

"Not finally?" said Gerald.

"Finally—finally—no," said Birkin.

"Nor I," said Gerald.

"And do you want to?" said Birkin.

Gerald looked with a long, twinkling, almost sardonic look into the eyes of the other man.

"I don't know," he said.

"I do—I want to love," said Birkin.

"You do?"

"Yes. I want the finality of love."

"The finality of love," repeated Gerald. And he waited for a moment.

"Just one woman?" he added. The evening light, flooding yellow along the fields, lit up Birkin's face with a tense, abstract steadfastness. Gerald still could not make it out.

"Yes, one woman," said Birkin.

But to Gerald it sounded as if he were insistent rather than confident.

"I don't believe a woman, and nothing but a woman, will ever make my life," said Gerald.

"Not the centre and core of it—the love between you and a woman?" asked Birkin.

Gerald's eyes narrowed with a queer dangerous smile as he watched the other man.

"I never quite feel it that way," he said.

"You don't? Then wherein does life centre, for you?"

"I don't know—that's what I want somebody to tell me.—As far as I can make out, it doesn't centre at all. It is artificially held together by the social mechanism."

Birkin pondered as if he would crack something.

"I know," he said, "it just doesn't centre. The old ideals are dead as nails—nothing there. It seems to me there remains only this perfect union with a woman—sort of ultimate marriage—and there isn't anything else."

"And you mean if there isn't the woman, there's nothing?" said Gerald.

"Pretty well that—seeing there's no God."

"Then we're hard put to it," said Gerald. And he turned to look out of the window at the flying, golden landscape.

Birkin could not help seeing how beautiful and soldierly his face was, with a certain courage to be indifferent.

"You think it's heavy odds against us?" said Birkin.

"If we've got to make our life up out of a woman, one woman, woman only, yes, I do," said Gerald. "I don't believe I shall ever make up *my* life, at that rate."

Birkin watched him almost angrily.

"You are a born unbeliever," he said.

"I only feel what I feel," said Gerald. And he looked again at Birkin almost sardonically, with his blue, manly, sharp-lighted eyes.

Birkin's eyes were at the moment full of anger. But swiftly they became troubled, doubtful, then full of a warm, rich affectionateness and laughter.

"It troubles me very much, Gerald," he said, wrinkling his brows.

"I can see it does," said Gerald, uncovering his mouth in a manly, quick, soldierly laugh.

Gerald was held unconsciously by the other man. He wanted to be near him, he wanted to be within his sphere of influence. There was something very congenial to him in Birkin. But yet, beyond this, he did not take much notice. He felt that he, himself, Gerald, had harder and more durable truths than any the other man knew. He felt himself older, more knowing. It was the quick-changing warmth and versatility* and brilliant warm utterance he loved in his friend. It was the rich play of words and quick interchange of feelings he enjoyed. The real content of the words he never really considered: he himself knew better.

Birkin knew this. He knew that Gerald wanted to be *fond* of him without taking him seriously. And this made him go hard and cold. As the train ran on, he sat looking at the land, and Gerald fell away, became as nothing to him.

Birkin looked at the land, at the evening, and was thinking: "Well, if mankind is destroyed, if our race is destroyed like Sodom,* and there is this beautiful evening with the luminous land and trees, I am satisfied. That which informs it all is there, and can never be lost. After all, what is mankind but just one expression of the incomprehensible. And if mankind passes away, it will only mean that this particular expression is completed and done. That which is expressed, and that which is to be expressed, cannot be diminished. There it is, in the shining evening. Let mankind pass away—time it did. The creative utterances will not cease, they will only be there. Humanity doesn't embody the utterance of the incomprehensible any more. Humanity is a dead letter. There will be a new embodiment, in a new way. Let humanity disappear as quick as possible."

Gerald interrupted him by asking,

"Where are you staying in London?"

Birkin looked up.

"With a man in Soho.* I pay part of the rent of a flat, and stop there when I like."

"Good idea—have a place more or less your own," said Gerald.

"Yes. But I don't care for it much. I'm tired of the people I am bound to find there."

"What kind of people?"

5   "Art—music—London Bohemia—the most pettifogging calculating Bohemia that ever reckoned its pennies.—But there are a few decent people, decent in some respects. They are really very thorough rejecters of the world—perhaps they live only in the gesture of rejection and negation—but negatively something, at any

10 rate."

"What are they?—painters, musicians?"

"Painters, musicians, writers—hangers-on, models, advanced young people, anybody who is openly at outs with the conventions, and belongs to nowhere particularly. They are often young fellows

15 down from the University,* and girls who are living their own lives, as they say."

"All loose?" said Gerald.

Birkin could see his curiosity was roused.

"In one way. Most bound, in another. For all their shockingness,

20 all on one note."

He looked at Gerald, and saw how his blue eyes were lit up with a little flame of curious desire. He saw too how good-looking he was. Gerald was attractive, his blood seemed fluid and electric. His blue eyes burned with a keen, yet cold light, there was a certain beauty, a

25 beautiful passivity in all his body, his moulding.

"We might see something of each other—I am in London for two or three days," said Gerald.

"Yes," said Birkin. "I don't want to go to the theatre, or the music hall—you'd better come round to the flat, and see what you make of

30 Halliday* and his crowd."

"Thanks—I should like to," laughed Gerald. "What are you doing tonight?"

"I promised to meet Halliday at the Pompadour.* It's a bad place, but there is nowhere else."

35   "Where is it?" asked Gerald.

"Piccadilly Circus."

"Oh yes—well, shall I come round there?"

"By all means, it might amuse you."

The evening was falling. They had passed Bedford. Birkin

40 watched the country, and was filled with a sort of hopelessness. He

always felt this, on approaching London. His dislike of mankind, of the mass of mankind, amounted almost to an illness.

> "'Where the quiet coloured end of evening smiles
> Miles and miles—'"

he was murmuring to himself, like a man condemned to death. Gerald, who was very subtly alert, wary in all his senses, leaned forward and asked, smilingly:

"What were you saying?"

Birkin glanced at him, laughed, and repeated:

> "'Where the quiet coloured end of evening smiles,
> Miles and miles,
> Over pastures where the something something sheep
> Half asleep—'"*

Gerald also looked now at the country. And Birkin, who, for some reason was now tired and dispirited, said to him:

"I always feel doomed when the train is running into London. I feel such a despair, so hopeless, as if it were the end of the world."

"Really!" said Gerald. "And does the end of the world frighten you?"

Birkin lifted his shoulders in a slow shrug.

"I don't know," he said. "It does while it hangs imminent and doesn't fall.—But people give me a bad feeling—very bad."

There was a roused glad smile in Gerald's eyes.

"Do they?" he said. And he watched the other man critically.

In a few minutes the train was running through the disgrace of outspread London. Everybody in the carriage was on the alert, waiting to escape. At last they were under the huge arch of the station, in the tremendous shadow of the town. Birkin shut himself together—he was in now.

The two men went together in a taxi-cab.

"Don't you feel like one of the damned?" asked Birkin, as they sat in the little, swiftly-running enclosure, and watched the hideous great street.

"No," laughed Gerald.

"It is real death," said Birkin.

Chapter VI

Crême de Menthe

They met again in the café several hours later. Gerald went through the push doors into the large, lofty room where the faces and heads of the drinkers showed dimly through the haze of smoke, reflected more dimly, and repeated ad infinitum in the great mirrors on the walls, so that one seemed to enter a vague, dim world of shadowy drinkers humming within an atmosphere of blue tobacco smoke. There was, however, the red plush of the seats to give substance within the bubble of pleasure.*

Gerald moved in his slow, observant, glistening-attentive motion down between the tables and the people whose shadowy faces looked up as he passed. He seemed to be entering in some strange element, passing into an illuminated new region, among a host of licentious souls. He was pleased, and entertained. He looked over all the dim, evanescent, strangely illuminated faces that bent across the tables. Then he saw Birkin rise and signal to him.

At Birkin's table was a girl with dark, soft, fluffy hair cut short in the artist fashion, hanging level and full almost like the Egyptian princes's.* She was small and delicately made, with warm colouring and large, dark, hostile eyes. There was a delicacy, almost a beauty in all her form,* and at the same time a certain attractive grossness of spirit, that made a little spark leap instantly alight in Gerald's eyes.

Birkin, who looked muted, unreal, his presence left out, introduced her as Miss Darrington. She gave her hand with a sudden, unwilling movement, looking all the while at Gerald with a dark, exposed stare. A glow came over him as he sat down.

The waiter appeared. Gerald glanced at the glasses of the other two. Birkin was drinking something green, Miss Darrington had a small liqueur glass that was empty save for a tiny drop.

"Won't you have some more—?"

"Brandy," she said, sipping her last drop and putting down the glass. The waiter disappeared.

"No," she said to Birkin. "He doesn't know I'm back. He'll be terwified when he sees me here."

She spoke her r's like w's, lisping with a slightly babyish pronunciation which was at once affected and true to her character. Her voice
was dull and toneless.

"Where is he then?" asked Birkin.

"He's doing a private show at Lady Snellgrove's," said the girl. 5
"Warens* is there too."

There was a pause.

"Well then," said Birkin, in a dispassionate protective manner,
"what do you intend to do?"

The girl paused sullenly. She hated the question. 10

"I don't intend to do anything," she replied. "I shall look for some
sittings tomorrow."

"Who shall you go to?" asked Birkin.

"I shall go to Bentley's* first. But I believe he's angwy with me for
running away." 15

"That is from the Madonna?"

"Yes. And then if he doesn't want me, I know I can get work with
Carmarthen."

"Carmarthen—?"

"Lord Carmarthen*—he does photographs." 20

"Chiffon and shoulders—"

"Yes. But he's awfully decent."

There was a pause.

"And what are you going to do about Julius?" he asked.

"Nothing," she said. "I shall just ignore him." 25

"You've done with him altogether?"

But she turned aside her face sullenly, and did not answer the
question.

Another young man came hurrying up to the table.

"Hallo Birkin! *Hallo Pussum*, when did you come back?" he said 30
eagerly.

"Today."

"Does Halliday know?"

"I don't know. I don't care either."

"Ha-ha! The wind still sits in that quarter,* does it? Do you mind 35
if I come over to this table?"

"I'm talking to Wupert, do you mind?" she replied, coolly and yet
appealingly, like a child.

"Open confession—good for the soul, eh?" said the young man.
"Well, so long." 40

And giving a sharp look at Birkin and at Gerald, the young man moved off, with a swing of his coat skirts.

All this time Gerald had been completely ignored. And yet he felt that the girl was physically aware of his proximity. He waited,
5 listened, and tried to piece together the conversation.

"Are you staying at the flat?" the girl asked, of Birkin.

"For three days," replied Birkin. "And you?"

"I don't know yet. I can always go to Bertha's."

There was a silence.
10 Suddenly the girl turned to Gerald, and said, in a rather formal, polite voice, with the distant manner of a woman who accepts her position as a social inferior, yet assumes an intimate *camaraderie* with the male she addresses:

"Do you know London well?"
15 "I can hardly say," he laughed. "I've been up a good many times, but I was never in this place before."

"You're not an artist, then?" she said, in a tone that placed him an outsider.

"No," he replied.
20 "He's a soldier, and an explorer,* and a Napoleon of industry," said Birkin, giving Gerald his credentials for Bohemia.

"Are you a soldier?" asked the girl, with a cold, yet lively curiosity.

"No, I resigned my commission," said Gerald, "some years ago."

"He was in the last war,"* said Birkin.
25 "Were you really?" said the girl.

"And then he explored the Amazon," said Birkin, "and now he is ruling over coal-mines."*

The girl looked at Gerald with steady, calm curiosity. He laughed, hearing himself described. He felt proud too, full of male strength.
30 His blue, keen eyes were lit up with laughter, his ruddy face with its sharp fair hair was full of satisfaction, and glowing with life. He piqued her.

"How long are you staying?" she asked him.

"A day or two," he replied. "But there is no particular hurry."
35 Still she stared into his face with that slow, full gaze which was so curious and so exciting to him. He was acutely and delightfully conscious of himself, of his own attractiveness. He felt full of strength, able to give off a sort of electric power. And he was aware of her dark, hot-looking eyes upon him. She had beautiful eyes, dark,
40 fully-opened, hot, naked in their looking at him. And on them there

seemed to float a film of disintegration, a sort of misery and sullenness, like oil on water. She wore no hat, in the heated café, her loose, simple jumper* was strung on a string round her neck. But it was made of rich peach-coloured crêpe-de-chine, that hung heavily and softly from her young throat and her slender wrists. Her appearance was simple and complete, really beautiful, because of her regularity and form, her soft dark hair falling full and level on either side of her head, her straight, small, softened features, Egyptian in the slight fulness of their curves, her slender neck, and the simple, rich-coloured smock hanging on her slender shoulders. She was very still, almost null, in her manner, apart and watchful.

She appealed to Gerald strongly. He felt an awful, enjoyable power over her, an instinctive cherishing very near to cruelty. For she was a victim. He felt that she was in his power, and he was generous. The electricity was turgid and voluptuously rich, in his limbs. He would be able to destroy her utterly in the strength of the discharge. But she was waiting in her separation, given.

They talked banalities for some time. Suddenly Birkin said:

"There's Julius!" and he half rose to his feet, motioning to the new-comer. The girl, with a curious, almost evil motion, looked round over her shoulder without moving her body. Gerald watched her dark, soft hair swing over her ears. He felt her watching intensely the man who was approaching, so he looked too. He saw a pale, full-built young man with rather long, solid fair hair hanging from under his black hat,* moving cumbrously down the room, his face lit up with a smile at once naive and warm, and vapid.* He approached straight towards Birkin, with a haste of welcome.

It was not till he was quite close that he perceived the girl. He recoiled, went pale, and said, in a high, squealing voice:

"Pussum, what are *you* doing here?"

The café looked up like animals when they hear a cry. Halliday hung motionless, an almost imbecile smile flickering palely on his face. The girl only stared at him with a black look in which flared an unfathomable hell of knowledge, and a certain impotence. She was limited by him.

"Why have you come back?" repeated Halliday, in the same high, hysterical voice. "I told you not to come back."

The girl did not answer, only stared in the same viscous, heavy fashion, straight at him, as he stood recoiled, as if for safety, against the next table.

"You know you wanted her to come back—come and sit down," said Birkin to him.

"No I didn't want her to come back, and I told her not to come back.—What have you come for, Pussum?"

"For nothing from *you*," she said in a heavy voice of resentment.

"Then why have you come back at *all*?" cried Halliday, his voice rising to a kind of squeal.

"She comes as she likes," said Birkin. "Are you going to sit down, or are you not?"

"No I won't sit down with Pussum," cried Halliday.

"I won't hurt you, you needn't be afwaid," she said to him, very curtly, and yet with a sort of protectiveness towards him, in her voice.

Halliday came and sat at the table, putting his hand on his heart, and crying:

"Oh, it's given me such a turn! Pussum, I wish you wouldn't do these things. Why did you come back?"

"Not for anything from you," she repeated.

"You've said that before," he cried in a high voice.

She turned completely away from him, to Gerald Crich, whose eyes were shining with a subtle amusement.

"Were you ever vewy much afwaid of the savages?" she asked in her calm, dull, childish voice.

"No—never very much afraid. On the whole they're harmless—they're not born yet, you can't feel really afraid of them. You know you can manage them."

"Do you weally? Aren't they very fierce?"

"Not very. There aren't many fierce things, as a matter of fact. There aren't many things, neither people nor animals, that have it in them to be really dangerous."

"Except in herds," interrupted Birkin.

"Aren't there really?" she said. "Oh, I thought savages were all so dangerous, they'd have your life before you could look round."

"Did you?" he laughed. "They are over-rated, savages. They're too much like other people, not exciting, after the first acquaintance."

"Oh, it's not so very wonderfully brave then, to be an explorer?"

"No. It's more a question of hardships than of terrors."

"Oh! And weren't you *ever* afraid?"

"In my life? I don't know. Yes, I'm afraid of some things—of being shut up, locked up anywhere—or being fastened. I'm afraid of being bound hand and foot." *like in marriage?*

She looked at him steadily with her dark eyes, that rested on him and roused him so deeply, that it left his upper self quite calm. It was rather delicious, to feel her drawing his self-revelations from him, as from the very innermost dark marrow of his body. She wanted to know. And her dark eyes seemed to be looking through into his naked organism. He felt, she was compelled to him, she was fated to come into contact with him, must have the seeing him and knowing him. And this roused a curious exultance. Also he felt, she must relinquish herself into his hands, and be subject to him. She was so profane, slave-like, watching him, absorbed by him. It was not that she was interested in what he said; she was absorbed by his self-revelation, by *him*, she wanted the secret of him, the experience of his male being.

Gerald's face was lit up with an uncanny smile, full of light and rousedness, yet unconscious. He sat with his arms on the table, his sun-browned, rather sinister hands, that were animal and yet very shapely and attractive, pushed forward towards her. And they fascinated her. And she knew, she watched her own fascination.

Other men had come to the table, to talk with Birkin and Halliday. Gerald said in a low voice, apart, to Pussum:

"Where have you come back from?"

"From the country," replied Pussum, in a very low, yet fully resonant voice. Her face closed hard. Continually she glanced at Halliday, and then a black flare came over her eyes. The heavy, fair young man ignored her completely; he was really afraid of her. For some moments she would be unaware of Gerald. He had not conquered her yet.

"And what has Halliday to do with it?" he asked, his voice still muted.

She would not answer for some seconds. Then she said, unwillingly:

"He made me go and live with him, and now he wants to throw me over. And yet he won't let me go to anybody else. He wants me to live hidden in the country. And then he says I persecute him, that he can't get rid of me."

"Doesn't know his own mind," said Gerald.

"He hasn't any mind, so he can't know it," she said. "He waits for what somebody tells him to do. He never does anything he wants to do himself—because he doesn't know what he wants. He's a perfect baby."

Gerald looked at Halliday for some moments, watching the soft, rather degenerate face of the young man. Its very softness was an attraction; it was a soft, warm, corrupt nature, into which one might plunge with gratification.

"But he has no hold over you, has he?" Gerald asked.

"You see he *made* me go and live with him, when I didn't want to," she replied. "He came and cried to me, tears, you never saw so many, saying *he couldn't* bear it unless I went back to him. And he wouldn't go away, he would have stayed for ever. He made me go back. Then every time he behaves in this fashion.—And now I'm going to have a baby,* he wants to give me a hundred pounds and send me into the country, so that he would never see me nor hear of me again. But I'm not going to do it, after—"

A queer look came over Gerald's face.

"Are you going to have a child?" he asked incredulous. It seemed, to look at her, impossible, she was so young and so far in spirit from any childbearing.

She looked full into his face, and her dark, inchoate eyes had now a furtive look, and a look of a knowledge of evil, dark and indomitable. A flame ran secretly to his heart.

"Yes," she said. "Isn't it beastly?"

"Don't you want it?" he asked.

"I don't," she replied, emphatically.

"But—" he said, "how long have you known?"

"Ten weeks," she said.

All the time she kept her dark, inchoate eyes full upon him. He remained silent, thinking. Then, switching off and becoming cold, he asked, in a voice full of considerate kindness:

"Is there anything we can eat here? Is there anything you would like?"

"Yes," she said. "I should adore some oysters."

"All right," he said. "We'll have oysters."

And he beckoned to the waiter.

Halliday took no notice, until the little plate was set before her. Then suddenly he cried:

"Pussum, you can't eat oysters when you're drinking brandy."

"What has it got to do with you?" she asked.

"Nothing, nothing," he cried. "But you can't eat oysters when you're drinking brandy."

"I'm not drinking brandy," she replied, and she sprinkled the last drops of her liqueur over his face. He gave an odd squeal. She sat looking at him, as if indifferent.

"Pussum, why do you do that?" he cried in panic. He gave Gerald the impression that he was terrified of her, and that he loved his terror. He seemed to relish his own horror and hatred of her, turn it over and extract every flavour from it, in real panic. Gerald thought him a strange fool, and yet piquant.

"But Pussum," said another man,* in a very small, quick, Eton voice, "you promised not to hurt him."

"I haven't hurt him," she answered.

"What will you drink?" the young man asked. He was dark, and smooth-skinned, and full of a stealthy vigour.

"I don't like porter, Maxim," she replied.

"You must ask for champagne," came the whispering, gentlemanly voice of the other.

Gerald suddenly realised that this was a hint to him.

"Shall we have champagne?" he asked, laughing.

"Yes please, dwy," she lisped, childishly.

Gerald watched her eating the oysters. She was delicate and finicking in her eating, her fingers were fine and seemed very sensitive in the tips, so she put her food apart with fine, small motions, she ate carefully, delicately. It pleased him very much to see her, and it irritated Birkin. They were all drinking champagne. Maxim, the prim young Russian with the smooth, warm-coloured face and black, oiled hair, was the only one who seemed to be perfectly calm and sober. Birkin was white and abstract, unnatural, Gerald was smiling with a constant bright, amused, cold light in his eyes, leaning a little protectively towards the Pussum, who was very handsome and soft, unfolded like some red lotus in dreadful flowering nakedness, vainglorious now, flushed with wine and with the excitement of men. Halliday looked foolish. One glass of wine was enough to make him drunk and giggling. Yet there was always a pleasant, warm naïveté about him, that made him attractive.

"I'm not afwaid of anything essept black-beetles," said the Pussum, looking up suddenly and staring with her black eyes, on which there seemed an unseeing film of flame, fully upon Gerald. He laughed dangerously, from the blood. Her childish speech caressed his nerves, and her burning, filmed eyes, turned now full upon him, oblivious of all her antecedents, gave him a sort of licence.

"I'm not," she protested. "I'm not afraid of other things. But black-beetles—ugh!—" she shuddered convulsively, as if the very thought were too much to bear.

"Do you mean," said Gerald, with the punctiliousness of a man who has been drinking, "that you are afraid of the sight of a black-beetle, or you are afraid of a black-beetle biting you, or doing you some harm?"

"Do they bite?" cried the girl.

"How perfectly loathsome!" exclaimed Halliday.

"I don't know," replied Gerald, looking round the table. "Do black-beetles bite?—But that isn't the point. Are you afraid of their biting, or is it a metaphysical antipathy?"

The girl was looking full upon him all the time with inchoate eyes.

"Oh, I think they're beastly, they're horrid," she cried. "If I see one, it gives me the creeps all over. If one were to crawl on me, I'm *sure* I should die—I'm sure I should."

"I hope not," whispered the young Russian.

"I'm sure I should, Maxim," she asseverated.

"Then one won't crawl on you," said Gerald, smiling and knowing. In some strange way, he understood her.

"It's metaphysical, as Gerald says," Birkin stated.

There was a little pause of uneasiness.

"And are you afraid of nothing else, Pussum?" asked the young Russian, in his quick, hushed, elegant manner.

"Not weally," she said. "I am afwaid of some things, but not weally the same. I'm not afwaid of *blood*."

"Not afwaid of blood!" exclaimed a young man* with a thick, pale, jeering face, who had just come to the table and was drinking whisky.

The Pussum turned on him a sulky look of dislike, low and ugly.

"Aren't you really afraid of blud?" the other persisted, a sneer all over his face.

"No, I'm not," she retorted.

"Why, have you ever seen blood, except in a dentist's spittoon?" jeered the young man.

"I wasn't speaking to you," she replied rather superbly.

"You can answer me, can't you?" he said.

For reply, she suddenly jabbed a knife across his thick, pale hand. He started up with a vulgar curse.

"Show's what you are," said the Pussum in contempt.

"Curse you,"* said the young man, standing by the table and looking down at her with acrid malevolence.

"Stop that," said Gerald, in quick, instinctive command.

The young man stood looking down at her with sardonic contempt, a cowed, self-conscious look on his thick, pale face. The blood began to flow from his hand.

"Oh, how horrible, take it away!" squealed Halliday, turning green and averting his face.

"D'you feel ill?" asked the sardonic young man, in some concern. "Do you feel ill, Julius? Garn, it's nothing man, don't give her the pleasure of letting her think she's performed a feat—don't give her the satisfaction, man,—it's just what she wants."

"Oh!" squealed Halliday.

"He's going to cat,* Maxim," said the Pussum warningly.

The suave young Russian rose and took Halliday by the arm, leading him away. Birkin, white and diminished, looked on as if he were displeased. The wounded, sardonic young man moved away, ignoring his bleeding hand in the most conspicuous fashion.

"He's an awful coward, really," said the Pussum to Gerald. "He's got such an influence over Julius."

"Who is he?" asked Gerald.

"He's a Jew, really. I can't bear him."

"Well, he's quite unimportant. But what's wrong with Halliday?"

"Julius's the most awful coward you've ever seen," she cried. "He always faints if I lift a knife—he's *tewwified* of me."

"Hm!" said Gerald.

"They're all afwaid of me," she said. "Only the Jew thinks he's going to show his courage. But he's the biggest coward of them all, really, because he's afwaid what people will think about him—and Julius doesn't care about that."

"They've a lot of valour between them," said Gerald good-humouredly.

The Pussum looked at him with a slow, slow smile. She was very handsome, flushed, and confident in dreadful knowledge. Two little points of light glinted on Gerald's eyes.

'Why do they call you Pussum, because you're like a cat?" he asked her.

"I expect so," she said.

The smile grew more intense on his face.

"You are, rather;—or a young, female panther."

"Oh god, Gerald!" said Birkin, in some disgust.

They both looked uneasily at Birkin.

"You're silent tonight, Wupert," she said to him, with a slight insolence, being safe with the other man.

5 Halliday was coming back, looking forlorn and sick.

"Pussum," he said, "I wish you wouldn't do these things—Oh!" he sank in his chair with a groan.

"You'd better go home," she said to him.

"I *will* go home," he said. "But won't you all come along. Won't 10 you come round to the flat?" he said to Gerald. "I should be so glad if you would. Do—that'll be splendid.—I say?" He looked round for a waiter. "Get me a taxi." Then he groaned again. "Oh I do feel—perfectly ghastly! Pussum, you see what you do to me."

"Then why are you such an idiot," she said with sullen calm.

15 "But I'm *not* an idiot! Oh, how awful! Do come, everybody, it will be *so* splendid. Pussum, you are coming.—What?—Oh but you *must* come, yes, you must. What?—Oh, my dear girl, don't make a fuss now, I feel perfectly—Oh, it's so ghastly—Hc!-er!—Oh!"

"You know you can't drink," she said to him, coldly.

20 "I tell you it isn't drink—it's your disgusting behaviour, Pussum, it's nothing else.—Oh, how awful! Libidnikov, *do* let us go."

"He's only drunk one glass—only one glass," came the rapid, hushed voice of the young Russian.

They all moved off to the door. The girl kept near to Gerald, and 25 seemed to be at one in her motion with him. He was aware of this, and filled with demon-satisfaction that his motion held good for two. He held her in the hollow of his will, and she was soft, secret, invisible in her stirring there.

They crowded five of them into the taxi-cab. Halliday lurched in 30 first, and dropped into his seat against the other window. Then the Pussum took her place, and Gerald sat next to her. They heard the young Russian giving orders to the driver, then they were all seated in the dark, crowded close together, Halliday groaning and leaning out of the window. They felt the swift, muffled motion of the car.

35 The Pussum sat near to Gerald, and she seemed to become soft, subtly to infuse herself into his bones, as if she were passing into him in a black, electric flow. Her being suffused into his veins like a magnetic darkness, and concentrated at the base of his spine like a fearful source of power. Meanwhile her voice sounded out reedy and 40 nonchalant, as she talked indifferently with Birkin and with Maxim.

Between her and Gerald was this silence and this black, electric comprehension in the darkness. Then she found his hand, and grasped it in her own firm, small clasp. It was so utterly dark, and yet such a naked statement, that rapid vibrations ran through his blood and over his brain, he was no longer responsible. Still her voice rang on like a bell, tinged with a tone of mockery. And as she swung her head, her fine mane of hair just swept his face, and all his nerves were on fire, as with a subtle friction of electricity. But the great centre of his force held steady, a magnificent pride to him, at the base of his spine.

They arrived at a large block of buildings,* went up in a lift, and presently a door was being opened for them by a Hindu. Gerald looked in surprise, wondering if he were a gentleman, one of the Hindus down from Oxford, perhaps. But no, he was the man-servant.

"Make tea, Hasan,"* said Halliday.

"There is a room for me?" said Birkin.

To both of which questions the man grinned, and murmured.

He made Gerald uncertain, because, being tall and slender and reticent, he looked like a gentleman.

"Who is your servant?" he asked of Halliday. "He looks a swell."

"Oh yes—that's because he's dressed in another man's clothes. He's anything but a swell, really. We found him in the road, starving. So I took him here, and another man gave him clothes. He's anything but what he seems to be—his only advantage is that he can't speak English and can't understand it, so he's perfectly safe."

"He's very dirty," said the young Russian swiftly and silently.

Directly, the man appeared in the doorway.

"What is it?" said Halliday.

The Hindu grinned, and murmured shyly:

"Want to speak to master."

Gerald watched curiously. The fellow in the doorway was good-looking and clean-limbed, his bearing was calm, he looked elegant, aristocratic. Yet he was half a savage, grinning foolishly. Halliday went out into the corridor to speak with him.

"What?" they heard his voice. "What? What do you say? Tell me again. What? Want money? Want *more* money? But what do you want money for?" There was the confused sound of the Hindu's talking, then Halliday appeared in the room, smiling also foolishly, and saying:

"He says he wants money to buy underclothing. Can anybody lend me a shilling? Oh thanks, a shilling will do to buy all the underclothes he wants." He took the money from Gerald and went out into the passage again, where they heard him saying, "You can't want more money, you had three and six yesterday. You mustn't ask for any more. Bring the tea in quickly."

Gerald looked round the room. It was an ordinary London sitting-room in a flat, evidently taken furnished, rather common and ugly. But there were several negro statues, wood-carvings from West Africa,* strange and disturbing, the carved negroes looked almost like the foetus of a human being. One was of a woman sitting naked in a strange posture, and looking tortured, her abdomen stuck out. The young Russian explained that she was sitting in childbirth,* clutching the ends of the band that hung from her neck, one in each hand, so that she could bear down, and help labour. The strange, transfixed, rudimentary face of the woman again reminded Gerald of a foetus, it was also rather wonderful, conveying the suggestion of the extreme of physical sensation, beyond the limits of mental consciousness.

"Aren't they rather obscene?" he asked, disapproving.

"I don't know," murmured the other rapidly. "I have never defined the obscene. I think they are very good."

Gerald turned away. There were one or two new pictures in the room, in the Futurist manner;* there was a large piano. And these, with some ordinary London lodging-house furniture of the better sort, completed the whole.

The Pussum had taken off her hat and coat, and was seated on the sofa. She was evidently quite at home in the house, but uncertain, suspended. She did not quite know her position. Her alliance for the time being was with Gerald, and she did not know how far this was admitted by any of the men. She was considering how she should carry off the situation. She was determined to have her experience. Now, at this eleventh hour, she was not to be balked. Her face was flushed as with battle, her eye was brooding but inevitable.

The man came in with tea and a bottle of Kümmel.* He set the tray on a little table before the couch.

"Pussum," said Halliday, "pour out the tea."

She did not move.

"Won't you do it?" Halliday repeated, in a state of nervous apprehension.

"I've not come back here as it was before," she said. "I only came because the others wanted me to, not for your sake."

"My dear Pussum, you know you are your own mistress. I don't want you to do anything but use the flat for your own convenience—you know it, I've told you so many times."

She did not reply, but silently, reservedly reached for the tea-pot. They all sat round and drank tea. Gerald could feel the electric connection between him and her so strongly, as she sat there quiet and withheld, that another set of conditions altogether had come to pass. Her silence and her immutability perplexed him. *How* was he going to come to her? And yet he felt it quite inevitable. He trusted completely to the current that held them. His perplexity was only superficial, new conditions reigned, the old were surpassed; here one did as one was possessed to do, no matter what it was.

Birkin rose. It was nearly one o'clock.

"I'm going to bed," he said. "Gerald, I'll ring you up in the morning at your place—or you ring me up here."

"Right," said Gerald, and Birkin went out.

When he was well gone, Halliday said in a stimulated voice, to Gerald:

"I say, won't you stay here—oh do!"

"You can't put everybody up," said Gerald.

"Oh but I can, perfectly—there are three more beds besides mine—do stay, won't you. Everything is quite ready—there is always somebody here—I always put people up—I love having the house crowded."

"But there are only two rooms," said the Pussum, in a cold, hostile voice, "now Rupert's here."

"I know there are only two rooms," said Halliday, in his odd, high way of speaking. "But what does that matter?"

He was smiling rather foolishly, and he spoke eagerly, with an insinuating determination.

"Julius and I will share one room," said the Russian in his discreet, precise voice. Halliday and he were friends since Eton.*

"It's very simple," said Gerald, rising and pressing back his arms, stretching himself. Then he went again to look at one of the pictures. Every one of his limbs was turgid with electric force, and his back was tense like a tiger's, with slumbering fire. He was very proud.

The Pussum rose. She gave a black look at Halliday, black and deadly, which brought the rather foolish, pleased smile to that young man's face. Then she went out of the room, with a cold Goodnight to them all generally.

There was a brief interval, they heard a door close, then Maxim said, in his refined voice:

5   "That's all right."

He looked significantly at Gerald, and said again, with a slight nod:

"That's all right—you're all right."

Gerald looked at the smooth, ruddy, comely face, and at the
10 strange, significant eyes, and it seemed as if the voice of the young Russian, so small and perfect, sounded in the blood rather than in the air.

"*I'm* all right then," said Gerald.

"Yes! Yes! You're all right," said the Russian.

15 Halliday continued to smile, and to say nothing.

Suddenly the Pussum appeared again in the door, her small, childish face looking sullen and vindictive.

"I know you want to catch me out," came her cold, rather resonant voice. "But I don't care, I don't care how much you catch me out."

20 She turned and was gone again. She had been wearing a loose dressing-gown of purple silk, tied round her waist. She looked so small and childish and vulnerable, almost pitiful. And yet the black looks of her eyes made Gerald feel drowned in some potent darkness that almost frightened him.

25 The men lit another cigarette and talked casually.

Chapter VII

Fetish*

In the morning Gerald woke late. He had slept heavily. Pussum was still asleep, sleeping childishly and pathetically. There was something small and curled up and defenceless about her, that roused an unsatisfied flame of passion in the young man's blood, a devouring, avid pity. He looked at her again. But it would be too cruel to wake her. He subdued himself, and went away.

Hearing voices coming from the sitting-room, Halliday talking to Libidnikov, he went to the door and glanced in, knowing he might go about in this bachelor establishment in his trousers and shirt.*

To his surprise he saw the two young men by the fire, stark naked. Halliday looked up, rather pleased.

"Good-morning," he said. "Oh—did you want towels?"

And stark naked, he went out into the hall, striding a strange, white figure between the unliving furniture. He came back with the towels, and took his former position, crouching seated before the fire on the fender.

"Don't you love to feel the fire on your skin?" he said.

"It *is* rather pleasant," said Gerald.

"How perfectly splendid it must be to be in a climate where one could do without clothing altogether," said Halliday.

"Yes," said Gerald, "if there weren't so many things that sting and bite."

"That's a disadvantage," murmured Maxim.

Gerald looked at him, and with a slight revulsion saw the human animal, golden skinned and bare, somehow humiliating. Halliday was different. He had a rather heavy, slack, broken beauty, white and firm. He was like a Christ in a Pietà. The animal was not there at all, only the heavy, broken beauty. And Gerald realised how Halliday's eyes were beautiful too, so blue and warm and confused, broken also in their expression. The fireglow fell on his heavy, rather bowed shoulders, he sat slackly crouched on the fender, his face was uplifted, degenerate, perhaps slightly disintegrate, and yet with a moving beauty of its own.

"Of course," said Maxim, "you've been in hot countries where the people go about naked."

"Oh really!" exclaimed Halliday. "Where?"

"South America—Amazon," said Gerald.

5   "Oh but how perfectly splendid! It's one of the things I want most to do—to live from day to day without *ever* putting on any sort of clothing whatever. If I could do that, I should feel I had lived."

"But why?" said Gerald. "I can't see that it makes so much difference."

10 "Oh, I think it would be perfectly splendid. I'm sure life would be entirely another thing—entirely different, and perfectly wonderful."

"But why?" asked Gerald. "Why should it?"

"Oh—one would *feel* things instead of merely looking at them. I should feel the air move against me, and feel the things I touched, 15 instead of having only to look at them. I'm sure life is all wrong because it has become much too visual—we can neither hear nor feel nor understand, we can only see. I'm sure that is entirely wrong."

"Yes, that is true, that is true," said the Russian.

Gerald glanced at him, and saw him, his suave, golden coloured 20 body with the black hair growing fine and freely, like tendrils, and his limbs like smooth plant-stems. He was so healthy and well-made, why did he make one ashamed, why did one feel repelled. Why should Gerald even dislike it, why did it seem to him to detract from his own dignity. Was that all a human being amounted to? So 25 uninspired! thought Gerald.

Birkin suddenly appeared in the doorway, also in a state of nudity, towel and sleeping suit over his arm. He was very narrow and white, and somehow apart.

"There's the bath-room now, if you want it," he said generally, 30 and was going away again, when Gerald called:

"I say, Rupert!"

"What?" The single white figure appeared again, a presence in the room.

"What do you think of that figure there? I want to know," Gerald 35 asked.

Birkin, white and strangely present, went over to the carved figure of the negro woman in labour. Her nude, protuberant body crouched in a strange, clutching posture, her hands gripping the ends of the band, above her breast.

40 "It is art," said Birkin.

"Very beautiful, it's very beautiful," said the Russian.

They all drew near to look. Gerald looked at the group of naked men, the Russian golden and like a water-plant, Halliday tall and heavily, brokenly beautiful, Birkin very white and immediate, not to be defined, as he looked closely at the carven woman. Strangely elated, Gerald also lifted his eyes to the face of the wooden figure. And his heart contracted.

He saw vividly, with his spirit, the grey, forward-stretching face of the negro woman, African and tense, abstracted in utter physical stress. It was a terrible face, void, peaked, abstracted almost into meaninglessness by the weight of sensation beneath. He saw the Pussum in it. As in a dream, he knew her.

"Why is it art?" Gerald asked, shocked, resentful.

"It conveys a complete truth," said Birkin. "It contains the whole truth of that state, whatever you feel about it."

"But you can't call it *high* art," said Gerald.

"High! There are centuries and hundreds of centuries of development in a straight line, behind that carving; it is an awful pitch of culture, of a definite sort."

"What culture?" Gerald asked, in opposition. He hated the sheer African thing.

"Pure culture in sensation, culture in the physical consciousness, really *ultimate* physical consciousness, mindless, utterly sensual. It is so sensual as to be final, supreme."

But Gerald resented it. He wanted to keep certain illusions, certain ideas like clothing.

"You like the wrong things, Rupert," he said, "things against yourself."

"Oh, I know, this isn't everything," Birkin replied, moving away.

When Gerald went back to his room from the bath, he also carried his clothes. It seemed bad form in this house, not to go about naked. And after all, it was rather nice, there *was* a real simplicity. Still, it was rather funny, everybody being so deliberately nude.

The Pussum lay in her bed, motionless, her round, dark eyes like black, unhappy pools. He could only see the black, bottomless pools of her eyes. Perhaps she suffered. The sensation of her inchoate suffering roused the old sharp flame in him, a mordant pity, a passion almost of cruelty.

"You are awake now," he said to her.

"What time is it?" came her muted voice.

She seemed to flow back, almost like liquid, from his approach, to sink helplessly away from him. Her inchoate look of a violated slave, whose fulfilment lies in her further and further violation, made his nerves quiver with acutely desirable sensation. After all, his was the only will, she was the passive substance of his will. He tingled with the subtle, biting sensation. And then he knew, he must go away from her, there must be pure separation between them.

It was a quiet and ordinary breakfast, the four men all looking very clean and bathed. Gerald and the Russian were both correct and *comme il faut* in appearance and manner, Birkin was gaunt and sick, and looked a failure in his attempt to be a properly dressed man, like Gerald and Maxim. Halliday wore tweeds and a green flannel shirt, and a rag of a tie, which was just right for him. The Hindu brought in a great deal of soft toast, and looked exactly the same as he had looked the night before, statically the same.

At the end of the breakfast the Pussum appeared, in a purple silk wrap with a shimmering sash. She had recovered herself somewhat, but was mute and lifeless still. It was a torment to her when anybody spoke to her. Her face was like a small, fine mask, sinister too, masked with unwilling suffering. It was almost midday. Gerald rose and went away to his business, glad to get out. But he had not finished. He was coming back again at evening, they were all dining together, and he had booked seats for the party, excepting Birkin, at a music-hall.

At night they came back to the flat very late again, again flushed with drink. Again the man-servant—who invariably disappeared between the hours of ten and twelve at night—came in silently and inscrutably with tea, bending in a slow, strange, leopard-like fashion to put the tray softly on the table. His face was immutable, aristocratic-looking, tinged slightly with grey under the skin; he was young and good-looking. But Birkin felt a slight sickness, looking at him, and feeling the slight greyness an ash of corruption,* the aristocratic inscrutability of expression a nauseating, bestial stupidity.

Again they talked cordially and rousedly together. But already a certain friability was coming over the party, Birkin was mad with irritation, Halliday was turning in an insane hatred against Gerald, the Pussum was becoming hard and cold, like a flint knife, and Halliday was laying himself out to her. And her intention, ultimately, was to capture Halliday, to have complete power over him.

In the morning they all stalked and lounged about again. But Gerald could feel a strange hostility to himself, in the air. It roused his obstinacy, and he stood up against it. He hung on for two more days. The result was a nasty and insane scene with Halliday on the fourth evening. Halliday turned with absurd animosity upon Gerald, in the Café. There was a row. Gerald was on the point of knocking-in Halliday's face; when he was filled with sudden disgust and indifference, and he went away, leaving Halliday in a foolish state of gloating triumph,* the Pussum hard and established, and Maxim standing clear. Birkin was absent, he had gone out of town again.

Gerald was piqued because he had left without giving the Pussum money. It was true, she did not care whether he gave her money or not, and he knew it. But she would have been glad of ten pounds, and he would have been *very* glad to give them to her. Now he felt in a false position. He went away chewing his lips to get at the ends of his short clipped moustache. He knew the Pussum was merely glad to be rid of him. She had got her Halliday, whom she wanted. She wanted him completely in her power. Then she would marry him. She wanted to marry him. She had set her will on marrying Halliday. She never wanted to hear of Gerald again; unless, perhaps, she were in difficulty. Because after all, Gerald was what she called a man, and these others, Halliday, Libidnikov, Birkin, the whole Bohemian set, they were only half men. But it was half men she could deal with. She felt sure of herself with them. The real men, like Gerald, put her in her place too much.

Still, she respected Gerald, she really respected him. She had managed to get his address, so that she could appeal to him in time of distress. She knew he wanted to give her money. She would perhaps write to him on that inevitable rainy day.

Chapter VIII

Breadalby

Breadalby was a Georgian house with Corinthian pillars, standing among the softer, greener hills of Derbyshire, not far from Cromford. In front, it looked over a lawn, over a few trees, down to a string of fish-ponds in the hollow of the silent park. At the back were trees, among which were to be found the stables, and the big kitchen garden, behind which was a wood.

It was a very quiet place, some miles from the high-road, back from the Derwent valley, outside the show scenery. Silent and forsaken, the golden stucco showed between the trees, the house-front looked down the park, unchanged and unchanging.

Of late, however, Hermione had lived a good deal at the house. She had turned away from London, away from Oxford, towards the silence of the country. Her father was mostly absent, abroad, she was either alone in the house, with her visitors, of whom there were always several, or she had with her her brother, a bachelor, and a Liberal member of Parliament.* He always came down when the House was not sitting, seemed always to be present in Breadalby, although he was most conscientious in his attendance to duty.

The summer was just coming in when Ursula and Gudrun went to stay the second time with Hermione. Coming along in the car, after they had entered the park, they looked across the dip, where the fish-ponds lay in silence, at the pillared front of the house, sunny and small like an English drawing of the old school,* on the brow of the green hill, against the trees. There were small figures on the green lawn, women in lavender and yellow moving to the shade of the enormous, beautifully balanced cedar tree.

"Isn't it complete!" said Gudrun. "It is as final as an old aquatint." She spoke with some resentment in her voice, as if she were captivated unwillingly, as if she must admire against her will.

"Do you love it?" asked Ursula.

"I don't *love* it, but in its way, I think it is quite complete."

The motor-car ran down the hill and up again in one breath, and they were curving to the side door. A parlour-maid appeared, and then Hermione, coming forward with her pale face lifted, and her hands outstretched, advancing straight to the new-comers, her voice singing:

"Here you are—I'm so glad to see you—" she kissed Gudrun— "—so glad to see you—" she kissed Ursula and remained with her arm round her. "Are you very tired?"

"Not at all tired," said Ursula.

"Are you tired, Gudrun?"

"Not at all, thanks," said Gudrun.

"No—" drawled Hermione. And she stood and looked at them. The two girls were embarrassed because she would not move into the house, but must have her little scene of welcome there on the path. The servants waited.

"Come in," said Hermione at last, having fully taken in the pair of them. Gudrun was the more beautiful and attractive, she had decided again, Ursula was more physical, more womanly. She admired Gudrun's dress more. It was of green poplin, with a loose coat above it, of broad, dark-green and dark-brown stripes. The hat was of a pale, greenish straw, the colour of new hay, and it had a plaited ribbon of black and orange, the stockings were dark green, the shoes black. It was a good get-up, at once fashionable and individual. Ursula, in dark blue, was more ordinary, though she also looked well.

Hermione herself wore a dress of prune-coloured silk, with coral beads and coral coloured stockings. But her dress was both shabby and soiled, even rather dirty.

"You would like to see your rooms now, wouldn't you! Yes. We will go up now, shall we?"

Ursula was glad when she could be left alone in her room. Hermione lingered so long, made such a stress on one. She stood so near to one, pressing herself near upon one, in a way that was most embarrassing and oppressive. She seemed to hinder one's workings.

Lunch was served on the lawn, under the great tree, whose thick, blackish boughs came down close to the grass. There were present a young Italian woman, slight and fashionable, a young, athletic-looking Miss Bradley, a learned, dry Baronet of fifty, who was always making witticisms and laughing at them heartily in a harsh, horse-laugh, there was Rupert Birkin, and then a woman secretary, a Fräulein März,* young and slim and pretty.

The food was very good, that was one thing. Gudrun, critical of

everything, gave it her full approval. Ursula loved the situation, the white table by the cedar tree, the scent of new sunshine, the little vision of the leafy park, with far-off deer feeding peacefully. There seemed a magic circle drawn about the place, shutting out the
5 present, enclosing the delightful, precious past, trees and deer and silence, like a dream.

But in spirit she was unhappy. The talk went on like a rattle of small artillery, always slightly sententious, with a sententiousness that was only emphasised by the continual crackling of a witticism,
10 the continual spatter of verbal jest, designed to give a tone of flippancy to a stream of conversation that was all critical and general, a canal of conversation rather than a stream.

The attitude was mental and very wearying. Only the elderly sociologist, whose mental fibre was so tough as to be insentient,
15 seemed to be thoroughly happy. Birkin was down in the mouth. Hermione appeared, with amazing persistence, to wish to ridicule him and make him look ignominious in the eyes of everybody. And it was surprising how she seemed to succeed, how helpless he seemed against her. He looked completely insignificant. Ursula and Gudrun,
20 both very unused, were mostly silent, listening to the slow, rhapsodic sing-song of Hermione, or the verbal sallies of Sir Joshua, or the prattle of Fräulein, or the responses of the other two women.

Luncheon was over, coffee was brought out on to the grass, the party left the table and sat about in lounge chairs, in the shade or in
25 the sunshine as they wished. Fräulein departed into the house, Hermione took up her embroidery, the little contessa took a book, Miss Bradley was weaving a basket out of fine grass, and there they all were on the lawn, in the early summer afternoon, working leisurely and spattering with half-intellectual, deliberate talk.
30 Suddenly there was the sound of the brakes and the shutting off of a motor-car.

"There's Salsie!"* sang Hermione, in her slow, amusing sing-song. And laying down her work, she rose slowly, and slowly passed over the lawn, round the bushes, out of sight.
35 "Who is it?" asked Gudrun.

"Mr Roddice—Miss Roddice's brother—at least, I suppose it's he," said Sir Joshua.

"Salsie, yes, it is her brother," said the little contessa, lifting her head for a moment from her book, and speaking as if to give
40 information, in her slightly deepened, guttural English.

They all waited. And then, round the bushes came the tall form of Alexander Roddice, striding romantically like a Meredith hero who remembers Disraeli.* He was cordial with everybody, he was at once a host, with an easy, off-hand hospitality that he had learned for Hermione's friends. He had just come down from London, from the House. At once the atmosphere of the House of Commons made itself felt over the lawn: the Home Secretary had said such and such a thing, and he, Roddice, on the other hand, thought such and such a thing, and had said so-and-so to the P. M.

Now Hermione came round the bushes with Gerald Crich. He had come along with Alexander. Gerald was presented to everybody, was kept by Hermione for a few moments in full view, then he was led away, still by Hermione. He was evidently her guest of the moment.

There had been a split in the Cabinet; the minister for Education had resigned owing to adverse criticism.* This started a conversation on education.

"Of course," said Hermione, lifting her face like a rhapsodist, "there *can* be no reason, no *excuse* for education, except the joy and beauty of knowledge in itself." She seemed to rumble and ruminate with subterranean thoughts for a minute, then she proceeded: "Vocational education *isn't* education, it is the close of education."

Gerald, on the brink of a discussion, sniffed the air with delight and prepared for action.

"Not necessarily," he said. "But isn't education really like gymnastics, isn't the end of education the production of a well-trained, vigorous, energetic mind?"

"Just as athletics produce a healthy body, ready for anything," cried Miss Bradley, in hearty accord.

Gudrun looked at her in silent loathing.

"Well—" rumbled Hermione, "I don't know. To me the pleasure of knowing is *so* great, so *wonderful*—nothing has meant so much to me in all life, as certain knowledge—no, I am sure—nothing."

"What knowledge, for example, Hermione?" asked Alexander.

Hermione lifted her face and rumbled—

"m- m- m- I don't know.———But one thing was the stars, when I really understood something about the stars. One feels so *uplifted*, so *unbounded*——————"

Birkin looked at her in a white fury.

"What do you want to feel unbounded for?" he said sarcastically. "You don't want to *be* unbounded."

Hermione recoiled in offence.

"Yes, but one does have that limitless feeling," said Gerald. "It's
5 like getting on top of the mountain and seeing the Pacific."

"Silent upon a peak in Dariayn,"* murmured the Italian, lifting her face for a moment from her book.

"Not necessarily in Darien," said Gerald, while Ursula began to laugh.

10 Hermione waited for the dust to settle, and then she said, untouched:

"Yes, it is the greatest thing in life—*to know*. It is really to be happy, to be *free*."

"Knowledge is, of course, liberty," said Malleson.

15 "In compressed tabloids," said Birkin, looking at the dry, stiff little body of the Baronet. Immediately Gudrun saw the famous sociologist as a flat bottle, containing tabloids of compressed liberty. That pleased her. Sir Joshua was labelled and placed forever in her mind.

20 "What does that mean, Rupert?" sang Hermione, in a calm snub.

"You can only have knowledge, strictly," he replied, "of things concluded, in the past.* It's like bottling the liberty of last summer in the bottled gooseberries."

25 "Can one have knowledge only of the past?" asked the baronet, pointedly. "Could we call our knowledge of the laws of gravitation,* for instance, knowledge of the past?"

"Yes," said Birkin.

"There is a most beautiful thing in my book," suddenly piped
30 the little Italian woman. "It says the man came to the door and threw his eyes down the street."

There was a general laugh in the company. Miss Bradley went and looked over the shoulder of the contessa.

"See!" said the contessa.

35 "Bazarov came to the door and threw his eyes hurriedly down the street,"* she read.

Again there was a loud laugh, the most startling of which was the Baronet's, which rattled out like a clatter of falling stones.

"What is the book?" asked Alexander, promptly.

40 "*Fathers and Sons*, by Turgenev," said the little foreigner, pro-

nouncing every syllable distinctly. She looked at the cover, to verify herself.

"An old American edition," said Birkin.

"Ha! of course—translated from the French," said Alexander, with a fine declamatory voice. "Bazarov ouvra la porte et jeta les yeux dans la rue."

He looked brightly round the company.

"I wonder what the 'hurriedly' was," said Ursula.

They all began to guess.

And then, to the amazement of everybody, the maid came hurrying with a large tea-tray. The afternoon had passed so swiftly.

After tea, they were all gathered for a walk.

"Would you like to come for a walk?" said Hermione to each of them, one by one. And they all said yes, feeling somehow like prisoners marshalled for exercise. Birkin only refused.

"Will you come for a walk, Rupert?"

"No, Hermione."

"But are you *sure*?"

"Quite sure."

There was a second's hesitation.

"And why not?" sang Hermione's question. It made her blood run sharp, to be thwarted in even so trifling a matter. She intended them all to walk with her in the park.

"Because I don't like trooping off in a gang," he said.

Her voice rumbled in her throat for a moment. Then she said, with a curious stray calm:

"Then we'll leave a little boy behind, if he's sulky."

And she looked really gay, while she insulted him. But it merely made him stiff.

She trailed off to the rest of the company, only turning to wave her handkerchief to him, and to chuckle with laughter, singing out:

"Goodbye, goodbye little boy."

"Goodbye impudent hag," he said to himself.

They all went through the park. Hermione wanted to show them the wild daffodils on a little slope. "This way, this way," sang her leisurely voice at intervals. And they had all to come this way. The daffodils were pretty, but who could see them? Ursula was stiff all over with resentment by this time, resentment of the whole atmosphere. Gudrun, mocking and objective, watched and registered everything.

They looked at the shy deer, and Hermione talked to the stag, as if he too were a boy she wanted to wheedle and fondle. He was male, so she must exert some kind of power over him. They trailed home by the fish-ponds, and Hermione told them about the quarrel of two
5 male swans, who had striven for the love of the one lady. She chuckled and laughed as she told how the ousted lover had sat with his head buried under his wing, on the gravel.

When they arrived back at the house, Hermione stood on the lawn and sang out, in a strange, small, high voice that carried very far:
10 "Rupert! Rupert!" The first syllable was high and slow, the second dropped down. "Roo-o-opert."

But there was no answer. A maid appeared.

"Where is Mr Birkin, Alice?" asked the mild, straying voice of Hermione. But under the straying voice, what a persistent, almost
15 insane *will*!

"I think he's in his room, my lady."*

"Is he."

Hermione went slowly up the stairs, along the corridor, singing out in her high, small call:
20 "Ru-oo-pert! Ru-oo-pert!"

She came to his door, and tapped, still crying: "Roo-pert."

"Yes," sounded his voice at last.

"What are you doing?"

The question was mild and curious.
25 There was no answer. Then he opened the door.

"We've come back," said Hermione. "The daffodils are *so* beautiful."

"Yes," he said, "I've seen them."

She looked at him with her long, slow, impassive look, along her
30 cheeks.

"Have you," she echoed. And she remained looking at him. She was stimulated above all things by this conflict with him, when he was like a sulky boy, helpless, and she had him safe at Breadalby. But underneath she knew the split was coming, and her hatred of him
35 was subconscious and intense.

"What were you doing?" she reiterated, in her mild, indifferent tone. He did not answer, and she made her way, almost unconsciously, into his room. He had taken a Chinese drawing of geese from the boudoir, and was copying it, with much skill and
40 vividness.*

"You are copying the drawing," she said, standing near the table and looking down at his work. "Yes—How beautifully you do it! You like it very much, don't you?"

"It's a marvellous drawing," he said.

"Is it? I'm so glad you like it, because I've always been fond of it.—The Chinese ambassador gave it me."

"I know," he said.

"But why do you copy it?" she asked, casual and sing-song. "Why not do something original?"

"I want to know it," he replied. "One gets more of China, copying this picture, than reading all the books."

"And what do you get?"

She was at once roused, she laid as it were violent hands on him, to extract his secrets from him. She *must* know. It was a dreadful tyranny, an obsession in her, to know all he knew. For some time he was silent, hating to answer her. Then, compelled, he began:

"I know what centres they live from—what they perceive and feel—the hot, stinging centrality of a goose in the flux* of cold water and mud—the curious bitter stinging heat of a goose's blood, entering their own blood like an inoculation of corruptive fire—fire of the cold-burning mud—the lotus mystery."

Hermione looked at him along her narrow, pallid cheeks. Her eyes were strange and drugged, heavy under their heavy, dropping lids. Her thin bosom shrugged convulsively. He stared back at her, devilish and unchanging. With another strange, sick convulsion, she turned away, as if she were sick, could feel dissolution setting-in in her body. For with her mind she was unable to attend to his words, he caught her, as it were, beneath all her defences, and destroyed her with some insidious occult potency.

"Yes," she said, as if she did not know what she were saying. "Yes." and she swallowed, and tried to regain her mind. But she could not, she was witless, decentralised. Use all her will as she might, she could not recover. She suffered the ghastliness of dissolution, broken and gone in a horrible corruption. And he stood and looked at her unmoved. She strayed out, pallid and preyed-upon like a ghost, like one attacked by the tomb-influences which dog us. And she was gone like a corpse, that has no presence, no connection. He remained hard and vindictive.

Hermione came down to dinner strange and sepulchral, her eyes heavy and full of sepulchral darkness, strength. She had put on a

dress of stiff old greenish brocade, that fitted tight and made her look tall and rather terrible, ghastly. In the gay light of the drawing-room she was uncanny and oppressive. But seated in the half-light of the dining-room, sitting stiffly before the shaded candles on the table,
5 she seemed a power, a presence. She listened and attended with a drugged attention.

The party was gay and extravagant in appearance, everybody had put on evening dress except Birkin and Joshua Malleson. The little Italian contessa wore a dress of tissue of orange and gold and black
10 velvet in soft wide stripes, Gudrun was emerald green with strange net-work of grey, Ursula was in yellow with dull silver veiling, Miss Bradley was crimson* and jet, Fräulein März wore pale blue. It gave Hermione a sudden convulsive sensation of pleasure, to see these rich colours under the candle-light. She was aware of the talk going
15 on, ceaselessly, Joshua's voice dominating; of the ceaseless pitter-patter of women's light laughter and responses; of the brilliant colours and the white table and the shadow above and below; and she seemed in a swoon of gratification, convulsed with pleasure, and yet sick, like a *revenant.** She took very little part in the conversation, yet
20 she heard it all, it was all hers.

They all went together into the drawing-room, as if they were one family, easily, without any attention to ceremony. Fräulein handed the coffee, everybody smoked cigarettes, or else long warden pipes* of white clay, of which a sheaf was provided.
25 "Wiill you smooke?—cigarettes or pipe?" asked Fräulein prettily.

There was a circle of people, Sir Joshua with his eighteenth-century appearance, Gerald the amused, handsome young Englishman, Alexander tall and the handsome politician, democratic and lucid, Hermione strange like a long Cassandra,* and the women
30 lurid with colour, all dutifully smoking their long white pipes, and sitting in a half-moon in the comfortable, soft-lighted drawing-room, round the logs that flickered on the marble hearth.

The talk was very often political or sociological, and interesting, curiously anarchistic. There was an accumulation of powerful force
35 in the room, powerful and destructive. Everything seemed to be thrown into the melting pot, and it seemed to Ursula they were all witches, helping the pot to bubble. There was an elation and a satisfaction in it all, but it was cruelly exhausting for the new-comers, this ruthless mental pressure, this powerful, consuming, destructive
40 mentality that emanated from Joshua and Hermione and Birkin, and dominated the rest.

But a sickness, a fearful nausea gathered possession of Hermione. There was a lull in the talk, as it was arrested by her unconscious but all-powerful will.

"Salsie, won't you play something?" said Hermione, breaking off completely. "Won't somebody dance? Gudrun, you will dance, won't 5 you? I wish you would. Anche tu, Palestra, ballerai?—si, per piacere.* You too, Ursula."

Hermione rose and slowly pulled the gold-embroidered band that hung by the mantel, clinging to it for a moment, then releasing it suddenly. Like a priestess she looked, unconscious, sunk in a heavy 10 half-trance. A servant came, and soon reappeared with armfuls of silk robes and shawls and scarves, mostly oriental, things that Hermione, with her love for beautiful extravagant dress, had collected gradually.*

"The three women will dance together," she said. 15

"What shall it be?" asked Alexander, rising briskly.

"Vergini Delle Rocchette,"* said the contessa at once.

"They are so languid," said Ursula.

"The three witches from Macbeth," suggested Fräulein usefully.

It was finally decided to do Naomi and Ruth and Orpah.* Ursula 20 was Naomi, Gudrun was Ruth, the contessa was Orpah. The idea was to make a little ballet, in the style of the Russian Ballet of Pavlova and Nijinsky.*

The contessa was ready first. Alexander went to the piano, a space was cleared, Orpah, in beautiful oriental clothes, began slowly to 25 dance the death of her husband. Then Ruth came, and they wept together, and lamented, then Naomi came to comfort them. It was all done in dumb show, the women danced their emotion in gesture and motion. The little drama went on for a quarter of an hour.

Ursula was beautiful as Naomi. All her men were dead, it 30 remained to her only to stand alone in indomitable assertion, demanding nothing. Ruth, woman-loving, loved her. Orpah, a vivid, sensational, subtle widow, would go back to the former life,* a repetition. The interplay between the women was real and rather frightening. It was strange to see how Gudrun clung with heavy, 35 desperate passion to Ursula, yet smiled with subtle malevolence against her, how Ursula accepted silently, unable to provide any more either for herself or for the other, but dangerous and indomitable, refuting her grief.

Hermione loved to watch. She could see the contessa's rapid, 40 stoat-like sensationalism, Gudrun's ultimate but treacherous cleaving* to the woman in her sister, Ursula's dangerous helplessness, as if she were helplessly weighted, and unreleased.

"That was very beautiful," everybody cried with one accord. But Hermione writhed in her soul, knowing what she could not know.
5 She cried out for more dancing, and it was her will that set the contessa and Birkin moving mockingly in Malbrouk.*

Gerald was excited by the desperate cleaving of Gudrun to Naomi. The essence of that female, subterranean recklessness and mockery penetrated his blood. He could not forget Gudrun's lifted,
10 offered, cleaving, reckless, yet withal mocking weight. And Birkin, watching like a hermit crab from its hole, had seen the brilliant frustration and helplessness of Ursula. She was rich, full of dangerous power. She was like a strange unconscious bud of powerful womanhood. He was unconsciously drawn to her. She was his
15 future.

Alexander played some Hungarian music,* and they all danced, seized by the spirit. Gerald was marvellously exhilarated at finding himself in motion, moving towards Gudrun, dancing with feet that could not yet escape from the waltz and the two-step, but feeling his
20 force stir along his limbs and his body, out of captivity. He did not know yet how to dance their convulsive, rag-time sort of dancing,* but he knew how to begin. Birkin, when he could get free from the weight of the people present, whom he disliked, danced rapidly and with a real gaiety. And how Hermione hated him for this irrespons-
25 ible gaiety.

"Now I see," cried the contessa excitedly, watching his purely gay motion, which he had all to himself. "Mr Birkin, he is a changer."

Hermione looked at her slowly, and shuddered, knowing that only a foreigner could have seen and have said this.
30 "Cosa vuol dire,* Palestra?" she asked, sing-song.

"Look," said the contessa, in Italian. "He is not a man, he is a chameleon, a creature of change."

"He is not a man, he is treacherous, not one of us," sang itself over in Hermione's consciousness. And her soul writhed in the black
35 subjugation to him, because of his power to escape, to exist, other than she did, because he was not consistent, not a man, less than a man. She hated him in a despair that shattered her and broke her down, so that she suffered sheer dissolution, like a corpse, and was unconscious of everything save the horrible sickness of dissolution
40 that was taking place within her, body and soul.

The house being full, Gerald was given the smaller room, really the dressing-room, communicating with Birkin's bedroom. When they all took their candles and mounted the stairs, where the lamps were burning subduedly, Hermione captured Ursula and brought her into her own bedroom, to talk to her. A sort of constraint came over Ursula, in the big, strange bedroom. Hermione seemed to be bearing down on her, awful and inchoate, making some appeal. They were looking at some Indian silk shirts, gorgeous and sensual in themselves, their shape, their almost corrupt gorgeousness. And Hermione came near, and her bosom writhed, and Ursula was for a moment blank with panic. And for a moment, Hermione's haggard eyes saw the fear on the face of the other, there was again a sort of crash, a crashing down. And Ursula picked up a shirt of rich red and blue silk, made for a young princess of fourteen, and was crying mechanically:

"Isn't it wonderful—who would dare to put those two strong colours together——"

Then Hermione's maid entered silently, and Ursula, overcome with dread, escaped, carried away by powerful impulse.

Birkin went straight to bed. He was feeling happy, and sleepy. Since he had danced he was happy. But Gerald would talk to him. Gerald, in evening dress, sat on Birkin's bed when the other lay down, and must talk.

"Who are those two Brangwens?" Gerald asked.

"They live in Beldover."

"In Beldover! Who are they, then?"

"Teachers in the Grammar School."

There was a pause.

"They are?" said* Gerald at length. "I thought I had seen them before."

"It disappoints you?" said Birkin.

"Disappoints me? No.—But how is it Hermione has them here?"

"She knew Gudrun in London—that's the younger one, the one with the darker hair—she's an artist—does sculpture and modelling."

"She's not a teacher in the Grammar School, then—only the other?"

"Both—Gudrun art mistress, Ursula a class mistress."

"And what's the father?"

"Handicraft instructor in the schools."*

"Really!"

"Class-barriers are breaking down!"

Gerald was always uneasy under the slightly jeering tone of the other.

5   "That their father is handicraft instructor in a school? What does it matter to me?"

Birkin laughed. Gerald looked at his face, as it lay there laughing and bitter and indifferent, on the pillow, and he could not go away.

"I don't suppose you will see very much more of Gudrun, at least.
10 She is a restless bird, she'll be gone in a week or two," said Birkin.

"Where will she go?"

"London, Paris, Rome—heaven knows. I always expect her to sheer off to Damascus or San Francisco; she's a bird of paradise. God knows what she's got to do with Beldover. It goes by contraries,
15 like dreams."

Gerald pondered for a few moments.

"How do you know her so well?" he asked.

"I knew her in London," he replied, "in the Algernon Strange set.* She'll know about Pussum and Libidnikov and the rest—even if
20 she doesn't know them personally.—She was never quite that set—more conventional, in a way. I've known her for two years, I suppose."

"And she makes money, apart from her teaching?" asked Gerald.

"Some—irregularly. She can sell her models. She has a certain
25 réclame."

"How much for?"

"A guinea—ten guineas—."

"And are they good? What are they?"

"I think sometimes they are marvellously good. That is hers, those
30 two wagtails in Hermione's boudoir—you've seen them—they are carved in wood and painted."

"I thought it was savage carving again."

"No, hers.—That's what they are—animals and birds, sometimes odd small people in everyday dress, really rather wonderful when
35 they come off. They have a sort of funniness that is quite unconscious and subtle."

"She might be a well-known artist one day?" mused Gerald.

"She might. But I think she won't. She drops her art if anything else catches her. Her contrariness prevents her taking it seriously—
40 she must never be too serious, she feels she gives herself away. And

she won't give herself away—she's always on the defensive. That's what I can't stand about her type.—By the way, how did things go off with Pussum after I left you? I haven't heard anything."

"Oh, rather disgusting. Halliday turned objectionable, and I only just saved myself from jumping in his stomach, in a real old-fashioned row."

Birkin was silent.

"Of course," he said, "Julius is really mad.* On the one hand he's a religious maniac, and on the other, he is fascinated by obscenity. Either he is a pure servant, washing the feet of Christ, or else he is making obscene drawings of Jesus—action and reaction—and between the two, nothing. He is really split mad. He wants a pure lily, another girl, with a baby face,—the good old chaste love—and at the same time he *must* have the Pussum, just to defile himself with her."*

"That's what I can't make out," said Gerald. "Does he love her, the Pussum, or doesn't he?"

"He neither does nor doesn't. She is the harlot, the actual harlot of adultery to him. And he's got a craving to throw himself away with her. Then he gets up and turns towards the lily of purity, the baby-faced girl, and so gets another thrill. It's the old game—action and reaction, and nothing between."

"I don't know," said Gerald, after a pause, "that he does insult the Pussum so very much. She strikes me as being rather foul."

"But I thought you liked her!" exclaimed Birkin. "I always felt fond of her.—I never had anything to do with her, personally, that's true."

"I liked her all right, for a couple of days," said Gerald. "But a week of her would have turned me over. There's a certain smell about the skin of those women, that in the end is sickening beyond words—even if you like it at first."

"I know," said Birkin. Then he added, rather fretfully, "But go to bed, Gerald. God knows what time it is."

Gerald looked at his watch, and at length rose off the bed, and went to his room. But he returned in a few minutes, in his shirt.

"One thing," he said, seating himself on the bed again; "we finished up rather stormily, and I never had time to give her anything."

"Money?" said Birkin. "She'll get what she wants from Halliday or from one of her acquaintances."

"But then," said Gerald, "I'd rather give her her dues, and settle the account."

"She doesn't care."

"No, perhaps not.—But one feels the account is left open, and one would rather it were closed."

"Would you?" said Birkin. He was looking at the white legs of Gerald, as the latter sat on the side of the bed in his shirt. They were white-skinned, full, muscular legs, handsome and decided. Yet they moved Birkin with a sort of pathos, tenderness, as if they were childish.

"I think I'd rather close the account," said Gerald, repeating himself vaguely.

"It doesn't matter, one way or another," said Birkin.

"You always say it doesn't matter," said Gerald, a little puzzled, looking down at the face of the other man affectionately.

"Neither does it," said Birkin.

"But she was a decent sort, really."

"Render unto Caesarina the things that are Caesarina's,"* said Birkin, turning aside. It seemed to him Gerald was talking for the sake of talking.

"Go away, it wearies me—it's too late at night," he said.

"I wish you'd tell me something that *did* matter," said Gerald, looking down all the time at the face of the other man, waiting for something. But Birkin turned his face aside.

"All right then, go to sleep," said Gerald, and he laid his hand affectionately on the other man's shoulder, and went away.

In the morning, when Gerald awoke and heard Birkin move, he called out:

"I still think I ought to give the Pussum ten pounds."

"Oh God," said Birkin, "don't be so matter-of-fact. Close the account in your own soul, if you like. It is there you can't close it."

"How do you know I can't?"

"Knowing you."

Gerald meditated for some moments.

"It seems to me the right thing to do, you know, with the Pussums, is to pay them."

"And the right thing for mistresses: keep them. And the right thing for wives: live under the same roof with them. Integer vitae scelerisque purus—"* said Birkin.

"There's no need to be nasty about it," said Gerald.

"It bores me. I'm not interested in your peccadilloes."

"And I don't care whether you are or not—I am."*

The morning was again sunny. The maid had been in and brought the water,* and had drawn the curtains. Birkin, sitting up in bed, looked lazily and pleasantly out on the park, that was so green and deserted, romantic, belonging to the past. He was thinking how lovely, how sure, how formed, how final all the things of the past were—the lovely accomplished past*—this house, so still and golden, the park slumbering its centuries of peace. And then, what a snare and a delusion, this beauty of static things—what a horrible, dead prison Breadalby really was, what an intolerable confinement, the peace! Yet it was better than the sordid scrambling conflict of the present. If only one might create the future after one's own heart—for a little pure truth, a little unflinching application of simple truth to life, the heart cried out ceaselessly.

"I can't see what you will leave me at all, to be interested in," came Gerald's voice from the lower room. "Neither the Pussums, nor the mines, nor anything else."

"You be interested in what you can, Gerald. Only I'm not interested myself," said Birkin.

"What am I to do at all, then?" came Gerald's voice.

"What you like.—What am I to do myself?"

In the silence Birkin could feel Gerald musing this fact.

"I'm blest if I know," came the good-humoured answer.

"You see," said Birkin, "part of you wants the Pussum, and nothing but the Pussum, part of you wants the mines, the business, and nothing but the business—and there you are—all in bits—"

"And part of me wants something else," said Gerald, in a queer quiet, real voice.

"What?" said Birkin, rather surprised.

"That's what I hoped you could tell me," said Gerald.

There was a silence for some time.

"I can't tell you—I can't find my own way, let alone yours. You might marry," Birkin replied.

"Who—the Pussum?" asked Gerald.

"Perhaps," said Birkin. And he rose and went to the window.

"That is your panacea," said Gerald. "But you haven't even tried it on yourself yet, and you are sick enough."

"I am," said Birkin. "Still, I shall come right."

"Through marriage?"

"Yes," Birkin answered obstinately.

"And no," added Gerald. "No, no, no, my boy."

There was a silence between them, and a strange tension of hostility. They always kept a gap, a distance between them, they wanted always to be free each of the other. Yet there was a curious heart-straining towards each other.

"Salvator femininus,"* said Gerald, satirically.

"Why not?" said Birkin.

"No reason at all," said Gerald, "if it really works. But whom will you marry?"

"A woman," said Birkin.

"Good," said Gerald.

Birkin and Gerald were the last to come down to breakfast. Hermione liked everybody to be early. She suffered when she felt her day was diminished, she felt she had missed her life. She seemed to grip the hours by the throat, to force her life from them. She was rather pale and ghastly, as if left behind, in the morning. Yet she had her power, her will was strangely pervasive. With the entrance of the two young men a sudden tension was felt.

She lifted her face, and said, in her amused sing-song:

"Good morning! Did you sleep well?—I'm so glad."

And she turned away, ignoring them. Birkin, who knew her well, saw that she intended to discount his existence.

"Will you take what you want from the sideboard," said Alexander, in a voice slightly suggesting disapprobation. "I hope the things aren't cold. Oh no!—Do you mind putting out the flame under the chafing-dish, Rupert? Thank you."

Even Alexander was rather authoritative where Hermione was cool. He took his tone from her, inevitably. Birkin sat down and looked at the table. He was so used to this house, to this room, to this atmosphere, through years of intimacy, and now he felt in complete opposition to it all, it had nothing to do with him. How well he knew Hermione, as she sat there, erect and silent and somewhat bemused, and yet so potent, so powerful! He knew her statically, so finally, that it was almost like a madness. It was difficult to believe one was not mad, that one was not a figure in the hall of kings in some Egyptian tomb,* where the dead all sat immemorial and tremendous. How utterly he knew Joshua Malleson, who was talking in his harsh, yet rather mincing voice, endlessly, endlessly, always with a strong mentality working, always interesting, and yet always known, everything he said known beforehand, however novel it was, and clever.

Alexander the up-to-date host, so bloodlessly free-and-easy, Fräulein so prettily chiming in just as she should, the little Italian countess taking no notice of anybody, only playing her little game, objective and cold, like a weasel watching everything, and extracting her own amusement, never giving herself in the slightest; then Miss Bradley, heavy and rather subservient, treated with cool, almost amused contempt by Hermione, and therefore slighted by everybody—how known it all was, like a game with the figures set out, the same figures, the Queen of chess, the knights, the pawns, the same now as they were hundreds of years ago, the same figures moving round in one of the innumerable permutations that make up the game. But the game is known, its going on is like a madness, it is so exhausted.

There was Gerald, an amused look on his face; the game pleased him. There was Gudrun, watching with steady, large, hostile eyes; the game fascinated her, and she loathed it. There was Ursula, with a slightly startled look on her face, as if she were hurt, and the pain were just outside her consciousness.

Suddenly Birkin got up and went out.

"That's enough," he said to himself, involuntarily.

Hermione knew his motion, though not in her consciousness. She lifted her heavy eyes and saw him lapse suddenly away, on a sudden, unknown tide, and the waves broke over her. Only her indomitable will remained static and mechanical, she sat at table making her musing, stray remarks. But the darkness had covered her, she was like a ship that has gone down. It was finished for her too, she was wrecked in the darkness. Yet the unfailing mechanism of her will worked on, she had that activity.

"Shall we bathe this morning?" she said, suddenly looking at them all.

"Splendid," said Joshua. "It is a perfect morning."

"Oh it is beautiful," said the Fräulein.

"Yes, let us bathe," said the Italian woman.

"We have no bathing suits," said Gerald.

"Have mine," said Alexander. "I must go to church and read the lessons. They expect me."

"Are you a Christian?" asked the Italian countess, with sudden interest.

"No," said Alexander. "I'm not. But I believe in keeping up the old institutions."

"They are so beautiful," said the Fräulein daintily.

"Oh they are," cried Miss Bradley.

They all trailed out on to the lawn. It was a sunny, soft morning in early summer, when life ran in the world subtly, like a reminiscence. The church bells were ringing a little way off, not a cloud was in the
5   sky, the swans were like lilies on the water below, the peacocks walked with long, prancing steps across the shadow and into the sunshine of the grass. One wanted to swoon into the by-gone perfection of it all.

"Goodbye," called Alexander, waving his gloves cheerily, and he
10 disappeared behind the bushes, on his way to church.

"Now," said Hermione, "shall we all bathe?"

"I won't," said Ursula.

"You don't want to?" said Hermione, looking at her slowly.

"No, I don't want to," said Ursula.

15 "Nor I," said Gudrun.

"What about my suit?" asked Gerald.

"I don't know," laughed Hermione, with an odd, amused intonation. "Will a handkerchief do—a large handkerchief?"

"That will do," said Gerald.

20 "Come along then," sang Hermione.

The first to run across the lawn was the little Italian, small and like a cat, her white legs twinkling as she went, ducking slightly her head, that was tied in a gold silk kerchief. She tripped through the gate and down the grass, and stood, like a tiny figure of ivory and bronze, at
25 the water's edge, having dropped off her towelling, watching the swans, which came up in surprise. Then out ran Miss Bradley, like a large, soft plum in her dark-blue suit. Then Gerald came, a scarlet silk kerchief round his loins, his towels over his arms. He seemed to flaunt himself a little in the sun, lingering and laughing, strolling
30 easily, looking white but natural in his nakedness. Then came Sir Joshua, in an overcoat, and lastly Hermione, striding with stiff grace from out of a great mantle of purple silk, her head tied up in purple and gold. Handsome was her stiff, long body, her straight-stepping white legs, there was a static magnificence about her as she let the
35 cloak float loosely away from her striding. She crossed the lawn like some strange memory, and passed slowly and statelily towards the water.

There were three ponds, in terraces descending the valley, large and smooth and beautiful, lying in the sun. The water ran over a little
40 stone wall, over small rocks, splashing down from one pond to the

level below. The swans had gone out on to the opposite bank, the reds smelled sweet, a faint breeze touched the skin.

Gerald had dived in, after Sir Joshua, and had swum to the end of the pond. There he climbed out and sat on the wall. There was a dive, and the little countess was swimming like a rat, to join him. They both sat in the sun, laughing and crossing their arms on their breasts. Sir Joshua swam up to them, and stood near them, up to his arm-pits in the water. Then Hermione and Miss Bradley swam over, and they sat in a row on the embankment.

"Aren't they terrifying? Aren't they really terrifying?" said Gudrun. "Don't they look saurian? They are just like great lizards. Did ever you see anything like Sir Joshua? But really, Ursula, he belongs to the primeval world, when great lizards crawled about."

Gudrun looked in dismay on Sir Joshua, who stood up to the breast in the water, his long, greyish hair washed down into his eyes, his neck set into thick, crude shoulders. He was talking to Miss Bradley, who, seated on the bank above, plump and big and wet, looked as if she might roll and slither in the water almost like one of the slithering sea-lions in the Zoo.

Ursula watched in silence. Gerald was laughing happily, between Hermione and the Italian. He reminded her of Dionysos, because his hair was really yellow,* his figure so full and laughing. Hermione, in her large, stiff, sinister grace, leaned near him, frightening, as if she were not responsible for what she might do. He knew a certain danger in her, a convulsive madness. But he only laughed the more, turning often to the little countess, who was flashing up her face at him.

They all dropped into the water, and were swimming together like a shoal of seals. Hermione was powerful and unconscious in the water, large and slow and powerful, Palestra was quick and silent as a water rat, Gerald wavered and flickered, a white natural shadow. Then, one after the other, they waded out, and went up to the house.

But Gerald lingered a moment to speak to Gudrun.

"You don't like the water?" he said.

She looked at him with a long, slow, inscrutable look, as he stood before her negligently, the water standing in beads all over his skin.

"I like it very much," she replied.

He paused, expecting some sort of explanation.

"And you swim?"

"Yes, I swim."

Still he would not ask her why she would not go in, then. He could feel something ironic in her. He walked away, piqued for the first time.

"Why wouldn't you bathe?" he asked her again, later, when he was once more the properly-dressed, correct young Englishman.

She hesitated a moment before answering, opposing his persistence.

"Because I didn't like the crowd," she replied.

He laughed, her phrase seemed to re-echo in his consciousness. The flavour of her slang was piquant to him. Whether he would or not, she signified the real world to him. He wanted to come up to her standards, fulfil her expectations. He knew that her criterion was the only one that mattered. The others were all outsiders, instinctively, whatever they might be socially. And Gerald could not help it, he was bound to strive to come up to her criterion, fulfil her idea of a man and a human-being.

After lunch, when all the others had withdrawn, Hermione and Gerald and Birkin lingered, finishing their talk. There had been some discussion, on the whole quite intellectual and artificial, about a new state, a new world of man. Supposing this old social state *were* broken and destroyed, then, out of the chaos, what then?

The great social idea, said Sir Joshua, was the *social* equality of man.* No, said Gerald, the idea was, that every man was fit for his own little bit of a task—let him do that, and then please himself. The unifying principle was the work in hand. Only work, the business of production, held men together. It was mechanical, but then society *was* a mechanism. Apart from work they were isolated, free to do as they liked.

"Oh!" cried Gudrun. "Then we shan't have names any more—we shall be like the Germans, nothing but Herr Obermeister and Herr Untermeister.* I can imagine it—'I am Mrs Colliery-Manager Crich—I am Mrs Member-of-Parliament Roddice, I am Miss Art-Teacher Brangwen.' Very pretty that."

"Things would work very much better, Miss Art-Teacher Brangwen," said Gerald.

"What things, Mr Colliery-Manager Crich? The relation between you and me, *par exemple?*"

"Yes, for example," cried the Italian. "That which is between men and women—!"

"That is non-social," said Birkin, sarcastically.

"Exactly," said Gerald. "Between me and a woman, the social question does not enter. It is my own affair."

"A ten-pound note on it," said Birkin.

"You don't admit that a woman is a social being?" asked Ursula of Gerald.

"She is both," said Gerald. "She is a social being, as far as society is concerned. But for her own private self, she is a free agent, it is her own affair, what she does."

"But won't it be rather difficult to arrange the two halves?" asked Ursula.

"Oh no," replied Gerald. "They arrange themselves naturally—we see it now, everywhere."

"Don't you laugh so pleasantly till you're out of the wood," said Birkin.

Gerald knitted his brows in momentary irritation.

"Was I laughing?" he said.

"*If*," said Hermione at last, "we could only realise, that in the *spirit* we are all one, all equal in the spirit, all brothers there—the rest wouldn't matter, there would be no more of this carping and envy and this struggle for power, which destroys, only destroys."

This speech was received in silence, and almost immediately the party rose from table. But when the others had gone, Birkin turned round in bitter declamation, saying:

"It is just the opposite, just the contrary, Hermione. We are all different and unequal in spirit—it is only the *social* differences that are based on accidental material conditions. We are all abstractly or mathematically equal, if you like. Every man has hunger and thirst, two eyes, one nose and two legs.* We're all the same in point of number. But spiritually, there is pure difference and neither equality nor inequality counts. It is upon these two bits of knowledge that you must found a state. Your democracy is an absolute lie—your brotherhood of man is a pure falsity, if you apply it further than the mathematical abstraction. We all drank milk first, we all eat bread and meat, we all want to ride in motor-cars—therein lies the beginning and the end of the brotherhood of man. But no equality.

"But I, myself, who am myself, what have I to do with equality—with any other man or woman? In the spirit, I am as separate as one star is from another, as different in quality and quantity. Establish a state on *that*. One man isn't any better than another, not because they are equal, but because they are intrinsically *other*, that there is no term of comparison. The minute you begin to compare, one man is seen to be far better than another, all the inequality you can imagine, is there by nature.

"I want every man to have his share in the world's goods, so that
5   I am rid of his importunity, so that I can tell him: 'Now you've got what you want—you've got your fair share of the world's gear. Now, you one-mouthed fool, mind yourself and don't obstruct me.'"

Hermione was looking at him with leering eyes, along her
10   cheeks. He could feel violent waves of hatred and loathing of all he said, coming out of her. It was dynamic hatred and loathing, coming strong and black out of the unconsciousness. She heard his words in her unconscious self, *consciously* she was as if deafened, she paid no heed to them.

15   "It *sounds* like megalomania, Rupert," said Gerald, genially.

Hermione gave a queer, grunting sound. Birkin stood back.

"Yes, let it," he said suddenly, the whole tone gone out of his voice, that had been so insistent, bearing everybody down. And he went away.

20   But he felt, later, a little compunction. He had been violent, cruel with poor Hermione. He wanted to recompense her, to make it up. He had hurt her, he had been vindictive. He wanted to be on good terms with her again.

He went into her boudoir, a remote and very cushiony place. She
25   was sitting at her table writing letters. She lifted her face abstractedly when he entered, watched him go to the sofa, and sit down. Then she looked down at her paper again.

He took a large volume,* which he had been reading before, and became minutely attentive to his author. His back was towards
30   Hermione. She could not go on with her writing. Her whole mind was a chaos, darkness breaking in upon it, and herself struggling to gain control with her will, as a swimmer struggles with the swirling water. But in spite of her efforts she was borne down, darkness seemed to break over her, she felt as if her heart was bursting. The
35   terrible tension grew stronger and stronger, it was most fearful agony, like being walled up.

And then she realised that his presence was the wall, his presence was destroying her. Unless she could break out, she must die most fearfully, walled up in horror. And he was the wall. She must
40   break down the wall—she must break him down before her, the

awful obstruction of him who obstructed her life to the last. It must be done, or she must perish most horribly.

Terrible shocks ran over her body, like shocks of electricity, as if many volts of electricity suddenly struck her down. She was aware of him sitting silently there, an unthinkable evil obstruction. Only this blotted out her mind, pressed out her very breathing, his silent, stooping back, the back of his head.

A terrible voluptuous thrill ran down her arms—she was going to know her voluptuous consummation. Her arms quivered and were strong, immeasurably and irresistibly strong. What delight, what delight in strength, what delirium of pleasure! She was going to have her consummation of voluptuous ecstasy at last. It was coming! In utmost terror and agony, she knew it was upon her now, in extremity of bliss. Her hand closed on a blue, beautiful ball of lapis lazuli* that stood on her desk for a paper-weight. She rolled it round in her hand as she rose silently. Her heart was a pure flame in her breast, she was purely unconscious in ecstasy. She moved towards him and stood behind him for a moment in ecstasy. He, closed within the spell, remained motionless and unconscious.

Then swiftly, in a flame that drenched down her body like fluid lightning, and gave her a perfect, unutterable consummation, unutterable satisfaction, she brought down the ball of jewel stone with all her force, crash on his head. But her fingers were in the way, and deadened the blow. Nevertheless down went his head on the table on which his book lay, the stone slid aside and over his ear, it was one convulsion of pure bliss for her, lit up by the crushed pain of her fingers. But it was not somehow complete. She lifted her arm high to aim once more, straight down on the head that lay dazed on the table. She must smash it, it must be smashed before her ecstasy was consummated, fulfilled for ever. A thousand lives, a thousand deaths mattered nothing now, only the fulfilment of this perfect ecstasy.

She was not swift, she could only move slowly. A strong spirit in him woke him and made him lift his face and twist to look at her. Her arm was raised, the hand clasping the ball of lapis lazuli. It was her left hand, he realised again with horror that she was left-handed.* Hurriedly, with a burrowing motion, he covered his head under the thick volume of Thucydides, and the blow came down, almost breaking his neck, and shattering his heart.

He was shattered, but he was not afraid. Twisting round to face her, he pushed the table over and got away from her. He was like a flask that is smashed to atoms, he seemed to himself that he was all fragments, smashed to bits. Yet his movements were perfectly coherent and clear, his soul was entire and unsurprised.

"No you don't, Hermione," he said in a low voice. "I don't let you."

He saw her standing tall and livid and attentive, the stone clenched tense in her hand.

"Stand away and let me go," he said, drawing near to her.

As if pressed back by some hand, she stood away, watching him all the time without changing, like a neutralised angel confronting him.

"It is no good," he said, when he had gone past her. "It isn't I who will die. You hear?"

He kept his face to her as he went out, lest she should strike again. While he was on his guard, she dared not move. And he was on his guard, she was powerless. So he had gone, and left her standing.

She remained perfectly rigid, standing as she was for a long time. Then she staggered to the couch and lay down, and went heavily to sleep. When she awoke, she remembered what she had done, but it seemed to her, she had only hit him, as any woman might do, because he tortured her. She was perfectly right. She knew that, spiritually, she was right. In her own infallible purity, she had done what must be done. She was right, she was pure. A drugged, almost sinister religious expression became permanent on her face.

Birkin, barely conscious, and yet perfectly direct in his motion, went out of the house and straight across the park, to the open country, to the hills. The brilliant day had become overcast, spots of rain were falling. He wandered on to a wild valley-side, where were thickets of hazel, many flowers, tufts of heather, and little clumps of young fir-trees, budding with soft paws. It was rather wet everywhere, there was a stream running down at the bottom of the valley, which was gloomy, or seemed gloomy. He was aware that he could not regain his consciousness, that he was moving in a sort of darkness.

Yet he wanted something. He was happy in the wet hill-side, that was overgrown and obscure with bushes and flowers. He wanted to touch them all, to saturate himself with the touch of them all. He took off his clothes, and sat down naked among the primroses, moving his feet softly among the primroses, his legs, his knees, his arms right up to the arm-pits, then lying down and letting them touch his belly, his breasts. It was such a fine, cool, subtle touch all over him, he seemed to saturate himself with their contact.

But they were too soft. He went through the long grass to a clump of young fir-trees, that were no higher than a man. The soft sharp boughs beat upon him, as he moved in keen pangs against them, threw little cold showers of drops on his belly, and beat his loins with their clusters of soft-sharp needles. There was a thistle which pricked him vividly, but not too much, because all his movements were too discriminate and soft. To lie down and roll in the sticky, cool young hyacinths, to lie on one's belly and cover one's back with handfuls of fine wet grass, soft as a breath, soft and more delicate and more beautiful than the touch of any woman; and then to sting one's thigh against the living dark bristles of the fir-boughs; and then to feel the light whip of the hazel on one's shoulders, stinging, and then to clasp the silvery birch-trunk against one's breast, its smoothness, its hardness, its vital knots and ridges—this was good, this was all very good, very satisfying. Nothing else would do, nothing else would satisfy, except this coolness and subtlety of vegetation travelling into one's blood. How fortunate he was, that there was this lovely, subtle, responsive vegetation, waiting for him, as he waited for it; how fulfilled he was, how happy!

As he dried himself a little with his handkerchief, he thought about Hermione and the blow. He could feel a pain on the side of his head. But after all, what did it matter? What did Hermione matter, what did people matter altogether? There was this perfect cool loneliness, so lovely and fresh and unexplored. Really, what a mistake he had made, thinking he wanted people, thinking he wanted a woman. He did not want a woman—not in the least. The leaves and the primroses and the trees, they were really lovely and cool and desirable, they really came into the blood and were added on to him. He was enrichened now immeasurably, and so glad.

It was quite right of Hermione to want to kill him. What had he to do with her?* Why should he pretend to have anything to do with human beings at all? Here was his world, he wanted nobody and nothing but the lovely, subtle, responsive vegetation, and himself, his own living self.

It was necessary to go back into the world. That was true. But that did not matter, so one knew where one belonged. He knew now where he belonged. He knew where to plant himself, his seed:—

along with the trees, in the folds of the delicious fresh growing leaves.* This was his place, his marriage place. The world was extraneous.

He climbed out of the valley, wondering if he were mad. But if so, he preferred his own madness, to the regular sanity. He rejoiced in his own madness, he was free. He did not want that old sanity of the world, which was become so repulsive. He rejoiced in the new-found world of his madness. It was so fresh and delicate and so satisfying.

As for the certain grief he felt at the same time, in his soul, that was only the remains of an old ethic, that bade a human-being adhere to humanity. But he was weary of the old ethic, of the human being, and of humanity. He loved now the soft, delicate vegetation, that was so cool and perfect. He would overlook the old grief, he would put away the old ethic, he would be free in his new state.

He was aware of the pain in his head becoming more and more difficult every minute. He was walking now along the road to the nearest station. It was raining and he had no hat. But then plenty of cranks went out nowadays without hats,* in the rain.

He wondered again how much of his heaviness of heart, a certain depression, was due to fear, fear lest anybody should have seen him naked lying with* the vegetation. What a dread he had of mankind, of other people! It amounted almost to horror, to a sort of dream terror—his horror of being observed by some other people. If he were on an island, like Alexander Selkirk,* with only the creatures and the trees, he would be free and glad, there would be none of this heaviness, this misgiving. He could love the vegetation and be quite happy and unquestioned, by himself.

He had better send a note to Hermione: she might trouble about him, and he did not want the onus of this. So at the station, he wrote saying:

"I will go on to town—I don't want to come back to Breadalby for the present. But it is quite all right—I don't want you to mind having biffed me, in the least. Tell the others it is just one of my moods. You were quite right, to biff me—because I know you wanted to. So there's the end of it."

In the train, however, he felt ill. Every motion was insufferable pain, and he was sick. He dragged himself from the station into a cab, feeling his way step by step, like a blind man, and held up only by a dim will.

For a week or two he was ill, but he did not let Hermione know, and she thought he was sulking, there was a complete estrangement between them. She became rapt, abstracted in her conviction of exclusive righteousness. She lived in and by her own self-esteem, conviction of her own rightness of spirit.

Chapter IX

Coal-Dust*

Going home from school in the afternoon, the Brangwen girls
descended the hill between the picturesque cottages of Willey
Green till they came to the railway crossing. There they found the
gate shut, because the colliery train was rumbling nearer. They
could hear the small locomotive panting hoarsely as it advanced
with caution between the embankments. The one-legged man in
the little signal-hut by the road stared out from his obscurity like a
crab from a snail-shell.

Whilst the two girls waited, Gerald Crich trotted up on a red
Arab mare. He rode well and softly, pleased with the delicate
quivering of the creature between his knees. And he was very
picturesque, at least in Gudrun's eyes, sitting soft and close on the
slender red mare, whose long tail flowed on the air. He saluted the
two girls, and drew up at the crossing to wait for the gate, looking
down the railway for the approaching train. In spite of her ironic
smile at his picturesqueness, Gudrun liked to look at him. He was
well-set and easy, his face with its warm tan showed up his whitish,
coarse moustache, and his blue eyes were full of sharp light, as he
watched the distance.

The locomotive chuffed slowly between the banks, hidden. The
mare did not like it. She began to wince away, as if hurt by the
unknown noise. But Gerald pulled her back and held her head to
the gate. The sharp blasts of the chuffing engine broke with more
and more force on her. The repeated sharp blows of unknown,
terrifying noise struck through her till she was rocking with terror.
She recoiled like a spring let go. But a glistening, half-smiling look
came into Gerald's* face. He brought her back again, inevitably.

The noise was released, the little locomotive with her clanking
steel connecting-rod emerged on the high-road, clanking sharply.
The mare rebounded like a drop of water from hot iron. Ursula and
Gudrun pressed back into the hedge, in fear. But Gerald was heavy
on the mare, and forced her back. It seemed as if he sank into her
magnetically, and could thrust her back, against herself.

"The fool," cried Ursula, loudly. "Why doesn't he ride away till it's gone by."

Gudrun was looking at him with black-dilated, spell-bound eyes. But he sat glistening and* obstinate, forcing the wheeling mare, which spun and swerved like a wind, and yet could not get out of the grasp of his will, nor escape from the mad clamour of terror that resounded through her, as the trucks thumped slowly, heavily, horrifying, one after the other, one pursuing the other, over the rails of the crossing.

The locomotive, as if wanting to see what could be done, put on the brakes, and back came the trucks rebounding on the iron buffers, striking like horrible cymbals, clashing nearer and nearer in frightful strident concussions. The mare opened her mouth and rose slowly, as if lifted up on a wind of terror. Then suddenly her fore feet struck out, as she convulsed herself utterly away from the horror. Back she went, and the two girls clung to each other, feeling she must fall backwards on top of him. But he leaned forward, his face shining with fixed amusement, and at last he brought her down, sank her down, and was bearing her back to the mark. But as strong as the pressure of his compulsion was the repulsion of her utter terror, throwing her back away from the railway, so that she spun round and round, on two legs, as if she were in the centre of some whirlwind. It made Gudrun faint with poignant dizziness, which seemed to penetrate to her heart.

"No—! No—! Let her go! Let her go, you fool, you *fool*——!" cried Ursula at the top of her voice, completely outside herself. And Gudrun hated her bitterly for being outside herself. It was unendurable that Ursula's voice was so powerful and naked.

A sharpened look came on Gerald's face. He bit himself down on the mare like a keen edge biting home, and *forced* her round. She roared as she breathed, her nostrils were two wide, hot holes, her mouth was apart, her eyes frenzied. It was a repulsive sight. But he held on her unrelaxed, with an almost mechanical relentlessness, keen as a sword pressing in to her. Both man and horse were sweating with violence. Yet he seemed calm as a ray of cold sunshine.

Meanwhile the eternal trucks were rumbling on, very slowly, threading one after the other, one after the other, like a disgusting dream that has no end. The connecting chains were grinding and squeaking as the tension varied, the mare pawed and struck away mechanically now, her terror fulfilled in her, for now the man encompassed her; her paws were blind and pathetic as she beat the air, the man closed round her, and brought her down, almost as if she were part of his own physique.

"And she's bleeding!—She's bleeding!" cried Ursula, frantic with
5 opposition and hatred of Gerald. She alone understood him perfectly, in pure opposition.

Gudrun looked and saw the trickles of blood on the sides of the mare, and she turned white. And then on the very wound the bright spurs came down, pressing relentlessly. The world reeled and
10 passed into nothingness for Gudrun, she could not know any more.

When she recovered, her soul was calm and cold, without feeling. The trucks were still rumbling by, the man and the mare were still fighting. But she herself was cold and separate, she had no more feeling for them. She was quite hard and cold and indifferent.

15   They could see the top of the hooded guard's-van approaching, the sound of the trucks was diminishing, there was hope of relief from the intolerable noise. The heavy panting of the half-stunned mare sounded automatically, the man seemed to be relaxing confidently, his will bright and unstained.

20   The guard's-van came up, and passed slowly, the guard staring out in his transition on the spectacle in the road. And, through the man in the closed wagon Gudrun could see the whole scene spectacularly, isolated and momentary, like a vision isolated in eternity.

25   Lovely, grateful silence seemed to trail behind the receding train. How sweet the silence is! Ursula looked with hatred on the buffers of the diminishing wagon. The gate-keeper stood ready at the door of his hut, to proceed to open the gate. But Gudrun sprang suddenly forward, in front of the struggling horse, threw off the latch and flung
30 the gates asunder, throwing one half to the keeper, and running with the other half, forwards. Gerald suddenly let go the horse and leaped forwards, almost on to Gudrun. She was not afraid. As he jerked aside the mare's head, Gudrun cried, in a strange, high voice, like a gull, or like a witch screaming out from the side of the road:

35   "I should think you're proud."

The words were distinct and formed. The man, twisting aside on his dancing horse, looked at her in some surprise, some wondering interest. Then the mare's hoofs had danced three times on the drum-like sleepers of the crossing, and man and horse were
40 bounding springily, unequally up the road.

The two girls watched them go. The gate-keeper hobbled thudding over the logs of the crossing, with his wooden leg. He had
fastened the gate. Then he also turned, and called to the girls:

"A masterful young jockey,* that;—'ll have his own road, if ever
anybody would." 5

"Yes," cried Ursula, in her hot, overbearing voice. "Why couldn't
he take the horse away, till the trucks had gone by? He's a fool, and a
bully. Does he think it's manly, to torture a horse? It's a living thing,
why should he bully it and torture it?"

There was a pause, then the gate-keeper shook his head, and 10
replied:

"Yes, it's as nice a little mare as you could set eyes on—beautiful
little thing, beautiful.—Now you wouldn't see his father treat any
animal like that—not you. They're as different as they welly* can be,
Gerald Crich and his father—two different men, different made." 15

There was a pause.

"But why does he do it?" cried Ursula, "why does he? Does he
think he's grand, when he's bullied a sensitive creature, ten times as
sensitive as himself?"

Again there was the cautious pause. Then again the man shook his 20
head, as if he would say nothing, but would think the more.

"I expect he's got to train the mare to stand to anything," he
replied. "A pure-bred Harab—not the sort of breed as is used to
round here—different sort from our sort altogether. They say as he
got her from Constantinople." 25

"He would!" said Ursula. "He'd better have left her to the Turks,
I'm sure they would have had more decency towards her."

The man went in to drink his can of tea, the girls went on down the
lane, that was deep in soft black dust. Gudrun was as if numbed in
her mind by the sense of indomitable soft weight of the man, bearing 30
down into the living body of the horse: the strong, indomitable*
thighs of the blond man clenching the palpitating body of the mare
into pure control; a sort of soft white magnetic domination from the
loins and thighs and calves, enclosing and encompassing the mare
heavily into unutterable subordination, soft blood-subordination, 35
terrible.

On the left, as the girls walked silently, the coal-mine lifted its
great mounds and its patterned head-stocks, the black railway with
the trucks at rest looked like a harbour just below, a large bay of
railroad with anchored wagons. 40

Near the second level-crossing, that went over many bright rails, was a farm belonging to the collieries, and a great round globe of iron, a disused boiler, huge and rusty and perfectly round, stood silently in a paddock by the road. The hens were pecking round it,
5 some chickens were balanced on the drinking trough, wagtails flew away in among trucks, from the water.

On the other side of the wide crossing, by the road-side, was a heap of pale-grey stones for mending the roads, and a cart standing, and a middle-aged man with whiskers round his face was leaning on
10 his shovel, talking to a young man in gaiters, who stood by the horse's head. Both men were facing the crossing.

They saw the two girls appear, small, brilliant figures in the near distance, in the strong light of the late afternoon. Both wore light, gay summer dresses, Ursula had an orange-coloured knitted coat,
15 Gudrun a pale yellow, Ursula wore canary yellow stockings, Gudrun bright rose, the figures of the two women seemed to glitter in progress over the wide bay of the railway crossing, white and orange and yellow and rose glittering in motion across a hot world silted with coal-dust.

20 The two men stood quite still in the heat, watching. The elder was a short, hard-faced, energetic man of middle age, the younger a laborer of twenty-three or so. They stood in silence watching the advance of the sisters. They watched whilst the girls drew near, and whilst they passed, and whilst they receded down the dusty road, that
25 had dwellings on one side, and dusty young corn on the other.

Then the elder man, with the whiskers round his face, said in a prurient manner to the young man:

"What price that, eh? She'll do, won't she?"

"Which?" asked the young man, eagerly, with a laugh.

30 "Her with the red stockings.—What d' you say?—I'd give my week's wages for five minutes;—what!—just for five minutes."

Again the younger man laughed.

"Your Missis 'ud have summat to say to you," he replied.

Gudrun had turned round and looked at the two men. They were
35 to her sinister creatures, standing watching after her, by the heap of pale grey slag. She loathed the man with whiskers round his face.

"You're first class, you are," the man said to her, and to the distance.

"Do you think it would be worth a week's wages?" said the
40 younger man, musing.

"Do I? I'd put 'em bloody-well down this second—"

The younger man looked after Gudrun and Ursula objectively, as if he wished to calculate what there might be, that was worth his week's wages. He shook his head with fatal misgiving.

"No," he said. "It's not worth that to me."

"Isn't?" said the old man. "By God, if it isn't to me!"

And he went on shovelling his stones.

The girls descended between the houses with slate roofs and blackish brick walls. The heavy gold glamour of approaching sunset lay over all the colliery district, and the ugliness overlaid with beauty was like a narcotic to the senses. On the roads silted with black dust, the rich light fell more warmly, more heavily; over all the amorphous squalor a kind of magic was cast, from the glowing close of day.

"It has a foul kind of beauty, this place," said Gudrun, evidently suffering from the fascination. "Can't you feel, in some way, a thick, hot attraction in it? *I* can. And it quite stupefies me."

They were passing between blocks of miners' dwellings. In the back yards of several dwellings, a miner could be seen washing himself in the open on this hot evening, naked down to the loins, his great trousers of moleskin slipping almost away. Miners already cleaned were sitting on their heels, with their backs near the walls, talking and silent in pure physical well-being, tired, and taking physical rest. Their voices sounded out with strong intonation, and the broad dialect was curiously caressing to the blood. It seemed to envelop Gudrun in a laborer's caress, there was in the whole atmosphere a resonance of physical men, a glamorous thickness of labour and maleness surcharged in the air. But it was universal in the district, and therefore unnoticed by the inhabitants.

To Gudrun, however, it was potent and half-repulsive. She could never tell why Beldover was so utterly different from London and the south, why one's whole feelings were different, why one seemed to live in another sphere. Now she realised that this was the world of powerful, underworld men who spent most of their time in the darkness. In their voices she could hear the voluptuous resonance of darkness, the strong, dangerous underworld, mindless, inhuman. They sounded also like strange machines, heavy, oiled. The voluptuousness was like that of machinery, cold and iron.

It was the same every evening when she came home, she seemed to move through a wave of disruptive force, that was given off from the presence of thousands of vigorous, underworld, half-automa-

tised colliers, and which went to the brain and the heart, awaking a
fatal desire, and a fatal callousness.

There came over her a nostalgia for the place. She hated it, she
knew how utterly cut off it was, how hideous and how sickeningly
mindless. Sometimes she beat her wings like a new Daphne,* turning not into a tree but a machine. And yet, she was overcome by
the nostalgia. She struggled to get more and more into accord with
the atmosphere of the place, she craved to get her satisfaction of it.

She felt herself drawn out at evening into the main street of the
town, that was uncreated and ugly, and yet surcharged with this same
potent atmosphere of intense, dark callousness. There were always
miners about. They moved with their strange, distorted dignity, a
certain beauty, an unnatural stillness in their bearing, a look of
abstraction and half-resignation in their pale, often gaunt faces.
They belonged to another world, they had a strange glamour, their
voices were full of an intolerable deep resonance, like a machine's
burring, a music more maddening than the siren's long ago.

She found herself, with the rest of the common women, drawn out
on Friday evenings to the little market. Friday was pay-day for the
colliers, and Friday night was market night. Every woman was
abroad, every man was out, shopping with his wife, or gathering with
his pals. The pavements were dark for miles around with people
coming in, the little market-place on the crown of the hill, and the
main street of Beldover were black with thickly-crowded men and
women.

It was dark, the market-place was hot with kerosene flares,* which
threw a ruddy light on the grave faces of the purchasing wives, and
on the pale abstract faces of the men. The air was full of the sound of
criers and of people talking, thick streams of people moved on the
pavements towards the solid crowd of the market. The shops were
blazing and packed with women, in the streets were men, mostly
men, miners of all ages. Money was spent with almost lavish
freedom.

The carts that came could not pass through. They had to wait, the
driver calling and shouting, till the dense crowd would make way.
Everywhere, young fellows from the outlying district were making
conversation with the girls, standing in the road and at the corners.
The doors of the public-houses were open and full of light, men
passed in and out in a continual stream, everywhere men were calling
out to one another, or crossing to meet one another, or standing in

little gangs and circles, discussing, endlessly discussing. The sense of talk, buzzing, jarring, half-secret, the endless mining and political wrangling, vibrated in the air like discordant machinery. And it was these* voices which affected Gudrun almost to swooning. They aroused a strange, nostalgic ache of desire, something almost demoniacal, never to be fulfilled.

Like any other common girl of the district, Gudrun strolled up and down, up and down the length of the brilliant two-hundred paces of the pavement nearest the market-place. She knew it was a vulgar thing to do; her father and mother could not bear it; but the nostalgia came over her, she must be among the people. Sometimes she sat among the louts in the cinema: rakish-looking, unattractive louts they were. Yet she must be among them.

And, like any other common lass, she found her 'boy'. It was an electrician,* one of the electricians introduced according to Gerald's new scheme. He was an earnest, clever man, a scientist with a passion for sociology. He lived alone in a cottage, in lodgings, in Willey Green. He was a gentleman, and sufficiently well-to-do. His landlady spread the reports about him: he *would* have a large wooden tub in his bedroom, and every time he came in from work, he *would* have pails and pails of water brought up, to bath in, then he put on clean shirt and underclothing *every* day, and clean silk socks; fastidious and exacting he was in these respects, but in every other way, most ordinary and unassuming.

Gudrun knew all these things. The Brangwens' house was one to which the gossip came naturally and inevitably. Palmer was in the first place a friend of Ursula's. But in his pale, elegant, serious face there showed the same nostalgia that Gudrun felt. He too must walk up and down the street on Friday evening. So he walked with Gudrun, and a friendship was struck up between them. But he was not in love with Gudrun; he *really* wanted Ursula, but for some strange reason, nothing could happen between her and him. He liked to have Gudrun about, as a fellow mind—but that was all. And she had no real feeling for him. He was a scientist, he had to have a woman to back him. But he was really impersonal, he had the fineness of an elegant piece of machinery. He was too cold, too destructive to care really for women, too great an egoist. He was polarised by the men. Individually he detested and despised them. In the mass they fascinated him, as machinery fascinated him. They were a new sort of machinery to him—but incalculable, incalculable.

So Gudrun strolled the streets with Palmer, or went to the cinema with him. And his long, pale, rather elegant face flickered as he made his sarcastic remarks. There they were, the two of them: two elegants, in one sense: in the other sense, two units, absolutely
5   adhering to the people, teeming with the distorted colliers. The same secret seemed to be working in the souls of all alike, Gudrun, Palmer, the rakish young bloods, the gaunt, middle-aged men. All had a secret sense of power, and of inexpressible destructiveness, and of fatal half-heartedness, a sort of rottenness in the will.
10   Sometimes Gudrun would start aside, see it all, see how she was sinking in. And then she was filled with a fury of contempt and anger. She felt she was sinking into one mass with the rest—all so close and intermingled and breathless. It was horrible. She stifled. She prepared for flight, feverishly she flew to her work. But soon she let
15   go. She started off into the country—the darkish, glamorous country. The spell was beginning to work again.

Chapter X

Sketch-Book*

One morning the sisters were sketching by the side of Willey Water, at the remote end of the lake. Gudrun had waded out to a gravelly shoal, and was seated like a Buddhist,* staring fixedly at the water-plants that rose succulent from the mud of the low shores. What she could see was mud, soft, oozy, watery mud, and from its festering chill,* water-plants rose up, thick and cool and fleshy, very straight and turgid, thrusting out their leaves at right angles, and having dark lurid colours, dark green and blotches of black-purple and bronze. But she could feel their turgid fleshy structure as in a sensuous vision, she *knew* how they rose out of the mud, she *knew* how they thrust out from themselves, how they stood stiff and succulent against the air.

Ursula was watching the butterflies, of which there were dozens near the water, little blue ones suddenly snapping out of nothingness into a jewel-life, a large black-and-red one standing upon a flower and breathing with his soft wings, intoxicatingly, breathing pure, ethereal sunshine; two white ones wrestling in the low air; there was a halo round them; ah, when they came tumbling nearer they were orange-tips, and it was the orange that had made the halo. Ursula rose and drifted away, unconscious like the butterflies.

Gudrun, absorbed in a stupor of apprehension of surging water-plants, sat crouched on the shoal, drawing, not looking up for a long time, and then staring unconsciously, absorbedly at the rigid, naked, succulent stems. Her feet were bare, her hat lay on the bank opposite.

She started out of her trance, hearing the knocking of oars. She looked round. There was a boat with a gaudy Japanese parasol, and a man in white, rowing. The woman was Hermione, and the man was Gerald. She knew it instantly. And instantly she perished in the keen *frisson* of anticipation, an electric vibration in her veins, intense, much more intense than that which was always humming low in the atmosphere of Beldover.

Gerald was her escape from the heavy slough of the pale,

underworld, automatic colliers—he started out of the mud. He was master. She saw his back, the movement of his white loins. But not that—it was the whiteness he seemed to enclose as he bent forwards, rowing. He seemed to stoop to something. His glistening, whitish hair seemed like the electricity of the sky.

"There's Gudrun," came Hermione's voice floating distinct over the water. "We will go and speak to her. Do you mind?"

Gerald looked round and saw the girl standing by the water's edge, looking at him. He pulled the boat towards her, magnetically, without thinking of her. In his world, his conscious world, she was still nobody. He knew that Hermione had a curious pleasure in treading down all the social differences, at least apparently, and he left it to her.

"How do you do, Gudrun?" sang Hermione, using the Christian name in the fashionable manner. "What are you doing?"

"How do you do, Hermione? I *was* sketching."

"Were you." The boat drifted nearer, till the keel ground on the bank. "May we see? I should like to *so* much."

It was no use resisting Hermione's deliberate intention.

"Well—" said Gudrun reluctantly, for she always hated to have her unfinished work exposed—"there's nothing in the least interesting."

"Isn't there. But let me see, will you?"

Gudrun reached out the sketch-book, Gerald stretched from the boat to take it. And as he did so, he remembered Gudrun's last words to him, and her face lifted up to him as he sat on the swerving horse. An intensification of pride went over his nerves, because he felt, in some way she was compelled by him. The exchange of feeling between them was strong and apart from their consciousness.

And as if in a spell, Gudrun was aware of his body, stretching and surging like the marsh-fire,* stretching towards her, his hand coming straight forward like a stem. Her voluptuous, acute apprehension of him made the blood faint in her veins, her mind went dim and unconscious. And he rocked on the water perfectly, like the rocking of phosphorescence. He looked round at the boat. It was drifting off a little. He lifted the oar to bring it back. And the exquisite pleasure of slowly arresting the boat, in the heavy-soft water, was complete as a swoon.

"*That's* what you have done," said Hermione, looking searchingly at the plants on the shore, and comparing with Gudrun's drawing.

Gudrun looked round in the direction of Hermione's long, pointing finger. "That is it, isn't it?" repeated Hermione, needing confirmation.

"Yes," said Gudrun automatically, taking no real heed.

"Let me look," said Gerald, reaching forward for the book. But Hermione ignored him, he must not presume, before she had finished. But he, his will as unthwarted and as unflinching as hers, stretched forward till he touched the book. A little shock, a storm of revulsion against him, shook Hermione unconsciously. She released the book when he had not properly got it, and it tumbled against the side of the boat and bounced into the water.

"There!" sang Hermione, with a strange ring of malevolent victory. "I'm so sorry, so awfully sorry. Can't you get it, Gerald?"

This last was said in a note of anxious sneering that made Gerald's veins tingle with fine hate for her. He leaned far out of the boat, reaching down into the water. He could feel his position was ridiculous, his loins exposed behind him.

"It is of no importance," came the strong, clanging voice of Gudrun. She seemed to touch him. But he reached further, the boat swayed violently. Hermione, however, remained unperturbed. He grasped the book, under the water, and brought it up, dripping.

"I'm so dreadfully sorry—so dreadfully sorry," repeated Hermione. "I'm afraid it was all my fault."

"It's of no importance—really, I assure you—it doesn't matter in the least," said Gudrun loudly, with emphasis, her face flushed scarlet. And she held out her hand impatiently for the wet book, to have done with the scene. Gerald gave it to her. He was not quite himself.

"I'm so dreadfully sorry," repeated Hermione, till both Gerald and Gudrun were exasperated. "Is there nothing that can be done?"

"In what way?" asked Gudrun, with cool irony.

"Can't we save the drawings?"

There was a moment's pause, wherein Gudrun made evident all her refutation of Hermione's persistence.

"I assure you," said Gudrun, with cutting distinctness, "the drawings are quite as good as ever they were, for my purpose. I want them only for reference."

"But can't I give you a new book? I wish you'd let me do that. I feel so truly sorry. I feel it was all my fault."

"As far as I saw," said Gudrun, "it wasn't your fault at all. If there was any *fault*, it was Mr Crich's. But the whole thing is *entirely* trivial, and it really is ridiculous to take any notice of it."

Gerald watched Gudrun closely, whilst she repulsed Hermione. There was a body of cold power in her. He watched her with an insight that amounted to clairvoyance. He saw her a dangerous, hostile spirit, that could stand undiminished and unabated. It was so finished, and of such perfect gesture, moreover.

"I'm awfully glad if it doesn't matter," he said; "if there's no real harm done."

She looked back at him, with her fine blue eyes, and signalled full into his spirit, as she said, her voice ringing with intimacy almost caressive now it was addressed to him:

"Of course it doesn't matter in the *least*."

The bond was established between them, in that look, in her tone. In her tone, she made the understanding clear—they were of the same kind, he and she, a sort of diabolic freemasonry subsisted between them. Henceforward, she knew, she had her power over him. Wherever they met, they would be secretly associated. And he would be helpless in the association with her. Her soul exulted.

"Goodbye! I'm so glad you forgive me. Gooood-byyye!" Hermione sang her farewell, and waved her hand. Gerald automatically took the oar and pushed off. But he was looking all the time, with a glimmering, subtly-smiling admiration in his eyes, at Gudrun, who stood on the shoal shaking the wet book in her hand. She turned away and ignored the receding boat. But Gerald looked back as he rowed, beholding her, forgetting what he was doing.

"Aren't we going too much to the left?" sang Hermione, as she sat ignored under her coloured parasol.

Gerald looked round without replying, the oars balanced and glancing in the sun.

"I think it's all right," he said good-humouredly, beginning to row again without thinking of what he was doing. And Hermione disliked him extremely for his good-humoured obliviousness, she was nullified, she could not regain ascendancy.

Chapter XI

An Island

Meanwhile Ursula had wandered on from Willey Water along the course of the bright little stream. The afternoon was full of larks' singing. On the bright hill-sides was a subdued smoulder of gorse. A few forget-me-nots flowered by the water. There was a rousedness and a glancing everywhere.

She strayed absorbedly on, over the brooks. She wanted to go to the mill-pond above. The big mill-house was deserted, save for a laborer and his wife, who lived in the kitchen. So she passed through the empty farm-yard and through the wilderness of a garden, and mounted the bank by the sluice. When she got to the top, to see the old, velvety surface of the pond before her, she noticed a man on the bank, tinkering with a punt. It was Birkin sawing and hammering away.

She stood at the head of the sluice, looking at him. He was unaware of anybody's presence. He looked very busy, like a wild animal active and intent. She felt she ought to go away, he would not want her. He seemed to be so much occupied. But she did not want to go away. Therefore she moved along the bank till he would look up.

Which he soon did. The moment he saw her, he dropped his tools and came forward, saying:

"How do you do! I'm making the punt water-tight. Tell me if you think it is right."

She went along with him.

"You are your father's daughter, so you can tell me if it will do," he said.

She bent to look at the patched punt.

"I am sure I am my father's daughter," she said, fearful of having to judge. "But I don't know anything about carpentry. It *looks* right, don't you think?"

"Yes, I think. I hope it won't let me to the bottom, that's all. Though even so, it isn't a great matter, I should come up again. Help me to get it into the water, will you?"

With combined efforts they turned over the heavy punt and set it afloat.

"Now," he said, "I'll try it, and you can watch what happens. Then if it carries I'll take you over to the island."

5 "Do," she cried, watching anxiously.

The pond was large, and had that perfect stillness and the dark lustre of very deep water. There were two small islands overgrown with bushes and a few trees, towards the middle. Birkin pushed himself off, and veered clumsily in the pond. Luckily the punt drifted 10 so that he could catch hold of a willow bough, and pull in to the island.

"Rather overgrown," he said, looking into the interior, "but very nice. I'll come and fetch you. The boat leaks a little."

In a moment he was with her again, and she stepped into the wet 15 punt.

"It'll float us all right," he said, and manoeuvred again to the island.

They landed under a willow tree. She shrank from the little jungle of rank plants before her, evil-smelling fig-wort and hemlock. But he 20 explored into it.

"I shall mow this down," he said, "and then it will be romantic— like *Paul et Virginie*."

"Yes, one could have lovely Watteau picnics* here," cried Ursula with enthusiasm.

25 His face darkened.

"I don't want Watteau picnics here," he said.

"Only your Virginie," she laughed.

"Virginie enough," he smiled wryly. "No, I don't want her either."

30 Ursula looked at him closely. She had not seen him since Breadalby. He was very thin and hollow, with a ghastly look in his face.

"You have been ill, haven't you?" she asked, rather repulsed.

"Yes." he replied coldly.*

35 They had sat down under the willow tree, and were looking at the pond, from their retreat on the island.

"Has it made you frightened?" she asked.

"What of?" he asked, turning his eyes to look at her. Something in him, inhuman and unmitigated, disturbed her, and shook her out of 40 her ordinary self.

"It *is* frightening to be very ill, isn't it?" she said.

"It isn't pleasant," he said. "Whether one is really afraid of death, or not, I have never decided. In one mood, not a bit, in another, very much."

"But doesn't it make you feel ashamed? I think it makes one so ashamed, to be ill—illness is so terribly humiliating, don't you think?"

He considered for some minutes.

"Maybe," he said. "Though one knows all the time one's life isn't really right, at the source. That's the humiliation. I don't see that the illness counts so much, after that. One is ill because one doesn't live properly—can't. It's the failure to live that makes one ill, and humiliates one."

"But do you fail to live?" she asked, almost jeering.

"Why yes—I don't make much of a success of my days. One seems always to be bumping one's nose against the blank wall ahead."

Ursula laughed. She was frightened, and when she was frightened she always laughed and pretended to be jaunty.

"Your poor nose!" she said, looking at that feature of his face.

"No wonder it's ugly," he replied.

She was silent for some minutes, struggling with her own self-deception. It was an instinct in her, to deceive herself.

"But *I'm* happy—I think life is *awfully* jolly," she said.

"Good," he answered, with a certain cold indifference.

She reached for a bit of paper which had wrapped a small piece of chocolate she had found in her pocket, and began making a boat. He watched her without heeding her. There was something strangely pathetic and tender in her moving, unconscious finger-tips, that were agitated and hurt, really.

"I *do* enjoy things—don't you?" she asked.

"Oh yes! But it infuriates me that I can't get right, at the really growing part of me. I feel all tangled and messed up, and I *can't* get straight anyhow. I don't know what really to *do*. One must do something somewhere."

"Why should you always be *doing*?" she retorted. "It is so plebeian. I think it is much better to be really patrician, and to do nothing but just be oneself, like a walking flower."

"I quite agree," he said, "if one has burst into blossom. But I can't get my flower into blossom anyhow. Either it is blighted in the bud, or has got the smother-fly,* or it isn't nourished. Curse it, it isn't even a bud. It is a contravened knot."

Again she laughed. He was so very fretful and exasperated. But she was anxious and puzzled. How was one to get out, anyhow.
5   There must be a way out somewhere.

There was a silence, wherein she wanted to cry. She reached for another bit of chocolate paper, and began to fold another boat.

"And why is it," she asked at length, "that there is no flowering, no dignity of human life now?"
10   "The whole idea is dead. Humanity itself is dry-rotten really. There are myriads of human beings hanging on the bush—and they look very nice and rosy, your healthy young men and women. But they are apples of Sodom, as a matter of fact, Dead Sea Fruit, gall-apples.* It isn't true that they have any significance—their
15   insides are full of bitter, corrupt ash."

"But there *are* good people," protested Ursula.

"Good enough for the life of today. But mankind is a dead tree, covered with fine brilliant galls of people."

Ursula could not help stiffening herself against this, it was too
20   picturesque and final. But neither could she help making him go on.

"And if it is so, *why* is it?" she asked, hostile. They were rousing each other to a fine passion of opposition.

"Why? Why are people all balls of bitter dust? Because they won't fall off the tree when they're ripe. They hang on to their old positions
25   when the position is overpast, till they become infested with little worms and dry-rot."

There was a long pause. His voice had become hot and very sarcastic. Ursula was troubled and bewildered, they were both oblivious of everything but their own immersion.
30   "But even if everybody is wrong—where are *you* right?" she cried. "Where are you any better?"

"I?—I'm not right," he cried back. "At least my only rightness lies in the fact that I know it. I detest what I am, outwardly. I loathe myself as a human being. Humanity is a huge aggregate lie, and a
35   huge lie is less than a small truth. Humanity is less, far less than the individual, because the individual may sometimes be capable of truth, and humanity is a tree of lies.——And they say that love is the greatest thing; they persist in *saying* this, the foul liars, and just look at what they do! Look at all the millions of people who repeat every
40   minute that love is the greatest, and charity is the greatest*—and see

what they are doing all the time. By their works ye shall know them,* for dirty liars and cowards, who daren't stand by their own actions, much less by their own words."

"But," said Ursula sadly, "that doesn't alter the fact that love is the greatest, does it? What they *do* doesn't alter the truth of what they 5 say, does it?"

"Completely. If* what they say *were* true, then they couldn't help fulfilling it. But they maintain a lie, and so they run amok at last. It's a lie to say that love is the greatest. You might as well say that hate is the greatest, since the opposite of everything balances.—What 10 people want is hate—hate and nothing but hate. And in the name of righteousness and love, they get it. They distil themselves into nitro-glycerine, all the lot of them, out of very love.—It's the lie that kills. If we want hate, let us have it—death, murder, torture, violent destruction—let us have it: but not in the name of love.—But I abhor 15 humanity, I wish it was swept away. It could go, and there would be no *absolute* loss, if every human being perished tomorrow. The reality would be untouched. Nay, it would be better. The real tree of life would then be rid of the most ghastly heavy crop of Dead Sea Fruit, the intolerable burden of myriad simulacra of people, an 20 infinite weight of mortal lies."

"So you'd like everybody in the world destroyed?" said Ursula.

"I should indeed."

"And the world empty of people."

"Yes truly. You yourself, don't you find it a beautiful clean 25 thought, a world empty of people, just uninterrupted grass, and a hare sitting up?"*

The pleasant sincerity of his voice made Ursula pause to consider her own proposition. And really it *was* attractive: a clean, lovely, humanless world. It was the *really* desirable.—Her heart hesitated, 30 and exulted.—But still, she was dissatisfied with *him*.

"But," she objected, "you'd be dead yourself, so what good would it do you?"

"I would die like a shot, to know that the earth would really be cleaned of *all* the people. It is the most beautiful and freeing thought. 35 Then there would *never* be another foul humanity created, for a universal defilement."

"No," said Ursula, "there would be nothing."

"What! Nothing? Just because humanity was wiped out? You flatter yourself. There'd be everything." 40

"But how, if there were no people?"

"Do you think that creation depends on *man*! It merely doesn't.—There are the trees and the grass and birds. I much prefer to think of the lark rising up in the morning upon a humanless world.—Man is a mistake, he must go.—There is the grass, and hares and adders, and the unseen hosts, actual angels that go about freely when a dirty humanity doesn't interrupt them—and good pure-tissued demons: very nice."

It pleased Ursula, what he said, pleased her very much, as a phantasy. Of course it was only a pleasant fancy. She herself knew too well the actuality of humanity, its hideous actuality. She knew it could not disappear so cleanly and conveniently. It had a long way to go yet, a long and hideous way. Her subtle, feminine, demoniacal soul knew it well.

"If only man was swept off the face of the earth, creation would go on so marvellously, with a new start, non-human. Man is one of the mistakes of creation—like the ichthyosauri.*—If only he were gone again, think what lovely things would come out of the liberated days; things straight out of the fire."

"But man will never be gone," she said, with insidious, diabolical knowledge of the horrors of persistence. "The world will go with him."

"Ah no," he answered, "not so. I believe in the proud angels and the demons that are our fore-runners. They will destroy us, because we are not proud enough. The ichthyosauri were not proud: they crawled and floundered as we do.—And besides, look at elder-flowers and bluebells—they are a sign that pure creation takes place—even the butterfly. But humanity never gets beyond the caterpillar stage—it rots in the chrysalis, it never will have wings. It is anti-creation, like monkeys and baboons."*

Ursula watched him as he talked. There seemed a certain impatient fury in him, all the while, and at the same time a great amusement in everything, and a final tolerance. And it was this tolerance she mistrusted, not the fury. She saw that, all the while, in spite of himself, he would have to be trying to save the world. And this knowledge, whilst it comforted her heart somewhere with a little self-satisfaction, stability, yet filled her with a certain sharp contempt and hate of him. She wanted him to herself, she hated the Salvator Mundi* touch. It was something diffuse and generalised about him, which she could not stand.—He would behave in the same way, say the same things, give himself as completely to anybody who came along, anybody and everybody who liked to appeal to him. It was despicable, a very insidious form of prostitution.

"But," she said, "you believe in individual love, even if you don't believe in loving humanity—?"

"I don't believe in love at all—that is, any more than I believe in hate, or in grief. Love is one of the emotions like all the others—and so it is all right whilst you feel it. But I can't see how it becomes an absolute. It is just part of human relationships, no more. And it is only part of *any* human relationship. And why one should be required *always* to feel it, any more than one always feels sorrow or distinct joy, I cannot conceive. Love isn't a desideratum—it is an emotion you feel or you don't feel, according to circumstance."

"Then why do you care about people at all?" she asked, "if you don't believe in love? Why do you bother about humanity?"

"Why do I? Because I can't get away from it."

"Because you love it," she persisted.

It irritated him.

"If I do love it," he said, "it is my disease."

"But it is a disease you don't want to be cured of," she said, with some cold sneering.

He was silent now, feeling she wanted to insult him.

"And if you don't believe in love, what *do* you believe in?" she asked, mocking. "Simply in the end of the world, and grass?"

He was beginning to feel a fool.

"I believe in the unseen hosts," he said.

"And nothing else?—You believe in nothing visible, except grass and birds?—Your world is a poor show."

"Perhaps it is," he said, cool and superior now he was offended, assuming a certain insufferable aloof superiority, and withdrawing into his distance.

Ursula disliked him. But also she felt she had lost something. She looked at him as he sat crouched on the bank. There was a certain priggish Sunday-school stiffness over him, priggish and detestable. And yet, at the same time, the moulding of him was so quick and attractive, it gave such a great sense of freedom: the moulding of his brows, his chin, his whole physique, something so alive, somewhere, in spite of the look of sickness.

And it was this duality in feeling which he created in her, that made a fine hate of him quicken in her bowels. There was his wonderful, desirable life-rapidity, the rare quality of an utterly desirable man: and there was at the same time this ridiculous, mean effacement into a Salvator Mundi and a Sunday-school teacher, a prig of the stiffest type.*

5 He looked up at her. He saw her face strangely enkindled, as if suffused from within by a powerful sweet fire. His soul was arrested in wonder. She was enkindled in her own living fire. Arrested in wonder and in pure, perfect attraction, he moved towards her. She sat like a strange queen, almost supernatural in her glowing smiling 10 richness.

"The point about love," he said, his consciousness quickly adjusting itself, "is that we hate the word because we have vulgarised it. It ought to be proscribed, tabooed from utterance, for many years, till we get a new, better idea."

15 There was a beam of understanding between them.

"But it always means the same thing," she said.

"Ah God, no, let it not mean that any more," he cried. "Let the old meanings go."

"But still it is love," she persisted. A strange, wicked yellow light 20 shone at him in her eyes.

He hesitated, baffled, withdrawing.

"No," he said, "it isn't. Spoken like that, never in the world. You've no business to utter the word."

"I must leave it to you, to take it out of the Ark of the Covenant at 25 the right moment,"* she mocked.

Again they looked at each other. She suddenly sprang up, turned her back to him, and walked away. He too rose slowly and went to the water's edge, where, crouching he began to amuse himself unconsciously. Picking a daisy he dropped it on the pond, so that the 30 stem was a keel, the flower floated like a little water lily, staring with its open face up to the sky. It turned slowly round, in a slow, slow dervish dance, as it veered away.

He watched it, then dropped another daisy into the water, and after that another, and sat watching them with bright, absolved eyes, 35 crouching near on the bank. Ursula turned to look. A strange feeling possessed her, as if something were taking place. But it was all intangible. And some sort of control was being put on her. She could not know. She could only watch the brilliant little discs of the daisies veering slowly in travel on the dark, lustrous water. The little flotilla 40 was drifting into the light, a company of white specks in the distance.

"Do let us go to the shore, to follow them," she said, afraid of being any longer imprisoned on the island. And they pushed off in the punt.

She was glad to be on the free land again. She went along the bank towards the sluice. The daisies were scattered broadcast on the pond, tiny radiant things, like an exaltation, points of exaltation here and there. Why did they move her so strongly and mystically?

"Look," he said, "your boat of purple paper is escorting them, and they are a convoy of rafts."

Some of the daisies came slowly towards her, hesitating, making a shy bright little cotillon on the dark clear water. Their gay bright candour moved her so much as they came near, that she was almost in tears.

"Why are they so lovely?" she cried. "Why do I think them so lovely?"

"They are nice flowers," he said, her emotional tones putting a constraint on him. "You know that a daisy is a company of florets, a concourse, become individual.* Don't the botanists put it highest in the line of development? I believe they do."

"The compositae, yes, I think so," said Ursula, who was never very sure of anything. Things she knew perfectly well, at one moment, seemed to become doubtful the next.

"Explain it so, then," he said. "The daisy is a perfect little democracy, so it's the highest of flowers, hence its charm."

"No," she cried, "no—never. It isn't democratic."

"No," he admitted. "It's the golden mob of the proletariat, surrounded by a showy white fence of the idle rich."

"How hateful—your hateful social orders!" she cried.

"Quite! It's a daisy—we'll leave it alone."

"Do. Let it be a dark horse for once," she said: "if anything can be a dark horse to you," she added satirically.

They stood aside, forgetful. As if a little stunned, they both were motionless, barely conscious. The little conflict into which they had fallen had torn their consciousness and left them like two impersonal forces, there in contact.

He became aware of the lapse. He wanted to say something, to get on to a new more ordinary footing.

"You know," he said, "that I am having rooms here at the mill? Don't you think we can have some good times?"

"Oh are you?" she said, ignoring all his implication of admitted intimacy.

He adjusted himself at once, became normally distant.

"If I find I can live sufficiently by myself," he continued, "I shall give up my work altogether. It has become dead to me. I don't believe in the humanity I pretend to be part of, I don't care a straw for the social ideals I live by, I hate the dying organic form of social mankind—so it can't be anything but trumpery,* to work at education. I shall drop it as soon as I am clear enough—tomorrow perhaps—and be by myself."

"Have you enough to live on?" asked Ursula.

"Yes—I've about four hundred a year.* That makes it easy for me."

There was a pause.

"And what about Hermione?" asked Ursula.

"That's over, finally—a pure failure, and never could have been anything else."

"But you still know each other?"

"We could hardly pretend to be strangers, could we?"

There was a stubborn pause.

"But isn't that a half-measure?" asked Ursula at length.

"I don't think so," he said. "You'll be able to tell me if it is."

Again there was a pause of some minutes duration. He was thinking.

"One must throw everything away, everything—let everything go, to get the one last thing one wants," he said.

"What thing?" she asked, in challenge.

"I don't know—freedom together," he said.

She had wanted him to say 'love.'

There was heard a loud barking of the dogs below. He seemed disturbed by it. She did not notice. Only she thought he seemed uneasy.

"As a matter of fact," he said, in rather a small voice, "I believe that is Hermione come now, with Gerald Crich. She wanted to see the rooms before they are furnished."

"I know," said Ursula. "She will superintend the furnishing for you."

"Probably. Does it matter?"

"Oh no, I should think not," said Ursula. "Though personally, I can't bear her. I think she is a lie, if you like, you who are always talking about lies." Then she ruminated for a moment, when she broke out: "Yes, and I do mind if she furnishes your rooms—I do mind. I mind that you keep her hanging on at all."

He was silent now, frowning.

"Perhaps," he said. "I don't *want* her to furnish the rooms here—and I don't keep her hanging on. Only, I needn't be churlish to her, need I?——At any rate, I shall have to go down and see them now. You'll come, won't you?"

"I don't think so," she said coldly and irresolutely.

"Won't you? Yes do. Come and see the rooms as well. Do come."

Chapter XII

Carpeting[*]

He set off down the bank, and she went unwillingly with him. Yet she would not have stayed away, either.

"We know each other well, you and I, already," he said. She did not answer.

In the large, darkish kitchen of the mill, the laborer's wife was talking shrilly to Hermione and Gerald, who stood, he in white and she in a glistening bluish foulard, strangely luminous in the dusk of the room; whilst from the cages on the walls, a dozen or more canaries sang at the top of their voices. The cages were all placed round a small square window at the back, where the sunshine came in, a beautiful beam, filtering through green leaves of a tree. The voice of Mrs Salmon[*] shrilled against the noise of the birds, which rose ever more wild and triumphant, and the woman's voice went up and up against them, and the birds replied with wild animation.

"Here's Rupert!" shouted Gerald in the midst of the din. He was suffering badly, being very sensitive in the ear.

"O-o-h them birds, they won't let you speak—!" shrilled the laborer's wife in disgust. "I'll cover them up."

And she darted here and there, throwing a duster, an apron, a towel, a table-cloth over the cages of the birds.

"Now will you stop it, and let a body speak for your row," she said, still in a voice that was too high.

The party watched her. Soon the cages were covered, they had a strange funereal look. But from under the towels odd defiant trills and bubblings still shook out.

"Oh, they won't go on," said Mrs Salmon reassuringly. "They'll go to sleep now."

"Really," said Hermione, politely.

"They will," said Gerald. "They will go to sleep automatically, now the impression of evening is produced."

"Are they so easily deceived?" cried Ursula.

"Oh yes," replied Gerald. "Don't you know the story of Fabre,

134

who, when he was a boy, put a hen's head under her wing, and she straight away went to sleep?* It's quite true."

"And did that make him a naturalist?" asked Birkin.

"Probably," said Gerald.

Meanwhile Ursula was peeping under one of the cloths. There sat the canary in a corner, bunched and fluffed up for sleep.

"How ridiculous!" she cried. "It really thinks the night has come! How absurd! Really, how can one have any respect for a creature that is so easily taken in!"

"Yes," sang Hermione, coming also to look. She put her hand on Ursula's arm and chuckled a low laugh. "Yes, doesn't he look comical?" she chuckled. "Like a stupid husband."

Then, with her hand still on Ursula's arm, she drew her away, saying, in her mild sing-song:

"How did you come here? We saw Gudrun too."

"I came to look at the pond," said Ursula, "and I found Mr Birkin there."

"Did you.——This is quite a Brangwen land, isn't it!"

"I'm afraid I hoped so," said Ursula. "I ran here for refuge, when I saw you down the lake just putting off."

"Did you!—And now we've run you to earth!"

Hermione's eyelids lifted with an uncanny movement, amused but overwrought. She had always her strange, rapt look, unnatural and irresponsible.

"I was going on," said Ursula. "Mr Birkin wanted me to see the rooms. Isn't it delightful to live here? It is perfect."

"Yes," said Hermione, abstractedly. Then she turned right away from Ursula, ceased to know her existence.

"How do you feel, Rupert?" she sang in a new, affectionate tone, to Birkin.

"Very well," he replied.

"Were you quite comfortable?" The curious, sinister, rapt look was on Hermione's face, she shrugged her bosom in a convulsed movement, and seemed like one half in a trance.

"Quite comfortable," he replied.

There was a long pause, whilst Hermione looked at him for a long time, from under her heavy, drugged eyelids.

"And you think you'll be happy here?" she said at last.

"I'm sure I shall."

"I'm sure I shall do anything for him as I can," said the laborer's wife. "And I'm sure our mester will; so I *hope* as he'll find himself comfortable."

Hermione turned and looked at her slowly.

"Thank you so much," she said, and then she turned completely away again. She recovered her position, and lifting her face towards him, and addressing him exclusively, she said:

"Have you measured the rooms?"

"No," he said, "I've been mending the punt."

"Shall we do it now?" she said slowly, balanced and dispassionate.

"Have you got a tape measure, Mrs Salmon?" he said, turning to the woman.

"Yes sir, I think I can find you one," replied the woman, bustling immediately to a basket. "This is the only one I've got, if it will do."

Hermione took it, though it was offered to him.

"Thank you so much," she said. "It will do very nicely. Thank you so much." Then she turned to Birkin, saying with a little gay movement: "Shall we do it now, Rupert?"

"What about the others, they'll be bored," he said reluctantly.

"Do you mind?" said Hermione, turning to Ursula and Gerald vaguely.

"Not in the least," they replied.

"Which room shall we do first?" she said, turning again to Birkin, with the same gaiety, now she was going to *do* something with him.

"We'll take them as they come," he said.

"Should I be getting your teas ready, while you do that?" said the laborer's wife, also gay because *she* had something to do.

"Would you?" said Hermione, turning to her with the curious motion of intimacy that seemed to envelop the woman, draw her almost to Hermione's breast, and which left the others standing apart. "I should be so glad. Where shall we have it?"

"Where you would like it, my lady!* Shall it be in here, or out on the grass?"

"Where shall we have tea?" sang Hermione to the company at large.

"On the bank by the pond. And *we'll* carry the things up, if you'll just get them ready, Mrs Salmon," said Birkin.

"All right," said the pleased woman.

The party moved down the passage into the front room. It was empty, but clean and sunny. There was a window looking on to the tangled front garden.

"This is the dining room," said Hermione. "We'll measure it this way, Rupert—you go down there—"

"Can't I do it for you," said Gerald, coming to take the end of the tape.

"No thank you," cried Hermione, stooping to the ground in her bluish, brilliant foulard. It was a great joy to her to *do* things, and to have the ordering of the job, with Birkin. He obeyed her subduedly. Ursula and Gerald looked on. It was a peculiarity of Hermione's, that at every moment, she had one intimate, and turned all the rest of those present into onlookers. This raised her into a state of triumph.

They measured and discussed in the dining-room, and Hermione decided what the floor coverings must be. It sent her into a strange, convulsed anger, to be thwarted. Birkin always let her have her way, for the moment.

Then they moved across, through the hall, to the other front room, that was a little smaller than the first.

"This is the study," said Hermione. "Rupert, I have a rug that I want you to have for here. Will you let me give it you? Do—I want to give it you."

"What is it like?" he asked ungraciously.

"You haven't seen it. It is chiefly rose red, then blue, a metallic, mid-blue, and a very soft dark blue. I think you would like it. Do you think you would?"

"It sounds very nice," he replied. "What is it? Oriental? With a pile?"

"Yes. Persian! It is made of camel's hair, silky. I think it is called Bergamos:*—twelve feet by seven—. Do you think it would do?"

"It would *do*," he said. "But why should you give me an expensive rug? I can manage perfectly well with my old Oxford Turkish."

"But may I give it you? Do let me."

"How much did it cost?"

She looked at him, and said:

"I don't remember. It was quite cheap."

He looked at her, his face set.

"I don't want to take it, Hermione," he said.

"Do let me give it to the rooms," she said, going up to him and putting her hand on his arm lightly, pleadingly. "I shall be so disappointed."

"You know I don't want you to give me things," he repeated helplessly.

"I don't want to give you *things*," she said teasingly. "But will you have this?"

"All right," he said, defeated, and she triumphed.

They went upstairs. There were two bedrooms to correspond with the rooms downstairs. One of them was half furnished, and Birkin had evidently slept there. Hermione went round the room carefully, taking in every detail, as if absorbing the evidence of his presence, in all the inanimate things. She felt the bed and examined the coverings.

"Are you *sure* you were quite comfortable?" she said, pressing the pillow.

"Perfectly," he replied coldly.

"And you were warm? There is no down quilt. I am sure you need one. You mustn't have a great pressure of clothes."

"I've got one," he said. "It is coming down."

They measured the rooms, and lingered over every consideration. Ursula stood at the window and watched the woman carrying the tea up the bank to the pond. She hated the palaver Hermione made, she wanted to drink tea, she wanted anything but this fuss and business.

At last they all mounted the grassy bank, to the picnic. Hermione poured out tea. She ignored now Ursula's presence. And Ursula, recovering from her ill-humour, turned to Gerald saying:

"Oh, I hated you so much the other day, Mr Crich."

"What for?" said Gerald, wincing slightly away.

"For treating your horse so badly. Oh, I hated you so much!"

"What did he do?" sang Hermione.

"He made his lovely sensitive Arab horse stand with him at the railway crossing whilst a horrible lot of trucks went by; and the poor thing, she was in a perfect frenzy, a perfect agony. It was the most horrible sight you can imagine."

"Why did you do it, Gerald?" asked Hermione, calm and interrogative.

"She must learn to stand—what use is she to me, in this country, if she shies and goes off every time an engine whistles."

"But why inflict unnecessary torture?" said Ursula. "Why make her stand all that time at the crossing? You might just as well have ridden back up the road, and saved all that horror. Her sides were bleeding where you had spurred her. It was too horrible—!"

Gerald stiffened.

"I have to use her," he replied. "And if I'm going to be sure of her at *all*, she'll have to learn to stand noises."

"Why should she?" cried Ursula in a passion. "She is a living creature, why should she stand anything, just because you choose to make her? She has as much right to her own being, as you have to yours."

"There I disagree," said Gerald. "I consider that mare is there for my use. Not because I bought her, but because that is the natural order. It is more natural for a man to take a horse and use it as he likes, than for him to go down on his knees to it, begging it to do as it wishes, and to fulfil its own marvellous nature."

Ursula was just breaking out, when Hermione lifted her face and began, in her musing sing-song:

"I do think—I do really think we must have the *courage* to use the lower animal life for our needs. I do think there is something wrong, when we look on every living creature as if it were ourself. I do feel, that it is false to project our own feelings on every animate creature. It is a lack of discrimination, a lack of criticism."

"Quite," said Birkin sharply. "Nothing is so detestable as the maudlin attributing of human feelings and consciousness to animals."

"Yes," said Hermione, wearily, "we must really take a position. Either we are going to use the animals, or they will use us."

"That's a fact," said Gerald. "A horse has got a will like a man, though it has no *mind*, strictly. And if your will isn't master, then the horse is master of you. And this is a thing I can't help. I can't help being master of the horse."

"If only we could learn how to use our will," said Hermione, "we could do anything. The will can cure anything, and put anything right. That I am convinced of—if only we use the will properly, intelligently."

"What do you mean by using the will properly?" said Birkin.

"A very great doctor taught me," she said, addressing Ursula and Gerald vaguely. "He told me, for instance, that to cure oneself of a bad habit, one should *force* oneself to do it, when one would not do it;—make oneself do it—and then the habit would disappear."

"How do you mean?" said Gerald.

"If you bite your nails, for example. Then, when you don't want to bite your nails, bite them—make yourself bite them. And you would find the habit was broken."

"Is that so?" said Gerald.

"Yes. And in so many things, I have *made* myself well. I was a very queer and nervous girl. And by learning to use my will, simply by using my will, I *made* myself right."

Ursula looked all the while at Hermione, as she spoke in her slow, dispassionate, and yet strangely tense voice. A curious thrill went over the younger woman. Some strange, dark, convulsive power was in Hermione, fascinating and repelling.

"It is fatal to use the will like that," cried Birkin harshly, "disgusting. Such a will is an obscenity."*

Hermione looked at him for a long time, with her shadowed, heavy eyes. Her face was soft and pale and thin, almost phosphorescent, her jaw was lean.

"I'm sure it isn't," she said at length. There always seemed an interval, a strange split between what she seemed to feel and experience, and what she actually said and thought. She seemed to catch her thoughts at length from off the surface of a maelström of chaotic black emotions and reactions, and Birkin was always filled with repulsion, she caught so infallibly, her will never failed her. Her voice was always dispassionate and tense, and perfectly confident. Yet she shuddered with a sense of nausea, a sort of sea-sickness that always threatened to overwhelm her mind. But her mind remained unbroken, her will was still perfect. It almost sent Birkin mad. But he would never, never dare to break her will, and let loose the maelström of her subconsciousness, and see her in her ultimate madness. Yet he was always striking at her.

"And of course," he said to Gerald, "horses *haven't* got a complete will, like human beings. A horse has no *one* will. Every horse, strictly, has two wills. With one will, it wants to put itself in the human power completely,—and with the other, it wants to be free, wild. The two wills sometimes lock—you know that, if ever you've felt a horse bolt, while you've been driving it."

"I have felt a horse bolt while I was driving it," said Gerald, "but it didn't make me know it had two wills. I only knew it was frightened."

Hermione had ceased to listen. She simply became oblivious when these subjects were started.

"Why should a horse want to put itself in the human power?" asked Ursula. "That is quite incomprehensible to me. I don't believe it ever wanted it."

"Yes it did. It's the last, perhaps highest, love-impulse: resign your will to the higher being," said Birkin.

"What curious notions you have of love," jeered Ursula.

"And woman is the same as horses: two wills act in opposition inside her. With one will, she wants to subject herself utterly. With the other she wants to bolt, and pitch her rider to perdition."

"Then I'm a bolter," said Ursula, with a burst of laughter.

"It's a dangerous thing to domesticate even horses, let alone women," said Birkin. "The dominant principle has some rare antagonists."

"Good thing too," said Ursula.

"Quite," said Gerald, with a faint smile. "There's more fun."

Hermione could bear no more. She rose, saying in her easy sing-song:

"Isn't the evening beautiful! I get filled sometimes with such a great sense of beauty, that I feel I can hardly bear it."

Ursula, to whom she had appealed, rose with her, moved to the last impersonal depths. And Birkin seemed to her almost a monster of hateful arrogance. She went with Hermione along the bank of the pond, talking of beautiful, soothing things, picking the gentle cowslips.

"Wouldn't you like a dress," said Ursula to Hermione, "of this yellow spotted with orange—a cotton dress?"

"Yes," said Hermione, stopping and looking at the flower, letting the thought come home to her and soothe her. "Wouldn't it be pretty? I should *love* it."

And she turned smiling to Ursula, in a feeling of real affection.

But Gerald remained with Birkin, wanting to probe him to the bottom, to know what he meant by the dual will in horses. A flicker of excitement danced on Gerald's face.

Hermione and Ursula strayed on together, united in a sudden bond of deep affection and closeness.

"I really do *not* want to be forced into all this criticism and analysis of life. I really *do* want to see things in their entirety, with their beauty left to them, and their wholeness, their natural holiness.—Don't you feel it, don't you feel you *can't* be tortured into any more knowledge?" said Hermione, stopping in front of Ursula, and turning to her with clenched fists thrust downwards.

"Yes," said Ursula. "I do. I am sick of all this poking and prying."

"I'm so glad you are. Sometimes," said Hermione, again stopping

arrested in her progress and turning to Ursula, "sometimes I wonder if I *ought* to submit to all this realisation, if I am not being weak in rejecting it.—But I feel I *can't*—I *can't*. It seems to destroy *everything*. All the beauty and the,—and the true holiness is destroyed,—and I
5 feel I can't live without them."

"And it would be simply wrong to live without them," cried Ursula. "No, it is so *irreverent* to think that everything must be realised in the head. Really, something must be left to the Lord, there always is and always will be."*

10 "Yes," said Hermione, reassured like a child, "it should, shouldn't it? And Rupert—" she lifted her face to the sky, in a muse—"he *can* only tear things to pieces. He really *is* like a boy who must pull everything to pieces to see how it is made. And I can't think it is right—it does seem so irreverent, as you say."

15 "Like tearing open a bud to see what the flower will be like," said Ursula.

"Yes. And that kills everything, doesn't it? It doesn't allow any possibility of flowering."

"Of course not," said Ursula. "It is purely destructive."

20 "It is, isn't it!"

Hermione looked long and slow at Ursula, seeming to accept confirmation from her. Then the two women were silent. As soon as they were in accord, they began mutually to mistrust each other. In spite of herself, Ursula felt herself recoiling from Hermione. It was
25 all she could do to restrain her revulsion.

They returned to the men, like two conspirators who have withdrawn to come to an agreement. Birkin looked up at them. Ursula hated him for his cold watchfulness. But he said nothing.

"Shall we be going?" said Hermione. "Rupert, you are coming to
30 Shortlands to dinner? Will you come at once, will you come now, with us?"

"I'm not dressed," replied Birkin. "And you know Gerald stickles for* the convention."

"I don't stickle for it," said Gerald. "But if you'd got as sick as I
35 have of rowdy go-as-you-please in the house, you'd prefer it if people were peaceful and conventional, at least at meals."

"All right," said Birkin.

"But can't we wait for you while you dress?" persisted Hermione.

"If you like."

40 He rose to go indoors. Ursula said she would take her leave.

"Only," she said, turning to Gerald, "I must say that, however man is lord of the beast and the fowl,* I still don't think he has any right to violate the feelings of the inferior creation. I still think it would have been much more sensible and nice of you if you'd trotted back up the road while the train went by, and been considerate."

"I see," said Gerald, smiling, but somewhat annoyed. "I must remember another time."

"They all think I'm an interfering female," thought Ursula to herself, as she went away. But she was in arms against them.

She ran home plunged in thought. She had been very much moved by Hermione, she had really come into contact with her, so that there was a sort of league between the two women. And yet she could not bear her. But she put the thought away. "She's really good," she said to herself. "She really wants what is right." And she tried to feel at one with Hermione, and to shut off from Birkin. She was strictly hostile to him. But she was held to him by some bond, some deep principle. This at once irritated her and saved her.

Only now and again, violent little shudders would come over her, out of her subconsciousness, and she knew it was the fact that she had stated her challenge to Birkin, and he had, consciously or unconsciously, accepted. It was a fight to the death between them—or to new life: though in what the conflict lay, no one could say.

Chapter XIII

Mino*

The days went by, and she received no sign. Was he going to ignore her, was he going to take no further notice of her secret? A dreary weight of anxiety and acrid bitterness settled on her. And yet Ursula knew she was only deceiving herself, that he *would* proceed. She said no word to anybody.

Then, sure enough, there came a note from him, asking if she would come to tea, with Gudrun, to his rooms in town.

"Why does he ask Gudrun as well?" she asked herself at once. "Does he want to protect himself, or does he think I would not go alone?"

She was tormented by the thought that he wanted to protect himself. But at the end of all, she only said to herself:

"I don't *want* Gudrun to be there, because I want him to say something more to me. So I shan't tell Gudrun anything about it, and I shall go alone. Then I shall know."

She found herself sitting on the tram-car, mounting up the hill going out of the town, to the place where he had his lodging. She seemed to have passed into a kind of dream world, absolved from the conditions of actuality. She watched the sordid streets of the town go by beneath her, as if she were a spirit disconnected from the material universe. What had it all to do with her? She was palpitating and formless within the flux of the ghost life. She could not consider any more, what anybody would say of her or think about her. People had passed out of her range, she was absolved. She had fallen strange and dim, out of the sheath of the material life, like a berry falls from the only world it has ever known, down out of the sheath on to the real unknown.*

Birkin was standing in the middle of the room, when she was shown in by the landlady. He too was moved outside himself. She saw him agitated and shaken, a frail, unsubstantial body silent like the node of some violent force, that came out from him and shook her almost into a swoon.

"You are alone?" he said.

144

"Yes—Gudrun couldn't come."

He instantly guessed why.

And they were both seated in silence, in the terrible tension of the room. She was aware that it was a pleasant room full of light and very restful in its form—aware also of a fuchsia tree, with dangling scarlet and purple flowers.

"How nice the fuchsias are!" she said, to break the silence.

"Aren't they!—Did you think I had forgotten what I said?"

A swoon went over Ursula's mind.

"I don't want you to remember it—if you don't want to," she struggled to say, through the dark mist that covered her.

There was silence for some moments.

"No," he said. "It isn't that. Only—if we are going to know each other, we must pledge ourselves for ever. If we are going to make a relationship, even of friendship, there must be something final and infallible about it."

There was a clang of mistrust and almost anger in his voice. She did not answer. Her heart was too much contracted. She could not have spoken.

Seeing she was not going to reply, he continued, almost bitterly, giving himself away:

"I can't say it is love I have to offer—and it isn't love I want. It is something much more impersonal and harder,—and rarer."

There was a silence, out of which she said:

"You mean you don't love me?"

She suffered furiously, saying that.

"Yes, if you like to put it like that.—Though perhaps that isn't true. I don't know. At any rate, I don't feel the emotion of love for you—no, and I don't want to. Because it gives out in the last issues."

"Love gives out in the last issues?" she asked, feeling numb to the lips.

"Yes, it does. At the very last, one is alone, beyond the influence of love. There is a real impersonal me, that is beyond love, beyond any emotional relationship. So it is with you. But we want to delude ourselves that love is the root. It isn't. It is only the branches. The root is beyond love, a naked kind of isolation, an isolated me, that does *not* meet and mingle, and never can."

She watched him with wide, troubled eyes. His face was incandescent in its abstract earnestness.

"And you mean you can't love?" she asked, in trepidation.

"Yes, if you like.—I have loved. But there is a beyond, where there is no love."

She could not submit to this. She felt it swooning over her. But she could not submit.

5   "But how do you know—if you have never *really* loved?" she asked.

"It is true, what I say: there is a beyond, in you, in me, which is further than love, beyond the scope, as stars are beyond the scope of vision, some of them."

10   "Then there *is* no love," cried Ursula.

"Ultimately, no, there is something else. But ultimately, there *is* no love."

Ursula was given over to this statement for some moments. Then she half rose from her chair, saying, in a final, repellant voice:

15   "Then let me go home—what am I doing here!"

"There is the door," he said. "You are a free agent."

He was suspended finely and perfectly in this extremity. She hung motionless for some seconds, then she sat down again.

"If there is no love, what is there?" she cried, almost jeering.

20   "Something," he said, looking at her, battling with his soul, with all his might.

"What?"

He was silent for a long time, unable to be in communication with her whilst she was in this state of opposition.

25   "There is," he said, in a voice of pure abstraction, "a final me which is stark and impersonal and beyond responsibility. So there is a final you. And it is there I would want to meet you—not in the emotional, loving plane—but there beyond, where there is no speech and no terms of agreement. There we are two stark, unknown

30   beings, two utterly strange creatures, I would want to approach you, and you me.—And there could be no obligation, because there is no standard for action there, because no understanding has been reaped from that plane. It is quite inhuman,—so there can be no calling to book, in any form whatsoever—because one is outside the

35   pale of all that is accepted, and nothing known applies. One can only follow the impulse, taking that which lies in front, and responsible for nothing, asked for nothing, giving nothing, only each taking according to the primal desire."

Ursula listened to this speech, her mind dumb and almost

40   senseless, that he said was so unexpected and so untoward.

"It is just purely selfish," she said.

"If it is pure, yes. But it isn't selfish at all. Because I don't *know* what I want of you. I deliver *myself* over to the unknown, in coming to you, I am without reserves or defences, stripped entirely into the unknown. Only there needs the pledge between us, that we will both cast off everything, cast off ourselves even, and cease to be, so that that which is perfectly ourselves can take place in us."

She pondered along her own line of thought.

"But it is because you love me, that you want me?" she persisted.

"No it isn't. It is because I believe in you—if I *do* believe in you."

"Aren't you sure?" she laughed, suddenly hurt.

He was looking at her steadfastly, scarcely heeding what she said.

"Yes, I must believe in you, or else I shouldn't be here saying this," he replied. "But that is all the proof I have. I don't feel any very strong belief at this particular moment."

She disliked him for his sudden relapse into weariness and faithlessness.*

"But don't you think me good-looking?" she persisted, in a mocking voice.

He looked at her, to see if he felt that she was good-looking.

"I don't *feel* that you're good-looking," he said.

"Not even attractive?" she mocked, bitingly.

He knitted his brows in sudden exasperation.

"Don't you see that it's not a question of visual appreciation in the least," he cried. "I don't *want* to see you. I've seen plenty of women, I'm sick and weary of seeing them. I want a woman I don't see."

"I'm sorry I can't oblige you by being invisible," she laughed.

"Yes," he said, "you are invisible to me, if you don't force me to be visually aware of you. But I don't want to see you or hear you."

"What did you ask me to tea for, then?" she mocked.

But he would take no notice of her. He was talking to himself.

"I want to find you, where you don't know your own existence, the you that your common self denies utterly. But I don't want your good looks, and I don't want your womanly feelings, and I don't want your thoughts nor opinions nor your ideas—they are all bagatelles to me."

"You are very conceited, Monsieur," she mocked. "How do you know what my womanly feelings are, or my thoughts or my ideas? You don't even know what I think of you now."

"Nor do I care in the slightest."

"I think you are very silly. I think you want to tell me you love me, and you go all this way round to do it."

"All right," he said, looking up with sudden exasperation. "Now go away then, and leave me alone. I don't want any more of your
5 meretricious persiflage."*

"Is it really persiflage?" she mocked, her face really relaxing into laughter. She interpreted it, that he had made a deep confession of love to her. But he was so absurd in his words, also.

They were silent for many minutes, she was pleased and elated
10 like a child. His concentration broke, he began to look at her simply and naturally.

"What I want is a strange conjunction with you—" he said quietly: "—not meeting and mingling;—you are quite right:—but an equilibrium, a pure balance of two single beings:—as the stars balance
15 each other."

She looked at him. He was very earnest, and earnestness was always rather ridiculous, commonplace, to her. It made her feel unfree and uncomfortable. Yet she liked him so much. But why drag in the stars!

20 "Isn't this rather sudden?"* she mocked.

He began to laugh.

"Best to read the terms of the contract, before we sign," he said.

A young grey cat that had been sleeping on the sofa jumped down and stretched, rising on its long legs, and arching its slim back. Then
25 it sat considering for a moment, erect and kingly. And then, like a dart, it had shot out of the room, through the open window-doors, and into the garden.

"What's he after?" said Birkin, rising.

The young cat trotted lordly down the path, waving his tail. He
30 was an ordinary tabby with white paws, a slender young gentleman. A crouching, fluffy, brownish-grey cat was stealing up the side of the fence. The Mino walked statelily up to her, with manly nonchalance. She crouched before him and pressed herself on the ground in humility, a fluffy soft outcast, looking up at him with wild eyes that
35 were green and lovely as great jewels. He looked casually down on her. So she crept a few inches further, proceeding on her way to the back door, crouching in a wonderful soft, self-obliterating manner, and moving like a shadow.

He, going statelily on his slim legs, walked after her, then
40 suddenly, for pure excess, he gave her a light cuff with his paw on the

side of her face. She ran off a few steps, like a blown leaf along the ground, then crouched unobtrusively, in submissive, wild patience. The Mino pretended to take no notice of her. He blinked his eyes superbly at the landscape. In a minute she drew herself together and moved softly, a fleecy brown-grey shadow, a few paces forward. She began to quicken her pace, in a moment she would be gone like a dream, when the young grey lord sprang before her, and gave her a light handsome cuff. She subsided at once, submissively.

"She is a wild cat," said Birkin. "She has come in from the woods."

The eyes of the stray cat flared round for a moment, like great green fires staring at Birkin. Then she had rushed in a soft swift rush, half way down the garden. There she paused to look round. The Mino turned his face in pure superiority to his master, and slowly closed his eyes, standing in statuesque young perfection. The wild cat's round, green, wondering eyes were staring all the while like uncanny fires. Then again, like a shadow, she slid towards the kitchen.

In a lovely springing leap, like a wind, the Mino was upon her, and had boxed her twice, very definitely, with a white, delicate fist. She sank and slid back, unquestioning. He walked after her, and cuffed her once or twice, leisurely, with sudden little blows of his magic white paws.

"Now why does he do that?" cried Ursula in indignation.

"They are on intimate terms," said Birkin.

"And is that why he hits her!" cried Ursula.

"Yes," laughed Birkin, "I think he wants to make it quite obvious to her."

"Isn't it horrid of him!" she cried; and going out into the garden she called to the Mino:

"Stop it, don't bully. Stop hitting her."

The stray cat vanished like a swift, invisible shadow. The Mino glanced at Ursula, then looked from her disdainfully to his master.

"Are you a bully, Mino?" Birkin asked.

The young slim cat looked at him, and slowly narrowed its eyes. Then it glanced away at the landscape, looking into the distance as if completely oblivious of the two human beings.

"Mino," said Ursula, "I don't like you. You are a bully like all the males."

"No," said Birkin, "he is justified. He is not a bully. He is only insisting to the poor stray that she shall acknowledge him as a sort of fate, her own fate: because you can see she is fluffy and promiscuous as the wind. I am with him entirely. He wants superfine stability."

"Yes, I know!" cried Ursula. "He wants his own way—I know what your fine words work down to—bossiness, I call it, bossiness."

The young cat again glanced at Birkin in disdain of the noisy woman.

"I quite agree with you, Miciotto,"* said Birkin to the cat. "Keep your male dignity, and your higher understanding."

Again the Mino narrowed his eyes as if he were looking at the sun. Then, suddenly affecting to have no connection at all with the two people, he went trotting off, with assumed spontaneity and gaiety, his tail erect, his white feet blithe.

"Now he will find the belle sauvage* once more, and entertain her with his superior wisdom," laughed Birkin.

Ursula looked at the man who stood in the garden with his hair blowing and his eyes smiling ironically, and she cried:

"Oh it makes me so cross, this assumption of male superiority! And it is such a lie! One wouldn't mind if there were any justification for it."

"The wild cat," said Birkin, "doesn't mind. She perceives that it is justified."

"Does she!" cried Ursula. "And tell it to the Horse Marines."*

"To them also."

"It is just like Gerald Crich with his horse—a lust for bullying—a real Wille zur Macht*—so base, so petty."

"I agree that the Wille zur Macht is a base and petty thing. But with the Mino, it is the desire to bring this female cat into a pure stable equilibrium, a transcendent and abiding *rapport* with the single male.—Whereas without him, as you see, she is a mere stray, a fluffy sporadic bit of chaos. It is a volonté de pouvoir,* if you like, a will to ability, taking pouvoir as a verb."

"Ah—! Sophistries! It's the old Adam."*

"Oh yes. Adam kept Eve in the indestructible paradise, when he kept her single with himself, like a star in its orbit."

"Yes—yes—" cried Ursula, pointing her finger at him. "There you are—a star in its orbit! A satellite!—a satellite of Mars*—that's what she is to be! There—there—you've given yourself away! You want a satellite, Mars and his satellite! You've said it—you've said it—you've dished yourself!"

He stood smiling in frustration and amusement and irritation and admiration and love. She was so quick, and so lambent, like discernible fire, and so vindictive, and so rich in her dangerous flamy sensitiveness.

"I've not said it at all," he replied, "if you will give me a chance to speak."

"No, no!" she cried. "I won't let you speak. You've said it, 'a satellite,' you're not going to wriggle out of it. You've said it."

"You'll never believe now that *I haven't* said it," he answered. "I neither implied nor indicated nor mentioned a satellite, nor intended a satellite, never."

"*You prevaricator!*" she cried, in real indignation.

"Tea is ready, sir," said the landlady from the doorway.

They both looked at her, very much as the cats had looked at them, a little while before.

"Thank you, Mrs Daykin."*

An interrupted silence fell over the two of them, a moment of breach.

"Come and have tea," he said.

"Yes, I should love it," she replied, gathering herself together.

They sat facing each other across the tea-table.

"I did not say, nor imply, a satellite. I meant two single equal stars balanced in conjunction—"

"You gave yourself away, you gave away your little game completely," she cried, beginning at once to eat. He saw that she would take no further heed of his expostulations, so he began to pour the tea.

"What *good* things to eat!" she cried.

"Take your own sugar," he said.

He handed her her cup. He had everything so nice, such pretty cups and plates, painted with mauve-lustre and green, also shapely bowls and glass plates, and old spoons, on a woven cloth of pale grey and black and purple. It was very rich and fine. But Ursula could see Hermione's influence.

"Your things are so lovely!" she said, almost angrily.

"*I* like them. It gives me real pleasure to use things that are attractive in themselves—pleasant things. And Mrs Daykin is good. She thinks everything is wonderful, for my sake."

"Really," said Ursula, "landladies are better than wives, nowadays. They certainly *care* a great deal more. It is much more beautiful and complete here now, than if you were married."

"But think of the emptiness within," he laughed.

"No," she said. "I am jealous that men have such perfect landladies and such beautiful lodgings. There is nothing left them to desire."

"In the house-keeping way, we'll hope not. It is disgusting, people marrying for a home."

"Still," said Ursula, "a man has very little need for a woman now, has he?"

"In outer things, maybe—except to share his bed and bear his children. But essentially, there is just the same need as ever there was. Only nobody takes the trouble to be essential."

"How essential?" she asked.

"I do think," he said, "that the world is only held together by the mystic conjunction, the ultimate unison between people—a bond. And the immediate bond is between man and woman."

"But it's such old hat," said Ursula. "Why should love be a bond?—No, I'm not having any."

"If you are walking westward," he said, "you forfeit the northern and eastward and southern direction.—If you admit a unison, you forfeit all the possibilities of chaos."

"But love is freedom," she declared.

"Don't cant to me," he replied. "Love is a direction which excludes all other directions. It's a freedom *together*, if you like."

"No," she said, "love includes everything."

"Sentimental cant," he replied. "You want the state of chaos, that's all. It is ultimate nihilism, this freedom-in-love business, this freedom which is love and love which is freedom.—As a matter of fact, if you enter into a pure unison, it is irrevocable, and it is never pure till it is irrevocable. And when it is irrevocable, it is one way, like the path of a star."

"Ha!" she cried bitterly. "It is the old dead morality."

"No," he said, "it is the law of creation. One is committed. One must commit oneself to a conjunction with the other—forever. But it is not selfless—it is a maintaining of the self in mystic balance and integrity—like a star balanced with another star."

"I don't trust you when you drag in the stars," she said. "If you were quite true, it wouldn't be necessary to be so far-fetched."

"Don't trust me then," he said, angry. "It is enough that I trust myself."

"And that is where you make another mistake," she replied. "You *don't* trust yourself. You don't fully believe yourself what you are saying. You don't really want this conjunction, otherwise you wouldn't talk so much about it, you'd get it."

He was suspended for a moment, arrested. 5

"How?" he said.

"By just loving," she retorted in defiance.

He was still a moment, in anger. Then he said:

"I tell you, I don't believe in love like that. I tell you, you want love to administer to your egotism, to subserve you. Love is a process of 10 subservience with you—and with everybody. I hate it."

"No," she cried, pressing back her head like a cobra, her eyes flashing. "It is a process of pride—I want to be proud—"

"Proud and subservient, proud and subservient, I know you," he retorted dryly. "Proud and subserved, then subservient to the 15 proud—I know you and your love. It is a tick-tack, tick-tack, a dance of opposites."

"Are you so sure?" she mocked wickedly, "what my love is?"

"Yes, I am," he retorted.

"So cocksure!" she said. "How can anybody ever be right, who is 20 so cocksure? It shows you are wrong."

He was silent in chagrin.

They had talked and struggled till they were both wearied out.

"Tell me about yourself and your people," he said.

And she told him about the Brangwens, and about her mother, 25 and about Skrebensky, her first love,* and about her later experiences. He sat very still, watching her as she talked. And he seemed to listen with reverence. Her face was beautiful and full of baffled light as she told him all the things that had hurt her or perplexed her so deeply. He seemed to warm and comfort his soul at the beautiful 30 light of her nature.

"If she *really* could pledge herself," he thought to himself, with passionate insistence but hardly any hope. Yet a curious little irresponsible laughter appeared in his heart.

"We have all suffered so much," he mocked, ironically. 35

She looked up at him, and a flash of wild gaiety went over her face, a strange flash of yellow light coming from her eyes.

"Haven't we!" she cried, in a high, reckless cry. "It is almost absurd, isn't it?"

"Quite absurd," he said. "Suffering bores me, any more." 40

"So it does me."

He was almost afraid of the mocking recklessness of her splendid face. Here was one who would go the whole lengths of heaven or hell, whichever she had to go. And he mistrusted her, he was afraid of a woman capable of such abandon, such dangerous thoroughness of destructivity. Yet he chuckled within himself also.

She came over to him and put her hand on his shoulder, looking down at him with strange golden-lighted eyes, very tender, but with a curious devilish look lurking underneath.

"Say you love me, say 'my love' to me," she pleaded.

He looked back into her eyes, and saw. His face flickered with sardonic comprehension.

"I love you right enough," he said, grimly. "But I want it to be something else."

"But why? But why?" she insisted, bending her wonderful luminous face to him. "Why isn't it enough?"

"Because we can go one better," he said, putting his arms round her.

"No, we can't," she said, in a strong, voluptuous voice of yielding. "We can only love each other. Say 'my love' to me, say it, say it."

She put her arms round his neck. He enfolded her, and kissed her subtly, murmuring in a subtle voice of love, and irony, and submission:

"Yes,—my love, yes,—my love. Let love be enough then.—I love you then—I love you. I'm bored by the rest."

"Yes," she murmured, nestling very sweet and close to him.

Chapter XIV

Water-Party

Every year Mr Crich gave a more-or-less public water-party on the lake. There was a little pleasure-launch on Willey Water, and several rowing boats,* and guests could take tea either in the marquee that was set up in the grounds of the house, or they could picnic in the shade of the great walnut tree at the boat-house by the lake. This year the staff of the Grammar School was invited, along with the chief officials of the firm. Gerald and the younger Criches did not care for this party, but it had become customary now, and it pleased the father, as being the only occasion when he could gather some people of the district together in festivity with him. For he loved to give pleasures to his dependents and to those poorer than himself. But his children preferred the company of their own equals in wealth. They hated their inferiors' humility or gratitude or awkwardness. Nevertheless they were willing to attend at this festival, as they had done almost since they were children, the more so, as they all felt a little guilty now, and unwilling to thwart their father any more, since he was so ill in health. Therefore, quite cheerfully Laura prepared to take her mother's place as hostess, and Gerald assumed responsibility for the amusements on the water.

Birkin had written to Ursula saying he expected to see her at the party, and Gudrun, although she scorned the patronage of the Criches, would nevertheless accompany her mother and father if the weather were fine.

The day came blue and full of sunshine, with little wafts of wind. The sisters both wore dresses of white cotton* crape, and hats of soft grass. But Gudrun had a sash of brilliant black and pink and yellow colour wound broadly round her waist, and she had pink silk stockings, and black and pink and yellow decoration on the brim of her hat, weighing it down a little. She carried also a yellow silk coat over her arm, so that she looked remarkable, like a painting from the Salon.* Her appearance was a sore trial to her father, who said angrily:

"Don't you think you might as well get yourself up for* a Christmas cracker, an' ha' done with it?"

But Gudrun looked handsome and brilliant, and she wore her clothes in pure defiance. When people stared at her, and giggled after her, she made a point of saying loudly, to Ursula:

"Regarde, regarde ces gens-là! Ne sont-ils pas des hiboux incroyables?"* And with the words of French in her mouth, she would look over her shoulder at the giggling party.

"No, really, it's impossible!" Ursula would reply distinctly.

And so the two girls took it out of their universal enemy. But their father became more and more enraged.

Ursula was all snowy white, save that her hat was pink, and entirely without trimming, and her shoes were dark red, and she carried an orange-coloured coat. And in this guise they were walking all the way to Shortlands, their father and mother* going in front.

They were laughing at their mother, who, dressed in a summer material of black and purple stripes, and wearing a hat of purple straw, was setting forth with much more of the shyness and trepidation of a young girl than her daughters ever felt, walking demurely beside her husband, who, as usual, looked rather crumpled in his best suit, as if he were the father of a young family and had been holding the baby whilst his wife got dressed.

"Look at the young couple in front," said Gudrun calmly. Ursula looked at her mother and father, and was suddenly seized with uncontrollable laughter. The two girls stood in the road and laughed till the tears ran down their faces, as they caught sight again of the shy, unworldly couple of their parents going on ahead.

"We are roaring at you, mother," called Ursula, helplessly following after her parents.

Mrs Brangwen turned round with a slightly puzzled, exasperated look.

"Oh indeed!" she said. "What is there so very funny about *me*, I should like to know?"

She could not understand that there could be anything amiss with her appearance. She had a perfect calm sufficiency, an easy indifference to any criticism whatsoever, as if she were beyond it. Her clothes were always rather odd, and as a rule slip-shod, yet she wore them with a perfect ease and satisfaction. Whatever she had on, so long as she was barely tidy, she was right, beyond remark; such an aristocrat she was by instinct.

"You look so stately, like a country Baroness," said Ursula, laughing with a little tenderness at her mother's naive puzzled air.

"*Just* like a country Baroness!" chimed in Gudrun.

Now the mother's natural hauteur became self-conscious, and the girls shrieked again.

"Go home, you pair of idiots, great giggling idiots!" cried the father inflamed with irritation.

"Mm-m-er!" booed Ursula, pulling a face at his crossness.

The yellow lights danced in his eyes, he leaned forward in real rage.

"Don't be so silly as to take any notice of the great gabies,"* said Mrs Brangwen, turning on her way.

"I'll see if I'm going to be followed by a pair of giggling yelling jackanapes—" he cried vengefully.

The girls stood still, laughing helplessly at his fury, upon the path beside the hedge.

"Why you're as silly as they are, to take any notice," said Mrs Brangwen also becoming angry now he was really enraged.

"There are some people coming, father," cried Ursula, with mocking warning. He glanced round quickly, and went on to join his wife, walking stiff with rage. And the girls followed, weak with laughter.

When the people had passed by, Brangwen cried in a loud, stupid voice:

"I'm going back home if there's any more of this. I'm damned if I'm going to be made a fool of in this fashion, in the public road."

He was really out of temper. At the sound of his blind, vindictive voice, the laughter suddenly left the girls, and their hearts contracted with contempt. They hated his words "in the public road." What did they care for the public road?—But Gudrun was conciliatory.

"But we weren't laughing to *hurt* you," she cried, with an uncouth gentleness which made her parents uncomfortable. "We were laughing because we're fond of you."

"We'll walk on in front, if they are *so* touchy," said Ursula, angry.

And in this wise* they arrived at Willey Water. The lake was blue and fair, the meadows sloped down in sunshine on one side, the thick dark woods dropped steeply on the other. The little pleasure-launch was fussing out from the shore, twanging its music, crowded with people, flapping its paddles. Near the boat-house was a throng of gaily-dressed persons, small in the distance. And on the high-road, some of the common people were standing along the hedge, looking at the festivity beyond, enviously, like souls not admitted to paradise.

"My eye!" said Gudrun, sotto voce, looking at the motley of guests, "there's a pretty crowd if you like! Imagine yourself in the midst of that, my dear."

Gudrun's apprehensive horror of people in the mass unnerved Ursula.

"It looks rather awful," she said anxiously.

"And imagine what they'll be like—*imagine!*" said Gudrun, still in that unnerving, subdued voice. Yet she advanced determinedly.

"I suppose we can get away from them," said Ursula anxiously.

"We're in a pretty fix if we can't," said Gudrun. Her extreme ironic loathing and apprehension was very trying to Ursula.

"We needn't stay," she said.

"I certainly shan't stay five minutes among that little lot," said Gudrun.

They advanced nearer, till they saw the policemen at the gates.

"Policemen to keep you in, too!" said Gudrun. "My word, this is a beautiful affair."

"We'd better look after father and mother," said Ursula anxiously.

"Mother's *perfectly* capable of getting through this little celebration," said Gudrun with some contempt.

But Ursula knew that her father felt uncouth and angry and unhappy, so she was far from her ease. They waited outside the gate till their parents came up. The tall, thin man in his crumpled clothes was unnerved and irritable as a boy, finding himself on the brink of this social function. He did not feel a gentleman, he did not feel anything except pure exasperation.

Ursula took her place at his side, they gave their tickets to the policemen, and passed in on to the grass, four abreast: the tall, hot, ruddy-dark man with his narrow boyish brow drawn with irritation, the fresh-faced, easy woman, perfectly collected though her hair was slipping on one side, then Gudrun, her eyes round and dark and staring, her full soft face impassive, almost sulky, so that she seemed to be backing away in antagonism even whilst she was advancing; and then Ursula, with the odd, brilliant, dazzled look on her face, that always came when she was in some false situation.

Birkin was the good angel. He came smiling to them with his affected social grace, that somehow was never *quite* right. But he took off his hat and smiled at them with a real smile in his eyes, so that Brangwen cried out heartily in relief:

"How do you do? You're better, are you?"

"Yes, I'm better. How do you do, Mrs Brangwen? I know Gudrun and Ursula very well."

His eyes smiled full of natural warmth. He had a soft, flattering manner with women, particularly with women who were not young.

"Yes," said Mrs Brangwen, cool but yet gratified. "I have heard speak of* you often enough."

He laughed. Gudrun looked aside, feeling she was being belittled. People were standing about in groups, some women were sitting in the shade of the walnut tree, with cups of tea in their hands, a waiter in evening dress was hurrying round, some girls were simpering with parasols, some young men, who had just come in from rowing, were sitting cross-legged on the grass, coatless, their shirt-sleeves rolled up in manly fashion, their hands resting on their white flannel trousers, their gaudy ties floating about, as they laughed and tried to be witty with the young damsels.

"Why," thought Gudrun churlishly, "don't they have the manners to put their coats on, and not to assume such intimacy in their appearance."

She abhorred the ordinary young man, with his hair plastered back, and his easy-going chumminess.

Hermione Roddice came up, in a handsome gown of white lace, trailing an enormous silk shawl blotched with great embroidered flowers, and balancing an enormous plain hat on her head. She looked striking, astonishing, almost macabre, so tall, with the fringe of her great cream-coloured vividly-blotched shawl trailing on the ground after her, her thick hair coming low over her eyes, her face strange and long and pale, and the blotches of brilliant colour drawn round her.

"Doesn't she look *weird*!" Gudrun heard some girls titter behind her. And she could have killed them.

"How do you do!" sang Hermione, coming up very kindly, and glancing slowly over Gudrun's father and mother. It was a trying moment, exasperating for Gudrun. Hermione was really so strongly entrenched in her class superiority, she could come up and know people out of simple curiosity, as if they were creatures on exhibition. Gudrun would do the same herself. But she resented being in the position when somebody might do it to her.

Hermione, very remarkable, and distinguishing the Brangwens very much, led them along to where Laura Crich stood receiving the guests.

"This is Mrs Brangwen," sang Hermione, and Laura, who wore a
5 stiff embroidered linen dress, shook hands and said she was glad to see her. Then Gerald came up, dressed in white, with a black-and-brown blazer, and looking handsome. He too was introduced to the Brangwen parents, and immediately he spoke to Mrs Brangwen as if she were a lady, and to Brangwen as if he were *not* a gentleman.
10 Gerald was so obvious in his demeanour. He had to shake hands with his left hand, because he had hurt his right, and carried it, bandaged up, in the pocket of his jacket. Gudrun was *very* thankful that none of her party asked him what was the matter with the hand.

The steam launch was fussing in, all its music jingling, people
15 calling excitedly from on board. Gerald went to see to the debarkation, Birkin was getting tea for Mrs Brangwen, Brangwen had joined a Grammar-School group, Hermione was sitting down by their mother, the girls went to the landing-stage to watch the launch come in.
20 She hooted and tooted gaily, then her paddles were silent, the ropes were thrown ashore, she drifted in with a little bump. Immediately the passengers crowded excitedly to come ashore.

"Wait a minute, wait a minute," shouted Gerald in sharp command.
25 They must wait till the boat was tight on the ropes, till the small gangway was put out. Then they streamed ashore, clamouring as if they had come from America.

"Oh it's *so* nice!" the young girls were crying. "It's quite lovely."

The waiters from on board ran out to the boat-house with baskets,
30 the captain* lounged on the little bridge. Seeing all safe, Gerald came to Gudrun and Ursula.

"You wouldn't care to go on board for the next trip, and have tea there?" he asked.

"No thanks," said Gudrun coldly.
35 "You don't care for the water?"

"For the water? Yes, I like it very much."

He looked at her, his eyes searching.

"You don't care for going on a launch, then?"

She was slow in answering, and then she spoke slowly.
40 "No," she said. "I can't say that I do."

Her colour was high, she seemed angry about something.

"Un peu trop de monde,"* said Ursula, explaining.

"Eh? *Trop de monde!*" He laughed shortly. "Yes, there's a fair number of 'em."

Gudrun turned on him brilliantly. 5

"Have you ever been from Westminster Bridge to Richmond on one of the Thames steamers?" she cried.

"No," he said, "I can't say I have."

"Well, it's one of the most *vile* experiences I've ever had." She spoke rapidly and excitedly, the colour high in her cheeks. "There 10 was absolutely nowhere to sit down, nowhere, a man just above sang 'Rocked in the Cradle of the Deep'* the *whole* way; he was blind and he had a small organ, one of those portable organs, and he expected money; so you can imagine what *that* was like; there came a constant smell of luncheon from below, and puffs of hot oily machinery; the 15 journey took hours and hours and hours; and for miles, literally for miles, dreadful boys ran with us on the shore, in that *awful* Thames mud, going in *up to the waist*—they had their trousers turned back, and they went up to their hips in that indescribable Thames mud, their faces always turned to us, and screaming, exactly like carrion 20 creatures, screaming ''Ere y'are sir, 'ere y'are sir, 'ere y'are sir,' exactly like some foul carrion objects, perfectly obscene; and paterfamilias on board, laughing when the boys went right down in that awful mud, occasionally throwing them a ha'penny. And if you'd seen the intent look on the faces of those boys, and the way they 25 darted in the filth when a coin was flung—really, no vulture or jackal could dream of approaching them, for foulness. I *never* would go on a pleasure boat again—never."*

Gerald watched her all the time she spoke, his eyes glittering with faint rousedness. It was not so much what she said: it was she herself 30 who roused him, roused him with a small, vivid pricking.

"Of course," he said, "every civilised body is bound to have its vermin."

"Why?" cried Ursula. "*I* don't have vermin."

"And it's not that—it's the *quality* of the whole thing—paterfami- 35 lias laughing and thinking it sport, and throwing the ha'pennies, and materfamilias spreading her fat little knees and eating, continually eating—" replied Gudrun.

"Yes," said Ursula. "It isn't the boys so much who are vermin; it's the people themselves, the whole body politic, as you call it." 40

Gerald laughed.

"Never mind," he said. "You shan't go on the launch."

Gudrun flushed quickly at his rebuke. There were a few moments of silence. Gerald, like a sentinel, was watching the
5   people who were going on to the boat. He was very good-looking and self-contained, but his air of soldierly alertness was rather irritating.

"Will you have tea here then, or go across to the house, where there's a tent on the lawn?" he asked.

10   "Can't we have a rowing boat, and get out?" asked Ursula, who was always rushing in too fast.

"To get out?" smiled Gerald.

"You see," cried Gudrun, flushing at Ursula's outspoken rudeness, "we don't know the people, we are almost *complete* strangers
15   here."

"Oh, I can soon set you up with a few acquaintances," he said easily.

Gudrun looked at him, to see if it were ill-meant. Then she smiled at him.

20   "Ah," she said, "you know what we mean. Can't we go up there, and explore that coast?" She pointed to a grove on a hillock of the meadow-side, near the shore, half way down the lake. "That looks perfectly lovely. We might even bathe. Isn't it beautiful in this light!—Really, it's like one of the reaches of the Nile—as one
25   imagines the Nile."

Gerald smiled at her factitious enthusiasm for the distant spot.

"You're sure it's far enough off?" he asked ironically, adding at once: "Yes, you might go there, if we could get a boat. They seem to be all out." He looked round the lake and counted the rowing
30   boats on its surface.

"How lovely it would be!" cried Ursula wistfully.

"And don't you want tea?" he said.

"Oh," said Gudrun, "we could just drink a cup, and be off."

He looked from one to the other, smiling. He was somewhat
35   offended—yet sporting.

"Can you manage a boat pretty well?" he asked.

"Yes," replied Gudrun, coldly, "pretty well."

"Oh yes," cried Ursula. "We can both of us row like water-spiders."

40   "You can?—There's a light little canoe of mine, that I didn't take

out for fear somebody should drown themselves. Do you think you'd be safe in that?"

"Oh perfectly," said Gudrun.

"What an angel!" cried Ursula.

"Don't, for *my* sake, have an accident—because I'm responsible for the water."

"Sure," pledged Gudrun.

"Besides, we can both swim quite well," said Ursula.

"Well—then I'll get them to put you up a tea-basket, and you can picnic all to yourselves,—that's the idea, isn't it?"

"How fearfully good! How frightfully nice if you could!" cried Gudrun warmly, her colour flushing up again. It made the blood stir in his veins, the subtle way she turned to him and infused her gratitude into his body.

"Where's Birkin?" he said, his eyes twinkling. "He might help me to get it down."

"But what about your hand? Isn't it hurt?" asked Gudrun, rather muted, as if avoiding the intimacy. This was the first time the hurt had been mentioned. The curious way she skirted round the subject sent a new, subtle caress through his veins. He took his hand out of his pocket. It was bandaged. He looked at it, then put it in his pocket again. Gudrun quivered at the sight of the wrapped up paw.

"Oh, I can manage with one hand. The canoe is as light as a feather," he said. "There's Rupert!—Rupert!"

Birkin turned from his social duties and came towards them.

"What have you done to it?" asked Ursula, who had been aching to put the question for the last half hour.

"To my hand?" said Gerald. "I trapped it in some machinery."

"Ugh!" said Ursula. "And did it hurt it much?"

"Yes," he said. "It did at the time. It's getting better now. It crushed the fingers."

"Oh," cried Ursula, as if in pain, "I hate people who hurt themselves. I can *feel* it." And she shook her hand.

"What do you want?" said Birkin.

The two men carried down the slim brown boat, and set it on the water.

"You're quite sure you'll be safe in it?" Gerald asked.

"Quite sure," said Gudrun. "I wouldn't be so mean as to take it, if there was the slightest doubt. But I've had a canoe at Arundel, and I assure you I'm perfectly safe."

So saying, having given her word like a man, she and Ursula entered the frail craft, and pushed gently off. The two men stood watching them. Gudrun was paddling. She knew the men were watching her, and it made her slow and rather clumsy. The colour
5   flew in her face like a flag.

"Thanks awfully," she called back to him, from the water, as the boat slid away. "It's lovely—like sitting in a leaf."

He laughed at the fancy. Her voice was shrill and strange, calling from the distance. He watched her as she paddled away. There was
10   something child-like about her, trustful and deferential, like a child. He watched her all the while, as she rowed. And to Gudrun it was a real delight, in make-believe, to be the child-like, clinging woman to the man who stood there on the quay, so good-looking and efficient in his white clothes, and moreover the most important man she knew
15   at the moment. She did not take any notice of the wavering, indistinct, lambent Birkin, who stood at his side. One figure at a time occupied the field of her attention.

The boat rustled lightly along the water. They passed the bathers whose striped tents stood between the willows of the meadow's edge,
20   and drew along the open shore, past the meadows that sloped golden in the light of the already late afternoon. Other boats were stealing under the wooded shore opposite, they could hear people's laughter and voices. But Gudrun rowed on towards the clump of trees that balanced perfect in the distance, in the golden light.
25   The sisters found a little place where a tiny stream flowed into the lake, with reeds and flowery marsh of pink willow herb, and a gravelly bank to the side. Here they ran delicately ashore, with their frail boat, the two girls took off their shoes and stockings and went through the water's edge to the grass. The tiny ripples of the lake
30   were warm and clear, they lifted their boat on to the bank, and looked round with joy. They were quite alone in a forsaken little stream-mouth, and on a knoll just behind was the clump of trees.

"We will bathe just for a moment," said Ursula, "and then we'll have tea."
35   They looked round. Nobody could notice them, or could come up in time to see them. In less than a minute Ursula had thrown off her clothes and had slipped naked into the water, and was swimming out. Quickly, Gudrun joined her. They swam silently and blissfully for a few minutes, circling round their little stream-mouth. Then they
40   slipped ashore and ran into the grove again, like nymphs.

"How lovely it is to be free," said Ursula, running swiftly here and there between the tree trunks, quite naked, her hair blowing loose. The grove was of beech-trees, big and splendid, a steel-grey scaffolding of trunks and boughs, with level sprays of strong green here and there, whilst through the northern side the distance glimmered open as through a window.*

When they had run and danced themselves dry, the girls quickly dressed and sat down to the fragrant tea. They sat on the northern side of the grove, in the yellow sunshine facing the slope of the grassy hill, alone in a little wild world of their own. The tea was hot and aromatic, there were delicious little sandwiches of cucumber and of caviare, and winy cakes.

"Are you happy, Prune?" cried Ursula in delight, looking at her sister.

"Ursula, I'm perfectly happy," replied Gudrun gravely, looking at the westering sun.

"So am I."

When they were together, doing the things they enjoyed, the two sisters were quite complete in a perfect world of their own. And this was one of the perfect moments of freedom and delight, such as children alone know, when all seems a perfect and blissful adventure.

When they had finished tea, the two girls sat on, silent and serene. Then Ursula, who had a beautiful strong voice, began to sing to herself, softly: "Ännchen von Tharau."* Gudrun listened, as she sat beneath the trees, and the yearning came into her heart. Ursula seemed so peaceful and sufficient unto herself, sitting there unconsciously crooning her song, strong and unquestioned at the centre of her own universe. And Gudrun felt herself outside. Always this desolating, agonised feeling, that she was outside of life, an onlooker, whilst Ursula was a partaker, caused Gudrun to suffer from a sense of her own negation, and made her, that she must always demand the other to be aware of her, to be in connection with her.

"Do you mind if I do Dalcroze* to that tune, Hurtler?" she asked in a curious muted tone, scarce moving her lips.

"What did you say?" asked Ursula, looking up in peaceful surprise.

"Will you sing while I do Dalcroze?" said Gudrun, suffering at having to repeat herself.

Ursula thought a moment, gathering her straying wits together. "While you do——?" she asked vaguely.

"Dalcroze movements," said Gudrun, suffering tortures of self-consciousness, even because of her sister.

"Oh Dalcroze! I couldn't catch the name. *Do*—I should love to see you," cried Ursula, with childish surprised brightness. "What shall I sing?"

"Sing anything you like, and I'll take the rhythm from it."

But Ursula could not for her life think of anything to sing. However, she suddenly began, in a laughing, teasing voice:

"My love——is a high-born lady—"*

Gudrun, looking as if some invisible chain weighed on her hands and feet, began slowly to dance in the eurythmic manner, pulsing and fluttering rhythmically with her feet, making slower, regular gestures with her hands and arms, now spreading her arms wide, now raising them above her head, now flinging them softly apart, and lifting her face, her feet all the time beating and running to the measure of the song, as if it were some strange incantation, her white, rapt form drifting here and there in a strange impulsive rhapsody, seeming to be lifted on a breeze of incantation, shuddering with strange little runs. Ursula sat on the grass, her mouth open in her singing, her eyes laughing as if she thought it was a great joke, but a yellow light flashing up in them, as she caught some of the unconscious ritualistic suggestion of the complex shuddering and waving and drifting of her sister's white form, that was clutched in pure, mindless, tossing rhythm, and a will set powerful in a kind of hypnotic influence.

"My love is a high-born lady—She is-s-s—rather dark than shady—" rang out Ursula's laughing, satiric song, and quicker, fiercer went Gudrun in the dance, stamping as if she were trying to throw off some bond, flinging her hands suddenly and stamping again, then rushing with face uplifted and throat full and beautiful, and eyes half closed, sightless. The sun was low and yellow, sinking down, and in the sky floated a thin, ineffectual moon.

Ursula was quite absorbed in her song, when suddenly Gudrun stopped and said mildly, ironically:

"Ursula!"

"Yes?" said Ursula, opening her eyes out of the trance.

Gudrun was standing still and pointing, a mocking smile on her face, towards the side.

"Ugh!" cried Ursula in sudden panic, starting to her feet.

"They're quite all right," rang out Gudrun's sardonic voice.

On the left stood a little cluster of Highland cattle, vividly coloured and fleecy in the evening light, their horns branching into the sky, pushing forward their muzzles inquisitively, to know what it was all about. Their eyes glittered through their tangle of hair, their naked nostrils were full of shadow.

"Won't they do anything?" cried Ursula in fear.

Gudrun, who was usually frightened of cattle, now shook her head in a queer, half-doubtful, half-sardonic motion, a faint smile round her mouth.

"Don't they look charming, Ursula?" cried Gudrun, in a high, strident voice, something like the scream of a sea-gull.

"Charming," cried Ursula in trepidation. "But won't they do anything to us?"

Again Gudrun looked back at her sister with an enigmatic smile, and shook her head.

"I'm sure they won't," she said, as if she had to convince herself also, and yet, as if she were confident of some secret power in herself, and had to put it to the test. "Sit down and sing again," she called in her high, strident voice.

"I'm frightened," cried Ursula, in a pathetic voice, watching the group of sturdy short cattle, that stood with their knees planted, and watched with their dark, wicked eyes, through the matted fringe of their hair. Nevertheless, she sank down again, in her former posture.

"They are quite safe," came Gudrun's high call. "Sing something, you've only to sing something."

It was evident she had a strange passion to dance before the sturdy, handsome cattle.

Ursula began to sing, in a false, quavering voice:

"Way down in Tennessee———"*

She sounded purely anxious. Nevertheless Gudrun, with her arms outspread and her face uplifted, went in a strange, palpitating dance towards the cattle, lifting her body towards them as if in a spell, her feet pulsing as if in some little frenzy of unconscious sensation, her arms, her wrists, her hands stretching and heaving and falling and reaching and reaching and falling, her breasts lifted and shaken towards the cattle, her throat exposed as in some voluptuous ecstasy towards them, whilst she drifted imperceptibly nearer, an uncanny white figure carried* away in its own rapt trance, ebbing in strange

fluctuations upon the cattle, that waited, and ducked their heads a little in sudden contraction from her, watching all the time as if hypnotised, their bare horns branching in the clear light, as the white figure of the woman ebbed upon them, in the slow, hypnotis-
5 ing convulsion of the dance. She could feel them just in front of her, it was as if she had the electric pulse from their breasts running into her hands. Soon she would touch them, actually touch them. A terrible shiver of fear and pleasure went through her. And all the while, Ursula spell-bound kept up her high-pitched thin,
10 irrelevant song, which pierced the fading evening like an incantation.

Gudrun could hear the cattle breathing heavily with helpless fear and fascination. Oh, they were brave little beasts, these wild Scotch bullocks, wild and fleecy. Suddenly one of them snorted, ducked its
15 head, and backed.

"Hue! Hi—eee!" came a sudden loud shout from the edge of the grove. The cattle broke and fell back quite spontaneously, went running up the hill, their fleece waving like fire to their motion. Gudrun stood suspended, out on the grass, Ursula rose to her feet.
20 It was Gerald and Birkin come to find them, and Gerald had cried out to frighten off the cattle.

"What do you think you're doing?" he now called, in a high, wondering, vexed tone.

"Why have you come—?" came back Gudrun's strident cry of
25 anger.

"What do you think you were doing?" Gerald repeated, automatically.

"We were doing eurythmics," laughed Ursula, in a shaken voice.

Gudrun stood aloof looking at them with large dark eyes of
30 resentment, suspended for a few moments. Then she walked away up the hill, after the cattle, which had gathered in a little, spellbound cluster higher up.

"Where are you going?" Gerald called after her. And he followed her up the hill-side. The sun had gone behind the hill, and
35 shadows were clinging to the earth, the sky above was full of travelling light.

"A poor song for a dance," said Birkin to Ursula, standing before her with a sardonic, flickering laugh on his face. And in another second, he was singing softly to himself, and dancing a
40 grotesque step-dance in front of her, his limbs and body shaking

loose, his face flickering palely, a constant thing, whilst his feet beat a rapid mocking tattoo, and his body seemed to hang all loose and quaking in between, like a shadow.

"I think we've all gone mad," she said, laughing rather frightened.

"Pity we aren't madder," he answered, as he kept up the incessant shaking dance. Then suddenly he leaned up to her and kissed her fingers lightly, putting his face to hers and looking into her eyes with a pale grin. She stepped back, affronted.

"Offended—?" he asked ironically, suddenly going quite still and reserved again. "I thought you liked the light fantastic."

"Not like that," she said, confused and bewildered, almost affronted. Yet somewhere inside her she was fascinated by the sight of his loose, vibrating body, perfectly abandoned to its own dropping and swinging, and by the pallid, sardonic-smiling face above. Yet automatically she stiffened herself away, and disapproved. It seemed almost an obscenity, in a man who talked as a rule so very seriously.

"Why not like that?" he mocked. And immediately he dropped again into the incredibly rapid, slack-waggling dance, watching her malevolently. And moving in the rapid, stationary dance, he came a little nearer, and reached forward with an incredibly mocking, satiric gleam on his face, and would have kissed her again, had she not started back.

"No, don't!" she cried, really afraid.

"Cordelia after all,"* he said satirically.

She was stung, as if this were an insult. She knew he intended it as such, and it bewildered her.

"And you," she cried in retort, "why do you always take your soul in your mouth, so frightfully full!"

"So that I can spit it out the more readily," he said, pleased by his own retort.

Gerald Crich, his face narrowing to an intent gleam, followed up the hill with quick strides, straight after Gudrun. The cattle stood with their noses together on the brow of a slope, watching the scene below, the men in white hovering about the white forms of the women, watching above all Gudrun, who was advancing slowly towards them. She stood a moment, glancing back at Gerald, and then at the cattle.

Then in a sudden motion, she lifted her arms and rushed sheer upon the long-horned bullocks, in shuddering irregular runs, pausing for a second and looking at them, then lifting her hands and running forward with a flash, till they ceased pawing the ground, and gave way, snorting with terror, lifting their heads from the ground and flinging themselves away, galloping off into the evening, becoming tiny in the distance, and still not stopping.

5   Gudrun remained staring after them, with a mask-like, defiant face.

"Why do you want to drive them mad?" asked Gerald, coming up with her.

She took no notice of him, only averted her face from him.

10   "It's not safe, you know," he persisted. "They're nasty, when they do turn."

"Turn where? Turn away?" she mocked loudly.

"No," he said, "turn against you."

"Turn against *me*?" she mocked.

15   He could make nothing of this.

"Any way, they gored one of the farmer's cows to death, the other day," he said.

"What do I care?" she said.

"*I* cared though," he replied, "seeing that they're my cattle."

20   "How are they yours! You haven't swallowed them. Give me one of them now," she said, holding out her hand.

"You know where they are," he said, pointing over the hill. "You can have one if you'd like it sent to you later on."

She looked at him inscrutably.

25   "You think I'm afraid of you and your cattle, don't you?" she asked.

His eyes narrowed dangerously. There was a faint domineering smile on his face.

"Why should I think that?" he said.

30   She was watching him all the time with her dark, dilated, inchoate eyes. She leaned forward and swung round her arm, catching him a light blow on the face with the back of her hand.

"That's why," she said, mocking.

And she felt in her soul an unconquerable desire for deep violence
35   against him. She shut off the fear and dismay that filled her conscious mind. She wanted to do as she did, she was not going to be afraid.

He recoiled from the slight blow on his face. He became deadly pale, and a dangerous flame darkened his eyes. For some seconds he
40   could not speak, his lungs were so suffused with blood, his heart

stretched almost to bursting with a great gush of ungovernable emotion. It was as if some reservoir of black emotion had burst within him, and swamped him.

"You have struck the first blow," he said at last, forcing the words from his lungs, in a voice so soft and low, it sounded like a dream within her, not spoken in the outer air.

"And I shall strike the last," she retorted involuntarily, with confident assurance. He was silent, he did not contradict her.

She stood negligently, staring away from him, into the distance. On the edge of her consciousness the question was asking itself, automatically, "Why *are* you behaving in this *impossible* and ridiculous fashion?" But she was sullen, she half shoved the question out of herself. She could not get it clean away, so she felt self-conscious.

Gerald, very pale, was watching her closely. His eyes were lit up with intent lights, absorbed and gleaming. She turned suddenly on him.

"It's you who make me behave like this, you know," she said, almost suggestive.

"I? How?" he said.

But she turned away, and set off towards the lake.* Below, on the water, lanterns were coming alight, faint ghosts of warm flame floating in the pallor of the first twilight. The earth was spread with darkness, like lacquer, overhead was a pale sky, all primrose, and the lake was pale as milk in one part. Away at the landing-stage, tiniest points of coloured rays were stringing themselves in the dusk. The launch was being illuminated. All round, shadow was gathering from the trees.

Gerald, white like a presence in his summer clothes, was following down the open grassy slope. Gudrun waited for him to come up. Then she softly put out her hand and touched him, saying softly:

"Don't be angry with me."

A flame flew over him, and he was unconscious. Yet he stammered:

"I'm not angry with you. I'm in love with you."

His mind was gone, he grasped for sufficient mechanical control, to save himself. She laughed a silvery little mockery, yet intolerably caressive.

"That's one way of putting it," she said.

The terrible swooning burden on his mind, the awful swooning, the loss of all his control, was too much for him. He grasped her arm in his one hand, as if his hand were iron.

"It's all right, then, is it?" he said, holding her arrested.

She looked at the face with the fixed eyes, set before her, and her
5   blood ran cold.

"Yes, it's all right," she said softly, as if drugged, her voice crooning and witch-like.

He walked on beside her, a striding, mindless body. But he recovered a little as he went. He suffered badly. He had killed his
10   brother when a boy, and was set apart, like Cain.

They found Birkin and Ursula sitting together by the boats, talking and laughing. Birkin had been teasing Ursula.

"Do you smell this little marsh?" he said, sniffing the air. He was very sensitive to scents, and quick in understanding them.
15   "It's rather nice," she said.

"No," he replied, "alarming."

"Why alarming?" she laughed.

"It seethes and seethes, a river of darkness," he said, "putting forth lilies and snakes, and the ignis fatuus, and rolling all the time
20   onward. That's what we never take into count—that it rolls onwards."

"What does?"

"The other river, the black river. We always consider the silver river of life, rolling on and quickening all the world to a brightness, on and on to heaven, flowing into a bright eternal sea, a heaven of
25   angels thronging.—But the other is our real reality—"*

"But what other? I don't see any other," said Ursula.

"It is your reality, nevertheless," he said; "the dark river of dissolution.—You see it rolls in us just as the other rolls—the black river of corruption. And our flowers are of this—our sea-born
30   Aphrodite,* all our white phosphorescent flowers of sensuous perfection, all our reality, nowadays."

"You mean that Aphrodite is really deathly?" asked Ursula.

"I mean she is the flowering mystery of the death-process, yes," he replied. "When the stream of synthetic creation lapses, we find
35   ourselves part of the inverse process, the flood of destructive creation. Aphrodite is born in the first spasm of universal dissolution—then the snakes and swans and lotus—marsh-flowers—and Gudrun and Gerald—born in the process of destructive creation."
40   "And you and me—?" she asked.

"Probably," he replied. "In part, certainly. Whether we are that, in toto, I don't yet know."

"You mean we are flowers of dissolution—fleurs du mal?*—I don't feel as if I were," she protested.

He was silent for a time.   5

"I don't feel as if we were, *altogether*," he replied. "Some people are pure flowers of dark corruption—lilies. But there ought to be some roses, warm and flamy.*—You know Herakleitos says 'a dry soul is best.'* I know so well what that means. Do you?"

"I'm not sure," Ursula replied. "But what if people *are* all flowers   10
of dissolution—when they're flowers at all—what difference does it make?"

"No difference—and all the difference. Dissolution rolls on, just as production does," he said. "It is a progressive process—and it ends in universal nothing—the end of the world, if you like.—But   15
why isn't the end of the world as good as the beginning?"

"I suppose it isn't," said Ursula, rather angry.

"Oh yes, ultimately," he said. "It means a new cycle of creation after—but not for us. If it is the end, then we are of the end—fleurs du mal if you like. If we are fleurs du mal, we are not roses of   20
happiness, and there you are."

"But I think I am," said Ursula. "I think I am a rose of happiness."

"Ready-made?" he asked ironically.

"No—real," she said, hurt.

"If we are the end, we are not the beginning," he said.   25

"Yes we are," she said. "The beginning comes out of the end."*

"After it, not out of it. After us, not out of us."

"You are a devil, you know, really," she said. "You want to destroy our hope. You *want* us to be deathly."

"No," he said, "I only want us to *know* what we are."   30

"Ha!" she cried in anger. "You only want us to know death."

"You're quite right," said the soft voice of Gerald, out of the dusk behind.

Birkin rose. Gerald and Gudrun came up. They all began to smoke, in the moments of silence. One after another, Birkin lighted   35
their cigarettes. The match flickered in the twilight, and they were all smoking peacefully by the water-side. The lake was dim, the light dying from off it, in the midst of the dark land. The air all round was intangible, neither here nor there, and there was an unreal noise of banjoes, or suchlike music.   40

As the golden swim of light overhead died out, the moon gained brightness, and seemed to begin to smile forth her ascendancy. The dark woods on the opposite shore melted into universal shadow. And amid this universal undershadow, there was a scattered intrusion of
5   lights. Far down the lake were fantastic pale strings of colour, like beads of wan fire, green and red and yellow. The music came out in a little puff, as the launch, all illuminated, veered into the great shadow, stirring her outlines of half-living lights, puffing out her music in little drifts.

10   All were lighting up. Here and there, close against the faint water, and at the far end of the lake, where the water lay milky in the last whiteness of the sky, and there was no shadow, solitary, frail flames of lanterns floated from the unseen boats. There was a sound of oars, and a boat passed from the pallor into the darkness under the wood,
15   where her lanterns seemed to kindle into fire, hanging in ruddy lovely globes. And again, in the lake, shadowy red gleams hovered in reflection about the boat. Everywhere were these noiseless ruddy creatures of fire drifting near the surface of the water, caught at by the rarest, scarce visible reflections.

20   Birkin brought the lanterns from the bigger boat, and the four shadowy white figures gathered round, to light them. Ursula held up the first, Birkin lowered the light from the rosy, glowing cup of his hands, into the depths of the lantern. It was kindled, and they all stood back to look at the great blue moon of light that hung from
25   Ursula's hand, casting a strange gleam on her face. It flickered, and Birkin went bending over the well of light. His face shone out like an apparition, so unconscious, and again, something demoniacal. Ursula was dim and veiled, looming over him.

"That is all right," said his voice softly.

30   She held up the lantern. It had a flight of storks streaming through a turquoise sky of light, over a dark earth.

"This is beautiful," she said.

"Lovely," echoed Gudrun, who wanted to hold one also, and lift it up full of beauty.

35   "Light one for me," she said. Gerald stood by her, incapacitated. Birkin lit the lantern she held up. Her heart beat with anxiety, to see how beautiful it would be. It was primrose yellow, with tall straight flowers growing darkly from their dark leaves, lifting their heads into the primrose day, while butterflies hovered about them, in the pure
40   clear light.

Gudrun gave a little cry of excitement, as if pierced with delight. "Isn't it beautiful, oh, isn't it beautiful!"

Her soul was really pierced with beauty, she was translated beyond herself. Gerald leaned near to her, into her zone of light, as if to see. He came close to her, and stood touching her, looking with her at the primrose-shining globe. And she turned her face to his, that was faintly bright in the light of the lantern, and they stood together in one luminous union, close together and ringed round with light, all the rest excluded.

Birkin looked away, and went to light Ursula's second lantern. It had a pale ruddy sea-bottom, with black crabs and sea-weed moving sinuously under a transparent sea, that passed into flamy ruddiness above.

"You've got the heavens above, and the waters under the earth,"* said Birkin to her.

"Anything but the earth itself," she laughed, watching his live hands that hovered to attend to the light.

"I'm dying to see what my second one is," cried Gudrun, in a vibrating rather strident voice, that seemed to repel the others from her.

Birkin went and kindled it. It was of a lovely deep blue colour, with a red floor, and a great white cuttle-fish flowing in white soft streams all over it. The cuttle-fish had a face that stared straight from the heart of the light, very fixed and coldly intent.

"How truly terrifying!" exclaimed Gudrun, in a voice of horror. Gerald, at her side, gave a low laugh.

"But isn't it really fearful!" she cried in dismay.

Again he laughed, and said:

"Change it with Ursula, for the crabs."

Gudrun was silent for a moment.

"Ursula," she said, "could you bear to have this fearful thing?"

"I think the colouring is *lovely*," said Ursula.

"So do I," said Gudrun. "But could you *bear* to have it swinging to your boat? Don't you want to destroy it *at once*?"

"Oh no," said Ursula. "I don't want to destroy it."

"Well—do you mind having it instead of the crabs? Are you sure you don't mind?"

Gudrun came forward to exchange lanterns.

"No," said Ursula, yielding up the crabs and receiving the cuttle-fish.

Yet she could not help feeling rather resentful at the way in which Gudrun and Gerald should assume a right over her, a precedence.

"Come then," said Birkin. "I'll put them on the boats."

He and Ursula were moving away to the big boat.

"I suppose you'll row me back, Rupert," said Gerald, out of the pale shadow of the evening.

"Won't you go with Gudrun in the canoe?" said Birkin. "It'll be more interesting."

There was a moment's pause. Birkin and Ursula stood dimly, with their swinging lanterns, by the water's edge. The world was all illusive.

"Is that all right?" said Gudrun to him.

"It'll suit *me* very well," he said. "But what about you, and the rowing? I don't see why you should pull me."

"Why not?" she said. "I can pull you as well as I could pull Ursula." By her tone he could tell she wanted to have him in the boat to herself, and that she was subtly gratified that she should have power over them both. He gave himself, in a strange, electric submission.

She handed him the lanterns, whilst she went to fix the cane at the end of the canoe. He followed after her, and stood with the lanterns dangling against his white-flannelled thighs, emphasising the shadow around.

"Kiss me before we go," came his voice softly from out of the shadow above.

She stopped her work in real, momentary astonishment.

"But why?" she exclaimed, in pure surprise.

"Why?" he echoed, ironically.

And she looked at him fixedly for some moments. Then she leaned forward and kissed him, with a slow, luxurious kiss, lingering on the mouth. And then she took the lanterns from him, while he stood swooning with the perfect fire that burned in all his joints.

They lifted the canoe into the water, Gudrun took her place, and Gerald pushed off.

"Are you sure you don't hurt your hand, doing that?" she asked, solicitous. "Because I could have done it *perfectly*."

"I don't hurt myself," he said in a low, soft voice, that caressed her with inexpressible beauty.

And she watched him as he sat near her, very near to her, in the stern of the canoe, his legs coming towards hers, his feet touching

hers. And she paddled softly, lingeringly, longing for him to say
something meaningful to her. But he remained silent.

"You like this, do you?" she said, in a gentle, solicitous voice.

He laughed shortly.

"There is a space between us," he said, in the same low, 5
unconscious voice, as if something were speaking out of him. And
she was as if magically aware of their being balanced in separation, in
the boat. She swooned with acute comprehension and pleasure.

"But I'm very near," she said caressively, gaily.

"Yet distant, distant," he said. Again she was silent with pleasure, 10
before she answered, speaking with a reedy, thrilled voice:

"Yet we cannot very well change, whilst we are on the water."—
She caressed him subtly and strangely, having him completely at her
mercy.

A dozen or more boats on the lake swung their rosy and moon-like 15
lanterns low on the water, that reflected as from a fire. In the
distance, the steamer twanged and thrummed and washed with her
faintly-splashing paddles, trailing her strings of coloured lights, and
occasionally lighting up the whole scene luridly with an effusion of
fireworks, Roman candles and sheafs of stars and other simple 20
effects, illuminating the surface of the water, and showing the boats
creeping round, low down. Then the lovely darkness fell again, the
lanterns and the little threaded lights glimmered softly, there was a
muffled knocking of oars and a waving of music.

Gudrun paddled almost imperceptibly. Gerald could see, not far 25
ahead, the rich blue and the rose globes of Ursula's lanterns swaying
softly cheek to cheek as Birkin rowed, and iridescent, evanescent
gleams chasing in the wake. He was aware, too, of his own delicately
coloured lights casting their softness behind him.

Gudrun rested her paddle and looked round. The canoe lifted 30
with the lightest ebbing of the water. Gerald's white knees were very
near to her.

"Isn't it beautiful!" she said softly, as if reverently.

She looked at him, as he leaned back against the faint crystal of the
lantern-light. She could see his face, although it was a pure shadow. 35
But it was a piece of twilight. And her breast was keen with passion
for him, he was so beautiful in his male stillness and mystery. It was a
certain pure effluence of maleness, like an aroma from his softly,
firmly moulded contours, a certain rich perfection of his presence,
that touched her with an ecstasy, a thrill of pure intoxication. She 40

loved to look at him. For the present she did not want to touch him, to know the further, satisfying substance of his living body. He was purely intangible, yet so near. Her hands lay on the paddle like slumber, she only wanted to see him like a crystal shadow, to feel his
5 essential presence.

"Yes," he said vaguely. "It is very beautiful."

He was listening to the faint near sounds, the dropping of water-drops from the oar-blades, the slight drumming of the lanterns behind him, as they rubbed against one another, the
10 occasional rustling of Gudrun's full skirt, an alien land noise. His mind was almost submerged, he was almost transfused, lapsed out for the first time in his life, into the things about him. For he always kept such a keen attentiveness, concentrated and unyielding in himself. Now he had let go, imperceptibly he was melting into
15 oneness with the whole. It was like pure, perfect sleep, his first great sleep of life. He had been so insistent, so guarded, all his life. But here was sleep, and peace, and perfect lapsing out.

"Shall I row to the landing-stage?" asked Gudrun wistfully.

"Anywhere," he answered. "Let it drift."

20 "Tell me then, if we are running into anything," she replied, in that very quiet, toneless voice of sheer intimacy.

"The lights will show," he said.

So they drifted almost motionless, in silence. He wanted silence, pure and whole. But she was uneasy yet for some word, for some
25 assurance.

"Nobody will miss you?" she asked, anxious for some communication.

"Miss me?" he echoed. "No! Why?"

"I wondered if anybody would be looking for you."

30 "Why should they look for me?" And then he remembered his manners. "But perhaps you want to get back," he said, in a changed voice.

"No, I don't want to get back," she replied. "No, I assure you."

35 "You're quite sure it's all right for you?"

"Perfectly all right."

And again they were still. The launch twanged and hooted, somebody was singing. Then as if the night smashed, suddenly there was a great shout, a confusion of shouting warring on the water, then
40 the horrid noise of paddles reversed and churned violently.

Gerald sat up, and Gudrun looked at him in fear.

"Somebody in the water," he said, angrily, and desperately, looking keenly across the dusk. "Can you row up?"

"Where, to the launch?" asked Gudrun, in nervous panic.

"Yes."

"You'll tell me if I don't steer straight," she said, in nervous apprehension.

"You keep pretty level," he said, and the canoe hastened forward. The shouting and the noise continued, sounding horrid through the dusk, over the surface of the water.

"Wasn't this *bound* to happen?" said Gudrun, with heavy, hateful irony.

But he hardly heard, and she glanced over her shoulder to see her way. The half-dark waters were sprinkled with lovely bubbles of swaying lights, the launch did not look far off. She was rocking her lights in the early night. Gudrun rowed as hard as she could. But now that it was a serious matter, she seemed uncertain and clumsy in her stroke, it was difficult to paddle swiftly. She glanced at his face. He was looking fixedly into the darkness, very keen and alert and single in himself, instrumental. Her heart sank, and she seemed to die a death. "Of course," she said to herself, "nobody will be drowned. Of course they won't. It would be too extravagant and sensational." But her heart was cold, because of his sharp, impersonal face. It was as if he belonged naturally to dread and catastrophe, as if he were himself again.

Then there came a child's voice, a girl's high, piercing shriek:

"*Di—Di—Di—Di—Oh Di—Oh Di—Oh Di*!"

The blood ran cold in Gudrun's veins.

"It's Diana, is it," muttered Gerald. "The young monkey, she'd have to be up to some of her tricks."

And he glanced again at the paddle, the boat was not going quickly enough for him. It made Gudrun almost helpless at the rowing, this nervous stress. She kept up with all her might. Still the voices were calling and answering. "Where, Where? There you are—that's it. Which? No—No-o-o. Damn it all, here, *here*—" Boats were hurrying from all directions to the scene, coloured lanterns could be seen waving close to the surface of the lake, reflections swaying after them in uneven haste. The steamer hooted again, for some unknown reason. Gudrun's boat was travelling quickly, the lanterns were swinging behind Gerald.

And then again came the child's high, screaming voice, with a note of weeping and impatience in it now:

"*Di—Oh Di—Oh Di—Di—*!"

It was a terrible sound, coming through the obscure air of the evening.

"You'd be better if you were in bed, Winnie," Gerald muttered to himself.

He was stooping unlacing his shoes, pushing them off with the foot. Then he threw his soft hat into the bottom of the boat.

"You can't go into the water with your hurt hand," said Gudrun, panting, in a low voice of horror.

"What?—It won't hurt."

He had struggled out of his jacket, and had dropped it between his feet. He sat bare-headed, all in white now. He felt the belt at his waist. They were nearing the launch, which stood still big above them, its myriad lamps making lovely darts, and sinuous running tongues of ugly red and green and yellow on the lustrous dark water, under the shadow.

"*Oh get her out! Oh Di, darling! Oh get her out! Oh Daddy, Oh Daddy!*" moaned the child's voice, in distraction. Somebody was in the water, with a life-belt. Two boats paddled near, their lanterns swinging ineffectually, the boats nosing round.

"Hi there—Rockley!—hi there!"

"Mr Gerald!" came the captain's terrified voice. "Miss Diana's in the water."

"Anybody gone in for her?" came Gerald's sharp voice.

"Young Doctor Brindell,* sir."

"Where?"

"Can't see no signs of them, sir. Everybody's looking, but there's nothing so far."

There was a moment's ominous pause.

"Where did she go in?"

"I think—about where that boat is," came the uncertain answer, "that one with red and green lights."

"Row there," said Gerald quietly to Gudrun.

"*Get her out, Gerald, Oh get her out,*" the child's voice was crying anxiously. He took no heed.

"Lean back that way," said Gerald to Gudrun, as he stood up in the frail boat. "She won't upset."

In another moment, he had dropped clean down, soft and plumb, into the water. Gudrun was swaying violently in her boat, the agitated water shook with transient lights, she realised that it was faintly moonlight, and that he was gone. So it was possible to be gone. A terrible sense of fatality robbed her of all feeling and thought. So* he was gone out of the world, there was merely the same world, and absence, his absence. The night seemed large and vacuous. Lanterns swayed here and there, people were talking in an undertone on the launch and in the boats. She could hear Winifred moaning: "*Oh do find her Gerald, do find her,*" and someone trying to comfort the child. Gudrun paddled aimlessly here and there. The terrible, massive, cold, boundless surface of the water terrified her beyond words. Would he never come back? She felt she must jump into the water too, to know the horror also.

She started, hearing someone say: "There he is." She saw the movement of his swimming, like a water-rat. And she rowed involuntarily to him. But he was near another boat, a bigger one. Still she rowed towards him. She must be very near. She saw him—he looked like a seal. He looked like a seal as he took hold of the side of the boat. His fair hair was washed down on his round head, his face seemed to glisten suavely. She could hear him panting.

Then he clambered into the boat. Oh, and the beauty of the subjection of his loins, white and dimly luminous as he climbed over the side of the boat, made her want to die, to die. The beauty of his dim and luminous loins as he climbed into the boat, his back rounded and soft—ah, this was too much for her, too final a vision. She knew it, and it was fatal. The terrible hopelessness of fate, and of beauty, such beauty!

He was not like a man to her, he was an incarnation, a great phase of life. She saw him press the water out of his face, and look at the bandage on his hand. And she knew it was all no good, and that she would never go beyond him, he was the final approximation of life to her.

"Put the lights out, we shall see better," came his voice, sudden and mechanical and belonging to the world of man. She could scarcely believe it. She could scarcely believe there was a world of man. She leaned round and blew out her lanterns. They were difficult to blow out. Everywhere the lights were gone, save the coloured points on the sides of the launch. The bluey-grey, early night spread level around, the moon was overhead, there were shadows of boats here and there.

Again there was a splash, and he was gone under. Gudrun sat, sick at heart, frightened of the great, level surface of the water, so heavy and deadly. She was so alone, with the level, unliving field of the water stretching beneath her. It was not a good isolation, it was a
5   terrible, cold separation of suspense. She was suspended upon the surface of the insidious reality until such time as she also should disappear beneath it.

Then she knew, by a stirring of voices, that he had climbed out again, into a boat. She sat wanting connection with him. Strenuously
10 she claimed her connection with him, across the invisible space of the water! But round her heart was an isolation unbearable, through which nothing would penetrate.

"Take the launch in. It's no use keeping her there. Get lines for the dragging," came the decisive, instrumental voice, that was full of
15 the sound of the world.

The launch began gradually to beat the waters.

"*Gerald*! *Gerald*?" came the wild crying voice of Winifred. He did not answer. Slowly the launch drifted round in a pathetic, clumsy circle, and slunk away to the land, retreating into the dimness. The
20 wash of her paddles grew duller. Gudrun rocked in her light boat, and dipped the paddle automatically to steady herself.

"Gudrun?" called Ursula's voice.

"Ursula!"

The boats of the two sisters pulled together.

25 "Where is Gerald?" said Gudrun.

"He's dived again," said Ursula plaintively. "And I know he ought not, with his hurt hand and everything."

"I'll take him in home this time," said Birkin.

The boats swayed again from the wash of the steamer. Gudrun
30 and Ursula kept a look-out for Gerald.

"There he is!" cried Ursula, who had the sharpest eyes. He had not been long under. Birkin pulled towards him, Gudrun following. He swam slowly, and caught hold of the boat with his wounded hand. It slipped, and he sank back.

35 "Why don't you help him?" cried Ursula sharply.

He came again, and Birkin leaned to help him in to the boat. Gudrun again watched Gerald climb out of the water, but this time slowly, heavily, with the blind clambering motions of an amphibious beast, clumsy. Again the moon shone with faint luminosity on his
40 white, wet figure, on the stooping back and the rounded loins. But it

looked defeated now, his body, it clambered and fell with slow clumsiness. He was breathing hoarsely too, like an animal that is suffering. He sat slack and motionless in the boat, his head blunt and blind like a seal's, his whole appearance inhuman, unknowing. Gudrun shuddered as she mechanically followed his boat. Birkin rowed without speaking to the landing-stage.

"Where are you going?" Gerald asked suddenly, as if just waking up.

"Home," said Birkin.

"Oh no!" said Gerald imperiously. "We can't go home while they're in the water. Turn back again, I'm going to find them." The women were frightened, his voice was so imperative and dangerous, almost mad, not to be opposed.

"No," said Birkin. "You can't." There was a strange fluid compulsion in his voice. Gerald was silent, in a battle of wills. It was as if he would kill the other man. But Birkin rowed evenly and unswerving, with an inhuman inevitability.

"Why should you interfere?" said Gerald, in hate.

Birkin did not answer. He rowed towards the land. And Gerald sat mute, like a dumb beast, panting, his teeth chattering, his arms inert, his head like a seal's head.

They came to the landing-stage. Wet and naked-looking, Gerald climbed up the few steps. There stood his father, in the night.

"Father!" he said.

"Yes my boy?—Go home and get those things off."

"We shan't save them, father," said Gerald.

"There's hope yet, my boy."

"I'm afraid not. There's no knowing where they are. You can't find them. And there's a current, as cold as hell."

"We'll let the water out," said the father. "Go home you and look to yourself. See that he's looked after, Rupert," he added in a neutral voice.

"Well father, I'm sorry. I'm sorry. I'm afraid it's my fault. But it can't be helped; I've done what I could for the moment. I could go on diving, of course—not much, though—and not much use—"

He moved away barefoot, on the planks of the platform. Then he trod on something sharp.

"Of course, you've got no shoes on," said Birkin.

"His shoes are here!" cried Gudrun from below. She was making fast her boat.

Gerald waited for them to be brought to him. Gudrun came with them. He pulled them on his feet.

"If you once die," he said, "then when it's over, it's finished. Why come to life again? There's room under that water there for
5   thousands."

"Two is enough," she said, murmuring.

He dragged on his second shoe. He was shivering violently, and his jaw shook as he spoke.

"That's true," he said, "maybe. But it's curious how much room
10 there seems, a whole universe under there; and as cold as hell, you're as helpless as if your head was cut off." He could scarcely speak, he shook so violently. "There's one thing about our family, you know," he continued. "Once anything goes wrong, it can never be put right again—not with us. I've noticed it all my life—you can't put a thing
15 right, once it has gone wrong."

They were walking across the high-road to the house.

"And do you know, when you are down there, it is so cold, actually, and so endless, so different really from what it is on top, so endless—you wonder how it is so many are alive, why we're all up
20 here.—Are you going? I shall see you again, shan't I? Goodnight, and thank you. Thank you very much."

The two girls waited a while, to see if there were any hope. The moon shone clearly overhead, an almost* impertinent brightness, the small dark boats clustered on the water, there were voices and
25 subdued shouts. But it was all to no purpose. Gudrun went home when Birkin returned.

He was commissioned to open the sluice that let out the water from the lake, which was pierced at one end, near the high-road, thus serving as a reservoir to supply with water the distant mines, in
30 case of necessity. "Come with me," he said to Ursula. "And then I will walk home* with you, when I've done this."

He called at the water-keeper's cottage and took the key of the sluice. They went through a little gate from the high-road, to the head of the water, where was a great stone basin which received the
35 overflow, and a flight of stone steps descended into the depths of the water itself. At the head of the steps was the lock of the sluice-gate.

The night was silver-grey and perfect, save for the scattered, restless sound of voices. The grey sheen of the moonlight caught the stretch of water, dark boats plashed and moved. But Ursula's mind
40 ceased to be receptive, everything was unimportant and unreal.

Birkin fixed the iron handle of the sluice, and turned it with a wrench. The cogs began slowly to rise. He turned and turned, like a slave, his white figure become distinct. Ursula looked away. She could not bear to see him winding heavily and laboriously, bending and rising mechanically like a slave, turning the handle.

Then, a real shock to her, there came a loud splashing of water from out of the dark, tree-filled hollow beyond the road, a splashing that deepened rapidly to a harsh roar, and then became a heavy, booming noise of a great body of water falling solidly all the time. It occupied the whole of the night, this great steady booming of water, everything was drowned within it, drowned and lost. Ursula seemed to have to struggle for her life. She put her hands over her ears, and looked at the high, bland moon.

"Can't we go now?" she cried to Birkin, who was watching the water on the steps, to see if it would get any lower. It seemed to fascinate him. He looked up at her and nodded.

The little dark boats had moved nearer, people were crowding curiously along the hedge by the high-road, to see what was to be seen. Birkin and Ursula went to the cottage with the key, then turned their backs on the lake. She was in great haste. She could not bear the terrible crushing boom of the escaping water.

"Do you think they are dead?" she cried in a high voice, to make herself heard.

"Yes," he replied.

"Isn't it horrible!"

He paid no heed. They walked up the hill, further and further away from the noise.

"Do you mind very much?" she asked him.

"I don't mind about the dead," he said, "once they are dead. The worst of it is, they cling on to the living, and won't let go."

She pondered for a time.

"Yes," she said. "The *fact* of death doesn't really seem to matter much, does it?"

"No," he said. "What does it matter if Diana Crich is alive or dead?"

"Doesn't it!" she said, shocked.

"No, why should it? Better she were dead—she'll be much more real. She'll be positive in death. In life she was a fretting, negated thing."

"You are rather horrible," murmured Ursula.

"No! I'd rather Diana Crich were dead. Her living, somehow, was all wrong. As for the young man, poor devil—he'll find his way out quickly instead of slowly. Death is all right—nothing better."

"Yet *you* don't want to die," she challenged him.

5 He was silent for a time. Then he said, in a voice that was frightening to her in its change:

"I should like to be through with it—I should like to be through with the death-process."

"And aren't you?" asked Ursula nervously.

10 They walked on for some way in silence, under the trees. Then he said, slowly, as if afraid:

"There is life which belongs to death, and there is life which isn't death. One is tired of the life that belongs to death—our kind of life. But whether it is finished, God knows. I want love that is like sleep,

15 like being born again, vulnerable as a baby that just comes into the world."

Ursula listened, half attentive, half avoiding what he said. She seemed to catch the drift of his statement, and then she drew away. She wanted to hear, but she did not want to be implicated. She was

20 reluctant to yield there, where he wanted her, to yield, as it were, her very identity.

"Why should love be like sleep?" she asked sadly.

"I don't know. So that it is like death—I *do* want to die from this life—and yet it is more than life itself. One is delivered over like a

25 naked infant from the womb, all the old defences and the old body gone, a new air around one, that has never been breathed before."

She listened, making out what he said. She knew, as well as he knew, that words themselves do not convey meaning, that they are but a gesture we make, a dumb show like any other. And she seemed

30 to feel his gesture through her blood, and she drew back, even though her desire sent her forward.

"But," she said gravely, "didn't you say you wanted something that was *not* love—something beyond love?"

He turned in confusion. There was always confusion in speech.

35 Yet it must be spoken. Whichever way one moved, if one were to move forwards, one must break a way through. And to know, to give utterance, was to break a way through the walls of the prison,* as the infant in labour strives through the walls of the womb. There is no new movement now, without the breaking through of the old body,

40 deliberately, in knowledge, in the struggle to get out.

"I don't want love," he said. "I don't want to know you. I want to be gone out of myself, and you to be lost to yourself, so we are found different.—One shouldn't talk when one is tired and wretched.— One Hamletises,* and it seems a lie.—Only believe me when I show a bit of healthy pride and insouciance. I hate myself serious." 5

"Why shouldn't you be serious?" she said.

He thought for a minute, then he said, sulkily:

"I don't know."

Then they walked on in silence, at outs. He was vague and lost.

"Isn't it strange," she said, suddenly putting her hand on his arm, 10 with a loving impulse, "how we always talk like this! I suppose we do love each other, in some way."

"Oh yes," he said; "too much."

She laughed almost gaily.

"You'd have to have it your own way, wouldn't you?" she teased. 15 "You could never take it on trust."

He changed, laughed softly, and turned and took her in his arms, in the middle of the road.

"Yes," he said softly.

And he kissed her face and brow, slowly, gently, with a sort of 20 delicate happiness which surprised her extremely, and to which she could not respond. They were soft, blind kisses, perfect in their stillness. Yet she held back from them. It was like strange moths, very soft and silent, settling on her from the darkness of her soul. She was uneasy. She drew away. 25

"Isn't somebody coming?" she said.

So they looked down the dark road, then set off again walking towards Beldover. Then suddenly, to show him she was no shallow prude, she stopped and held him tight, hard against her, and covered his face with hard, fierce kisses of passion. In spite of his otherness, 30 the old blood beat up in him.

"Not this, not this," he whimpered to himself, as the first perfect mood of softness and sleep-loveliness ebbed back away from the rushing of passion that came up his limbs and over his face as she drew him. And soon he was a perfect hard flame of passionate desire 35 for her. Yet in the small core of the flame was an unyielding anguish of another thing. But this also was lost; he only wanted her, with an extreme desire that seemed inevitable as death, beyond question.

Then,* satisfied and shattered, fulfilled and destroyed, he went home away from her, drifting vaguely through the darkness, lapsed 40

into the old fire of burning passion. Far away, far away, there seemed
to be a small lament in the darkness. But what did it matter? What
did it matter, what did anything matter save this ultimate and
triumphant experience of physical passion, that had blazed up anew
5 like a new spell of life. "I was becoming quite dead-alive, nothing but
a word-bag,"* he said in triumph, scorning his other self. Yet
somewhere far off and small, the other hovered.

The men were still dragging the lake when he got back. He stood
on the bank and heard Gerald's voice. The water was still booming
10 in the night, the moon was fair, the hills beyond were elusive. The
lake was sinking. There came the raw smell of the banks, in the night
air.

Up at Shortlands there were lights in the windows, as if nobody
had gone to bed. On the landing-stage was the old doctor, the father
15 of the young man who was lost. He stood quite silent, waiting. Birkin
also stood and watched. Gerald came up in a boat.

"You still here, Rupert?" he said. "We can't get them. The
bottom slopes, you know, very steep. The water lies between two
very sharp slopes, with little branch valleys, and God knows where
20 the drift will take you. It isn't as if it was a level bottom. You never
know where you are, with the dragging."

"Is there any need for you to be working?" said Birkin. "Wouldn't
it be much better if you went to bed?"

"To bed! Good God, do you think I should sleep? We'll find 'em,
25 before I go away from here."

"But the men would find them just the same without you—why
should you insist?"

Gerald looked up at him. Then he put his hand affectionately on
Birkin's shoulder, saying:

30 "Don't you bother about me, Rupert. If there's anybody's
health to think about, it's yours, not mine. How do you feel yourself?"

"Very well.—But you, you spoil your own chance of life—you
waste your best self."

35 Gerald was silent for a moment. Then he said:

"Waste it? What else is there to do with it?"

"But leave this, won't you? You force yourself into horrors, and
put a mill-stone of beastly memories round your neck! Come away
now."

40 "A mill-stone of beastly memories!" Gerald repeated. Then he

put his hand again affectionately on Birkin's shoulder. "God, you've got such a telling way of putting things, Rupert, you have."

Birkin's heart sank. He was irritated and weary of having a telling way of putting things.*

"Won't you leave it? Come over to my place—?" he urged, as one urges a drunken man.

"No," said Gerald coaxingly, his arm across the other man's shoulder. "Thanks very much, Rupert—I shall be glad to come tomorrow, if that'll do. You understand, don't you? I want to see this job through. But I'll come tomorrow, right enough. Oh, I'd rather come and have a chat with you than—than do anything else, I verily believe. Yes, I would. You mean a lot to me, Rupert, more than you know."

"What do I mean, more than I know?" asked Birkin irritably. He was acutely aware of Gerald's hand on his shoulder. And he did not want this altercation. He wanted the other man to come out of the ugly misery.

"I'll tell you another time," said Gerald, coaxingly.

"Come along with me now—I want you to come," said Birkin.

There was a pause, intense and real. Birkin wondered why his own heart beat so heavily.—Then Gerald's fingers gripped hard and communicative into Birkin's shoulder, as he said:

"No, I'll see this job through, Rupert. Thank you—I know what you mean. We're all right, you know, you and me."

"I may be all right, but I'm sure you're not, mucking about here," said Birkin.

And he went away.

The bodies of the dead were not recovered till towards dawn. Diana had her arms tight round the neck of the young man, choking him.

"She killed him," said Gerald.

The moon sloped down the sky and sank at last, the lake was sunk to quarter size, it had horrible raw banks of clay, that smelled of raw rottenish water. Dawn roused faintly behind the eastern hill. The water still boomed through the sluice.

As the birds were whistling for the first morning, and the hills at the back of the desolate lake stood radiant with new mists, there was a straggling procession up to Shortlands, men bearing the bodies on a stretcher, Gerald going beside them, the two grey-bearded fathers following in silence. Indoors the family was all sitting up, waiting.

Somebody must go to tell the mother, in her room. The doctor in secret struggled to bring back his son, till he himself was exhausted.

Over all the outlying district was a hush of dreadful excitement on that Sunday morning. The colliery people felt as if this catastrophe had happened directly to themselves, indeed they were more shocked and frightened than if their own men had been killed. Such a tragedy at Shortlands, the high home of the district! One of the young mistresses, persisting in dancing on the cabin roof of the launch,* wilful young madam, drowned in the midst of the festival, with the young doctor! Everywhere, on the Sunday morning, the colliers wandered about, discussing the calamity. At all the Sunday dinners of the people, there seemed a strange presence. It was as if the angel of death were very near, there was a sense of the supernatural in the air. The men had excited, startled faces, the women looked solemn, some of them had been crying. The children enjoyed the excitement at first. There was an intensity in the air, almost magical. Did all enjoy it? Did all enjoy the thrill?

Gudrun had wild ideas of rushing to comfort Gerald. She was thinking all the time of the perfect comforting, reassuring thing to say to him. She was shocked and frightened, but she put that away, thinking of how she should deport herself with Gerald: act her part. That was the real thrill: how she should act her part.

Ursula was deeply and passionately in love with Birkin, and she was capable of nothing. She was perfectly callous about all the talk of the accident, but her estranged air looked like trouble. She merely sat by herself, whenever she could, and longed to see him again. She wanted him to come to the house—she would not have it otherwise, he must come at once. She was waiting for him. She stayed indoors all the day, waiting for him to knock at the door. Every minute, she glanced automatically at the window. He would be there.

Chapter XV

Sunday Evening

As the day wore on, the life-blood seemed to ebb away from Ursula, and within the emptiness a heavy despair gathered. Her passion seemed to bleed to death, and there was nothing. She sat suspended in a state of complete nullity, harder to bear than death.

"Unless something happens," she said to herself, in the perfect lucidity of final suffering, "I shall die. I am at the end of my line of life."

She sat crushed and obliterated in a darkness that was the border of death. She realised how all her life she had been drawing nearer and nearer to this brink, where there was no beyond, from which one had to leap like Sappho into the unknown.* The knowledge of the imminence of death was like a drug. Darkly, without thinking at all, she knew that she was near to death. She had travelled all her life along the line of fulfilment, and it was nearly concluded. She knew all she had to know, she had experienced all she had to experience, she was fulfilled in a kind of bitter ripeness, there remained only to fall from the tree into death. And one must fulfil one's development to the end, must carry the adventure to its conclusion. And the next step was over the border into death. So it was then! There was a certain peace in the knowledge.

After all, when one was fulfilled, one was happiest in falling into death, as a bitter fruit plunges in its ripeness downwards. Death is a great consummation, a consummating experience. It is a development from life. That we know, while we are yet living. What then need we think for further? One can never see beyond the consummation. It is enough that death is a great and conclusive experience. Why should we ask what comes after the experience, when the experience is still unknown to us? Let us die, since the great experience is the one that follows now upon all the rest, death, which is the next great crisis in front of which we have arrived. If we wait, if we balk the issue, we do but hang about the gates in undignified uneasiness. There it is, in front of us, as in front of Sappho, the illimitable space. Thereinto goes the journey. Have we not the courage to go on with our journey, must we cry 'I daren't.'? On ahead we will go, into death, and whatever death may mean. If a man can see the next step to be taken, why should he fear the next but one? Why ask about the next but one? Of the next step we are certain. It is

5 the step into death.

"I shall die—I shall quickly die," said Ursula to herself, clear as if in a trance, clear, calm, and certain beyond human certainty. But somewhere behind, in the twilight, there was a bitter weeping and a hopelessness. That must not be attended to. One must go where the

10 unfaltering spirit goes, there must be no balking the issue, because of fear. No balking the issue, no listening to the lesser voices. If the deepest desire be now, to go on into the unknown of death, shall one forfeit the deepest truth for one more shallow?

"Then let it end," she said to herself. It was a decision. It was not a

15 question of taking one's life—she would *never* kill herself, that was repulsive and violent. It was a question of *knowing* the next step. And the next step led into the space of death. Did it?—or was there————?

Her thoughts drifted into unconsciousness, she sat as if asleep

20 beside the fire. And then the thought came back. The space of death! Could she give herself to it? Ah yes—it was a sleep. She had had enough. So long she had held out and resisted. Now was the time to relinquish, not to resist any more.

In a kind of spiritual trance, she yielded, she gave way, and all was

25 dark. She could feel, within the darkness, the terrible assertion of her body, the unutterable anguish of dissolution, the only anguish that is too much, the far-off, awful nausea of dissolution set in within the body.

"Does the body correspond so immediately with the spirit?" she

30 asked herself. And she knew, with the clarity of ultimate knowledge, that the body is only one of the manifestations of the spirit, the transmutation of the integral spirit is the transmutation of the physical body as well.—Unless I set my will, unless I absolve myself from the rhythm* of life, fix myself and remain static, cut off from

35 living, absolved within my own will. But better die than live mechanically a life that is a repetition of repetitions. To die is to move on with the invisible. To die is also a joy, a joy of submitting to that which is greater than the known, namely, the pure unknown. That is a joy. But to live mechanised and cut off within the motion of

40 the will, to live as an entity absolved from the unknown, that is

shameful and ignominious. There is no ignominy in death. There is complete ignominy in an unreplenished, mechanised life. Life indeed may be ignominious, shameful to the soul. But death is never a shame. Death itself, like the illimitable space, is beyond our sullying.

Tomorrow was Monday. Monday, the beginning of another school-week! Another shameful, barren school-week, mere routine and mechanical activity. Was not the adventure of death infinitely preferable? Was not death infinitely more lovely and noble than such a life? A life of barren routine, without inner meaning, without any real significance. How sordid life was, how it was a terrible shame to the soul, to live now! How much cleaner and more dignified to be dead! One could not bear any more of this shame of sordid routine and mechanical nullity. One might come to fruit in death. She had had enough. For where was life to be found? No flowers grow upon busy machinery, there is no sky to a routine, there is no space to a rotary motion. And all life was a rotary motion, mechanised, cut off from reality. There was nothing to look for from life—it was the same in all countries and all peoples. The only window was death. One could look out on to the great dark sky of death with elation, as one had looked out of the class-room window as a child, and seen perfect freedom in the outside. Now one was not a child, and one knew that the soul was a prisoner within this sordid vast edifice of life, and there was no escape, save in death.

But what a joy! What a gladness to think that whatever humanity did, it could not seize hold of the kingdom of death, to nullify that. The sea they turned into a murderous alley and a soiled road of commerce, disputed like the dirty land of a city every inch of it. The air they claimed too, shared it up, parcelled it out to certain owners, they trespassed in the air to fight for it.* Everything was gone, walled in, with spikes on top of the walls, and one must ignominiously creep between the spiky walls through a labyrinth of life.

But the great, dark, illimitable kingdom of death, there humanity was put to scorn. So much they could do upon earth, the multifarious little gods that they were. But the kingdom of death put them all to scorn, they dwindled into their true vulgar silliness in face of it.

How beautiful, how grand and perfect death was, how good to look forward to. There one would wash off all the lies and ignominy and dirt that had been put upon one here, a perfect bath of cleanness and glad refreshment, and go unknown, unquestioned, unabased.*

After all, one was rich, if only in the promise of perfect death. It was a gladness above all, that this remained to look forward to, the pure inhuman otherness of death. Whatever life might be, it could not take away death, the inhuman transcendent death. Oh, let us ask no question of it, what it is or is not. To know is human, and in death we do not know, we are not human. And the joy of this compensates for all the bitterness of knowledge and the sordidness of our humanity. In death we shall not be human, and we shall not know. The promise of this is our heritage, we look forward like heirs to their majority.

Ursula sat quite still and quite forgotten, alone by the fire in the drawing-room. The children were playing in the kitchen, all the others were gone to church. And she was gone into the ultimate darkness of her own soul.

She was startled by hearing the bell ring, away in the kitchen, the children came scudding along the passage in delicious alarm.

"Ursula, there's somebody."

"I know. Don't be silly," she replied. She too was startled, almost frightened. She dared hardly go to the door.

Birkin stood on the threshold, his rain-coat turned up to his ears. He had come now, now she was gone far away. She was aware of the rainy night behind him.

"Oh is it you?" she said.

"I am glad you are at home," he said in a low voice, entering the house.

"They are all gone to church."

He took off his coat and hung it up. The children were peeping at him round the corner.

"Go and get undressed now, Billy and Dora,"* said Ursula. "Mother will be back soon, and she'll be disappointed if you're not in bed."

The children, in a sudden angelic mood, retired without a word. Birkin and Ursula went into the drawing-room. The fire burned low. He looked at her, and wondered at the luminous delicacy of her beauty, and the wide shining of her eyes. He watched from a distance, with wonder in his heart, she seemed transfigured with light.

"What have you been doing all day?" he asked her.

"Only sitting about," she said.

He looked at her. There was a change in her. But she was separate from him. She remained apart, in a kind of brightness. They both sat silent in the soft light of the lamp. He felt he ought to go away again, he ought not to have come. Still he did not gather enough resolution to move. But he was *de trop*, her mood was absent and separate.

Then there came the voices of the two children calling shyly outside the door, softly, with self-excited timidity:

"Ursula! Ursula!"

She rose and opened the door. On the threshold stood the two children in their long nightgowns, with wide-eyed, angelic faces. They were being very good for the moment, playing the rôle perfectly of two obedient children.

"Shall you take us to bed!" said Billy, in a loud whisper.

"Why, you *are* angels tonight," she said softly. "Won't you come and say goodnight to Mr Birkin?"

The children merged shyly into the room, on bare feet. Billy's face was wide and grinning, but there was a great solemnity of being good in his round blue eyes. Dora, peeping from the floss of her fair hair, hung back like some tiny Dryad, that has no soul.

"Will you say goodnight to me?" asked Birkin, in a voice that was strangely soft and smooth. Dora drifted away at once, like a leaf lifted on a breath of wind. But Billy went softly forward, slow and willing, lifting his pinched-up mouth implicitly to be kissed. Ursula watched the full, gathered lips of the man gently touch those of the boy, so gently. Then Birkin lifted his fingers and touched the boy's round, confiding cheek, with a faint touch of love. Neither spoke. Billy seemed angelic like a cherub boy, or like an acolyte, Birkin was a tall, grave angel looking down to him.

"Are you going to be kissed?" Ursula broke in, speaking to the little girl. But Dora edged away like a tiny Dryad that will not be touched.

"Won't you say Goodnight to Mr Birkin? Go, he's waiting for you," said Ursula. But the girl-child only made a little motion away from him.

"Silly Dora, silly Dora!" said Ursula.

Birkin felt some mistrust and antagonism in the small child. He could not understand it.

"Come then," said Ursula. "Let us go before mother comes."

"Who'll hear us say our prayers?" asked Billy anxiously.

"Whom you like."

"Won't *you*?"

"Yes, I will."

"Ursula?"

"Well Billy?"

"Is it *whom* you like."

"That's it."

5   "Well what is *whom?*"

"It's the accusative of who."

There was a moment's contemplative silence, then the confiding: "Is it?"

Birkin smiled to himself as he sat by the fire. When Ursula came
10 down he sat motionless, with his arms on his knees. She saw him, how he was motionless and ageless, like some crouching idol, some image of a deathly religion. He looked round at her, and his face, very pale and unreal, seemed to gleam with a whiteness almost phosphorescent.

15   "Don't you feel well?" she asked, in indefinable repulsion.

"I hadn't thought about it."

"But don't you know without thinking about it?"

He looked at her, his eyes dark and swift, and he saw her revulsion. He did not answer her question.

20   "Don't you know whether you are unwell or not, without thinking about it?" she persisted.

"Not always," he said coldly.

"But don't you think that's very wicked?"

"Wicked?"

25   "Yes. I think it's *criminal* to have so little connection with your own body that you don't even know when you are ill."

He looked at her darkly.

"Yes," he said.

"Why don't you stay in bed when you are seedy? You look per-
30 fectly ghastly."

"Offensively so?" he asked ironically.

"Yes, quite offensive. Quite repelling."

"Ah!—Well that's unfortunate."

"And it's raining, and it's a horrible night. Really, you shouldn't
35 be forgiven for treating your body like it—you *ought* to suffer, a man who takes as little notice of his body as that."

"—takes as little notice of his body as that," he echoed mechanically.

This cut her short, and there was silence.

40   The others came in from church, and the two had the girls to

face, then the mother and Gudrun, and then the father and the boy.

"Good-evening," said Brangwen, faintly surprised. "Came to see me, did you?"

"No," said Birkin, "not about anything in particular, that is. The day was dismal, and I thought you wouldn't mind if I called in."

"It *has* been a depressing day," said Mrs Brangwen sympathetically. At that moment the voices of the children were heard calling from upstairs: "Mother! Mother!" She lifted her face and answered mildly into the distance: "I shall come up to you in a minute Doysie." Then to Birkin: "There is nothing fresh at Shortlands, I suppose?—Ah," she sighed, "no, poor things, I should think not."

"You've been over there today, I suppose?" asked the father.

"Gerald came round to tea with me, and I walked back with him. The house is overexcited and unwholesome, I thought."

"I should think they were people who hadn't much restraint,"* said Gudrun.

"Or too much," Birkin answered.

"Oh yes, I'm sure," said Gudrun, almost vindictively; "One or the other."

"They all feel they ought to behave in some unnatural fashion," said Birkin. "When people are in grief, they would do better to cover their faces and keep in retirement, as in the old days."

"Certainly!" cried Gudrun, flushed and inflammable. "What can be worse than this public grief—what is more horrible, more false! If *grief* is not private, and hidden, what is?"

"Exactly," he said. "I felt ashamed when I was there and they were all going about in a lugubrious false way, feeling they must not be natural or ordinary."

"Well—" said Mrs Brangwen, offended at this criticism, "it isn't so easy to bear a trouble like that."

And she went upstairs to the children.

He remained only a few minutes longer, then took his leave. When he was gone Ursula felt such a poignant hatred of him, that all her brain seemed turned into a sharp crystal of fine hatred. Her whole nature seemed sharpened and intensified into a pure dart of hate. She could not imagine what it was. It merely took hold of her, the most poignant and ultimate hatred, pure and clear and beyond thought. She could not think of it at all, she was translated beyond herself. It was like a possession. She felt she was possessed. And for several days she went about possessed by this exquisite force of hatred against him. It surpassed anything she had ever known before, it seemed to throw her out of the world into some terrible region where nothing of her old life held good. She was quite lost and dazed, really dead to her own life.

5　　　It was so completely incomprehensible and irrational. She did not know *why* she hated him, her hate was quite abstract.* She had only realised with a shock that stunned her, that she was overcome by this pure transportation. He was the enemy, fine as a diamond, and as hard and jewel-like, the quintessence of all that was inimical.

10　　　She thought of his face, white and purely wrought, and of his eyes that had such a dark, constant will of assertion, and she touched her own forehead, to feel if she were mad, she was so transfigured in white flame of essential hate.

It was not temporal, her hatred, she did not hate him for this or for 15　that; she did not want to do anything to him, to have any connection with him. Her relation was ultimate and utterly beyond words, the hate was so pure and gem-like. It was as if he were a beam of essential enmity, a beam of light that did not only destroy her, but denied her altogether, revoked her whole world. She saw him as a 20　clear stroke of uttermost contradiction, a strange gem-like being whose existence defined her own non-existence. When she heard he was ill again, her hatred only intensified itself a few degrees, if that were possible. It stunned her and annihilated her, but she could not escape it. She could not escape this transfiguration of hatred that had 25　come upon her.

Chapter XVI

Man to Man

He lay sick and unmoved, in pure opposition to everything. He knew how near to breaking was the vessel that held his life. He knew also how strong and durable it was. And he did not care. Better a thousand times take one's chance with death, than accept a life one did not want. But best of all to persist and persist and persist for ever, till one were satisfied in life.

He knew that Ursula was referred back to him. He knew his life rested with her. But he would rather not live than accept the love she proffered. The old way of love seemed a dreadful bondage, a sort of conscription.* What it was in him he did not know, but the thought of love, marriage, and children, and a life lived together, in the horrible privacy of domestic and connubial satisfaction, was repulsive. He wanted something clearer, more open, cooler, as it were. The hot narrow intimacy between man and wife was abhorrent. The way they shut their doors, these married people, and shut themselves in to their own exclusive alliance with each other, even in love, disgusted him. It was a whole community of mistrustful couples insulated in private houses or private rooms, always in couples, and no further life, no further immediate, no disinterested relationship admitted: a kaleidoscope of couples, disjoined, separatist, meaningless entities of married couples. True, he hated promiscuity even worse than marriage, and a liaison was only another kind of coupling, reactionary from the legal marriage. Reaction was a greater bore than action.

On the whole, he hated sex, it was such a limitation. It was sex that turned a man into a broken half of a couple, the woman into the other broken half. And he wanted to be single in himself, the woman single in her self. He wanted sex to revert to the level of the other appetites, to be regarded as a functional process, not as a fulfilment. He believed in sex marriage. But beyond this, he wanted a further conjunction, where man had being and woman had being, two pure beings, each constituting the freedom of the other, balancing each other like two poles of one force, like two angels, or two demons.

He wanted so much to be free, not under the compulsion of any

need for unification, or tortured by unsatisfied desire. Desire and aspiration should find their object without all this torture, as now, in a world of plenty of water, simple thirst is inconsiderable, satisfied almost unconsciously. And he wanted to be with Ursula as free as
5 with himself, single and clear and cool, yet balanced, polarised with her. The merging, the clutching, the mingling of love was become madly abhorrent to him.

But it seemed to him, woman was always so horrible and clutching, she had such a lust for possession, a greed of self-
10 importance in love. She wanted to have, to own, to control, to be dominant. Everything must be referred back to her, to Woman, the Great Mother of everything, out of whom proceeded everything and to whom everything must finally be rendered up.

It filled him with almost insane fury, this calm assumption of the
15 Magna Mater, that all was hers, because she had borne it. Man was hers, because she had borne him. A Mater Dolorosa,* she had borne him, a Magna Mater, she now claimed him again, soul and body, sex, meaning, and all. He had a horror of the Magna Mater, she was detestable.

20 She was on a very high horse again, was woman, the Great Mother. Did he not know it in Hermione. Hermione, the humble, the subservient, what was she all the while but the Mater Dolorosa, in her subservience claiming, with horrible, insidious arrogance and female tyranny, her own again, claiming back the man she had borne
25 in suffering. By her very suffering and humility she bound her son with chains, she held him her everlasting prisoner.

And Ursula, Ursula was the same—or the inverse. She too was the awful, arrogant queen of life, as if she were a queen bee* on whom all the rest depended. He saw the yellow flare in her eyes, he knew the
30 unthinkable overweening assumption of primacy in her. She was unconscious of it herself. She was only too ready to knock her head on the ground before a man. But this was only when she was so certain of her man, that she could worship him as a woman worships her own infant, with a worship of perfect possession.

35 It was intolerable, this possession at the hands of woman. Always a man must be considered as the broken-off fragment of a woman, and the sex was the still aching scar of the laceration.* Man must be added on to a woman, before he had any real place or wholeness.

And why? Why should we consider ourselves, men and women, as
40 broken fragments of one whole. It is not true. We are not broken

fragments of one whole. Rather we are the singling away into purity and clear being, of things that were mixed. Rather the sex is that which remains in us of the mixed, the unresolved. And passion is the further separating of this mixture, that which is manly being taken into the being of the man, that which is womanly passing to the woman, till the two are clear and whole as angels, the admixture of sex in the highest sense surpassed, leaving two single beings, constellated together like two stars.

In the old age, before sex was, we were mixed, each one a mixture. The process of singling into individuality resulted in the great polarisation of sex. The womanly drew to one side, the manly to the other. But the separation was imperfect even then. And so our world-cycle passes. There is now to come the new day, where we are beings each of us, fulfilled in difference. The man is pure man, the woman pure woman, they are perfectly polarised. But there is no longer any of the horrible merging, mingling, self-abnegation of love. There is only the pure duality of polarisation, each one free from any contamination of the other. In each, the individual is primal, sex is subordinate, but perfectly polarised. Each has a single, separate being, with its own laws. The man has his pure freedom, the woman hers. Each acknowledges the perfection of the polarised sex-circuit. Each admits the different nature in the other.

So Birkin meditated whilst he was ill. He liked sometimes to be ill enough to take to his bed. For then he got better very quickly, and things came to him clear and sure.

Whilst he was laid up, Gerald came to see him. The two men had a deep, uneasy feeling for each other. Gerald's eyes were quick and restless, his whole manner tense and impatient, he seemed strung up to some activity. According to conventionality, he wore black clothes, he looked formal, handsome and *comme il faut*. His hair was fair almost to whiteness, sharp like splinters of light, his face was keen and ruddy, his body seemed full of northern energy.

Gerald really loved Birkin, though he never quite believed in him. Birkin was too unreal;—clever, whimsical, wonderful, but not practical enough. Gerald felt that his own understanding was much sounder and safer. Birkin was delightful, a wonderful spirit, but after all, not to be taken seriously, not quite to be counted as a man among men.

"Why are you laid up again?" he asked, kindly, taking the sick man's hand. It was always Gerald who was protective, offering the warm shelter of his physical strength.

"For my sins, I suppose," Birkin said, smiling a little ironically.

"For your sins? Yes, probably that is so.—You should sin less, and keep better in health."

"You'd better teach me," said Birkin.

He looked at Gerald with ironic eyes.

"How are things with you?" asked Birkin.

"With me?" Gerald looked at Birkin, saw he was serious, and a warm light came into his eyes. "I don't know that they're any different. I don't see how they could be. There's nothing to change."

"I suppose you are conducting the business as successfully as ever, and ignoring the demands of the soul."

"That's it," said Gerald; "at least as far as the business is concerned. I couldn't say about the soul, I'm sure."

"No."

"Surely you don't expect me to?" laughed Gerald.

"No.—How are the rest of your affairs progressing, apart from the business?"

"The rest of my affairs? What are those? I couldn't say; I don't know what you refer to."

"Yes you do," said Birkin. "Are you gloomy or cheerful?—And what about Gudrun Brangwen?"

"What about her?" A confused look came over Gerald. "Well," he added, "I don't know. I can only tell you, she gave me a hit over the face the last time I saw her."

"A hit over the face! What for?"

"That I couldn't tell you, either."

"Really!—But when?"

"The night of the party—when Diana was drowned. She was driving the cattle up the hill, and I went after her—you remember."

"Yes, I remember. But what made her do that? You didn't definitely ask her for it, I suppose?"

"I? No, not that I know of. I merely said to her, that it was dangerous to drive those Highland bullocks—as it *is*. She turned in such a way, and said—'I suppose you think I'm afraid of you and your cattle, don't you?'—So I asked her 'Why—?'—And for answer she flung me a back-hander across the face."

Birkin laughed quickly, as if it pleased him. Gerald looked at him, wondering, and began to laugh as well, saying:

"I didn't laugh at the time, I assure you. I was never so taken aback in my life."

"And weren't you furious?"

"Furious? I should think I was. I'd have murdered her for two pins."

"Hm!" ejaculated Birkin. "Poor Gudrun, wouldn't she suffer afterwards for having given herself away!" He was hugely delighted.

"Would she suffer?" asked Gerald, also amused now.

Both men smiled in malice and amusement.

"Badly, I'm sure;* seeing how self-conscious she is."

"She is self-conscious is she? Then what made her do it? For I certainly think it was quite uncalled for, and quite unjustified."

"I suppose it was a sudden impulse."

"Yes, but how do you account for her having such an impulse? I'd done her no hurt."

Birkin shook his head.

"The Amazon suddenly came up in her I suppose," he said.

"Well," replied Gerald, "I'd rather it had been the Orinoco."

They both laughed at the poor joke. Gerald was thinking how Gudrun had said she would strike the last blow too. But some reserve made him keep this back from Birkin.

"And you resent it?" Birkin asked.

"I don't *resent* it. I don't care a tinker's curse about it." He was silent a moment, then he added, laughing, "No, I'll see it through, that's all. She seemed sorry afterwards."

"Did she? You've not met since that night?"

Gerald's face clouded.

"No," he said. "We've been—you can imagine how it's been, since the accident."

"Yes. Is it calming down?"

"I don't know. It's a shock, of course. But I don't believe mother minds. I really don't believe she takes any notice. And what's so funny, she used to be all for the children—nothing mattered, nothing whatever mattered but the children. And now, she doesn't take any more notice than if it was one of the servants."

"No? Did it upset *you* very much?"

"It's a shock. But I don't feel it very much, really. I don't feel any different. We've all got to die, and it doesn't seem to make any great difference, anyhow, whether you die or not. I can't feel any *grief*, you know. It leaves me cold. I can't quite account for it."

"You don't care if you die or not?" asked Birkin.

Gerald looked at him with eyes blue as the blue-fibred steel of a weapon. He felt awkward, but indifferent. As a matter of fact, he did care terribly, with a great fear.

5 "Oh," he said, "I don't want to die, why should I? But I never trouble. The question doesn't seem to be on the carpet for me at all. It doesn't interest me, you know."

"'Timor mortis conturbat me',"* quoted Birkin, adding—"No, death doesn't really seem the point any more. It curiously doesn't
10 concern one. It's like an ordinary tomorrow."

Gerald looked closely at his friend. The eyes of the two men met, and an unspoken understanding was exchanged.

Gerald narrowed his eyes, his face was cool and unscrupulous as he looked at Birkin, impersonally, with a vision that ended in a point
15 in space, strangely keen-eyed and yet blind.

"If death isn't the point," he said, in a strangely abstract, cold, fine voice—"what is?" He sounded as if he had been found out.

"What is?" re-echoed Birkin. And there was a mocking silence.

"There's a long way to go, after the point of intrinsic death, before
20 we disappear," said Birkin.

"There is," said Gerald. "But what sort of way?" He seemed to press the other man for knowledge which he himself knew far better than Birkin did.

"Right down the slopes of degeneration—mystic, universal
25 degeneration.—There are many stages of pure degradation to go through: agelong. We live on long after our death, and progressively, aeons of progressive devolution."*

Gerald listened with a faint, fine smile on his face, all the time, as if, somewhere, he knew so much better than Birkin, all about this: as
30 if his own knowledge were direct and personal, whereas Birkin's was a matter of observation and inference, not quite hitting the nail on the head:—though aiming near enough at it.—But he was not going to give himself away. If Birkin could get at the secrets, let him. Gerald would never help him. Gerald would be a dark horse to the
35 end.

"Of course," he said, with a startling change of conversation, "it is father who really feels it. It will finish him. For him the world collapses.—All his care now is for Winnie—he must save Winnie.—He says she ought to be sent away to school, but she won't
40 hear of it, and he'll never do it.—Of course she *is* in rather a queer

way. We're all of us curiously bad at living. We can do things—but we can't get on with life at all.—It's curious—a family failing."

"She oughtn't to be sent away to school," said Birkin, who was considering the new proposition.

"She oughtn't? Why?"

"She's a queer child—a special child, more special even than you. And in my opinion special children should never be sent away to school. Only moderately ordinary children should be sent to school,—so it seems to me."

"I'm inclined to think just the opposite. I think it would probably make her more normal if she went away and mixed with other children."

"She wouldn't mix, you see. *You* never really mixed, did you? And she wouldn't be willing even to pretend to. She's proud, and solitary, and naturally apart. If she has a single nature, why do you want to make her gregarious?"

"No, I don't want to make her anything. But I think school would be good for her."

"Was it good for *you?*"

Gerald's eyes narrowed uglily. School had been torture to him. Yet he had not questioned whether one should go through this torture. He seemed to believe in education through subjection and torment.

"I hated it at the time, but I can see it was necessary," he said. "It brought me into line a bit—and you can't live unless you do come into line somewhere."

"Well," said Birkin, "I begin to think that you can't live unless you keep entirely out of the line. It's no good trying to toe the line, when your one impulse is to smash up the line.—Winnie is a special nature, and for special natures you must give a special world."

"Yes, but where's your special world?" said Gerald.

"Make it.—Instead of chopping yourself down to fit the world, chop the world down to fit yourself.—As a matter of fact, two exceptional people make another world. You and I, we make another, separate world.—You don't *want* a world same as your brothers-in-law.—It's just the special quality you value. Do you *want* to be normal or ordinary?—It's a lie. You want to be free and extraordinary, in an extraordinary world of liberty."

Gerald looked at Birkin with subtle eyes of knowledge. But he would never openly admit what he felt. He knew more than Birkin, in

one direction—much more. And this gave him his gentle love for
the other man, as if Birkin were in some way young, innocent,
child-like: so amazingly clever, but incurably innocent.

"Yet you are so banal as to consider me chiefly a freak," said
5 Birkin pointedly.

"A freak!" exclaimed Gerald, startled. And his face opened suddenly, as if lighted with simplicity, as when a flower opens out of the
cunning bud. "No—I never consider you a freak." And he watched
the other man with strange eyes, that Birkin could not understand.
10 "I feel," Gerald continued, "that there is always an element of
uncertainty about you—perhaps you are uncertain about yourself.
But I'm never sure of you. You can go away and change as easily as
if you had no soul."

He looked at Birkin with penetrating eyes. Birkin was amazed.
15 He thought he had all the soul in the world. He stared in amazement. And Gerald, watching, saw the amazing attractive goodliness
of his eyes, a young, spontaneous goodness that attracted the other
man infinitely, yet filled him with bitter chagrin, because he mistrusted it so much. He knew Birkin could do without him—could
20 forget, and not suffer. This was always present in Gerald's
consciousness, filling him with bitter unbelief: this consciousness of
the young, animal-like spontaneity of detachment. It seemed almost
like hypocrisy and lying, sometimes, oh, often, on Birkin's part, to
talk so deeply and importantly.
25   Quite other things were going through Birkin's mind. Suddenly
he saw himself confronted with another problem—the problem of
love and eternal conjunction between two men. Of course this was
necessary—it had been a necessity inside himself all his life—to
love a man purely and fully. Of course he had been loving Gerald all
30 along, and all along denying it.

He lay in the bed and wondered, whilst his friend sat beside him,
lost in brooding. Each man was gone in his own thoughts.

"You know how the old German knights used to swear a Blutbrüderschaft,"* he said to Gerald, with quite a new happy activity in
35 his eyes.

"Make a little wound in their arms, and rub each other's blood
into the cut?" said Gerald.

"Yes—and swear to be true to each other, of one blood, all their
lives.—That is what we ought to do. No wounds, that is
40 obsolete.—But we ought to swear to love each other, you and I,

implicitly and perfectly, finally, without any possibility of going back
on it."

He looked at Gerald with clear, happy eyes of discovery. Gerald
looked down at him, attracted, so deeply bondaged in fascinated
attraction, that he was mistrustful, resenting the bondage, hating the
attraction.

"We will swear to each other, one day, shall we?" pleaded Birkin.
"We will swear to stand by each other—be true to each other—
ultimately—infallibly—given to each other, organically—without
possibility of taking back."

Birkin sought hard to express himself. But Gerald hardly listened.
His face shone with a certain luminous pleasure. He was pleased.
But he kept his reserve. He held himself back.

"Shall we swear to each other, one day?" said Birkin, putting out
his hand towards Gerald.

Gerald just touched the extended fine, living hand, as if withheld
and afraid.

"We'll leave it till I understand it better," he said, in a voice of
excuse.

Birkin watched him. A little sharp disappointment, perhaps a
touch of contempt came into his heart.

"Yes," he said. "You must tell me what you think, later. You know
what I mean? not sloppy emotionalism. An impersonal union that
leaves one free."

They lapsed both into silence. Birkin was looking at Gerald all the
time. He seemed now to see, not the physical, animal man, which he
usually saw in Gerald, and which usually he liked so much, but the
man himself, complete, and as if fated, doomed, limited. This
strange sense of fatality in Gerald, as if he were limited to one form
of existence, one knowledge, one activity, a sort of fatal halfness,
which to himself seemed wholeness, always overcame Birkin after
their moments of passionate approach, and filled him with a sort of
contempt, or boredom. It was the insistence on the limitation which
so bored Birkin in Gerald. Gerald could never fly away from himself,
in real indifferent gaiety. He had a clog, a sort of monomania.

There was silence for a time. Then Birkin said, in a lighter tone,
letting the stress of the contact pass:

"Can't you get a good governess for Winifred?—somebody
exceptional?"

"Hermione Roddice suggested we should ask Gudrun to teach

her to draw and to model in clay. You know Winnie is astonishingly
clever with that plasticine stuff. Hermione declares she is an artist."
Gerald spoke in the usual animated, chatty manner, as if nothing
unusual had passed. But Birkin's manner was full of reminder.

5   "Really! I didn't know that.—Oh well then, if Gudrun *would* teach
her, it would be perfect—couldn't be anything better—if Winifred is
an artist. Because Gudrun somewhere is one. And every true artist is
the salvation of every other."

"I thought they got on so badly, as a rule."

10   "Perhaps. But only artists produce for each other the world that is
fit to live in. If you can arrange *that* for Winifred, it is perfect."

"But you think she wouldn't come?"

"I don't know. Gudrun is rather self-opinionated. She won't go
cheap, anywhere. Or if she does, she'll pretty soon take herself back.

15   So whether she would condescend to do private teaching, particularly here, in Beldover, I don't know. But it would be just the
thing. Winifred has got a special nature. And if you can put into her
way the means of being self-sufficient, that is the best thing
possible.—She'll never get on with the ordinary life. You find it

20   difficult enough yourself, and she is several skins thinner than you
are. It is awful to think what her life will be like unless she does find a
means of expression, some way of fulfilment. You can see what mere
leaving it to fate brings. You can see how much marriage is to be
trusted to—look at your own mother."

25   "Do you think mother is abnormal?"

"No! I think she only wanted something more, or other than the
common run of life. And not getting it, she has gone wrong,
perhaps."

"After producing a brood of wrong children," said Gerald

30   gloomily.

"No more wrong than any of the rest of us," Birkin replied. "The
most normal people have the worst subterranean selves, take them
one by one."

"Sometimes I think it is a curse to be alive," said Gerald, with

35   sudden impotent anger.

"Well," said Birkin, "why not! Let it be a curse sometimes to be
alive—at other times it is anything but a curse. You've got plenty of
zest in it really."

"Less than you'd think," said Gerald, revealing a strange poverty

40   in his look at the other man.

There was silence, each thinking his own thoughts.

"She's a teacher already, isn't she?" said Gerald.* "I don't see what she has to distinguish between teaching at the Grammar School, and coming to teach Win."

"The difference between a public servant and a private one. The only nobleman today, king and only aristocrat, is the public, the public. You are quite willing to serve the public—but to be a private tutor—"

"I don't want to serve either—"

"No! And Gudrun will probably feel the same."

Gerald thought for a few minutes. Then he said:

"At all events, father won't make her feel like a private servant. He will be fussy and grateful enough."

"So he ought—and so ought all of you.—Do you think you can hire a woman like Gudrun Brangwen with money?—She is your equal like anything—probably your superior."

"Is she!" said Gerald.

"Yes. And if you haven't the guts to know it, I hope she'll leave you to your own devices."

"Nevertheless," said Gerald, "if she is my equal, I wish she weren't a teacher, because I don't think teachers as a rule are my equal."

"Nor do I, damn them. But am I a teacher because I teach, or a parson because I preach?—It bores me—."

Gerald laughed. He was always uneasy on this score. He did not *want* to claim social superiority, yet he *would* not* claim intrinsic personal superiority, because he would never base his standard of values on pure being. So he wobbled upon a tacit assumption of social standing. Now Birkin wanted him to accept the fact of intrinsic difference between human beings, which he did not intend to accept. It was against his social honor, his principle. He rose to go.

"I've been neglecting my business all this while," he said, smiling.

"I ought to have reminded you before," Birkin replied, laughing and mocking.

"I knew you'd say something like that," laughed Gerald, rather uneasily.

"Did you!"

"Yes, Rupert. It wouldn't do for us all to be like you are—we should soon be in the cart. When I am above the world, I shall ignore all businesses."

"Of course, we're not in the cart now," said Birkin, satirically.

"Not as much as you make out. At any rate, we have enough to eat and drink—"

"And be satisfied," added Birkin.

5   Gerald came near the bed, and stood looking down at Birkin whose throat was exposed, whose tossed hair fell attractively on the warm brow, above the eyes that were so unchallenged and still in the satirical face. Gerald, full-limbed and turgid with energy, stood unwilling to go, he was held by the presence of the other man. He

10 had not the power to go away.

"So," said Birkin, "goodbye." And he reached out his hand from under the bed-clothes, smiling with a glimmering look.

"Goodbye," said Gerald, taking the warm hand of his friend in a firm grasp. "I shall come again. I miss you down at the mill."

15 "I'll be there in a few days," said Birkin.

The eyes of the two men met again. Gerald's, that were keen as a hawk's, were suffused now with warm light and with unadmitted love, Birkin looked back as out of the darkness, unsounded and unknown, yet with a kind of warmth, that seemed to flow over

20 Gerald's brain like a fertile sleep.

"Goodbye then. There's nothing I can do for you?"

"Nothing, thanks."

Birkin watched the black-clothed form of the other man move out of the door, the bright head was gone, he turned over to sleep.

Chapter XVII

The Industrial Magnate*

In Beldover, there was both for Ursula and for Gudrun an interval. It seemed to Ursula as if Birkin had gone out of her for the time, he had lost his significance, he scarcely mattered in her world. She had her own friends, her own activities, her own life. She turned back to the old ways with zest, away from him.

And Gudrun, after feeling every moment in all her veins conscious of Gerald Crich, connected even physically with him, was now almost indifferent to the thought of him. She was nursing new schemes for going away and trying a new form of life. All the time, there was something in her urging her to avoid the final establishing of a relationship with Gerald. She felt it would be wiser and better to have no more than a casual acquaintance with him.

She had a scheme for going to St. Petersburg, where she had a friend who was a sculptor like herself, and who lived with a wealthy Russian whose hobby was jewel-making. The emotional, rather rootless life of the Russians appealed to her. She did not want to go to Paris. Paris was dry, and essentially boring. She would like to go to Rome, Munich, Vienna, or to St. Petersburg or Moscow. She had a friend in St. Petersburg and a friend in Munich. To each of these she wrote, asking about rooms.

She had a certain amount of money. She had come home partly to save, and now she had sold several pieces of work, she had been praised in various shows. She knew she could become quite the "go,"* if she went to London. But she knew London, she wanted something else. She had seventy pounds, of which nobody knew anything. She would move soon, as soon as she heard from her friends. Her nature, in spite of her apparent placidity and calm, was profoundly restless.

The sisters happened to call in a cottage in Willey Green to buy honey. Mrs Kirk, a stout, pale, sharp-nosed woman, sly, honied, with something shrewish and cat-like beneath, asked the girls into her too-cosy, too tidy kitchen. There was a cat-like comfort and cleanliness everywhere.

"Yes, Miss Brangwen," she said, in her slightly whining, insinuating voice, "and how do you like being back in the old place then?"

Gudrun, whom she addressed, hated her at once.

"I don't care for it," she replied abruptly.

5 "You don't? Ay, well, I suppose you find a difference from London. You like life, and big, grand places. Some of us has to be content with Willey Green and Beldover.—And what do you think of our Grammar School, as there's so much talk about?"

"What do I think of it?" Gudrun looked round at her slowly. "Do
10 you mean, do I think it's a good school?"

"Yes. What is your opinion of it?"

"I *do* think it's a good school."

Gudrun was very cold and repelling. She knew the common people hated the school.

15 "Ay, you do, then! I've heard so much, one way and the other. It's nice to know what those that's in it feel. But opinions vary, don't they? Mr Crich up at Shortlands* is all for it. Ay, poor man, I'm afraid he's not long for this world. He's very poorly."

"Is he worse?" asked Ursula.

20 "Eh, yes—since they lost Miss Diana. He's gone off to a shadow. Poor man, he's had a world of trouble."

"Has he?" asked Gudrun, faintly ironic.

"He has, a world of trouble. And as nice and kind a gentleman as ever you could wish to meet.—His children don't take after him."

25 "I suppose they take after their mother?" said Ursula.

"In many ways." Mrs Kirk lowered her voice a little. "She was a proud, haughty lady when she came into these parts—my word, she was that! She mustn't be looked at, and it was worth your life to speak to her."

30 The woman made a dry, sly face.*

"Did you know her when she was first married?"

"Yes, I knew her. I nursed three of her children.* And proper little terrors they were, little fiends—that Gerald was a demon if ever there was one, a proper demon, ay, at* six month's old."

35 A curious malicious, sly tone came into the woman's voice.

"Really!" said Gudrun.

"That wilful, masterful—he'd mastered one nurse at six months. Kick, and scream, and struggle like a demon! Many's the time I've pinched his little bottom for him, when he was a child in arms.—Ay,
40 and he'd have been better if he'd had it pinched oftener. But she

wouldn't have them corrected—no-o, wouldn't hear of it. I can remember the rows she had with Mr Crich, my word!—When he'd got worked up, properly worked up till he could stand no more, he'd lock the study door and whip them. But she paced up and down all the while like a tiger outside, like a tiger, with very murder in her face. She had a face that could *look* death. And when the door was opened, she'd go in with her hands lifted—'What have you been doing to *my* children, you coward.'—She was like one out of her mind. I believe he was frightened of her;—he had to be driven mad before he'd lift a finger. Didn't the servants have a life of it! And didn't we used to be thankful when one of them caught it. They were the torment of your life."

"Really!" said Gudrun.

"In every possible way. If you wouldn't let them smash their pots on the table, if you wouldn't let them drag the kitten about with a string round its neck, if you wouldn't give them whatever they asked for, every mortal thing—then there was a shine* on, and their mother coming in asking—'What's the matter with him? What have you done to him? What is it, Darling?' And then she'd turn on you as if she'd trample you under her feet.—But she didn't trample on me. I was the only one that could do anything with her demons—for she wasn't going to be bothered with them herself. No, *she* took no trouble for them. But they must just have their way, they mustn't be spoken to. And master Gerald was the beauty. I left when he was a year and a half, I could stand no more. But I pinched his little bottom for him when he was in arms, I did, when there was no holding him—and I'm not sorry I did—."

Gudrun went away in fury and loathing. The phrase, 'I pinched his little bottom for him,' sent her into a white, stony fury. She could not bear it, she wanted to have the woman taken out at once and strangled. And yet there the phrase was lodged in her mind for ever, beyond escape. She felt, one day, she would *have* to tell him, to see how he took it. And she loathed herself for the thought.

But at Shortlands the life-long struggle was coming to a close. The father was ill and was going to die. He had bad internal pains, which took away all his attentive life, and left him with only a vestige of his consciousness. More and more a silence came over him, he was less and less acutely aware of his surroundings. The pain seemed to absorb his activity. He knew it was there, he knew it would come again. It was like something lurking in the darkness within him.

And he had not the power, or the will, to seek it out and to know it. There it remained in the darkness, the great pain, tearing him at times, and then lying silent. And when it tore him he crouched in silent subjection under it, and when it left him alone again, he refused to know of it. It was within the darkness, let it remain unknown. So he never admitted it, except in a secret corner of himself, where all his never-revealed fears and secrets were accumulated. For the rest, he had a pain, it went away, it made no difference. It even stimulated him, excited him.

But it gradually absorbed his life. Gradually it drew away all his potentiality, it bled him into the dark, it weaned him of life and drew him away into the darkness. And in this twilight of his life, little remained visible to him. The business, his work, that was gone entirely. His public interests had disappeared as if they had never been. Even his family had become extraneous to him, he could only remember, in some slight, non-essential part of himself, that such and such were his children. It was superficial fact, not vital to him. He had to make an effort to know their relation to him. Even his wife barely existed. She indeed was like the darkness, like the pain within him. By some strange association, the darkness that contained the pain and the darkness that contained his wife were identical. All his thoughts and understandings became blurred and fused, and now his wife and the consuming pain were the same dark secret power against him, that he never faced. He never drove the dread out of its lair within him. He only knew that there was a dark place, and something inhabiting this darkness which issued from time to time and rent him. But he dared not penetrate and drive the beast into the open. He had rather ignore its existence. Only, in his vague way, the dread was his wife, the destroyer, and it was the pain, the destruction, a darkness which was one and both.

He very rarely saw his wife. She kept her room. Only occasionally she came forth, with her head stretched forward, and in her low, possessed voice, she asked him how he was. And he answered her, in the habit of more than thirty years: "Well, I don't think I'm any the worse, dear." But he was frightened of her, underneath this safeguard of habit, frightened almost to the verge of death.

But all his life, he had been so constant to his lights, he had never broken down. He would die even now without breaking down, without knowing what his feelings were, towards her. All his life, he had said: "Poor Christiana, she has such a strong temper." With unbroken will, he had stood by his position with regard to her, he had substituted pity for all his hostility, pity had been his shield and his safeguard, and his infallible weapon. And still, in his consciousness, he was sorry for her, her nature was so violent and so impatient.

But now his pity, with his life, was wearing thin, and the dread, almost amounting to horror, was rising into being. But before the armour of his pity really broke, he would die, as an insect when its shell is cracked. This was his final resource. Others would live on, and know the living death, the ensuing process of hopeless chaos. He would not. He denied death its victory.

He had been so constant to his lights, so constant to charity, and to his love for his neighbour. Perhaps he had loved his neighbour even better than himself*—which is going one further than the commandment. Always, this flame had burned in his heart, sustaining him through everything, the welfare of the people. He was a large employer of labour, he was a great mine-owner. And he had never lost this from his heart, that in Christ he was one with his workmen. Nay, he had felt inferior to them, as if they, through poverty and labour, were nearer to God than he. He had always the unacknowledged belief, that it was his workmen, the miners, who held in their hands the means of salvation. To move nearer to God, he must move towards his miners, his life must gravitate towards theirs. They were, unconsciously, his idol, his God made manifest. In them he worshipped the highest, the great, sympathetic, mindless Godhead of humanity.

And all the while, his wife had opposed him like one of the great demons of hell. Strange, like a bird of prey, with the fascinating beauty and abstraction of a hawk, she had beat against the bars of his philanthropy, and like a hawk in a cage, she had sunk into silence. By force of circumstance, because all the world combined to make the cage unbreakable, he had been too strong for her, he had kept her prisoner. And because she was his prisoner, his passion for her had always remained keen as death. He had always loved her, loved her with intensity. Within the cage, she was denied nothing, she was given all licence.

But she had gone almost mad. Of wild and overweening temper, she could not bear the humiliation of her husband's soft, half-appealing kindness to everybody. He was not deceived by the poor. He knew they came and sponged on him, and whined to him, the worse sort; the majority, luckily for him, were much too proud to ask

for anything, much too independent to come knocking at his door. But in Beldover, as everywhere else, there were the whining, parasitic, foul human beings who come crawling after charity, and feeding on the living body of the public like lice. A kind of fire would
5 go over Christiana Crich's brain, as she saw two more pale-faced, creeping women in objectionable black clothes, cringing lugubriously up the drive to the door. She wanted to set the dogs on them, "Hi Rip! Hi Ring! Ranger! At 'em boys, set 'em off." But Crowther, the butler, with all the rest of the servants, was Mr Crich's man.
10 Nevertheless, when her husband was away, she would come down like a wolf on the crawling supplicants; "What do you people want? There is nothing for you here. You have no business on the drive at all. Crowther,* drive them away, and let no more of them through the gate."

15 The servants had to obey her. And she would stand watching with an eye like the eagle's, whilst the groom in clumsy confusion drove the lugubrious persons down the drive, as if they were rusty fowls scuttling before him.

But they learned to know, from the lodge-keeper, when Mr Crich
20 was away, and they timed their visits. How many times, in the first years, would Crowther knock softly at the door: "Person to see you, sir."

"What name?"

"Grocock, sir."

25 "What do they want?" The question was half impatient, half gratified. He liked hearing appeals to his charity.

"About a child, sir."

"Show them into the library, and tell them they shouldn't come after eleven o'clock in the morning."

30 "Why do you get up from dinner?—send them off," his wife would say abruptly.

"Oh, I can't do that. It's no trouble just to hear what they have to say."

"How many more have been here today? Why don't you establish
35 open house for them? They would soon oust me and the children."

"You know dear, it doesn't hurt me to hear what they have to say. And if they really are in trouble—well, it is my duty to help them out of it."

"It's your duty to invite all the rats in the world to gnaw at your
40 bones."

"Come, Christiana, it isn't like that. Don't be uncharitable."

But she suddenly swept out of the room, and out to the study. There sat the meagre charity-seekers, looking as if they were at the doctor's.

"Mr Crich can't see you. He can't see you at this hour. Do you think he is your property, that you can come whenever you like? You must go away, there is nothing for you here."

The poor people rose in confusion. But Mr Crich, pale and black-bearded and deprecating, came behind her, saying:

"Yes, I don't like you coming as late as this. I'll hear any of you in the morning part of the day, but I can't really do with you after.—What's amiss then, Gittins? How is your Missis?"

"Why, she's sunk very low, Mester Crich, she's a'most gone, she is—"

Sometimes, it seemed to Mrs Crich as if her husband were some subtle funeral bird, feeding on the miseries of the people. It seemed to her he was never satisfied unless there was some sordid tale being poured out to him, which he drank in with a sort of mournful, sympathetic satisfaction. He would have no *raison d'être* if there were no lugubrious miseries in the world, as an undertaker would have no meaning if there were no funerals.

Mrs Crich recoiled back upon herself, she recoiled away from this world of creeping democracy. A band of tight, baleful exclusion fastened round her heart, her isolation was fierce and hard, her antagonism was passive but terribly pure, like that of a hawk in a cage. As the years went on, she lost more and more count of the world, she seemed rapt in some glittering abstraction, almost purely unconscious. She would wander about the house and about the surrounding country, staring keenly and seeing nothing. She rarely spoke, she had no connection with the world. And she did not even think. She was consumed in a fierce tension of opposition, like the negative pole of a magnet.

And she bore many children. For, as time went on, she never opposed her husband in word or deed. She took no notice of him, externally. She submitted to him, let him take what he wanted and do as he wanted with her. She was like a hawk that sullenly submits to everything. The relation between her and her husband was wordless and unknown, but it was deep, awful, a relation of utter interdestruction. And he, who triumphed in the world, he became more and more hollow in his vitality, the vitality was bled from within him, as by some hemorrhage. She was hulked like a hawk in a cage, but her heart was fierce and undiminished within her, though her mind was destroyed.

So to the last he would go to her and hold her in his arms, 5 sometimes, before his strength was all gone. The terrible white, destructive light that burned in her eyes only excited and roused him. Till he was bled to death, and then he dreaded her more than anything. But he always said to himself, how happy he had been, how he had loved her with a pure and consuming love ever since he had 10 known her. And he thought of her as pure, chaste, the white flame which was known to him alone, the flame of her sex, was a white flower of snow to his mind. She was a wonderful white snow-flower, which he had desired infinitely. And now he was dying with all his ideas and interpretations intact. They would only collapse when the 15 breath left his body. Till then they would be pure truths for him. Only death would show the perfect completeness of the lie. Till death, she was his white snow-flower. He had subdued her, and her subjugation was to him an infinite chastity in her, a virginity which he could never break, and which dominated him as by a spell.

20 She had let go the outer world, but within herself she was unbroken and unimpaired. She only sat in her room like a moping, dishevelled hawk, motionless, mindless. Her children, for whom she had been so fierce in her youth, now meant scarcely anything to her. She had lost all that, she was quite by herself. Only Gerald, the 25 gleaming, had some existence for her. But of late years, since he had become head of the business, he too was forgotten.

Whereas the father, now he was dying, turned for compassion to Gerald. There had always been opposition between the two of them. Gerald had feared and despised his father, and to a great extent had 30 avoided him all through boyhood and young manhood. And the father had felt very often a real dislike of his eldest son, which, never wanting to give way to, he had refused to acknowledge. He had ignored Gerald as much as possible, leaving him alone.

Since, however, Gerald had come home and assumed responsi-35 bility in the firm, and had proved such a wonderful director, the father, tired and weary of all outside concerns, had put all his trust of these things in his son, implicitly, leaving everything to him, and assuming a rather touching dependence on the young enemy. This immediately roused a poignant pity and allegiance in Gerald's heart, 40 always shadowed by contempt and by the unadmitted enmity. For

Gerald was in reaction against Charity, yet he was dominated by it; it assumed supremacy in the inner life, and he could not confute it. So he was partly subject to that which his father stood for, but he was in reaction against it. Now he could not save himself. A certain pity and grief and tenderness for his father overcame him, in spite of the deeper, more sullen hostility.

The father won shelter from Gerald through compassion. But for love he had Winifred. She was his youngest child, she was the only one of his children whom he had ever closely loved. And her he loved with all the great, overweening, sheltering love of a dying man. He wanted to shelter her infinitely, infinitely, to wrap her in warmth and love and shelter, perfectly. If he could save her she should never know one pain, one grief, one hurt. He had been so right all his life, so constant in his kindness and his goodness. And this was his last passionate righteousness, his love for the child Winifred. Some things troubled him yet. The world had passed away from him, as his strength ebbed. There were no more poor and injured and humble to protect and succour. These were all lost to him. There were no more sons and daughters to trouble him, and to weigh on him as an unnatural responsibility. These too had faded out of reality. All these things had fallen out of his hands, and left him free.

There remained the covert fear and horror of his wife, as she sat mindless and strange in her room, or as she came forth with slow, prowling step, her head bent forward. But this he put away. Even his life-long righteousness, however, would not quite deliver him from the inner horror. Still, he could keep it sufficiently at bay. It would never break forth openly. Death would come first.

Then there was Winifred! If only he could be sure about her, if only he could be sure. Since the death of Diana, and the development of his illness, his craving for surety with regard to Winifred amounted almost to obsession. It was as if, even dying, he must have some anxiety, some responsibility of love, of Charity, upon his heart.

She was an odd, sensitive, inflammable child, having her father's dark hair and quiet bearing, but being quite detached, momentaneous. She was like a changeling indeed, as if her feelings did not matter to her, really. She often seemed to be talking and playing like the gayest and most childish of children, she was full of the warmest, most delightful affection for a few things—for her father, and for her animals in particular. But if she heard that her beloved kitten Leo had been run over by the motor-car, she put her

head on one side, and replied, with a faint contraction like
resentment on her face: "Has he?" Then she took no more notice.
She only disliked the servant who would force bad news on her, and
wanted her to be sorry. She wished not to know, and that seemed her
chief motive. She avoided her mother, and most of the members of
her family. She *loved* her Daddy, because he wanted her always to be
happy, and because he seemed to become young again, and irresponsible in her presence. She liked Gerald, because he was so
self-contained. She loved people who would make life a game for
her. She had an amazing instinctive critical faculty, and was a pure
anarchist, a pure aristocrat at once. For she accepted her equals
wherever she found them, and she ignored with blithe indifference
her inferiors, whether they were her brothers and sisters, or whether
they were wealthy guests of the house, or whether they were the
common people or the servants. She was quite single and by herself,
deriving from nobody. It was as if she were cut off from all purpose
or continuity, and existed simply moment by moment.

The father, as by some strange final illusion, felt as if all his fate
depended on his ensuring to Winifred her happiness. She who could
never suffer, because she never formed vital connections, she who
could lose the dearest things of her life and be just the same the next
day, the whole memory dropped out, as if deliberately, she whose
will was so strangely and easily free, anarchistic, almost nihilistic,
who like a soulless bird flits on its own will, without attachment or
responsibility beyond the moment, who in her every motion snapped
the threads of serious relationship, with blithe, free hands, really
nihilistic, because never troubled, she must be the object of her
father's final passionate solicitude.

When Mr Crich heard that Gudrun Brangwen might come to help
Winifred with her drawing and modelling he saw a road to salvation
for his child. He believed that Winifred had talent, he had seen
Gudrun, he knew that she was an exceptional person. He could give
Winifred into her hands as into the hands of a right being. Here was
a direction and a positive force to be lent to his child, he need not
leave her directionless and defenceless. If he could but graft the girl
on to some tree of utterance before he died, he would have fulfilled
his responsibility. And here it could be done. He did not hesitate to
appeal to Gudrun.

Meanwhile, as the father drifted more and more out of life, Gerald
experienced more and more a sense of exposure. His father after all

had stood for the living world to him. Whilst his father lived, Gerald
was not responsible for the world. But now his father was passing
away, Gerald found himself left exposed and unready before the
storm of living, like the mutinous first mate of a ship that has lost its
captain, and who sees only a terrible chaos in front of him. He did   5
not inherit an established order and a living idea. The whole unifying
idea of mankind seemed to be dying with his father, the centralising
force that had held the whole together seemed to collapse with his
father, the parts were ready to go asunder in terrible disintegration.
Gerald was as if left on board of a ship that was going asunder   10
beneath his feet, he was in charge of a vessel whose timbers were all
coming apart.

He knew that all his life he had been wrenching at the frame of life
to break it apart. And now, with something of the terror of a
destructive child, he saw himself on the point of inheriting his own   15
destruction. And during the last months, under the influence of
death, and of Birkin's talk, and of Gudrun's penetrating being, he
had lost entirely that mechanical certainty that had been his triumph.
Sometimes spasms of hatred came over him, against Birkin and
Gudrun and that whole set. He wanted to go back to the dullest   20
conservatism, to the most stupid of conventional people. He wanted
to revert to the strictest Toryism. But the desire did not last long
enough to carry him into action.

During his childhood and his boyhood he had wanted a sort of
savage freedom. The days of Homer were his ideal, when a man was   25
chief of an army of heroes, or spent his years in wonderful Odyssey.
He hated remorselessly the circumstances of his own life, so much
so that he never really saw Beldover and the colliery valley. He
turned his face entirely away from the blackened mining region that
stretched away on the right hand of Shortlands, he turned entirely to   30
the country and the woods beyond Willey Water. It was true that the
panting and rattling of the coal-mines could always be heard at
Shortlands. But from his earliest childhood, Gerald had paid no
heed to this. He had ignored the whole of the industrial sea which
surged in coal-blackened tides against the grounds of the house.   35
The world was really a wilderness where one hunted and swam and
rode. He rebelled against all authority. Life was a condition of savage
freedom.

Then he had been sent away to school, which was so much death
to him. He refused to go to Oxford, choosing a German university.   40

He had spent a certain time at Bonn, at Berlin, and at Frankfurt.*
There, a curiosity had been aroused in his mind. He wanted to see
and to know, in a curious objective fashion, as if it were an
amusement to him. Then he must try war. Then he must travel into
5   the savage regions that had so attracted him.

The result was, he found humanity very much alike everywhere,
and to a mind like his, curious and cold, the savage was duller, less
exciting than the European. So he took hold of all kinds of
sociological ideas, and ideas of reform. But they never went more
10   than skin-deep, they were never more than a mental amusement.
Their interest lay chiefly in the reaction against the positive order,
the destructive reaction.

He discovered at last a real adventure in the coal-mines. His
father asked him to help in the firm. Gerald had been educated in the
15   science of mining, and it had never interested him. Now, suddenly,
with a sort of exultation, he laid hold of the world.

There was impressed photographically on his consciousness the
great industry. Suddenly, it was real, he was part of it. Down the
valley ran the colliery railway, linking mine with mine. Down the
20   railway ran the trains, short trains of heavily-laden trucks, long trains
of empty wagons, each one bearing in big white letters the initials:
"C. B. & Co."*

These white letters on all the wagons he had seen since his first
childhood, and it was as if he had never seen them, they were so
25   familiar, and so ignored. Now at last he saw his own name written on
the wall. Now he had a vision of power.

So many wagons, bearing his initial, running all over the country.
He saw them as he entered London in the train, he saw them at
Dover. So far his power ramified. He looked at Beldover, at Selby, at
30   Whatmore, at Lethley Bank, the great colliery villages which
depended entirely on his mines. They were hideous and sordid,
during his childhood they had been sores in his consciousness. And
now he saw them with pride. Four raw new towns, and many ugly
industrial hamlets were crowded under his dependence. He saw the
35   stream of miners flowing along the causeways from the mines at the
end of the afternoon, thousands of blackened, slightly distorted
human beings with red mouths, all moving subjugate to his will. He
pushed slowly in his motor-car through the little market-top on
Friday nights in Beldover, through a solid mass of human beings that
40   were making their purchases and doing their weekly spending. They

were all subordinate to him. They were ugly and uncouth, but they were his instruments. He was the God of the machine. They made way for his motor-car automatically, slowly.

He did not care whether they made way with alacrity, or grudgingly. He did not care what they thought of him. His vision had suddenly crystallised. Suddenly he had conceived the pure instrumentality of mankind. There had been so much humanitarianism, so much talk of sufferings and feelings. It was ridiculous. The sufferings and feelings of individuals did not matter in the least. They were mere conditions, like the weather. What mattered was the pure instrumentality of the individual. As a man as of a knife: does it cut well? Nothing else mattered.

Everything in the world has its function, and is good or not good in so far as it fulfils this function more or less perfectly.* Was a miner a good miner? Then he was complete. Was a manager a good manager? That was enough. Gerald himself, who was responsible for all this industry, was he a good director? If he were, he had fulfilled his life. The rest was by-play.

The mines were there, they were old. They were giving out, it did not pay to work the seams. There was talk of closing down two of them.* It was at this point that Gerald arrived on the scene.

He looked around. There lay the mines. They were old, obsolete. They were like old lions, no more good. He looked again. Pah! the mines were nothing but the clumsy efforts of impure minds. There they lay, abortions of a half-trained mind. Let the idea of them be swept away. He cleared his brain of them, and thought only of the coal in the under earth. How much was there?

There was plenty of coal. The old workings could not get at it, that was all. Then break the neck of the old workings. The coal lay there in its seams, even though the seams were thin. There it lay, inert matter, as it had always lain, since the beginning of time, subject to the will of man. The will of man was the determining factor. Man was the arch-god of earth. His mind was obedient to serve his will. Man's will was the absolute, the only absolute.

And it was his will to subjugate Matter to his own ends. The subjugation itself was the point, the fight was the be-all, the fruits of victory were mere results. It was not for the sake of money that Gerald took over the mines. He did not care about money, fundamentally. He was neither ostentatious nor luxurious, neither did he care about social position, not finally. What he wanted was the pure

fulfilment of his own will in the struggle with the natural conditions. His will was now, to take the coal out of the earth, profitably. The profit was merely the condition of victory, but the victory itself lay in the feat achieved. He vibrated with zest before the challenge. Every
5 day he was in the mines, examining, testing, he consulted experts, he gradually gathered the whole situation into his mind, as a general grasps the plan of his campaign.

Then there was need for a complete break. The mines were run on an old system, an obsolete idea. The initial idea had been, to
10 obtain as much money from the earth as would make the owners comfortably rich, would allow the workmen sufficient wages and good conditions, and would increase the wealth of the country altogether. Gerald's father, following in the second generation,* having a sufficient fortune, had thought only of the men. The mines,
15 for him, were primarily great fields to produce bread and plenty for all the hundreds of human beings gathered about them. He had lived and striven with his fellow owners to benefit the men every time. And the men had been benefited in their fashion. There were few poor, and few needy. All was plenty, because the mines were good and easy
20 to work. And the miners, in those days, finding themselves richer than they might have expected, felt glad and triumphant. They thought themselves well-off, they congratulated themselves on their good-fortune, they remembered how their fathers had starved and suffered, and they felt that better times had come. They were
25 grateful to those others, the pioneers, the new owners, who had opened out the pits, and let forth this stream of plenty.

But man is never satisfied, and soon* the miners, from gratitude to their owners, passed on to murmuring. Their sufficiency decreased with knowledge, they wanted more. Why should the masters be so
30 out-of-all-proportion rich?

There was a crisis when Gerald was a boy, when the Masters' Federation closed down the mines because the men would not accept a reduction.* This lock-out had forced home the new conditions to Thomas Crich. Belonging to the Federation, he had
35 been compelled by his honor to close the pits against his men. He, the father, the patriarch, was forced to deny the means of life to his sons, his people. He, the rich man who would hardly enter heaven because of his possessions,* must now turn upon the poor, upon those who were nearer Christ than himself, those who were humble
40 and despised and closer to perfection, those who were manly and

noble in their labours, and must say to them: "Ye shall neither labour nor eat bread."*

It was this recognition of the state of war which really broke his heart. He wanted his industry to be run on love, Oh, he wanted love to be the directing power even of the mines. And now, from under the cloak of love, the sword was cynically drawn, the sword of mechanical necessity.

This really broke his heart. He must have the illusion—and now the illusion was destroyed.—The men were not against *him*, but they were against the masters. It was war, and willy nilly he found himself on the wrong side, in his own conscience. Seething masses of miners met daily, carried away by a new religious impulse. The idea flew through them: "All men are equal on earth," and they would carry the idea to its material fulfilment. After all, is it not the teaching of Christ? And what is an idea, if not the germ of action in the material world. "All men are equal in spirit, they are all sons of God. Whence then this obvious disquality?"* It was a religious creed pushed to its material conclusion. Thomas Crich at least had no answer. He could but admit, according to his sincere tenets, that the disquality was wrong. But he could not give up his goods, which were the stuff of disquality. So the men would fight for their rights. The last impulses of the last religious passion left on earth, the passion for equality, inspired them.

Seething mobs of men marched about, their faces lighted up as for holy war, with a smoke of cupidity. How disentangle the passion for equality from the passion of cupidity, when begins the fight for equality of possessions? But the God was the machine. Each man claimed equality in the Godhead of the great productive machine. Every man equally was part of this Godhead.—But somehow, somewhere, Thomas Crich knew this was false. When the machine is the Godhead, and production or work is worship, then the most mechanical mind is purest and highest, the representative of God on earth—and the rest are subordinate, each according to his degree.

Riots broke out, Whatmore pit-head was in flames. This was the pit furthest in the country, near the woods. Soldiers came. From the windows of Shortlands, on that fatal day, could be seen the flare of fire in the sky not far off, and now the little colliery train, with the workmen's carriages which were used to convey the miners to the distant Whatmore, was crossing the valley full of soldiers, full of red-coats. Then there was the far-off sound of firing, then the later news that the mob was dispersed, one man was shot dead, the fire was put out.*

Gerald, who was a boy, was filled with the wildest excitement and delight. He longed to go with the soldiers to shoot the men. But he was not allowed to go out of the lodge gates. At the gates were stationed sentries with guns. Gerald stood near them in delight, whilst gangs of derisive miners strolled up and down the lanes, calling and jeering:

"Now then, three ha'porth o' coppers,* let's see thee shoot thy gun." Insults were chalked on the walls and the fences, the servants left.

And all this while Thomas Crich was breaking his heart, and giving away hundreds of pounds in charity. Everywhere there was free food, a surfeit of free food. Anybody could have bread for asking, and a loaf cost only three-ha'pence. Every day there was a free tea somewhere, the children had never had so many treats in their lives. On Friday afternoon great basketfuls of buns and cakes were taken into the schools,* and great pitchers of milk, the school-children had what they wanted. They were sick with eating too much cake and milk.

And then it came to an end, and the men went back to work. But it was never the same as before. There was a new situation created, a new idea reigned. Even in the machine, there should be equality. No part should be subordinate to any other part: all should be equal. The instinct for chaos had entered. Mystic equality lies in abstraction, not in having or in doing, which are processes. In function and process, one man, one part, must of necessity be subordinate to another. It is a condition of being.—But the desire for chaos had risen, and the idea of mechanical equality was the weapon of disruption which should execute the will of man, the will for chaos.

Gerald was a boy at the time of the strike, but he longed to be a man, to fight the colliers.—The father however was trapped between two half-truths, and broken. He wanted to be a pure Christian, one and equal with all men. He even wanted to give away all he had, to the poor.*—Yet he was a great promoter of industry, and he knew perfectly that he must keep his goods and keep his authority. This was as divine a necessity in him, as the need to give away all he possessed—more divine, even, since this was the necessity he acted upon. Yet because he did *not* act on the other ideal, it dominated him, he was dying of chagrin because he must forfeit it. He wanted to be a father of loving-kindness and sacrificial benevolence. The colliers shouted to him about his thousands a year. They would not be deceived.

When Gerald grew up in the ways of the world, he shifted the position. He did not care about the equality. The whole Christian attitude of love and self-sacrifice was old hat. He knew that position and authority were the right thing in the world, and it was useless to cant about it. They were the right thing, for the simple reason that they were functionally necessary. They were not the be-all and the end-all. It was like being part of a machine. He himself happened to be a controlling, central part, the masses of men were the parts variously controlled. This was merely as it happened. As well get excited because a central hub drives a hundred outer wheels—or because the whole universe wheels round the sun. After all, it would be mere silliness to say that the moon and the earth and Saturn and Jupiter and Venus have just as much right to be the centre of the universe, each of them separately, as the sun. Such an assertion is made merely in the desire of chaos.

Without bothering to *think* to a conclusion, Gerald jumped to a conclusion. He abandoned the whole democratic-equality problem as a problem of silliness. What mattered was the great social productive machine. Let that work perfectly, let it produce a sufficiency of everything, let every man be given a rational portion, greater or less according to his functional degree or magnitude, and then, provision made, let the devil supervene, let every man look after his own amusements and appetites, so long as he interfered with nobody.

So Gerald set himself to work, to put the great industry in order. In his travels, and in his accompanying readings, he had come to the conclusion that the essential secret of life was harmony. He did not define to himself at all clearly what harmony was. The word pleased him, he felt he had come to his own conclusions. And he proceeded to put his philosophy into practice by forcing order into the established world, translating the mystic word harmony into the practical word organisation.

Immediately he *saw* the firm, he realised what he could do. He had a fight to fight with Matter, with the earth and the coal it enclosed. This was the sole idea, to turn upon the inanimate matter of the underground, and reduce it to his will. And for this fight with matter, one must have perfect instruments in perfect organisation, a

mechanism so subtle and harmonious in its workings that it represents the single mind of man, and by its relentless repetition of given
movement, will accomplish a purpose irresistibly, inhumanly. It was
this inhuman principle in the mechanism he wanted to construct that
5 inspired Gerald with an almost religious exaltation. He, the man,
could interpose a perfect, changeless, godlike medium between
himself and the Matter he had to subjugate. There were two
opposites, his will and the resistant Matter of the earth. And between
these he could establish the very expression of his will, the incar-
10 nation of his power, a great and perfect machine, a system, an activity
of pure order, pure mechanical repetition, repetition ad infinitum,
hence eternal and infinite. He found his eternal and his infinite in
the pure machine-principle of perfect co-ordination into one pure,
complex, infinitely repeated motion, like the spinning of a wheel; but
15 a productive spinning, as the revolving of the universe may be called
a productive spinning, a productive repetition through eternity, to
infinity. And this is the God-motion, this productive repetition ad
infinitum. And Gerald was the God of the Machine, Deus ex
Machina.* And the whole productive will of man was the Godhead.
20 He had his life-work now, to extend over the earth a great and
perfect system in which the will of man ran smooth and unthwarted,
timeless, a Godhead in process. He had to begin with the mines.
The terms were given: first the resistant Matter of the underground;
then the instruments of its subjugation, instruments human and
25 metallic; and finally his own pure will, his own mind. It would need a
marvellous adjustment of myriad instruments, human, animal,
metallic, kinetic, dynamic, a marvellous casting of myriad tiny wholes
in to one great perfect entirety. And then, in this case there was
perfection attained, the will of the highest was perfectly fulfilled, the
30 will of mankind was perfectly enacted; for was not mankind mystically contradistinguished against inanimate Matter, was not the
history of mankind just the history of the conquest of the one by the
other?
The miners were overreached. While they were still in the toils of
35 divine equality of man, Gerald had passed on, granted essentially
their case, and proceeded in his quality of human being to fulfil the
will of mankind as a whole. He merely represented the miners in a
higher sense when he perceived that the only way to fulfil perfectly
the will of man was to establish the perfect, inhuman machine. But
40 he represented them very essentially, they were far behind, out of

date, squabbling for their material equality. The desire had already transmuted into this new and greater desire, for a perfect intervening mechanism between man and Matter, the desire to translate the Godhead into pure mechanism.

As soon as Gerald entered the firm, the convulsion of death ran 5 through the old system. He had all his life been tortured by a furious and destructive demon, which possessed him sometimes like an insanity. This temper now entered like a virus into the firm, and there were cruel eruptions. Terrible and inhuman were his examinations into every detail; there was no privacy he would spare, no old 10 sentiment but he would turn it over. The old grey managers, the old grey clerks, the doddering old pensioners, he looked at them, and removed them* as so much lumber. The whole concern seemed like a hospital of invalid employees. He had no emotional qualms. He arranged what pensions were necessary, he looked for efficient 15 substitutes, and when these were found, he substituted them for the old hands.

"I've a pitiful letter here from Letherinton," his father would say, in a tone of deprecation and appeal. "Don't you think the poor fellow might keep on a little longer. I always fancied he did very well." 20

"I've got a man in his place now, father. He'll be happier out of it, believe me. You think his allowance is plenty, don't you?"

"It is not the allowance that he wants, poor man. He feels it very much, that he is superannuated. Says he thought he had twenty more years of work in him yet." 25

"Not of this kind of work I want. He doesn't understand."

The father sighed. He wanted not to know any more. He believed the pits would have to be overhauled if they were to go on working. And after all, it would be worst in the long run for everybody, if they must close down. So he could make no answer to the appeals of his 30 old and trusty servants, he could only repeat "Gerald says."

So the father withdrew more and more out of the light. The whole frame of the real life was broken for him. He had been right according to his lights. And his lights had been those of the great religion. Yet they seemed to have become obsolete, to be superseded 35 in the world. He could not understand. He only withdrew his lights into an inner room, into the silence. The beautiful candles of belief, that would not do to light the world any more, they would still burn sweetly and sufficiently in the inner room of his soul, and in the silence of his retirement. 40

Gerald rushed into the reform of the firm, beginning with the office. It was needful to economise severely, to make possible the great alterations he must introduce.

"What are these widows' coals?" he asked.

5   "We have always allowed all widows of men who worked for the firm a load of coals every three months."

"They must pay cost price henceforward. The firm is not a charity institution, as everybody seems to think."

Widows, these stock figures of sentimental humanitarianism, he 10 felt a dislike at* the thought of them. They were almost repulsive. Why were they not immolated on the pyre of the husband, like the sati in India?* At any rate, let them pay the cost of their coals.

In a thousand ways he cut down the expenditure, in ways so fine as to be hardly noticeable to the men. The miners must pay for the 15 cartage of their coals, heavy cartage too; they must pay for their tools, for the sharpening, for the care of lamps, for many trifling things that made the bill of charges against every man mount up to a shilling or so in the week. It was not grasped very definitely by the miners, though they were sore enough. But it saved hundreds of pounds 20 every week for the firm.

Gradually Gerald got hold of everything. And then began the great reform. Expert engineers were introduced in every department. An enormous electric plant was installed, both for lighting and for haulage underground, and for power. The electricity was carried 25 to every mine. New machinery was brought from America, such as the miners had never seen before, great iron men, as the cutting machines were called, and unusual appliances. The working of the pits was thoroughly changed,* all the control was taken out of the hands of the miners, the butty system was abolished.* Everything 30 was run on the most accurate and delicate scientific method, educated and expert men were in control everywhere, the miners were reduced to mere mechanical instruments. They had to work hard, much harder than before, the work was terrible and heart-breaking in its mechanicalness.

35   But they submitted to it all.* The joy went out of their lives, the hope seemed to perish as they became more and more mechanised. And yet they accepted the new conditions. They even got a further satisfaction out of them. At first they hated Gerald Crich, they swore to do something to him, to murder him. But as time went on, they 40 accepted everything with some fatal satisfaction. Gerald was their

high priest, he represented the religion they really felt. His father was forgotten already. There was a new world, a new order, strict, terrible, inhuman, but satisfying in its very destructiveness. The men were satisfied to belong to the great and wonderful machine, even whilst it destroyed them. It was what they wanted, it was the highest that man had produced, the most wonderful and super-human. They were exalted by belonging to this great and super-human system which was beyond feeling or reason, something really godlike. Their hearts died within them, but their souls were satis-fied. It was what they wanted. Otherwise Gerald could never have done what he did. He was just ahead of them in giving them what they wanted, this participation in a great and perfect system that subjected life to pure mathematical principles. This was a sort of freedom, the sort they really wanted. It was the first great step in undoing, the first great phase of chaos, the substitution of the mechanical principle for the organic, the destruction of the organic purpose, the organic unity, and the subordination of every organic unit to the great mechanical purpose. It was pure organic disintegra-tion and pure mechanical organisation. This is the first and finest state of chaos.

Gerald was satisfied. He knew the colliers said they hated him. But he had long ceased to hate them. When they streamed past him at evening, their heavy boots slurring on the pavement wearily, their shoulders slightly distorted, they took no notice of him, they gave him no greeting whatever, they passed in a grey-black stream of unemotional acceptance. They were not important to him, save as instruments, nor he to them, save as a supreme instrument of control. As miners they had their being, he had his being as director. He admired their qualities. But as men, personalities, they were just accidents, sporadic little unimportant phenomena.—And tacitly, the men agreed to this. For Gerald agreed to it in himself.

He had succeeded. He had converted the industry into a new and terrible purity. There was a greater output of coal than ever,* the wonderful and delicate system ran almost perfectly. He had a set of really clever engineers, both mining and electrical, and they did not cost much. A highly educated man cost very little more than a workman. His managers, who were all rare men, were no more expensive than the old bungling fools of his father's day, who were merely colliers promoted. His chief manager, who had twelve hundred a year, saved the firm at least five thousand. The whole system was now so perfect that Gerald was hardl necessary any more.

It was so perfect, that sometimes, a strange fear came over him, and he did not know what to do. He went on for some years in a sort of trance of activity. What he was doing seemed supreme, he was almost like a divinity. He was a pure and exalted activity.

But now he had succeeded—he had finally succeeded. And once or twice lately, when he was alone in the evening and had nothing to do, he had suddenly stood up in terror, not knowing what he was. And he went to the mirror and looked long and closely at his own face, at his own eyes, seeking for something. He was afraid, in mortal dry fear, but he knew not what of. He looked at his own face. There it was, shapely and healthy and the same as ever, yet somehow, it was not real, it was a mask. He dared not touch it, for fear it should prove to be only a composition mask. His eyes were blue and keen as ever, and as firm in their sockets. Yet he was not sure that they were not blue false bubbles that would burst in a moment and leave clear annihilation. He could see the darkness in them, as if they were only bubbles of darkness. He was afraid that one day he would break down and be a purely meaningless babble lapping round a darkness.

But his will yet held good, he was able to go away and read, and think about things. He liked to read books about the primitive man, books of anthropology, and also works of speculative philosophy. His mind was very active. But it was like a bubble floating in the darkness. At any moment it might burst and leave him in chaos. He would not die. He knew that. He would go on living, but the meaning would have collapsed out of him, his divine reason would be gone. In a strangely indifferent, sterile way, he was frightened. But he could not react even to the fear. It was as if his centres of feeling were drying up. He remained calm, calculative and healthy, and quite freely deliberate, even whilst he felt, with faint, small, but final, sterile horror, that his mystic reason was breaking, giving way now, at this crisis.

And it was a strain. He knew there was no equilibrium. He would have to go in some direction, shortly, to find relief. Only Birkin kept the fear definitely off him, saved him his quick sufficiency in life, by the odd mobility and changeableness which seemed to contain the quintessence of faith. But then Gerald must always come away from Birkin, as from a church service, back to the outside real world of work and life. There it was, it did not alter, and words were futilities.

He had to keep himself in reckoning with the world of work and material life. And it became more and more difficult, such a strange pressure was upon him, as if the very middle of him were a vacuum, and outside were an awful tension.

He had found his most satisfactory relief in women. After a debauch with some desperate woman, he went on quite easy and forgetful. The devil of it was, it was so hard to keep up his interest in women nowadays. He didn't care about them any more. A Pussum was all right in her way, but she was an exceptional case, and even she mattered extremely little. No, women, in that sense, were useless to him any more. He felt that his *mind* needed acute stimulation, before he could be physically roused.

Chapter XVIII

Rabbit

Gudrun knew that it was a critical thing for her to go to Shortlands. She knew it was equivalent to accepting Gerald Crich as a lover. And though she hung back, disliking the condition, yet she knew she would go on. She equivocated. She said to herself, in torment recalling the blow and the kiss, "After all, what is it? What is a kiss? What even is a blow? It is an instant, vanished at once. I can go to Shortlands just for a time, before I go away, if only to see what it is like." For she had an insatiable curiosity to see and to know everything.

She also wanted to know what Winifred was really like. Having heard the child calling from the steamer in the night, she felt some mysterious connection with her.

Gudrun talked with the father in the library. Then he sent for his daughter. She came accompanied by Mademoiselle.*

"Winnie, this is Miss Brangwen, who will be so kind as to help you with your drawing and making models of your animals," said the father.

The child looked at Gudrun for a moment with interest, before she came forward and with face averted offered her hand. There was a complete sang froid and indifference under Winifred's childish reserve, a certain irresponsible callousness.

"How do you do?" said the child, not lifting her face.

"How do you do," said Gudrun.

Then Winifred stood aside, and Gudrun was introduced to Mademoiselle.

"You have a fine day for your walk," said Mademoiselle, in a bright manner.

"*Quite* fine," said Gudrun.

Winifred was watching from her distance. She was as if amused, but rather unsure as yet what this new person was like. She saw so many new persons, and so few who became real to her. Mademoiselle was of no count whatever, the child merely put up with her, calmly and easily, accepting her little authority with faint scorn, compliant out of childish arrogance of indifference.

234

"Well Winifred," said the father, "aren't you glad Miss Brangwen has come? She makes animals and birds in wood and in clay, that the people in London write about in the papers, praising them to the skies."

Winifred smiled slightly.

"Who told you, Daddy?" she asked.

"Who told me? Hermione told me, and Rupert Birkin."

"Do you know them?" Winifred asked, of Gudrun, turning to her with faint challenge.

"Yes," said Gudrun.

Winifred readjusted herself a little. She had been ready to accept Gudrun as a sort of servant. Now she saw it was on terms of friendship they were intended to meet. She was rather glad. She had so many half inferiors, whom she tolerated with perfect good-humour.

Gudrun was very calm. She also did not take these things very seriously. A new occasion was mostly spectacular to her. However, Winifred was a detached, ironic child, she would never attach herself. Gudrun liked her and was intrigued by her. The first meetings went off with a certain humiliating clumsiness. Neither Winifred nor her instructress had any social grace.

Soon however, they met in a kind of make-believe world. Winifred did not notice human beings, unless they were like herself, playful and slightly mocking. She would accept nothing but the world of amusement, and the serious people of her life were the animals she had for pets. On those she lavished, almost ironically, her affection and her companionship. To the rest of the human scheme she submitted with a faint bored indifference.

She had a pekinese dog called Looloo, which she loved.

"Let us draw Looloo," said Gudrun, "and see if we can get his Looliness, shall we?"

"Darling!" cried Winifred, rushing to the dog, that sat with contemplative sadness on the hearth, and kissing its bulging brow. "Darling one, will you be drawn? Shall its mummy draw its portrait?" Then she chuckled gleefully, and turning to Gudrun, said: "Oh let's!"

They proceeded to get pencils and paper, and were ready.

"Beautifullest," cried Winifred, hugging the dog, "sit still while its mummy draws its beautiful portrait." The dog looked up at her with grievous resignation in its large, prominent eyes. She kissed it fervently, and said: "I wonder what mine will be like. It's sure to be awful."

As she sketched she chuckled to herself, and cried out at times: "Oh darling, you're so beautiful!"

5 And* again chuckling, she rushed to embrace the dog, in penitence, as if she were doing him some subtle injury. He sat all the time with the resignation and fretfulness of ages on his dark velvety face. She drew slowly, with a wicked concentration in her eyes, her head on one side, an intense stillness over her. She was as if working the 10 spell of some enchantment. Suddenly she had finished. She looked at the dog, and then at her drawing, and then cried, with real grief for the dog, and at the same time a wicked exultation:

"My beautiful, why did they?"

She took her paper to the dog, and held it under his nose. He 15 turned his head aside as in chagrin and mortification, and she impulsively kissed his velvety bulging forehead.

"'s a Loolie, 's a little Loozie! Look at his portrait, darling, look at his portrait, that his mother has done of him." She looked at her paper and chuckled. Then, kissing the dog once more, she rose and 20 came gravely to Gudrun, offering her the paper.

It was a grotesque little diagram of a grotesque little animal, so wicked and so comical, a slow smile came over Gudrun's face, unconsciously. And at her side Winifred chuckled with glee, and said:

25 "It isn't like him, is it? He's much lovelier than that. He's *so* beautiful—mmm, Looloo, my sweet darling." And she flew off to embrace the chagrined little dog. He looked up at her with reproachful, saturnine eyes, vanquished in his extreme agedness of being. Then she flew back to her drawing, and chuckled with 30 satisfaction.

"It isn't like him, is it?" she said to Gudrun.

"Yes, it's very like him," Gudrun replied.

The child treasured her drawing, carried it about with her, and showed it, with a silent embarrassment, to everybody.

35 "Look," she said, thrusting the paper into her father's hand.

"Why that's Looloo!" he exclaimed. And he looked down in surprise, hearing the almost inhuman chuckle of the child at his side.

Gerald was away from home when Gudrun first came to Shortlands. But the first morning he came back he watched for her. It was 40 a sunny, soft morning, and he lingered in the garden paths, looking at

the flowers that had come out during his absence. He was clean and
fit as ever, shaven, his fair hair scrupulously parted at the side, bright
in the sunshine, his short, fair moustache closely clipped, his eyes
with their humorous kind twinkle, which was so deceptive. He was
dressed in black, his clothes sat well on his well-nourished body. Yet   5
as he lingered before the flower-beds in the morning sunshine,
there was a certain isolation, a fear about him, as of something
wanting.

Gudrun came up quickly, unseen. She was dressed in blue, with
woollen yellow stockings, like the Blue coat boys.* He glanced up in   10
surprise. Her stockings always disconcerted him, the pale-yellow
stockings and the rather heavy black shoes. Winifred, who had been
playing about the garden with Mademoiselle and the dogs, came
flitting towards Gudrun. The child wore a dress of black-and-white
stripes. Her hair was rather short, cut round and hanging level in   15
her neck.

"We're going to do Bismarck, aren't we?" she said, linking her
hand through Gudrun's arm.

"Yes, we're going to do Bismarck. Do you want to?"

"Oh yes—Oh I do! I want most awfully to do Bismarck. He looks   20
so splendid this morning, so *fierce*. He's almost as big as a lion." And
the child chuckled sardonically at her own hyperbole. "He's a real
king, he really is."

"Bonjour mademoiselle," said the little French governess,
wavering up with a slight bow, a bow of the sort that Gudrun   25
loathed, insolent.

"Winifred veut tant faire* le portrait de Bismarck—! Oh, mais
toute la matinée c'est*—'We will do Bismarck this morning!'—
Bismarck, Bismarck, toujours Bismarck! C'est un lapin, n'est-ce
pas, mademoiselle?"   30

"Oui, c'est un grand lapin blanc et noir. Vous ne l'avez pas vu?"
said Gudrun in her good, but rather heavy French.

"Non, mademoiselle, Winifred n'a jamais voulu me le faire voir.
Tant de fois je le lui ai demandé, 'Qu'est-ce donc que ce Bismarck,
Winifred?' Mais elle n'a pas voulu me le dire. Son Bismarck, c'était   35
un mystère."

"Oui, c'est un mystère, vraiment un mystère! Miss Brangwen, say
that Bismarck is a mystery," cried Winifred.

"Bismarck is a mystery, Bismarck, c'est un mystère, der Bismarck, er ist ein Wunder," said Gudrun, in mocking incantation.   40

"Ja, er ist ein Wunder," repeated Winifred, with odd seriousness, under which lay a wicked chuckle.

"Ist er auch ein Wunder?" came the slightly insolent sneering of Mademoiselle.

"Doch!" said Winifred briefly, indifferent.

"Doch ist er nicht ein König. Beesmarck, he was not a king, Winifred, as you have said. He was only—il n'était que chancelier."

"Qu'est-ce qu'un chancelier?"* said Winifred, with slightly contemptuous indifference.

"A chancelier is a chancellor, and a chancellor is I believe, a sort of judge,"* said Gerald coming up and shaking hands with Gudrun. "You'll have made a song of Bismarck soon," said he.

Mademoiselle waited, and discreetly made her inclination, and her greeting.

"So they wouldn't let you see Bismarck, Mademoiselle?" he said.

"Non monsieur."

"Ah, very mean of them. What are you going to do to him, Miss Brangwen? I want him sent to the kitchen and cooked."

"Oh no," cried Winifred.

"We're going to draw him," said Gudrun.

"Draw him and quarter him* and dish him up," he said, being purposely fatuous.

"Oh *no!*" cried Winifred with emphasis, chuckling.

Gudrun detected the tang of mockery in him, and she looked up and smiled into his face. He felt his nerves caressed. Their eyes met in knowledge.

"How do you like Shortlands?" he asked.

"Oh, very much," she said, with nonchalance.

"Glad you do. Have you noticed these flowers?"

He led her along the path. She followed intently. Winifred came, and the governess lingered in the rear. They stopped before some veined salpiglossis flowers.

"Aren't they wonderful!" she cried, looking at them absorbedly. Strange how her reverential, almost ecstatic admiration of the flowers caressed his nerves. She stooped down, and touched the trumpets, with infinitely fine and delicate-touching finger-tips. It filled him with ease to see her. When she rose, her eyes, hot with the beauty of the flowers, looked into his.

"What are they?" she asked.

"Sort of petunia, I suppose," he answered. "I don't really know them."

"They are quite strangers to me," she said.

They stood together in a false intimacy, a nervous contact. And he was in love with her.

She was aware of Mademoiselle standing near, like a little French beetle, observant and calculative.* She moved away with Winifred, saying they would go to find Bismarck.

Gerald watched them go, looking all the while at the soft, full, still body of Gudrun, in its silky cashmere. How silky and rich and soft her body must be. An access of worship* came over his mind, she was the all-desirable, the all-beautiful. He wanted only to come to her, nothing more. He was only this, this being that should come to her, and be given to her.

At the same time he was finely and acutely aware of Mademoiselle's neat, brittle finality of form. She was like some elegant beetle with thin ankles, perched on her high heels, her glossy black dress perfectly correct, her dark hair done high and admirably. How repulsive her completeness and her finality was! He loathed her.

Yet he did admire her. She was perfectly correct. And it did rather annoy him, that Gudrun came dressed in startling colours, like a macaw, when the family was in mourning. Like a macaw she was! He watched the lingering way she took her feet from the ground. And her ankles were pale yellow, and her dress a deep blue. Yet it pleased him. It pleased him very much. He felt the challenge in her very attire—she challenged the whole world. And he smiled as to the note of a trumpet.

Gudrun and Winifred went through the house to the back, where were the stables and the out-buildings. Everywhere was still and deserted. Mr Crich had gone out for a short drive, the stable-man had just led round Gerald's horse. The two girls went to the hutch that stood in a corner, and looked at the great black-and-white rabbit.

"Isn't he beautiful! Oh, do look at him listening! Doesn't he look silly!" she laughed quickly, then added "Oh, do let's do him listening, do let us, he listens with so much of himself;—don't you darling Bismarck?"

"Can we take him out?" said Gudrun.

"He's very strong. He really is *extremely* strong." She looked at Gudrun, her head on one side, in odd calculating mistrust.

"But we'll try, shall we?"

"Yes, if you like. But he's a *fearful* kicker!"

They took the key to unlock the door. The rabbit exploded in a wild rush round the hutch.

5   "He scratches most awfully sometimes," cried Winifred in excitement. "Oh do look at him, isn't he wonderful!" The rabbit tore round the hutch in a flurry. "Bismarck!" cried the child, in rousing excitement. "How *dreadful* you are! You are beastly." Winifred looked up at Gudrun with some misgiving in her wild excitement.

10 Gudrun smiled sardonically with her mouth. Winifred made a strange crooning noise of unaccountable excitement. "Now he's still!" she cried, seeing the rabbit settled down in a far corner of the hutch.—"Shall we take him now?" she whispered excitedly, mysteriously, looking up at Gudrun and edging very close. "Shall we get

15 him now?"—She chuckled wickedly to herself.

They unlocked the door of the hutch. Gudrun thrust in her arm and seized the great, lusty rabbit as it crouched still, she grasped its long ears. It set its four feet flat, and thrust back. There was a long scraping sound as it was hauled forward, and in another instant it was

20 in mid-air, lunging wildly, its body flying like a spring coiled and released, as it lashed out, suspended from the ears. Gudrun held the black-and-white tempest at arms' length, averting her face. But the rabbit was magically strong, it was all she could do to keep her grasp. She almost lost her presence of mind.

25   "Bismarck, Bismarck, you are behaving *terribly*," said Winifred in a rather frightened voice, "Oh do put him down, he's beastly."

Gudrun stood for a moment astounded by the thunder-storm that had sprung into being in her grip. Then her colour came up, a heavy rage came over her like a cloud. She stood shaken as a house in a

30 storm, and utterly overcome. Her heart was arrested with fury at the mindlessness and the bestial stupidity of this struggle, her wrists were badly scored by the claws of the beast, a heavy cruelty welled up in her.

Gerald came round as she was trying to capture the flying rabbit

35 under her arm. He saw, with subtle recognition, her sullen passion of cruelty.

"You should let one of the men do that for you," he said, hurrying up.

"Oh he's *so* horrid!" cried Winifred, almost frantic.

40   He held out his nervous, sinewy hand and took the rabbit by the ears, from Gudrun.

"It's most *fearfully* strong," she cried, in a high voice, like the crying of a seagull, strange and vindictive.

The rabbit made itself into a ball in the air, and lashed out, flinging itself into a bow. It really seemed demoniacal. Gudrun saw Gerald's body tighten, saw a sharp blindness come into his eyes.

"I know these beggars of old," he said.

The long, demon-like beast lashed out again, spread on the air as if it were flying, looking something like a dragon, then closing up again, inconceivably powerful and explosive. The man's body, strung to its efforts, vibrated strongly. Then a sudden sharp, white-edged wrath came up in him. Swift as lightning he drew back and brought his free hand down like a hawk on the neck of the rabbit. Simultaneously, there came the unearthly, abhorrent scream of a rabbit in the fear of death. It made one immense writhe, tore his wrists and his sleeves in a final convulsion, all its belly flashed white in a whirlwind of paws, and then he had slung it round and had it under his arm, fast. It cowered and skulked. His face was gleaming with a smile.

"You wouldn't think there was all that force in a rabbit," he said, looking at Gudrun. And he saw her eyes black as night in her pallid face, she looked almost unearthly. The scream of the rabbit, after the violent tussle, seemed to have torn the veil of her consciousness. He looked at her, and the whitish, electric gleam in his face intensified.

"I don't really like him," Winifred was crooning. "I don't care for him as I do for Loozie. He's hateful really—."

A smile twisted Gudrun's face, as she recovered. She knew she was revealed.

"Don't they make the most fearful noise when they scream?" she cried, the high note in her voice, like a seagull's cry.

"Abominable," he said.

"He shouldn't be so silly, when he has to be taken out," Winifred was saying, putting out her hand and touching the rabbit tentatively, as it skulked under his arm, motionless as if it were dead.

"He's not dead, is he Gerald?" she asked.

"No, he ought to be," he said.

"Yes, he ought!" cried the child with a sudden flash of amusement. And she touched the rabbit with more confidence. "His heart is beating *so* fast. Isn't he funny? He really is."

"Where do you want him?" asked Gerald.

"In the little green court," she said.

Gudrun looked at Gerald with strange, darkened eyes, strained with underworld knowledge, almost supplicating, like those of a

creature which is at his mercy, yet which is his ultimate victor. He did
not know what to say to her. He felt the mutual hellish recognition.
And he felt he ought to say something, to cover it. He had the power
of lightning in his nerves, she seemed like a soft recipient of his
5 magical, hideous white fire. He was unconfident, he had qualms of
fear.

"Did he hurt you?" he asked.

"No," she said.

"He's an insensible beast," he said, turning his face away.

10 They came to the little court, which was shut in by old red walls, in
whose crevices wall-flowers were growing. The grass was soft and
fine and old, a level floor carpeting the court, the sky was blue
overhead. Gerald tossed the rabbit down. It crouched still and would
not move. Gudrun watched it with faint horror.

15 "Why doesn't it move?" she cried.

"It's skulking," he said.

She looked up at him, and a slight sinister smile contracted her
white face.

"Isn't it a *fool*!" she cried. "Isn't it a sickening *fool*?"

20 The vindictive mockery in her voice made his brain quiver.
Glancing up at him, into his eyes, she revealed again the mocking,
white-cruel recognition. There was a league between them, abhorrent to them both. They were implicated with each other in
abhorrent mysteries.

25 "How many scratches have you?" he asked, showing his hard
forearm, white and hard and torn in red gashes.

"How really vile!" she cried, flushing with a sinister vision. "Mine
is nothing."

She lifted her arm and showed a deep red score down the silken
30 white flesh.

"What a devil!" he exclaimed. But it was as if he had had
knowledge of her* in the long red rent of her forearm, so silken and
soft. He did not want to touch her. He would have to make himself
touch her, deliberately. The long, shallow red rip seemed torn across
35 his own brain, tearing the surface of his ultimate consciousness,
letting through the forever unconscious, unthinkable red ether* of
the beyond, the obscene beyond.

"It doesn't hurt you very much, does it?" he asked, solicitous.

"Not at all," she cried.

40 And suddenly the rabbit, which had been crouching as if it were a

flower, so still and soft, suddenly burst into life. Round and round
the court it went, as if shot from a gun, round and round like a furry
meteorite, in a tense hard circle that seemed to bind their brains.
They all stood in amazement, smiling uncannily, as if the rabbit were
obeying some unknown incantation. Round and round it flew, on the 5
grass under the old red walls, like a storm.

And then quite suddenly it settled down, hobbled among the
grass, and sat considering, its nose twitching like a bit of fluff in the
wind. After having considered for a few minutes, a soft bunch with a
black, open eye, which perhaps was looking at them, perhaps was 10
not, it hobbled calmly forward and began to nibble the grass with that
mean motion of a rabbit's quick eating.

"It's mad," said Gudrun. "It is most decidedly mad."

He laughed.

"The question is," he said, "what is madness? I don't suppose it is 15
rabbit-mad."

"Don't you think it is?" she asked.

"No. That's what it is to be a rabbit."

There was a queer, faint, obscene smile over his face. She looked
at him and saw him, and knew that he was initiate as she was initiate. 20
This thwarted her, and contravened her, for the moment.

"God be praised we aren't rabbits," she said, in a high, shrill
voice.

The smile intensified a little, on his face.

"Not rabbits?" he said, looking at her fixedly. 25

Slowly her face relaxed into a smile of obscene recognition.

"Ah Gerald," she said, in a strong, slow, almost man-like way.
"—All that, and more." Her eyes looked up at him with shocking
nonchalance.

He felt again as if she had hit him across the face—or rather, as if 30
she had torn him across the breast, dully, finally. He turned aside.

"Eat, eat my darling!" Winifred was softly conjuring the rabbit,
and creeping forward to touch it. It hobbled away from her. "Let its
mother stroke its fur then, darling, because it is so mysterious— —"

Chapter XIX

Moony*

After his illness Birkin went to the south of France for a time. He did not write, nobody heard anything of him. Ursula, left alone, felt as if everything were lapsing out. There seemed to be no hope in the world. One was a tiny little rock with the tide of nothingness rising higher and higher. She herself was real, and only herself—just like a rock in a wash of flood-water. The rest was all nothingness. She was hard and indifferent, isolated in herself.

There was nothing for it now, but contemptuous, resistant indifference. All the world was lapsing into a grey wish-wash of nothingness, she had no contact and no connection anywhere. She despised and detested the whole show. From the bottom of her heart, from the bottom of her soul, she despised and detested people, adult people. She loved only children and animals: children she loved passionately, but coldly. They made her want to hug them, to protect them, to give them life. But this very love, based on pity and despair, was only a bondage and a pain to her. She loved best of all the animals, that were single and unsocial as she herself was. She loved the horses and cows in the field. Each was single and to itself, magical. It was not referred away to some detestable social principle. It was incapable of soulfulness and tragedy, which she detested so profoundly.

She could be very pleasant and flattering, almost subservient, to people she met. But no one was taken in. Instinctively each felt her contemptuous mockery of the human being in himself, or herself. She had a profound grudge against the human being. That which the word "human" stood for was despicable and repugnant to her.

Mostly her heart was closed in this hidden, unconscious strain of contemptuous ridicule. She thought she loved, she thought she was full of love. This was her idea of herself. But the strange brightness of her presence, a marvellous radiance of intrinsic vitality, was a luminousness of supreme repudiation, repudiation, nothing but repudiation.

Yet, at moments, she yielded and softened, she wanted pure love,

244

only pure love. This other, this state of constant unfailing repudiation, was a strain, a suffering also. A terrible desire for pure love
overcame her again.

She went out one evening, numbed by this constant essential
suffering. Those who are timed for destruction must die now. The
knowledge of this reached a finality, a finishing in her. And the
finality released her. If fate would carry off in death or downfall all
those who were timed to go, why need she trouble, why repudiate
any further. She was free of it all, she could seek a new union
elsewhere.

Ursula set off to Willey Green, towards the mill. She came to
Willey Water. It was almost full again, after its period of emptiness.
Then she turned off through the woods. The night had fallen, it was
dark. But she forgot to be afraid, she who had such great sources of
fear. Among the trees, far from any human beings, there was a sort
of magic peace. The more one could find a pure loneliness, with no
taint of people, the better one felt. She was in reality terrified,
horrified in her apprehension of people.

She started, noticing something on her right hand, between the
tree trunks. It was like a great presence, watching her, dodging her.
She started violently. It was only the moon, risen through the thin
trees. But it seemed so mysterious, with its white and deathly smile.
And there was no avoiding it. Night or day, one could not escape the
sinister face, triumphant and radiant like this moon, with a high
smile. She hurried on, cowering from the white planet. She would
just see the pond at the mill before she went home.

Not wanting to go through the yard, because of the dogs, she
turned off along the hill-side to descend on the pond from above.
The moon was transcendent over the bare, open space, she suffered
from being exposed to it. There was a glimmer of nightly rabbits
across the ground. The night was as clear as crystal, and very still.
She could hear a distant coughing of a sheep.

So she swerved down to the steep, tree-hidden bank above the
pond, where the alders twisted their roots. She was glad to pass into
the shade out of the moon. There she stood, at the top of the
fallen-away bank, her hand on the rough trunk of a tree, looking at
the water, that was perfect in its stillness, floating the moon upon it.*
But for some reason she disliked it. It did not give her anything. She
listened for the hoarse rustle of the sluice. And she wished for
something else out of the night, she wanted another night, not this

moon-brilliant hardness. She could feel her soul crying out in her, lamenting desolately.

She saw a shadow moving by the water. It would be Birkin. He had come back then, unawares. She accepted it without remark, nothing mattered to her. She sat down among the roots of the alder tree, dim and veiled, hearing the sound of the sluice like dew distilling audibly into the night. The islands were dark and half revealed, the reeds were dark also, only some of them had a little frail fire of reflection. A fish leaped secretly, revealing the light in the pond. This fire of the chill night breaking constantly on to the pure darkness, repelled her. She wished it were perfectly dark, perfectly, and noiseless and without motion. Birkin, small and dark also, his hair tinged with moonlight, wandered nearer. He was quite near, and yet he did not exist in her. He did not know she was there. Supposing he did something he would not wish to be seen doing, thinking he was quite private? But there, what did it matter? What did the small privacies matter? How could it matter, what he did? How can there be any secrets, we are all the same organisms? How can there be any secrecy, when everything is known to all of us?

He was touching unconsciously the dead husks of flowers as he passed by, and talking disconnectedly to himself.

"You can't go away," he was saying. "There *is* no away. You only withdraw upon yourself."

He threw a dead flower-husk on to the water.

"An antiphony—they lie, and you sing back at them.—There wouldn't have to be any truth, if there weren't any lies—then one needn't assert anything—"

He stood still, looking at the water, and throwing upon it the husks of the flowers.

"Cybele—curse her! The accursed Syria Dea!*—Does one begrudge it her?—What else is there—?"

Ursula wanted to laugh loudly and hysterically, hearing his isolated voice speaking out. It was so ridiculous.

He stood staring at the water. Then he stooped and picked up a stone, which he threw sharply at the pond. Ursula was aware of the bright moon leaping and swaying, all distorted, in her eyes. It seemed to shoot out arms of fire like a cuttle-fish, like a luminous polyp, palpitating strongly before her.

And his shadow on the border of the pond, was watching for a few moments, then he stooped and groped on the ground. Then again

there was a burst of sound, and a burst of brilliant light, the moon
had exploded on the water, and was flying asunder in flakes of white
and dangerous fire.* Rapidly, like white birds, the fires all broken
rose across the pond, fleeing in clamorous confusion, battling with
the flock of dark waves that were forcing their way in. The furthest   5
waves of light, fleeing out, seemed to be clamouring against the shore
for escape, the waves of darkness came in heavily, running under
towards the centre. But at the centre, the heart of all, was still a vivid,
incandescent quivering of a white moon not quite destroyed, a white
body of fire writhing and striving and not even now broken open, not   10
yet violated. It seemed to be drawing itself together with strange,
violent pangs, in blind effort. It was getting stronger, it was
re-asserting itself, the inviolable moon. And the rays were hastening
in in thin lines of light, to return to the strengthened moon, that
shook upon the water in triumphant reassumption.   15

Birkin stood and watched, motionless, till the pond was almost
calm, the moon was almost serene. Then, satisfied of so much, he
looked for more stones. She felt his invisible tenacity. And in a
moment again, the broken lights scattered in explosion over her face,
dazzling her; and then, almost immediately, came the second shot.   20
The moon leapt up white and burst through the air. Darts of bright
light shot asunder, darkness swept over the centre. There was no
moon, only a battlefield of broken lights and shadows, running close
together. Shadows, dark and heavy, struck again and again across the
place where the heart of the moon had been, obliterating it alto-   25
gether. The white fragments pulsed up and down, and could not find
where to go, apart and brilliant on the water like the petals of a rose
that a wind has blown far and wide.

Yet again, they were flickering their way to the centre, finding the
path blindly, enviously. And again, all was still, as Birkin and Ursula 30
watched. The waters were loud on the shore. He saw the moon
regathering itself insidiously, saw the heart of the rose intertwining
vigorously and blindly, calling back the scattered fragments, winning
home the fragments, in a pulse and an effort of return.

And he was not satisfied. Like a madness, he must go on. He got   35
large stones, and threw them, one after the other, at the white-
burning centre of the moon, till there was nothing but a rocking of
hollow noise, and a pond surged up, no moon any more, only a few
broken flakes tangled and glittering broadcast in the darkness,
without aim or meaning, a darkened confusion, like a black and   40

white kaleidoscope tossed at random. The hollow night was rocking and crashing with noise, and from the sluice came sharp, regular flashes of sound. Flakes of light appeared here and there, glittering tormented among the shadows, far off, in strange places, among the dripping shadow of the willow on the island. Birkin stood and listened, and was satisfied.

Ursula was dazed, her mind was all gone. She felt she had fallen to the ground and was spilled out, like water on the earth. Motionless and spent, she remained in the gloom. Though even now she was aware, unseeing, that in the darkness was a little tumult of ebbing flakes of light, a cluster dancing secretly in a round, twining and coming stealthily together. They were gathering a heart again, they were coming once more into being. Gradually the fragments caught together, re-united, heaving, rocking, dancing, falling back as in panic, but working their way home again persistently, making semblance of fleeing away when they had advanced, but always flickering nearer, a little closer to the mark, the cluster growing mysteriously larger and brighter, as gleam after gleam fell in with the whole, until a ragged rose, a distorted, frayed moon was shaking upon the waters again, re-asserted, renewed, trying to recover from its convulsion, to get over the disfigurement and the agitation, to be whole and composed, at peace.

Birkin lingered vaguely by the water. Ursula was afraid that he would stone the moon again. She slipped from her seat and went down to him, saying:

"You won't throw stones at it any more, will you?"

"How long have you been there?" he asked.

"All the time. You won't throw any more stones, will you?"

"I wanted to see if I could make it be quite gone off the pond," he said.

"Yes, it was horrible, really. Why should you hate the moon? It hasn't done you any harm, has it?"

"Was it hate?" he said.

And they were silent for a few minutes.

"When did you come back?" she said.

"Today."

"Why did you never write?"

"I could find nothing to say."

"Why was there nothing to say?"

"I don't know. Why are there no daffodils now?"

"No."*

Again there was a space of silence. Ursula looked at the moon. It had gathered itself together, and was quivering slightly.

"Was it good for you, to be alone?" she asked.

"Perhaps. Not that I know much. But I got over a good deal. Did you do anything important?"

"No. I looked at England, and thought I'd done with it."

"Why England?" he asked in surprise.

"I don't know, it came like that."

"It isn't a question of nations," he said. "France is far worse."

"Yes, I know. I felt I'd done with it all."

They went and sat down on the roots of the trees, in the shadow. And being silent, he remembered the beauty of her eyes, which were sometimes filled with light, like spring, suffused with wonderful promise. So he said to her, slowly, with difficulty:

"There is a golden light in you, which I wish you would give me." It was as if he had been thinking of this for some time.

She was startled, she seemed to leap clear of him. Yet also she was pleased.

"What kind of a light?" she asked.

But he was shy, and did not say any more. So the moment passed for this time. And gradually a feeling of sorrow came over her.

"My life is so unfulfilled," she said.

"Yes," he answered briefly, not wanting to hear this.

"And I feel as if nobody would ever really love me," she said.

But he did not answer.

"You think, don't you," she said slowly, "that I only want physical things? It isn't true. I want you to serve my spirit."

"I know you do. I know you don't want physical things by themselves.—But, I want you to give me—to give your spirit to me—that golden light which is you—which you don't know—give it me—"

After a moment's silence she replied:

"But how can I, you don't love me! You only want your own ends. You don't want to serve *me*, and yet you want me to serve you. It is so one-sided."

It was a great effort to him to maintain this conversation, and to press for the thing he wanted from her, the surrender of her spirit.

"It is different," he said. "The two kinds of service are so different. I serve you in another way—not through *yourself*,— somewhere else.—But I want us to be together without bothering about ourselves—to be really together because we *are* together, as if it were a phenomenon, not a thing we have to maintain by our own effort."

"No," she said, pondering. "You are just egocentric.—You never
5 have any enthusiasm, you never come out with any spark, towards me. You want yourself, really, and your own affairs. And you want me just to be there, to serve you."

But this only made him shut off from her.

"Ah well," he said, "words make no matter, any way. The thing *is*
10 between us, or it isn't."

"You don't even love me," she cried.

"I do," he said angrily. "But I want—" His mind saw again the lovely golden light of spring transfused through her eyes, as through some wonderful window. And he wanted her to be with him there, in
15 this world of proud indifference. But what was the good of telling her he wanted this company in proud indifference. What was the good of talking, any way? It must happen beyond the sound of words. It was merely ruinous to try to work her by conviction. This was a paradisal bird that could never be netted, it must fly by itself to the heart.

20 "I always think I am going to be loved—and then I am let down. You *don't* love me, you know. You don't want to serve me. You only want yourself."

A shiver of rage went over his veins, at this repeated: "You don't want to serve me." All the paradisal disappeared from him.

25 "No," he said, irritated, "I don't want to serve you, because there is nothing there to serve. What you want me to serve, is nothing, mere nothing. It isn't even you, it is your mere female quality. And I wouldn't give a straw for your female ego—it's a rag doll."

"Ha!" she laughed in mockery. "That's all you think of me, is it?
30 And then you have the impudence to say you love me!"

She rose in anger, to go home.

"You want the paradisal unknowing," she said, turning round on him as he still sat half-visible in the shadow. "I know what that means, thank you. You want me to be your thing, never to criticise
35 you or to have anything to say for myself. You want me to be a mere *thing* for you! No thank you! *If* you want that, there are plenty of women who will give it you. There are plenty of women who will lie down for you to walk over them—*go* to them then, if that's what you want—go to them."

40 "No," he said, outspoken with anger. "I want you to drop your

assertive *will*, your frightened apprehensive self-insistence, that is what I want.—I want you to trust yourself so implicitly, that you can let yourself go."

"Let myself go!" She re-echoed in mockery. "*I* can let myself go, easily enough. It is you who can't let yourself go, it is you who hang on to yourself as if it were your only treasure. *You*—*you* are the Sunday school teacher—*you*—you preacher."

The amount of truth that was in this made him stiff and unheeding of her.

"I don't mean let yourself go in the Dionysic ecstatic way,"* he said. "I know you can do that. But I hate ecstasy, Dionysic or any other. It's like going round in a squirrel cage.—I want you not to care about yourself, just to be there and not to care about yourself, not to insist—be glad and sure and indifferent."

"Who insists?" she mocked. "Who is it that keeps on insisting?— It isn't *me*!"

There was a weary, mocking bitterness in her voice. He was silent for some time.

"I know," he said. "While ever either of us insists to the other, we are all wrong.—But there we are, the accord doesn't come."

They sat in stillness under the shadow of the trees by the bank. The night was white around them, they were in the darkness, barely conscious.

Gradually, the stillness and peace came over them. She put her hand tentatively on his. Their hands clasped softly and silently, in peace.

"Do you really love me?" she said.

He laughed.

"I call that your war-cry," he replied, amused.

"Why!" she cried, amused and really wondering.

"Your insistence—your war-cry—'A Brangwen, A Brangwen,' an old battle-cry.—Yours is 'Do you love me?—Yield knave, or die.'"

"No," she said, pleading, "not like that. Not like that. But I must know that you love me, mustn't I?"

"Well then, know it and have done with it."

"But do you?"

"Yes, I do. I love you, and I know it's final. It is final, so why say any more about it."

She was silent for some moments, in delight and doubt.

"Are you sure?" she said, nestling happily near to him.

"Quite sure—so now have done—accept it and have done."
She was nestled quite close to him.
"Have done with what?" she murmured, happily.
"With bothering," he said.

5   She clung nearer to him. He held her close, and kissed her softly, gently. It was such peace and heavenly freedom, just to fold her and kiss her gently, and not to have any thoughts or any desires or any will, just to be still with her, to be perfectly still and together, in a peace that was not sleep, but content in bliss. To be content in bliss,
10   without desire or insistence anywhere, this was heaven: to be together in happy stillness.

For a long time she nestled to him, and he kissed her softly, her hair, her face, her ears, gently, softly, like dew falling. But his warm breath on her ears disturbed her again, kindled the old destructive
15   fires. She cleaved to him, and he could feel his blood changing like quicksilver.

"But we'll be still, shall we?" he said.
"Yes," she said, as if submissively.
And she continued to nestle against him.
20   But in a little while she drew away and looked at him.
"I must be going home," she said.
"Must you—how sad," he replied.
She leaned forward and put up her mouth to be kissed.
"Are you really sad?" she murmured, smiling.
25   "Yes," he said. "I wish we could stay as we were, always."
"Always! Do you?" she murmured, as he kissed her. And then, out of a full throat, she crooned "Kiss me! Kiss me!" And she cleaved close to him. He kissed her many times. But he too had his idea and his will. He wanted only gentle communion, no other, no passion
30   now.—So that soon she drew away, put on her hat and went home.

The next day, however, he felt wistful and yearning. He thought he had been wrong, perhaps. Perhaps he had been wrong to go to her with an idea of what he wanted. Was it really only an idea, or was it the interpretation of a profound yearning?—If the latter, how was it
35   he was always talking about sensual fulfilment. The two did not agree very well.

Suddenly he found himself face to face with a situation. It was as simple as this: fatally simple. On the one hand, he knew he did want a further sensual experience—something deeper, darker than ordi-
40   nary life could give. He remembered the African fetishes he had

seen at Halliday's so often. There came back to him one, a statuette
about two feet high, a tall, slim, elegant figure from West Africa, in
dark wood, glossy and suave. It was a woman, with hair dressed high,
like a melon-shaped dome. He remembered her vividly: she was one
of his soul's intimates. Her body was long and elegant, her face was 5
crushed tiny like a beetle's, she had rows of round heavy collars, like
a column of quoits, on her neck. He remembered her: her
astonishing cultured elegance, her diminished, beetle face, the
astounding long elegant body, on short, ugly legs, with such
protuberant buttocks, so weighty and unexpected below her slim 10
long loins.* She knew what he himself did not know. She had
thousands of years of purely sensual, purely unspiritual knowledge
behind her. It must have been thousands of years since her race had
died, mystically: that is, since the relation between the senses and the
outspoken mind had broken, leaving the experience all in one sort, 15
mystically sensual. Thousands of years ago, that which was
imminent in himself must have taken place in these Africans: the
goodness, the holiness, the desire for creation and productive
happiness must have lapsed, leaving the single impulse for knowledge in one sort, mindless progressive knowledge through the 20
senses, knowledge arrested and ending in the senses, mystic knowledge in disintegration and dissolution, knowledge such as the
beetles have, which live purely within the world of corruption and
cold dissolution. This was why her face looked like a beetle's: this
was why the Egyptians worshipped the ball-rolling scarab:* because 25
of the principle of knowledge in dissolution and corruption.

There is a long way we can travel, after the death-break: after that
point where the soul in intense suffering breaks, breaks away from its
organic hold like a leaf that falls. We fall from the connection with
life and hope, we lapse from pure integral being, from creation and 30
liberty, and we fall into the long, long African process of purely
sensual understanding, knowledge in the mystery of dissolution.

He realised now that this is a long process—thousands of years it
takes, after the death of the creative spirit. He realised that there
were great mysteries to be unsealed, sensual, mindless, dreadful 35
mysteries, far beyond the phallic cult. How far, in their inverted
culture, had these West Africans gone beyond phallic knowledge?
Very, very far. Birkin recalled again the female figure: the elongated,
long, long body, the curious, unexpected heavy buttocks, the long,
imprisoned neck, the face with tiny features like a beetle's. This was 40

far beyond any phallic knowledge, sensual subtle realities far beyond the scope of phallic investigation.

There remained this way, this awful African process, to be fulfilled. It would be done differently by the white races. The white races, having the arctic north behind them, the vast abstraction of ice and snow, would fulfil a mystery of ice-destructive knowledge, snow-abstract annihilation. Whereas the West Africans, controlled by the burning death-abstraction of the Sahara, had been fulfilled in sun-destruction, the putrescent mystery of sun-rays.

Was this then all that remained? Was there left now nothing but to break off from the happy creative being, was the time up? Is our day of creative life finished? Does there remain to us only the strange, awful afterwards of the knowledge in dissolution, the African knowledge, but different in us, who are blond and blue-eyed from the north?

Birkin thought of Gerald. He was one of these strange white wonderful demons from the north, fulfilled in the destructive frost-mystery. And was he fated to pass away in this knowledge, this one process of frost-knowledge, death by perfect cold? Was he a messenger, an omen of the universal dissolution into whiteness and snow?

Birkin was frightened. He was tired too, when he had reached this length of speculation. Suddenly his strange, strained attention gave way, he could not attend to these mysteries any more.—There was another way, the way of freedom. There was the Paradisal entry into pure, single being, the individual soul taking precedence over love and desire for union, stronger than any pangs of emotion, a lovely state of free proud singleness, which accepts the obligation of the permanent connection with others, and with the other, submits to the yoke and leash of love, but never forfeits its own proud individual singleness, even while it loves and yields.

This was the other way, the remaining way. And he must run to follow it. He thought of Ursula, how sensitive and delicate she really was, her skin so over-fine, as if one skin were wanting. She was really so marvellously gentle and sensitive. Why did he ever forget it? He must go to her at once. He must ask her to marry him. They must marry at once, and so make a definite pledge, enter into a definite communion. He must set out at once and ask her, this moment. There was no moment to spare.

He drifted on swiftly to Beldover, half-unconscious of his own movement. He saw the town on the slope of the hill, not straggling, but as if walled-in with the straight, final streets of miners-dwellings, making a great square, and it looked like Jerusalem to his fancy.* The world was all strange and transcendent.

Rosalind opened the door to him. She started slightly, as a young girl will, and said:

"Oh, I'll tell father."

With which she disappeared, leaving Birkin in the hall, looking at some reproductions from Picasso,* lately introduced by Gudrun. He was admiring the almost wizard, sensuous apprehension of the earth, when Will Brangwen appeared, rolling down his shirt-sleeves.

"Well," said Brangwen, "I'll get a coat." And he too disappeared for a moment. Then he returned, and opened the door of the drawing-room, saying:

"You must excuse me, I was just doing a bit of work in the shed. Come inside, will you."

Birkin entered and sat down. He looked at the bright, reddish face of the other man, at the narrow brow and the very bright eyes, and at the rather sensual lips that unrolled wide and expansive under the black cropped moustache. How curious it was that this was a human being! What Brangwen thought himself to be, how meaningless it was, confronted with the reality of him. Birkin could see only a strange, inexplicable, almost patternless collection of passions and desires and suppressions and traditions and mechanical ideas, all cast unfused and disunited into this slender, bright-faced man of nearly fifty, who was as unresolved now as he was at twenty, and as uncreated. How could he be the parent of Ursula, when he was not created himself? He was not a parent. A slip of living flesh had been transmitted through him, but the spirit had not come from him. The spirit had not come from any ancestor, it had come out of the unknown. A child is the child of the mystery, or it is uncreated.

"The weather's not so bad as it has been," said Brangwen, after waiting a moment. There was no connection between the two men.

"No," said Birkin. "It was full moon two days ago."

"Oh! You believe in the moon then, affecting the weather?"

"No, I don't think I do. I don't really know enough about it."

"You know what they say?—The moon and the weather may change together, but the change of the moon won't change the weather."

"Is that it?" said Birkin. "I hadn't heard it."

There was a pause. Then Birkin said:

"Am I hindering you? I called to see Ursula, really. Is she at home?"

"I don't believe she is. I believe she's gone to the library. I'll just see."

Birkin could hear him enquiring in the dining-room.

"No," he said, coming back. "But she won't be long. You wanted to speak to her?"

Birkin looked across at the other man with curious calm, clear eyes.

"As a matter of fact," he said, "I wanted to ask her to marry me."

A point of light came on the golden-brown eyes of the elder man.

"O-oh?" he said, looking at Birkin, then dropping his eyes before the calm, steadily watching look of the other: "Was she expecting you then?"

"No," said Birkin.

"No?—I didn't know anything of—of this sort was on foot—."*

Brangwen smiled awkwardly.

Birkin looked back at him, and said to himself: "I wonder why it should be 'on foot'!" Aloud he said:

"No, it's perhaps rather sudden." At which, thinking of his relationship with Ursula, he added—"but I don't know—"

"Quite sudden, is it?—Oh!" said Brangwen, rather baffled and annoyed.

"In one way," replied Birkin, "—not in another."

There was a moment's pause, after which Brangwen said:

"Well, she pleases herself—"

"Oh yes!" said Birkin, calmly.

A vibration came into Brangwen's strong voice, as he replied:

"Though I shouldn't want her to be in too big a hurry, either. It's no good looking round afterwards, when it's too late."

"Oh, it need never be too late," said Birkin, "as far as that goes."

"How do you mean?" asked the father.

"If one repents being married, the marriage is at an end," said Birkin.

"You think so?"

"Certainly."*

"Ay, well that may be your way of looking at it."

Birkin, in silence, thought to himself: "So it may. As for *your* way of looking at it, William Brangwen, it needs a little explaining."

"I suppose," said Brangwen, "you know what sort of people we are?—What sort of a bringing-up she's had?"

"'*She*'," thought Birkin to himself, remembering his childhood's corrections, "is the cat's mother."*

"*Do* I know what sort of a bringing-up she's had?" he asked simply.

He seemed to annoy Brangwen intentionally.

"Well," he said, "she's had everything that's right for a girl to have—as far as was possible, as far as we could give it her."

"I'm sure she has," said Birkin.

Which caused a most perilous full-stop. The father was becoming exasperated. There was something naturally irritant to him in Birkin's mere presence.

"And I don't want to see her going back on it all," he said, in a clanging voice.

"Why?" said Birkin.

This monosyllable exploded in Brangwen's brain like a shot.

"Why!" he repeated. "Why don't I? Because I don't believe in your new-fangled ways and your new-fangled ideas—in and out like a frog in a gallipot.* It would never do for me."

Birkin watched him with steady, emotionless eyes. The radical antagonism in the two men was rousing.

"Yes, but are my ways and ideas new-fangled?" asked Birkin.

"Are they?" Brangwen caught himself up. "I'm not speaking of you in particular," he said. "What I mean is that my children have been brought up to think and do according to the religion I was brought up in myself, and I don't want to see them going away from that."

There was a dangerous pause.

"And beyond this—?" asked Birkin.

The father hesitated. He was in a nasty position.

"Eh? What do you mean?—All I want to say, is that my daughter—" he tailed off into silence, overcome by futility. He knew that in some way he was off the track.

"Of course," said Birkin, "I don't want to hurt anybody or influence anybody. Ursula does exactly as she pleases."

There was a complete silence, because of the utter failure in mutual understanding. Birkin felt bored. Her father was not a coherent human being, he was a roomful of old echoes. The eyes of the younger man rested on the face of the elder. Brangwen looked up, and saw Birkin looking at him. His face was covered with inarticulate anger and humiliation and sense of inferiority in strength.

"And as for beliefs, that's one thing," he said. "But I'd rather see
5 my daughters dead tomorrow than that they should be at the beck and call of the first man that likes to come and whistle after them."

A queer, painful light came into Birkin's eyes.

"As to that," he said, "I only know that it's much more likely that it's I who am at the beck and call of the woman, than she at mine."
10 Again there was a pause. The father was somewhat bewildered.

"I know," he said, "she'll please herself—she always has done. I've done my best for them—but that doesn't matter. They've got themselves to please, and if they can help it they'll please nobody *but* themselves. But she's a right to consider her mother, and me as
15 well—"

Brangwen was thinking his own thoughts.

"And I tell you this much, I would rather bury them, than see them getting into a lot of loose ways such as you see everywhere nowadays.—I'd rather bury them—"
20 "Yes but, you see," said Birkin slowly, rather wearily, bored again by this new turn, "they won't give either you or me the chance to bury them, because they're not to be buried."

Brangwen looked at him in a sudden flare of impotent anger.

"Now, Mr Birkin," he said, "I don't know what you've come here
25 for, and I don't know what you're asking for.—But my daughters are my daughters—and it's my business to look after them while I can."

Birkin's brows knitted suddenly, his eyes concentrated in mockery. But he remained perfectly stiff and still. There was a pause.
30 "I've nothing against you marrying Ursula," Brangwen began again at length. "It's got nothing to do wi' me. She'll do as she likes, me or no me."

Birkin turned away, looking out of the window and letting go his consciousness. After all, what good was this? It was hopeless to keep
35 it up. He would sit on till Ursula came home, then speak to her, then go away. He would not accept trouble at the hands of her father. It was all unnecessary, and he himself need not have provoked it.

The two men sat in complete silence, Birkin almost unconscious of his own whereabouts. He had come to ask her to marry him—well
40 then, he would wait on, and ask her. As for what she said, whether

she accepted or not, he did not think about it. He would say what he had come to say, and that was all he was conscious of. He accepted the complete insignificance of this household, for him. But everything now was as if fated. He could see one thing ahead, and no more. From the rest, he was absolved entirely for the time being. It had to be left to fate and chance to resolve the issues.

At length they heard the gate. They saw her coming up the steps with a bundle of books under her arm. Her face was bright and abstracted as usual, with the abstraction, that look of being not quite *there*, not quite present to the facts of reality, that galled her father so much. She had a maddening faculty of assuming a light of her own, which excluded the reality, and within which she looked radiant as if in sunshine.

They heard her go into the dining-room, and drop her armful of books on the table.

"Did you bring me that 'Girl's Own'?"* cried Rosalind.

"Yes, I brought it. But I forgot which one it was you wanted."

"You would," cried Rosalind angrily.—"It's right, for a wonder."

Then they heard her say something in a lowered tone.

"Where?" cried Ursula.

Again her sister's voice was muffled.

Brangwen opened the door, and called, in his strong, brazen voice:

"Ursula."

She appeared in a moment, wearing her hat.

"Oh how do you do!" she cried, seeing Birkin, and all dazzled as if taken by surprise. He wondered at her, knowing she was aware of his presence. She had her queer, radiant, breathless manner, as if confused by the actual world, unreal to it, having a complete bright world of her self alone.

"Have I interrupted a conversation?" she asked.

"No, only a complete silence," said Birkin.

"Oh," said Ursula, vaguely, absent. Their presence was not vital to her, she was withheld, she did not take them in. It was a subtle insult that never failed to exasperate her father.

"Mr Birkin came to speak to *you*, not to me," said her father.

"Oh, did he!" she exclaimed vaguely, as if it did not concern her. Then, recollecting herself, she turned to him rather radiantly, but still quite superficially, and said: "Was it anything special?"

"I hope so," he said, ironically.

"—To propose to you, according to all accounts," said her father.

"Oh," said Ursula.

"Oh," mocked her father, imitating her. "Have you nothing more to say?"

5 She winced as if violated.

"Did you really come to propose to me?" she asked of Birkin, as if it were a joke.

"Yes," he said. "I suppose I came to 'propose.'" He seemed to fight shy of the last word.

10 "Did you!" she cried, with her vague radiance. He might have been saying anything whatsoever. She seemed pleased.

"Yes," he answered. "I wanted to—I wanted you to agree to marry me."

She looked at him. His eyes were flickering with mixed lights, 15 wanting something of her, yet not wanting it. She shrank a little, as if she were exposed to his eyes, and as if it were a pain to her. She darkened, her soul clouded over, she turned aside. She had been driven out of her own radiant, single world. And she dreaded contact, it was almost unnatural to her at these times.

20 "Yes," she said vaguely, in a doubting, absent voice.

Birkin's heart contracted swiftly, in a sudden fire of bitterness. It all meant nothing to her. He had been mistaken again. She was in some self-satisfied world of her own. He and his hopes were accidentals, violations to her. It drove her father to a pitch of mad 25 exasperation. He had had to put up with this all his life, from her.

"Well, what do you say?" he cried.

She winced. Then she glanced down at her father, half-frightened, and she said:

"I didn't speak, did I?" as if she were afraid she might have 30 committed herself.

"No," said her father, exasperated. "But you needn't look like an idiot. You've got your wits, haven't you?"

She ebbed away in silent hostility.

"I've got my wits, what does that mean?" she repeated, in a sullen 35 voice of antagonism.

"You heard what was asked you, didn't you?" cried her father in anger.

"Of course I heard."

"Well then, can't you answer?" thundered her father.

40 "Why should I?"

At the impertinence of this retort, he went stiff. But he said nothing.

"No," said Birkin, to help out the occasion, "there's no need to answer at once. You can say when you like."

Her eyes flashed with a powerful yellow light.

"Why should I say anything?" she cried. "You do this off your *own* bat, it has nothing to do with me. Why do you both want to bully me!"

"Bully you! Bully you!" cried her father, in bitter, rancorous anger. "Bully you! Why, it's a pity you can't be bullied into some sense and decency. Bully you! *You'll* see to that, you self-willed bargust."*

She stood suspended in the middle of the room, her face glimmering and dangerous. She was set in satisfied defiance. Birkin looked up at her. He too was angry.

"But no-one is bullying you," he said, in a very soft, dangerous voice also.

"Oh yes," she cried. "You both want to force me into something."

"That is an illusion of yours," he said ironically.

"Illusion!" cried her father. "A self-opinionated fool, that's what she is."

Birkin rose, saying:

"However, we'll leave it for the time being."

And without another word, he walked out of the house.

"You fool!—You fool!" her father cried to her, with extreme bitterness. She left the room, and went upstairs, singing to herself. But she was terribly fluttered, as after some dreadful fight. From her window, she could see Birkin going up the road. He went in such a blithe drift of rage, that her mind wondered over him. He was ridiculous, but she was afraid of him. She was as if escaped from some danger.

Her father sat below, powerless in humiliation and chagrin. It was as if he were possessed with all the devils, after one of these unaccountable conflicts with Ursula. He hated her as if his only reality were in hating her to the last degree. He had all hell in his heart. But he went away, to escape himself. He knew he must despair, yield, give in to despair, and have done.

Ursula's face closed, she completed herself against them all. Recoiling upon herself, she became hard and self-completed, like a jewel. She was bright and invulnerable, quite free and happy, perfectly liberated in her self-possession. Her father had to learn not to see her blithe obliviousness, or it would have sent him mad. She was so radiant with all things, in her possession of perfect hostility.

She would go on now for days like this, in this bright frank state of seemingly pure spontaneity, so essentially oblivious of the existence of anything but herself, but so ready and facile in her interest. Ah it was a bitter thing for a man to be near her, and her father cursed his fatherhood. But he must learn not to see her, not to know.

She was perfectly stable in resistance when she was in this state: so bright and radiant and attractive in her pure opposition, so very pure, and yet mistrusted by everybody, disliked on every hand. It was her voice, curiously clear and repellant, that gave her away. Only Gudrun was in accord with her. It was at these times that the intimacy between the two sisters was most complete, as if their intelligence were one. They felt a strong, bright bond of understanding between them, surpassing everything else. And during all these days of blind bright abstraction and intimacy of his two daughters, the father seemed to breathe an air of death, as if he were destroyed in his very being. He was irritable to madness, he could not rest, his daughters seemed to be destroying him. But he was inarticulate and helpless against them. He was forced to breathe the air of his own death. He cursed them in his soul, and only wanted, that they should be removed from him.

They continued radiant in their easy female transcendency, beautiful to look at. They exchanged confidences, they were intimate in their revelations to the last degree, giving each other at last every secret. They withheld nothing, they told everything, till they were over the border of evil. And they armed each other with knowledge, they extracted the subtlest flavours from the apple of knowledge. It was curious how their knowledge was complementary, that of each to that of the other.

Ursula saw her men as sons, pitied their yearning and admired their courage, and wondered over them as a mother wonders over her child, with a certain delight in their novelty. But to Gudrun, they were the opposite camp. She feared them and despised them, and respected their activities even overmuch.

"Of course," she said easily, "there is a quality of life in Birkin which is quite remarkable. There is an extraordinary rich spring of life in him, really amazing, the way he can give himself to things. But there are so many things in life that he simply doesn't know. Either he is not aware of their existence at all, or he dismisses them as merely negligible—things which are vital to the other person. In a way, he is not clever enough, he is too intense in spots."

"Yes," cried Ursula, "too much of a preacher. He is really a priest."

"Exactly! He can't hear what anybody else has to say—he simply cannot hear. His own voice is so loud." 5

"Yes. He cries you down."

"He cries you down," repeated Gudrun. "And by mere force of violence. And of course it is hopeless. Nobody is convinced by violence. It makes talking to him impossible—and living with him I should think would be more than impossible." 10

"You don't think one could live with him?" asked Ursula.

"I think it would be too wearing, too exhausting. One would be shouted down every time, and rushed into his way without any choice. He would want to control you entirely. He cannot allow that there is any other mind than his own. And then the real clumsiness of 15 his mind is its lack of self-criticism—. No, I think it would be perfectly intolerable."

"Yes," assented Ursula vaguely. She only half agreed with Gudrun. "The nuisance is," she said, "that one would find almost any man intolerable after a fortnight." 20

"It's perfectly dreadful," said Gudrun. "But Birkin—he is too positive. He couldn't bear it if you called your soul your own. Of him that is strictly true."

"Yes," said Ursula. "You must have *his* soul."

"Exactly! And what can you conceive more deadly?" 25

This was all so true, that Ursula felt jarred to the bottom of her soul, with ugly distaste. She went on, with the discord jarring and jolting through her, in the most barren of misery.

Then there started a revulsion from Gudrun. She finished life off so thoroughly, she made things so ugly and so final. As a matter of 30 fact, even if it were as Gudrun said, about Birkin, other things were true as well. But Gudrun would draw two lines under him and cross him out like an account that is settled. There he was, summed up, paid for, settled, done with. And it was such a lie. This finality of Gudrun's, this dispatching of people and things in a sentence, it was 35 all such a lie. Ursula began to revolt from her sister.

One day as they were walking along the lane, they saw a robin sitting on the top twig of a bush, singing shrilly. The sisters stood to look at him. An ironical smile flickered on Gudrun's face.

"Doesn't he feel important?" smiled Gudrun. 40

"Doesn't he!" exclaimed Ursula, with a little ironical grimace. "Isn't he a little Lloyd George* of the air!"

"Isn't he! Little Lloyd Georges of the air! That's just what they are," cried Gudrun in delight. Then for days, Ursula saw the persistent, obtrusive birds as stout, short politicians lifting up their voices from the platform, little men who must make themselves heard at any cost.

But even from this there came the revulsion. Some yellow-ammers* suddenly shot along the road in front of her. And they looked to her so uncanny and inhuman, like flaring yellow barbs shooting through the air on some weird, living errand, that she said to herself: "After all, it is impudence to call them little Lloyd Georges. They are really unknown to us, they are the unknown forces. It is impudence to look at them as if they were the same as human beings. They are of another world. How stupid anthropomorphism is! Gudrun is really impudent, insolent, making herself the measure of everything, making everything come down to human standards. Rupert is quite right, human beings are boring, painting the universe with their own image. The universe is non-human, thank God." It seemed to her irreverence, destructive of all true life, to make little Lloyd Georges of the birds. It was such a lie towards the robins, and such a defamation. Yet she had done it herself. But under Gudrun's influence: so she exonerated herself.

So she withdrew away from Gudrun and from that which she stood for, she turned in spirit towards Birkin again. She had not seen him since the fiasco of his proposal. She did not want to, because she did not want the question of her acceptance thrust upon her. She knew what Birkin meant when he asked her to marry him; vaguely, without putting it into speech, she knew. She knew what kind of love, what kind of surrender he wanted. And she was not at all sure that this was the kind of love that she herself wanted. She was not at all sure that it was this mutual unison in separateness that she wanted. She wanted unspeakable intimacies. She wanted to have him, utterly, finally to have him as her own, oh, so unspeakably, in intimacy. To drink him down—ah, like a life-draught. She made great professions, to herself, of her willingness to warm his foot-soles between her breasts, after the fashion of the nauseous Meredith poem.* But only on condition that he, her lover, loved her absolutely, with complete self-abandon. And subtly enough, she knew he would never abandon himself *finally* to her. He did not

believe in final self-abandonment. He said it openly. It was his
challenge. She was prepared to fight him for it. For she believed in
an absolute surrender to love. She believed that love by far surpassed
the individual. He said the individual was *more* than love, or than any
relationship. For him, the bright, single soul accepted love as one of 5
its conditions, a condition of its own equilibrium. She believed that
love was *everything*. Man must render himself up to her: he must be
quaffed to the dregs by her. Let him be *her man* utterly, and she in
return would be his humble slave—whether he wanted it or not.

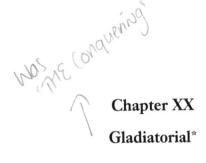

was THE conquering

Chapter XX

Gladiatorial*

After the fiasco of the proposal, Birkin had hurried blindly away from Beldover, in a whirl of fury. He felt he had been a complete fool, that the whole scene had been a farce of the first water. But that did not trouble him at all. He was deeply, mockingly angry that Ursula persisted always in this old cry: "Why do you want to bully me?", and in her bright, insolent abstraction.

He went straight to Shortlands. There he found Gerald standing with his back to the fire, in the library, as motionless as a man is, who is completely and emptily restless, utterly hollow. He had done all the work he wanted to do—and now there was nothing. He could go out in the car, he could run to town. But he did not want to go out in the car, he did not want to run to town, he did not want to call on the Thirlbys.* He was suspended motionless, in an agony of inertia, like a machine that is without power.

This was very bitter to Gerald, who had never known what boredom was, who had gone from activity to activity, never at a loss. Now, gradually, everything seemed to be stopping in him. He did not want any more to do the things that offered. Something dead within him just refused to respond to any suggestion. He cast over in his mind, what it would be possible to do, to save himself from this misery of nothingness, relieve the stress of this hollowness. And there were only three things left, that would rouse him, make him live. One was to drink or smoke hashish, the other was to be soothed by Birkin, and the third was woman. And there was no one for the moment to drink with. Nor was there a woman. And he knew Birkin was out. So there was nothing to do but to bear the stress of his own emptiness.

When he saw Birkin his face lit up in a sudden, wonderful smile:

"By God, Rupert," he said, "I'd just come to the conclusion that nothing in the world mattered except somebody to take the edge off one's being alone: the right somebody."

The smile in his eyes was very astonishing, as he looked at the other man. It was the pure gleam of relief. His face was pallid and even haggard.

"The right woman, I suppose you mean," said Birkin spitefully.

"Of course, for choice. Failing that, an amusing man."

He laughed as he said it. Birkin sat down near the fire.

"What were you doing?" he asked.

"I? Nothing. I'm in a bad way just now, everything's on edge, and I can neither work nor play. I don't know whether it's a sign of old age, I'm sure."

"You mean you're bored?"

"Bored! I don't know.—I can't apply myself. And I feel the devil is either very present inside me, or dead."

Birkin glanced up and looked in his eyes.

"You should try hitting something," he said.

Gerald smiled.

"Perhaps," he said. "So long as it was something worth hitting."

"Quite!" said Birkin, in his soft voice.

There was a long pause, during which each man* could feel the presence of the other.

"One has to wait," said Birkin.

"Ah God! Waiting! What are we waiting for?"

"Some old Johnny says there are three cures for *ennui*: sleep, drink, and travel,"* said Birkin.

"All cold eggs,"* said Gerald. "In sleep, you dream, in drink you curse, and in travel you yell at a porter.—No, work and love are the two. When you're not at work you should be in love."

"Be it then," said Birkin.

"Give me the object," said Gerald. "The possibilities of love exhaust themselves."

"Do they? And then what?"

"Then you die," said Gerald.

"So you ought," said Birkin.

"I don't see it," replied Gerald. He took his hands out of his trousers pockets, and reached for a cigarette. He was tense and nervous. He lit the cigarette over a lamp, reaching forward and drawing steadily. He was dressed for dinner, as usual in the evening, although he was alone.

"There's a third one even to your two," said Birkin. "Work, love, and fighting. You forget the fight."

"I suppose I do," said Gerald. "Did you ever do any boxing—?"

"No, I don't think I did," said Birkin.

"Ay—" Gerald lifted his head and blew the smoke slowly into the air.

"Why?" said Birkin.

5 "Nothing.—I thought we might have a round. It is perhaps true, that I want something to hit. It's a suggestion."

"So you think you might as well hit me?" said Birkin.

"You? Well—! Perhaps—! In a friendly kind of way, of course."

"Quite!" said Birkin, bitingly.

10 Gerald stood leaning back against the mantel-piece. He looked down at Birkin, and his eyes flashed with a sort of terror, like the eyes of a stallion, that are bloodshot and overwrought, turned glancing backwards in a stiff terror.

"I feel that if I don't watch myself, I shall find myself doing 15 something silly," he said.

"Why not do it?" said Birkin coldly.*

Gerald listened with quick impatience. He kept glancing down at Birkin, as if looking for something from the other man.

"I used to do some Japanese wrestling," said Birkin. "A Jap lived 20 in the same house with me in Heidelberg, and he taught me a little. But I was never much good at it."

"You did!" exclaimed Gerald. "That's one of the things I've never even seen done. You mean jiu-jitsu, I suppose?"

"Yes. But I am no good at those things—they don't interest me."

25 "They don't? They do me.—What's the start?"

"I'll show you what I can, if you like," said Birkin.

"You will?" A queer, smiling look tightened Gerald's face for a moment, as he said, "Well, I'd like it very much."

"Then we'll try jiu-jitsu. Only you can't do much in a starched 30 shirt."

"Then let us strip, and do it properly.—Half a minute—" He rang the bell, and waited for the butler.

"Bring a couple of sandwiches and a syphon," he said to the man, "and then don't trouble me any more tonight—or let anybody else."

35 The man went. Gerald turned to Birkin with his eyes lighted.

"And you used to wrestle with a Jap?" he said. "Did you strip?"

"Sometimes."

"You did! What was he like then, as a wrestler?"

"Good, I believe. I am no judge. He was very quick and slippery 40 and full of electric fire. It is a remarkable thing, what a curious sort of fluid force they seem to have in them, those people—not like a human grip—like a polyp—"

Gerald nodded.

"I should imagine so," he said, "to look at them. They repel me, rather."

"Repel and attract, both. They are very repulsive when they are cold, and they look grey. But when they are hot and roused, there is a definite attraction—a curious kind of full electric fluid—like eels."*

"Well—, yes—, probably."

The man brought in the tray and set it down.

"Don't come in any more," said Gerald.

The door was closed.

"Well then," said Gerald; "shall we strip and begin? Will you have a drink first?"

"No, I don't want one."

"Neither do I."

Gerald fastened the door and pushed the furniture aside. The room was large, there was plenty of space, it was thickly carpeted. Then he quickly threw off his clothes, and waited for Birkin. The latter, white and thin, came over to him. Birkin was more a presence than a visible object; Gerald was aware of him completely, but not really visually. Whereas Gerald himself was concrete and notice-able, a piece of pure final substance.

"Now," said Birkin, "I will show you what I learned, and what I remember. You let me take you so—" And his hands closed on the naked body of the other man. In another moment, he had Gerald swung over lightly and balanced against his knee, head downwards. Relaxed, Gerald sprang to his feet with eyes glittering.

"That's smart," he said. "Now try again."

So the two men began to struggle together. They were very dissimilar. Birkin was tall and* narrow, his bones were very thin and fine. Gerald was much heavier and more plastic.* His bones were strong and round, his limbs were rounded, all his contours were beautifully and fully moulded. He seemed to stand with a proper, rich weight on the face of the earth, whilst Birkin seemed to have the centre of gravitation in his own middle. And Gerald had a rich, frictional kind of strength, rather mechanical, but sudden and invincible, whereas Birkin was abstract as to be almost intangible. He impinged invisibly upon the other man, scarcely seeming to

touch him, like a garment, and then suddenly piercing in a tense
fine grip that seemed to penetrate into the very quick of Gerald's
being.

5   They stopped, they discussed methods, they practised grips and
throws, they became more accustomed to each other, to each other's
rhythm, they got a kind of mutual physical understanding. And then
again they had a real struggle. They seemed to drive their white flesh
deeper and deeper against each other, as if they would break into a
oneness. Birkin had a great subtle energy, that would press upon the
10 other man with an uncanny force, weigh him like a spell put upon
him. Then it would pass, and Gerald would heave free, with white,
heaving, dazzling movements.

So the two men entwined and wrestled with each other, working
nearer and nearer. Both were white and clear, but Gerald flushed
15 smart red where he was touched, and Birkin remained white and
tense. He seemed to penetrate into Gerald's more solid, more
diffuse bulk, to interfuse his body through the body of the other, as if
to bring it subtly into subjection, always seizing with some rapid
necromantic foreknowledge every motion of the other flesh, con-
20 verting and counteracting it, playing upon the limbs and trunk of
Gerald like some hard wind. It was as if Birkin's whole physical
intelligence interpenetrated into Gerald's body, as if his fine,
sublimated energy entered into the flesh of the fuller man, like some
potency, casting a fine net, a prison, through the muscles into the
25 very depths of Gerald's physical being.

So they wrestled swiftly, rapturously, intent and mindless at last,
two essential white figures ever working into a tighter, closer oneness
of struggle, with a strange, octopus-like knotting and flashing of
limbs in the subdued light of the room; a tense white knot of flesh
30 gripped in silence between the walls of old brown books. Now and
again came a sharp gasp of breath, or a sound like a sigh, then the
rapid thudding of movement on the thickly-carpeted floor, then the
strange sound of flesh escaping under flesh. Often, in the white,
interlaced knot of violent living being that swayed silently, there was
35 no head to be seen, only the swift, tight limbs, the solid white backs,
the physical junction of two bodies clinched* into oneness. Then
would appear the gleaming, ruffled head of Gerald, as the struggle
changed, then for a moment the dun-coloured, shadow-like head of
the other man would lift up from the conflict, the eyes wide and
40 dreadful and sightless.

At length Gerald lay back inert on the carpet, his breast rising in great slow panting, whilst Birkin kneeled over him, almost unconscious. Birkin was much more exhausted. He caught little, short breaths, he could scarcely breathe any more. The earth seemed to tilt and sway, and a complete darkness was coming over his mind. He did not know what happened. He slid forward quite unconscious, over Gerald, and Gerald did not notice. Then he was half-conscious again, aware only of the strange tilting and sliding of the world. The world was sliding, everything was sliding off into the darkness. And he was sliding endlessly, endlessly away.

He came to consciousness again, hearing an immense knocking outside. What could be happening, what was it, the great hammer-strokes resounding through the house? He did not know. And then it came to him that it was his own heart beating. But that seemed impossible, the noise was outside. No, it was inside himself, it was his own heart. And the beating was painful, so strained, surcharged. He wondered if Gerald heard it. He did not know whether he were standing or lying or falling.

When he realised that he was fallen prostrate upon Gerald's body he wondered, he was surprised. But he sat up, steadying himself with his hand and waiting for his heart to become stiller and less painful. It hurt very much, and took away his consciousness.

Gerald however was still less conscious than Birkin. They waited dimly, in a sort of not-being, for many uncounted, unknown minutes.

"Of course—" panted Gerald, "I didn't have to be rough—with you—I had to keep back—my force—"

Birkin heard the sound as if his own spirit stood behind him, outside him, and listened to it. His body was in a trance of exhaustion, his spirit heard thinly. His body could not answer. Only he knew his heart was getting quieter. He was divided entirely between his spirit, which stood outside, and knew, and his body, that was a plunging, unconscious stroke of blood.

"I could have thrown you—using violence—" panted Gerald. "But you beat me right enough."

"Yes," said Birkin, hardening his throat and producing the words in the tension there, "You're much stronger than I—you could beat me—easily."

Then he relaxed again to the terrible plunging of his heart and his blood.

"It surprised me," panted Gerald, "what strength you've got. Almost—supernatural."

"For a moment," said Birkin.

He still heard as if it were his own disembodied spirit hearing, standing at some distance behind him. It drew nearer however, his spirit. And the violent striking of blood in his chest was sinking quieter, allowing his mind to come back. He realised that he was leaning with all his weight on the soft body of the other man. It startled him, because he thought he had withdrawn. He recovered himself, and sat up. But he was still vague and unestablished. He put out his hand to steady himself. It touched the hand of Gerald, that was lying out on the floor. And Gerald's hand closed warm and sudden over Birkin's, they remained exhausted and breathless, the one hand clasped closely over the other. It was Birkin whose hand, in swift response, had closed in a strong, warm clasp over the hand of the other. Gerald's clasp had been sudden and momentaneous.

The normal consciousness however was returning, ebbing back. Birkin could breathe almost naturally again. Gerald's hand slowly withdrew, Birkin slowly, dazedly rose to his feet and went towards the table. He poured out a whisky and soda. Gerald also came for a drink.

"It was a real set-to, wasn't it?" said Birkin, looking at Gerald with darkened eyes.

"God, yes," said Gerald. He looked at the delicate body of the other man, and added: "It wasn't too much for you, was it?"

"No. One ought to wrestle and strive and be physically close. It makes one sane."

"You do think so?"

"I do. Don't you?"

"Yes," said Gerald, "it's life for me—"

There were long spaces of silence between their words. The wrestling had some deep meaning to them—an unfinished meaning.

"We are mentally, spiritually intimate, therefore we should be more or less physically intimate too—it is more whole."

"Certainly it is," said Gerald. Then he laughed pleasantly, adding: "It's rather wonderful to me."

He stretched out his arms handsomely.

"Yes," said Birkin. "—I don't know why one should have to justify oneself."

"No."

The two men began to dress.

"I think also that you are beautiful," said Birkin to Gerald, "and that is enjoyable too. One should enjoy what is given."

"You think I am beautiful—how do you mean, physically?" asked Gerald, his eyes glistening.

"Yes. You have a northern kind of beauty, like light refracted from snow—and a beautiful plastic form. Yes, that is there to enjoy as well. We should enjoy everything."

Gerald laughed in his throat, and said:

"That's certainly one way of looking at it.—I can say this much, I feel better. It has certainly helped me.—Is this the Brüderschaft you wanted?"

"Perhaps. Do you think this pledges anything?"

"I don't know," laughed Gerald.

"At any rate, one feels freer and more open now—and that is what we want."

"Certainly," said Gerald.

They drew to the fire, with the decanters and the glasses and the food.

"I always eat a little before I go to bed," said Gerald. "I sleep better."

"I should not sleep so well," said Birkin.

"No? There you are, we are not alike.—I'll put a dressing-gown on." Birkin remained alone, looking at the fire. His mind had reverted to Ursula. She seemed to return again into his consciousness. Gerald came down wearing a gown of broad-barred, thick black-and-green silk, brilliant and striking.

"You are very fine," said Birkin, looking at the full robe.

"It was a caftan in Bokhara,"* said Gerald. "I like it."

"I like it too."

Birkin was silent, thinking how scrupulous Gerald was in his attire, how expensive too. He wore silk socks, and studs of fine workmanship, and silk underclothing, and silk braces. Curious! This was another of the differences between them. Birkin was careless and unimaginative about his own appearance.

"Of course you," said Gerald, as if he had been thinking; "there's something curious about you. You're curiously strong. One doesn't expect it, it is rather surprising."

Birkin laughed. He was looking at the handsome figure of the other man, blond and comely in the rich robe, and he was half thinking of the difference between it and himself—so different; as far, perhaps, apart as man from woman, yet in another direction. But really it was Ursula, it was the woman who was gaining ascendance over Birkin's being, at this moment. Gerald was becoming dim again, lapsing out of him.

"Do you know," he said suddenly, "I went and proposed to Ursula Brangwen tonight, that she should marry me."

He saw the blank shining wonder come over Gerald's face.

"You did?"

"Yes. Almost formally—speaking first to her father, as it should be, in the world—though that was accident—or mischief."

Gerald only stared in wonder, as if he did not grasp.

"You don't mean to say that you seriously went and asked her family to let you marry her?"

"Yes," said Birkin, "I did."

"What, had you spoken to her before about it, then?"

"No, not a word. I suddenly thought I would go there and ask her—and her father happened to come instead of her—so I asked him first."

"If you could have her?" concluded Gerald.

"Ye-es, that."

"And you didn't speak to her?"

"Yes. She came in afterwards. So it was put to her as well."

"It was!—And what did she say then?—You're an engaged man?"

"No,—she only said she didn't want to be bullied into answering."

"She what?"

"Said she didn't want to be bullied into answering."

"'Said she didn't want to be bullied into answering!' Why what did she mean by that?"

Birkin raised his shoulders.—"Can't say," he answered. "Didn't want to be bothered just then, I suppose."

"But is this really so?—And what did you do then?"

"I walked out of the house and came here."

"You came straight here?"

"Yes."

Gerald stared in amazement and amusement. He could not take it in.

"But is this really true, as you say it now?"

"Word for word."

"It is?"

He leaned back in his chair, filled with delight and amusement.

"Well that's good," he said. "And so you came here to wrestle with your good angel,* did you?"

"Did I?" said Birkin.

"Well it looks like it. Isn't that what you did?"

Now Birkin could not follow Gerald's meaning.

"And what's going to happen?" said Gerald. "You're going to keep open the proposition, so to speak?"

"I suppose so. I vowed to myself I would see them all to the devil. But I suppose I shall ask her again, in a little while."

Gerald watched him steadily.

"So you're fond of her then?" he asked.

"I think—I love her," said Birkin, his face going very still and fixed.

Gerald glistened for a moment with pleasure, as if it were something done specially to please him. Then his face assumed a fitting gravity, and he nodded his head slowly.

"You know," he said, "I always believed in love—true love.—But where does one find it, nowadays?"

"I don't know," said Birkin.

"Very rarely," said Gerald. Then, after a pause, "I've never felt it myself—not what I should call love. I've gone after women—and been keen enough over some of them. But I've never felt *love*. I don't believe I've ever felt as much *love* for a woman, as I have for you—not *love*. You understand what I mean?"

"Yes. I'm sure you've never loved a woman."

"You feel that, do you?—And do you think I ever shall? You understand what I mean?" He put his hand to his breast, closing his fist there, as if he would draw something out.* "I mean that—that——I can't express what it is, but I know it."

"What is it, then?" asked Birkin.

"You see, I can't put it into words. I mean, at any rate, something abiding, something that can't change——"

His eyes were bright and puzzled.

"Now do you think I shall ever feel that for a woman?" he asked, anxiously.

Birkin looked at him, and shook his head.

"I don't know," he said. "I could not say."

Gerald had been on the *qui vive*, as awaiting his fate. Now he drew back in his chair.

"No," he said, "and neither do I, and neither do I."

"We are different, you and I," said Birkin. "I can't tell your life."

"No," said Gerald, "no more can I. But I tell you—I begin to doubt it."

5 "That you will ever love a woman?"

"Well—yes—what you would truly call *love*—"

"You doubt it?"

"Well—I begin to."

There was a long pause.

10 "Life has all kinds of things," said Birkin. "There isn't only one road."

"Yes, I believe that too. I believe it.—And mind you, I don't care how it is with me—I don't care how it is—so long as I don't feel—" he paused, and a blank, barren look passed over his face, to express 15 his feeling—"so long as I feel I've *lived*, somehow—and I don't care how it is—but I want to feel that—"

"Fulfilled," said Birkin.

"We-ell, perhaps it is, fulfilled;—I don't use the same words as you."

20 "It is the same."

Chapter XXI

Threshold

Gudrun was away in London, having a little show of her work, with a friend, and looking round, preparing for flight from Beldover. Come what might, she would be on the wing in a very short time. She received a letter from Winifred Crich, ornamented with drawings.

"Father also has been to London, to be examined by the doctors. It made him very tired. They say he must rest a very great deal, so he is mostly in bed. He brought me a lovely tropical parrot in faïence, of Dresden ware, also a man ploughing, and two mice climbing up a stalk, also in faïence. The mice are Copenhagen ware.* They are the best, but mice don't shine so much, otherwise they are very good, their tails are slim and long. They all shine nearly like glass. Of course it is the glaze, but I don't like it. Gerald likes the man ploughing the best, his trousers are torn, he is ploughing with an ox, being I suppose a German peasant. It is all grey and white, white shirt and grey trousers, but very shiny and clean. Mr Birkin likes the girl best, under the hawthorn blossom, with a lamb, and with daffodils painted on her skirts, in the drawing room. But that is silly, because the lamb is not a real lamb, and she is silly too.

"Dear Miss Brangwen are you coming back soon, you are very much missed here. I enclose a drawing of father sitting up in bed. He says he hopes you are not going to forsake us. Oh dear Miss Brangwen, I am sure you won't. Do come back and draw the ferrets, they are the most lovely noble darlings in the world. We might carve them in holly-wood, playing against a background of green leaves. Oh do let us, for they are most beautiful.

"Father says we might have a studio. Gerald says we could easily have a beautiful one over the stables, it would only need windows to be put in the slant of the roof, which is a simple matter. Then you could stay here all day and work, and we could live in the studio, like two real artists, like the man in the picture in the hall, with the frying-pan and the walls all covered with drawings. I long to be free, to live the free life of an artist. Even Gerald told father that only an artist is free, because he lives in a creative world of his own.———"

Gudrun caught the drift of the family intentions, in this letter. Gerald wanted her to be attached to the household at Shortlands, he was using Winifred as his stalking-horse. The father thought only of his child, he saw a rock of salvation in Gudrun. And Gudrun

admired him for his perspicacity. The child, moreover, was really exceptional. Gudrun was quite content. She was quite willing, given a studio, to spend her days at Shortlands. She disliked the Grammar School already thoroughly, she wanted to be free. If a studio were
5 provided, she would be free to go on with her work, she would await the turn of events with complete serenity. And she was really interested in Winifred, she would be quite glad to understand the girl.

So there was quite a little festivity on Winifred's account, the day Gudrun returned to Shortlands.

10 "You should make a bunch of flowers to give to Miss Brangwen when she arrives," Gerald said smiling to his sister.

"Oh no," cried Winifred, "it's silly."

"Not at all. It is a very charming and ordinary attention."

"Oh, it *is* silly," protested Winifred, with all the extreme *mauvaise*
15 *honte** of her years. Nevertheless, the idea appealed to her. She wanted very much to carry it out. She flitted round the green-houses and the conservatory looking wistfully at the flowers on their stems. And the more she looked, the more she *longed* to have a bunch of the blossoms she saw, the more fascinated she became with her little
20 vision of ceremony, and the more consumedly shy and self-conscious she grew, till she was almost beside herself. She could not get the idea out of her mind. It was as if some haunting challenge prompted her, and she had not enough courage to take it up. So again she drifted into the green-houses, looking at the lovely roses in
25 their pots, and at the virginal cyclamens, and at the mystic white clusters of a creeper. The beauty, oh the beauty of them, and oh the paradisal bliss, if she should have a perfect bouquet and could give it to Gudrun the next day. Her passion and her complete indecision almost made her ill.

30 At last she slid to her father's side.

"Daddy—" she said.

"What my precious?"

But she hung back, the tears almost coming to her eyes, in her sensitive confusion. Her father looked at her, and his heart ran hot
35 with tenderness, an anguish of poignant love.

"What do you want to say to me, my love?"

"Daddy—!" her eyes smiled laconically—"isn't it silly if I give Miss Brangwen some flowers when she comes?"

The sick man looked at the bright, knowing eyes of his child, and
40 his heart burned with love.

"No, darling, that's not silly. It's what they do to queens."

This was not very reassuring to Winifred. She half suspected that queens in themselves were a silliness. Yet she so wanted her little romantic occasion.

"Shall I then?" she asked.

"Give Miss Brangwen some flowers? Do, Birdie. Tell Wilson* I say you are to have what you want."

The child smiled a small, subtle, unconscious smile to herself, in anticipation of her way.

"But I won't get them till tomorrow," she said.

"Not till tomorrow, Birdie.—Give me a kiss then—"

Winifred silently kissed the sick man, and drifted out of the room. She again went the round of the green-houses and the conservatory, informing the gardener, in her high, peremptory, simple fashion, of what she wanted, telling him all the blooms she had selected.

"What do you want these for?" Wilson asked her.

"I want them," she said. She wished servants did not ask questions.

"Ay, you've said as much. But what do you want them for, for decoration, or to send away, or what?"

"I want them for a presentation bouquet."

"A presentation bouquet! Who's coming then?—the Duchess of Portland?"*

"No."

"Oh, not her?—Well you'll have a rare poppy-show* if you put all the things you've mentioned into your bouquet."

"Yes, I want a rare poppy-show."

"You do! Then there's no more to be said."

The next day Winifred, in a dress of silvery velvet, and holding a gaudy bunch of flowers in her hand, waited with keen impatience in the schoolroom, looking down the drive for Gudrun's arrival. It was a wet morning. Under her nose was the strange fragrance of hot-house flowers, the bunch was like a little fire to her, she seemed to have a strange new fire in her heart. This slight sense of romance stirred her like an intoxicant.

At last she saw Gudrun coming, and she ran downstairs to warn her father and Gerald. They, laughing at her anxiety and gravity, came with her into the hall. The man-servant came hastening to the door, and there he was, relieving Gudrun of her umbrella, and then of her raincoat. The welcoming party hung back till their visitor entered the hall.

Gudrun was flushed with the rain, her hair was blown in loose little curls, she was like a flower just opened in the rain, the heart of the blossom just newly visible, seeming to emit a warmth of retained sunshine. Gerald winced in spirit, seeing her so beautiful and unknown. She was wearing a soft blue dress, and her stockings were of dark red.

Winifred advanced with odd, stately formality.

"We are so glad you've come back," she said. "These are your flowers."

She presented the bouquet.

"Mine!" cried Gudrun. She was suspended for a moment, then a vivid flush* went over her, she was as if blinded for a moment with a flame of pleasure. Then her eyes, strange and flaming, lifted and looked at the father, and at Gerald. And again Gerald shrank in spirit, as if it would be more than he could bear, as her hot, exposed eyes rested on him. There was something so revealed, she was revealed beyond bearing, to his eyes. He turned his face aside. And he felt he would not be able to avert her. And he writhed under the imprisonment.

Gudrun put her face into the flowers.

"But how beautiful they are!" she said, in a muffled voice. Then, with a strange, suddenly revealed passion, she stooped and kissed Winifred.

Mr Crich went forward with his hand held out to her.

"I was afraid you were going to run away from us," he said, playfully.

Gudrun looked up at him with a luminous, roguish, unknown face.

"Really!" she replied. "No, I didn't want to stay in London."

Her voice seemed to imply that she was glad to get back to Shortlands, her tone was warm and subtly caressing.

"That is a good thing," smiled the father. "You see you are very welcome here among us."

Gudrun only looked into his face with dark-blue, warm, shy eyes. She was unconsciously carried away by her own power.

"And you look as if you came home in every possible triumph," Mr Crich continued, holding her hand.

"No," she said, glowing strangely. "I haven't had any triumph till I came here."

"Ah come come! We're not going to hear any of those tales. Haven't we read notices in the paper, Gerald?"

"You came off pretty well," said Gerald to her, shaking hands. "Did you sell anything?"

"No," she said, "not much."

"Just as well," he said.

She wondered what he meant. But she was all aglow with her reception, carried away by this little flattering ceremonial on her behalf.

"Winifred," said the father, "have you a pair of shoes for Miss Brangwen?—You had better change at once—"

Gudrun went out with her bouquet in her hand.

"Quite a remarkable young woman," said the father to Gerald, when she had gone.

"Yes," replied Gerald briefly, as if he did not like the observation.

Mr Crich liked Gudrun to sit with him for half an hour. Usually he was ashy and wretched, with all the life gnawed out of him. But as soon as he rallied, he liked to make-belief that he was just as before, quite well and in the midst of life—not of the outer world, but in the midst of a strong essential life. And to this belief, Gudrun contributed perfectly. With her, he could get by stimulation those precious half-hours of strength and exaltation and pure freedom, when he seemed to live more than he had ever lived.

She came to him as he lay propped up in the library. His face was like yellow wax, his eyes darkened, as it were sightless. His black beard, now streaked with grey, seemed to spring out of the waxy flesh of a corpse. Yet the atmosphere about him was energetic and playful. Gudrun subscribed to this, perfectly. To her fancy, he was just an ordinary man. Only his rather terrible appearance was photographed upon her soul, away beneath her consciousness. She knew that, in spite of his playfulness, his eyes could not change from their darkened vacancy, they were the eyes of a man who is dead.

"Ah, this is Miss Brangwen," he said, suddenly rousing as she entered, announced by the man-servant. "Thomas, put Miss Brangwen a chair here—that's right." He looked at her soft, fresh face with pleasure. It gave him the illusion of life. "Now, you will have a glass of sherry and a little piece of cake.—Thomas——"

"No thank you," said Gudrun. And as soon as she had said it, her heart sank horribly. The sick man seemed to fall into a gap of death, at her contradiction. She ought to play up to him, not to contravene him. In an instant she was smiling her rather roguish smile.

"I don't like sherry very much," she said. "But I like almost anything else."

The sick man caught at this straw instantly.

"Not sherry! No! Something else! What then? What is there Thomas?"

"Port wine—curaçao——"

"I would love some curaçao—" said Gudrun, looking at the sick man confidingly.

"You would. Well then Thomas, curaçao—and a little cake, or a biscuit?"

"A biscuit," said Gudrun. She did not want anything, but she was wise.

"Yes."

He waited till she was settled with her little glass and her biscuit. Then he was satisfied.

"You have heard the plan," he said with some excitement, "for a studio for Winifred, over the stables?"

"No!" exclaimed Gudrun, in mock wonder.

"Oh!—I thought Winnie wrote it to you, in her letter?"

"Oh—yes—of course.—But I thought perhaps it was only her own little idea—" Gudrun smiled subtly, indulgently.

The sick man smiled also, elated.

"Oh no. It is a real project. There is a good room under the roof of the stables—with sloping rafters. We had thought of converting it into a studio."

"How *very* nice that would be!" cried Gudrun with excited warmth. The thought of the rafters stirred her.

"You think it would? Well, it can be done."

"But how perfectly splendid for Winifred! Of course, it is just what is needed, if she is to work at all seriously. One must have one's workshop, otherwise one never ceases to be an amateur."

"Is that so? Yes.—Of course.—Of course, I should like you to share it with Winifred."

"Thank you *so* much."

Gudrun knew all these things already, but she must look shy and very grateful, as if overcome.

"Of course, what I should like best, would be if you could give up your work at the Grammar School, and just avail yourself of the studio, and work there—well, as much or as little as you liked—"

He looked at Gudrun with dark, vacant eyes. She looked back at him as if full of gratitude. These phrases of a dying man were so complete and natural, coming like echoes through his dead mouth.

"And as to your earnings—you don't mind taking from me what you have taken from the Education Committee, do you? I don't want you to be a loser."

"Oh," said Gudrun, "if I can have the studio and work there, I can earn money enough, really I can."

"Well," he said, pleased to be the benefactor, "we can see about all that.—You wouldn't mind spending your days here?"

"If there were a studio to work in," said Gudrun, "I could ask for nothing better."

"Is that so?"

He was really very pleased. But already he was getting tired. She could see the grey, awful semi-consciousness of mere pain and dissolution coming over him again, the torture coming into the vacancy of his ·darkened eyes. It was not over yet, this process of death. She rose softly, saying:

"Perhaps you will sleep. I must look for Winifred."

She went out, telling the nurse that she had left him. Day by day the tissue of the sick man was further and further reduced, nearer and nearer the process came, towards the last knot which held the human being in its unity. But this knot was hard and unrelaxed, the will of the dying man never gave way. He might be dead in nine-tenths, yet the remaining tenth remained unchanged, till it too was torn apart. With his will he held the unit of himself firm, but the circle of his power was ever and ever reduced, it would be reduced to a point at last, then swept away.

To adhere to life, he must adhere to human relationships, and he caught at every straw. Winifred, the butler, the nurse, Gudrun, these were the people who meant all to him, in these last resources. Gerald, in his father's presence, stiffened with repulsion. It was so, to a less degree, with all the other children except Winifred. They could not see anything but the death, when they looked at their father. It was as some subterranean dislike overcame them. They could not see the familiar face, hear the familiar voice. They were overwhelmed by the antipathy of visible and audible death. Gerald could not breathe in his father's presence. He must get out at once. And so, in the same way, the father could not bear the presence of his son. It sent a final irritation through the soul of the dying man.

The studio was made ready, Gudrun and Winifred moved in.

They enjoyed so much the ordering and the appointing of it. And now they need hardly be in the house at all. They had their meals in the studio, they lived there safely. For the house was becoming dreadful. There were two nurses in white, flitting silently about, like heralds of
5   death. The father was confined to his bed, there was a come and go of sotto-voce sisters and brothers and children.

Winifred was her father's constant visitor. Every morning, after breakfast, she went into his room when he was washed and propped up in bed, to spend half an hour with him.

10   "Are you better, Daddy?" she asked him invariably.

And invariably he answered:

"Yes, I think I'm a little better, pet."

She held his hand in both her own, lovingly and protectively. And this was very dear to him.

15   She ran in again as a rule at lunchtime, to tell him the course of events, and every evening, when the curtains were drawn, and his room was cosy, she spent a long time with him. Gudrun was gone home, Winifred was alone in the house, she liked best to be with her father. They talked and prattled at random, he always as if he were
20   well, just the same as when he was going about. So that Winifred, with a child's subtle instinct for avoiding the painful things, behaved as if nothing serious was the matter. Instinctively, she withheld her attention, and was happy. Yet in her remoter soul, she knew as well as the adults knew: perhaps better.

25   Her father was quite well in his make-belief with her. But when she went away, he relapsed under the misery of his dissolution. But still there were these bright moments, though as his strength waned, his faculty for attention grew weaker, and the nurse had to send Winifred away, to save him from exhaustion.

30   He never admitted that he was going to die. He knew it was so, he knew it was the end. Yet even to himself he did not admit it. He hated the fact, mortally. His will was rigid. He could not bear being overcome by death. For him, there was no death. And yet, at times, he felt a great need to cry out and to wail and complain. He would
35   have liked to cry aloud to Gerald, so that his son should be horrified out of his composure. Gerald was instinctively aware of this, and he recoiled, to avoid any such thing. This uncleanness of death repelled him too much. One should die quickly, like the Romans, one should be master of one's fate* in dying as in living. He was convulsed in the
40   clasp of this death of his father's, as in the coils of the great serpent of

Laocoön.* The great serpent had got the father, and the son was dragged into the embrace of horrifying death along with him. He resisted always. And in some strange way, he was a tower of strength to his father.

The last time the dying man asked to see Gudrun he was grey with near death. Yet he must see someone, he must, in the intervals of consciousness, catch into connection with the living world, lest he should have to accept his own situation. Fortunately he was most of his time dazed and half gone. And he spent many hours dimly thinking of the past, as it were, dimly re-living his old experiences. But there were times even to the end when he was capable of realising what was happening to him in the present, the death that was on him. And these were the times when he called in outside help, no matter whose. For to realise this death that he was dying was a death beyond death, never to be borne. It was an admission never to be made.

Gudrun was shocked by his appearance, and by the darkened, almost disintegrated eyes, that still were unconquered and firm.

"Well," he said in his weakened voice, "and how are you and Winifred getting on?"

"Oh, very well indeed," replied Gudrun.

There were slight dead gaps in the conversation, as if the ideas called up were only elusive straws floating on the dark chaos of the sick man's dying.

"The studio answers all right?" he said.

"Splendid. It couldn't be more beautiful and perfect," said Gudrun.

She waited for what he would say next.

"And you think Winifred has the makings of a sculptor?"

It was strange how hollow the words were, meaningless.

"I'm sure she has. She will do good things one day."

"Ah! Then her life won't be altogether wasted, you think?"

Gudrun was rather surprised.

"Sure* it won't!" she exclaimed softly.

"That's right."

Again Gudrun waited for what he would say.

"You find life pleasant, it is good to live, isn't it?" he asked, with a pitiful faint smile that was almost too much for Gudrun.

"Yes," she smiled—she would lie at random—"I get a pretty good time I believe."

"That's right. A happy nature is a great asset."

Again Gudrun smiled, though her soul was dry with repulsion. Did one have to die like this, having the life extracted forcibly from one, whilst one smiled and made conversation to the end? Was there
5 no other way? Must one go through all the horror of this victory over death, the triumph of the integral will, that would not be broken till it disappeared utterly? One must, it was the only way. She admired the self-possession and the control of the dying man exceedingly. But she loathed the death itself. She was glad the everyday world held
10 good, and she need not recognise anything beyond.

"You are quite all right here?—nothing we can do for you?—nothing you find wrong in your position?"

"Except that you are too good to me," said Gudrun.

"Ah, well, the fault of that lies with yourself," he said, and he felt a
15 little exultation, that he had made this speech. He was still so strong and living! But the nausea of death began to creep back on him, in reaction.

Gudrun went away, back to Winifred. Mademoiselle had left, Gudrun stayed a good deal at Shortlands, and a tutor came in to
20 carry on Winifred's education. But he did not live in the house, he was connected with the Grammar School.

One day, Gudrun was to drive with Winifred and Gerald and Birkin to town, in the car. It was a dark, showery day. Winifred and Gudrun were ready and waiting at the door. Winifred was very quiet,
25 but Gudrun had not noticed. Suddenly the child asked, in a voice of unconcern:

"Do you think my father is going to die, Miss Brangwen?"

Gudrun started.

"I don't know," she replied.

30 "Don't you truly?"

"Nobody knows for certain. He *may* die, of course."

The child pondered a few moments, then she asked:

"But do you *think* he will die?"

It was put almost like a question in geography or science, insistent,
35 as if she would force an admission from the adult. The watchful, slightly triumphant child was almost diabolical.

"Do I think he will die?" repeated Gudrun. "Yes, I do."

But Winifred's large eyes were fixed on her, and the girl did not move.

40 "He is very ill," said Gudrun.

A small smile came over Winifred's face, subtle and sceptical.

"*I* don't believe he will," the child asserted mockingly, and she moved away into the drive. Gudrun watched the isolated figure, and her heart stood still. Winifred was playing with a little rivulet of water, absorbedly, as if nothing had been said.

"I've made a proper dam," she cried, out of the moist distance.

Gerald came to the door from out of the hall behind.

"It is just as well she doesn't choose to believe it," he said.

Gudrun looked at him. Their eyes met; and they exchanged a sardonic understanding.

"Just as well," said Gudrun.

He looked at her again, and a fire flickered up in his eyes.

"Best to dance while Rome burns,* since it must burn, don't you think?" he said.

She was rather taken aback. But, gathering herself together, she replied:

"Oh—better dance than wail, certainly."

"So I think."

And they both felt the subterranean desire to let go, to fling away everything, and lapse into a sheer unrestraint, brutal and licentious. A strange black passion surged up pure in Gudrun. She felt strong. She felt her hands so strong, as if she could tear the world asunder with them. She remembered the abandonments of Roman licence,* and her heart grew hot. She knew she wanted this herself also—or something, something equivalent. Ah, if that which was unknown and suppressed in her were once let loose, what an orgiastic and satisfying event it would be. And she wanted it, she trembled slightly from the proximity of the man, who stood just behind her, suggestive of the same black licentiousness that rose in herself. She wanted it with him, this unacknowledged frenzy. For a moment the clear perception of this preoccupied her, distinct and perfect in its final reality. Then she shut it off completely, saying:

"We might as well go down to the lodge after Winifred—we can get in the car there."

"So we can," he answered, going with her.

They found Winifred at the lodge admiring the litter of pure-bred white puppies. The girl looked up, and there was a rather ugly, unseeing cast in her eyes as she turned to Gerald and Gudrun. She did not want to see them.

"Look!" she cried. "Three new puppies! Marshall* says this one

seems perfect. Isn't it a sweetling? But it isn't so nice as its mother."
She turned to caress the fine white bull-terrier bitch that stood
uneasily near her.

"My dearest Lady Crich," she said, "you are beautiful as an angel
5 on earth. Angel—angel—*don't* you think she's good enough and
beautiful enough to go to heaven, Gudrun?—They will be in heaven,
won't they—and *especially* my darling Lady Crich!—Mrs
Marshall,—I say!"

"Yes Miss Winifred?" said the woman, appearing at the door.

10 "Oh do call this one Lady Winifred, if she turns out perfect, will
you? Do tell Marshall to call it Lady Winifred."

"I'll tell him—but I'm afraid that's a gentleman puppy, Miss
Winifred."

"Oh *no*!" There was the sound of a car. "There's Rupert!" cried
15 the child, and she ran to the gate.

Birkin, driving his car, pulled up outside the lodge gate.

"We're ready!" cried Winifred. "I want to sit in front with you,
Rupert. May I?"

"I'm afraid you'll fidget about and fall out," he said.

20 "No I won't. I do want to sit in front next to you. It makes my feet
so lovely and warm, from the engines."

Birkin helped her up, amused at sending Gerald to sit by Gudrun
in the body of the car.

"Have you any news, Rupert?" Gerald called, as they rushed
25 along the lanes.

"News?" exclaimed Birkin.

"Yes." Gerald looked at Gudrun, who sat by his side, and he said,
his eyes narrowly laughing, "I want to know whether I ought to
congratulate him, but I can't get anything definite out of him."

30 Gudrun flushed deeply.

"Congratulate him on what?" she asked.

"There was some mention of an engagement—at least, he said
something to me about it."

Gudrun flushed darkly.

35 "You mean with Ursula?" she said, in challenge.

"Yes. That is so, isn't it?"

"I don't think there's any engagement," said Gudrun coldly.

"That so?—Still no developments, Rupert?" he called.

"Where? Matrimonial? No."

40 "How's that?" called Gudrun.

Birkin glanced quickly round. There was irritation in his eyes also.

"Why?"* he replied. "What do you think of it, Gudrun?"

"Oh," she cried, determined to fling her stone also into the pool, since they had begun, "I don't think she wants an engagement. Naturally, she's a bird that prefers the bush."* Gudrun's voice was clear and gong-like. It reminded Rupert of her father's, so strong and vibrant.

"And I," said Birkin, his face playful but yet determined, "I want a binding contract, and am not keen on love, particularly free love."

They were both amused. *Why* this public avowal? Gerald seemed suspended a moment, in amusement.

"Love isn't good enough for you?" he called.

"No!" shouted Birkin.

"Ha, well that's being over-refined," said Gerald, and the car ran on through the mud.

"What's the matter, really?" said Gerald, turning to Gudrun.

This was an assumption of a sort of intimacy that irritated Gudrun almost like an affront. It seemed to her that Gerald was deliberately insulting her, and infringing on the decent privacy of them all.

"What is it?" she said, in her high, repellant voice. "Don't ask me!—I know nothing about *ultimate* marriage, I assure you: or even penultimate."

"Only the ordinary unwarrantable brand!" replied Gerald. "Just so—same here. I am no expert on marriage, and degrees of ultimateness. It seems to be a bee that buzzes loudly in Rupert's bonnet."

"Exactly! But that is his trouble, exactly! Instead of wanting a woman for herself, he wants his *ideas* fulfilled. Which, when it comes to actual practice, is not good enough."

"Oh no. Best go slap for what's womanly in woman, like a bull at a gate." Then he seemed to glimmer in himself. "—You think love is the ticket,* do you?" he asked.

"Certainly, while it lasts—you only can't insist on *permanency*," came Gudrun's voice, strident above the noise.

"Marriage or no marriage, ultimate or penultimate or just so-so?—take the love as you find it."

"As you please, or as you don't please," she echoed.* "Marriage is a social arrangement, I take it, and has nothing to do with the question of love."

His eyes were flickering on her all the time. She felt as if he were kissing her freely and malevolently. It made the colour burn in her cheeks, but her heart was quite firm and unfailing.

"You think Rupert is off his head a bit?" Gerald asked.

Her eyes flashed with acknowledgement.

5 "As regards a woman, yes," she said, "I do. There *is* such a thing as two people being in love for the whole of their lives—perhaps. But marriage is neither here nor there, even then.—If they are in love, well and good. If not—why break eggs about it!"

"Yes," said Gerald. "That's how it strikes me. But what about 10 Rupert?"

"I can't make out—neither can he nor anybody. He seems to think that if you marry you can get through marriage into a third heaven, or something—all very vague."

"Very! And who wants a third heaven?—As a matter of fact, 15 Rupert has a great yearning to be *safe*—to tie himself to the mast."*

"Yes. It seems to me he's mistaken there too," said Gudrun. "I'm sure a mistress is more likely to be faithful than a wife—just because she is her *own* mistress. No—he says he believes that a man and wife can go further than any other two beings—but *where*, is not 20 explained. They can know each other, heavenly and hellish, but particularly hellish, so perfectly that they go beyond heaven and hell—into—there it all breaks down—into nowhere—"

"Into Paradise, he says," laughed Gerald.

Gudrun shrugged her shoulders.

25 "*Je m'en fiche* of your Paradise!" she said.

"Not being a Mohammedan,"* said Gerald. Birkin sat motionless, driving the car, quite unconscious of what they said. And Gudrun, sitting immediately behind him, felt a sort of ironic pleasure in thus exposing him.

30 "He says," she added, with a grimace of irony, "that you can find an eternal equilibrium in marriage, if you accept the unison, and still leave yourself separate, don't try to fuse."

"Doesn't inspire me," said Gerald.

"That's just it," said Gudrun.

35 "I believe in love, in a real *abandon*, if you're capable of it," said Gerald.

"So do I," said she.

"And so does Rupert, too—though he is always shouting."

"No," said Gudrun. "He won't abandon himself to the other 40 person. You can't be sure of him. That's the trouble, I think."

"Yet he wants marriage!—Marriage—*et puis?*"

"Le paradis!"* mocked Gudrun.

Birkin, as he drove, felt a creeping of the spine, as if somebody was threatening his neck. But he shrugged with indifference. It began to rain. Here was a change. He stopped the car and got down to put up 5
the hood.

Chapter XXII

Woman to Woman

They came to the town, and left Gerald at the railway station. Gudrun and Winifred were to come to tea with Birkin, who expected Ursula also. In the afternoon, however, the first person to turn up was Hermione. Birkin was out, so she went in the drawing-room, looking at his books and papers, and playing on the piano. Then Ursula arrived. She was surprised, unpleasantly so, to see Hermione, of whom she had heard nothing for some time.

"It is a surprise to see you," she said.

"Yes," said Hermione—"I've been away at Aix—"*

"Oh, for your health?"

"Yes."

The two women looked at each other. Ursula resented Hermione's long, grave, downward-looking face. There was something of the stupidity and the unenlightened self-esteem of a horse in it. "She's got a horse-face," Ursula said to herself, "she runs between blinkers." It did seem as if Hermione, like the moon, had only one side to her penny. There was no obverse. She stared out all the time on the narrow, but to her, complete world of the extant consciousness. In the darkness, she did not exist. Like the moon, one half of her was lost to life. Her self was all in her head, she did not know what it was spontaneously to run or move, like a fish in the water, or a weasel on the grass. She must always *know*.

But Ursula only suffered from Hermione's one-sidedness. She only felt Hermione's cool confidence, which seemed to put her down as nothing. Hermione, who brooded and brooded till she was exhausted with the ache of her effort at consciousness, spent and ashen in her body, who gained so slowly and with such effort her final and barren conclusions of knowledge, was apt, in the presence of other women, whom she thought simply female, to wear the conclusions of her bitter assurance like jewels which conferred on her an unquestionable distinction, established her in a higher order of life. She was apt, mentally, to condescend to women such as Ursula, whom she regarded as purely emotional. Poor Hermione, it was her one possession, this aching certainty of hers, it was her only justification. She must be confident here, for God knows, she felt rejected and deficient enough elsewhere. In the life of thought, of the spirit, she was one of the elect. And she wanted to be universal. But there was a devastating cynicism at the bottom of her. She did not believe in her own universals—they were sham. She did not believe in the inner life—it was a trick, not a reality. She did not believe in the spiritual world—it was an affectation. In the last resort, she believed in Mammon, the flesh, and the devil*—these at least were not sham. She was a priestess without belief, without conviction, suckled in a creed outworn,* and condemned to the reiteration of mysteries that were not divine to her. Yet there was no escape. She was a leaf upon a dying tree. What help was there then, but to fight still for the old, withered truths, to die for the old, outworn belief, to be a sacred and inviolate priestess of desecrated mysteries? The old great truths *had* been true. And she was a leaf of the old great tree of knowledge, that was withering now. To the old and last truth then she must be faithful, even though cynicism and mockery took place at the bottom of her soul.

"I am so glad to see you," she said to Ursula, in her slow voice, that was like an incantation. "—You and Rupert have become quite friends?"

"Oh yes," said Ursula. "He is always somewhere in the background."

Hermione paused before she answered. She saw perfectly well the other woman's vaunt: it seemed truly vulgar.

"Is he!" she said slowly, and with perfect equanimity. "And do you think you will marry?"

The question was so calm and mild, so simple and bare and dispassionate that Ursula was somewhat taken aback, rather attracted. It pleased her almost like a wickedness. There was some delightful naked irony in Hermione.

"Well," replied Ursula, "*he* wants to, awfully, but I'm not so sure."

Hermione watched her with slow calm eyes. She noted this new expression of vaunting. How she envied Ursula a certain unconscious positivity! even her vulgarity!

"Why aren't you sure?" she asked, in her easy sing-song. She was perfectly at her ease, perhaps even rather happy in this conversation. "You don't really love him?"

Ursula flushed a little at the mild impertinence of this question. And yet she could not definitely take offence. Hermione seemed so calmly and sanely candid. After all, it was rather great to be able to be so sane.

5 "He says it isn't love he wants," she replied.

"What is it then?" Hermione was slow and level.

"He wants me really to accept him in marriage."

Hermione was silent for some time, watching Ursula with slow, pensive eyes.

10 "Does he," she said at length, without expression. Then, rousing, "And what is it you don't want? You don't want marriage?"

"No—I don't—not really. I don't want to give the sort of *submission* he insists on. He wants me to give myself up—and I simply don't feel that I *can* do it."*

15 Again there was a long pause, before Hermione replied:

"Not if you don't want to." Then again there was silence. Hermione shuddered with a strange desire. Ah, if only he had asked *her* to subserve him, to be his slave! She shuddered with desire.

"You see I can't—"

20 "But exactly in what does—"

They had both begun at once, they both stopped. Then Hermione, assuming priority of speech, resumed as if wearily:

"To what does he want you to submit?"

"He says he wants me to accept him non-emotionally, and 25 finally——I really don't know *what* he means. He says he wants the demon part of himself to be mated—physically—not the human being.—You see he says one thing one day, and another the next—and he always contradicts himself—"

"And always thinks about himself, and his own dissatisfaction," 30 said Hermione slowly.

"Yes," cried Ursula. "As if there were no-one but himself concerned.—That makes it so impossible."

But immediately she began to retract.

"He insists on my accepting God knows what in *him*," she 35 resumed. "He wants me to accept *him* as—as an absolute—But it seems to me he doesn't want to *give* anything. He doesn't want real warm intimacy—he won't have it—he rejects it. He won't let me think, really, and he won't let me *feel*—he hates feelings."

There was a long pause, bitter for Hermione. Ah, if only he would 40 have made this demand of her! Her he *drove* into thought, drove inexorably into knowledge—and then execrated her for it.

"He wants me to sink myself in him," Ursula resumed, "not to have any being of my own— —"

"Then why doesn't he marry an odalisk?" said Hermione in her mild sing-song, "if it is that he wants." Her long face looked sardonic and amused.

"Yes," said Ursula vaguely.—After all, the tiresome thing was, he did *not* want an odalisk, he did not want a slave. Hermione would have been his slave—there was in her a horrible desire to prostrate herself before a man—a man who worshipped her, however, and admitted her as the supreme thing.—He did not want an odalisk. He wanted a woman to *take* something from him, to give herself up so much that she could take the last realities of him, the last facts, the last physical facts, physical and unbearable.

And if she did, would he acknowledge her? Would he be able to acknowledge her through everything, or would he use her just as an instrument, use her for his own private satisfactions, not admitting her? That was what the other men had done. They had wanted their own show, and they would not admit her, they turned all she was into nothingness. Just as Hermione now betrayed herself as a woman. Hermione was like a man, she believed only in men's things. She betrayed the woman in herself.—And Birkin, would he acknowledge, or would he deny her?

"Yes," said Hermione, as each woman came out of her own separate reverie. "It would be a mistake—I think it would be a mistake—"

"To marry him?" asked Ursula.

"Yes," said Hermione slowly—"I think you need a man—soldierly, strong-willed—" Hermione held out her hand and clenched it with rhapsodic intensity. "You should have a man like the old heroes—you need to stand behind him as he goes into battle, you need to *see* his strength, and to *hear* his shout— —You need a man physically strong, and *virile* in his will, *not* a sensitive man— —" there was a break, as if the pythoness had uttered the oracle, and now the woman went on, in a rhapsody-wearied voice: "And you see, Rupert isn't this, he isn't. He is frail in health and body, he needs great, great care. Then he is so changeable and unsure of himself—it requires the greatest patience and understanding to help him. And I don't think you are patient. You would have to be prepared to suffer—dreadfully. I can't *tell* you how much suffering it would take to make him happy. He lives an *intensely* spiritual life, at times—too, too wonderful. And then come the reactions.—I can't speak of what I

have been through with him.——We have been together so long, I
really do know him, I *do* know what he is.——And I feel I must say it;
I feel it would be perfectly *disastrous* for you to marry him—for you
even more than for him."—Hermione lapsed into bitter reverie.—

5 "He is so uncertain, so unstable—he wearies, and then reacts. I
couldn't *tell* you what his reactions are. I couldn't *tell* you the agony of
them.——That which he affirms and loves one day—a little later he
turns on it in a fury of destruction.——He is never constant, always
this awful, dreadful reaction.——Always the quick change from

10 good to bad, bad to good—And nothing is so devastating,
nothing——"

"Yes," said Ursula humbly, "you must have suffered."

An unearthly light came on Hermione's face. She clenched her
hand like one inspired.

15 "And one must be willing to suffer—willing to suffer for him
hourly, daily—if you are going to help him, if he is to keep true to
anything at all——"

"And I don't *want* to suffer hourly and daily," said Ursula.
"I don't, I should be ashamed. I think it is degrading not to be

20 happy."

Hermione stopped and looked at her a long time.

"Do you," she said at last. And this utterance seemed to her a
mark of Ursula's far distance from herself. For to Hermione
suffering was the greatest reality, come what might. Yet she too had a

25 creed of happiness.

"Yes," she said. "One *should* be happy—." But it was a matter of
will.

"Yes," said Hermione, listlessly now, "I can only feel that it would
be disastrous, disastrous——at least, to marry in a hurry. Can't you

30 be together without marriage? Can't you go away and live somewhere
without marriage?—I do feel that marriage would be fatal, for both of
you. I think for you even more than for him—and I think of his
health——"

"Of course," said Ursula, "*I* don't care about marriage—it isn't

35 really important to me—it's he who wants it."

"It is his idea for the moment," said Hermione, with that weary
finality, and a sort of *si jeunesse savait** infallibility.

There was a pause. Then Ursula broke into faltering challenge.

"You think I'm merely a physical woman, don't you?"

40 "No indeed," said Hermione. "No indeed! But I think you are

vital and *young*—it isn't a question of years, or even of experience—
it is almost a question of race. Rupert is race-old, he comes of an old
race—and you seem to me so young, you come of a young,
inexperienced race."

"Do I!" said Ursula.—"But I think he is awfully young, on one
side."

"Yes, perhaps—childish in many respects. Nevertheless——"

They both lapsed into silence. Ursula was filled with deep
resentment and a touch of hopelessness. "It isn't true," she said to
herself, silently addressing her adversary. "It isn't true. And it is *you*
who want a physically strong, bullying man, not I. It is you who
want an unsensitive man, not I. You *don't* know anything about
Rupert, not really, in spite of the years you have had him. You
don't give him a woman's love, you give him an ideal love, and that is
why he reacts away from you. You *don't* know. You only know the
dead things. Any kitchen maid would know something about him,
you don't know. What do you think your knowledge is but dead
understanding, that doesn't mean a thing. You are so false, and
untrue, how could you know anything? What is the good of your
talking about love—you untrue spectre of a woman! How can you
know anything, when you don't believe? You don't believe in yourself
and your own womanhood, so what good is your conceited, shallow
cleverness—!"

The two women sat on in antagonistic silence. Hermione felt
injured, that all her good intention, all her offering, only left the
other woman in vulgar antagonism. But then, Ursula could not
understand, never would understand, could never be more than the
usual jealous and unreasonable female, with a good deal of powerful
female emotion, female attraction, and a fair amount of female
understanding, but no mind. Hermione had decided long ago that
where there was no mind, it was useless to appeal for reason—one
had merely to ignore the ignorant. And Rupert—he had now reacted
towards the strongly female, healthy, selfish woman—it was his
reaction for the time being—there was no helping it all. It was all a
foolish backward and forward, a violent oscillation that would at
length be too violent for his coherency, and he would smash and be
dead. There was no saving him. This violent and directionless
reaction between animalism and spiritual truth would go on in him
till he tore himself in two between the opposite directions, and
disappeared meaninglessly out of life. It was no good——he too was

without unity, without *mind*, in the ultimate stages of living; not quite
man enough to make a destiny for a woman.

They sat on till Birkin came in and found them together. He felt at
once the antagonism in the atmosphere, something radical and
5 insuperable, and he bit his lip. But he affected a bluff manner.

"Hello, Hermione, are you back again? How do you feel?"

"Oh, better. And how are you—you don't look well—"

"Oh?—I believe Gudrun and Winnie Crich are coming in to tea.
At least they said they were. We shall be a tea-party. What train did
10 you come by, Ursula?"

It was rather annoying to see him trying to placate both women at
once. Both women watched him, Hermione with deep resentment
and pity for him, Ursula very impatient. He was nervous and
apparently in quite good spirits, chattering the conventional common-
15 places. Ursula was amazed and indignant at the way he made
small-talk; he was adept as any *fat** in Christendom. She became
quite stiff, she would not answer. It all seemed to her so false and so
belittling. And still Gudrun did not appear.

"I think I shall go to Florence for the winter,"* said Hermione at
20 length.

"Will you?" he answered. "But it is so cold there."

"Yes, but I shall stay with Palestra. It is quite comfortable."

"What takes you to Florence?"

"I don't know," said Hermione slowly. Then she looked at him
25 with her slow, heavy gaze. "Barnes is starting his school of aesthetics,
and Olandese is going to give a set of discourses on the Italian
national policy—"*

"Both rubbish," he said.

"No, I don't think so," said Hermione.
30 "Which do you admire, then?"

"I admire both. Barnes is a pioneer.—And then I am interested in
Italy, in her coming to national consciousness."

"I wish she'd come to something different from national
consciousness, then," said Birkin; "especially as it only means a sort
35 of commercial-industrial consciousness. I hate Italy and her national
rant.—And I think Barnes is an amateur."

Hermione was silent for some moments, in a state of hostility. But
yet, she had got Birkin back again into her world! How subtle her
influence was, she seemed to start his irritable attention into her
40 direction exclusively, in one minute. He was her creature.

"No," she said, "you are wrong." Then a sort of tension came over her, she raised her face like the pythoness inspired with oracles, and went on, in rhapsodic manner: "il Sandro mi scrive che ha accolto il più grande entusiasmo, tutti i giovani, e fanciulle e ragazzi, sono appassionati, appassionati per l'Italia, e vogliono assolutamente imparare tutto———"* She went on in Italian, as if, in thinking of the Italians she thought in their language.

He listened with a shade of distaste to her rhapsody, then he said:

"For all that, I don't like it. Their nationalism is just industrialism,—that, and a shallow jealousy I detest so much."

"I think you are wrong—I think you are wrong—" said Hermione. "It seems to me purely spontaneous and beautiful, the modern Italian's *passion*, for it is a passion, for Italy, L'Italia—"

"Do you know Italy well?" Ursula asked of Hermione. Hermione hated to be broken in upon in this manner. Yet she answered mildly:

"Yes, pretty well.——I spent several years of my girlhood there, with my mother.——My mother died in Florence."*

"Oh."

There was a pause, painful to Ursula and to Birkin. Hermione however seemed abstracted and calm. Birkin was white, his eye glowed as if he were in a fever, he was far too overwrought. How Ursula suffered in this tense atmosphere of strained wills! Her head seemed bound round by iron bands.

Birkin rang the bell for tea. They would not wait for Gudrun any longer. When the door was opened, the cat walked in.

"Micio! Micio!" called Hermione, in her slow, deliberate singsong. The young cat turned to look at her, then, with his slow and stately walk he advanced to her side.

"Vieni—vieni qua," Hermione was saying, in her strange caressive, protective voice, as if she were always the elder, the mother superior. "Vieni dire Buon Giorno alla zia. Mi ricorde, mi ricorde bene—non è vero, piccolo? È vero che mi ricordi? È vero?"* And slowly she rubbed his head, slowly and with ironic indifference.

"Does he understand Italian?" said Ursula, who knew nothing of the language.

"Yes," said Hermione at length. "His mother was Italian. She was born in my waste-paper basket, in Florence, on the morning of Rupert's birthday. She was his birthday present."

Tea was brought in. Birkin poured out for them. It was strange how inviolable was the intimacy which existed between him and

Hermione. Ursula felt that she was an outsider. The very tea-cups and the old silver was a bond between Hermione and Birkin. It seemed to belong to an old, past world which they inhabited together, and in which Ursula was a foreigner. She was almost a
5 parvenue in their old cultured milieu. Her convention was not their convention, their standards were not her standards. But theirs were established, they had the sanction and the grace of age. He and she together, Hermione and Birkin, were people of the same old tradition, the same withered, deadening culture. And she, Ursula,
10 was an intruder. So they always made her feel.

Hermione poured a little cream into a saucer. The simple way she assumed her rights in Birkin's room maddened and discouraged Ursula. There was a fatality about it, as if it were bound to be. Hermione lifted the cat and put the cream before him. He planted
15 his two paws on the edge of the table and bent his graceful young head to drink.

"Siccuro che capisce italiano," sang Hermione, "non l'avrà dimenticato, la lingua della Mamma."

She lifted the cat's head with her long, slow, white fingers, not
20 letting him drink, holding him in her power. It was always the same, this joy in power she manifested, peculiarly in power over any male being. He blinked forbearingly, with a male, bored expression, licking his whiskers. Hermione laughed in her short, grunting fashion.
25 "Ecco, il bravo ragazzo, come è superbo, questo!"*

She made a vivid picture, so calm and strange with the cat. She had a true static impressiveness, she was a social artist in some ways.

The cat refused to look at her, indifferently avoided her fingers, and began to drink again, his nose down to the cream, perfectly
30 balanced, as he lapped with his odd little click.

"It's bad for him, teaching him to eat at table," said Birkin.

"Yes," said Hermione, easily assenting.

Then, looking down at the cat, she resumed in her old, mocking, humorous sing-song:
35 "Ti imparano fare brutte cose, brutte cose——"

She lifted the Mino's white chin on her fore-finger, slowly. The young cat looked round with a supremely forbearing air, avoided seeing anything, withdrew his chin, and began to wash his face with his paw. Hermione grunted her laughter, pleased.
40 "Bel giovanotto——"* she said.

The cat reached forward again and put his fine white paw on the edge of the saucer. Hermione lifted it down with delicate slowness. This deliberate, delicate carefulness of movement reminded Ursula of Gudrun.

"No! Non è permesso di mettere il zampino nel tondinetto. Non piace al babbo. Un signor gatto così selvatico—!"*

And she kept her finger on the softly planted paw of the cat, and her voice had the same whimsical, humorous note of bullying.

Ursula had her nose out of joint. She wanted to go away now. It all seemed no good. Hermione was established for ever, she herself was ephemeral and had not yet even arrived.

"I will go now," she said suddenly.

Birkin looked at her almost in fear—he so dreaded her anger.

"But there is no need for such hurry," he said.

"Yes," she answered. "I will go." And turning to Hermione, before there was time to say any more, she held out her hand and said: "Goodbye."

"Goodbye—" sang Hermione, detaining the hand. "Must you really go now?"

"Yes, I think I'll go," said Ursula, her face set, and averted from Hermione's eyes.

"You think you will——"

But Ursula had got her hand free. She turned to Birkin with a quick, almost jeering: "Goodbye," and she was opening the door before he had time to do it for her.

When she got outside the house she ran down the road in fury and agitation. It was strange, the unreasoning rage and violence Hermione roused in her, by her very presence. Ursula knew she gave herself away to the other woman, she knew she looked ill-bred, uncouth, exaggerated. But she did not care. She only ran up the road, lest she should go back and jeer in the faces of the two she had left behind. For they outraged her.

Chapter XXIII

Excurse*

Next day Birkin sought Ursula out. It happened to be the half-day at the Grammar School. He appeared towards the end of the morning, and asked her, would she drive with him in the afternoon. She consented. But her face was closed and unresponding, and his heart sank.

The afternoon was fine and dim. He was driving the motor-car, and she sat beside him. But still her face was closed against him, unresponding. When she became like this, like a wall against him, his heart contracted.

His life now seemed so reduced, that he hardly cared any more. At moments it seemed to him he did not care a straw whether Ursula or Hermione or anybody else existed or did not exist. Why bother! Why strive for a coherent, satisfied life? Why not drift on in a series of accidents—like a picaresque novel? Why not? Why bother about human relationships? Why take them seriously—male or female? Why form any serious connections at all? Why not be casual, drifting along, taking all for what it was worth?

And yet, still, he was damned and doomed to the old effort at serious living.

"Look," he said, "what I bought." The car was running along a broad white road, between autumn trees.

He gave her a little bit of screwed-up paper. She took it and opened it.

"How lovely!" she cried.

She examined the gift.

"How perfectly lovely!" she cried again. "But why do you give them me?" She put the question offensively.

His face flickered with bored irritation. He shrugged his shoulders slightly.

"I wanted to," he said, coolly.

"But why? Why should you?"

"Am I called on to find reasons?" he asked.

There was a silence, whilst she examined the rings that had been screwed up in the paper.

"I think they are *beautiful*," she said, "especially this. This is wonderful—"

It was a round opal, red and fiery,* set in a circle of tiny rubies.

"You like that best?" he said.

"I think I do."

"I like the sapphire," he said.

"This?"

It was a rose-shaped, beautiful sapphire, with small brilliants.

"Yes," she said, "it *is* lovely." She held it in the light. "Yes, perhaps it *is* the best—"

"The blue—" he said.

"Yes, wonderful—"

He suddenly swung the car out of the way of a farm-cart. It tilted on the bank. He was a careless driver, yet very quick. But Ursula was frightened. There was always that something regardless in him which terrified her. She suddenly felt he might kill her, by making some dreadful accident with the motor-car. For a moment she was stony with fear.

"Isn't it rather dangerous, the way you drive?" she asked him.

"No, it isn't dangerous," he said. And then, after a pause: "Don't you like the yellow ring at all?"

It was a squarish topaz set in a frame of steel, or some other similar mineral, finely wrought.

"Yes," she said, "I do like it. But why did you buy three rings?"

"I wanted them. They are second-hand."

"You bought them for yourself?"

"No. Rings look wrong on my hands."

"Why did you buy them then?"

"I bought them to give to you."

"But why? Surely you ought to give them to Hermione! You belong to her."

He did not answer. She remained with the jewels shut in her hand. She wanted to try them on her finger, but something in her would not let her. And moreover, she was afraid her hands were too large, she shrank from the mortification of a failure to put them on any but her little finger. They travelled in silence through the empty lanes.

Driving in a motor-car excited her, she forgot his presence even.

"Where are we?" she asked suddenly.

"Not far from Worksop."*

"And where are we going?"

"Anywhere."

5

10

15

20

25

30

35

40

It was the answer she liked.

She opened her hand to look at the rings. They gave her *such* pleasure, as they lay, the three circles, with their knotted jewels, entangled in her palm. She would have to try them on. She did so
5 secretly, unwilling to let him see, so that he should not know her finger was too large for them. But he saw nevertheless. He always saw, if she wanted him not to. It was another of his hateful, watchful characteristics.

Only the opal, with its thin wire loop, would go on her ring finger.
10 And she was superstitious.* No, there was ill-portent enough, she would not accept this ring from him in pledge.

"Look," she said, putting forward her hand, that was half-closed and shrinking. "The others don't fit me."

He looked at the red-glinting, soft stone, on her over-sensitive
15 skin.

"Yes," he said.

"But opals are unlucky, aren't they?" she said wistfully.

"No. I prefer unlucky things. Luck is vulgar. Who wants what *luck* would bring? I don't."

20 "But why?" she laughed.

And, consumed with desire to see how the other rings would look on her hand, she put them on her little finger.

"They can be made a little bigger," he said.

"Yes," she replied, doubtfully. And she sighed. She knew that, in
25 accepting the rings, she was accepting a pledge. Yet fate seemed more than herself. She looked again at the jewels. They were very beautiful to her eyes—not as ornament, or wealth, but as tiny fragments of loveliness.

"I'm glad you bought them," she said, putting her hand, half
30 unwillingly, gently on his arm.

He smiled, slightly. He wanted her to come to him. But he was angry at the bottom of his soul, and indifferent. He knew she had a passion for him, really. But it was not finally interesting. There were depths of passion where one became impersonal and indifferent,
35 unemotional. Whereas Ursula was still at the emotional personal level—always so abominably personal.—He had taken her as he had never been taken himself. He had taken her at the roots of her darkness and shame—like a demon, laughing over the fountain of mystic corruption which was one of the sources of her being, laughing,
40 shrugging, accepting, accepting finally.—As for her, when would she so much go beyond herself as to accept him at the quick of death?

She now became quite happy. The motor-car ran on, the afternoon was soft and dim, she talked with lively interest, analysing people and their motives—Gudrun, Gerald. He answered vaguely. He was not very much interested any more in personalities and in people—people were all different, but they were all enclosed 5 nowadays in a definite limitation he said; there were only about two great ideas, two great streams of activity remaining, with various forms of reaction therefrom. The reactions were all varied in various people, but they followed a few great laws, and intrinsically there was no difference. They acted and re-acted involuntarily according to a 10 few great laws, and once the laws, the great principles, were known, people were no longer mystically interesting. They were all essentially alike, the differences were only variations on a theme. None of them transcended the given terms.

Ursula did not agree—people were still an adventure to her— 15 but—perhaps not as much as she tried to persuade herself. Perhaps there was something mechanical, now, in her interest. Perhaps also her interest was destructive, her analysing was a real tearing to pieces. There was an under-space in her where she did not care for people and their idiosyncrasies, even to destroy them. She seemed to 20 touch for a moment this undersilence in herself, she became still, and she turned for a moment purely to Birkin.

"Won't it be lovely to go home in the dark?" she said. "We might have tea rather late—shall we?—and have high tea?—wouldn't that be rather nice?"
25
"I promised to be at Shortlands for dinner," he said.

"But—it doesn't matter—you can go tomorrow—."

"Hermione is there," he said, in rather an uneasy voice. "She is going away in two days. I suppose I ought to say goodbye to her—I shall never see her again."
30
Ursula drew away, closed in a violent silence. He knitted his brows, and his eyes began to sparkle again in anger.

"You don't mind, do you?" he asked irritably.

"No, I don't care—why should I—Why should I mind?"

Her tone was jeering and offensive.
35
"That's what I ask myself," he said; "why *should* you mind! But you seem to." His brows were tense with violent irritation.

"I *assure* you I don't, I don't mind in the least. Go where you belong—it's what I want you to do."

"Ah you fool!" he cried, "with your 'go where you belong.' It's 40 finished between Hermione and me. She means much more to *you*, if it comes to that, than she does to me. For you can only revolt in pure reaction from her—and to be her opposite is to be her counterpart."

"Ah, opposite!" cried Ursula. "I know your dodges. I am not taken in by your word-twisting. You belong to Hermione and her dead show.—Well, if you do, you do. I don't blame you. But then you've nothing to do with me."

In his inflamed, overwrought exasperation, he stopped the car, and they sat there, in the middle of the country lane, to have it out. It was a crisis of war between them, so they did not see the ridiculousness of their situation.

"If you weren't a fool, if only you weren't a fool," he cried in bitter despair, "you'd see that one could be decent, even where one has been wrong. I *was* wrong to go on all those years with Hermione—it was a deathly process. But after all, one can have a little human decency.—But no, you would tear my soul out with your jealousy, at the very mention of Hermione's name."

"I jealous! *I*—jealous! You *are* mistaken if you think that. I'm not jealous in the least of Hermione, she is nothing to me, not *that*!" And Ursula snapped her fingers. "No, it's you who are a liar. It's you who must return, like a dog to his vomit. It is what Hermione *stands for* that I *hate*, I *hate* it, it is lies, it is false, it is death.—But you want it, you can't help it, you can't help yourself. You belong to that old, deathly way of living—then go back to it.—But don't come to me, for I've nothing to do with it."

And in the stress of her violent emotion, she got down from the car and went to the hedgerow, picking unconsciously some flesh-pink spindle berries, some of which were burst, showing their orange seeds.

"Ah, you are a fool," he cried, bitterly, with some contempt.

"Yes, I am. I *am* a fool. And thank God for it. I'm too big a fool to swallow your clevernesses, God be praised. You go to your women—go to them—they are your sort. You've always had a string of them trailing after you—and you always will. Go to your spiritual brides—but don't come to me as well, because I'm not having any, thank you.—You're not satisfied, aren't you? Your spiritual brides can't give you what you want, they aren't common and fleshly enough for you, aren't they? So you come to me, and keep them in the background! You will marry me, for daily use. But you'll keep yourself well provided with spiritual brides, in the background.—I

know your dirty little game." Suddenly a flame ran over her, and she stamped her foot madly on the road, and he winced, afraid she would strike him. "And *I*, *I'm* not spiritual enough, *I'm* not as spiritual as that Hermione—!" Her brows knitted, her eyes blazed like a tiger's. "Then *go* to her, that's all I say, *go* to her, *go*.—Ha, she spiritual— 5
spiritual, she! A dirty materialist as she is. *She* spiritual?—What does she care for, what *is* her spirituality? What *is* it?" Her fury seemed to blaze out and burn his face. He shrank a little. "I tell you it's *dirt, dirt*, and nothing *but* dirt.—And it's dirt you want, you crave for it.—Spiritual! Is *that* spiritual, her bullying, her conceit, her sordid 10
materialism? She's a fishwife,* a fishwife, she is such a materialist. And all so sordid. What does she work out to, in the end, with all her social passion, as you call it. Social passion—what social passion has she?—show it me!—where is it? She wants petty, immediate *power*, she wants the illusion that she is a great woman, that is all.—In her 15
soul she's a devilish unbeliever, common as dirt. That's what she is at the bottom. And all the rest is *pretence*—but you love it. You love the sham spirituality, it's your food. And why?—Because of the dirt underneath.—Do you think I don't know the foulness of your sex life—and hers?—I do. And it's that foulness you want, you liar. Then 20
have it, have it.—You're such a liar."

She turned away, spasmodically tearing the twigs of spindle berry from the hedge, and fastening them, with vibrating fingers, in the bosom of her coat.

He stood watching in silence. A wonderful tenderness burned 25
in him, at the sight of her quivering, so sensitive fingers: and at the same time he was full of rage and callousness.

"This is a degrading exhibition," he said coolly.

"Yes, degrading indeed," she said. "But more to me than to you."

"Since you choose to degrade yourself," he said. Again the flash 30
came over her face, the yellow lights concentrated in her eyes.

"*You!*" she cried. "You! You truth-lover! you purity-monger! It *stinks*, your truth and your purity. It stinks of the offal you feed on, you scavenger dog, you eater of corpses.—You are foul, *foul*—and you must know it. Your purity, your candour, your goodness—yes 35
thank you, we've had some. What you are is a foul, deathly thing, obscene, that's what you are, obscene and perverse.—You, and love! You may well say you don't want love. No, you want *yourself*, and dirt, and death—that's what you want. You are so *perverse*, so death-eating. And then—"

40

re's a bicycle coming," he said, writhing under her loud
ciation.

e glanced down the road.

don't care," she cried.

Nevertheless she was silent. The cyclist, having heard the voices
raised in altercation, glanced curiously at the man, and the woman,
and at the standing motor-car, as he passed.

"—Afternoon," he said, cheerfully.

"Good-afternoon," replied Birkin coldly.

10 They were silent as the man passed into the distance.

A clearer look had come over Birkin's face. He knew she was in
the main right. He knew he was perverse, so spiritual on the one
hand, and in some strange way, degraded, on the other. But was she
herself any better? Was anybody any better?

15 "It may all be true, lies and stink and all," he said. "But
Hermione's spiritual intimacy is no rottener than your emotional-
jealous intimacy.—One can preserve the decencies, even to one's
enemies: for one's own sake. Hermione is my enemy—to her last
breath. That's why I must bow her off the field."

20 "You! You and your enemies and your bows! A pretty picture you
make of yourself. But it takes nobody in but yourself. I, *jealous*! *I*!
What I say," her voice sprang into flame, "I say because it is *true*, do
you see, because you are *you*, a foul and false liar, a whited sepulchre.
That's why I say it. And *you*, hear it."

25 "And be grateful," he added, with a satirical grimace.

"Yes," she cried, "and if you have a spark of decency in you, be
grateful."

"Not having a spark of decency, however—" he retorted.

"No," she cried, "you haven't a *spark*. And so you can go your way,
30 and I'll go mine. It's no good, not the slightest.—So you can leave me
now, I don't want to go any further with you—leave me—."

"You don't even know where you are," he said.

"Oh, don't bother, I assure you I shall be all right. I've got ten
shillings in my purse, and that will take me back from anywhere *you*
35 have brought me to." She hesitated. The rings were still on her
fingers, two on her little finger, one on her ring finger. Still she
hesitated.

"Very good," he said. "The only hopeless thing is a fool."

"You are quite right," she said.

40 Still she hesitated. Then an ugly, malevolent look came over her

face, she pulled the rings from her fingers, and tossed them at him. One touched his face, the others hit his coat, and they scattered into the mud.

"And take your rings," she said, "and go and buy yourself a female elsewhere—there are plenty to be had, who will be quite glad to share your spiritual mess,—or to have your physical mess, and leave your spiritual mess to Hermione."

With which she walked away, desultorily, up the road. He stood motionless, watching her sullen, rather ugly walk. She was sullenly picking and pulling at the twigs of the hedge as she passed. She grew smaller, she seemed to pass out of his sight. A darkness came over his mind. Only a small, mechanical speck of consciousness hovered near him.

He felt tired and weak. Yet also he was relieved. He gave up his old position. He went and sat on the bank. No doubt Ursula was right. It was true, really, what she said. He knew that his spirituality was concomitant of a process of depravity, a sort of pleasure in self-destruction. There really *was* a certain stimulant in self-destruction, for him—especially when it was translated spiritually.—But then he knew it—he knew it, and had done. And was not Ursula's way of emotional intimacy, emotional and physical, was it not just as dangerous as Hermione's abstract spiritual intimacy? Fusion, fusion, this horrible fusion of two beings, which every woman, and most men insisted on, was it not nauseous and horrible anyhow, whether it was a fusion of the spirit or of the emotional body? Hermione saw herself as the perfect Idea, to which all men must come: and Ursula was the perfect Womb, the bath of birth, to which all men must come! And both were horrible. Why could they not remain individuals, limited by their own limits? Why this dreadful all-comprehensiveness, this hateful tyranny? Why not leave the other being free, why try to absorb, or melt, or merge? One might abandon oneself utterly to the *moment*, but not to any other being.

He could not bear to see the rings lying in the pale mud of the road. He picked them up, and wiped them unconsciously on his hands. They were the little tokens of the reality of beauty, the reality of happiness in warm creation.—But he had made his hands all dirty and gritty.

There was a darkness over his mind. The terrible knot of consciousness that had persisted there like an obsession was broken, gone, his life was dissolved in darkness over his limbs and his body.

But there was a point of anxiety in his heart now. He wanted her to come back. He breathed lightly and regularly like an infant, that breathes innocently, beyond the touch of responsibility.

She was coming back. He saw her drifting desultorily under the high hedge, advancing towards him slowly. He did not move, he did not look again. He was as if asleep, at peace, slumbering and utterly relaxed.

She came up and stood before him, hanging her head.

"See what a flower I found you," she said, wistfully, holding a piece of purple-red bell-heather under his face. He saw the clump of coloured bells, and the tree-like, tiny branch: also her hands, with their over-fine, over-sensitive skin.

"Pretty!" he said, looking up at her with a smile, taking the flower. Everything had become simple again, quite simple, the complexity gone into nowhere. But he badly wanted to cry: except that he was weary and bored by emotion.

Then a hot passion of tenderness for her filled his heart. He stood up and looked into her face. It was new and oh, so delicate in its luminous wonder and fear. He put his arms round her, and she hid her face on his shoulder.

It was peace, just simply peace, as he stood folding her quietly there on the open lane. It was peace at last. The old, detestable world of tension had passed away at last, his soul was strong and at ease.

She looked up at him. The wonderful yellow light in her eyes now was soft and yielded, they were at peace with each other. He kissed her, softly, many, many times. A laugh came into her eyes.

"Did I abuse you?" she asked.

He smiled too, and took her hand, that was so soft and given.

"Never mind," she said, "it is all for the good."

He kissed her again, softly, many times.

"Isn't it?" she said.

"Certainly," he replied. "Wait! I shall have my own back."

She laughed suddenly, with a wild catch in her voice, and flung her arms round him.

"You are mine, my love, aren't you?" she cried, straining him close.

"Yes," he said, softly.

His voice was so soft and final, she went very still, as if under a fate which had taken her. Yes, she acquiesced—but it was accomplished without her acquiescence. He was kissing her quietly, repeatedly, with a soft, still happiness that almost made her heart stop beating.

"My love!" she cried, lifting her face and looking with frightened, gentle wonder of bliss. Was it all real? But his eyes were beautiful and soft and immune from stress or excitement, beautiful and smiling lightly to her, smiling with her. She hid her face on his shoulder, hiding before him, because he could see her so completely. She knew he loved her, and she was afraid, she was in a strange element, a new heaven round about her. She wished he were passionate, because in passion she was at home. But this was so still and frail, as space is more frightening than force.

Again, quickly, she lifted her head.

"Do you love me?" she said, quickly, impulsively.

"Yes," he replied, not heeding her motion, only her stillness.

She knew it was true. She broke away.

"So you ought," she said, turning round to look at the road. "Did you find the rings?"

"Yes."

"Where are they?"

"In my pocket."

She put her hand into his pocket and took them out.

She was restless.

"Shall we go," she said.

"Yes," he answered. And they mounted the car* once more, and left behind them this memorable battle-field.

They drifted through the mild, late afternoon, in a beautiful motion that was smiling and transcendent. His mind was sweetly at ease, the life flowed through him as from some new fountain, he was as if born out of the cramp of a womb.

"Are you happy?" she asked him, in her strange, delighted way.

"Yes," he said.

"So am I," she cried in sudden ecstasy, putting her arm round him and clutching him violently against her, as he steered the motor-car.

"Don't drive much more," she said. "I don't want you to be always doing something."

"No," he said. "We'll finish this little trip, and then we'll be free."

"We will, my love, we will," she cried in delight, kissing him as he turned to her.

He drove on in a strange new wakefulness, the tension of his consciousness broken. He seemed to be conscious all over, all his body awake with a simple, glimmering awareness, as if he had just come awake, like a thing that is born, like a bird when it comes out of an egg, into a new universe.

They dropped down a long hill in the dusk, and suddenly Ursula
5 recognised on her right hand, below in the hollow, the form of Southwell Minster.*

"Are we here!" she cried with pleasure.

The rigid, sombre, ugly cathedral was settling under the gloom of the coming night, as they entered the narrow town, the golden lights
10 showed like slabs of revelation, in the shop-windows.

"Father came here with mother," she said, "when they first knew each other. He loves it—he loves the minster. Do you?"

"Yes. It looks like quartz crystals sticking up out of the dark hollow. We'll have our high tea at the Saracen's Head."*

15 As they descended, they heard the Minster bells playing a hymn, when the hour had struck six.

> "Glory to thee my God this night
> For all the blessings of the light— —"*

So, to Ursula's ear, the tune fell out, drop by drop, from the unseen
20 sky on to the dusky town. It was like dim, bygone centuries sounding. It was all so far off. She stood in the old yard of the inn, smelling of straw and stables and petrol. Above, she could see the first stars. What was it all? This was no actual world, it was the dream-world of one's childhood—a great circumscribed reminiscence. The world
25 had become unreal. She herself was a strange, transcendent reality.

They sat together in a little parlour by the fire.

"Is it true?" she said, wondering.*

"What?"

"Everything—is everything true?"

30 "The best is true," he said, grimacing at her.

"Is it?" she replied, laughing, but unassured.

She looked at him. He seemed still so separate. New eyes were opened in her soul, she saw a strange creature from another world, in him. It was as if she were enchanted, and everything were metamor-
35 phosed. She recalled again the old magic of the Book of Genesis, where the Sons of God saw the daughters of men, that they were fair.* And he was one of these, one of these strange creatures from the beyond, looking down at her, and seeing she was fair.

He stood on the hearth-rug looking at her, at her face that was

upturned exactly like a flower, a fresh, luminous flower, glinting
faintly golden with the dew of the first light. And he was smiling
faintly as if there were no speech in the world, save the silent delight
of flowers in each other. Smilingly they delighted in each other's
presence, pure presence, not to be thought of, even known. But his 5
eyes had a faintly ironical contraction.

And she was drawn to him strangely, as in a spell. Kneeling on the
hearth-rug before him, she put her arms round his loins, and put her
face against his thighs. Riches! Riches? She was overwhelmed with a
sense of a heavenful of riches. 10

"We love each other," she said in delight.

"More than that," he answered, looking down at her with his
glimmering, easy face.

Unconsciously, with her sensitive finger-tips, she was tracing the
back of his thighs, following some mysterious life-flow* there. She 15
had discovered something, something more than wonderful, more
wonderful than life itself. It was the strange mystery of his life-
motion, there, at the back of the thighs, down the flanks. It was a
strange reality of his being, the very stuff of being, there in the
straight downflow of the thighs. It was here she discovered him one 20
of the Sons of God such as were in the beginning of the world, not a
man, something other, something more.

This was release at last. She had had lovers, she had known
passion. But this was neither love nor passion. It was the daughters of
men coming back to the Sons of God, the strange inhuman Sons of 25
God who are in the beginning.*

Her face was now one dazzle of released, golden light, as she
looked up at him, and laid her hands full on his thighs, behind, as he
stood before her. He looked down at her with a rich bright brow like
a diadem above his eyes. She was beautiful as a new marvellous 30
flower opened at his knees, a paradisal flower she was, beyond
womanhood, such a flower of luminousness. Yet something was tight
and unfree in him. He did not like this crouching, this radiance—not
altogether.

It was all achieved, for her. She had found one of the Sons of God 35
from the Beginning, and he had found one of the first most luminous
daughters of men.

She traced with her hands the line of his loins and thighs, at the
back, and a living fire ran through her, from him, darkly. It was a
dark flood of electric passion she released from him, drew into 40

herself. She had established a rich new circuit, a new current of passional electric energy, between the two of them, released from the darkest poles of the body and established in perfect circuit. It was a dark fire of electricity that rushed from him to her, and flooded them both with rich peace, satisfaction.

"My love," she cried, lifting her face to him, her eyes, her mouth open in transport.

"My love," he answered, bending and kissing her, always kissing her.

She closed her hands over the full, rounded body of his loins, as he stooped over her, she seemed to touch the quick of the mystery of darkness that was bodily him. She seemed to faint beneath, and he seemed to faint, stooping over her. It was a perfect passing away for both of them, and at the same time the most intolerable accession into being, the marvellous fulness of immediate gratification, over-whelming, outflooding from the Source of the deepest life-force, the darkest, deepest, strangest life-source of the human body, at the back and base of the loins.

After a lapse of stillness, after the rivers of strange dark fluid richness had passed over her, flooding, carrying away her mind and flooding down her spine and down her knees, past her feet, a strange flood, sweeping away everything and leaving her an essential new being, she was left quite free, she was free in complete ease, her complete self. So she rose, stilly and blithe, smiling at him. He stood before her, glimmering, so awfully real, that her heart almost stopped beating. He stood there in his strange, whole body, that had its marvellous fountains, like the bodies of the Sons of God who were in the beginning. There were strange fountains of his body, more mysterious and potent than any she had imagined or known, more satisfying, ah, finally, mystically-physically satisfying. She had thought there was no source deeper than the phallic source. And now, behold, from the smitten rock* of the man's body, from the strange marvellous flanks and thighs, deeper, further in mystery than the phallic source, came the floods of ineffable darkness and ineffable riches.

They were glad, and they could forget perfectly. They laughed, and went to the meal provided. There was a venison pasty, of all things, a large broad-faced cut ham, eggs and cresses and red beet-root, and medlars and apple-tart, and tea.

"What *good* things!" she cried with pleasure. "How noble it looks!—Shall I pour out the tea?—"

She was usually nervous and uncertain at performing these public duties, such as giving tea. But today she forgot, she was at her ease, entirely forgetting to have misgivings. The tea-pot poured beautifully from a proud slender spout. Her eyes were warm with smiles as she gave him his tea. She had learned at last to be still and perfect. 5

"Everything is ours," she said to him.

"Everything," he answered.

She gave a queer little crowing sound of triumph.

"I'm so glad!" she cried, with unspeakable relief.

"So am I," he said. "But I'm thinking. We'd better get out of our 10 responsibilities as quick as we can."

"What responsibilities?" she asked, wondering.

"We must drop our jobs, like a shot."

A new understanding dawned into her face.

"Of course," she said, "there's that." 15

"We must get out," he said. "There's nothing for it but to get out, quick."

She looked at him doubtfully across the table.

"But where?" she said.

"I don't know," he said. "We'll just wander about for a bit." 20

Again she looked at him quizzically.

"I should be perfectly happy at the Mill," she said.

"It's very near the old thing," he said. "Let us wander a bit."

His voice could be so soft and happy-go-lucky, it went through her veins like an exhilaration. Nevertheless she dreamed of a valley, 25 and wild gardens, and peace. She had a desire too for splendour—an aristocratic extravagant splendour. Wandering seemed to her like restlessness, dissatisfaction.

"Where will you wander to?" she asked.

"I don't know. I feel as if I would just meet you and we'd set 30 off—just towards the distance."

"But where can one go?" she asked, anxiously. "After all, there *is* only the world, and none of it is very distant."

"Still," he said, "I should like to go with you—nowhere. It would be rather wandering just to nowhere. That's the place to get 35 to—nowhere. One wants to wander away from the world's some- wheres, into our own nowhere."

Still she meditated.

"You see, my love," she said, "I'm so afraid that while we are only people, we've got to take the world that's given—because there isn't 40 any other."

"Yes there is," he said. "There's somewhere where we can be free—somewhere where one needn't wear much clothes—none even— —where one meets a few people who have gone through enough, and can take things for granted—where you be yourself, without bothering. There is somewhere—there are one or two people—"

"But where—?" she sighed.

"Somewhere—anywhere. Let's wander off. That's the thing to do—let's wander off."

"Yes—" she said, thrilled at the thought of travel. But to her it was only travel.

"To be free," he said. "To be free, in a free place, with a few other people!"

"Yes," she said wistfully. Those "few other people" depressed her.

"It isn't really a locality, though," he said. "It's a perfected relation between you and me, and others—the perfection relation—so that we are free together."

"It is, my love, isn't it," she said. "It's you and me. It's you and me, isn't it?" She stretched out her arms to him. He went across, and stooped to kiss her face. Her arms closed round him again, her hands spread upon his shoulders, moving slowly there, moving slowly on his back, down his back slowly, with a strange recurrent, rhythmic motion, yet moving slowly down, pressing mysteriously over his loins, over his flanks. The sense of the awfulness of riches that could never be impaired flooded her mind like a swoon, a death in most marvellous possession, mystic-sure. She possessed him so utterly and intolerably, that she herself lapsed out. And yet she was only sitting still in the chair, with her hands pressed upon him, and lost.

Again he softly kissed her.

"We shall never go apart again," he murmured quietly.

And she did not speak, but only pressed her hands firmer down upon the source of darkness in him.

They decided, when they woke again from the pure swoon, to write their resignations from the world of work there and then. She wanted this.

He rang the bell, and ordered note-paper without a printed address. The waiter cleared the table.

"Now then," he said, "yours first. Put your home address, and the date—then 'Director of Education, Town Hall—Sir—' Now

then!—I don't know how one really stands—I suppose one could get
out of it in less than a month—Anyhow 'Sir—I beg to resign my post
as class-mistress in the Willey Green Grammar School. I should be
very grateful if you would liberate me as soon as possible, without
waiting for the expiration of the month's notice.'—That'll do. Have
you got it? Let me look. 'Ursula Brangwen.' Good! Now I'll write
mine. I ought to give them three months, but I can plead health. I can
arrange it all right."

He sat and wrote out his formal resignation.

"Now," he said, when the envelopes were sealed and addressed,
"shall we post them here, both together?—I know Jackie will say
'Here's a coincidence!', when he receives them in all their identity.
Shall we let him say it, or not?"

"I don't care," she said.

"No—?" he said, pondering.

"It doesn't matter, does it?" she said.

"Yes," he replied. "Their imaginations shall not work on us. I'll
post yours here, mine after.—I cannot be implicated in their
imaginings."

He looked at her with his strange, non-human singleness.

"Yes, you are right," she said.

She lifted her face to him, all shining and open. It was as if he
might enter straight in to the source of her radiance. His face became
a little distracted.

"Shall we go?" he said.

"As you like," she replied.

They were soon out of the little town, and running through the
uneven lanes of the country. Ursula nestled near him, into his
constant warmth, and watched the pale-lit revelation racing ahead,
the visible night. Sometimes it was a wide old road, with grass-
spaces on either side, flying magic and elvin* in the greenish
illumination, sometimes it was trees looming overhead, sometimes it
was bramble bushes, sometimes the walls of a crew-yard* and the
butt of a barn.

"Are you going to Shortlands to dinner?" Ursula asked him
suddenly. He started.

"Good God!" he said. "Shortlands. Never again. Not that.—
Besides we should be too late."

"Where are we going then—to the Mill?"

"If you like.—Pity to go anywhere on this good dark night. Pity to come out of it, really. Pity we can't stop in the good darkness. It is better than anything ever would be—this good immediate darkness."

She sat wondering. The car lurched and swayed. She knew there was no leaving him, the darkness held them both and contained them, it was not to be surpassed. Besides she had a full mystic knowledge of his suave loins of darkness, dark-clad and suave, and in this knowledge there was some of the inevitability and the beauty of fate, fate which one asks for, which one accepts in full.

He sat still like an Egyptian Pharaoh, driving the car. He felt as if he were seated in immemorial potency, like the great carven statues of real Egypt, as real and as fulfilled with subtle strength, as these are, with a vague inscrutable smile on the lips. He knew what it was to have the strange and magical current of force in his back and loins, and down his legs, force so perfect that it stayed him immobile, and left his face subtly, mindlessly smiling. He knew what it was to be awake and potent in that other basic mind, the deepest physical mind. And from this source he had a pure and magic control, magical, mystical, a force in darkness, like electricity.

It was very difficult to speak, it was so perfect to sit in this pure living silence, subtle, full of unthinkable knowledge and unthinkable force, upheld immemorially in timeless force, like the immobile, supremely potent Egyptians, seated forever in their living, subtle silence.

"We need not go home," he said. "This car has seats that let down and make a bed, and we can lift the hood."

She was glad and frightened. She cowered near to him.

"But what about them at home?" she said.

"Send a telegram."

Nothing more was said. They ran on in silence. But with a sort of second consciousness he steered the car towards a destination. For he had the free intelligence to direct his own ends. His arms and his breast and his head were rounded and living like those of the Greek, he had not the unawakened straight arms of the Egyptian,* nor the sealed, slumbering head. A lambent intelligence played secondarily above his pure Egyptian concentration in darkness.

They came to a village that lined along the road. The car crept slowly along, until he saw the post-office. Then he pulled up.

"I will send a telegram to your father," he said. "I will merely say 'spending the night in town,' shall I?"

"Yes," she answered. She did not want to be disturbed into taking thought.

She watched him move into the post-office. It was also a shop, she saw. Strange, he was. Even as he went into the lighted, public place he remained dark and magic, the living silence seemed the body of reality in him, subtle, potent, indiscoverable. There he was! In a strange uplift of elation she saw him, the being never to be revealed, awful in its potency, mystic and real. This dark, subtle reality of him, never to be translated, liberated her into perfection, her own perfected being. She too was dark and fulfilled in silence.

He came out, throwing some packages into the car.

"There is some bread, and cheese, and raisins, and apples, and hard chocolate," he said, in his voice that was as if laughing, because of the unblemished stillness and force which was the reality in him. She would have to touch him. To speak, to see, was nothing. It was a travesty to look and to comprehend the man there. Darkness and silence must fall perfectly on her, then she could know mystically, in unrevealed touch. She must lightly, mindlessly connect with him, have the knowledge which is death of knowledge, the reality of surety in not-knowing.

Soon they had run on again into the darkness. She did not ask where they were going, she did not care. She sat in a fulness and a pure potency that was like apathy, mindless and immobile. She was next to him, and hung in a pure rest, as a star is hung, balanced unthinkably.—Still there remained a dark lambency of anticipation. She would touch him. With perfect fine finger-tips of reality she would touch the reality in him, the suave, pure, untranslateable reality of his loins of darkness. To touch, mindlessly in darkness to come in pure touching upon the living reality of him, his suave perfect loins and thighs of darkness, this was her sustaining anticipation.

And he too waited in the magical steadfastness of suspense, for her to take this knowledge of him as he had taken it of her. He knew her darkly, with the fulness of dark knowledge. Now she would know him, and he too would be liberated. He would be night-free, like an Egyptian, steadfast in perfectly suspended equilibrium, pure mystic nodality of physical being. They would give each other this star-equilibrium which alone is freedom.

She saw that they were running among trees—great old trees with dying bracken undergrowth. The palish, gnarled trunks showed ghostly, and like old priests in the hovering distance, the fern rose magical and mysterious. It was a night all darkness, with low cloud. The motor-car advanced slowly.

"Where are we?" she whispered.

5   "In Sherwood Forest."*

It was evident he knew the place. He drove softly, watching. Then they came to a green road between the trees. They turned cautiously round, and were advancing between the oaks of the forest, down a green lane. The green lane widened into a little circle of grass, where 10 there was a small trickle of water at the bottom of a sloping bank. The car stopped.

"We will stay here," he said, "and put out the lights."

He extinguished the lamps at once, and it was pure night, with shadows of trees like realities of other, nightly being. He threw a rug 15 on to the bracken, and they sat in stillness and mindless silence. There were faint sounds from the wood, but no disturbance, no possible disturbance, the world was under a strange ban, a new mystery had supervened.

They threw off their clothes, and he gathered her to him, and 20 found her, found the pure lambent reality of her forever invisible flesh. Quenched, inhuman, his fingers upon her unrevealed nudity were the fingers of silence upon silence, the body of mysterious night upon the body of mysterious night, the night masculine and femin- ine, never to be seen with the eye, or known with the mind, only 25 known as a palpable revelation of living otherness.

She had her desire of him, she touched, she received the maximums of unspeakable communication in touch, dark, subtle, positively silent, a magnificent gift and give again, a perfect accept- ance and yielding, a mystery, the reality of that which can never be 30 known, vital, sensual reality that can never be transmuted into mind content, but remains outside, living body of darkness and silence and subtlety, the mystic body of reality. She had her desire fulfilled, he had his desire fulfilled. For she was to him what he was to her, the immemorial magnificence of mystic, palpable, real otherness.

35   They slept the chilly night through under the hood of the car, a night of unbroken sleep. It was already high day when he awoke. They looked at each other and laughed, then looked away, filled with darkness and secrecy. Then they kissed and remembered the magnificence of the night. It was so magnificent, such an inheritance 40 of a universe of dark reality, that they were afraid to, seem to remember. They hid away the remembrance and the knowledge.

Chapter XXIV

Death and Love

Thomas Crich died slowly, terribly slowly. It seemed impossible to everybody, that the thread of life could be drawn out so thin, and yet not break. The sick man lay unutterably weak and spent, kept alive by morphia and by drinks, which he sipped slowly. He was only half conscious—a thin strand of consciousness linking the darkness of death with the light of day. Yet his will was unbroken, he was integral, complete. Only he must have perfect stillness about him.

Any presence but that of the nurses, was a strain and an effort to him now. Every morning, Gerald went into the room, hoping to find his father passed away at last. Yet always he saw the same transparent face, the same weary dark hair on the waxen forehead, and the awful, inchoate dark eyes, which seemed to be decomposing into formless darkness, having only a tiny grain of vision within them.

And always, as the dark, inchoate eyes turned to him, there passed through Gerald's bowels a burning stroke of revolt, that seemed to resound through his whole being, threatening to break his mind with its clangour, and make him mad.

Every morning, the son stood there, erect and taut with life, gleaming in his blondness. The gleaming blondness of his strange, imminent being put the father into a fever of fretful irritation. He could not bear to meet the uncanny, downward look of Gerald's blue eyes. But it was only for a moment. Each on the brink of departure, the father and son looked at each other, then parted.

For a long time Gerald preserved a perfect sang froid, he remained quite collected. But at last, fear undermined him. He was afraid of some horrible collapse in himself. He had to stay and see this thing through. Some perverse will made him watch his father drawn over the borders of life. And yet, now, every day, the great red-hot stroke of horrified fear through the bowels of the son struck a further inflammation, Gerald went about all day with a tendency to cringe, as if there were the point of a sword of Damocles* pricking the nape of his neck.

There was no escape—he was bound up with his father, he had to see him through. And the father's will never relaxed or yielded to death. It would have to snap when death at last snapped it,—if it did not persist after physical death. In the same way, the will of the son never yielded. He stood firm and immune, he was outside this death and this dying.

5 It was a trial by ordeal. Could he stand and see his father slowly dissolve and disappear in death, without once yielding his will, without once relenting before the omnipotence of death. Like a Red Indian undergoing torture,* Gerald would experience the whole process of slow death without wincing or flinching. He even
10 triumphed in it. He somehow *wanted* this death, even forced it. It was as if he himself were dealing the death, even when he most recoiled in horror. Still, he would deal it, he would triumph through death.

But in the stress of this ordeal, Gerald too lost his hold on the
15 outer, daily life. That which was much to him, came to mean nothing. Work, pleasure—it was all left behind. He went on more or less mechanically with his business, but this activity was all extraneous. The real activity was this ghastly wrestling for death, in his own soul. And his own will should triumph. Come what might, he
20 would not bow down or submit or acknowledge a master. He had no master in death.

But as the fight went on, and all that he had been and was continued to be destroyed, so that life was a hollow shell all round him, roaring and clattering like the sound of the sea, a noise in which
25 he participated externally, and inside this hollow shell was all the darkness and fearful space of death, he knew he would have to find reinforcements, otherwise he would collapse inwards upon the great dark void which circled at the centre of his soul. His will held his outer life, his outer mind, his outer being unbroken and unchanged.
30 But the pressure was too great. He would have to find something to make good the equilibrium. Something must come with him into the hollow void of death in his soul, fill it up, and so equalise the pressure within to the pressure without. For day by day he felt more and more like a bubble filled with darkness,* round which whirled the irides-
35 scence of his consciousness, and upon which the pressure of the outer world, the outer life, roared vastly.

In this extremity his instinct led him to Gudrun. He threw away everything now—he only wanted the relation established with her. He would follow her to the studio, to be near her, to talk to her. He
40 would stand about the room, aimlessly picking up the implements,

the lumps of clay, the little figures she had cast—they were whimsical and grotesque—looking at them without perceiving them. And she felt him following her, dogging her heels like a doom. She held away from him, and yet she knew he drew always a little nearer, a little nearer.

"I say," he said to her one evening, in an odd, unthinking, uncertain way, "won't you stay to dinner tonight?—I wish you would."

She started slightly. He spoke to her like a man making a request of another man.

"They'll be expecting me at home," she said.

"Oh, they won't mind, will they?" he said. "I should be awfully glad if you'd stay."

Her long silence gave consent at last.

"I'll tell Thomas, shall I?" he said.

"I must go almost immediately after dinner," she said.

It was a dark, cold evening. There was no fire in the drawing-room, they sat in the library. He was mostly silent, absent, and Winifred talked little. But when Gerald did rouse himself, he smiled and was pleasant and ordinary with her. Then there came over him again the long blanks, of which he was not aware.

She was very much attracted by him. He looked so pre-occupied, and his strange, blank silences, which she could not read, moved her and made her wonder over him, made her feel reverential towards him.

But he was very kind. He gave her the best things at the table, he had a bottle of slightly sweet, delicious golden wine brought out for dinner, knowing she would prefer it to the burgundy. She felt herself esteemed, needed almost.

As they took coffee in the library, there was a soft, very soft knocking at the door. He started, and called "Come in." The timbre of his voice, like something vibrating at high pitch, unnerved Gudrun. A nurse in white entered, half hovering in the doorway like a shadow. She was very good-looking, but strangely enough, shy and self-mistrusting.

"The doctor would like to speak to you, Mr Crich," she said, in her low, discreet voice.

"The doctor!" he said, starting up. "Where is he?"

"He is in the dining room."

"Tell him I'm coming."

He drank up his coffee, and followed the nurse, who had dissolved like a shadow.

"Which nurse was that?" asked Gudrun.

"Miss Inglis—I like her best," replied Winifred.

After a while Gerald came back, looking absorbed by his own thoughts, and having some of that tension and abstraction which is seen in a slightly drunken man. He did not say what the doctor had wanted him for, but stood before the fire, with his hands behind his back, and his face open and as if rapt. Not that he was really thinking—he was only arrested in pure suspense inside himself, and thoughts wafted through his mind without order.

"I must go now and see Mama," said Winifred, "and see Dadda before he goes to sleep."

She bade them both goodnight.

Gudrun also rose to take her leave.

"You needn't go yet, need you?" said Gerald, glancing quickly at the clock. "It is early yet. I'll walk down with you when you go. Sit down, don't hurry away."

Gudrun sat down, as if, absent as he was, his will had power over her. She felt almost mesmerised. He was strange to her, something unknown. What was he thinking, what was he feeling, as he stood there rapt,* saying nothing? He kept her—she could feel that. He would not let her go. She watched him in humble submissiveness.

"Had the doctor anything new to tell you?" she asked softly, at length, with that gentle, timid sympathy which touched a keen fibre in his heart.

He lifted his eyebrows with a negligent, indifferent expression.

"No—nothing new," he replied, as if the question were quite casual, trivial. "He says the pulse is very weak indeed, very intermittent—but that doesn't necessarily mean much, you know."

He looked down at her. Her eyes were dark and soft and unfolded, with a stricken look that roused him.

"No," she murmured at length. "—I don't understand anything about these things."

"Just as well not," he said.—"I say, won't you have a cigarette?—do!" He quickly fetched the box, and held her a light. Then he stood before her on the hearth again.

"No," he said, "we've never had much illness in the house, either—not till father." He seemed to meditate a while. Then, looking down at her, with strangely communicative blue eyes, that filled her with dread, he continued: "It's something you don't reckon with, you know, till it is there. And then you realise that it was there all the time—it was always there—you understand what I mean?—the possibility of this incurable illness, this slow death."

He moved his feet uneasily on the marble hearth, and put his cigarette to his mouth, looking up at the ceiling.

"I know," murmured Gudrun; "it is dreadful."

He smoked without knowing. Then he took the cigarette from his lips, bared his teeth, and putting the tip of his tongue between his teeth, spat off a grain of tobacco, turning slightly aside, like a man who is alone, or who is lost in thought.

"I don't know what the effect actually *is*, on one," he said, and again he looked down at her. Her eyes were dark and stricken with knowledge, looking into his. He saw her submerged, and he turned aside his face. "But I absolutely am not the same. There's nothing left, if you understand what I mean. You seem to be clutching at the void—and at the same time you are void yourself.—And so you don't know what to *do*."

"No," she murmured. A heavy thrill ran down her nerves, heavy, almost pleasure, almost pain. "What can be done?" she added.

He turned, and flipped the ash from his cigarette on to the great marble hearth-stone, that lay bare to the room, without fender or bar.

"I don't know, I'm sure," he replied. "But I do think you've got to find some way of resolving the situation—not because you want to, but because you've *got* to, otherwise you're done. The whole of everything, and yourself included, is just on the point of caving in, and you are just holding it up with your hands.—Well, it's a situation that obviously can't continue. You can't stand holding the roof up with your hands, for ever. You know that sooner or later you'll *have* to let go.—Do you understand what I mean?—And so something's got to be done, or there's a universal collapse—as far as you yourself are concerned."

He shifted slightly on the hearth, crunching a cinder under his heel. He looked down at it. Gudrun was aware of the beautiful old marble panels of the fireplace, swelling softly carved, round him and above him. She felt as if she were caught at last by fate, imprisoned in some horrible and fatal trap.

"But what *can* be done?" she murmured humbly. "You must use me if I can be of any help at all—but how can I? I don't see how I *can* help you."

He looked down at her critically.

"I don't want you to *help*," he said, slightly irritated, "because there's nothing to be *done*. I only want sympathy, do you see: I want somebody I can talk to sympathetically. That eases the strain. And there *is* nobody to talk to sympathetically. That's the curious thing. There *is* nobody. There's Rupert Birkin. But then he *isn't* sympathetic, he wants to *dictate*. And that is no use whatsoever."

She was caught in a strange snare. She looked down at her hands.

Then there was the sound of the door softly opening. Gerald started. He was chagrined. It was his starting that really startled Gudrun. Then he went forward, with quick, graceful, intentional courtesy.

"Oh, mother!" he said. "How nice of you to come down. How are you?"

The elderly woman, loosely and bulkily wrapped in a purple gown, came forward silently, slightly hulked, as usual. Her son was at her side. He pushed her up a chair, saying:

"You know Miss Brangwen, don't you?"

The mother glanced at Gudrun indifferently.

"Yes," she said. Then she turned her wonderful, forget-me-not blue eyes up to her son, as she slowly sat down in the chair he had brought her.

"I came to ask you about your father," she said, in her rapid, scarcely-audible voice. "I didn't know you had company."

"No? Didn't Winifred tell you?—Miss Brangwen stayed to dinner, to make us a little more lively—"

Mrs Crich turned slowly round to Gudrun, and looked at her, but with unseeing eyes.

"I'm afraid it would be no treat to her." Then she turned again to her son. "Winifred tells me the doctor had something to say about your father. What is it?"

"Only that the pulse is very weak—misses altogether a good many times—so that he might not last the night out," Gerald replied.

Mrs Crich sat perfectly impassive, as if she had not heard. Her bulk seemed hunched in the chair, her fair hair hung slack over her ears. But her skin was clear and fine, her hands, as she sat with them forgotten and folded, were quite beautiful, full of potential energy. A great mass of energy seemed decaying up in that silent, hulking form.

She looked up at her son, as he stood, keen and soldierly, near to her. Her eyes were most wonderfully blue, bluer than forget-me-nots. She seemed to have a certain confidence in Gerald, and to feel a certain motherly mistrust of him.

"How *are* you?" she muttered, in her strangely quiet voice, as if nobody should hear but him. "You're not getting into a state, are you? You're not letting it make you hysterical?"

The curious challenge in the last words startled Gudrun.

"I don't think so, mother," he answered, rather coldly cheery. "Somebody's got to see it through, you know."

"Have they? Have they?" answered his mother rapidly. "Why should *you* take it on yourself? What have *you* to do, seeing it through?* It will see itself through. You are not needed."

"No, I don't suppose I can do any good," he answered. "It's just how it affects us, you see."

"You like to be affected—don't you? It's quite nuts* for you? You would have to be important. You have no need to stop at home. Why don't you go away?"

These sentences, evidently the ripened grain of many dark hours, took Gerald by surprise.

"I don't think it's any good going away now, mother, at the last minute," he said, coldly.

"You take care," replied his mother. "You mind *yourself*, that's your business. You take too much on yourself.—You mind *yourself*, or you'll find yourself in Queer Street, that's what will happen to you. You're hysterical, always were."

"I'm all right, mother," he said. "There's no need to worry about *me*, I assure you."

"Let the dead bury their dead*—don't go and bury yourself along with them—that's what I tell you. I know you well enough."

He did not answer this, not knowing what to say. The mother sat bunched up in silence, her beautiful white hands, that had no rings whatsoever, clasping the pommels of her arm-chair.

"You can't do it," she said, almost bitterly. "You haven't the nerve. You're as weak as a cat, really—always were.—Is this young woman staying here?"

"No," said Gerald. "She is going home tonight."

"Then she'd better have the dog-cart. Does she go far?"

"Only to Beldover."

"Ah." The elderly woman never looked at Gudrun, yet she seemed to take knowledge of her presence.

"You are inclined to take too much on yourself, Gerald," said the mother, pulling herself to her feet, with a little difficulty.

"Will you go, mother?" he asked politely.

"Yes, I'll go up again," she replied. Turning to Gudrun, she bade her "Goodnight." Then she went slowly to the door, as if she were unaccustomed to walking. At the door she lifted her face to him, implicitly. He kissed her.

"Don't come any farther with me," she said, in her barely audible voice. "I don't want you any farther."

He bade her goodnight, watched her cross to the stairs and mount slowly. Then he closed the door and came back to Gudrun. Gudrun rose also, to go.

"A queer being, my mother," he said.

"Yes," replied Gudrun.

"She has her own thoughts."

"Yes," said Gudrun.

Then they were silent.

"You want to go?" he asked. "Half a minute, I'll just have a horse put in—"

"No," said Gudrun, "I want to walk."

He had promised to walk with her down the long, lonely mile of drive, and she wanted this.

"You might *just* as well drive," he said.

"I'd *much rather* walk," she asserted, with emphasis.

"You would?—Then I will come along with you.—You know where your things are?—I'll put boots on."

He put on a cap, and an overcoat over his evening dress. They went out into the night.

"Let us light a cigarette," he said, stopping in a sheltered angle of the porch. "You have one too."

So, with the scent of tobacco on the night air, they set off down the dark drive, that ran between close-cut hedges through sloping meadows.

He wanted to put his arm round her. If he could put his arm round her, and draw her against him as they walked, he would equilibrate himself. For now he felt like a pair of scales, the half of which tips down and down into an infinite void. He must recover some sort of balance. And here was the hope and the perfect recovery.

Blind to her, thinking only of himself, he slipped his arm softly round her waist, and drew her to him. Her heart fainted, feeling herself taken. But then, his arm was so strong, she quailed under its powerful close grasp. She died a little death, and was drawn against him as they walked down the stormy darkness. He seemed to balance her perfectly in opposition to himself, in their dual motion of walking. So, suddenly, he was liberated and perfect, strong, heroic.

He put his hand to his mouth and threw his cigarette away, a gleaming point, into the unseen hedge. Then he was quite free to balance her.

"That's better," he said, with exultancy.

The exultation in his voice was like a sweetish, poisonous drug to her. Did she then mean so much to him? She sipped the poison.

"Are you happier?" she asked, wistfully.

"Much better," he said, in the same exultant voice, "and I *was* rather far gone."

She nestled against him. He felt her all soft and warm, she was the rich, lovely substance of his being. The warmth and motion of her walk suffused through him wonderfully.

"I'm *so* glad if I help you," she said.

"Yes," he answered. "There's nobody else could do it, if you wouldn't."

"That is true," she said to herself, with a thrill of strange, fatal elation.

As they walked, he seemed to lift her nearer and nearer to himself, till she moved upon the firm vehicle of his body. He was so strong, so sustaining, and he could not be opposed. She drifted along in a wonderful interfusion of physical motion, down the dark, blowy hill-side. Across,* shone the little yellow lights of Beldover, many of them, spread in a thick patch on another dark hill. But he and she were walking in perfect, isolated darkness, outside the world.

"But how much do you care for me?" came her voice, almost querulous. "You see, I don't know, I don't understand."

"How much!" His voice rang with a painful elation. "I don't know either—but everything." He was startled by his own declaration. It was true. So, he stripped himself of every safeguard, in making this admission to her. He cared everything for her—she was everything.

"But I can't believe it," said her low voice, amazed, trembling. She was trembling with doubt and exultance. This was the thing she wanted to hear, only this. Yet now she heard it, heard the strange clapping vibration of truth in his voice as he said it, she could not believe. She could not believe—she did not believe. Yet she believed, triumphantly, with fatal exultance.

"Why not?" he said. "Why don't you believe it?—It's true. It is true, as we stand at this moment—" he stood still with her in the wind; "I care for nothing on earth, or in heaven, outside this spot where we are. And it isn't my own presence I care about, it is all yours. I'd sell my soul a hundred times—but I couldn't bear not to have you here. I couldn't bear to be alone. My brain would burst. It is true."

He drew her closer to him, with definite movement.

"No," she murmured, afraid. Yet this was what she wanted. Why did she so lose courage?

They resumed their strange walk. They were such strangers—and yet they were so frightfully, unthinkably near. It was like a madness. Yet it was what she wanted, it was what she wanted.

They had descended the hill, and now they were coming to the square arch where the road passed under the colliery railway. The arch, Gudrun knew, had walls of squared stone, mossy on one side with water that trickled down, dry on the other side. She had stood under it to hear the train rumble thundering over the logs overhead. And she knew that under this dark and lonely bridge the young colliers stood in the darkness with their sweethearts, in rainy weather. And so she wanted to stand under the bridge with *her* sweetheart, and be kissed under the bridge in the invisible darkness. Her steps dragged as she drew near.

So, under the bridge, they came to a standstill, and he lifted her upon his breast. His body vibrated taut and powerful as he closed upon her and crushed her, breathless and dazed and destroyed, crushed her upon his breast. Ah, it was terrible, and perfect. Under this bridge, the colliers pressed their lovers to their breast. And now, under the bridge, the master of them all pressed her to himself! And how much more powerful and terrible was his embrace, than theirs, how much more concentrated and supreme his love was, than theirs, in the same sort! She felt she would swoon, die, under the vibrating, inhuman tension of his arms and his body—she would pass away. Then the unthinkable, high vibration slackened and became more undulating, he slackened and drew her with him to stand with his back to the wall.

She was almost unconscious. So, the colliers' lovers would stand with their backs to the walls, holding their sweethearts and kissing them as she was being kissed.—Ah, but would their kisses be fine and powerful as the kisses of the firm-mouthed master? Even the keen, short-cut moustache—the colliers would not have that.

And the colliers' sweethearts would, like herself, hang their heads back limp over their shoulder, and look out from the dark archway, at the close patch of yellow lights on the unseen hill in the distance, or at the vague form of trees, and at the buildings of the colliery wood-yard, in the other direction.

His arms were fast round her, he seemed to be gathering her into himself, her warmth, her softness, her adorable weight, drinking in the suffusion of her physical being, avidly. He lifted her, and seemed to pour her into himself, like wine into a cup.

"This is worth everything," he said, in a strange, penetrating voice.

So she relaxed, and seemed to melt, to flow into him, as if she were some infinitely warm and precious suffusion filling into his veins, like an intoxicant. Her arms were round his neck, he kissed her and held her perfectly suspended, she was all slack and flowing in to him, and he was the firm, strong cup that receives the wine of her life. So she lay cast upon him, stranded, lifted up against him, melting and melting under his kisses, melting into his limbs and bones, as if he were soft iron becoming surcharged with her electric life.

Till she seemed to swoon, gradually her mind went, and she passed away, everything in her was melted down and fluid, and she lay still, become contained by him, sleeping in him as lightning sleeps in a pure, soft stone. So she was passed away and gone in him, and he was perfected.

When she opened her eyes again, and saw the patch of lights in the distance, it seemed to her strange that the world still existed, that she was standing under the bridge resting her head on Gerald's breast. Gerald—who was he? He was the exquisite adventure, the desirable unknown to her.

She looked up, and in the darkness saw his face above her, his shapely, male face. There seemed a faint, white light emitted from him, a white aura, as if he were visitor from the unseen. She reached up, like Eve reaching to the apples on the tree of knowledge, and she kissed him, though her passion was a transcendent fear of the thing he was, touching his face with her infinitely delicate, encroaching, wondering fingers. Her fingers went over the mould of his face, over his features. How perfect and foreign he was—ah how dangerous!

Her soul thrilled with complete knowledge. This was the glistening, forbidden apple, this face of a man. She kissed him, putting her fingers over his face, his eyes, his nostrils, over his brows and his ears, to his neck, to know him, to gather him in by touch. He was so
5 firm and shapely, with such satisfying, inconceivable shapeliness, strange yet unutterably clear. He was such an unutterable enemy, yet glistening with uncanny white fire. She wanted to touch him and touch him and touch him, till she had him all in her hands, till she had strained him into her knowledge. Ah, if she could have the
10 precious *knowledge* of him, she would be filled, and nothing could deprive her of this. For he was so unsure, so risky in the common world of day.

"You are so *beautiful*," she murmured in her throat.

He wondered, and was suspended. But she felt him quiver, and
15 come down involuntarily nearer upon her.* He could not help himself. Her fingers had him under their power. The fathomless, fathomless desire they could evoke in him was deeper than death, where he had no choice.

But she knew now, and it was enough. For the time, her soul was
20 destroyed with the exquisite shock of his invisible fluid lightning. She knew. And this knowledge was a death from which she must recover. How much more of him was there to know? Ah much, much, many days harvesting for her large, yet perfectly subtle and intelligent hands, upon the field of his living, radio-active* body. Ah,
25 her hands were eager, greedy for knowledge. But for the present it was enough, enough, as much as her soul could bear. Too much, and she would shatter herself, she would fill the fine vial of her soul too quickly, and it would break. Enough now—enough for the time being. There were all the afterdays when her hands, like birds, could
30 feed upon the fields of his mystical plastic form. Till then enough.

And even he was glad to be checked, rebuked, held back. For to desire is better than to possess, the finality of the end was dreaded as deeply as it was desired.

They walked on towards the town, towards where the lamps
35 threaded singly, at long intervals down the dark high-road of the valley. They came at length to the gate of the drive.

"Don't come any further," she said.

"You'd rather I didn't?" he asked, relieved. He did not want to go up the public streets with her, his soul all naked and alight as it
40 was.

"Much rather—goodnight." She held out her hand. He grasped it, then touched the perilous, potent fingers with his lips.

"Goodnight," he said. "Tomorrow."

And they parted. He went home full of the strength and the power of living desire.

But the next day, she did not come, she sent a note, that she was kept indoors by a cold. Here was a torment! But he possessed his soul in some sort of patience, writing a brief answer, telling her how sorry he was not to see her.

The day after this, he stayed at home—it seemed so futile to go down to the offices. His father could not live the week out. And he wanted to be at home, suspended.

Gerald sat on a chair by the window in his father's room. The landscape outside was black and winter-sodden. His father lay grey and ashen on the bed, a nurse moved silently in her white dress, neat and elegant, even beautiful. There was a scent of eau-de-cologne in the room.* The nurse went out of the room, Gerald was alone with death, facing the winter-black landscape.

"Is there much more water in Denley?" came the faint voice, determined and querulous, from the bed. The dying man was asking about a leakage from Willey Water into one of the pits.

"Some more—we shall have to run off the lake," said Gerald.

"Will you—?" The faint voice filtered to extinction.

There was dead stillness. The grey-faced, sick man lay with eyes closed, more dead than death. Gerald looked away. He felt his heart was seared, it would perish if this went on much longer.

Suddenly he heard a strange noise. Turning round, he saw his father's eyes wide open, strained and rolling in a frenzy of inhuman struggling. Gerald started to his feet, and stood transfixed in horror.

"Wha—a—ah-h-h—" came a horrible choking rattle from his father's throat, the fearful, frenzied eye, rolling awfully in its wild fruitless search for help, passed blindly over Gerald, then up came the dark blood and mess pumping over the face of the agonised being, the tense body relaxed, the head fell aside, down the pillow.

Gerald stood transfixed, his soul echoing in horror. He would move, but he could not. He could not move his limbs. His brain seemed to re-echo,* like a pulse.

The nurse in white softly entered. She glanced at Gerald, then at the bed.

"Ah!" came her soft, whimpering cry, and she hurried forward to

the dead man. "Ah—h!" came the slight sound of her agitated distress, as she stood bending over the bedside. Then she recovered, turned, and came for towel and sponge. She was wiping the dead face carefully, and murmuring, almost whimpering, very softly:
5   "Poor Mr Crich!—Poor Mr Crich!—Oh poor Mr Crich!"

"Is he dead?" clanged Gerald's sharp voice.

"Oh yes, he's gone," replied the soft, moaning voice of the nurse, as she looked up at Gerald's face. She was young and beautiful and quivering. A strange sort of grin went over Gerald's face, over the
10 horror. And he walked out of the room.

He was going to tell his mother. On the landing he met his brother Basil.

"He's gone, Basil," he said, scarcely able to subdue his voice, not to let an unconscious, frightening exultation sound through.
15   "What?" cried Basil, going pale.

Gerald nodded. Then he went on to his mother's room.

She was sitting in her purple gown, sewing, very slowly sewing, putting in a stitch, then another stitch. She looked up at Gerald with her blue, undaunted eyes.
20   "Father's gone," he said.

"He's dead? Who says so?"

"Oh, you know, mother, if you see him."

She put her sewing down, and slowly rose.

"Are you going to see him?" he asked.
25   "Yes," she said.

By the bedside the children already stood in a weeping group.

"Oh mother—!" cried the daughters, almost in hysterics, weeping loudly.

But the mother went forward. The dead man lay in repose, as if
30 gently asleep, so gently, so peacefully, like a young man sleeping in purity. He was still warm.

She stood looking at him in gloomy, heavy silence, for some time.

"Ay," she said bitterly, at length, speaking as if to the unseen witnesses of the air.* "You're dead." She stood for some minutes in
35 silence, looking down. "Beautiful," she asserted, "beautiful as if life had never touched you—never touched you.—God send I look different.—I hope I shall look my years, when I am dead.—Beautiful, beautiful," she crooned over him. "You can see him in his teens, with his first beard on his face.—A beautiful soul, beautiful—" Then
40 there was a tearing in her voice as she cried: "None of you look like

this, when you are dead! Don't let it happen again." It was a strange, wild command from out of the unknown. Her children moved unconsciously together, in a nearer group, at the dreadful command in her voice. The colour was flushed bright in her cheek, she looked awful and wonderful. "Blame me, blame me if you like, that he lies 5 there like a lad in his teens, with his first beard on his face. Blame me if you like. But you none of you know." She was silent in intense silence. Then there came, in a low, tense voice: "If I thought that the children I bore would lie looking like that in death, I'd strangle them when they were infants, yes—" 10

"No mother," came the strange, clarion voice of Gerald from the background, "we are different, we don't blame you."

She turned and looked full in his eyes. Then she lifted her hands in a strange half-gesture of mad despair.

"Pray!" she said strongly. "Pray for yourselves to God, for there's 15 no help for you from your parents."

"Oh mother!" cried her daughters wildly.

But she had turned and gone, and they all went quickly away from each other.

When Gudrun heard that Mr Crich was dead, she felt rebuked. 20 She had stayed away lest Gerald should think her too easy of winning. And now, he was in the midst of trouble, whilst she was cold.

The following day she went up as usual to Winifred, who was glad to see her, glad to get away into the studio. The girl had wept, and 25 then, too frightened, had turned aside to avoid any more tragic eventuality. She and Gudrun resumed work as usual, in the isolation of the studio, and this seemed an immeasurable happiness, a pure world of freedom, after the aimlessness and misery of the house— Gudrun stayed on till evening. She and Winifred had dinner brought 30 up to the studio, where they ate in freedom, away from all the people in the house.

After dinner Gerald came up. The great high studio was full of shadow and a fragrance of coffee, Gudrun and Winifred had a little table near the fire at the far end, with a white lamp whose light did 35 not travel far. They were a tiny world to themselves, the two girls, surrounded by lovely shadows, the beams and rafters shadowy overhead, the benches and implements shadowy down the studio.

"You are cosy enough here," said Gerald, going up to them.

There was a low brick fireplace full of fire, an old blue turkish rug, 40 the little oak table with the lamp and the white-and-blue cloth and the dessert, and Gudrun making coffee in an odd brass coffee-maker, and Winifred scalding a little milk in a tiny saucepan.

"Have you had coffee?" said Gudrun.

5   "I have—but I'll have some more with you," he replied.

"Then you must have it in a glass—there are only two cups," said Winifred.

"It is the same to me," he said, taking a chair and coming into the charmed circle of the girls. How happy they were, how cosy and
10 glamorous it was with them, in a world of lofty shadows! The outside world, in which he had been transacting funeral business all the day, was completely wiped out. In an instant he snuffed glamour and magic.

They had all their things very dainty, two odd and lovely little
15 cups, scarlet and solid gilt, and a little black jug with scarlet discs, and the curious coffee-machine, whose spirit-flame flowed steadily, almost invisible. There was the effect of rather sinister richness, in which Gerald at once escaped himself.

They all sat down, and Gudrun carefully poured out the coffee.
20 "Will you have milk?" she asked, calmly, yet nervously poising the little black jug with its big red dots. She was always so completely controlled, yet so bitterly nervous.

"No, I won't," he replied.

So, with a curious humility, she placed him the little cup of coffee,
25 and herself took the awkward tumbler. She seemed to want to serve him.

"Why don't you give me the glass—it is so clumsy for you," he said. He would much rather have had it, and seen her daintily served. But she was silent, pleased with the disparity, with her self-
30 abasement.

"You are quite *en ménage*,"* he said.

"Yes. We aren't really at home to visitors," said Winifred.

"You're not? Then I'm an intruder."

For once he felt his conventional dress was out of place, he was an
35 outsider.

Gudrun was very quiet. She did not feel drawn to talk to him. At this stage, silence was best—or mere light words. It was best to leave serious things aside. So they talked gaily and lightly, till they heard the man below lead out the horse, and call it to "back—back!" into
40 the dog-cart* that was to take Gudrun home. So she put on her

things, and shook hands with Gerald, without once meeting his eyes. And she was gone.

The funeral was detestable. Afterwards, at the tea-table, the daughters kept saying—"He was a good father to us—the best father in the world"—or else "We shan't easily find another man as good as father was."

Gerald acquiesced in all this. It was the right conventional attitude, and, as far as the world went, he believed in the conventions. He took it as a matter of course. But Winifred hated everything, and hid in the studio, and cried her heart out, and wished Gudrun would come.

Luckily everybody was going away. The Criches never stayed long at home. By dinner-time, Gerald was left quite alone. Even Winifred was carried off to London for a few days, with her sister Laura.

But when Gerald was really left alone, he could not bear it. One day passed by, and another. And all the time he was like a man hung in chains over the edge of an abyss. Struggle as he might, he could not turn himself to the solid earth, he could not get footing. He was suspended on the edge of a void, writhing. Whatever he thought of, was the abyss—whether it were friends or strangers, or work or play, it all showed him only the same bottomless void, in which his heart swung perishing. There was no escape, there was nothing to grasp hold of. He must writhe on the edge of the chasm, suspended in chains of invisible physical life.

At first he was quiet, he kept still, expecting the extremity to pass away, expecting to find himself released into the world of the living, after this extremity of penance. But it did not pass, and a crisis gained upon him.

As the evening of the third day came on, his heart rang with fear. He could not bear another night. Another night was coming on, for another night he was to be suspended in chains of physical life, over the bottomless pit of nothingness. And he could not bear it. He could not bear it. He was frightened deeply, and coldly, frightened in his soul. He did not believe in his own strength any more. He could not fall into this infinite void, and rise again. If he fell, he would be gone for ever. He must withdraw, he must seek reinforcements. He did not believe in his own single self, any further than this.

After dinner, faced with the ultimate experience of his own nothingness, he turned aside. He pulled on his boots, put on his coat, and set out to walk in the night.

It was dark and misty. He went through the wood, stumbling and feeling his way, to the Mill. Birkin was away. Good—he was half glad. He turned up the hill, and stumbled blindly over the wild slopes, having lost the path in the complete darkness. It was boring.
5 Where was he going? No matter. He stumbled on till he came to a path again. Then he went on through another wood. His mind became dark, he went on automatically. Without thought or sensation, he stumbled unevenly on, out into the open again, fumbling for stiles, losing the path, and going along the hedges of the fields till he
10 came to the outlet.

And at last he came to a high-road. It had distracted him to struggle blindly through the maze of darkness. But now, he must take a direction. And he did not even know where he was. But he must take a direction now. Nothing would be resolved by merely
15 walking, walking away. He had to take a direction.

He stood still on the road, that was high in the utterly dark night, and he did not know where he was. It was a strange sensation: his heart beating, and ringed round with the utterly unknown darkness. So he stood for some time.

20 Then he heard footsteps, and saw a small, swinging light. He immediately went towards this. It was a miner.

"Can you tell me," he said, "where this road goes?"

"Road?—Ay, it goos ter Whatmore."

"Whatmore! Oh thank you, that's right. I thought I was wrong.
25 Goodnight."

"Goodnight," replied the broad voice of the miner.

Gerald guessed where he was. At least, when he came to Whatmore, he would know. He was glad to be on a high-road. He walked forward as in a sleep of decision.

30 That was Whatmore village—? Yes, the Kings Head—and there the hall gates. He descended the steep hill almost running. Winding through the hollow, he passed the Grammar School, and came to Willey Green Church. The churchyard! He halted.

Then in another moment he had clambered up the wall and was
35 going among the graves. Even in this darkness he could see the heaped pallor of old white flowers at his feet. This then was the grave. He stooped down. The flowers were cold and clammy: there was a raw scent of chrysanthemums and tube-roses, deadened. He felt the clay beneath, and shrank, it was so horribly cold and sticky.
40 He stood away in revulsion.

Here was one centre then, here in the complete darkness beside the unseen, raw grave. But there was nothing for him here. No, he had nothing to stay here for. He felt as if some of the clay were sticking cold and unclean, on his heart. No, enough of this.

Where then?—home? Never! It was no use going there. That was less than no use. It could not be done. There was somewhere else to go. Where?

A dangerous resolve formed in his heart, like a fixed idea. There was Gudrun.—She would be safe in her home.—But he could get at her—he *would* get at her. He would not go back tonight till he had come to her, if it cost him his life. He staked his all on this throw.

He set off walking straight across the fields towards Beldover. It was so dark, nobody could ever see him. His feet were wet and cold, heavy with clay. But he went on persistently, like a wind, straight forward, as if to his fate. There were great gaps in his consciousness. He was conscious that he was at Winthorpe hamlet, but quite unconscious how he had got there. And then, as in a dream, he was in the long street of Beldover, with its street-lamps.

There was a noise of voices, and of a door shutting loudly, and of men talking in the night. The "Lord Nelson" had just closed, and the drinkers were going home. He had better ask one of these where she lived—for he did not know the side streets at all.

"Can you tell me where Somerset Drive is?" he asked of one of the uneven men.

"Where what?" replied the tipsy miner's voice.

"Somerset Drive."

"Somerset Drive!—I've heerd o' such a place, but I couldn't for my life say wheer it is.—Who might you be wanting?"

"Mr Brangwen—William Brangwen."

"William Brangwen—?—?"

"Who teaches at the Grammar School, at Willey Green—his daughter teaches there too."

"OO—O—O—Oh, Brangwen! *Now* I've got you. Of *course*, William Brangwen! Yes, Yes, he's got two lasses as teaches, aside hisself. Ay, that's him!—that's him!—Why certainly I know where he lives, back your life I do! Yi—*what* place do they ca' it?"

"Somerset Drive," repeated Gerald patiently. He knew his own colliers fairly well.

"Somerset Drive, for certain!" said the collier, swinging his arm

as if catching something up. "Somerset Drive—yi!—I couldn't for
my life lay hold o' the lercality o'* the place. Yis, I know the place, to
be sure I do—"

He turned unsteadily on his feet, and pointed up the dark,
5 nigh-deserted road.

"You go up theer—an' you ta'e th' first—yi, th' first turnin' on
your left—o' that side—past Withamses tuffy shop—"

"*I* know," said Gerald.

"Ay! You go down a bit, past wheer th' water-man lives—and then
10 Somerset Drive, as they ca' it, branches off on 't right-hand
side—an' there's nowt but* three houses in it, no more than three, I
believe—an' I'm a'most certain as theirs is th' last—th' last o' th'
three—you see—"

"Thank you very much," said Gerald. "Goodnight."

15 And he started off, leaving the tipsy man there standing rooted.

Gerald went past the dark shops and houses, most of them
sleeping now, and twisted round to the little blind road that ended on
a field of darkness. He slowed down, as he neared his goal, not
knowing how he should proceed. What if the house were closed in
20 darkness?

But it was not. He saw a big lighted window, and heard voices,
then a gate banged. His quick ears caught the sound of Birkin's
voice, his keen eyes made out Birkin, with Ursula standing in a pale
dress on the step of the garden path. Then Ursula stepped down,
25 and came along the road, holding Birkin's arm.

Gerald went across into the darkness and they dawdled past him,
talking happily, Birkin's voice low, Ursula's high and distinct. Gerald
went quickly to the house.

The blinds were drawn before the big, lighted window of the
30 dining-room. Looking up the path at the side, he could see the door
left open, shedding a soft, coloured light from the hall lamp. He went
quickly and silently up the path, and looked up into the hall. There
were pictures on the walls, and the antlers of a stag—and the stairs
going up on one side—and just near the foot of the stairs the
35 half-opened door of the dining-room.

With heart drawn fine, Gerald stepped into the hall, whose floor
was of coloured tiles, went quickly and looked into the large, pleasant
room. In a chair by the fire, the father sat asleep, his head tilted back
against the side of the big oak chimney piece, his ruddy face seen
40 foreshortened, the nostrils open, the mouth fallen a little. It would
take the merest sound to wake him.

Gerald stood a second suspended. He glanced down the passage behind him. It was all dark. Again he was suspended. Then he went swiftly upstairs. His senses were so finely, almost supernaturally keen, that he seemed to cast his own will over the half-unconscious house.

He came to the first landing. There he stood, scarcely breathing. Again, corresponding to the door below, there was a door ajar. That would be the mother's room. He could hear her moving about in the candle-light. She would be expecting her husband to come up. He looked along the dark landing.

Then silently, on infinitely careful feet, he went along the passage, feeling the wall with the extreme tips of his fingers. There was a door. He stood and listened. He could hear two people's breathing. It was not that. He went stealthily forward. There was another door, slightly open. The room was in darkness. Empty. Then there was the bathroom, he could smell the soap and the heat. Then at the end was another bedroom—one soft breathing. This was she.

With an almost occult carefulness he turned the door handle, and opened the door an inch. It creaked slightly. Then he opened it another inch—then another. His heart did not beat, he seemed to create a silence about himself, an obliviousness.

He was in the room. Still the sleeper breathed softly. It was very dark. He felt his way forward inch by inch, with his feet and hands. He touched the bed, he could hear the sleeper. He drew nearer, bending close as if his eyes would disclose whatever there was. And then, very near his face, to his fear, he saw the round, dark head of a boy.

He recovered, turned round, saw the door afar, a faint light revealed. And he retreated swiftly, drew the door to without fastening it, and passed rapidly down the passage. At the head of the stairs he hesitated. There was still time to flee.

But it was unthinkable. He would maintain his will. He turned past the door of the parental bedroom like a shadow, and was climbing the second flight of stairs. They creaked under his weight—it was exasperating. Ah what disaster, if the mother's door opened just beneath him, and she saw him! It would have to be, if it were so. He held the control still.

He was not quite up these stairs when he heard a quick running of feet below, the outer door was closed and locked, he heard Ursula's voice, then the father's sleepy exclamation. He pressed on swiftly to the upper landing.

Again a door was ajar, a room was empty. Feeling his way forward, with the tips of his fingers, travelling rapidly, like a blind man, anxious lest Ursula should come upstairs, he found another door. There, with his preternaturally fine senses alert, he listened. He
5 heard someone moving in bed. This would be she.

Softly now, like one who has only one sense, the tactile sense, he turned the latch. It clicked. He held still. The bed-clothes rustled. His heart did not beat. Then again he drew the latch back, and very gently pushed the door. It made a sticking noise as it gave.
10 "Ursula?" said Gudrun's voice, frightened. He quickly opened the door and pushed it behind him.

"Is it you, Ursula?" came Gudrun's frightened voice. He heard her sitting up in bed. In another moment she would scream.

"No, it's me," he said, feeling his way towards her. "It is I,
15 Gerald."

She sat motionless in her bed in sheer astonishment. She was too astonished, too much taken by surprise, even to be afraid.

"Gerald!" she echoed, in blank amazement.

He had found his way to the bed, and his outstretched hand
20 touched her warm breast, blindly. She shrank away.

"Let me make a light," she said, springing out.

He stood perfectly motionless. He heard her touch the match-box, he heard her fingers in their movement. Then he saw her in the light of a match, which she held to the candle. The light rose in the
25 room, then sank to a small dimness, as the flame sank down on the candle, before it mounted again.

She looked at him, as he stood near the other side of the bed. His cap was pulled low over his brow, his black overcoat was buttoned close up to his chin. His face was strange and luminous. He was
30 inevitable as a supernatural being. When she had seen him, she knew. She knew there was something fatal in the situation, and she must accept it. Yet she must challenge him.

"How did you come up?" she asked.

"I walked up the stairs—the door was open." She looked at him.
35 "I haven't closed this door, either," he said. She walked swiftly across the room, and closed her door, softly, and locked it. Then she came back.

She was wonderful, with startled eyes and flushed cheeks, and her plait of hair rather short and thick down her back, and her long, fine
40 white night-dress falling to her feet.

She saw that his boots were all clayey, even his trousers were plastered with clay. And she wondered if he had made footprints all the way up. He was a very strange figure, standing in her bedroom, near the tossed bed.

"Why have you come?" she asked, almost querulous. 5

"I wanted to," he replied.

And this she could see, from his face. It was fate.

"You are so muddy," she said, in distaste, but gently.

He looked down at his feet.

"I was walking in the dark," he replied. But he felt vividly elated. 10 There was a pause. He stood on one side of the tumbled bed, she on the other. He did not even take his cap from his brows.

"And what do you want of me," she challenged.

He looked aside, and did not answer. Save for the extreme beauty and mystic attractiveness of his distinct, strange face, she would have 15 sent him away. But his face was too wonderful and undiscovered to her. It fascinated her with the fascination of pure beauty, cast a spell on her, like nostalgia, an ache.

"What do you want of me?" she repeated, in an estranged voice.

He pulled off his cap, in a movement of dream-liberation, and 20 went across to her. But he could not touch her, because she stood barefoot in her night-dress, and he was muddy and damp. Her eyes, wide and large and wondering, watched him, and asked him the ultimate question.

"I came—because I must," he said. "Why do you ask?" 25

She looked at him in doubt and wonder.

"I must ask," she said.

He shook his head slightly.

"There is no answer," he replied, with strange vacancy.

There was about him a curious, and almost godlike air of 30 simplicity and naive directness. He reminded her of an apparition, the young Hermes.*

"But why did you come to me?" she persisted.

"Because—it has to be so.—If there weren't you in the world, then *I* shouldn't be in the world, either." 35

She stood looking at him, with large, wide, wondering, stricken eyes. His eyes were looking steadily into hers all the time, and he seemed fixed in an odd supernatural steadfastness. She sighed. She was lost now. She had no choice.

"Won't you take off your boots," she said. "They must be wet." 40

He dropped his cap on a chair, unbuttoned his overcoat, lifting up his chin to unfasten the throat buttons. His short, keen hair was ruffled. He was so beautifully blond, like wheat. He pulled off his overcoat.

5   Quickly he pulled off his jacket, pulled loose his black tie, and was unfastening his studs, which were headed each with a pearl. She listened, watching, hoping no one would hear the starched linen crackle. It seemed to snap like pistol-shots.

He had come for vindication. She let him hold her in his arms, 10 clasp her close against him. He found in her an infinite relief. Into her he poured all his pent-up darkness and corrosive death, and he was whole again. It was wonderful, marvellous, it was a miracle. This was the ever-recurrent miracle of his life, at the knowledge of which he was lost in an ecstasy of relief and wonder. And she, subject, 15 received him as a vessel filled with his bitter potion of death. She had no power at this crisis to resist. The terrible frictional violence of death filled her, and she received it in an ecstasy of subjection, in throes of acute, violent sensation.

As he drew nearer to her, he plunged deeper into her enveloping 20 soft warmth, a wonderful creative heat that penetrated his veins and gave him life again. He felt himself dissolving and sinking to rest in the bath of her living strength. It seemed as if her heart in her breast were a second unconquerable sun, into the glow and creative strength of which he plunged further and further. All his veins, that 25 were murdered and lacerated, healed softly as life came pulsing in, stealing invisibly in to him as if it were the all-powerful effluence of the sun. His blood, which seemed to have been drawn back into death, came ebbing on the return, surely, beautifully, powerfully.

He felt his limbs growing fuller and flexible with life, his body 30 gained an unknown strength. He was a man again, strong and rounded. And he was a child, so soothed and restored and full of gratitude.

And she, she was the great bath of life, he worshipped her. Mother and substance of all life she was. And he, child and man, received of 35 her and was made whole. His pure body was almost killed. But the miraculous, soft effluence of her breast suffused over him, over his seared, damaged brain, like a healing lymph, like a soft, soothing flow of life itself, perfect as if he were bathed in the womb again.

His brain was hurt, seared, the tissue was as if destroyed. He had 40 not known how hurt he was, how his tissue, the very tissue of his brain was damaged by the corrosive flood of death. Now, as the healing lymph of her effluence flowed through him, he knew how destroyed he was, like a plant whose tissue is burst from inwards by a frost.

He buried his small, hard head between her breasts, and pressed her breasts against him with his hands. And she with quivering hands pressed his head against her, as he lay suffused out, and she lay fully conscious. The lovely, creative warmth flooded through him like a sleep of fecundity within the womb. Ah if only she would grant him the flow of this living effluence, he would be restored, he would be complete again. He was afraid she would deny him before it was finished. Like a child at the breast, he cleaved intensely to her, and she could not put him away. And his seared, ruined membrane relaxed, softened, that which was seared and stiff and blasted yielded again, became soft and flexible, palpitating with new life.* He was infinitely grateful, as to God, or as an infant is at its mother's breast. He was glad and grateful like a delirium, as he felt his own wholeness come over him again, as he felt the full, unutterable sleep coming over him, the sleep of complete exhaustion and restoration.

But Gudrun lay wide awake, destroyed into perfect consciousness. She lay motionless, with wide eyes staring motionless into the darkness, whilst he was sunk away in sleep, his arms round her.

She seemed to lie hearing waves break on a hidden shore, long, slow, gloomy waves breaking with the rhythm of fate, so monotonously that it seemed eternal. This endless breaking of slow, sullen waves of fate held her like a possession, whilst she lay with dark, wide eyes looking into the darkness. She could see so far, as far as eternity—yet she saw nothing. She was suspended in perfect consciousness—and of what was she conscious?

This mood of extremity, when she lay staring into eternity, utterly suspended, and conscious of everything, to the last limits, passed, and left her uneasy. She had lain so long motionless. She moved, she became self-conscious. She wanted to look at him, to see him.

But she dared not make a light, because she knew he would wake, and she did not want to break his perfect sleep, that she knew he had got of her.

She disengaged herself, softly, and rose up a little to look at him. There was a faint light, it seemed to her, in the room. She could just distinguish his features, as he slept the perfect sleep. In this darkness, she seemed to see him so distinctly. But he was far off, in

another world. Ah, she could shriek with torment, he was so far off, and perfected, in another world. She seemed to look at him as at a pebble far away under clear, dark water. And here was she, left with all the anguish of consciousness, whilst he was sunk deep into the
5 other element of mindless, remote, living shadow-gleam. He was beautiful, far-off, and perfected. They would never be together. Ah, this awful, inhuman distance which would always be interposed between her and the other being!

There was nothing to do but to lie still and endure. She felt an
10 overwhelming tenderness for him, and a dark understirring of jealous hatred, that he should lie so perfect and immune, in an otherworld, whilst she was tormented with violent wakefulness, cast out in the outer darkness.

She lay in intense and vivid consciousness, an exhausting super-
15 consciousness. The church clock struck the hours, it seemed to her, in quick succession. She heard them distinctly in the tension of her vivid consciousness. And he slept as if time were one moment, unchanging and unmoving.

She was exhausted, wearied. Yet she must continue in this state of
20 violent active superconsciousness. She was conscious of every-thing—her childhood, her girlhood, all the forgotten incidents, all the unrealised influences and all the happenings she had not understood, pertaining to herself, to her family, to her friends, her lovers, her acquaintances, everybody. It was as if she drew a
25 glittering rope of knowledge out of the sea of darkness, drew and drew and drew it out of the fathomless depths of the past, and still it did not come to an end, there was no end to it, she must haul and haul at the rope of glittering conscious, pull it out phosphorescent from the endless depths of the unconsciousness, till she was weary,
30 aching, exhausted, and fit to break, and yet she had not done.

Ah, if only she might wake him! She turned uneasily. When could she rouse him and send him away? When could she disturb him? And she relapsed into her activity of automatic consciousness, that would never end.

35 But the time was drawing near when she could wake him. It was like a release. The clock had struck four, outside in the night. Thank God the night had passed almost away. At five he must go, and she would be released. Then she could relax and fill her own place. Now she was driven up against his perfect sleeping motion like a knife
40 white-hot on a grindstone. There was something monstrous about him, about his juxtaposition against her.

The last hour was the longest. And yet, at last, it passed. Her heart leapt with relief—yes, there was the slow, strong stroke of the church clock—at last, after this night of eternity. She waited to catch each slow, fatal reverberation—"Three———four———*five!*" There, it was finished. A weight rolled off her.

She raised herself, leaned over him tenderly, and kissed him. She was sad to wake him. After a few moments, she kissed him again. But he did not stir. The darling, he was so deep in sleep! What a shame to take him out of it. She let him lie a little longer. But he must go—he must really go.

With full over-tenderness she took his face between her hands, and kissed his eyes. The eyes opened, he remained motionless, looking at her. Her heart stood still. To hide her face from his dreadful opened eyes, in the darkness, she bent down and kissed him, whispering:

"You must go, my love."

But she was sick with terror, sick.

He put his arms round her. Her heart sank.

"But you must go, my love. It's late."

"What time is it?" he said.

Strange, his man's voice. She quivered. It was an intolerable oppression to her.

"Past five o'clock," she said.

But he only closed his arms round her again. Her heart cried within her in torture. She disengaged herself firmly.

"You really must go," she said.

"Not for a minute," he said.

She lay still, nestling against him, but unyielding.

"Not for a minute," he repeated, clasping her closer.

"Yes," she said, unyielding. "I'm afraid if you stay any longer."

There was a certain coldness in her voice that made him release her, and she broke away, rose and lit the candle. That then was the end.

He got up. He was warm and full of life and desire. Yet he felt a little bit ashamed, humiliated, putting on his clothes before her, in the candle-light. For he felt revealed, exposed to her, at a time when she was in some way against him. It was all very difficult to understand. He dressed himself quickly, without collar or tie. Still he felt full and complete, perfected.—She thought it humiliating to see a man dressing: the ridiculous shirt, the ridiculous trousers and braces. But again an idea saved her.

"It is like a workman getting up to go to work," thought Gudrun. "And I am like a workman's wife." But an ache like nausea was upon her: a nausea of him.

He pushed his collar and tie into his overcoat pocket. Then he sat down and pulled on his boots. They were sodden, as were his socks and trouser-bottoms. But he himself was quick and warm.

"Perhaps you ought to have put your boots on downstairs," she said.

At once, without answering, he pulled them off again, and stood holding them in his hand. She had thrust her feet into slippers, and flung a loose robe round her. She was ready. She looked at him as he stood waiting, his black coat buttoned to the chin, his cap pulled down, his boots in his hand. And the passionate almost hateful fascination revived in her for a moment. It was not exhausted. His face was so warm-looking, wide-eyed and full of newness, so perfect. She felt old, old. She went to him heavily, to be kissed. He kissed her quickly. She wished his warm, expressionless beauty did not so fatally put a spell on her, compel her and subjugate her. It was a burden upon her, that she resented but could not escape. Yet when she looked at his straight, man's brows, and at his rather small, well-shaped nose, and at his blue, indifferent eyes, she knew her passion for him was not yet satisfied, perhaps never to be satisfied. Only now she was weary, with an ache like nausea. She wanted him gone.

They went downstairs quickly. It seemed they made a prodigious noise. He followed her as, wrapped in her vivid green wrap, she preceded him with the light. She suffered badly with fear, lest her people should be roused. He hardly cared. He did not care now who knew.—And she hated this in him. One *must* be cautious: one must preserve oneself.

She led the way to the kitchen. It was neat and tidy, as the woman had left it. He looked up at the clock—twenty minutes past five! Then he sat down on a chair to put on his boots. She waited, watching his every movement. She wanted it to be over, it was a great nervous strain on her.

He stood up—she unbolted the back door, and looked out. A cold, raw night, not yet dawn, with a piece of a moon in the vague sky. She was glad she need not go out.

"Goodbye then," he murmured.

"I'll come to the gate," she said.

And again she hurried on in front, to warn him of the steps. And at the gate, once more she stood on the step whilst he stood below her.

"Goodbye," she whispered.

He kissed her, dutifully, and turned away. She suffered torments hearing his firm tread going so distinctly down the road. Ah, the insensitiveness of that firm tread!

She closed the gate, and crept quickly and noiselessly back to bed. When she was in her room, and the door closed, and all safe, she breathed freely, and a great weight fell off her. She nestled down in bed, in the groove his body had made, in the warmth he had left. And, excited, worn-out, yet still satisfied, she fell soon into a deep, heavy sleep.

Gerald walked quickly through the raw darkness of the coming dawn. He met nobody. His mind was beautifully still and thoughtless, like a still pool, and his body full and warm and rich. He went quickly along towards Shortlands, in a grateful self-sufficiency.

Chapter XXV

Marriage or Not

The Brangwen family was going to move from Beldover. It was necessary now for the father to be in town.

Birkin had taken out a marriage licence,* yet Ursula deferred from day to day. She would not fix any definite time—she still wavered. Her month's notice to leave the Grammar School was in its third week. Christmas was not far off.

Gerald waited for the Ursula–Birkin marriage. It was something crucial to him.

"Shall we make it a double-barrelled affair?" he said to Birkin one day.

"Who for the second shot?" asked Birkin.

"Gudrun and me," said Gerald, the venturesome twinkle in his eyes.

Birkin looked at him steadily, as if somewhat taken aback.

"Serious—or joking?" he asked.

"Oh, serious.—Shall I? Shall Gudrun and I rush in along with you?"

"Do by all means," said Birkin.—"I didn't know you'd got that length."

"What length?" said Gerald, looking at the other man, and laughing. "Oh yes, we've gone all the lengths."

"There remains to put it on a broad social basis, and to achieve a high moral purpose," said Birkin.

"Something like that: the length and breadth and height of it," replied Gerald, smiling.

"Oh well," said Birkin, "it's a very admirable step to take, I should say."

Gerald looked at him closely.

"Why aren't you enthusiastic?" he asked. "I thought you were such dead nuts on marriage."

Birkin lifted his shoulders.

"One might as well be dead nuts on noses.—There are all sorts of noses, snub and otherwise—"

Gerald laughed.

"And all sorts of marriage, also snub and otherwise?" he said.

"That's it."

"And you think if I marry, it will be snub?" asked Gerald quizzically, his head a little on one side.

Birkin laughed quickly.

"How do I know what it will be!" he said. "Don't lambaste me with my own parallels—"

Gerald pondered a while.

"But I should like to know your opinion, exactly," he said.

"On your marriage?—or marrying?—why should you want my opinion? I've got no opinions. I'm not interested in legal marriage, one way or another.—It's a mere question of convenience."

Still Gerald watched him closely.

"More than that, I think," he said seriously. "However you may be bored by the ethics of marriage, yet really to marry, in one's own personal case, is something critical, final—"

"You mean there is something final in going to the registrar with a woman?"

"If you're coming back with her, I do," said Gerald. "It is in some way irrevocable."

"Yes, I agree," said Birkin.

"No matter how one regards legal marriage, yet to enter into the married state, in one's own personal instance, is final—"

"I believe it is," said Birkin, "somewhere."

"The question remains then, should one do it," said Gerald.

Birkin watched him narrowly, with amused eyes.

"You are like Lord Bacon,* Gerald," he said. "You argue it like a lawyer—or like Hamlet's to-be-or-not-to-be.—If I were you I would *not* marry: but ask Gudrun, not me. You're not marrying me, are you?"

Gerald did not heed the latter part of this speech.

"Yes," he said, "one must consider it coldly.—It is something critical.—One comes to the point where one must take a step in one direction or another. And marriage is one direction—"

"And what is the other?" asked Birkin quickly.

Gerald looked up at him with hot, strangely-conscious eyes, that the other man could not understand.

"I can't say," he replied. "If I knew *that*—." He moved uneasily on his feet, and did not finish.

"You mean if you knew the alternative?" asked Birkin. "And since you don't know it, marriage is a *pis aller*."

Gerald looked up at Birkin with the same hot, constrained eyes.

"One does have the feeling that marriage is a *pis aller*," he admitted.

"Then don't do it," said Birkin. "I tell you," he went on, "the same as I've said before, marriage in the old sense seems to me
5 repulsive. *Egoïsme à deux** is nothing to it. It's a sort of tacit hunting in couples: the world all in couples, each couple in its own little house, watching its own little interests, and stewing in its own little privacy—it's the most repulsive thing on earth."

"I quite agree," said Gerald. "There's something inferior about it.
10 But as I say, what's the alternative."

"One should avoid this *home* instinct. It's not an instinct, it's a habit of cowardliness. One should never have a *home*."

"I agree really," said Gerald. "But there's no alternative."

"We've got to find one.—I do believe in a permanent union
15 between a man and a woman. Chopping about is merely an exhaustive process.—But a permanent relation between a man and a woman isn't the last word—it certainly isn't."

"Quite," said Gerald.

"In fact," said Birkin, "because the relation between man and
20 woman is made the supreme and exclusive relationship, that's where all the tightness and meanness and insufficiency comes in."

"Yes, I believe you," said Gerald.

"You've got to take down the love-and-marriage ideal from its pedestal. We want something broader.—I believe in the *additional*
25 perfect relationship between man and man—additional to marriage."*

"I can never see how they can be the same," said Gerald.

"Not the same—but equally important, equally creative, equally sacred, if you like."
30 Gerald moved uneasily.—"You know, I can't feel that," said he. "Surely there can never be anything as strong between man and man as sex love is between man and woman. Nature doesn't provide the basis."

"Well, of course, I think she does. And I don't think we shall ever
35 be happy till we establish ourselves on this basis. You've got to get rid of the *exclusiveness* of married love. And you've got to admit the unadmitted love of man for man. It makes for a greater freedom for everybody, a greater power of individuality both in men and women."*
40 "I know," said Gerald, "you believe something like that. Only I

can't *feel* it, you see." He put his hand on Birkin's arm, with a sort of deprecating affection. And he smiled as if triumphantly.

He was ready to be doomed. Marriage was like a doom to him. He was willing to condemn himself in marriage, to become like a convict condemned to the mines of the underworld, living no life in the sun, but having a dreadful subterranean activity. He was willing to accept this. And marriage was the seal of his condemnation. He was willing to be sealed thus in the underworld, like a soul damned but living forever in damnation.—But he would not make any pure relationship with any other soul. He could not. Marriage was not the committing of himself into a relationship with Gudrun. It was a committing of himself in acceptance of the established world, he would accept the established order, in which he did not livingly believe, and then he would retreat to the underworld for his life. This he would do.

The other way was to accept Rupert's offer of love, to enter into the bond of pure trust and love with the other man, and then subsequently with the woman. If he pledged himself with the man he would later be able to pledge himself with the woman: not merely in legal marriage, but in absolute, mystic marriage.*

Yet he could not accept the offer. There was a numbness upon him, a numbness either of unborn, absent volition, or of atrophy. Perhaps it was the absence of volition. For he was strangely elated at Rupert's offer. Yet he was still more glad to reject it, not to be committed.

Chapter XXVI

A Chair

There was a jumble market every Monday afternoon in the old market-place in town. Ursula and Birkin strayed down there one afternoon. They had been talking of furniture, and they wanted to see if there was any fragment they would like to buy, amid the heaps of rubbish collected on the cobble-stones.

The old market square was not very large, a mere bare patch of granite setts, usually, with a few fruit-stalls under a wall. It was in a poor quarter of the town. Meagre houses stood down one side, there was a hosiery factory, a great blank with myriad oblong windows, at the end, a street of little shops with flagstone pavement down the other side, and, for a crowning monument, the public baths, of new red brick, with a clock-tower. The people who moved about seemed stumpy and sordid, the air seemed to smell rather dirty, there was a sense of many mean streets ramifying off into warrens of meanness. Now and again a great chocolate-and-yellow tram-car ground round a difficult bend under the hosiery factory.

Ursula was superficially thrilled when she found herself out among the common people, in the jumbled place piled with old bedding, heaps of old iron, shabby crockery in pale lots, muffled lots of unthinkable clothing. She and Birkin went unwillingly down the narrow aisles between the rusty wares. He was looking at the goods, she at the people.

She excitedly watched a young woman, who was going to have a baby, and who was turning over a mattress and making a young man, down-at-heel and dejected, feel it also. So secretive and active and anxious the young woman seemed, so reluctant, slinking, the young man. He was going to marry her because she was having a child.

When they had felt the mattress, the young woman asked the old man seated on a stool among his wares, how much it was. He told her, and she turned to the young man. The latter was ashamed and self-conscious, he turned his face away, though he left his body standing there, and muttered aside. And again the young woman anxiously and actively fingered the mattress and added up in her mind

354

and bargained with the old, unclean man. All the while, the young man stood by, shamefaced and down-at-heel, submitting.

"Look," said Birkin, "there is a pretty chair."

"Charming!" cried Ursula. "Oh charming."

It was an arm-chair of simple wood, probably birch, but of such fine delicacy of grace, standing there on the sordid stones, it almost brought tears to the eyes. It was square in shape, of the purest, slender lines, and four short lines of wood in the back, that reminded Ursula of harp-strings.

"It was once," said Birkin, "gilded—and it had a cane seat. Somebody has nailed this wooden seat in.—Look, here is a trifle of the red that underlay the gilt. The rest is all black, except where the wood is worn pure and glossy.—It is the fine unity of the lines that is so attractive—look, how they run and meet and counteract.—But of course the wooden seat is wrong—it destroys the perfect lightness and unity in tension the cane gave.—I like it though—"

"Ah yes," said Ursula, "so do I."

"How much is it?" Birkin asked the man.

"Ten shillings."

"And you will send it—?"

It was bought.*

"So beautiful, so pure!" Birkin said. "It almost breaks my heart." They walked along between the heaps of rubbish. "My beloved country—it had something to express even when it made that chair."

"And hasn't it now?" asked Ursula. She was always angry when he took this tone.

"No, it hasn't.—When I see that clear, beautiful chair, and I think of England, even Jane Austen's England—it had living thoughts to unfold even then, and pure happiness in unfolding them. And now, we can only fish among the rubbish heaps for the remnants of their old expression. There is no production in us now, only sordid and foul mechanicalness."

"It isn't true," cried Ursula. "Why must you always praise the past, at the expense of the present?—*Really*, I don't think so much of Jane Austen's England. It was materialistic enough, if you like—"

"It could afford to be materialistic," said Birkin, "because it had the power to be something other—which we haven't. We are materialistic because we haven't the power to be anything else—try as we may, we can't bring off anything but materialism: mechanism, the very soul of materialism."

Ursula was subdued into angry silence. She did not heed what he said. She was rebelling against something else.

"And I hate your past—I'm sick of it," she cried. "I believe I even hate that old chair, though it *is* beautiful.—It isn't *my* sort of beauty.—I wish it had been smashed up when its day was over, not left to preach the beloved past at us—I'm sick of the beloved past."

"Not so sick as I am of the accursed present," he said.

"Yes—just the same. I hate the present—but I don't want the past to take its place—I don't want that old chair."

He was rather angry for a moment. Then he looked at the sky shining beyond the tower of the public baths, and he seemed to get over it all. He laughed.

"All right," he said, "then let us not have it. I'm sick of it all, too. At any rate one can't go on living on the old bones of beauty."

"One can't," she cried. "I *don't* want old things."

"The truth is, we don't want things at all," he replied. "The thought of a house and furniture of my own is hateful to me."

This startled her, for a moment. Then she replied:

"So it is to me.—But one must live somewhere."

"Not somewhere—anywhere," he said. "One should just live anywhere—not have a definite place. I don't want a definite place.—As soon as you get a room, and it is *complete*, you want to run from it.—Now my rooms at the Mill are quite complete, I want them at the bottom of the sea. It is a horrible tyranny of a fixed milieu, where each piece of furniture is a commandment-stone."

She clung to his arm as they walked away from the market.

"But what are we going to do," she said. "We must live somehow. And I do want some beauty in my surroundings. I want a sort of natural *grandeur* even, *splendour*."

"You'll never get it in houses and furniture—or even clothes. Houses and furniture and clothes, they are all terms of an old base world, a detestable society of man. And if you have a Tudor house and old, beautiful furniture, it is only the past perpetuated on top of you, horrible.—And if you have a perfect modern house done for you by Poiret,* it is something else perpetuated on top of you. It is all horrible. It is all possessions, possessions, bullying you and turning you into a generalisation.—You have to be like Rodin, Michael Angelo, and leave a piece of raw rock unfinished* to your figure. You must leave your surroundings sketchy, unfinished, so that you are never contained, never confined, never dominated from the outside."

She stood in the street contemplating.

"And we are never to have a complete place of our own—never a home?" she said.

"Pray God, in this world, no," he answered.

"But there's only this world," she objected.

He spread out his hands with a gesture of indifference.

"Meanwhile, then, we'll avoid having things of our own," he said.

"But you've just bought a chair," she said.

"I can tell the man I don't want it," he replied.

She pondered again. Then a queer little movement twitched her face.

"No," she said, "we don't want it. I'm sick of old things."

"New ones as well," he said.

They retraced their steps.

There, in front of some furniture, stood the young couple, the woman who was going to have a baby, and the narrow-faced youth. She was fair, rather short, stout. He was of medium height, attractively built. His dark hair fell sideways over his brow, from under his cap, he stood strangely aloof, like one of the damned.

"Let us give it to *them*," whispered Ursula. "Look, they are getting a home together."

"*I* won't aid and abet them in it," he said petulantly, instantly sympathising with the aloof, furtive youth, against the active, procreant female.

"Oh yes," cried Ursula. "It's right for them—there's nothing else, for them."

"Very well," said Birkin, "you offer it them—I'll watch."

Ursula went rather nervously to the young couple, who were discussing an iron washstand—or rather, the man was glancing furtively and wonderingly, like a prisoner, at the abominable article, whilst the woman was arguing.

"We bought a chair," said Ursula, "and we don't want it. Would you have it? We should be glad if you would."

The young couple looked round on her, not believing that she could be addressing them.

"Would you care for it?" repeated Ursula. "It's really *very* pretty—but—but—" she smiled rather dazzlingly.

The young couple only stared at her, and looked significantly at each other, to know what to do. And the man curiously obliterated himself, as if he could make himself invisible, as a rat can.

"We wanted to *give* it you," explained Ursula, now overcome with confusion and dread of them. She was attracted by the young man.
5 He was a still, mindless creature, hardly a man at all, a creature that the towns have produced, strangely pure-bred and fine in one sense, furtive, quick, subtle. His lashes were dark and long and fine over his eyes, that had no mind in them, only a dreadful kind of subject, inward consciousness, glazed and dark. His dark brows, and all his
10 lines, were finely drawn. He would be a dreadful, but wonderful lover to a woman, so marvellously contributed.* His legs would be marvellously subtle and alive, under the shapeless trousers, he had some of the fineness and stillness and silkiness of a dark-eyed, silent rat.
15   Ursula had apprehended him with a fine *frisson* of attraction. The full-built woman was staring offensively. Again Ursula forgot him.

"Won't you have the chair?" she said.

The man looked at her with a sideways look of appreciation, yet far-off, almost insolent. The woman drew herself up. There was a
20 certain coster-monger richness about her. She did not know what Ursula was after, she was on her guard, hostile. Birkin approached, smiling wickedly at seeing Ursula so nonplussed and frightened.

"What's the matter?" he said, smiling.

His eyelids had dropped slightly, there was about him the same
25 suggestive, mocking secrecy that was in the bearing of the two city creatures.—The man jerked his head a little on one side, indicating Ursula, and said, with curious amiable, jeering warmth:

"What she warnt?*—Eh!" An odd smile writhed his lips.

Birkin looked at him from under his slack, ironical eyelids.
30 "To give you a chair—that—with the label on it," he said, pointing.

The man looked at the object indicated. There was a curious hostility in male, outlawed understanding between the two men.

"What's she warnt to give it *us* for, guvnor," he replied, in a tone of
35 free intimacy that insulted Ursula.

"Thought you'd like it—it's a pretty chair. We bought it, and don't want it. No need for you to have it, don't be frightened," said Birkin, with a wry smile.

The man glanced up at him, half inimical, half recognising.
40 "Why don't you want it for yourselves, if you've just bought it?"

asked the woman coolly. "'Taint good enough for you, now you've had a look at it.—Frightened it's got something in it, eh?"

She was looking at Ursula, admiringly, but with some resentment.

"I'd never thought of that," said Birkin. "But no, the wood's too thin everywhere."

"You see," said Ursula, her face luminous and pleased. "*We* are just going to get married, and we thought we'd buy things. Then we decided, just now, that we wouldn't have furniture, we'd go abroad."

The full built, slightly blowsy city girl looked at the fine face of the other woman, with appreciation. They appreciated each other. The youth stood aside, his face expressionless and timeless, the thin line of the black moustache drawn strangely suggestive over his rather wide, closed mouth. He was impassive, abstract, like some dark suggestive presence, a gutter-presence.

"It's all right to be some folks," said the city girl, turning to her own young man. He did not look at her, but he smiled with the lower part of his face, putting his head aside in an odd gesture of assent. His eyes were unchanging, glazed with darkness.

"Cawsts something to chynge your mind," he said, in an incredibly low accent.

"Only ten shillings this time," said Birkin.

The man looked up at him with a grimace of a smile, furtive, unsure.

"Cheap at 'arf a quid,* guvnor," he said. "Not like getting divawced."

"We're not married yet," said Birkin.

"No, no more aren't we," said the young woman loudly. "But we shall be, a Saturday."

Again she looked at the young man with a determined, protective look, at once overbearing and very gentle. He grinned sicklily, turning away his head. She had got his manhood, but Lord, what did he care! He had a strange furtive pride and slinking singleness.

"Good luck to you," said Birkin.

"Same to you," said the young woman. Then, rather tentatively: "When's yours coming off, then?"

Birkin looked round at Ursula.

"It's for the lady to say," he replied. "We go to the registrar the moment she's ready."

Ursula laughed, covered with confusion and bewilderment.

"No 'urry," said the young man, grinning suggestive.

"Oh, don't break your neck to get there," said the young woman.
"'Slike when you're dead—you're a long time married."*

The young man turned aside as if this hit him.

"The longer the better, let us hope," said Birkin.

5 "That's it, guvnor," said the young man admiringly. "Enjoy it
while it larsts—niver whip a dead donkey."*

"Only when he's shamming dead," said the young woman,
looking at her young man with caressive tenderness of authority.

"Aw, there's a difference," he said satirically.

10 "What about the chair?" said Birkin.

"Yes, all right," said the woman.

They trailed off to the dealer, the handsome but abject young
fellow hanging a little aside.

"That's it," said Birkin. "Will you take it with you, or have the
15 address altered?"

"Oh, Fred can carry it. Make him do what he can for the dear old
'ome."

"Mike* use of 'im," said Fred, grimly humorous, as he took the
chair from the dealer. His movements were graceful, yet curiously
20 abject, slinking.

"'Ere's mother's cosy chair," he said. "Warnts a cushion."

And he stood it down on the market stones.

"Don't you think it's pretty?" laughed Ursula.

"Oh, I do," said the young woman.

25 "'Ave a sit in it, you'll wish you'd kept it," said the young man.

Ursula promptly sat down in the middle of the market-place.

"Awfully comfortable," she said. "But rather hard.—You try it."
She invited the young man to a seat. But he turned uncouthly,
awkwardly aside, glancing up at her with quick bright eyes, oddly
30 suggestive, like a quick, live rat.

"Don't spoil him," said the young woman. "He's not used to
arm-chairs, 'e isn't."

The young man turned away, and said, with averted grin:

"Only warnts legs on 'is."

35 The four parted. The young woman thanked them.

"Thank you for the chair—it'll last till it gives way."

"Keep it for an ornment," said the young man.

"Good afternoon—good afternoon," said Ursula and Birkin.

"Goo'—luck to you," said the young man, glancing and avoiding
40 Birkin's eyes, as he turned aside his head.

The two couples went asunder, Ursula clinging to Birkin's arm. When they had gone some distance, she glanced back and saw the young man going beside the full, easy young woman. His trousers sank over his heels, he moved with a sort of slinking evasion, more crushed with odd self-consciousness now he had the slim old arm-chair to carry, his arm over the back, the four fine, square, tapering legs swaying perilously near the granite setts of the pavement. And yet he was somewhere indomitable and separate, like a quick, vital rat. He had a queer, subterranean beauty, repulsive too.

"How strange they are!" said Ursula.

"Children of men," he said. "They remind me of Jesus' 'The meek shall inherit the earth.'"*

"But they aren't the meek," said Ursula.

"Yes, I don't know why, but they are," he replied.

They waited for the tram-car. Ursula sat on top and looked out on the town. The dusk was just dimming the hollows of crowded houses.

"And are they going to inherit the earth?" she said.

"Yes—they."

"Then what are we going to do?" she asked. "We're not like them—are we?—We're not the meek?"

"No.—We've got to live in the chinks they leave us."

"How horrible!" cried Ursula. "I don't want to live in chinks."

"Don't worry," he said. "They are the children of men, they like market-places and street-corners best. That leaves plenty of chinks."

"All the world," she said.

"Ah no—but some room."

The tram-car mounted slowly up the hill, where the ugly winter-grey masses of houses looked like a vision of hell that is cold and angular. They sat and looked. Away in the distance was an angry redness of sunset. It was all cold, somehow small, crowded, and like the end of the world.

"I don't mind it even then," said Ursula, looking at the repulsiveness of it all. "It doesn't concern me."

"No more it does," he replied, holding her hand. "One needn't see. One goes one's way. In my world it is sunny and spacious—"

"It is, my love, isn't it," she cried, hugging near to him on the top of the tram-car, so that the other passengers stared at them.

"And we will wander about on the face of the earth," he said, "and we'll look at the world beyond just this bit."

There was a long silence. Her face was radiant like gold, as she sat thinking.

"I don't want to inherit the earth," she said. "I don't want to inherit anything."

He closed his hand over hers.

"Neither do I. I want to be disinherited."

She clasped his fingers closely.

"We won't care about *anything*," she said.

He sat still, and laughed.

"And we'll be married, and have done with them," she added.

—Again he laughed.

"It's one way of getting rid of everything," she said, "to get married."

"And one way of accepting the whole* world," he added.

"A whole other world, yes," she said happily.

"Perhaps there's Gerald—and Gudrun—" he said.

"If there is there is, you see," she said. "It's no good our worrying. We can't really alter them, can we?"

"No," he said. "One has no right to try—not with the best intentions in the world."

"Do you try to force them?" she asked.

"Perhaps," he said. "Why should I want him to be free, if it isn't his business?"

She paused for a time.

"We can't *make* him happy, anyhow," she said. "He'd have to be it of himself."

"I know," he said. "But we want other people with us, don't we?"

"Why should we?" she asked.

"I don't know," he said uneasily. "One has a hankering after a sort of further fellowship."

"But why?" she insisted. "Why should you hanker after other people? Why should you need them?"

This hit him right on the quick. His brows knitted.

"Does it end with just our two selves?" he asked, tense.

"Yes—what more do you want? If anybody likes to come along, let them. But why must you run after them?"

His face was tense and unsatisfied.

"You see," he said, "I always imagine our being really happy with some few other people—a little freedom with people."

She pondered for a moment.

"Yes, one does want that. But it must *happen*. You can't do anything for it with your will. You always seem to think you can *force* the flowers to come out. People must love us because they love us—you can't *make* them."

"I know," he said. "But must one take no steps at all? Must one just go as if one were alone in the world—the only creature in the world?"

"You've got me," she said. "Why should you *need* others? Why must you *force* people to agree with you? Why can't you be single by yourself, as you are always saying?—You try to bully Gerald—as you tried to bully Hermione.—You must learn to be alone.—And it's so horrid of you. You've got me. And yet you want to force other people to love you as well. You do try to bully them to love you.—And even then, you don't want their love."

His face was full of real perplexity.

"Don't I?" he said. "It's the problem I can't solve. I *know* I want a perfect and complete relationship with you: and we've nearly got it—we really have.—But beyond that. *Do* I want a real, ultimate relationship with Gerald. Do I want a final, almost extra-human relationship with him—a relationship in the ultimates of me and him—or don't I?"

She looked at him for a long time, with strange bright eyes, but she did not answer.

Chapter XXVII

Flitting

That evening Ursula returned home very bright-eyed and wondrous—which irritated her people. Her father came home at supper-time, tired after the evening class, and the long journey home. Gudrun was reading, the mother sat in silence.

Suddenly Ursula said, to the company at large, in a bright voice: "Rupert and I are going to be married tomorrow."

Her father turned round, stiffly.

"You what?" he said.

"Tomorrow!" echoed Gudrun.

"Indeed!" said the mother.

But Ursula only smiled wonderfully, and did not reply.

"Married tomorrow!" cried her father harshly. "What are you talking about!"

"Yes," said Ursula. "Why not?" Those two words, from her, always drove him mad. "Everything is all right—we shall go to the registrar's office—"

There was a second's hush in the room, after Ursula's blithe vagueness.

"*Really*, Ursula!" said Gudrun.

"Might we ask why there has been all this secrecy?" demanded the mother, rather superbly.

"But there hasn't," said Ursula. "You knew."

"Who knew?" now cried her father. "Who knew? What do you mean, by your '*you knew*'?" He was in one of his stupid rages, she instantly closed against him.

"Of course you knew," she said coolly. "You knew we were going to get married."

There was a dangerous pause.

"We knew you were going to get married, did we? Knew! Why when* does anybody know anything about *you*, you shifty bitch!"

"Father!" cried Gudrun, flushing deep in violent remonstrance. Then, in a cold, but gentle voice, as if to remind her sister to be tractable. "But isn't it a *fearfully* sudden decision, Ursula?" she asked.

"No, not really," replied Ursula, with the same maddening cheerfulness. "He's been *wanting* me to agree, for weeks—he's had the licence ready. Only I—I wasn't ready in myself. Now I am ready—is there anything to be disagreeable about?"

"Certainly not," said Gudrun, but in a tone of cold reproof. "You are perfectly free to do as you like."

"'Ready in yourself'—*yourself*, that's all that matters, isn't it! 'I wasn't ready in myself,'" he mimicked her phrase offensively. "You and *yourself*, you're of some importance, aren't you?"

She drew herself up and set back her throat, her eyes shining yellow and dangerous.

"I am to myself," she said, wounded and mortified. "I know I am not to anybody else. You only wanted to *bully* me—you never cared for my happiness."

He was leaning forward watching her, his face intense like a spark.

"Ursula, what are you saying? Keep your tongue still," cried her mother. Ursula swung round, and the lights in her eyes flashed.

"No I won't," she cried. "I won't hold my tongue and be bullied.—What does it matter which day I get married—what does it *matter*! It doesn't affect anybody but myself."

Her father was tense and gathered together like a cat about to spring.

"Doesn't it?" he cried, coming nearer to her. She shrank away.

"No, how can it?" she replied, shrinking but stubborn.

"It doesn't matter to *me* then, what you do—what becomes of you—?" he cried, in a strange voice like a cry.

The mother and Gudrun stood back as if hypnotised.

"No," stammered Ursula. Her father was very near to her. "You only want to——"

She knew it was dangerous, and she stopped. He was gathered together, every muscle ready.

"What—?" he challenged.

"Bully me," she muttered, and even as her lips were moving, his hand had caught her smack at the side of the face and she was sent up against the door.

"Father!" cried Gudrun in a high voice—"It is *impossible*!"

He stood unmoving. Ursula recovered, her hand was on the door handle. She slowly drew herself up. He seemed doubtful now.

"It's true," she declared, with brilliant tears in her eyes, her head lifted up in defiance. "What has your love meant—what did it ever mean?—bullying, and denial—it did—"

He was advancing again with strange, tense movements, and clenched fist, and the face of a murderer. But swift as lightning she had flashed out of the door, and they heard her running upstairs.

He stood for a moment looking at the door. Then, like a defeated animal, he turned and went back to his seat by the fire.

Gudrun was very white. Out of the intense silence, the mother's voice was heard saying, cold and angry:

"Well, you shouldn't take so much notice of her."

Again the silence fell, each followed a separate set of emotions and thoughts.

Suddenly the door opened again: Ursula, dressed in hat and furs, with a small valise in her hand:

"Goodbye!" she said, in her maddening, bright, almost mocking tone. "I'm going."

And in the next instant the door was closed, they heard the outer door, then her quick steps down the garden path, then the gate banged, and her light footfall was gone. There was a silence like death in the house.

Ursula went straight to the station, hastening heedlessly, on winged feet. There was no train, she must walk on to the junction. As she went through the darkness, she began to cry, and she wept bitterly, with a dumb, heart-broken, child's anguish, all the way on the road, and in the train. Time passed unheeded and unknown, she did not know where she was, nor what was taking place. Only she wept from fathomless depths of hopeless, hopeless grief, the terrible grief of a child, that knows no extenuation.

Yet her voice had the same defensive brightness as she spoke to Birkin's landlady at the door.

"Good evening! Is Mr Birkin in? Can I see him?"

"Yes, he's in. He's in his study."

Ursula stepped past the woman. His door opened. He had heard her voice.

"Hello!" he exclaimed in surprise, seeing her standing there with the valise in her hand, and marks of tears on her face. She was one who wept without showing many traces, like a child.

"Do I look a sight?" she said, shrinking.

"No—why? Come in," he took the bag from her hand and they went into the study.

There, immediately, her lips began to tremble like those of a child that remembers again, and the tears came rushing up.

"What's the matter?" he asked, taking her in his arms. She sobbed violently on his shoulder, whilst he held her still, waiting.

"What's the matter?" he said again, when she was quieter. But she only pressed her face further into his shoulder, in pain, like a child that cannot tell.

"What is it, then?" he asked.

Suddenly she broke away, wiped her eyes, regained her composure, and went and sat in a chair.

"Father hit me," she announced, sitting bunched up, rather like a ruffled bird, her eyes very bright.

"What for?" he said.

She looked away, and would not answer. There was a pitiful redness about her sensitive nostrils, and her quivering lips.

"Why?" he repeated, in his strange, soft, penetrating voice.

She looked round at him, rather defiantly.

"Because I said I was going to be married tomorrow, and he bullied me."

"Why did he bully you?"

Her mouth dropped again, she remembered the scene once more, the tears came up.

"Because I said he didn't care—and he doesn't, it's only his domineeringness that's hurt—" she said, her mouth pulled awry by her weeping, all the time she spoke, so that he almost smiled, it seemed so childish. Yet it was not childish, it was a mortal conflict, a deep wound.

"It isn't quite true," he said. "And even so, you shouldn't *say* it."

"It *is* true—it *is* true," she wept. "And I won't be bullied by his pretending it's love—when it *isn't*—he doesn't care, how can he—no, he can't—."

He sat in silence. She moved him beyond himself.

"Then you shouldn't rouse him, if he can't," replied Birkin quietly.

"And I *have* loved him, I have," she wept, "I've loved him always, and he's always done this to me, he has—."

"It's been a love of opposition, then," he said. "Never mind—it will be all right. It's nothing desperate."

"Yes," she wept, "it is, it is."

"Why?"

"I shall never see him again——"

"Not immediately—Don't cry, you had to break with him, it had to be—don't cry."

He went over to her and kissed her fine, fragile hair, touching her wet cheeks gently.

"Don't cry," he repeated, "don't cry any more."

He held her head close against him, very close and quiet.

At last she was still. Then she looked up, her eyes wide and frightened.

"Don't you want me?" she asked.

"Want you?" His darkened, steady eyes puzzled her and did not give her play.

"Do you wish I hadn't come?" she asked, anxious now again, for fear she might be out of place.

"No," he said. "I wish there hadn't been the violence—so much ugliness—but perhaps it was inevitable."

She watched him in silence. He seemed deadened.

"But where shall I stay?" she asked, feeling humiliated.

He thought for a moment.

"Here, with me," he said. "We're married as much today as we shall be tomorrow."

"But—"

"I'll tell Mrs Varley," he said. "Never mind now."

He sat looking at her. She could feel his darkened, steady eyes looking at her all the time. It made her a little bit frightened. She pushed her hair off her forehead nervously.

"Do I look ugly?" she said.

And she blew her nose again.

A small smile came round his eyes.

"No," he said, "fortunately."

And he went across to her, and gathered her like a belonging in his arms. She was so tenderly beautiful, he could not bear to see her, he could only bear to hide her against himself. Now, washed all clear by her tears, she was new and frail like a flower just unfolded, a flower so new, so tender, so made perfect by inner light, that he could not bear to look on her, he must hide her against himself, cover his eyes against her. She had the perfect candour of creation, something translucent and simple, like a radiant, shining flower that moment unfolded in primal blessedness. She was so new, so wonder-clear, so undimmed. And he was so old, so steeped in heavy memories. Her soul was new, undefined and glimmering with the unseen. And his soul was dark and gloomy, it had only one grain of living hope, like a grain of mustard seed.* But this one living grain in him matched the perfect youth in her.

"I love you," he whispered as he kissed her, and trembled with pure hope, like a man who is born again to a wonderful, lovely hope far exceeding the bounds of death.

She could not know how much it meant to him, how much he meant by the few words. Almost childish, she wanted proof, and statement, even overstatement. For everything seemed still uncertain, unfixed to her.

But the passion of gratitude with which he received her into his soul, the extreme, unthinkable gladness of knowing himself living and fit to unite with her, he, who was so nearly dead, who was so near to being gone with the rest of his race down the slope of mechanical death, could never be understood by her. He worshipped her as age worships youth, he gloried in her because, in his one grain of faith, he was young as she, he was her proper mate. This marriage with her was his resurrection and his life.*

All this she could not know. She wanted to be made much of, to be adored. There were infinite distances of silence between them. How could he tell her of the immanence of her beauty, that was not form or weight or colour, but something like a strange golden light! How could he know himself what her beauty lay in, for him. He said "Your nose is beautiful, your chin is adorable." But it sounded like lies, and she was disappointed, hurt. Even when he said, whispering with truth, "I love you, I love you," it was not the real truth. It was something beyond love, such a gladness of having surpassed oneself, of having transcended the old existence. How could he say 'I', when he was something new and unknown, not himself at all? This I, this old formula of the ego, was a dead letter.

In the new, superfine bliss, a peace superseding knowledge, there was no I and you, there was only the third, unrealised wonder, the wonder of existing not as oneself, but in a consummation of my being and of her being in a new One, a new, paradisal unit regained from the duality. How* can I say "I love you", when I have ceased to be, and you have ceased to be, we are both caught up and transcended into a new oneness where everything is silent, because there is nothing to answer, all is perfect and at one. Speech travels between the separate parts. But in the perfect One there is perfect silence of bliss.

They were married by law on the next day, and she did as he bade her, she wrote to her father and mother. Her mother replied, not her father.

She did not go back to school. She stayed with Birkin in his rooms, or at the Mill, moving with him as he moved. But she did not see anybody, save Gudrun and Gerald. She was all strange and wondering as yet, but relieved as by dawn.

Gerald sat talking to her one afternoon, in the warm study down at the Mill. Rupert had not yet come home.

"You are happy?" Gerald asked her, with a smile.

"Very happy!" she cried, shrinking a little in her brightness.

"Yes, one can see it."

"Can one?" cried Ursula, in surprise.

He looked up at her with a communicative smile.

"Oh yes, plainly."

She was pleased. She meditated a moment.

"And can you see that Rupert is happy as well?"

He lowered his eyelids, and looked aside.

"Oh yes," he said.

"Really?"

"Oh yes."

He was very quiet, as if it were something not to be talked about by him. He seemed sad.

She was very sensitive to suggestion. She asked the question he wanted her to ask.

"Why don't you be happy as well?" she said. "You could be just the same."

He paused a moment.

"With Gudrun?" he asked.

"Yes!" she cried, her eyes glowing. But there was a strange tension, an emphasis, as if they were asserting their wishes, against the truth.

"You think Gudrun would have me, and we should be happy?" he said.

"Yes, I'm *sure!*" she cried.

Her eyes were round with delight. Yet underneath she was constrained, she knew her own insistence.

"Oh, I'm *so* glad," she added.

He smiled.

"What makes you glad?" he said.

"For *her* sake," she replied. "I'm sure you'd—you're the right man for her."

"You are?" he said. "And do you think she would agree with you?"

"Oh yes!" she exclaimed hastily. Then, upon reconsideration, very uneasy: "Though Gudrun isn't so very simple, is she? One doesn't know her in five minutes, does one? She's not like me in that."

She laughed at him with her strange, open, dazzled face.

"You think she's not much like you?" Gerald asked.

She knitted her brows.

"Oh, in many ways she is.—But I never know what she will do when anything new comes."

"You don't?" said Gerald. He was silent for some moments. Then he moved tentatively. "I was going to ask her, in any case, to go away with me at Christmas," he said, in a very small, cautious voice.

"Go away with you? For a time, you mean?"

"As long as she likes," he said, with a deprecating movement.

They were both silent for some minutes.

"Of course," said Ursula at last, "she *might* just be willing to rush into marriage. You can see."

"Yes," smiled Gerald, "I can see.—But in case she won't—do you think she would go abroad with me for a few days—or for a fortnight?"

"Oh yes," said Ursula. "I'd ask her."

"Do you think we might all go together?"

"All of us?" Again Ursula's face lighted up. "It would be rather fun, don't you think?"

"Great fun," he said.

"And then you could see," said Ursula.

"What?"

"How things went.—I think it is best to take the honeymoon before the wedding—don't you?"

She was pleased with this *mot*. He laughed.

"In certain cases," he said. "I'd rather it were so in my own case."

"Would you!" exclaimed Ursula. Then doubtingly, "Yes, perhaps you're right.—One should please oneself."

Birkin came in a little later, and Ursula told him what had been said.

"Gudrun!" exclaimed Birkin. "She's a born mistress, just as Gerald is a born lover—*amant en titre.** If as somebody says all women are either wives or mistresses,* then Gudrun is a mistress."

"And all men either lovers or husbands?" cried Ursula. "But why not both?"

"The one excludes the other," he laughed.

"Then I want a lover," cried Ursula.

"No you don't," he said.

"But I do," she wailed.

5   He kissed her, and laughed.

It was two days after this that Ursula was to go to fetch her things from the house in Beldover. The removal had taken place, the family had gone. Gudrun had rooms in Willey Green.

Ursula had not seen her parents since her marriage. She wept over 10 the rupture, yet what was the good making it up! Good or not good, she could not go to them. So her things had been left behind, and she and Gudrun were to walk over for them, in the afternoon.

It was a wintry afternoon, with red in the sky, when they arrived at the house. The windows were dark and blank, already the place was 15 frightening. A stark, void entrance-hall struck a chill to the hearts of the girls.

"I don't believe I dare have come in alone," said Ursula. "It frightens me."

"Ursula!" cried Gudrun. "Isn't it amazing? Can you believe you 20 lived in this place and never felt it? How I lived here a day without dying of terror, I cannot conceive!"

They looked in the big dining-room. It was a good-sized room, but now, a cell would have been lovelier. The large bay windows were naked, the floor was stripped, and a border of dark polish went 25 round the tract of pale boarding. In the faded wall-paper were dark patches where furniture had stood, where pictures had hung. The sense of walls, dry, thin, flimsy-seeming walls, and a flimsy flooring, pale with its artificial black edges, was neutralising to the mind. Everything was null to the senses, there was enclosure without 30 substance, for the walls were dry and papery. Where were they standing, on earth, or suspended in some cardboard box? In the hearth was burnt paper, and scraps of half-burnt paper.

"Imagine that we passed our days here!" said Ursula.

"I know," cried Gudrun. "It is too appalling. What *must* we be 35 like, if* we are the contents of *this*!"

"Vile!" said Ursula. "It really is."

And she recognised half-burnt covers of "Vogue"*—half-burnt representations of women in gowns—lying under the grate.

They went to the drawing-room. Another piece of shut-in air, 40 without weight or substance, only a sense of intolerable papery

imprisonment in nothingness. The kitchen did look more substantial, because of the red-tiled floor and the stove, but it was cold
and horrid.

The two girls tramped hollowly up the bare stairs. Every sound
re-echoed under their hearts. They tramped down the bare corridor. 5
Against the wall of Ursula's bedroom were her things—a trunk, a
work-basket, some books, loose coats, a hat-box, standing desolate
in the universal emptiness of the dusk.

"A cheerful sight, aren't they?" said Ursula, looking down at her
forsaken possessions. 10

"Very cheerful," said Gudrun.

The two girls set to, carrying everything down to the front door.
Again and again they made the hollow, re-echoing transit. The
whole place seemed to resound about them with a noise of hollow,
empty futility. In the distance the empty, invisible rooms sent forth a 15
vibration almost of obscenity. They almost fled with the last articles,
into the out-of-doors.

But it was cold. They were waiting for Birkin, who was coming
with the car. They went indoors again, and upstairs to their parents'
front bedroom, whose windows looked down on the road, and across 20
the country at the black-barred sunset, black and red barred, without
light.

They sat down in the window-seat, to wait. Both girls were
looking over the room. It was void, with a meaninglessness that was
almost dreadful. 25

"Really," said Ursula, "this room *couldn't* be sacred, could it?"

Gudrun looked over it with slow eyes.

"Impossible," she replied.

"When I think of their lives—father's and mother's—their love,
and their marriage, and all us children, and our bringing-up—would 30
you have such a life, Prune?"

"I wouldn't, Ursula."

"It all seems so *nothing*—their two lives—there's no *meaning* in
it.—Really, if they had *not* met, and *not* married, and *not* lived
together—it wouldn't have mattered, would it?" 35

"Of course—you can't tell," said Gudrun.

"No.—But if I thought my life was going to be like it—Prune,"
she caught Gudrun's arm, "I should run."

Gudrun was silent for a few moments.

"As a matter of fact, one cannot contemplate the ordinary 40

life—one cannot contemplate it," replied Gudrun. "With you,
Ursula, it is quite different. You will be out of it all, with Birkin. He's
a special case.—But with the ordinary man, who has his life fixed in
one place, marriage is just impossible.—There may be, and there
5 *are*, thousands of women who want it, and could conceive of nothing
else. But the very thought of it sends me *mad*.—One must be free,
above all, one must be free. One may forfeit everything else, but one
must be free—one must not become 7 Pinchbeck Street*—or
Somerset Drive—or Shortlands.—No man will be sufficient to
10 make that good—no man!—To marry, one must have a free lance, or
nothing, a comrade-in-arms, a Glücksritter.* A man with a position
in the social world—well, it is just impossible, impossible!"

"What a lovely word—a Glücksritter!" said Ursula. "So much
nicer than a soldier of fortune."

15 "Yes, isn't it!" said Gudrun. "I'd tilt the world with a Glücksritter.
But a home, an establishment—Ursula, what would it mean?—
think!"

"I know," said Ursula. "We've had one home—that's enough for
me."

20 "Quite enough," said Gudrun.

"The little grey home in the west,"* quoted Ursula ironically.

"*Doesn't* it sound grey, too!" said Gudrun grimly.

They were interrupted by the sound of the car. There was
Birkin—Ursula was surprised that she felt so lit up, that she became
25 suddenly so free from the problems of grey homes in the west.

They heard his heels click on the hall pavement below.

"Hello!" he called, his voice echoing alive through the house.
Ursula smiled to herself. *He* was frightened of the place too.

"Hello! Here we are," she called downstairs.

30 And they heard him quickly running up.

"This is a ghostly situation," he said.

"These houses don't have ghosts—they've never had any personality, and only a place with personality can have a ghost," said
Gudrun.

35 "I suppose so. Are you both weeping over the past?"

"We are," said Gudrun grimly.

Ursula laughed.

"Not weeping that it's gone—but weeping that it ever *was*," she
said.

40 "Oh," he replied, relieved.

He sat down for a moment. There was something in his presence, Ursula thought, lambent and alive. It made even the impertinent structure of this null house disappear.

"Gudrun says she could not bear to be married and put into a house," said Ursula, meaningful—they knew this referred to Gerald.

He was silent for some moments.

"Well," he said, "if you know beforehand you couldn't stand it, you're safe."

"Quite!" said Gudrun.

"Why *does* every woman think her aim in life is to have a hubby and a little grey home in the west? Why is this the goal of life? Why should it be?" asked Ursula.

"Il faut avoir le respect de ses bêtises," said Birkin.

"But you needn't have the respect for the bêtise before you've committed it," laughed Ursula.

"Ah then: 'il faut avoir le respect des bêtises du papa'."

"Et de la maman," added Gudrun satirically.

"Et des voisins,"* said Ursula.

They all laughed, and rose. It was getting dark. They carried the things to the car. Gudrun locked the door of the empty house. Birkin had lighted the lamps of the automobile. It all seemed very happy, as if they were setting out.

"Do you mind stopping at Coulsons.* I have to leave the key there," said Gudrun.

"Right," said Birkin, and they moved off.

They stopped in the main street. The shops were just lighted, the last miners were passing home along the causeways, half-visible shadows in their grey pit-dirt, moving through the blue air. But their feet rang harshly, in manifold sound, along the pavement.

How pleased Gudrun was to come out of the shop, and enter the car, and be borne swiftly away into the down-hill of palpable dusk, with Ursula and Birkin! What an adventure life seemed at this moment! How deeply, how suddenly she envied Ursula! Life for her was so quick, and an open door—so reckless, as if not only this world, but the world that was gone and the world to come were nothing to her. Ah, if she could be *just like that*, it would be perfect.

For always, except in her moments of excitement, she felt a want within herself, she was unsure. She had felt that now, at last, in Gerald's strong and violent love, she was living fully and finally. But

when she compared herself with Ursula, already her soul was
jealous, unsatisfied. She was not satisfied—she was never to be
satisfied.

What was she short of now? It was marriage—it was the wonderful
stability of marriage. She did want it, let her say what she might. She
had been lying. The old idea of marriage was right even now—
marriage and the home. Yet her mouth gave a little grimace at the
words. She thought of Gerald and Shortlands—marriage and the
home! Ah well, let it rest! He meant a great deal to her—but—!
Perhaps it was not in her to marry. She was one of life's outcasts, one
of the drifting lives that have no root. No, no—it could not be so. She
suddenly conjured up a rosy room, with herself in a beautiful gown,
and a handsome man in evening dress who held her in his arms in the
firelight, and kissed her. This picture she entitled "Home." It would
have done for the Royal Academy.

"Come with us to tea—*do*," said Ursula, as they ran nearer to the
cottages of Willey Green.

"Thanks awfully—but I *must* go in—" said Gudrun. She wanted
very much to go on with Ursula and Birkin. That seemed like life
indeed to her. Yet a certain perversity would not let her.

"Do come—yes, it would be so nice," pleaded Ursula.

"I'm awfully sorry—I should love to—but I can't—really—"
She descended from the car in trembling haste.

"Can't you really!" came Ursula's regretful voice.

"No, really I can't," responded Gudrun's pathetic, chagrined
words out of the dusk.

"All right, are you?" called Birkin.

"Quite!" said Gudrun. "Goodnight!"

"Goodnight," they called.

"Come whenever you like, we shall be glad," called Birkin.

"Thank you very much," called Gudrun, in the strange, twanging
voice of lonely chagrin that was very puzzling to him. She turned
away to her cottage gate, and they drove on. But immediately she
stood to watch them, as the car ran vague into the distance. And as
she went up the path to her strange house, her heart was full of
incomprehensible bitterness.

In her parlour was a long-case clock, and inserted into its dial was
a ruddy, round, slant-eyed, joyous-painted face, that wagged over
with the most ridiculous ogle when the clock ticked, and back again
with the same absurd glad eye at the next tick. All the time the absurd
smooth, brown-ruddy face gave her an obtrusive "glad eye." She

stood for minutes, watching it, till a sort of maddened disgust overcame her, and she laughed at herself, hollowly. And still it rocked, and gave her the glad eye from one side, then from the other, from one side, then from the other. Ah, how unhappy she was! In the midst of her most active happiness, ah, how unhappy she was! She glanced at the table. Gooseberry jam, and the same home-made cake with too much soda* in it! Still, gooseberry jam was good, and one so rarely got it.

All the evening she wanted to go to the Mill. But she coldly refused to allow herself. She went the next afternoon instead. She was happy to find Ursula alone. It was a lovely, intimate, secluded atmosphere. They talked endlessly and delightedly. "Aren't you *fearfully* happy here?" said Gudrun to her sister, glancing at her own bright eyes in the mirror. She always envied, almost with resentment, the strange positive fulness that subsisted in the atmosphere around Ursula and Birkin.

"How really beautifully this room is done," she said aloud. "This hard plaited matting—what a lovely colour it is, the colour of cool light!"

And it seemed to her perfect.

"Ursula," she said at length, in a voice of question and detachment, "did you know that Gerald Crich had suggested our going away all together at Christmas?"

"Yes, he's spoken to Rupert."

A deep flush dyed Gudrun's cheek. She was silent a moment, as if taken aback, and not knowing what to say.

"But don't you think," she said at last, "it is *amazingly cool*!"

Ursula laughed.

"I liked him for it," she said.

Gudrun was silent. It was evident that, whilst she was almost mortified by Gerald's taking the liberty of making such a suggestion to Birkin, yet the idea itself attracted her strongly.

"There's a rather lovely simplicity about Gerald, I think," said Ursula. "So defiant, somehow!—Oh, I think he's *very* lovable."

Gudrun did not reply for some moments. She had still to get over the feeling of insult at the liberty* taken with her freedom.

"What did Rupert say—do you know?" she asked.

"He said it would be most awfully jolly," said Ursula.

Again Gudrun looked down, and was silent.

"Don't you think it would?" said Ursula, tentatively. She was never quite sure how many defences Gudrun was having round herself.

Gudrun raised her face with difficulty, and held it averted.

"I think it *might* be awfully jolly, as you say," she replied. "But don't you think it was an unpardonable liberty to take—to talk of such a thing to Rupert—who after all—You see what I mean, Ursula—they might have been two men arranging an outing with
5 some little *type** they'd picked up. Oh, I think it's unforgiveable, quite!"—She used the French word, '*type*.'

Her eye flashed, her soft face was flushed and sullen. Ursula looked on, rather frightened, frightened most of all because she thought Gudrun seemed rather common, really like a little *type*. But
10 she had not the courage quite to think this—not right out—

"Oh no," she cried, stammering. "Oh no—not at all like that—oh no!—No, I think it's rather beautiful, the friendship between Rupert and Gerald. They just are simple—they say anything to each other, like brothers."

15 Gudrun flushed deeper. She could not *bear* it that Gerald gave her away—even to Birkin.

"But do you think even brothers have any right to exchange confidences of that sort?" she asked, with deep anger.

"Oh yes," said Ursula. "There's never anything said that isn't
20 perfectly straightforward.—No, the thing that's amazed me most in Gerald—how perfectly simple and direct he can be!—And you know, it takes rather a big man. Most of them *must* be indirect, they are such cowards."

But Gudrun was still silent with anger. She wanted the absolutest
25 secrecy kept, with regard to her movements.

"Won't you go?" said Ursula. "Do, we might all be so happy!—There is something I *love* about Gerald—he's *much* more lovable than I thought him. He's free, Gudrun, he really is."

Gudrun's mouth was still closed sullen and ugly. She opened it at
30 length.

"Do you know where he proposes to go?" she asked.

"Yes—to the Tyrol, where he used to go when he was in Germany—a lovely place where students go, small and rough and lovely, for winter sport!"

35 Through Gudrun's mind went the angry thought—"they know everything."

"Yes," she said aloud, "about forty kilometers from Innsbruck,* isn't it?"

"I don't know exactly where—but it would be lovely, don't you
40 think, high in the perfect snow—?"

"Very lovely!" said Gudrun, sarcastically.

Ursula was put out.

"Of course," she said, "I think Gerald spoke to Rupert so that it *shouldn't* seem like a little outing with a *type*—"

"I know, of course," said Gudrun, "that he quite commonly does take up with that sort."

"Does he!" said Ursula. "Why how do you know?"

"I know of a model in Chelsea," said Gudrun coldly.

Now Ursula was silent.

"Well," she said at last, with a doubtful laugh, "I hope he has a good time with her." At which Gudrun only looked more glum.

Chapter XXVIII

Gudrun in the Pompadour*

Christmas drew near, all four prepared for flight. Birkin and Ursula
were busy packing their few personal things, making them ready to
5 be sent off, to whatever country and whatever place they might
choose at last. Gudrun was very much excited. She loved to be on the
wing.

She and Gerald, being ready first, set off via London and Paris to
Innsbruck, where they would meet Ursula and Birkin. In London
10 they stayed one night. They went to a music-hall, and afterwards to
the Pompadour Café.

Gudrun hated the Café, yet she always went back to it, as did most
of the artists of her acquaintance. She loathed its atmosphere of petty
vice and petty jealousy and petty art. Yet she always called in again,
15 when she was in town. It was as if she *had* to return to this small,
slow, central whirlpool of disintegration and dissolution: just give it a
look.

She sat with Gerald drinking some sweetish liqueur, and staring
with black, sullen looks at the various groups of people at the tables.
20 She would greet nobody, but young men nodded to her frequently,
with a kind of sneering familiarity. She cut them all. And it gave her
pleasure to sit there, cheeks flushed, eyes black and sullen, seeing
them all objectively, as put away from her, like creatures in some
menagerie of apish, degraded souls. God, what a foul crew they
25 were! Her blood beat black and thick in her veins with rage and
loathing. Yet she must sit and watch, watch. One or two people came
to speak to her. From every side of the Café, eyes turned half
furtively, half jeeringly at her, men looking over their shoulders,
women under their hats.

30 The old crowd was there, Carlyon* in his corner with his pupils
and his girl, Halliday and Libidnikov and the Pussum—they were all
there. Gudrun watched Gerald. She watched his eyes linger a
moment on Halliday, on Halliday's party. These last were on the
look-out—they nodded to him, he nodded again. They giggled
35 and whispered among themselves. Gerald watched them with the

steady twinkle in his eyes. They were urging the Pussum to
something.

She at last rose. She was wearing a curious dress of dark silk
splashed and spattered with different colours, a curious motley
effect.* She was thinner, her eyes were perhaps hotter, more
disintegrated. Otherwise she was just the same. Gerald watched her
with the same steady twinkle in his eyes as she came across.

She held out her thin brown hand to him.

"How are you?" she said.

He shook hands with her, but remained seated, and let her stand
near him, against the table. She nodded blackly to Gudrun, whom
she did not know to speak to, but well enough by sight and
reputation.

"I am very well," said Gerald. "And you—?"

"Oh I'm all wight.—What about Wupert?"

"Rupert?—He's very well too."

"Yes, I don't mean that. What about him being married?"

"Oh—yes, he is married."

The Pussum's eyes had a hot flash.

"Oh, he's weally bwought it off then, has he? When was he
married?"

"A week or two ago."

"Weally! He's never written."

"No."

"No.—Don't you think it's too bad?"

This last was in a tone of challenge. The Pussum let it be known,
by her tone, that she was aware of Gudrun's listening.

"I suppose he didn't feel like it," replied Gerald.

"But why didn't he?" pursued the Pussum.

This was received in silence. There was an ugly mocking persistence in the small, beautiful figure of the short-haired girl, as she
stood near Gerald.

"Are you staying in town long?" she asked.

"Tonight only."

"Oh, only tonight.—Are you coming over to speak to Julius?"

"Not tonight."

"Oh very well. I'll tell him then." Then came her touch of
diablerie. "You're looking awf'lly fit."

"Yes—I feel it." Gerald was quite calm and easy, a spark of satiric
amusement in his eye.

"Are you having a good time?"

This was a direct blow for Gudrun, spoken in a level, toneless voice of callous ease.

"Yes," he replied, quite colourlessly.

5   "I'm awf'lly sorry you aren't coming round to the flat.—You aren't very faithful to your fwiends."

"Not very," he said.

She nodded them both 'Goodnight', and went back slowly to her own set. Gudrun watched her curious walk, stiff and jerking at the
10 loins. They heard her level, toneless voice distinctly.

"He won't come over;—he is otherwise engaged," it said.

There was more laughter and lowered voices and mockery at the table.

"Is she a friend of yours?" said Gudrun, looking calmly at Gerald.

15   "I've stayed at Halliday's flat with Birkin," he said, meeting her slow, calm eyes. And she knew that the Pussum was one of his mistresses—and he knew she knew.

She looked round, and called for the waiter. She wanted an iced cocktail, of all things. This amused Gerald—he wondered what was
20 up.

The Halliday party was tipsy, and malicious. They were talking out loudly about Birkin, ridiculing him on every point, particularly on his marriage.

"Oh, *don't* make me think of Birkin," Halliday was squealing. "He
25 makes me perfectly sick. He is as bad as Jesus. 'Lord, *what* must I do to be saved'."*

He giggled to himself tipsily.

"Do you remember," came the quick voice of the Russian, "the letters he used to send. 'Desire is holy—'"*

30   "Oh yes!" cried Halliday. "Oh, how perfectly splendid! Why, I've got one in my pocket. I'm sure I have."

He took out various papers from his pocket book.

"I'm sure I've—*hic!*—*Oh dear!*—got one."

Gerald and Gudrun were watching absorbedly.

35   "Oh yes, how perfectly—*hic!*—splendid!—Don't make me laugh, Pussum, it gives me the hiccup. Hic!—" They all giggled.

"What did he say in that one?" the Pussum asked, leaning forward, her dark, soft hair falling and swinging against her face. There was something curiously indecent, obscene, about her small,
40 longish, dark skull, particularly when the ears showed.

"Wait—oh do wait! *No—o*, I won't give it you, I'll read it aloud. I'll read you the choice bits—*hic*! Oh dear! Do you think if I drank water it would take off this hiccup? *Hic!* Oh, I feel perfectly helpless."

"Isn't that the letter about uniting the dark and the light—and the Flux of Corruption?" asked Maxim, in his precise, quick voice.

"I believe so," said the Pussum.   5

"Oh is it? I'd forgotten—*hic*!—it was that one," Halliday said, opening the letter. "*Hic*!—Oh yes. How perfectly splendid! This is one of the best.—'There is a phase in every race—'" he read in the sing-song, slow, distinct voice of a clergyman reading the Scriptures,* "'when the desire for destruction overcomes every other   10 desire. In the individual, this desire is ultimately a desire for destruction in the self'—*hic*!—" he paused and looked up.

"I hope he's going ahead with the destruction of himself," said the quick voice of the Russian. Halliday giggled, and lolled his head back, vaguely.   15

"There's not much to destroy in him," said the Pussum. "He's so thin already, there's only a fag-end to start on."

"Oh, isn't it beautiful! I love reading it! I believe it has cured my hiccup!" squealed Halliday. "Do let me go on.—'It is a desire for the reduction process in oneself, a reducing back to the origins, a return   20 along the Flux of Corruption, to the original rudimentary conditions of being—' Oh, but I *do* think it is wonderful. It *almost* supersedes the Bible—"

"Yes—Flux of Corruption," said the Russian. "I remember that phrase."   25

"Oh, he was always talking about Corwuption," said the Pussum. "He must be corwupt himself, to have it so much on his mind."

"Exactly!" said the Russian.

"Do let me go on! Oh, this is a perfectly wonderful piece! But do listen to this. 'And in the great retrogression, the reducing back of   30 the created body of life, we get knowledge, and beyond knowledge, the phosphorescent ecstasy of acute sensation.'—Oh, I do think those phrases are too absurdly wonderful. Oh but don't you think they *are*—they're nearly as good as Jesus.—'—and if, Julius, you want this ecstasy of reduction with the Pussum, you must go on till it   35 is fulfilled. But surely there is in you also, somewhere, the living desire for positive creation, relationships in ultimate faith, when all this process of active corruption, with all its flowers of mud, is transcended, and more or less finished—'—I do wonder what the flowers of mud are. Pussum, you are a flower of mud."   40

"Thank you—and what are you?"

"Oh, I'm another, surely, according to this letter! We're all flowers of mud.—Fleurs—*hic!*—du mal!—It's perfectly wonderful, Birkin harrowing Hell—harrowing the Pompadour—*Hic!*"

"Go on—go on," said Maxim. "What comes next. It's really very interesting."

"I think it's awful cheek to write like that," said the Pussum.

"Yes—yes, so do I," said the Russian. "He is a megalomaniac, of course—it is a form of religious mania. He thinks he is the saviour of man—go on reading."

"Surely," Halliday intoned, "Surely goodness and mercy hath followed me all the days of my life—"* he broke off, and giggled. Then he began again, intoning like a clergyman. "Surely there will come an end in us to this desire—for the constant going apart,—this passion for putting asunder—everything—ourselves, reducing ourselves part from part,—reacting in intimacy only for destruction,—using sex as a great reducing agent, by friction between the two great elements of male and female obtaining a frenzy of sensual satisfaction—reducing the old ideas, going back to the savages for our sensations, always seeking to *lose* ourselves in some ultimate black sensation, mindless and infinite—burning only with destructive fires, raging on with the hope of being burnt out utterly—"*

"I want to go," said Gudrun to Gerald, as she signalled the waiter. Her eyes were flashing, her cheeks were flushed. The strange effect of Birkin's letter read aloud in a perfect clerical sing-song, clear and resonant, phrase by phrase, made the blood mount into her head as if she were mad.

She rose, whilst Gerald was paying the bill, and walked over to Halliday's table. They all glanced up at her.

"Excuse me," she said. "Is that a genuine letter you are reading?"

"Oh yes," said Halliday. "Quite genuine."

"May I see?"

Smiling foolishly he handed it to her, as if hypnotised.

"Thank you," she said.

And she turned and walked out of the Café with the letter,* all down the brilliant room, between the tables, in her measured fashion. It was some moments before anybody realised what was happening.

From Halliday's table came half articulate cries, then somebody booed, then all the far end of the place began booing after Gudrun's retreating form. She was fashionably dressed in blackish-green and silver, her hat was brilliant green, like the sheen on an insect, but the brim was soft dark green, a falling edge with fine silver, her coat was dark green,* lustrous, with a high collar of grey fur, and great fur cuffs, the edge of her dress showed silver and black velvet, her stockings and shoes were silver grey. She moved with slow, fashion- 5 able indifference to the door. The porter opened obsequiously for her, and, at her nod, hurried to the edge of the pavement and whistled for a taxi. The two lights of a vehicle almost immediately curved round towards her, like two eyes.

Gerald had followed in wonder, amid all the booing, not having 10 caught her misdeed. He heard the Pussum's voice saying:

"Go and get it back from her! I never heard of such a thing! Go and get it back from her.—Tell Gerald Crich—there he goes—go and make him give it up."

Gudrun stood at the door of the taxi, which the man held open for 15 her.

"To the hôtel?" she asked, as Gerald came out, hurriedly.

"Where you like," he answered.

"Right!" she said. Then, to the driver: "Wagstaff's—Barton Street."* 20

The driver bowed his head, and put down the flag.*

Gudrun entered the taxi, with the deliberate, cold movement of a woman who is well-dressed and contemptuous in her soul. Yet she was frozen with overwrought feeling. Gerald followed her.

"You've forgotten the man," she said coolly, with a slight nod of 25 her hat. Gerald gave the porter a shilling. The man saluted. They were in motion.

"What was all the row about?" asked Gerald, in wondering excitement.

"I walked away with Birkin's letter," she said, and he saw the 30 crushed paper in her hand.

His eyes glittered with satisfaction.

"Ah!" he said. "Splendid!—A set of jackasses!"

"I could have *killed* them!" she cried in passion. "*Dogs!*—they *are* dogs!*—Why is Rupert such a *fool* as to write such letters to them? 35 *Why* does he give himself away to such canaille? It's a thing that *cannot be borne*—"

Gerald wondered over her strange passion.

And she could not rest any longer in London. They must go by the morning train from Charing Cross. As they drew over the bridge, in 40 the train, having glimpses of the river between the great iron girders, she cried:

"I feel I could *never* see this *foul* town again—. I couldn't *bear* to come back to it."

Chapter XXIX

Continental*

Ursula went on in an unreal suspense, the last weeks before going away. She was not herself—she was not anything. She was something that is going to be—soon—soon—very soon. But as yet, she was only imminent.

She went to see her parents. It was a rather stiff, sad meeting, more like a verification of separateness than a reunion. But they were all vague and indefinite with one another, stiffened in the fate that moved them apart.

She did not really come to, until she was on the ship crossing from Dover to Ostend. Dimly she had come down to London with Birkin, London had been a vagueness, so had the train-journey to Dover. It was all like a sleep.

And now, at last, as she stood in the stern of the ship, in a pitch-dark, rather blowy night, feeling the motion of the sea, and watching the small, rather desolate little lights that twinkled on the shores of England, as on the shores of nowhere, watched them sinking smaller and smaller on the profound and living darkness, she felt her soul stirring to awake from its anaesthetic sleep.

"Let us go forward, shall we?" said Birkin. He wanted to be at the tip of their projection. So they left off looking at the faint sparks that glimmered out of nowhere, in the far distance, called England, and turned their faces to the unfathomed night in front.

They went right to the bows of the softly plunging vessel. In the complete obscurity, Birkin found a comparatively sheltered nook, where a great rope was coiled up. It was quite near the very point of the ship, near the black, unpierced space ahead. Here they sat down, folded together, folded round with the same rug, creeping in nearer and ever nearer to one another, till it seemed they had crept right in to each other, and become one substance. It was very cold, and the darkness was palpable.

One of the ship's crew came along the deck, dark as the darkness, not really visible. They then made out the faintest pallor of his face. He felt their presence, and stopped, unsure—then bent forward.

When his face was near them, he saw the faint pallor of their faces. Then he withdrew, like a phantom. And they watched him without making any sound.

They seemed to fall away into the profound darkness. There was
5   no sky, no earth, only one unbroken darkness, into which, with a soft, sleeping motion, they seemed to fall, like one closed seed of life falling through dark, fathomless space.

They had forgotten where they were, forgotten all that was and all that had been, conscious only in their heart, and there conscious only
10 of this pure trajectory through the surpassing darkness. The ship's prow cleaved on, with a faint noise of cleavage, into the complete night, without knowing, without seeing, only surging on.

In Ursula the sense of the unrealised world ahead triumphed over everything. In the midst of this profound darkness, there seemed to
15 glow on her heart the effulgence of a paradise unknown and unrealised. Her heart was full of the most wonderful light, golden like honey of darkness, sweet like the warmth of day, a light which was not shed on the world, only on the unknown paradise towards which she was going, a sweetness of habitation, a delight of living
20 quite unknown, but hers infallibly.

In her transport she lifted her face suddenly to him, and he touched it with his lips. So cold, so fresh, so sea-clear her face was, it was like kissing a flower that grows near the surf.

But he did not know the ecstasy of bliss in foreknowledge,* that
25 she knew. To him, the wonder of this transit was overwhelming. He was falling through a gulf of infinite darkness, like a meteorite plunging across the chasm between the worlds. The world was torn in two, and he was plunging like an unlit star through the ineffable rift. What was beyond was not yet for him. He was overcome by the
30 trajectory.

In a trance he lay enfolding Ursula round about. His face was against her fine, fragile hair, he breathed its fragrance with the sea and the profound night. And his soul was at peace; yielded, as he fell into the unknown. This was the first time that an utter and
35 absolute peace had entered his heart, now, in this final transit out of life.

When there came some stir on the deck, they roused. They stood up. How stiff and cramped they were, in the night-time! And yet the paradisal glow on her heart, and the unutterable peace of darkness in
40 his, this was the all-in-all.

They stood up and looked ahead. Low lights were seen down the darkness. This was the world again. It was not the bliss of her heart, nor the peace of his. It was the superficial unreal world of fact. Yet not quite the old world. For the peace and the bliss in their hearts was enduring. 5

Strange, and desolate above all things, like disembarking from the Styx into the desolated underworld, was this landing at night. There was the raw, half-lighted, covered-in vastness of the dark place, boarded and hollow underfoot, with only desolation everywhere. Ursula had caught sight of the big pallid, mystic letters 10 "OSTEND," standing in the darkness. Everybody was hurrying with a blind, insect-like intentness through the dark grey air, porters were calling in unEnglish English, then trotting with heavy bags, their colourless blouses looking ghostly as they disappeared; Ursula stood at a long, low, zinc-covered barrier, along with hundreds of 15 other spectral people, and all the way down the vast, raw darkness was this low stretch of open bags and spectral people, whilst, on the other side of the barrier, pallid officials in peaked caps and moustaches were turning the underclothing in the bags, then scrawling a chalk-mark. 20

It was done. Birkin snapped the hand bags, off they went, the porter coming behind. They were through a great doorway and* in the open night again—ah, a railway platform! Voices were still calling in inhuman agitation through the dark-grey air, spectres were running along the darkness between the trains. 25

"Köln—Berlin—" Ursula made out on the boards hung on the high train on one side.

"Here we are," said Birkin. And on her side she saw:

"ELSASS—LOTHRINGEN—Luxembourg, Metz—BASEL."*

That was it, Basle! 30

The porter came up:

"A Bâle—deuxième classe?—Voilà."*

And he clambered into the high train. They followed. The compartments were already some of them taken. But many were dim and empty. The luggage was stowed, the porter was tipped. 35

"Nous avons encore—?" said Birkin, looking at his watch and at the porter.

"Encore une demi-heure."* With which, in his blue blouse, he disappeared. He was ugly and insolent.

"Come," said Birkin. "It is cold. Let us eat." 40

There was a coffee-wagon on the platform. They drank hot, watery coffee, and ate the long rolls, split, with ham between, which were such a wide bite that it almost dislocated Ursula's jaw; and they walked beside the high trains. It was all so strange, so extremely
5 desolate, like the underworld, grey, grey, dirt-grey, desolate, forlorn, nowhere—grey, dreary nowhere.

At last they were moving through the night. In the darkness Ursula made out the flat fields, the wet flat dreary darkness of the continent. They pulled up surprisingly soon—Bruges! Then on
10 through the level darkness, with glimpses of sleeping farms and thin poplar trees and deserted high-roads. She sat dismayed, hand in hand with Birkin. He, pale, immobile, like a *revenant* himself, looked sometimes out of the window, sometimes closed his eyes. Then his eyes opened again, dark as the darkness outside.

15 A flash of a few lights on the darkness—Ghent station! A few more spectres moving outside on the platform—then the bell—then motion again through the level darkness.

Ursula saw a man with a lantern come out of a farm by the railway, and cross to the dark farm-buildings. She thought of the Marsh, the
20 old, intimate farm-life at Cossethay.* My God, how far was she projected from her childhood, how far was she still to go! In one life-time one travelled through aeons. The great chasm of memory, from her childhood in the intimate country surroundings of Cosse-thay and the Marsh Farm—she remembered the servant Tilly,* who
25 used to give her bread and butter sprinkled with brown sugar, in the old living-room where the grandfather clock had two pink roses in a basket painted above the figures on the face—and now, when she was travelling into the unknown with Birkin, an utter stranger—was so great, that it seemed she had no identity, that the child she had
30 been, playing in Cossethay churchyard, was a little creature of history, not really herself.

They were at Brussels—half an hour for breakfast. They got down. On the great station clock it said six o'clock. They had coffee and rolls and honey in the vast, desert refreshment room, so dreary,
35 always so dreary, dirty, so spacious, such desolation of space. But she washed her face and hands in hot water, and combed her hair—that was a blessing.

Soon they were in the train again and moving on. The greyness of dawn began. There were several people in the compartment, large,

florid Belgian business-men with long brown beards, talking in-
cessantly in an ugly French she was too tired to follow.

It seemed the train ran by degrees out of the darkness into a faint
light, then beat after beat into the day. Ah, how weary it was! Faintly,
the trees showed, like shadows. Then a house, white, had a curious
distinctness. How was it? Then she saw a village—there were always
houses passing.

This was an old world she was still journeying through, winter-
heavy and dreary. There was plough-land and pasture, and copses of
bare trees, copses of bushes, and homesteads naked and work-bare.
No new earth had come to pass.

She looked at Birkin's face. It was white and still and eternal, too
eternal. She linked her fingers imploringly in his, under the cover of
her rug. His fingers responded, his eyes looked back at her. How
dark, like a night, his eyes were, like another world beyond! Oh, if he
were the world as well, if only the world were he! If only he could call
a world into being, that should be their own world!

The Belgians left, the train ran on, through Luxembourg, through
Alsace-Lorraine, through Metz. But she was blind, she could see no
more. Her soul did not look out.

They came at last to Basle, to the hotel. It was all a drifting trance,
from which she never came to. They went out in the morning, before
the train departed. She saw the streets, the river, she stood on the
bridge. But it all meant nothing. She remembered some shops—one
full of pictures, one with orange velvet and ermine. But what did
these signify?—nothing.

She was not at ease till they were in the train again. Then she was
relieved. So long as they were moving onwards, she was satisfied.
They came to Zürich, then, before very long, ran under the
mountains, that were deep in snow. At last she was drawing near.
This was the other world, now.

Innsbruck was wonderful, deep in snow, and evening. They drove
in an open sledge over the snow: the train had been so hot and
stifling. And the hotel, with the golden light glowing under the
porch, seemed like a home.

They laughed with pleasure when they were in the hall. The place
seemed full and busy.

"Do you know if Mr and Mrs Crich—English—from Paris, have
arrived?" Birkin asked in German.

The porter* reflected a moment, and was just going to answer, when Ursula caught sight of Gudrun sauntering down the stairs, wearing her dark glossy coat, with grey fur.

"Gudrun! Gundrun!" she called, waving up the well of the
5 staircase: "Yu-hu!"*

Gudrun looked over the rail, and immediately lost her sauntering, diffident air. Her eyes flashed.

"Really—Ursula!" she cried.

And she began to move downstairs as Ursula ran up. They met at a
10 turn and kissed with laughter and exclamations inarticulate and stirring.

"But!" cried Gudrun, mortified. "We thought it was *tomorrow* you were coming! I wanted to come to the station."

"No, we've come today!" cried Ursula. "Isn't it lovely here!"

15 "Adorable!" said Gudrun. "Gerald's just gone out to get something.—Ursula, aren't you *fearfully* tired?"

"No, not so very. But I look a filthy sight, don't I?"

"No, you don't. You look almost perfectly fresh.—I like that fur cap *immensely*!"

20 She glanced over Ursula, who wore a big soft coat with a collar of deep, soft, blond fur, and a soft blond cap of fur.

"And you!" cried Ursula. "What do you think *you* look like!"

Gudrun assumed an unconcerned, expressionless face.

"Do you like it?" she said.

25 "It's *very* fine!" cried Ursula, perhaps with a touch of satire.

"Go up—or come down," said Birkin.

For there the sisters stood, Gudrun with her hand on Ursula's arm, on the turn of the stairs half way to the first landing, blocking the way, and affording full entertainment to the whole of
30 the hall below, from the door porter to the plump Jew in black clothes.

The two young women slowly mounted, followed by Birkin and the porter.

"First floor?" asked Gudrun, looking back over her shoulder.

35 "Second madam—the lift—!" the porter replied, and he darted to the elevator, to forestall the two women. But they ignored him, as, chattering without heed, they set to mount the second flight. Rather chagrined, the porter followed.

It was curious, the delight of the sisters in each other, at this
40 meeting. It was as if they met in exile, and united their solitary forces

against all the world. Birkin looked on with some mistrust and wonder.

When they had bathed and changed, Gerald came in. He looked shining like the sun on frost.

"Go with Gerald and smoke," said Ursula to Birkin. "Gudrun and I want to talk."

Then the sisters sat in Gudrun's bedroom, and talked clothes, and experiences. Gudrun told Ursula the experience of the Birkin letter in the café, Ursula was shocked and frightened.

"Where is the letter?" she asked.

"I kept it," said Gudrun.

"You'll give it me, won't you?" she said. But Gudrun was silent for some moments, before she replied:

"Do you really want it, Ursula?"

"I want to read it," said Ursula.

"Certainly," said Gudrun.

Even now, she could not admit, to Ursula, that she wanted to keep it, as a memento, or a symbol. But Ursula knew, and was not pleased. So the subject was switched off.

"What did you do in Paris?" asked Ursula.

"Oh," said Gudrun laconically—"the usual things. We had a *fine* party one night in Fanny Rath's studio."*

"Did you? And you and Gerald were there! Who else? Tell me about it."

"Well," said Gudrun. "There's nothing particular to tell. You know Fanny is *frightfully* in love with that painter, Billy Macfarlane.* *He* was there—so Fanny spared nothing, she spent *very* freely.—It was really remarkable! Of course, everybody got fearfully drunk— but in an interesting way, not like that filthy London crowd. The fact is, these were all people that matter, which makes all the difference. There was a Roumanian,* a fine chap. He got completely drunk, and climbed to the top of a high studio ladder, and gave the most marvellous address—really, Ursula, it was wonderful! He began in French—La vie, c'est une affaire d'âmes impériales*—in a most beautiful voice—he was a fine-looking chap—but he had got into Roumanian before he had finished, and not a soul understood. But Donald Gilchrist* was worked to a frenzy. He dashed his glass to the ground, and declared, by God, he was glad he had been born, by God, it was a miracle to be alive.—And do you know, Ursula, so it was—" Gudrun laughed rather hollowly.

"But how was Gerald among them all?" asked Ursula.

"Gerald! Oh, my word, he came out like a dandelion in the sun! *He's* a whole Saturnalia in himself, once he is roused. I shouldn't like to say whose waist his arm did not go round.—Really, Ursula, he seems to reap the women like a harvest: there wasn't one that would have resisted him. It was too amazing! Can you understand it?"

Ursula reflected, and a dancing light came into her eyes.

"Yes," she said, "I can. He is such a whole-hogger."*

"Whole-hogger!—I should think so!" exclaimed Gudrun. "But it is true, Ursula, every woman in the room was ready to surrender to him—Chanticleer* isn't in it—even Fanny Rath, who is genuinely in love with Billy Macfarlane! I never was more amazed in my life!—And you know, afterwards—I felt I was a whole *roomful* of women. I was no more myself to him, than I was Queen Victoria. I was a whole roomful of women at once. It was most astounding!— But my eye, I'd caught a Sultan* that time—"

Gudrun's eyes were flashing, her cheek was hot, she looked strange, exotic, satiric. Ursula was fascinated at once—and yet uneasy.

They had to get ready for dinner. Gudrun came down in a daring gown of vivid green silk and tissue of gold, with green velvet bodice, and a strange black-and-white band round her hair. She was really brilliantly beautiful, and everybody noticed her. Gerald was in that full-blooded, gleaming state when he was most handsome. Birkin watched them with quick, laughing, half-sinister eyes, Ursula quite lost her head. There seemed a spell, almost a blinding spell, cast round their table, as if they were lighted up more strongly than the rest of the dining-room.

"Don't you love to be in this place?" cried Gudrun. "Isn't the snow wonderful! Do you notice how it exalts everything? It is simply marvelous. One really does feel übermenschlich*—more than human."

"One does," cried Ursula. "But isn't that partly the being out of England?"

"Oh, of course," cried Gudrun. "One could never feel like this in England, for the simple reason that the damper is *never* lifted off one, there. It is quite impossible really to let go, in England, of that I am assured."

And she turned again to the food she was eating. She was fluttering with vivid intensity.

"It's quite true," said Gerald, "it never is *quite* the same in England.—But perhaps we don't want it to be—perhaps it's like bringing the light a little too near the powder-magazine, to let go altogether, in England. One is afraid what might happen, if *everybody else* let go."

"My God!" cried Gudrun. "But wouldn't it be wonderful, if all England *did* suddenly go off like a display of fireworks."

"It couldn't," said Ursula. "They are all too damp, the powder is damp in them."

"I'm not so sure of that," said Gerald.

"Nor I," said Birkin. "When the English really begin to go off, *en masse*, it'll be time to shut your ears, and run."

"They never will," said Ursula.

"We'll see," he replied.

"Isn't it marvellous," said Gudrun, "how thankful one can be, to be out of one's country. I cannot believe myself, I am so transported, the moment I set foot on a foreign shore. I say to myself 'here steps a new creature into life.'"

"Don't be too hard on poor old England," said Gerald. "Though we curse it, we love it really."

To Ursula, there seemed a fund of cynicism in these words.

"We may." said Birkin. "But it's a damnably uncomfortable love: like a love for an aged parent who suffers horribly from a complication of diseases, for which there is no hope."

Gudrun looked at him with dilated dark eyes.

"You think there is no hope?" she asked, in her pertinent fashion.

But Birkin backed away. He would not answer such a question.

"Any hope of England's becoming real? God knows. It's a great actual unreality now, an aggregation into unreality.—It might be real, if there were no Englishmen."

"You think the English will have to disappear?" persisted Gudrun. It was strange, her pointed interest in his answer. It might have been her own fate she was inquiring after. Her dark, dilated eyes rested on Birkin, as if she could conjure the truth of the future out of him, as out of some instrument of divination.

He was pale. Then, reluctantly, he answered:

"Well—what else is in front of them, but disappearance?— They've got to disappear from their own special brand of Englishness, anyhow."

Gudrun watched him as if in a hypnotic state, her eyes wide and fixed on him.

"But in what way do you mean, disappear?—" she persisted.

"Yes, do you mean a change of heart?" put in Gerald.

5 "I don't mean anything, why should I?" said Birkin. "I'm an Englishman, and I've paid the price of it. I can't talk about England—I can only speak for myself."

"Yes," said Gudrun slowly, "You love England immensely, *immensely*, Rupert."

10 "And leave her,"* he replied.

"No, not for good. You'll come back," said Gerald, nodding sagely.

"They say the lice crawl off a dying body," said Birkin, with a glare of bitterness. "So I leave England."

15 "Ah, but you'll come back," said Gudrun, with a sardonic smile.

"*Tant pis pour moi*,"* he replied.

"Isn't he angry with his mother country!" laughed Gerald, amused.

"Ah, a patriot!" said Gudrun, with something like a sneer.

20 Birkin refused to answer any more.

Gudrun watched him still for a few seconds. Then she turned away. It was finished, her spell of divination in him. She felt already purely cynical. She looked at Gerald. He was wonderful like a piece of radium to her. She felt she could consume herself and know *all*, by 25 means of this fatal, living metal.* She smiled to herself at her fancy. And what would she do with herself, when she had destroyed herself? For if spirit, if integral being is destructible, Matter is indestructible.

He was looking bright and abstracted, puzzled, for the moment. 30 She stretched out her beautiful arm, with its fluff of green tulle, and touched his chin with her subtle, artist's fingers.

"What are they then?" she asked, with a strange, knowing smile.

"What?" he replied, his eyes suddenly dilating with wonder.

"Your thoughts."

35 Gerald looked like a man coming awake.

"I think I had none," he said.

"Really!" she said, with grave laughter in her voice.

And to Birkin, it was as if she killed Gerald, with that touch.

"Ah but," cried Gudrun, "let us drink to Britannia—let us drink 40 to Britannia."

It seemed there was wild despair in her voice. Gerald laughed, and filled the glasses.

"I think Rupert means," he said "that *nationally* all Englishmen must die, so that they can exist individually and—"

"Super-nationally—" put in Gudrun, with a slight ironic grimace, raising her glass.

Chapter XXX

Snow*

The next day, they descended at the tiny railway station of Hohen-hausen, at the end of the tiny valley railway.* It was snow everywhere, a white, perfect cradle of snow, new and frozen, sweeping up up on either side, black crags and white sweeps of silver towards the blue pale heavens.

As they stepped out on to the naked platform, with only snow around and above, Gudrun shrank as if it chilled her heart.

"My God, Jerry," she said, turning to Gerald with sudden intimacy, "you've done it now."

"What?"

She made a faint gesture, indicating the world on either hand. "Look at it!"

She seemed afraid to go on. He laughed.

They were in the heart of the mountains. From high above, on either side, swept down the white fold of snow, so that one seemed small and tiny in a valley of pure concrete heaven, all strangely radiant and changeless* and silent.

"It makes one feel so small and alone," said Ursula, turning to Birkin and laying her hand on his arm.

"You're not sorry you've come, are you?" said Gerald to Gudrun.

She looked doubtful. They went out of the station between banks of snow.

"Ah," said Gerald, sniffing the air in elation, "this is perfect.—There's our sledge.—We'll walk a bit—we'll run up the road."

Gudrun, always doubtful, dropped her heavy coat on the sledge, as he did his, and they set off. Suddenly she threw up her head and set off scudding along the road of snow, pulling her cap down over her ears. Her blue, bright dress fluttered in the wind, her thick scarlet stockings were brilliant above the whiteness. Gerald watched her: she seemed to be rushing towards her fate, and leaving him behind. He let her get some distance, then, loosening his limbs, he went after her.

Everywhere was deep and silent snow. Great snow-eaves weighed down the broad-roofed Tyrolese houses, that were sunk to the window-sashes in snow. Peasant-women, full-skirted, wearing each a cross-over shawl, and thick snowboots, turned in the way to look at the soft, determined girl running with such heavy fleetness from the man, who was overtaking her, but not gaining any power over her. 5

They passed the inn with its painted shutters and balcony, a few cottages half buried in the snow; then the snow-buried silent saw-mill by the roofed bridge, which crossed the hidden stream, over which they ran into the very depth of the untouched sheets of 10 snow. It was a silence and a sheer whiteness exhilarating to madness. But the perfect silence was most terrifying, isolating the soul, surrounding the heart with frozen air.

"It's a marvellous place, for all that," said Gudrun, looking into his eyes with a strange, meaning look. His soul leapt. 15

"Good!" he said.

A fierce, electric energy seemed to flow over all his limbs, his muscles were surcharged, his hands felt hard with strength. They walked along rapidly up the snow-road, that was marked by withered branches of trees stuck in at intervals. He and she were separate, like 20 opposite poles of one fierce energy. But they felt powerful enough to leap over the confines of life into the forbidden places, and back again.

Birkin and Ursula were running along also, over the snow. He had disposed of the luggage, and they had a little start of the sledges. 25 Ursula was excited and happy, but she kept turning suddenly to catch hold of Birkin's arm, to make sure of him.

"This is something I never expected," she said. "It is a different world, here."

They went on into a snow meadow. There they were overtaken by 30 the sledge, that came tinkling through the silence. It was another mile before they came upon Gudrun and Gerald, on the steep up-climb, beside the pink, half-buried shrine.

Then they passed into a gulley,* where were walls of black rock, and a river filled with snow, and a still blue sky above. Through a 35 covered bridge they went, drumming roughly over the boards, crossing the snow-bed once more, then slowly up and up, the horses walking swiftly, the driver cracking his long whip as he walked beside, and calling his strange wild *heu-heu!*, the walls of rock passing slowly by, till they emerged again between slopes and masses 40

of snow. Up and up, gradually, they went, through the cold
shadow-radiance of the afternoon, silenced by the imminence of the
mountains, the luminous, dazing sides of snow that rose above them
and fell away beneath.

5   They came forth at last in a little high table-land of snow, where
stood the last peaks of snow like the heart petals of an open rose. In
the midst of the last deserted valleys of heaven stood a lonely
building* with brown wooden walls and white-heavy roof, deep and
deserted in the waste of snow, like a dream. It stood like a rock that
10 had rolled down from the last steep slopes, a rock that had taken the
form of a house, and was now half buried. It was unbelievable that
one could live there uncrushed by all this terrible waste of whiteness
and silence and clear, upper, ringing cold.

    Yet the sledges ran up in fine style, people came to the door
15 laughing and excited, the floor of the hostel rang hollow, the passage
was wet with snow, it was a real, warm interior.

    The new-comers tramped up the bare wooden stairs, following
the serving woman. Gudrun and Gerald took the first bedroom. In a
moment they found themselves alone in a bare, smallish, close-shut
20 room that was all of golden-coloured wood, floor, walls, ceiling,
door, all of the same warm-gold panelling of oiled pine. There was a
window opposite the door, but low down, because the roof sloped.
Under the slope of the ceiling were the table with wash-hand bowl
and jug, and across, another table with mirror. On either side the
25 door were two beds piled high with an enormous blue-checked
overbolster,* enormous.

    This was all—no cupboard, none of the amenities of life. Here
they were shut up together in this cell of golden-coloured wood, with
two blue-checked beds. They looked at each other and laughed,
30 frightened by this naked nearness of isolation.

    A man knocked and came in with the luggage. He was a sturdy
fellow with flattish cheek-bones, rather pale, and with coarse fair
moustache. Gudrun watched him put down the bags, in silence, then
tramp heavily out.

35   "It isn't too rough, is it?" Gerald asked.

    The bedroom was not very warm, and she shivered slightly.

    "It is wonderful," she equivocated. "Look at the colour of this
panelling—it's wonderful, like being inside a nut."

    He was standing watching her, feeling his short-cut moustache,
40 leaning back slightly and watching her with his keen, undaunted

eyes, dominated by the constant passion, that was like a doom upon him.

She went and crouched down in front of the window, curious.

"Oh, but this—!" she cried involuntarily, almost in pain.

In front was a valley shut in under the sky, the last huge slopes of snow and black rock, and at the end, like the navel of the earth, a white-folded wall, and two peaks glimmering in the late light. Straight in front ran the cradle of silent snow, between the great slopes, that were fringed with a little roughness of pine-trees, like hair, round the base. But the cradle of snow ran on to the eternal closing-in, where the walls of snow and rock rose impenetrable, and the mountain peaks above were in heaven immediate. This was the centre, the knot, the navel of the world, where the earth belonged to the skies, pure, unapproachable, impassable.

It filled Gudrun with a strange rapture. She crouched in front of the window, clenching her face in her hands, in a sort of trance. At last she had arrived, she had reached her place. Here at last she folded her venture and settled down like a crystal in the navel of snow, and was gone.

Gerald bent above her and was looking out over her shoulder. Already he felt he was alone. She was gone. She was completely gone, and there was icy vapour round his heart. He saw the blind valley, the great cul de sac of snow and mountain peaks, under the heaven. And there was no way out. The terrible silence and cold and the glamorous whiteness of the dusk wrapped him round, and she remained crouching before the window, as at a shrine, a shadow.

"Do you like it?" he asked, in a voice that sounded detached and foreign. At least she might acknowledge he was with her. But she only averted her soft, mute face a little from his gaze. And he knew that there were tears in her eyes, her own tears, tears of her strange religion, that put him to nought.

Quite suddenly, he put his hand under her chin and lifted up her face to him. Her dark blue eyes, in their wetness of tears, dilated as if she was startled in her very soul. They looked at him through their tears in terror and a little horror. His light blue eyes were keen, small-pupilled and unnatural in their vision. Her lips parted, as she breathed with difficulty.

The passion came up in him, stroke after stroke, like the ringing of a bronze bell, so strong and unflawed and indomitable. His knees tightened to bronze, as he hung above her soft face, whose lips parted and whose eyes dilated in a strange violation. In the grasp of his hand her chin was unutterably soft and silken. He felt strong as winter, his hands were living metal, invincible and not to be turned aside. His heart rang like a bell clanging inside him.

5 He took her up in his arms. She was soft and inert, motionless. All the while her eyes, in which the tears had not yet dried, were dilated as if in a kind of swoon of fascination and helplessness. He was superhumanly strong, and unflawed, as if invested with supernatural force.

10 He lifted her close and folded her against him. Her softness, her inert, relaxed weight lay against his own surcharged, bronze-like limbs in a heaviness of desirability that would destroy him, if he were not fulfilled. She moved convulsively, recoiling away from him. His heart went up like a flame of ice, he closed over her like steel. He

15 would destroy her rather than be denied.

But the overweening power of his body was too much for her. She relaxed again, and lay loose and soft, panting in a little delirium. And to him, she was so sweet, she was such bliss of release, that he would have suffered a whole eternity of torture rather than forego one

20 second of this pang of unsurpassable bliss.

"My God," he said to her, his face drawn and strange, trans-figured, "what next?"

She lay perfectly still, with a still, child-like face and dark eyes, looking at him. She was lost, fallen right away.

25 "I shall always love you," he said, looking at her.

But she did not hear. She lay looking at him as at something she could never understand, never: as a child looks at a grown-up person, without hope of understanding, only submitting.

He kissed her, kissed her eyes shut, so that she should not look any

30 more. He wanted something now, some recognition, some sign, some admission. But she only lay silent and child-like and remote, like a child that is overcome and cannot understand, only feels lost. He kissed her again, giving up.

"Shall we go down and have coffee and Kuchen?"* he asked.

35 The twilight was falling slate-blue at the window. She closed her eyes, closed away the monotonous level of dead wonder, and opened them again to the everyday world.

"Yes," she said briefly, regaining her will with a click.

She went again to the window. Blue evening had fallen over the

40 cradle of snow and over the great pallid slopes. But in the heaven the

peaks of snow were rosy, glistening like transcendent, radiant spikes
of blossom in the heavenly upper-world, so lovely and beyond.

Gudrun saw all their loveliness, she *knew* how immortally beautiful they were, great pistils of rose-coloured, snow-fed fire in the blue
twilight of the heaven. She could *see* it, she knew it, but she was not of   5
it. She was divorced, debarred, a soul shut out.

With a last look of remorse, she turned away, and was doing her
hair. He had unstrapped the luggage, and was waiting, watching her.
She knew he was watching her. It made her a little hasty and feverish
in her precipitation.   10

They went downstairs, both with a strange, other-world look on
their faces, and with a glow in their eyes. They saw Birkin and Ursula
sitting at the long table in a corner, waiting for them.

"How good and simple they look together," Gudrun thought,
jealously. She envied them some spontaneity, a childish sufficiency   15
to which she herself could never approach. They seemed such
children to her.

"Such *good* Kranzkuchen!" cried Ursula greedily. "So *good*!"

"Right," said Gudrun. "Can we have Kaffee mit Kranzkuchen?"*
she added, to the waiter.   20

And she seated herself on the bench, beside Gerald. Birkin,
looking at them, felt a pain of tenderness for them.

"I think the place is really wonderful, Gerald," he said; "prachtvoll and wunderbar and wunderschön and unbeschreiblich* and all
the other German adjectives."   25

Gerald broke into a slight smile.

"*I* like it," he said.

The tables, of white scrubbed wood, were placed round three
sides of the room, as in a Gasthaus.* Birkin and Ursula sat with
their backs to the wall, which was of oiled wood, and Gerald and   30
Gudrun sat in the corner next them, near to the stove. It was a fairly
large place, with a tiny bar, just like a country inn, but quite simple
and bare, and all of oiled wood, ceilings and walls and floor, the only
furniture being the tables and benches going round three sides, the
great green stove,* and the bar and the doors on the fourth side.   35
The windows were double, and quite uncurtained. It was early
evening.

The coffee came—hot and good—and a whole ring of cake.

"A whole Kuchen!" cried Ursula. "They give you more than us! I
want some of yours."   40

There were other people in the place, ten altogether, so Birkin had found out: two artists, three students, a man and wife, and a Professor and two daughters,—all Germans. The four English people, being new-comers, sat in their coign of vantage* to watch.

5 The Germans peeped in at the door, called a word to the waiter, and went away again. It was not meal-time, so they did not come into this dining-room, but betook themselves, when their boots were changed, to the Reunionsaal.*

The English visitors could hear the occasional twanging of a 10 zither, the strumming of a piano, snatches of laughter and shouting and singing, a faint vibration of voices. The whole building being of wood, it seemed to carry every sound, like a drum, but instead of increasing each particular noise, it decreased it, so that the sound of the zither seemed tiny, as if a diminutive zither were playing 15 somewhere, and it seemed the piano must be a small one, like a little spinet.

The host came when the coffee was finished. He was a Tyrolese, broad, rather flat-cheeked, with a pale, pock-marked skin and flourishing moustaches.

20 "Would you like to go to the Reunionsaal and be introduced to the other ladies and gentlemen?" he asked, bending forward and smiling, showing his large, strong teeth. His blue eyes went quickly from one to the other—he was not quite sure of his ground with these English people. He was unhappy too because he spoke no 25 English, and he was not sure whether to try his French.

"Shall we go to the Reunionsaal and be introduced to the other people?" repeated Gerald, laughing.

There was a moment's hesitation.

"I suppose we'd better—better break the ice," said Birkin.

30 The women rose, rather flushed. And the Wirt's* black, beetle-like, broad-shouldered figure went on ignominiously in front, towards the noise. He opened the door and ushered the four strangers into the play-room.

Instantly a silence fell, a slight embarrassment came over the 35 company. The new-comers had a sense of many blond faces looking their way. Then the host* was bowing to a short, energetic-looking man with large moustaches, and saying in a low voice:

"Herr Professor, darf ich Sie vorstellen—"*

The Herr Professor was prompt and energetic. He bowed low to 40 the English people, smiling, and began to be a comrade at once.

"Nehmen die Herrschaften teil an unserer Unterhaltung?"* he said, with a vigorous suavity, his voice curling up in the question.

The four English people smiled, lounging with an attentive uneasiness in the middle of the room. Gerald, who was spokesman, said that they would willingly take part in the entertainment. Gudrun and Ursula, laughing, excited, felt the eyes of all the men upon them, and they lifted their heads and looked nowhere, and felt royal.

The Professor announced the names of those present, sans cérémonie, there was a bowing to the wrong people and to the right people. Everybody was there, except the man and wife. The two tall, clear-skinned, athletic daughters of the professor, with their plain-cut, dark blue blouses and loden* skirts, their rather long, strong necks, their clear blue eyes and carefully banded hair, and their blushes, bowed and stood back; the three students bowed very low, in the humble hope of making an impression of extreme good-breeding; then there was a small,* dark-skinned man with full eyes, an odd creature, like a child, and like a troll, quick, detached: he bowed slightly; his companion, a large fair young man, stylishly dressed, blushed to the eyes and bowed very low.

It was over.

"Herr Loerke* was giving us a recitation in the Cologne dialect," said the Professor.

"He must forgive us for interrupting him," said Gerald, "we should like very much to hear it."

There was instantly a bowing and an offering of seats. Gudrun and Ursula, Gerald and Birkin sat in the deep sofas against the wall. The room was of naked oiled panelling, like the rest of the house. It had a piano, sofas and chairs, and a couple of tables with books and magazines. In its complete absence of decoration, save for the big blue stove, it was cosy and pleasant.

Herr Loerke was the little man with the boyish figure, and the round, full, sensitive-looking head, and the quick, full eyes, like a mouse's. He glanced swiftly from one to the other of the strangers, and held himself aloof.

"Please, go on with the recitation," said the Professor, suavely, with his slight authority. Loerke, who was sitting hunched on the piano stool, blinked and did not answer.

"It would be a great pleasure," said Ursula, who had been getting the sentence ready, in German, for some minutes.

Then suddenly, the small, unresponding man swung aside,

towards his previous audience, and broke forth, exactly as he had broken off, in a controlled, mocking voice, giving an imitation of a quarrel between an old Cologne woman and a railway guard.

5 His body was slight and unformed, like a boy's, but his voice was mature, sardonic, its movement had the flexibility of essential energy, and of a mocking, penetrating understanding. Gudrun could not understand a word of his monologue, but she was spell-bound watching him. He must be an artist: nobody else could have such fine adjustment and singleness. The Germans were doubled up with

10 laughter, hearing his strange, droll words, his droll phrases of dialect. And in the midst of their paroxysms, they glanced with deference at the four English strangers, the elect. Gudrun and Ursula were forced to laugh. Then the room rang with shouts of laughter, the blue eyes of the Professor's daughters were swimming

15 over with laughter-tears, their clear cheeks were flushed crimson with mirth, their father broke out in the most astonishing peals of hilarity, the students bowed their heads on their knees in excess of joy. Ursula looked round amazed, the laughter was bubbling out of her involuntarily. She looked at Gudrun, Gudrun looked at her: and

20 the two sisters burst out laughing, carried away. Loerke glanced at them swiftly, with his full eyes. Birkin was sniggering involuntarily, Gerald Crich sat erect, with a glistening look of amusement on his face. And the laughter crashed out again, in wild paroxysms, the Professor's daughters were reduced to shaking helplessness, the

25 veins in the Professor's neck were swollen, his face was purple, he was strangled in ultimate silent spasms of laughter, the students were shouting half-articulated words that tailed off in helpless explosions. Then suddenly the rapid patter of the artist ceased, there were little whoops of subsiding mirth, Ursula and Gudrun were wiping their

30 eyes, and the Professor was crying loudly:

"Ja, das war merkwürdig, das war famos—"

"Wirklich famos!" echoed his exhausted daughters, faintly.

"And we couldn't understand it," cried Ursula.

"Oh leider, leider," cried the Professor.

35 "You couldn't understand it?" cried the students, let loose at last in speech with the new-comers. "Ja, das ist wirklich schade, das ist schade, gnädige Frau. Wissen Sie———"*

The mixture was made, the new-comers were stirred into the party, like new ingredients, the whole room was alive. Gerald was in

40 his element, he talked freely and excitedly, his face glistened with a

strange amusement. Perhaps even Birkin, in the end, would break forth. He was shy and withheld, though full of attention.

Ursula was prevailed upon to sing "Annie Lowrie,"* as the Professor called it. There was a hush of *extreme* deference. She had never been so flattered in her life. Gudrun accompanied her on the piano, playing from memory.

Ursula had a beautiful ringing voice, but usually no confidence, she spoiled everything. This evening she felt conceited and untrammelled. Birkin was well in the background, she shone almost in reaction, the Germans made her feel fine and infallible, she was liberated into overweening self-confidence. She felt like a bird flying in the air, as her voice soared out, enjoying herself extremely in the balance and flight of the song, like the motion of a bird's wings that is up in the wind, sliding and playing on the air, she played with sentimentality, supported by rapturous attention. She was very happy, singing that song by herself, full of a conceit of emotion and power, working upon all those people, and upon herself, exerting herself with gratification, giving immeasurable gratification to the Germans.

At the end, the Germans were all touched with admiring, delicious melancholy, they praised her in soft, reverent voices, they could not say too much.

"Wie schön, wie rührend! Ach, die Schottischen Lieder, sie haben so viel Stimmung! Aber die gnädige Frau hat eine *wunderbare* Stimme; die gnädige Frau ist wirklich eine Künstlerin, aber wirklich!"*

She was dilated and brilliant, like a flower in the morning sun. She felt Birkin looking at her, as if he were jealous of her, and her breasts thrilled, her veins were all golden. She was as happy as the sun that has just opened above clouds. And everybody seemed so admiring and radiant, it was perfect.

After dinner she wanted to go out for a minute, to look at the world. The company tried to dissuade her—it was so terribly cold. But just to look, she said.

They all four wrapped up warmly, and found themselves in a vague, unsubstantial outdoors of dim snow and ghosts of an upper-world, that made strange shadows before the stars. It was indeed cold, bruisingly, frighteningly, unnaturally cold. Ursula could not believe the air in her nostrils. It seemed conscious, malevolent, purposive in its intense, murderous coldness.

Yet it was wonderful, an intoxication, a silence of dim, unrealised snow, of the invisible intervening between her and the visible, between her and the flashing stars. She could see Orion sloping up.*
How wonderful he was, wonderful enough to make one cry aloud.

5 And all around was this cradle of snow, and there was firm snow underfoot, that struck with heavy cold through her boot-soles. It was night, and silence. She imagined she could hear the stars. She imagined distinctly she could hear the celestial, musical motion of the stars, quite near at hand. She seemed like a bird flying amongst
10 their harmonious motion.

And she clung close to Birkin. Suddenly, she realised she did not know what he was thinking. She did not know where he was ranging.

"My love!" she said, stopping to look at him.

His face was pale, his eyes dark, there was a faint spark of starlight
15 on them. And he saw her face soft and upturned to him, very near. He kissed her softly.

"What then?" he asked.

"Do you love me?" she asked.

"Too much," he answered, quietly.

20 She clung a little closer.

"Not too much," she pleaded.

"Far too much—" he said, almost sadly.

"And does it make you sad, that I am everything to you?" she asked, wistful.

25 He held her close, kissing her, and saying, scarcely audible:

"No, but I feel like a beggar—I feel poor."

She was silent, looking at the stars now. Then she kissed him.

"Don't be a beggar," she pleaded, wistfully. "It isn't ignominious, that you love me."

30 "It is ignominious to feel poor, isn't it?" he replied.

"Why?—why should it be?" she asked. He only stood still, in the terribly cold air that moved invisibly over the mountain tops, folding her round with his arms.

"I couldn't bear this cold, eternal place without you," he said. "I
35 couldn't bear it, it would kill the quick of my life."

She kissed him again, suddenly.

"Do you hate it?" she asked, puzzled, wondering.

"If I couldn't come near to you, if you weren't here, I should hate it, I couldn't bear it," he answered.

40 "But the people are nice," she said.

"I mean the snow, the stillness, the cold, the frozen eternality," he said.

She wondered. Then her spirit came home to him, nestling unconscious in him.

"Yes, it is good we are warm and together," she said. 5

And they turned home again. They saw the golden lights of the hotel glouring* out in the night of snow-silence, small in the hollow, like a cluster of yellow berries. It seemed like a bunch of sun-sparks, tiny and orange in the midst of the snow-darkness. Behind, was a high shadow of a peak, blotting out the stars, like a ghost. 10

They drew near to their home. They saw a man come from the dark building, with a lighted lantern which swung golden, and made that his dark feet walked in a halo of snow. He was a small, dark figure in the darkened snow. He unlatched the door of an outhouse. A smell of cows, hot, animal, almost like beef, came out on the 15 heavily cold air. There was a glimpse of two cattle in their dark stalls, then the door was shut again, and not a chink of light showed. It had reminded Ursula again of home, of the Marsh, of her childhood, and of the journey to Brussels, and, strangely enough, of Anton Skrebensky. 20

Oh God, could one bear it, this past which was gone down the abyss? Could she bear, that it ever had been! She looked round this silent, upper world of snow and stars and powerful cold. There was another world, like views on a magic lantern: the Marsh, Cossethay, Ilkeston,* lit up with a common, unreal light. There was a shadowy, 25 unreal Ursula, a whole shadow-play of an unreal life. It was as unreal, and circumscribed, as a magic-lantern show. She wished the slides could all be broken. She wished it could be gone for ever, like a lantern-slide which is broken. She wanted to have no past. She wanted to have come down from the slopes of heaven to this place, 30 with Birkin, not to have toiled out of the murk of her childhood and her upbringing, slowly, all soiled. She felt that memory was a dirty trick played upon her. What was this decree, that she should 'remember'! Why not a bath of pure oblivion, a new birth, without any recollections or blemish of a past life. She was with Birkin, she 35 had just come into life, here in the high snow, against the stars. What had she to do with parents and antecedents? She knew herself new and unbegotten, she had no father, no mother,* no anterior connec-tions, she was herself, pure and silvery, she belonged only to the oneness with Birkin, a oneness that struck deeper notes, sounding 40 into the heart of the universe, the heart of reality, where she had never existed before.

Even Gudrun was a separate unit, separate, separate, having nothing to do with this self, this Ursula, in her new world of reality. That old shadow-world, the actuality of the past—ah, let it go! She rose free on the wings of her new condition.

Gudrun and Gerald had not come in. They had walked up the valley straight in front of the house, not like Ursula and Birkin, on to the little hill at the right. Gudrun was driven by a strange desire. She wanted to plunge on and on, till she came to the end of the valley of snow. Then she wanted to climb the wall of white finality, climb over, into the peaks that sprang up like sharp petals in the heart of the frozen, mysterious navel of the world. She felt that there, over the strange, blind, terrible wall of rocky snow, there in the navel of the mystic world, among the final cluster of peaks, there, in the infolded navel of it all, was her consummation. If she could but come there, alone, and pass into the infolded navel of eternal snow and of uprising, immortal peaks of snow and rock, she would be a oneness with all, she would be herself the eternal, infinite silence, the sleeping, timeless, frozen centre of the All.

They went back to the house, to the Reunionsaal. She was curious to see what was going on. The men there made her alert, roused her curiosity. It was a new taste of life for her, they were so prostrate before her, yet so full of life.

The party was boisterous; they were dancing all together, dancing the Schuhplatteln,* the Tyrolese dance of the clapping hands and tossing the partner in the air at the crisis. The Germans were all proficient—they were from Munich chiefly. Gerald also was quite passable. There were three zithers twanging away in a corner. It was a scene of great animation and confusion. The professor was initiating Ursula into the dance, stamping, clapping, and swinging her high, with amazing force and zest, when the crisis came. Birkin* was behaving manfully with one of the professor's fresh, strong daughters, who was exceedingly happy. Everybody was dancing, there was the most boisterous turmoil.

Gudrun looked on with delight. The solid wooden floor resounded to the knocking heels of the men, the air quivered with the clapping hands and the zither music, there was a golden dust about the hanging lamps.

Suddenly the dance finished, Loerke and the students rushed out

to bring in drinks. There was an excited clamour of voices, a
chinking of mug-lids, a great crying of "Prosit—Prosit!"* Loerke
was everywhere at once, like a gnome—suggesting drinks for the
women, making an obscure, slightly risky joke with the men,
confusing and mystifying the waiter.   5

He wanted very much to dance with Gudrun. From the first
moment he had seen her, he wanted to make a connection with her.
Instinctively she felt this, and she waited for him to come up. But a
kind of sulkiness kept him away from her, so she thought he disliked
her.   10

"Will you schuhplattern, gnädige Frau?" said the large, fair youth,
Loerke's companion. He was too soft, too humble for Gudrun's
taste. But she wanted to dance, and the fair youth, who was called
Leitner,* was handsome enough, in his uneasy, slightly abject
fashion, a humility that covered a certain fear. She accepted him as a 15
partner.

The zithers sounded out again, the dance began. Gerald led them,
laughing, with one of the Professor's daughters. Ursula danced with
one of the students, Birkin with the other daughter of the Professor,
the Professor with Frau Kramer, and the rest of the men danced   20
together, with quite as much zest as if they had had women partners.

Because Gudrun had danced with the well-built, soft youth, his
companion, Loerke was more pettish and exasperated than ever, and
would not even notice her existence in the room. This piqued her,
but she made up to herself by dancing with the professor, who was   25
strong as a mature, well-seasoned bull, and as full of coarse energy.
She could not bear him, critically, and yet she enjoyed being rushed
through the dance, and tossed up into the air, on his coarse, powerful
impetus. The professor enjoyed it too, he eyed her with strange,
large blue eyes, full of galvanic fire. She hated him for the seasoned, 30
semi-paternal animalism with which he regarded her, but she
admired his weight of strength.

The room was charged with excitement and strong, animal
emotion. Loerke was kept away from Gudrun, to whom he wanted to
speak, as by a hedge of thorns, and he felt a sardonic, ruthless hatred 35
for his young love-companion, Leitner, who was his penniless
dependent. He mocked the youth, with an acid ridicule, that made
Leitner red in the face and impotent with resentment.

Gerald, who had now got the dance perfectly, was dancing again
with the younger of the Professor's daughters, who was almost dying 40

of virgin excitement, because she thought Gerald so handsome, so superb. He had her in his power, as if she were a palpitating bird, a fluttering, flushing, bewildered creature. And it made him smile, as she shrank convulsively between his hands, violently, when he must throw her into the air. At the end, she was so overcome with prostrate love for him, that she could scarcely speak sensibly at all.

Birkin was dancing with Ursula. There were odd little fires playing in his eyes, he seemed to have turned into something wicked and flickering, mocking, suggestive, quite impossible. Ursula was frightened of him, and fascinated. Clear, before her eyes, as in a vision, she could see the sardonic, licentious mockery of his eyes, he moved towards her with subtle, animal, indifferent approach. The strangeness of his hands, which came quick and cunning, inevitably to the vital place beneath her breasts, and, lifting with mocking, suggestive impulse, carried her through the air as if without strength, through black-magic, made her swoon with fear. For a moment she revolted, it was horrible. She would break the spell. But before the resolution had formed she had submitted again, yielded to her fear. He knew all the time what he was doing, she could see it in his smiling, concentrated eyes. It was his responsibility, she would leave it to him.

When they were alone in the darkness, she felt the strange licentiousness of him hovering upon her. She was troubled and repelled. Why should he turn like this?

"What is it?" she asked in dread.

But his face only glistened on her, unknown, horrible. And yet she was fascinated. Her impulse was to repel him violently, break from this spell of mocking brutishness. But she was too fascinated, she wanted to submit, she wanted to know. What would he do to her?

He was so attractive, and so repulsive at once. The sardonic suggestivity that flickered over his face and looked from his narrowed eyes, made her want to hide, to hide herself away from him, and watch him from somewhere unseen.

"Why are you like this?" she demanded again, rousing against him with sudden force and animosity.

The flickering fires in his eyes concentrated as he looked into her eyes. Then the lids drooped with a faint motion of satiric contempt. Then they rose again to the same remorseless suggestivity. And she gave way, he might do as he would. His licentiousness was repulsively attractive. But he was self-responsible, she would see what it was.

They might do as they liked—this she realised as she went to sleep. How could anything that gave one satisfaction be excluded? What was degrading?—Who cared? Degrading things were real, with a different reality. And he was so unabashed and unrestrained. Wasn't it rather horrible, a man who could be so soulful and spiritual, now to be so—she balked at her own thoughts and memories: then she added—so bestial? So bestial, they two!—so degraded! She winced.—But after all, why not? She exulted as well. Why not be bestial, and go the whole round of experience? She exulted in it. She was bestial. How good it was to be really shameful! There would be no shameful thing she had not experienced.—Yet she was unabashed, she was herself. Why not?—She was free, when she knew everything, and no dark shameful things were denied her.

Gudrun, who had been watching Gerald in the Reunionsaal, suddenly thought:

"He should have all the women he can—it is his nature. It is absurd to call him monogamous—he is naturally promiscuous. That is his nature."*

The thought came to her involuntarily. It shocked her somewhat. It was as if she had seen some new Mene! Mene! upon the wall.* Yet it was merely true. A voice seemed to have spoken it to her so clearly, that for the moment she believed in inspiration.

"It is really true," she said to herself again.

She knew quite well she had believed it all along. She knew it implicitly. But she must keep it dark—almost from herself. She must keep it completely secret. It was knowledge for her alone, and scarcely even to be admitted to herself.

The deep resolve formed in her, to combat him. One of them must triumph over the other. Which should it be? Her soul steeled itself with strength. Almost she laughed within herself, at her confidence. It woke a certain keen, half contemptuous pity, tenderness for him: she was so ruthless.

Everybody retired early. The professor and Loerke went into a small lounge to drink. They both watched Gudrun go along the landing, by the railing, upstairs.

"Ein schönes Frauenzimmer," said the Professor.

"Ja!"* assented Loerke, shortly.

Gerald walked with his queer, long wolf-steps across the bedroom

to the window, stooped and looked out, then rose again, and turned
to Gudrun, his eyes sharp with an abstract smile. He seemed very tall
to her, she saw the glisten of his whitish eyebrows, that met between
his brows.

5   "How do you like it?" he said.

He seemed to be laughing inside himself, quite unconsciously.
She looked at him. He was a phenomenon to her, not a human being:
a sort of creature, greedy.

"I like it very much," she replied.

10   "Who do you like best downstairs?" he asked, standing tall and
glistening above her, with his glistening stiff hair erect.

"Who do I like best?" she repeated, wanting to answer his
question, and finding it difficult to collect herself. "Why I don't
know, I don't know enough about them yet, to be able to say. Whom
15 do *you* like best?"

"Oh I don't care—I don't like or dislike any of them. It doesn't
matter about me. I wanted to know about you."

"But why?" she asked, going rather pale.

The abstract, unconscious smile in his eyes was intensified.

20   "I wanted to know," he said.

She turned aside, breaking the spell. In some strange way, she felt
he was getting power over her.

"Well I can't tell you already," she said.

She went to the mirror to take out the hairpins from her hair. She
25 stood before the mirror every night for some minutes, brushing her
fine dark hair. It was part of the inevitable ritual of her life.

He followed her, and stood behind her. She was busy, with bent
head, taking out the pins and shaking her warm hair loose. When she
looked up, she saw him in the glass, standing behind her, watching
30 unconsciously, not consciously seeing her, and yet watching, with
fine-pupilled eyes that *seemed* to smile, and which were not really
smiling.

She started. It took all her courage for her to continue brushing
her hair, as usual, for her to pretend she was at her ease. She was far,
35 far from being at her ease with him. She beat her brains wildly for
something to say to him.

"What are your plans for tomorrow?" she asked, nonchalant,*
whilst her heart was beating so furiously, her eyes were so bright with
strange nervousness, she felt he could not but observe. But she knew
40 also that he was completely blind, blind as a wolf looking at her. It

was a strange battle between her ordinary consciousness and his uncanny, black-art consciousness.

"I don't know," he replied; "what would you like to do?"

He spoke emptily, his mind was sunk away.

"Oh," she said, with easy protestation, "I'm ready for anything—anything will be fine for *me*, I'm sure."

And to herself she was saying:

"God, why am I so nervous,—why are you so *nervous*, you fool. If he sees it I'm done for for ever—you *know* you're done for for ever, if he sees the absurd state you're in."

And she smiled to herself as if it were all child's play. Meanwhile her heart was plunging, she was almost fainting. She could see him, in the mirror, as he stood there behind her, tall and over-arching—blond and terribly frightening. She glanced at his reflection with furtive eyes, willing to give anything to save him from knowing she could see him. He did not know she could see his reflection. He was looking unconsciously, glisteningly down at her head, from which the hair fell loose, as she brushed it with wild, nervous hand. She held her head aside and brushed and brushed her hair madly. For her life, she could not turn round and face him. For her life, *she could not*. And the knowledge made her almost sink to the ground in a faint, helpless, spent. She was aware of his frightening, impending figure standing close behind her, she was aware of his hard, strong, unyielding chest, close upon her back. And she felt she could not bear it any more, in a few minutes she would fall down at his feet, grovelling at his feet, and letting him destroy her.

The thought pricked up all her sharp intelligence and presence of mind. She dared not turn round to him—and there he stood motionless, unbroken. Summoning all her strength, she said in a full, resonant, nonchalant voice, that was forced out with all her remaining self-control:

"Oh would you mind looking in that bag behind there and giving me my———"

Here her power fell inert. "My what—my what—?" she screamed in silence to herself.

But he had started round, surprised and startled that she should ask him to look in her bag, which she always kept so *very* private to herself. She turned now, her face white, her dark eyes blazing with uncanny, overwrought excitement. She saw him stooping to the bag, undoing the loosely buckled strap. She had conquered him, he was stooping down, servile.*

"Your what?" he asked.

"Oh, a little enamel box—yellow—with a design of a cormorant plucking her breast—"*

She went towards him, stooping her beautiful, bare arm, and deftly turned some of her things, disclosing the box, which was exquisitely painted.

"That is it, see," she said, taking it from under his eyes.

And he was baffled now. He was left to fasten up the bag, whilst she swiftly did up her hair for the night, and sat down to unfasten her shoes. She would not turn her back to him any more.

He was baffled, frustrated, but unconscious. She had the whip hand over him now. She knew he had not realised her terrible panic. Her heart was beating heavily still. Fool, fool that she was, to get into such a state! How she thanked God for Gerald's obtuse blindness. Thank God he could see nothing.

She sat slowly unlacing her shoes, and he too commenced to undress. Thank God that crisis was over. She felt almost fond of him now, almost in love with him.

"Ah Gerald," she laughed, caressively, teasingly, "Ah, what a fine game you played with the Professor's daughter—didn't you now?"

"What game?" he asked, looking round.

"*Isn't* she in love with you—oh *dear*, isn't she in love with you!" said Gudrun, smiling in her gayest, most attractive mood.

"I shouldn't think so," he said.

"'Shouldn't think so!'" she teased. "Why the poor girl is lying at this moment overwhelmed, dying with love for you. She thinks you're *wonderful*—oh marvellous, beyond what man has ever been.—*Really*, isn't it funny?"

"Why funny, what is funny?" he asked.

"Why to see you working it on her," she said, with a half reproach that confused the male conceit in him. "Really Gerald, the poor girl——!"

"I did nothing to her," he said.

"Oh, it was too shameful, the way you simply swept her off her feet."

"That was Schuhplatteln," he replied, with a bright grin.

"Ha—ha—ha!" laughed Gudrun.

Her mockery quivered through his muscles with curious re-echoes. When he slept he seemed to crouch down in the bed, lapped up in his own strength, that yet was hollow.

And Gudrun slept strongly, a victorious sleep. Suddenly, she was almost fiercely awake. The small timber room glowed with the dawn, that came upwards from the low window. She could see down the valley when she lifted her head: the snow with a pinkish, half-revealed magic, the fringe of pine-trees at the bottom of the slope. And one tiny figure moved over the vaguely-illumined space.

She glanced at his watch: it was seven o'clock. He was still completely asleep. And she was so hard awake, it was almost frightening—a hard, metallic wakefulness. She lay looking at him.

He slept in the subjection of his own health and defeat. She was overcome by a sincere regard for him. Till now, she was afraid before him. She lay and thought about him, what he was, what he represented in the world. A fine, independent will, he had. She thought of the revolution he had worked in the mines, in so short a time. She knew that, if he were confronted with any problem, any hard actual difficulty, he would overcome it. If he laid hold of any idea, he would carry it through. He had the faculty of making order out of confusion. Only let him grip hold of a situation, and he would bring to pass an inevitable conclusion.

For a few moments she was borne away on the wild wings of ambition. Gerald, with his force of will and his power for comprehending the actual world, should be set to solve the problems of the day, the problem of industrialism in the modern world. She knew he would, in the course of time, effect the changes he desired, he could re-organise the industrial system. She knew he could do it. As an instrument, in these things, he was marvellous, she had never seen any man with his potentiality. He was unaware of it, but she knew.

He only needed to be hitched on, he needed that his hand should be set to the task, because he was so unconscious. And this she could do. She would marry him, he would go into Parliament in the Conservative interest, he would clear up the great muddle of labour and industry. He was so superbly fearless, masterful, he knew that every problem could be worked out, in life as in geometry. And he would care neither about himself nor about anything but the pure working out of the problem. He was very pure, really.

Her heart beat fast, she flew away on wings of elation, imagining a future. He would be a Napoleon of peace, or a Bismarck—and she the woman behind him. She had read Bismarck's letters,* and had been deeply moved by them. And Gerald would be freer, more dauntless than Bismarck.

But even as she lay in fictitious transport, bathed in the strange, false sunshine of hope in life, something seemed to snap in her, and a terrible cynicism began to gain upon her, blowing in like a wind. Everything turned to irony with her: the last flavour of everything, was ironical. When she felt her pang of undeniable reality, this was when she knew the hard irony of hopes and ideas.

She lay and looked at him, as he slept. He was sheerly beautiful, he was a perfect instrument. To her mind, he was a pure, inhuman, almost superhuman instrument. His instrumentality appealed so strongly to her, she wished she were God, to use him as a tool.

And at the same instant, came the ironical question: "What for?" She thought of the colliers' wives, with their linoleum and their lace curtains and their little girls in high-laced boots. She thought of the wives and daughters of the pit-managers, their tennis-parties, and their terrible struggles to be superior each to the other, in the social scale. There was Shortlands with its meaningless distinction, the meaningless crowd of the Criches. There was London, the House of Commons, the extant social world. My God!

Young as she was, Gudrun had touched the whole pulse of social England, she had no ideals of rising in the world. She knew, with the perfect cynicism of cruel youth, that to rise in the world meant to have one outside show instead of another, the advance was like having a spurious half-crown instead of a spurious penny. The whole coinage of valuation was spurious. Yet of course, her cynicism knew well enough that, in a world where spurious coin was current, a bad sovereign was better than a bad farthing. But rich and poor, she despised both alike.

Already she mocked at herself for her dreams. They could be fulfilled easily enough. But she recognised too well, in her spirit, the mockery of her own impulses. What did she care, that Gerald had created a richly-paying industry out of an old worn-out concern? What did she care? The worn-out concern, and the rapid, splendidly-organised industry, they were alike indifferent to her, they were bad money.—Yet of course, she cared a great deal, outwardly—and outwardly was all that mattered, for inwardly was a bad joke.

Everything was intrinsically a piece of irony to her. She leaned over Gerald and said in her heart, with compassion:

"Oh, my dear, my dear, the game isn't worth even you. You are a fine thing really—why should you be used on such a poor show!"

Her heart was breaking with pity and grief for him. And at the same moment, a grimace came over her mouth, of mocking irony at her own unspoken tirade. Ah, what a farce it was! She thought of Parnell and Katherine O'Shea.* Parnell! After all, who can take the nationalisation of Ireland* seriously? Who can take political Ireland really seriously, whatever it does? And who can take political England seriously? Who can? Who can care a straw, really, how the old, patched-up Constitution is tinkered at any more? Who cares a button for our national ideals, any more than for our national bowler hat? Aha, it is all old hat, it is all old bowler hat?

That's all it is, Gerald, my young hero. At any rate we'll spare ourselves the nausea of stirring the old broth any more. You be beautiful, my Gerald, and reckless. There *are* perfect moments. Wake up, Gerald, wake up, convince me of the perfect moments, oh convince me, I need it.

He opened his eyes, and looked at her. She greeted him with a mocking, enigmatic smile in which was a poignant gaiety. Over his face went the reflection of the smile, he smiled too, purely unconsciously.

That filled her with extraordinary delight, to see the smile cross his face, reflected from her face. She remembered, that was how a baby smiled. It filled her with extraordinary radiant delight.

"You've done it," she said.

"What?" he asked, dazed.

"Convinced me."

And she bent down, kissing him passionately, passionately, so that he was bewildered. He did not ask her of what he had convinced her, though he meant to. He was glad she was kissing him. She seemed to be feeling for his very heart, to touch the quick of him. And he wanted her to touch the quick of his being, he wanted that most of all.

Outside, somebody was singing, in a manly, reckless, handsome voice:

> "Mach mir auf, mach mir auf, du Stolze,
> Mach mir ein Feuer von Holze
> Vom Regen bin ich nass
> Vom Regen bin ich nass—"*

Gudrun knew, that that song would sound through her eternity, sung in a manly, reckless, mocking voice. It marked one of her supreme moments, the supreme pangs of her nervous gratification. There it was, fixed in eternity for her.

The day came fine and bluish. There was a light wind blowing among the mountain-tops, keen as a rapier where it touched, carrying with it a fine dust of snow-powder. Gerald went out with the fine, blind face of a man who is in his state of fulfilment. Gudrun and he were in perfect static unity this morning, both unseeing and unwitting. They went out with a toboggan, leaving Ursula and Birkin to follow.

Gudrun was all scarlet and royal blue—a scarlet jersey and cap, and a royal blue skirt and stockings. She went gaily over the white snow, with Gerald beside her, in white and grey, pulling the little toboggan. They grew small in the distance of snow, climbing the steep slope.

For Gudrun herself, she seemed to pass altogether into the whiteness of the snow, she became a pure, thoughtless crystal. When she reached the top of the slope, in the wind, she looked round, and saw peak beyond peak of rock and snow, bluish, transcendent in heaven. And it seemed to her like a garden, with the peaks for pure flowers, and her heart gathering them. She had no separate consciousness for Gerald.

She held on to him as they went sheering down over the keen slope. She felt as if her senses were being whetted on some fine grindstone, that was keen as flame. The snow sprinted on either side, like sparks from a blade that is being sharpened, the whiteness round about ran swifter, swifter, in pure flame the white slope flew against her, and she fused like one molten, dancing globule, rushed through a white intensity. Then there was a great swerve at the bottom, when they swung as it were in a fall to earth, in the diminishing motion.

They came to rest. But when she rose to her feet, she could not stand. She gave a strange cry, turned and clung to him, sinking her face on his breast, fainting in him. Utter oblivion came over her, as she lay for a few moments abandoned against him.

"What is it?" he was saying. "Was it too much for you?"

But she heard nothing.

When she came to, she stood up and looked round, astonished. Her face was white, her eyes brilliant and large.

"What is it?" he repeated. "Did it upset you?"

She looked at him with her brilliant eyes, that seemed to have undergone some transfiguration, and she laughed, with a terrible merriment.

"No," she cried, with triumphant joy. "It was the complete moment of my life."

And she looked at him with her dazzling, overweening laughter, like one possessed. A fine blade seemed to enter his heart, but he did not care, or take any notice.

But they climbed up the slope again, and they flew down through the white flame again, splendidly, splendidly. Gudrun was laughing and flashing, powdered with snow-crystals, Gerald worked perfectly. He felt he could guide the toboggan to a hair's-breadth, almost he could make it pierce into the air and right into the very heart of the sky. It seemed to him the flying sledge was but his strength spread out, he had but to move his arms, the motion was his own. They explored the great slopes, to find another slide. He felt there must be something better than they had known. And he found what he desired, a perfect long, fierce sweep, sheering past the foot of a rock and into the trees at the base. It was dangerous, he knew. But then he knew also he could direct the sledge* between his fingers.

The first days passed in an ecstasy of physical motion, sleighing, ski-ing, skating, moving in an intensity of speed and white light that surpassed life itself, and carried the souls of the human beings beyond into an inhuman abstraction of velocity and weight and eternal, frozen snow.

Gerald's eyes became hard and strange, and as he went by on his skis he was more like some powerful, fateful sigh than a man, his muscles elastic in a perfect, soaring trajectory, his body projected in pure flight, mindless, soulless, whirling along one perfect line of force.

Luckily there came a day of snow, when they must all stay indoors: otherwise, Birkin said, they would all lose their faculties, and begin to utter themselves in cries and shrieks, like some strange, unknown species of snow-creatures.

It happened in the afternoon that Ursula sat in the Reunionsaal talking to Loerke. The latter had seemed unhappy lately. He was lively and full of mischievous humour, as usual. But Ursula had thought he was sulky about something. His partner, too, the big, fair, good-looking youth, was ill at ease, going about as if he belonged to nowhere, and was kept in some sort of subjection, against which he was rebelling.

Loerke had hardly talked to Gudrun. His associate, on the other hand, had paid her constantly a soft, over-deferential attention. Gudrun wanted to talk to Loerke. He was a sculptor, and she wanted to hear his view of his art. And his figure attracted her. There was the
5   look of a little wastrel about him, that intrigued her, and an old man's look, that interested her, and then, beside this, an uncanny single-ness, a quality of being by himself, not in contact with anybody else, that marked out an artist to her. He was a chatterer, a mag-pie, a maker of mischievous word-jokes, that were sometimes very clever,
10 but which often were not—And she could see in his brown, gnome's eyes, the black look of inorganic misery, which lay behind all his small buffoonery.

His figure interested her—the figure of a boy, almost of a street arab. He made no attempt to conceal it. He always wore a simple
15 loden suit, with knee breeches. His legs were thin, and he made no attempt to disguise the fact: which was of itself remarkable, in a German. And he never ingratiated himself anywhere, not in the slightest, but kept to himself, for all his apparent playfulness.

Leitner, his companion, was a great sportsman, very handsome
20 with his big limbs and his blue eyes. Loerke would go tobogganing, or ski-ing, or skating, in little snatches, but he was indifferent. And his fine, thin nostrils, the nostrils of a pure-bred street arab, would quiver with contempt at Leitner's splothering gymnastic displays. It was evident that the two men, who had travelled and lived together in
25 the last degree of intimacy,* had now reached the stage of loathing. Leitner hated Loerke with an injured, writhing, impotent hatred, and Loerke treated Leitner with a fine-quivering contempt and sarcasm. Soon the two would have to go apart.

Already they were rarely together. Leitner ran attaching himself to
30 somebody or other, always deferring, Loerke was a good deal alone. Out of doors he wore a Westphalian cap, a close brown-velvet head with big brown-velvet flaps down over his ears,* so that he looked like a lop-eared rabbit, or a troll. His face was brown-red, with a dry, bright skin, that seemed to crinkle with his mobile expressions. His
35 eyes were arresting—brown, full, like a rabbit's, or like a troll's, or like the eyes of a lost being, having a strange, dumb, depraved look of knowledge, and a quick spark of uncanny fire. Whenever Gudrun had tried to talk to him he had shied away unresponsive, looking at her with his watchful dark eyes, but entering into no relation with
40 her. He had made her feel that her slow French, and her slower

German, were hateful to him. As for his own inadequate English, he was much too awkward to try it at all. But he understood a good deal of what was said, nevertheless. And Gudrun, piqued, left him alone.

This afternoon, however, she came into the lounge as he was talking to Ursula. His fine, black hair somehow reminded her of a bat, thin as it was on his full, sensitive-looking head, and worn away at the temples, he sat hunched up, as if his spirit were bat-like. And Gudrun could see he was making some slow confidence to Ursula, unwilling, a slow, grudging, scanty self-revelation. She went and sat by her sister.

He looked at her, then looked away again, as if he took no notice of her. But as a matter of fact, she interested him deeply.

"Isn't it interesting, Prune," said Ursula, turning to her sister, "Herr Loerke is doing a great frieze for a factory in Cologne,* for the outside, the street."

She looked at him, at his thin, brown, nervous hands, that were prehensile, and somehow like talons, like 'griffes,' inhuman.

"What in?" she asked.

"*Aus was?*" repeated Ursula.

"*Granit,*"* he replied.

It had become immediately a laconic series of question and answer between fellow craftsmen.

"What is the relief?" asked Gudrun.

"Alto rilievo."*

"And at what height?"

It was very interesting to Gudrun, to think of his making the great granite frieze for a great granite factory in Cologne. She got from him some notion of the design. It was a representation of a fair, with peasants and artizans in an orgy of enjoyment, drunk and absurd in their modern dress, whirling ridiculously in roundabouts, gaping at shows, kissing and staggering and rolling in knots, swinging in swing-boats and firing down shooting galleries, a frenzy of chaotic motion.

There was a swift discussion of technicalities. Gudrun was very much impressed.

"But how wonderful, to have such a factory!" cried Ursula. "Is the whole building fine?"

"Oh yes," he replied. "The frieze is part of the whole architecture. Yes, it is a colossal thing."

Then he seemed to stiffen, shrugged his shoulders, and went on:

"Sculpture and architecture must go together. The day for irrelevant statues, as for wall pictures, is over. As a matter of fact sculpture is always part of an architectural conception.* And since churches are all museum stuff, since industry is our business, now,

5 then let us make our places of industry our art—our factory-area our Parthenon—ecco!"*

Ursula pondered.

"I suppose," she said, "there is no *need* for our great works to be so hideous."

10 Instantly he broke into motion.

"There you are!" he cried, "there you are! There is not only *no need* for our places of work to be ugly, but their ugliness ruins the work, in the end. Men will not go on submitting to such intolerable ugliness. In the end it will hurt too much, and they will wither

15 because of it. And this will wither the *work* as well. They will think the work itself is ugly: the machines, the very act of labour. Whereas machinery and the acts of labour are extremely, maddeningly beautiful.* But this will be the end of our civilisation, when people will not work because work has become so intolerable to their

20 senses, it nauseates them too much, they would rather starve. *Then* we shall see the hammer used only for smashing, then we shall see it.—Yet here we are—we have the opportunity to make beautiful factories, beautiful machine-houses—we have the opportunity—"

Gudrun could only partly understand. She could have cried with

25 vexation.

"What does he say?" she asked Ursula. And Ursula translated, stammering and brief. Loerke watched Gudrun's face, to see her judgment.

"And do you think then," said Gudrun, "that art should serve

30 industry?"

"Art should *interpret* industry, as art once interpreted religion," he said.

"But does your fair interpret industry?" she asked him.

"Certainly. What is man doing, when he is at a fair like this? He is

35 fulfilling the counterpart of labour—the machine works him, instead of he the machine. He enjoys the mechanical motion, in his own body."*

"But is there nothing but work—mechanical work?" said Gudrun.

"Nothing but work!" he repeated, leaning forward, his eyes two

40 darknesses, with needle-points of light. "No, it is nothing but this,

serving a machine, or enjoying the motion of a machine—motion, that is all.—You have never worked for hunger, or you would know what God governs us."

Gudrun quivered and flushed. For some reason she was almost in tears.

"No, I have not worked for hunger," she replied. "But I have worked?"

"Travaillé—lavorato?" he cried. "E che lavoro—che lavoro? Quel travail est-ce que vous avez fait?"*

He broke into a mixture of Italian and French, instinctively using a foreign language when he spoke to her.

"You have never worked as the world works," he said to her, with sarcasm.

"Yes," she said, "I have. And I do—I work now for my daily bread."*

He paused, looked at her steadily, then dropped the subject entirely. She seemed to him to be trifling.

"But have *you* ever worked as the world works?" Ursula asked him.

He looked at her untrustful.

"Yes," he replied, with a surly bark. "I have known what it was to lie in bed for three days, because I had nothing to eat."

Gudrun was looking at him with large, grave eyes, that seemed to draw the confession from him as the marrow from his bones. All his nature held him back from confessing. And yet her large, grave eyes upon him seemed to open some valve in his veins, and involuntarily he was telling.

"My father was a man who did not like work, and we had no mother. We lived in Austria, Polish Austria.* How did we live? Ha!—somehow! Mostly in a room with three other families—one set in each corner—and the W.C. in the middle of the room—a pan with a plank on it—ha! I had two brothers and a sister—and there might be a woman with my father. He was a free being, in his way—would fight with any man in the town—a garrison town—and was a little man too. But he wouldn't work for anybody—set his heart against it, and wouldn't."

"And how did you live then?" asked Ursula.

He looked at her—then, suddenly, at Gudrun.

"Do you understand?" he asked.

"Enough," she replied.

Their eyes met for a moment. Then he looked away. He would say
no more.

"And how did you become a sculptor?" asked Ursula.

"How did I become a sculptor—" he paused. "Dunque—"* he
resumed, in a changed manner, and beginning to speak French—"I
became old enough—I used to steal from the market-place. Later, I
went to work—I imprinted the stamp on clay bottles, before they
were baked. It was an earthenware-bottle factory. There I began
making models. One day, I had had enough. I lay in the sun and did
not go to work. Then I walked to Munich—then I walked to
Italy—begging, begging everything.

"The Italians were very good to me—they were good and
honorable to me. From Bozen to Rome, almost every night, I had a
meal and a bed, perhaps of straw, with some peasant. I love the
Italian people, with all my heart.

"Dunque, adesso—maintenant*—I earn a thousand pounds in a
year, or I earn two thousand—."

He looked down at the ground, his voice tailing off into silence.

Gudrun looked at his fine, thin, shiny skin, reddish-brown from
the sun, drawn tight over his full temples; and at his thin hair—, and
at the thick, coarse, brush-like moustache, cut short above his
mobile, rather shapeless mouth.

"How old are you?" she asked.

He looked up at her with his full, elvin eyes, startled.

"*Wie alt?*"* he repeated. And he hesitated. It was evidently one of
his reticencies.

"How old are *you?*" he replied, without answering.

"I am twenty-six," she answered.

"Twenty-six," he repeated, looking into her eyes. He paused.
Then he said:

"Und Ihr Herr Gemahl, wie alt ist er?"*

"Who?" asked Gudrun.

"Your husband," said Ursula, with a certain irony.

"I haven't got a husband," said Gudrun in English. In German
she answered.

"He is thirty-one."

But Loerke was watching closely, with his uncanny, full, suspicious eyes. Something in Gudrun seemed to accord with him. He
was really like one of the "little people" who have no soul, who has
found his mate in a human being. But he suffered in his discovery.

She too was fascinated by him, fascinated, as if some strange creature, a rabbit or a bat or a brown seal, had begun to talk to her.* But also, she knew what he was unconscious of, his tremendous power of understanding, of apprehending her living motion. He did not know his own power. He did not know how, with his full, submerged, watchful eyes, he could look into her and see her, what she was, see her secrets. He would only want her to be herself.—He knew her verily, with a subconscious, sinister knowledge, devoid of illusions and hopes.

To Gudrun, there was in Loerke the rock-bottom of all life. Everybody else had their illusion, must have their illusion, their before and after. But he, with a perfect stoicism, did without any before and after, dispensed with all illusion. He did not deceive himself, in the last issue. In the last issue he cared about nothing, he was troubled about nothing, he made not the slightest attempt to be at one with anything. He existed a pure, unconnected will, stoical and momentaneous. There was only his work.

It was curious too how his poverty, the degradation of his earlier life, attracted her. There was something insipid and tasteless to her, in the idea of a gentleman, a man who had gone the usual course through school and university. A certain violent sympathy, however, came up in her for this mud-child. He seemed to be the very stuff of the underworld of life. There was no going beyond him.

Ursula too was attracted by Loerke. In both sisters he commanded a certain homage. But there were moments when to Ursula he seemed indescribably inferior, false, a vulgarism.

Both Birkin and Gerald disliked him, Gerald ignoring him with some contempt, Birkin exasperated.

"What do the women find so impressive in that little brat?" Gerald asked.

"God above knows," replied Birkin; "unless it's some sort of appeal he makes to them, which flatters them and has such a power over them."

Gerald looked up in surprise.

"*Does* he make an appeal to them?" he asked.

"Oh yes," replied Birkin. "He is the perfectly subjected being, existing almost like a criminal. And the women rush towards that, like a current of air towards a vacuum."

"Funny they should rush to that," said Gerald.

"Makes one mad, too," said Birkin. "But he has the fascination of pity and repulsion for them, a little obscene monster of the darkness that he is."

Gerald stood still, suspended in thought.

"What *do* women want, at the bottom?" he asked.

Birkin shrugged his shoulders.

"God knows," he said. "Some satisfaction in basic repulsion, it seems to me. They seem to creep down some ghastly tunnel of darkness, and will never be satisfied till they've come to the end."

Gerald looked out into the mist of fine snow that was blowing by. Everywhere was blind today, horribly blind.

"And what *is* the end?" he asked.

Birkin shook his head.

"I've not got there yet, so I don't know. Ask Loerke, he's pretty near. He is a good many stages further than either you or I can go."

"Yes, but stages further in what?" cried Gerald, irritated.

Birkin sighed, and gathered his brows into a knot of anger.

"Stages further in social hatred," he said. "He lives like a rat, in the river of corruption,* just where it falls over into the bottomless pit. He's further on than we are. He hates the ideal more acutely. He *hates* the ideal utterly, yet it still dominates him. I expect he is a Jew—or part Jewish."*

"Probably," said Gerald.

"He is a gnawing little negation, gnawing at the roots of life."

"But why does anybody care about him?" cried Gerald.

"Because they hate the ideal also, in their souls. They want to explore the sewers, and he's the wizard rat that swims ahead."

Still Gerald stood and stared at the blind haze of snow outside.

"I don't understand your terms, really," he said, in a flat, doomed voice. "But it sounds a rum sort of desire."

"I suppose we want the same," said Birkin. "Only we want to take a quick jump downwards, in a sort of ecstasy—and he ebbs with the stream, the sewer stream."

Meanwhile Gudrun and Ursula waited for the next opportunity to talk to Loerke. It was no use beginning when the men were there. Then they could get into no touch with the isolated little sculptor. He had to be alone with them. And he preferred Ursula to be there, as a sort of transmitter to Gudrun.

"Do you do nothing but architectural sculpture?" Gudrun asked him one evening.

"Not now," he replied. "I have done all sorts—except portraits—I never did portraits. But other things—"

"What kind of thing?" asked Gudrun.

He paused a moment, then rose, and went out of the room. He returned almost immediately with a little roll of paper, which he handed to her. She unrolled it. It was a photogravure reproduction of a statuette, signed F. Loerke.

"That is quite an early thing—*not* mechanical," he said, "more popular."

The statuette was of a naked girl, small, finely made, sitting on a great naked horse. The girl was young and tender, a mere bud. She was sitting sideways on the horse, her face in her hands, as if in shame and grief, in a little abandon. Her hair, which was short and must be flaxen, fell forward, divided, half covering her hands.

Her limbs were young and tender. Her legs, scarcely formed yet, the legs of a maiden just passing towards cruel womanhood, dangled childishly over the side of the powerful horse, pathetically, the small feet folded one over the other, as if to hide. But there was no hiding. There she was exposed naked on the naked flank of the horse.

The horse stood stock still, stretched in a kind of start. It was a massive, magnificent stallion, rigid with pent up power. Its neck was arched and terrible, like a sickle, its flanks were pressed back, rigid with power.

Gudrun went pale, and a darkness came over her eyes, like shame, she looked up with a certain supplication, almost slave-like. He glanced at her, and jerked his head a little.

"How big is it?" she asked, in a toneless voice, persisting in appearing casual and unaffected.

"How big?" he replied, glancing again at her. "Without pedestal—so high—" he measured with his hand—"with pedestal, so—"

He looked at her steadily. There was a little brusque, turgid contempt for her in his swift gesture, and she seemed to cringe a little.

"And what is it done in?" she asked, throwing back her head and looking at him with affected coldness.

He still gazed at her steadily, and his dominance was not shaken. "Bronze—green bronze."

"Green bronze!" repeated Gudrun, coldly accepting his challenge. She was thinking of the slender, immature, tender limbs of the girl, smooth and cold in green bronze.

"Yes, beautiful," she murmured, looking up at him with a certain dark homage.

He closed his eyes and looked aside, triumphant.

"Why," said Ursula, "did you make the horse so stiff? It is as stiff as a block."

"Stiff!" he repeated, in arms at once.

5 "Yes. *Look* how stock and stupid and brutal it is. Horses are sensitive, quite delicate and sensitive, really."

He raised his shoulders, spread his hands in a shrug of slow indifference, as much as to inform her she was an amateur and an impertinent nobody.

10 "Wissen Sie," he said, with an insulting patience and condescension in his voice, "that horse is a certain *form*, part of a whole form. It is part of a work of art, a piece of form. It is not a picture of a friendly horse to which you give a lump of sugar, do you see—it is part of a work of art, it has no relation to anything outside that work of art."*

15 Ursula, angry at being treated quite so insultingly *de haut en bas*,* from the height of esoteric art to the depth of general exoteric amateurism, replied hotly, flushing and lifting her face:

"But it *is* a picture of a horse, nevertheless."

He lifted his shoulders in another shrug.

20 "As you like—it is not the picture of a cow, certainly."

Here Gudrun broke in, flushed and brilliant, anxious to avoid any more of this, any more of Ursula's foolish persistence in giving herself away.

"What do you mean by 'it is a picture of a horse'?" she cried at her 25 sister. "What do you mean by a horse? You mean an idea you have in *your* head, and which you want to see represented. This is another idea altogether, quite another idea. Call it a horse if you like, or say it is not a horse. I have just as much right to say that *your* horse isn't a horse, that it is a falsity of your own make-up."

30 Ursula wavered, baffled. Then her words came.

"But why does he have this idea of a horse?" she said. "I know it is his idea. I know it is a picture of himself, really—"

Loerke snorted with rage.

"A picture of myself!" he repeated, in derision. "Wissen Sie, 35 gnädige Frau, that is a Kunstwerk, a work of art. It is a work of art, it is a picture of nothing, of absolutely nothing. It has nothing to do with anything but itself, it has no relation with the everyday world of this and the other, there is no connection between them, absolutely none, they are two different and distinct planes of existence, and to 40 translate one into the other is worse than foolish, it is a darkening of all counsel, a making confusion everywhere. Do you see, you *must not* confuse the relative world of action, with the absolute world of art. That you *must not do*."

"That is quite true," cried Gudrun, let loose in a sort of rhapsody. "The two things are quite and permanently apart, they have nothing to do with one another. *I* and my art, they have *nothing* to do with each other. My art stands in another world,* I am in this world."

Her face was flushed and transfigured. Loerke, who was sitting with his head ducked, like some creature at bay, looked up at her swiftly, almost furtively, and murmured:

"Ja—so ist es, so ist es."*

Ursula was silent after this outburst. She was furious. She wanted to poke a hole into them both.

"It isn't a word of it true, of all this harangue you have made me," she replied flatly. "The horse is a picture of your own stock stupid brutality, and the girl was a girl you loved and tortured and then ignored."

He looked up at her with a small smile of contempt in his eyes. He would not trouble to answer this last charge. Gudrun too was silent in exasperated contempt. Ursula *was* such an insufferable outsider, rushing in where angels would fear to tread. But there—fools must be suffered, if not gladly.*

But Ursula was persistent too.

"As for your world of art and your world of reality," she replied; "you have to separate the two, because you can't bear to know what you are. You can't bear to realise what a stock, stiff, hide-bound brutality you *are* really, so you say 'it's the world of art.' The world of art is only the truth about the real world, that's all—but you are too far gone to see it."

She was white and trembling, intent. Gudrun and Loerke sat in stiff dislike of her. Gerald too, who had come up in the beginning of the speech, stood looking at her in complete disapproval and opposition. He felt she was undignified, she put a sort of vulgarity over the esotericism which gave man his last distinction. He joined his forces with the other two. They all three wanted her to go away. But she sat on in silence, her soul weeping, throbbing violently, her fingers twisting her handkerchief.

The others maintained a dead silence, letting the display of Ursula's obtrusiveness pass by. Then Gudrun asked, in a voice that was quite cool and casual, as if resuming a casual conversation:

"Was the girl a model?"

"Nein, sie war kein Modell. Sie war eine kleine Malschülerin."*

"An art-student!" replied Gudrun.

And how the situation revealed itself to her! She saw the girl
5   art-student, unformed and of pernicious recklessness, too young,
her straight flaxen hair cut short, hanging just into her neck, curving
inwards slightly, because it was rather thick; and Loerke, the
well-known master-sculptor, and the girl, probably well-brought-up
and of good family, thinking herself so great to be his mistress. Oh
10 how well she knew the common callousness of it all. Dresden, Paris,
or London, what did it matter? She knew it.

"Where is she now?" Ursula asked.

Loerke raised his shoulders, to convey his complete ignorance and
indifference.

15   "That is already six years ago," he said; "she will be twenty-three
years old, no more good."

Gerald had picked up the picture and was looking at it. It attracted
him also. He saw on the pedestal, that the piece was called "Lady
Godiva."

20   "But this isn't Lady Godiva," he said, smiling good-humouredly.
"She was the middle-aged wife of some Earl or other,* who covered
herself with her long hair."

"A la Maud Allan,"* said Gudrun, with a mocking grimace.

"Why Maud Allan?" he replied. "Isn't it so?—I always thought the
25 legend was that."

"Yes, Gerald dear, I'm quite *sure* you've got the legend perfectly."
She was laughing at him, with a little, mock-caressive contempt.

"To be sure, I'd rather see the woman than the hair," he laughed
in return.

30   "Wouldn't you just!" mocked Gudrun.

Ursula rose and went away, leaving the three together.

Gudrun took the picture again from Gerald, and sat looking at it
closely.

"Of course," she said, turning to tease Loerke now, "you
35 *understood* your little Malschülerin."

He raised his eyebrows and his shoulders in a complacent shrug.

"The little* girl?" asked Gerald, pointing to the figure. Gudrun
was sitting with the picture in her lap. She looked up at Gerald, full
into his eyes, so that he seemed to be blinded.

40   "*Didn't* he understand her!" she said to Gerald, in a slightly

mocking, humourous playfulness. "You've only to look at the feet—*aren't* they darling, so pretty and tender—oh, they're really wonderful, they are really—"

She lifted her eyes slowly, with a hot, flaming look into Loerke's eyes. His soul was filled with her burning recognition, he seemed to grow more uppish and lordly.

Gerald looked at the small, sculptured feet. They were turned together, half covering each other in pathetic shyness and fear. He looked at them a long time, fascinated. Then, in some pain, he put the picture away from him. He felt full of barrenness.

"What was her name?" Gudrun asked Loerke.

"Annette von Weck," Loerke replied, reminiscent. "Ja, sie war hübsch.* She was pretty—but she was tiresome. She was a nuisance—not for a minute would she keep still—not until I'd slapped her hard and made her cry—then she'd sit for five minutes."

He was thinking over the work, his work, the all-important to him.

"Did you really slap her?" asked Gudrun, coolly. He glanced back at her, reading her challenge.

"Yes, I did," he said, nonchalant, "harder than I have ever beat anything in my life.—I had to, I had to.—It was the only way I got the work done."

Gudrun watched him with large, dark-filled eyes, for some moments. She seemed to be considering his very soul. Then she looked down, in silence.

"Why did you have such a young Godiva then?" asked Gerald. "She is so small, besides, on the horse—not big enough for it—such a child."

A queer spasm went over Loerke's face.

"Yes," he said, "I don't like them any bigger, any older. Then they are beautiful, at sixteen, seventeen, eighteen—after that, they are no use to me."

There was a moment's pause.

"Why not?" asked Gerald.

Loerke shrugged his shoulders.

"I don't find them interesting—or beautiful—they are no good to me, for my work."

"Do you mean to say a woman isn't beautiful after she is twenty?" asked Gerald.

"For me, no. Before twenty, she is small and fresh and tender and slight. After that—let her be what she likes, she has nothing for me. The Venus of Milo* is a bourgeoise—so are they all."

"And you don't care for women at all after twenty?" asked Gerald.

"They are no good to me, they are of no use in my art," Loerke
5 repeated impatiently. "I don't find them beautiful."

"You are an epicure," said Gerald, with a slight sarcastic laugh.

"And what about men?" asked Gudrun suddenly.

"Yes, they are good at all ages," replied Loerke. "A man should be big and powerful—whether he is old or young is of no account, so he
10 has the size, something of massiveness and stupid form."*

Ursula went out alone into the world of pure, new snow. But the dazzling whiteness seemed to beat upon her till it hurt her, she felt the cold was slowly strangling her soul. Her head felt dazed and numb.

15 Suddenly, she wanted to go away. It occurred to her, like a miracle, that she might go away into another world. She had felt so doomed up here in the eternal snow, as if there were no beyond.

Now suddenly, as by a miracle, she remembered that away beyond, below her, lay the dark fruitful earth, that towards the south
20 there were stretches of land dark with orange trees and cypress, grey with olives, that ilex trees lifted wonderful plumy tufts in shadow against a blue sky. Miracle of miracles!—this utterly silent, frozen world of the mountain-tops was not universal! One might leave it and have done with it. One might go away.

25 She wanted to realise the miracle at once. She wanted at this instant to have done with the snow-world, the terrible static, ice-built mountain-tops. She wanted to see the dark earth, to smell its earthy fecundity, to see the patient wintry vegetation, to feel the sunshine touch a response in the buds.

30 She went back gladly to the house, full of hope. Birkin was reading, lying in bed.

"Rupert," she said, bursting in on him, "I want to go away."

He looked up at her slowly.

"Do you?" he replied mildly.

35 She sat by him and put her arms round his neck. It surprised her that he was so little surprised.

"Don't *you?*" she asked, troubled.

"I hadn't thought about it," he said. "But I'm sure I do."

She sat up, suddenly erect.

40 "I hate it," she said. "I hate this snow, and the unnaturalness of it,

the unnatural light it throws on everybody, the ghastly glamour, the unnatural feelings it makes everybody have."

He lay still, and laughed, meditating.

"Well," he said, "we can *go* away—we can go tomorrow. We'll go tomorrow to Verona, and find Romeo and Juliet, and sit in the amphitheatre*—shall we?"

Suddenly she hid her face against his shoulder with perplexity and shyness. He lay so untrammelled.

"Yes," she said softly, filled with relief. She felt her soul had new wings, now he was so uncaring. "I shall love to be Romeo and Juliet," she said.—"My love!"

"Though a fearfully cold wind blows in Verona," he said, "from out of the Alps. We shall have the smell of the snow in our noses."

She sat up and looked at him.

"Are you glad to go?" she asked, troubled. His eyes were inscrutable and laughing. She hid her face against his neck, clinging close to him, pleading:

"Don't laugh at me—don't laugh at me."

"Why—how's that?" he laughed, putting his arms round her.

"Because I don't want to be laughed at," she whispered.

He laughed more, as he kissed her delicate, finely perfumed hair.

"Do you love me?" she whispered, in wild seriousness.

"Yes," he answered, laughing.

Suddenly she lifted her mouth to be kissed. Her lips were taut and quivering and strenuous, his were soft, deep and delicate. He waited a few moments in the kiss. Then a shade of sadness went over his soul.

"Your mouth is so hard," he said, in faint reproach.

"And yours is so soft and nice," she said gladly.

"But why do you always grip your lips?" he asked, regretful.

"Never mind," she said swiftly. "It is my way."

She knew he loved her; she was sure of him. Yet she could not let go a certain hold over herself, she could not bear him to question her. She gave herself up in delight to being loved by him. She knew that, in spite of his joy when she abandoned herself, he was a little bit saddened too. She could give herself up to his activity. But she could not be herself, she *dared* not come forth quite nakedly to his nakedness, abandoning all adjustment, lapsing in pure faith with him. She abandoned herself to *him*, or she took hold of him and gathered her joy of him. And she enjoyed him fully. But they were never *quite* together, at the same moment, one was always a little left out. Nevertheless she was glad in hope, glorious and free, full of life and liberty. And he was still and soft and patient, for the time.

They made their preparations to leave the next day. First they went to Gudrun's room, where she and Gerald were just dressed ready for the evening indoors.

"Prune," said Ursula. "I think we shall go away tomorrow. I can't stand the snow any more. It hurts my skin and my soul."

"Does it really hurt your soul, Ursula?" asked Gudrun in some surprise. "I can quite believe it hurts your skin—it is *terrible*. But I thought it was *admirable* for the soul."

"No, not for mine. It just injures it," said Ursula.

"Really!" cried Gudrun.

There was a silence in the room. And Ursula and Birkin could feel that Gudrun and Gerald were relieved by their going.

"You will go south?" said Gerald, a little ring of uneasiness in his voice.

"Yes," said Birkin, turning away.

There was a queer, indefinable hostility between the two men, lately. Birkin was on the whole dim and indifferent, drifting along in a dim, easy flow, unnoticing and patient, since he came abroad, whilst Gerald, on the other hand, was intense and gripped into white light, agonistes.* The two men revoked one another.

Gerald and Gudrun were very kind to the two who were departing, solicitous for their welfare as if they were two children. Gudrun came to Ursula's bedroom with three pairs of the coloured stockings for which she was notorious, and she threw them on the bed. But these were thick silk stockings, vermilion, cornflower blue, and grey, bought in Paris. The grey ones were knitted, seamless and heavy. Ursula was in raptures. She knew Gudrun must be feeling *very* loving, to give away such treasures.

"I can't take them from you Prune," she cried. "I can't possibly deprive you of them—the jewels."

"*Aren't* they jewels!" cried Gudrun, eying her gifts with an envious eye. "*Aren't* they real lambs!"

"Yes, you *must* keep them," said Ursula.

"I don't *want* them, I've got three more pairs. I *want* you to keep them—I want you to have them—they're yours, there—."

And with trembling, excited hands she put the coveted stockings under Ursula's pillow.

"One gets the greatest joy of all out of really lovely stockings," said Ursula.

"One does," replied Gudrun; "the greatest joy of all."

And she sat down in the chair. It was evident she had come for a last talk. Ursula, not knowing what she wanted, waited in silence.

"Do you *feel*, Ursula," Gudrun began, rather sceptically, "that 'you are going away for ever, never to return—'* sort of thing?"

"Oh, we shall come back," said Ursula. "It isn't a question of train-journeys."

"Yes, I know. But spiritually, so to speak, you are going away from us all?"

Ursula quivered.

"I don't know a bit what is going to happen," she said. "I only know we are going somewhere."

Gudrun waited.

"And you are glad?" she asked.

Ursula meditated for a moment.

"I believe I am *very* glad," she replied.

But Gudrun read the unconscious brightness on her sister's face, rather than the uncertain tones of her speech.

"But don't you think you'll *want* the old connection with the world—Father and the rest of us, and all that it means, England and the world of thought—don't you think you'll *need* that, really to make a world?"

Ursula was silent, trying to imagine.

"I think," she said at length, involuntarily, "that Rupert is right—one wants a new space to be in, and one falls away from the old."

Gudrun watched her sister with impassive face and steady eyes.

"One wants a new space to be in, I quite agree," she said. "But *I* think that a new world is a development from this world, and that to isolate oneself with one other person, isn't to find a new world at all, but only to secure oneself in one's illusions."

Ursula looked out of the window. In her soul she began to wrestle, and she was frightened. She was always frightened of words, because she knew that mere word-force could always make her believe what she did not believe.

"Perhaps," she said, full of mistrust, of herself and everybody. "But," she added, "I do think that one can't have anything new whilst one cares for the old—do you know what I mean?—even

fighting the old is belonging to it.—I know, one is tempted to stop
with the world, just to fight it.—But then it isn't worth it."

Gudrun considered herself.

"Yes," she said. "In a way, one is of the world if one lives in it. But
5 isn't it really an illusion, to think you can get out of it? After all, a
cottage in the Abruzzi, or wherever it may be, isn't a new world.—
No, the only thing to do with the world, is to see it through."

Ursula looked away. She was so frightened of argument.

"But there *can* be something else, can't there?" she said. "One can
10 see it through in one's soul, long enough before it sees itself through
in actuality. And then, when one has seen in one's soul, one is
something else."

"*Can* one see it through in one's soul?" asked Gudrun. "If you
mean that you can see to the end of what will happen, I don't
15 agree.—I really can't agree.—And anyhow, you can't suddenly fly off
on to a new planet, because you think you can see to the end of *this*."

Ursula suddenly straightened herself.

"Yes," she said, "yes—one knows. One has no more connections
here. One has a sort of other self, that belongs to a new planet, not to
20 this.—You've got to hop off."

Gudrun reflected for a few moments. Then a smile of ridicule,
almost of contempt, came over her face.

"And what will happen when you find yourself in space?" she
cried in derision. "After all, the great ideas of the world are the same
25 there. You above everybody can't get away from the fact that love, for
instance, is the supreme thing, in space as well as on earth."

"No," said Ursula, "it isn't. Love is too human and little. I believe
in something inhuman, of which love is only a little part. I believe
what we must fulfil comes out of the Unknown to us, and it is
30 something infinitely more than love. It isn't so merely *human*."

Gudrun looked at Ursula with steady, balancing eyes. She
admired and despised her sister so much, both. Then suddenly she
averted her face, saying coldly, uglily:

"Well, I've got no further than love, yet."

35 Over Ursula's mind flashed the thought: "Because you never *have*
loved, you can't get beyond it."

Gudrun rose, came over to Ursula and put her arm round her
neck.

"Go and find your new world, dear," she said, her voice clanging
40 with false benignity. "After all, the happiest voyage is the quest of
Rupert's Blessed Isles."*

Her arm rested round Ursula's neck, her fingers on Ursula's cheek, for a few moments. Ursula was supremely uncomfortable meanwhile. There was an insult in Gudrun's protective patronage that was really too hurting. Feeling her sister's resistance, Gudrun drew awkwardly away, turned over the pillow and disclosed the stockings again.

"Ha—ha!" she laughed, rather hollowly. "How we do talk indeed—new worlds and old—!"

And they passed to the familiar, worldly subjects.

Gerald and Birkin had walked on ahead, waiting for the sledge to overtake them, conveying the departing guests.

"How much longer will you stay here?" asked Birkin, glancing up at Gerald's very red, almost blank face.

"Oh I can't say," Gerald replied. "Till we get tired of it."

"You're not afraid of the snow melting first?" asked Birkin. Gerald laughed.

"Does it melt?" he said.

"Things are all right with you then?" said Birkin.

Gerald screwed up his eyes a little.

"All right?" he said. "I never know what those common words mean. All right and all wrong, don't they become synonymous, somewhere?"

"Yes, I suppose.—How about going back?" asked Birkin.

"Oh, I don't know. We may never get back. I don't look before and after," said Gerald.

"*Nor* pine for what is not,"* said Birkin.

Gerald looked into the distance, with the small-pupilled, abstract eyes of a hawk.

"No. There's something final about this. And Gudrun seems like the end, to me. I don't know—but she seems so soft, her skin like silk, her arms heavy and soft. And it withers my consciousness, somehow, it burns the pith of my mind." He went on a few paces, staring ahead, his eyes fixed, looking like a mask used in ghastly religions of the barbarians. "It blasts your soul's eye," he said, "and leaves you sightless. Yet you *want* to be sightless, you *want* to be blasted, you don't want it any different."

He was speaking as if in a trance, verbal and blank. Then suddenly he braced himself up with a kind of rhapsody, and looked at Birkin with vindictive, cowed eyes, saying:

"Do you know what it is to suffer when you are with a woman? She's so beautiful, so perfect, you find her *so good*, it tears you like

a silk, and every stroke and bit cuts hot—ha, that perfection, when you blast yourself, you blast yourself!—And then—" he stopped on the snow and suddenly opened his clenched hands—"it's nothing—your brain might have gone charred as rags—and"—he
5 looked round into the air with a queer histrionic movement—"it's blasting—you understand what I mean—it is a great experience, something final—and then—you're shrivelled as if struck by electricity."

He walked on in silence. It seemed like bragging, but like a man in
10 extremity bragging truthfully.

"Of course," he resumed, "I wouldn't *not* have had it: it's a complete experience. And she's a wonderful woman. But—how I hate her somewhere!—It's curious—"

Birkin looked at him, at his strange, scarcely conscious face.
15 Gerald seemed blank before his own words.

"But you've had enough now?" said Birkin. "You have had your experience. Why work on an old wound?"

"Oh," said Gerald, "I don't know. It's not finished—"

And the two walked on.

20 "I've loved you, as well as Gudrun, don't forget," said Birkin bitterly. Gerald looked at him strangely, abstractedly.

"Have you?" he said, with icy scepticism. "Or do you think you have?" He was hardly responsible for what he said.

The sledge came. Gudrun dismounted and they all made their
25 farewells. They wanted to go apart, all of them. Birkin took his place, and the sledge drove away leaving Gudrun and Gerald standing on the snow, waving. Something froze Birkin's heart, seeing them standing there in the isolation of the snow, growing smaller and more isolated.

Chapter XXXI

Snowed Up

When Ursula and Birkin were gone, Gudrun felt herself free in her contest with Gerald. As they grew more used to each other, he seemed to press upon her more and more. At first she could manage him, so that her own will was always left free. But very soon, he began to ignore her female tactics, he dropped his respect for her whims and her privacies, he began to exert his own will, blindly, without submitting to hers.

Already a vital conflict had set in, which frightened them both. But he was alone, whilst already she had begun to cast round for external resource.

When Ursula had gone, Gudrun felt her own existence had become stark and elemental. She went and crouched alone in her bedroom, looking out of the window at the big, flashing stars. In front was the faint shadow of the mountain-knot. That was the pivot. She felt strange and inevitable, as if she were centred upon the pivot of all existence, there was no further reality.

Presently Gerald opened the door. She knew he would not be long before he came. She was rarely alone now, he pressed upon her like a frost, deadening her.

"Are you alone in the dark?" he said. And she could tell by his tone he resented it, he resented the isolation she had drawn round herself. Yet, feeling static and inevitable, she was kind towards him.

"Would you like to light the candle?" she asked.

He did not answer, but came and stood behind her, in the darkness.

"Look," she said, "at that lovely star up there. Do you know its name?"

He crouched beside her, to look through the low window.

"No," he said. "It is very fine."

"*Isn't* it beautiful? Do you notice how it darts different coloured fires—it flashes really superbly—"

They remained in silence. With a mute, heavy gesture she put her hand on his knee, and took his hand.

"Are you regretting Ursula?" he asked.

"No, not at all," she said. Then, in a slow mood, she asked:

"How much do you love me?"

He stiffened himself further against her.

"How much do you think I do?" he asked.

"I don't know," she replied.

5   "But what is your opinion?" he asked.

There was a pause. At length, in the darkness, came her voice, hard and indifferent:

"Very little indeed," she said coldly, almost flippant. His heart went icy at the sound of her voice.

10   "Why don't I love you?" he asked, as if admitting the truth of her accusation, yet hating her for it.

"I don't know why you don't—I've been good to you. You were in a *fearful* state, when you came to me."

Her heart was beating to suffocate her, yet she was stony and

15   unrelenting.

"When was I in a fearful state?" he asked.

"When you first came to me. I *had* to take pity on you.—But it was never love."

It was that statement 'It was never love,' which sounded in his ears

20   with madness.

"Why must you repeat it so often, that there is no love?" he said in a voice strangled with rage.

"Well you don't *think* you love, do you?" she asked.

He was silent with cold passion of anger.

25   "You don't think you *can* love me, do you?" she repeated,* almost with a sneer.

"No," he said.

"You know you never *have* loved me, don't you?"

"I don't know what you mean by the word 'love'," he replied.

30   "Yes you do.—You know all right that you have never loved me. Have you, do you think?"

"No," he said, prompted by some barren spirit of truthfulness and obstinacy.

"And you never *will* love me," she said finally. "Will you?"

35   There was a diabolic coldness in her, too much to bear.

"No," he said.

"Then," she replied, "what have you against me!"

He was silent in cold, frightened rage and despair. "If only I could kill her," his heart was whispering repeatedly. "If only I could kill

40   her—I should be free." It seemed to him that death was the only severing of this Gordian knot.

"Why do you torture me?" he said.

She flung her arms round his neck.

"Ah, I don't want to torture you," she said pityingly, as if she were comforting a child. The impertinence made his veins go cold, he was insensible. She held her arms round his neck, in a triumph of pity. And her pity for him was as cold as stone, its deepest motive was hate of him, and fear of his power over her, which she must always counterfoil.

"Say you love me," she pleaded. "Say you will love me for ever— won't you—won't you?"

But it was her voice only that coaxed him. Her senses were entirely apart from him, cold and destructive of him. It was her overbearing *will* that insisted.

"Won't you say you'll love me always?" she coaxed. "Say it, even if it isn't true—say it Gerald, do."

"I will love you always," he repeated, in real agony, forcing the words out.

She gave him a quick kiss.

"Fancy your actually having said it," she said, with a touch of raillery.

He stood as if he had been beaten.

"Try to love me a little more, and to want me a little less," she said, in a half contemptuous, half coaxing tone.

The darkness seemed to be swaying in waves across his mind, great waves of darkness plunging across his mind. It seemed to him he was degraded at the very quick, made of no account.

"You mean you don't want me?" he said.

"You are so insistent, and there is so little grace in you, so little fineness. You are so crude. You break me—you only waste me—it is horrible to me."

"Horrible to you?" he repeated.

"Yes. Don't you think I might have a room to myself, now Ursula has gone? You can say you want a dressing-room."

"You do as you like—you can leave altogether if you like," he managed to articulate.

"Yes I know that," she replied. "So can you. You can leave me whenever you like—without notice even."

The great tides of darkness were swinging across his mind, he could hardly stand upright. A terrible weariness overcame him, he felt he must lie on the floor. Dropping off his clothes, he got into bed, and lay like a man suddenly overcome by drunkenness, the darkness lifting and plunging as if he were lying upon a black, giddy sea. He lay still in this strange, horrific reeling for some time, purely unconscious.

At length she slipped from her own bed and came over to him.
5 He remained rigid, his back to her. He was all but unconscious.

She put her arms round his terrifying, insentient body, and laid her cheek against his hard shoulder.

"Gerald," she whispered. "Gerald."

There was no change in him. She caught him against her. She
10 pressed her breasts against his shoulders, she kissed his shoulder, through the sleeping-jacket. Her mind wondered, over his rigid, unliving body. She was bewildered and insistent, only her will was set for him to speak to her.

"Gerald, my dear!" she whispered, bending over him, kissing his
15 ear.

Her warm breath playing, flying rhythmically over his ear, seemed to relax the tension. She could feel his body gradually relaxing a little, losing its terrifying, unnatural rigidity. Her hands clutched his limbs, his muscles, going over him spasmodically.
20 The hot blood began to flow again through his veins, his limbs relaxed.

"Turn round to me," she whispered, forlorn with insistence and triumph.

So at last he was given again, warm and flexible. He turned and
25 gathered her in his arms. And feeling her soft against him, so perfectly and wondrously soft and recipient, his arms tightened on her, she was as if crushed powerless in him. His brain seemed hard and invincible now like a jewel, there was no resisting him.

His passion was awful to her, tense and ghastly and impersonal,
30 like a destruction, ultimate.* She felt it would kill her, she was being killed.

"My God, my God!" she cried in anguish, in his embrace, feeling her life being killed within her. And when he was kissing her, soothing her, her breath came slowly, as if she were really spent,
35 dying.

"Shall I die, shall I die?" she repeated to herself.

And in the night, and in him, there was no answer to the question.

And yet, next day, the fragment of her which was not destroyed remained intact and hostile, she did not go away, she remained to
40 finish the holiday, admitting nothing. He scarcely ever left her alone,

but followed her like a shadow, he was like a doom upon her, a continual 'thou shalt', 'thou shalt not'.* Sometimes it was he who seemed strongest, whilst she was almost gone, creeping near the earth like a spent wind; sometimes it was the reverse. But always it was this eternal see-saw, one destroyed that the other might exist, one ratified because the other was nulled.

"In the end," she said to herself, "I shall go away from him."

"I can be free of her," he said to himself in his paroxysms of suffering.

And he set himself to be free. He even prepared to go away, to leave her in the lurch. But for the first time there was a flaw in his will.

"Where shall I go?" he asked himself.

"Can't you be self-sufficient?" he replied to himself, putting himself upon his pride.

"Self-sufficient?" he repeated.

It seemed to him that Gudrun was sufficient unto herself, closed round and completed, like a thing in a case. In the calm, static reason of his soul, he recognised this, and admitted it was her right, to be closed round upon herself, self-complete, without desire. He realised it, he admitted it, it only needed one last effort on his own part, to win for himself the same completeness. He knew that it only needed one convulsion of his will for him to be able to turn upon himself also, to close upon himself as a stone fixes upon itself, and is impervious, self-completed, a thing isolated.

This knowledge threw him into a terrible chaos. Because, however much he might mentally *will* to be immune and self-complete, the desire for this state was lacking, and he could not create it. He could see that, to exist at all, he must be perfectly free of Gudrun, leave her if she wanted to be left, demand nothing of her, have no claim upon her.

But then, to have no claim upon her, he must stand by himself, in sheer nothingness. And his brain turned to nought at the idea. It was a state of nothingness.—On the other hand, he might give in, and fawn to her.—Or, finally, he might kill her.—Or he might become just indifferent, purposeless, dissipated, momentaneous.—But his nature was too serious, not gay enough or subtle enough for mocking licentiousness.

A strange rent had been torn in him; like a victim that is torn open and given to the heavens, so he had been torn apart and given to

Gudrun. How should he close again? This wound, this strange, infinitely-sensitive opening of his soul, where he was exposed, like an open flower, to all the universe, and in which he was given to his complement, the other, the unknown, this wound, this disclosure,
5   this unfolding of his own covering, leaving him incomplete, limited, unfinished, like an open flower under the sky, this was his cruelest joy. Why then should he forego it. Why should he close up and become impervious, immune, like a partial thing in a sheath, when he had broken forth, like a seed that has germinated, to issue forth in
10 being,* embracing the unrealised heavens.

He would keep the unfinished bliss of his own yearning even through the torture she inflicted upon him. A strange obstinacy possessed him. He would not go away from her whatever she said or did. A strange, deathly yearning carried him along with her. She was
15 the determinating influence of his very being. Though she treated him with contempt, repeated rebuffs and denials, still he would never be gone, since in being near her, even, he felt the quickening, the going forth in him, the release, the knowledge of his own limitation and the magic of the promise, as well as the mystery of his
20 own destruction and annihilation.

She tortured the open heart of him even as he turned to her. And she was tortured herself. It may have been her will was stronger. She felt, with horror, as if he tore at the bud of her heart, tore it open, like an irreverent, persistent being. Like a boy who pulls off a fly's wings,
25 or tears open a bud to see what is in the flower, he tore at her privacy, at her very life, he would destroy her as an immature bud, torn open, is destroyed.

She might open towards him, a long while hence, in her dreams, when she was a pure spirit. But now she was not to be violated and
30 ruined. She closed against him fiercely.

They climbed together, at evening, up the high slope, to see the sun set. In the finely breathing, keen wind they stood and watched the yellow sun sink in crimson and disappear. Then in the east the peaks and ridges glowed with living rose, incandescent like immortal
35 flowers against a brown-purple sky, a miracle, whilst down below the world was a bluish shadow, and above, like an annunciation, hovered a rosy transport in mid air.

To her it was so beautiful, it was a delirium, she wanted to gather the glowing, eternal peaks to her breast, and die. He saw them, saw
40 they were beautiful. But there arose no clamour in his breast, only a

bitterness that was visionary in itself. He wished the peaks were grey and unbeautiful, so that she should not get her support from them. Why did she betray the two of them so terribly, in embracing the glow of evening? Why did she leave him standing there, with the ice-wind blowing through his heart, like death, to gratify herself among the rosy snow-tips?

"What does the twilight matter?" he said. "Why do you grovel before it? Is it so important to you?"

She winced in violation and in fury.

"Go away," she cried, "and leave me to it. It is beautiful, beautiful," she sang, in strange, rhapsodic tones. "It is the most beautiful thing I have ever seen in my life. Don't try and come between it and me. Take yourself away, you are out of place—"

He stood back a little, and left her standing there, statue-like, transported into the mystic glowing east. Already the rose was fading, large white stars were flashing out. He waited. He would forego everything but the yearning.

"That was the most perfect thing I have ever seen," she said in cold, brutal tones, when at last she turned round to him. "It amazes me that you should want to destroy it. If you can't see it yourself, why try to debar me?" But in reality, he had destroyed it for her, she was straining after a dead effect.

"One day," he said, softly, looking up at her, "I shall destroy *you*, as you stand looking at a sunset; because you are such a liar."

There was a soft, voluptuous promise to himself in the words. She was chilled, but arrogant.

"Ha!" she said. "I am not afraid of your threats!"

She denied herself to him, she kept her room rigidly private to herself. But he waited on, in a curious patience, belonging to his yearning for her.

"In the end," he said to himself, with real voluptuous promise, "when it reaches that point, I shall do away with her." And he trembled delicately in every limb, in anticipation, as he trembled in his most violent accesses of passionate approach to her, trembling with too-much desire.

She had a curious sort of allegiance with Loerke, all the while, now, something insidious and traitorous. Gerald knew of it. But in the unnatural state of patience, and the unwillingness to harden himself against her, in which he found himself, he took no notice, although her soft kindliness to the other man, whom he hated as a noxious insect, made him shiver again with an access of the strange shuddering that came over him repeatedly.

He left her alone only when he went ski-ing, a sport he loved, and which she did not practise. Then he seemed to sweep out of life, to be a projectile into the beyond. And often, when he went away, she talked to the little German sculptor. They had an invariable topic, in their art.

They were almost of the same ideas. He hated Mestrovic, was not satisfied with the Futurists, he liked the West African wooden figures, the Aztec art, Mexican and Central American.* He saw the grotesque, and a curious sort of mechanical motion intoxicated him, a confusion in nature.

They had a curious game with each other, Gudrun and Loerke, of infinite suggestivity, strange and leering, as if they had some esoteric understanding of life, that they alone were initiated into the fearful central secrets, that the world dared not know. Their whole correspondence was in a strange, barely comprehensible suggestivity, they kindled themselves at the subtle lusts of the Egyptians or the Mexicans.* The whole game was one of subtle inter-suggestivity, and they wanted to keep it on the plane of suggestion. From their verbal and physical *nuances* they got the highest satisfaction in the nerves, from a queer interchange of half-suggested ideas, looks, expressions and gestures, which were quite intolerable, though incomprehensible, to Gerald. He had no terms in which to think of their commerce, his terms were much too gross.

The suggestion of primitive art was their refuge, and the inner mysteries of sensation their object of worship. Art and Life were to them the Reality and the Unreality.

"Of course," said Gudrun, "life doesn't *really* matter—it is one's art which is central. What one does in one's life has *peu de rapport*,* it doesn't signify much."

"Yes, that is so, exactly," replied the sculptor. "What one does in one's art, that is the breath of one's being. What one does in one's life, that is a bagatelle for the outsiders to fuss about."

It was curious what a sense of elation and freedom Gudrun found in this communication. She felt established for ever. Of course Gerald was *bagatelle*—love was one of the temporal things in her life, except in so far as she was an artist. She thought of Cleopatra— Cleopatra must have been an artist; she reaped the essential from a man, she harvested the ultimate sensation, and threw away the husk;

and Mary Stuart, and Eleonora Duse, panting with her lovers* after the theatre, these were the exoteric exponents of love. After all, what was the lover but fuel for the transport of this subtle knowledge, for a female art, the art of pure, perfect knowledge in sensuous understanding.

One evening Gerald was arguing with Loerke about Italy and Tripoli.* The Englishman was in a strange, inflammable state, the German was excited. It was a contest of words, but it meant a conflict in spirit between the two men. And all the while Gudrun could see in Gerald an arrogant, English contempt for a foreigner. Although Gerald was quivering, his eyes flashing, his face flushed, in his argument there was a brusqueness, a savage contempt in his manner, that made Gudrun's blood flare up, and made Loerke keen and mortified. For Gerald came down like a sledge-hammer with his assertions, anything the little German said was merely contemptible rubbish.

At last Loerke turned to Gudrun, raising his hands in helpless irony, a shrug of ironical dismissal, something appealing and childlike:

"Sehen Sie, Gnädige Frau—" he began.

"Bitte sagen Sie nicht immer gnädige Frau,"* cried Gudrun, her eyes flashing, her cheeks burning. She looked like a vivid Medusa.* Her voice was loud and clamorous, the other people in the room were startled.

"Please don't call me Mrs Crich," she cried aloud.

The name, in Loerke's mouth particularly, had been an intolerable humiliation and constraint upon her, these many days.

The two men looked at her in amazement. Gerald went white at the cheek-bones.

"What shall I say, then?" asked Loerke, with soft, mocking insinuation.

"Sagen Sie nur nicht das,"* she muttered, her cheeks flushed crimson. "Not that, at least."

She saw, by the dawning look on Loerke's face, that he had understood. She was *not* Mrs Crich! So-o-o, that explained a great deal.

"Soll ich Fräulein sagen?"* he asked, malevolently.

She looked at him with some aversion.

"I am not married," she said, with some hauteur.

Her heart was fluttering now, beating like a bewildered bird. She knew she had dealt a cruel wound, and she could not bear it.

Gerald sat erect, perfectly still, his face pale and calm, like the face of a statue. He was unaware of her, or of Loerke, or anybody. He sat perfectly still, in an unalterable calm. Loerke, meanwhile, was crouching and glancing up from under his ducked head.

5   Gudrun was tortured for something to say, to relieve the suspense. She twisted her face in a smile, and glanced knowingly, almost sneering, at Gerald.

"Truth is best," she said to him, with a grimace.

But now again, she was under his domination; now, because she
10 had dealt him this blow, because she had destroyed him, and she did not know how he had taken it. She watched him. He was interesting to her. She had lost her interest in Loerke.

Gerald rose at length, and went over, in a leisurely, still movement, to the professor. The two began a conversation on
15 Goethe.

She was rather piqued by the simplicity of Gerald's demeanour this evening. He did not seem angry or disgusted, only he looked curiously innocent and pure, really beautiful. Sometimes it came upon him, this look of clear distance, and it always fascinated her.
20 She waited, troubled, throughout the evening. She thought he would avoid her, or give some sign. But he spoke to her simply and unemotionally, as he would to anyone else in the room. A certain peace, an abstraction possessed his soul.

She went to his room, hotly, violently in love with him. He was so
25 beautiful and inaccessible. He kissed her, he was a lover to her. And she had extreme pleasure of him. But he did not come to, he remained remote and candid, unconscious. She wanted to speak to him. But this innocent beautiful state of unconsciousness that had come upon him prevented her. She felt tormented and dark.
30 In the morning, however, he looked at her with a little aversion, some horror and some hatred darkening into his eyes. She withdrew on to her old ground. But still he would not gather himself together, against her.

Loerke was waiting for her now. The little artist, isolated in his
35 own complete envelope, felt that here at last was a woman from whom he could get something. He was uneasy all the while, waiting to talk with her, subtly contriving to be near her. Her presence filled him with keenness and excitement, he gravitated cunningly towards her, as if she had some unseen force of attraction.
40 He was not in the least doubtful of himself, as regards Gerald.

Gerald was one of the outsiders. Loerke only hated him for being rich and proud and of fine appearance. All these things, however, riches, pride of social standing, handsome physique, were externals. When it came to the relation with a woman such as Gudrun, he, Loerke, had an approach and a power that Gerald never dreamed of.

How should Gerald hope to satisfy a woman of Gudrun's calibre? Did he think that pride or masterful will or physical strength would help him? Loerke knew a secret beyond these things. The greatest power is the one that is subtle and adjusts itself, not the one which blindly attacks. And he, Loerke, had understanding where Gerald was a calf. He, Loerke, could penetrate into depths far out of Gerald's knowledge, Gerald was left behind like a postulant in the ante-room of this temple of mysteries, this woman. But he, Loerke, could he not penetrate into the inner darkness, find the spirit of the woman in its inner recess, and wrestle with it there, the central serpent that is coiled at the core of life.*

What was it, after all, that a woman wanted? Was it mere social effect, fulfilment of ambition in the social world, in the community of mankind? Was it even a union in love and goodness? Did she want "goodness"? Who but a fool would accept this of Gudrun? This was but the street view of her wants. Cross the threshold, and you found her completely, completely cynical about the social world and its advantages. Once inside the house of her soul, and there was a pungent atmosphere of corrosion, an inflamed darkness of sensation, and a vivid, subtle, critical consciousness, that saw the world distorted, horrific.

What then, what next? Was it sheer blind force of passion that would satisfy her now? Not this, but the subtle thrills of extreme sensation in reduction. It was an unbroken will reacting against her unbroken will in a myriad subtle thrills of reduction, the last subtle activities of analysis and breaking-down carried out in the darkness of her, whilst the outside form, the individual, was utterly unchanged, even sentimental in its poses.

But between two particular people, any two people on earth, the range of pure sensational experience is limited. The climax of sensual reaction, once reached in any direction, is reached finally, there is no going on. There is only repetition possible, or the going apart of the two protagonists, or the subjugating of the one will to the other, or death.

Gerald had penetrated all the outer places of Gudrun's soul. He was to her the most crucial instance of the existing world, the ne plus ultra of the world of man as it existed for her. In him she knew the world, and had done with it. Knowing him finally she was the Alexander seeking new worlds.*—But there *were* no new worlds, there were no more *men*, there were only creatures, little, ultimate *creatures* like Loerke. The world was finished now, for her. There was only the inner, individual darkness, sensation within the ego, the obscene religious mystery of ultimate reduction, the mystic frictional activities of diabolic reducing down, disintegrating the vital organic body of life.

All this Gudrun knew in her subconsciousness, not in her mind. She knew her next step—she knew what she should move on to, when she left Gerald. She was afraid of Gerald, that he might kill her. But she did not intend to be killed. A fine thread still united her to him. It should not be *her* death which broke it.—She had further to go, a further, slow, exquisite experience to reap, unthinkable subtleties of sensation to know, before she was finished.

Of the last series of subtleties Gerald was not capable. He could not touch the quick of her. But where his ruder blows could not penetrate, the fine, insinuating blade of Loerke's insect-like comprehension could. At least, it was time for her now to pass over to the other, the creature, the final craftsman. She knew that Loerke, in his innermost soul, was detached from everything, for him there was neither heaven nor earth nor hell. He admitted no allegiance, he gave no adherence anywhere. He was single and, by abstraction from the rest, absolute in himself.

Whereas in Gerald's soul there still lingered some attachment to the rest, to the whole.* And this was his limitation. He was limited, *borné,** subject to his necessity, in the last issue, for goodness, for righteousness, for oneness with the ultimate purpose. That the ultimate purpose might be the perfect and subtle experiencing of the process of death, the will being kept unimpaired, that was not allowed in him. And this was his limitation.

There was a hovering triumph in Loerke, since Gudrun had denied her marriage with Gerald. The artist seemed to hover like a creature on the wing, waiting to settle. He did not approach Gudrun violently, he was never ill-timed. But, carried on by a sure instinct in the complete darkness of his soul, he corresponded mystically with her, imperceptibly, but palpably.

For two days, he talked to her, continued the discussions of art, of life, in which they both found such pleasure. They praised the by-gone things, they took a sentimental, childish delight in the achieved perfections of the past. Particularly they liked the late eighteenth century, the period of Goethe and of Shelley, and Mozart.*

They played with the past, and with the great figures of the past, a sort of little game of chess, or marionettes, all to please themselves. They had all the great men for their marionettes, and they two were the god of the show, working it all. As for the future, that they never mentioned except one laughed out some mocking dream of the destruction of the world by a ridiculous catastrophe of man's invention: a man invented such a perfect explosive that it blew the earth in two, and the two halves set off in different directions through space, to the dismay of the inhabitants: or else the people of the world divided into two halves, and each half decided *it* was perfect and right, the other half was wrong and must be destroyed; so another end of the world. Or else, Loerke's dream of fear, the world went cold, and snow fell everywhere, and only white creatures, polar-bears, white foxes, and men like awful white snow-birds, persisted in ice cruelty.

Apart from these stories, they never talked of the future. They delighted most either in mocking imaginations of destruction, or in sentimental, fine marionette-shows of the past. It was a sentimental delight to reconstruct the world of Goethe at Weimar, or of Schiller and poverty and faithful love, or to see again Jean Jacques in his quakings, or Voltaire at Ferney, or Frederick the Great reading his own poetry.*

They talked together for hours, of literature and sculpture and painting, amusing themselves with Flaxman and Blake and Fuseli, with tenderness, and with Feuerbach and Böcklin.* It would take them a life-time, they felt, to live again, in petto,* the lives of the great artists. But they preferred to stay in the eighteenth and the nineteenth centuries.

They talked in a mixture of languages. The groundwork was French, in either case. But he ended most of his sentences in a stumble of English and a conclusion of German, she skilfully wove herself to her end in whatever phrase came to her. She took a peculiar delight in this conversation. It was full of odd, fantastic expression, of double meanings, of evasions, of suggestive vagueness. It was a real physical pleasure to her to make this thread of conversation out of the different-coloured strands of three languages.

And all the while they two were hovering, hesitating round the flame of some invisible declaration. He wanted it, but was held back
5 by some inevitable reluctance. She wanted it also, but she wanted to put it off, to put it off indefinitely. She still had some pity for Gerald, some connection with him. And the most fatal of all, she had the reminiscent sentimental compassion for herself in connection with him. Because of what *had* been, she felt herself held to him by
10 immortal, invisible threads—because of what *had* been, because of his coming to her that first night, into her own house, in his extremity, because——.

Gerald was gradually overcome with a revulsion of loathing for Loerke. He did not take the man seriously, he despised him merely,
15 except as he felt in Gudrun's veins the influence of the little creature. It was this that drove Gerald wild, the feeling in Gudrun's veins of Loerke's presence, Loerke's being, flowing dominant through her.

"What makes you so smitten with that little vermin?" he asked, really puzzled. For he, man-like, could not see anything attractive or
20 important *at all* in Loerke. Gerald expected to find some handsomeness or nobleness, to account for a woman's subjection. But he saw none here, only an insect-like repulsiveness.

Gudrun flushed deeply. It was these attacks she would never forgive.
25 "What do you mean?" she replied. "My God, what a mercy I am *not* married to you!"

Her voice of flouting and contempt scotched him. He was brought up short. But he recovered himself.

"Tell me, only tell me," he reiterated, in a dangerous, narrowed
30 voice—"tell me what it is that fascinates you in him."

"I am not fascinated," she said, with cold, repelling innocence.

"Yes you are. You are fascinated by that little dry snake, like a bird gaping ready to fall down its throat."

She looked at him with black fury.
35 "I don't choose to be discussed by you," she said.

"It doesn't matter whether you choose or not," he replied, "that doesn't alter the fact that you are ready to fall down and kiss the feet of that little insect. And I don't want to prevent you—do it, fall down and kiss his feet. But I want to know, what it is that fascinates
40 you—what is it?"

She was silent, suffused with black rage.

"How *dare* you come brow-beating me," she cried, "how dare you, you little squire, you bully. What right have you over me, do you think?"

His face was white and gleaming, she knew by the light in his eyes that she was in his power—the wolf. And because she was in his power, she hated him with a power* that she wondered did not kill him. In her will she killed him as he stood, effaced him.

"It's not a question of right," said Gerald, sitting down on a chair. She watched the change in his body: she saw his clenched, mechanical body moving there like an obsession. Her hatred of him was tinged with fatal contempt. "It's not a question of my right over you—though I *have* some right, remember. I* want to know, I only want to know what it is that subjugates you to that little scum of a sculptor downstairs, what it is that brings you down like a humble maggot, in worship of him. I want to know what you creep after."

She stood over against the window, listening. Then she turned round.

"Do you?" she said, in her most easy, most cutting voice. "Do you want to know what it is in him? It's because he has some understanding of a woman, because he is not stupid, that's* why it is."

A queer, sinister, animal-like smile came over Gerald's face.

"But what understanding is it?" he said. "The understanding of a flea, a hopping flea with a proboscis. Why should you crawl abject before the understanding of a flea?"

There passed through Gudrun's mind Blake's representation of the soul of a flea.* She wanted to fit it to Loerke. Blake was a clown too. But it was necessary to answer Gerald.

"Don't you think the understanding of a flea is more interesting than the understanding of a fool—?" she asked.

"A fool?" he repeated—

"A fool, a conceited fool—a Dummkopf," she replied, adding the German word.

"Do you call me a fool?" he replied. "Well, wouldn't I rather be the fool I am, than that flea downstairs?"

She looked at him. A certain blunt, blind stupidity in him palled on her soul, limiting her.

"You give yourself away by that last," she said.

He sat and wondered.

"I shall go away soon," he said.

She turned on him.

"Remember," she said, "I am completely independent of you—completely. You make your arrangements, I make mine."

He pondered this.

5 "You mean we are strangers from this minute?" he asked.

She halted and flushed. He was putting her in a trap, forcing her hand. She turned round on him.

"Strangers," she said, "we can never be. But if you *want* to make any movement apart from me, then I wish you to know you are
10 perfectly free to do so. Do not consider me in the slightest."

Even so slight an implication that she needed him and was depending on him still was sufficient to rouse his passion. As he sat, a change came over his body, the hot, molten stream mounted involuntarily through his veins. He groaned inwardly, under its
15 bondage, but he loved it. He looked at her with clear eyes, waiting for her.

She knew at once, and was shaken with cold revulsion. *How* could he look at her with those clear, warm, waiting eyes, waiting for her, even now? What had been said between them, was it not enough to
20 put them worlds asunder, to freeze them forever apart? And yet he was all transfused and roused, waiting for her.

It confused her. Turning her head aside, she said:

"I shall always *tell* you, whenever I am going to make any change—"

25 And with this she moved out of the room.

He sat suspended in a fine recoil of disappointment, that seemed gradually to be destroying his understanding. But the unconscious state of patience persisted in him. He remained motionless, without thought or knowledge, for a long time. Then he rose, and went
30 downstairs, to play at chess with one of the students. His face was open and clear, with a certain innocent *laisser-aller** that troubled Gudrun most, made her almost afraid of him, whilst she disliked him deeply for it.

It was after this that Loerke, who had never yet spoken to her
35 personally, began to ask her of her state.

"You are not married at all, are you?" he asked.

She looked full at him.

"Not in the least," she replied, in her measured way.

Loerke laughed, wrinkling up his face oddly. There was a thin
40 wisp of his hair straying on his forehead, she noticed that his skin was

of a clear brown colour, his hands, his wrists. And his hands seemed
closely prehensile. He seemed like topaz, so strangely brownish and
pellucid.

"Good," he said.

Still it needed some courage for him to go on.

"Was Mrs Birkin your sister?" he asked.

"Yes."

"And was *she* married?"

"She was married."

"Have you parents, then?"

"Yes," said Gudrun, "we have parents."

And she told him, briefly, laconically, her position. He watched
her closely, curiously all the while.

"So!" he exclaimed with some surprise. "And the Herr Crich, is
he rich?"

"Yes, he is rich, a coal-owner."

"How long has your friendship with him lasted?"

"Some months."

There was a pause.

"Yes, I am surprised," he said at length. "The English, I thought
they were so—cold.—And what do you think to do when you leave
here?"

"What do I think to do?" she repeated.

"Yes. You cannot go back to the teaching. No—" he shrugged his
shoulders—"that is impossible. Leave that to the *canaille* who can do
nothing else. You, for your part—you know, you are a remarkable
woman, eine seltsame Frau.* Why deny it—why make any question
of it? You are an extraordinary woman, why should you follow the
ordinary course, the ordinary life?"

Gudrun sat looking at her hands, flushed. She was pleased that he
said, so simply, that she was a remarkable woman. He would not say
that to flatter her—he was far too self-opinionated and objective by
nature. He said it as he would say, a piece of sculpture was
remarkable, because he knew it was so.

And it gratified her to hear it from him. Other people had such a
passion to make everything of one degree, of one pattern. In England
it was chic to be perfectly ordinary. And it was a relief to her to be
acknowledged extraordinary. Then she need not fret about the
common standards.*

"You see," she said, "I have no money whatsoever."

"Ach, money!" he cried, lifting his shoulders. "When one is grown up, money is lying about at one's service. It is only when one is young that it is rare. Take no thought for money—that always lies to hand."

5   "Does it?" she said, laughing.

"Always. The Gerald will give you a sum, if you ask him for it—"

She flushed deeply.

"I will ask anybody else," she said, with some difficulty—"but not him."

10   Loerke looked closely at her.

"Good," he said. "Then let it be somebody else. Only don't go back to that England, that school. No, that is stupid."

Again there was a pause. He was afraid to ask her outright to go with him, he was not even quite sure he wanted her; and she was

15   afraid to be asked. He begrudged his own isolation, was *very* chary of sharing his life, even for a day.

"The only other place I know is Paris," she said, "and I can't stand that."

She looked with her wide, steady eyes full at Loerke. He lowered

20   his head and averted his face.

"Paris, no!" he said. "Between the *religion d'amour*, and the latest 'ism', and the new turning to Jesus,* one had better ride on a carrousel all day. But come to Dresden. I have a studio there—I can give you work—Oh, that would be easy enough. I haven't seen any of

25   your things, but I believe in you. Come to Dresden—that is a fine town to be in, and as good a life as you can expect of a town. You have everything there, without the foolishness of Paris or the beer of Munich."

He sat and looked at her, coldly. What she liked about him was

30   that he spoke to her simple and flat, as to himself. He was a fellow craftsman, a fellow being to her, first.

"No—Paris," he resumed, "it makes me sick. Pah—l'amour. I detest it. L'amour, l'amore, die Liebe*—I detest it in every language. Women and love, there is no greater tedium," he cried.

35   She was slightly offended. And yet, this was her own basic feeling. Men, and love—there was no greater tedium.

"I think the same," she said.

"A bore," he repeated.* "What does it matter, whether I wear this hat or another. So love! I needn't wear a hat at all, only for

40   convenience. Neither need I love, except for convenience.—I tell

you what, gnädige Frau—" and he leaned towards her—then he
made a quick, odd gesture, as of striking something aside—
"gnädiges Fräulein, never mind.—I tell you what, I would give
everything, everything, all your love, for a little companionship in
intelligence—" his eyes flickered darkly, evilly at her.—"You under- 5
stand?" he asked, with a faint smile. "It wouldn't matter if she was a
hundred years old, a thousand—it would be all the same to me, so
that she can *understand*." He shut his eyes with a little snap.

Again Gudrun was rather offended. Did he not think her good-
looking, then? Suddenly she laughed. 10

"I shall have to wait about eighty years to suit you, at that," she
said. "I am ugly enough, aren't I?"

He looked at her with an artist's sudden, critical, estimating eye.

"You are beautiful," he said, "and I am glad of it. But it isn't
that—it isn't that," he cried, with emphasis that flattered her. "It is 15
that you have a certain wit, it is the kind of understanding. For me, I
am little, chétif,* insignificant. Good! Do not ask me to be strong and
handsome, then. But it is the *me*—" he put his fingers to his mouth,
oddly—"it is the *me* that is looking for a mistress, and my *me* is
waiting for the *thee** of the mistress, for the match to my particular 20
intelligence—You understand?"

"Yes," she said. "I understand."

"As for the other, this amour—" he made a gesture, dashing his
hand aside, as if to dash away something troublesome—"it is
unimportant, unimportant. Does it matter, whether I drink white 25
wine this evening, or whether I drink nothing? It *does not matter*, it
does not matter. So this love, this amour, this *baiser*. Yes or no, soit
ou soit pas,* today, tomorrow, or never, it is all the same, it does not
matter—no more than the white wine."

He ended with an odd dropping of the head in a desperate 30
negation. Gudrun watched him steadily. She had gone pale.

Suddenly she stretched over and seized his hand in her own.

"That is true," she said, in rather a high, vehement voice, "that is
true for me too. It is the understanding that matters."

He looked up at her almost frightened, furtive. Then he nodded, a 35
little sullenly. She let go his hand: he had made not the slightest
response. And they sat in silence.

"Do you know," he said, suddenly looking at her with dark,
self-important, prophetic eyes, "your fate and mine, they will run
together, till—" and he broke off in a little grimace. 40

"Till when?" she asked, blenched, her lips going white. She was terribly susceptible to these evil prognostications. But he only shook his head.

"I don't know," he said, "I don't know."

5   Gerald did not come in from his ski-ing until night-fall, he missed the coffee and cake that she took at four o'clock. The snow was in perfect condition, he had travelled a long way, by himself, among the snow ridges, on his skis. He had climbed high, so high that he could see over the top of the pass, five miles distant, could see the Marienhütte, the hostel on the crest of the pass,* half buried in snow, and over into the deep valley beyond, to the dark of the pine-trees. One could go that way home; but he shuddered with nausea at the thought of home;—one could travel on skis down there, and come to the old Imperial road, below the pass.* But why come to any road? He revolted at the thought of finding himself in the world again. He must stay up there in the snow forever. He had been happy by himself, high up there alone, travelling swiftly on skis, taking far flights, and skimming past the dark rocks veined with brilliant snow.

But he felt something icy gathering at his heart. This strange mood of patience and innocence which had persisted in him for some days, was passing away, he would be left again a prey to the horrible passions and tortures.

So he came down reluctantly, snow-burned, snow-estranged, to the house in the hollow, between the knuckles of the mountain-tops. He saw its lights shining yellow, and he held back, wishing he need not go in, to confront those people, to hear the turmoil of voices and to feel the confusion of other presences. He was isolated as if there were a vacuum round his heart, or a sheath of pure ice.

The moment he saw Gudrun, something jolted in his soul. She was looking rather lofty and superb, smiling slowly and graciously to the Germans. A sudden desire leapt in his heart, to kill her. He thought, what a perfect voluptuous fulfilment it would be, to kill her. His mind was absent all the evening, estranged by the snow and his passion. But he kept the idea constant within him, what a perfect voluptuous consummation it would be to strangle her, to strangle every spark of life out of her, till she lay completely inert, soft, relaxed for ever, a soft heap lying dead between his hands, utterly dead. Then he would have had her finally and for ever, there would be such a perfect voluptuous finality.

40   Gudrun was unaware of what he was feeling, he seemed so quiet

and amiable, as usual. His amiability even made her feel brutal towards him.

She went into his room where he was partially undressed. She did not notice the curious, glad gleam of pure hatred, with which he looked at her. She stood near the door, with her hand behind her.

"I have been thinking, Gerald," she said, with an insulting nonchalance, "that I shall not go back to England."

"Oh," he said. "Where will you go then?"

But she ignored his question. She had her own logical statement to make, and it must be made as she had thought it.

"I can't see the use of going back," she continued. "It is over between me and you—"

She paused for him to speak. But he said nothing. He was only talking to himself, saying 'Over, is it? I believe it is over. But it isn't finished. Remember, it isn't finished. We must put some sort of a finish on it. There must be a conclusion, there must be finality.'

So he talked to himself, but aloud, he said nothing whatever.

"What has been has been," she continued. "There is nothing that I regret. I hope you regret nothing—"

She waited for him to speak.

"Oh, I regret nothing," he said, accommodatingly.

"Good then," she answered, "good then. Then neither of us cherishes any regrets, which is as it should be."

"Quite as it should be," he said aimlessly.

She paused, to gather up her thread again.

"Our attempt has been a failure," she said. "But we can try again, elsewhere."

A little flicker of rage ran through his blood. It was as if she were rousing him, goading him. Why must she do it?

"Attempt at what?" he asked.

"At being lovers, I suppose," she said, a little baffled, yet so trivial she made it all seem.

"Our attempt at being lovers has been a failure?" he repeated aloud.

To himself, he was saying: 'I ought to kill her here. There is only this left, for me to kill her.' A heavy, overcharged desire, to bring about her death, possessed him.

She was unaware.

"Hasn't it?" she asked. "Do you think it has been a success?"

Again the insult of the flippant question ran through his blood like a current of fire.

"It had some of the elements of success, our relationship," he replied. "It—might have come off."

5 But he paused before concluding the last phrase. Even as he began the sentence, he did not believe in what he was going to say. He knew it never could have been a success.

"No," she replied. "You cannot love."

"And you?" he asked.

10 Her wide, dark-filled eyes were fixed on him, like two moons of darkness.

"I couldn't love *you*," she said, with stark cold truth.

A blinding flash went over his brain, his body jolted. His heart had burst into flame. His consciousness was gone into his wrists, into his 15 hands. He was one blind, incontinent desire, to kill her. His wrists were bursting, there would be no satisfaction, till his hands had closed on her.

But even before his body swerved forward on her, a sudden, cunning comprehension was expressed on her face, and in a flash 20 she was out of the door. She ran in one flash to her room and locked herself in. She was afraid, but confident. She knew her life trembled on the edge of an abyss. But she was curiously sure of her footing. She knew her cunning could outwit him.

She trembled, as she stood in her room, with excitement and awful 25 exhilaration. She knew she could outwit him. She could depend on her presence of mind, and on her wits. But it was a fight to the death, she knew it now. One slip, and she was lost. She had a strange, tense, exhilarated sickness in her body, as one who is in peril of falling from a great height, but who does not look down, does not admit the fear.

30 "I will go away the day after tomorrow," she said.

She only did not want Gerald to think that she was afraid of him, that she was running away because she was afraid of him. She was not afraid of him, fundamentally. She knew it was her safeguard to avoid his physical violence. But even physically she was not afraid of 35 him. She wanted to prove it to him. When she had proved it, that, whatever he was, she was not afraid of him; when she had proved *that*, she could leave him forever. But meanwhile the fight between them, terrible as she knew it to be, was inconclusive. And she wanted to be confident in herself. However many terrors she might have, she 40 would be unafraid, uncowed by him. He could never cow her, nor

dominate her, nor have any right over her; this she would maintain
until she had proved it. Once it was proved, she was free of him for
ever.

But she had not proved it yet, neither to him nor to herself. And
this was what still bound her to him. She was bound to him, she 5
could not live beyond him. She sat up in bed, closely wrapped up,
for many hours, thinking endlessly to herself. It was as if she would
never have done weaving the great provision of her thoughts.

"It isn't as if he really loved me," she said to herself. "He doesn't.
Every woman he comes across, he wants to make her in love with 10
him. He doesn't even know that he is doing it. But there he is,
before every woman he unfurls his male attractiveness, displays his
great desirability, he tries to make every woman think how wonderful it would be to have him for a lover. His very ignoring of the
women is part of the game: he is never *unconscious* of them. He 15
should have been a cockerel, so he could strut before fifty females,
all his subjects. But really, his Don Juan does *not* interest me. I
could play Doña Juanita a million times better than he plays Juan.
He bores me, you know. His maleness bores me. Nothing is so
boring as the phallus,* so inherently stupid and stupidly conceited. 20
Really, the fathomless conceit of these men, it is ridiculous—the
little strutters.

"They are all alike. Look at Birkin. Built out of the limitation of
conceit they are, and nothing else. Really, nothing but their ridiculous limitation and intrinsic insignificance could make them so con- 25
ceited.

"As for Loerke, there is a thousand times more in him than in a
Gerald. Gerald is so limited, there is a dead end to him. He would
grind on at the old mills* forever. And really, there is no corn
between the mill-stones any more. They grind on and on, when 30
there is nothing to grind—saying the same things, believing the
same things, acting the same things—Oh my God, it would wear
out the patience of a stone.

"I don't worship Loerke, but at any rate, he is a free individual.
He is not stiff with conceit of his own maleness. He is not grinding 35
dutifully at the old mills. Oh God, when I think of Gerald, and his
work—those offices at Beldover, and the mines—it makes my heart
sick. What *have* I to do with it—and him thinking he can be a lover
to a woman! One might as well ask it of a self-satisfied
lamp-post.—These men, with their eternal jobs—and their eternal 40

mills of God that keep on grinding at nothing! It is too boring, just boring. However did I come to take him seriously at all!

"At least, in Dresden, one will have one's back to it all. And there will be amusing things to do. It will be amusing to go to these
5 eurythmic displays, and the German opera, the German theatre. It *will* be amusing to take part in German Bohemian life. And Loerke *is* an artist, he is a free individual. One will escape from so much—that is the chief thing—escape so much hideous boring repetition of vulgar actions, vulgar phrases, vulgar postures. I don't delude myself
10 that I shall find an elixir of life in Dresden. I know I shan't. But I shall get away from people who have their own homes and their own children and their own acquaintances and their own this and their own that. I shall be among people who *don't* own things and who *haven't* got a home and a domestic servant in the back-ground, who
15 *haven't* got a standing and a status and a degree and a circle of friends of the same. Oh God, the wheels within wheels of people—it makes one's head tick like a clock, with a very madness of dead mechanical monotony and meaninglessness. How I *hate* life, how I hate it. How I hate the Geralds, that they can offer one nothing else.

20 "Shortlands!—Heavens! Think of living there, one week, then the next, and *then the third*——

"No, I won't think of it—it is too much——"

And she broke off, really terrified, really unable to bear any more. The thought of the mechanical succession of day following day, day
25 following day, ad infinitum, was one of the things that made her heart palpitate with a real approach of madness. The terrible bondage of this tick-tack of time, this twitching of the hands of the clock, this eternal repetition of hours and days,—Oh God, it was too awful to contemplate. And there was no escape from it, no escape.

30 She almost wished Gerald were with her, to save her from the terror of her own thoughts. Oh, how she suffered, lying there alone, confronted by the terrible clock, with its eternal tick-tack. All life, all life resolved itself into this: tick-tack, tick-tack, tick-tack; then the striking of the hour; then the tick-tack, tick-tack, and the twitching
35 of the clock-fingers.

Gerald could not save her from it. He, his body, his motion, his life—it was the same ticking, the same twitching across the dial, a horrible, mechanical twitching forward over the face of the hours. What were his kisses, his embraces. She could hear their tick-tack,
40 tick-tack.

Ha—ha—she laughed to herself, so frightened that she was trying to laugh it off—ha—ha, how maddening it was, to be sure, to be sure!

Then, with a fleeting self-conscious motion, she wondered if she would be very much surprised, on rising in the morning, to realise 5 that her hair *had* turned white. She had *felt* it turning white so often, under the intolerable burden of her thoughts and her sensations. Yet there it remained, brown as ever, and there she was herself, looking a picture of health.

Perhaps she was healthy. Perhaps it was only her unabateable 10 health that left her so exposed to the truth. If she were sickly she would have illusions,* imaginations. As it was, there was no escape. She must always see and know and never escape. She could never escape. There she was, placed before the clock-face of life. And if she turned round, as in a railway station, to look at the book-stall, still 15 she could see, with her very spine she could see the clock, always the great white clock-face. In vain she fluttered the leaves of books, or made statuettes in clay. She knew she was not *really* reading, she was not *really* working. She was watching the fingers twitch across the eternal, mechanical, monotonous clock-face of time. She never 20 really lived, she only watched. Indeed, she was like a little, twelve-hour clock, vis-à-vis with the enormous clock of eternity—there she was, like Dignity and Impudence,* or Impudence and Dignity.

The picture pleased her. Didn't her face really look like a clock-dial—rather roundish, and often pale, and impassive. She 25 would have got up to look, in the mirror, but the thought of the sight of her own face, that was like a twelve-hour clock-dial, filled her with such deep terror, that she hastened to think of something else.

Oh, why wasn't somebody kind to her? Why wasn't there somebody who would take her in their arms, and hold her to their breast, 30 and give her rest, pure, deep, healing rest. Oh why wasn't there somebody to take her in their arms and fold her safe and perfect, for sleep. She wanted so much this perfect enfolded sleep. She lay always so unsheathed in sleep. She would lie always unsheathed in sleep, unrelieved, unsaved. Oh how could she bear it, this endless 35 unrelief, this eternal unrelief.

Gerald! Could *he* fold her in his arms and sheathe her in sleep? Ha! He needed putting to sleep himself—poor Gerald. That was all he needed. What did he do, he made the burden for her greater, the burden of her sleep was the more intolerable, when he was there. He 40 was an added weariness upon her unripening nights, her unfruitful slumbers. Perhaps he got some repose from her. Perhaps he did. Perhaps this was what he was always dogging her for, like a child that is famished crying for the breast. Perhaps this was the secret of his passion, his forever unquenched desire for her—that he needed her to put him to sleep, to give him repose.

What then! Was she his mother? Had she asked for a child, whom she must nurse through the nights, for her lover. She despised him, she despised him, she hardened her heart. An infant crying in the night,* this Don Juan.

Yes,* but how she hated the infant crying in the night. She would murder it gladly. She would stifle it and bury it, like* Hetty Sorrell did. No doubt Hetty Sorrell's infant cried in the night—no doubt Arthur Donnithorne's infant* would. Ha—the Arthur Donnithornes, the Geralds of this world. So manly by day, yet all the while, such a crying of infants in the night. Let them turn into mechanisms, let them. Let them become instruments, pure machines, pure wills that work like clock-work, in perpetual repetition. Let them be this, let them be taken up entirely in their work, let them be perfect parts of a great machine, having a slumber of constant repetition. Let Gerald manage his firm. There he would be satisfied, as satisfied as a wheel-barrow that goes backwards and forwards along a plank all day—she had seen it.

The wheel-barrow—the one humble wheel—the unit of the firm. Then the cart, with two wheels; then the truck, with four; then the donkey-engine,* with eight; then the winding-engine, with sixteen, and so on, till it came to the miner, with a thousand wheels, and then the electrician, with three thousand, and the underground manager, with twenty thousand, and the general manager, with a hundred thousand little wheels working away to complete his make-up, and then Gerald, with a million wheels and cogs and axles.

Poor Gerald, such a lot of little wheels to his make-up! He was more intricate than a chronometer-watch.* But oh heavens, what weariness! What weariness, God above! A chronometer-watch—a beetle—her soul fainted with utter ennui, from the thought. So many wheels to count and consider and calculate! Enough, enough—there was an end to man's capacity for complications, even. Or perhaps there was no end.

Meanwhile Gerald sat in his room, reading. When Gudrun was gone, he was left stupefied with arrested desire. He sat on the side of the bed for an hour, stupefied, little strands of consciousness appearing and reappearing. But he did not move, for a long time he remained inert, his head dropped on his breast.

Then he looked up and realised that he was going to bed. He was cold. Soon he was lying down in the dark.

But what he could not bear, was the darkness. The solid darkness confronting him drove him mad. So he rose, and made a light. He remained seated for a while, staring in front. He did not think of Gudrun, he did not think of anything.

Then suddenly he went downstairs for a book. He had all his life been in terror of the nights that should come, when he could not sleep. He knew that this would be too much for him, to have to face nights of sleeplessness and of horrified watching the hours.

So he sat for hours in bed, like a statue, reading. His mind, hard and acute, read on rapidly, his body understood nothing. In a state of rigid unconsciousness, he read on through the night, till morning, when, weary and disgusted in spirit, disgusted most of all with himself, he slept for two hours.

Then he got up, hard and full of energy. Gudrun scarcely spoke to him, except at coffee she said:

"I shall be leaving tomorrow."

"We will go together as far as Innsbruck, for appearances sake?" he asked.

"Perhaps," she said.

She said 'Perhaps' between the sips of her coffee. And the sound of her taking her breath in the word, was nauseous to him. He rose quickly, to be away from her.

He went and made arrangements for the departure on the morrow. Then, taking some food, he set out for the day on the skis. Perhaps, he said to the Wirt, he would go up to the Marienhütte, perhaps to the village below.

To Gudrun, this day was full of a promise like spring. She felt an approaching release, a new fountain of life rising up in her. It gave her pleasure to dawdle through her packing, it gave her pleasure to dip into books, to try on her different garments, to look at herself in the glass. She felt a new lease of life was come upon her, and she was happy like a child, very attractive and beautiful to everybody, with her soft, luxuriant figure and her happiness. Yet underneath was death itself.

In the afternoon she had to go out with Loerke. Her tomorrow was

perfectly vague before her. This was what gave her pleasure. She might be going to England with Gerald, she might be going to Dresden with Loerke, she might be going to Munich,* to a girl-friend she had there. Anything might come to pass on the morrow.
5   And today was the white, snowy, iridescent threshold of all possibility. All possibility—that was the charm to her, the lovely, iridescent, indefinite charm—pure illusion. All possibility—because death was inevitable, and *nothing* was possible but death.

She did not want things to materialise, to take any definite shape.
10   She wanted, suddenly, at one moment of the journey tomorrow, to be wafted into an utterly new course, by some utterly unforeseen event, or motion. So that, although she wanted to go out with Loerke for the last time into the snow, she did not want to be serious or business-like.

15   And Loerke was not a serious figure. In his brown-velvet cap, that made his head as round as a chestnut, with the brown-velvet flaps loose and wild over his ears, and a wisp of elf-like, thin black hair blowing above his full, elf-like dark eyes, the shiny, transparent brown skin crinkling up into odd grimaces on his small-featured
20   face, he looked an odd little boy-man, a bat. But in his figure, in the greeny loden suit, he looked chétif and puny, though still strangely different from the rest.

He had taken a little toboggan, for the two of them, and they trudged between the blinding slopes of snow, that burned their now
25   hardening faces, laughing in an endless sequence of quips and jests and polyglot fancies. The fancies were the reality to both of them, they were both so happy, tossing about the little coloured balls of verbal humour and whimsicality. Their natures seemed to sparkle in full interplay, they were enjoying a pure game. And they wanted
30   to keep it on the level of a game, their relationship: *such* a fine game.

Loerke did not take the tobogganing very seriously. He put no fire and intensity into it, as Gerald did. Which pleased Gudrun. She was weary, oh so weary of Gerald's gripped intensity of
35   physical motion. Loerke let the sledge go wildly and gaily, like a flying leaf, and when, at a bend, he pitched both her and him out into the snow, he only waited for them both to pick themselves up unhurt off the keen white ground, to be laughing and pert as a pixie. She knew he would be making ironical, playful remarks as he
40   wandered in hell—if he were in the humour. And that pleased her

immensely. It seemed like a rising above the dreariness of actuality, the monotony of contingencies.

They played till the sun went down, in pure amusement, careless and timeless. Then, as the little sledge twirled riskily to rest at the bottom of the slope,

"Wait!" he said suddenly, and he produced from somewhere a large thermos flask, a packet of Kekse, and a bottle of Schnapps.*

"Oh Loerke," she cried, "what an inspiration! What a comble de joie* indeed! What is the Schnapps?"

He looked at it, and laughed.

"Heidelbeer!" he said.

"No! From the bilberries under the snow. Doesn't it look as if it were distilled from snow. Can you—" she sniffed, and sniffed at the bottle—"can you smell bilberries? *Isn't* it wonderful! It is exactly as if one could smell them through the snow."

She stamped her foot lightly on the ground. He kneeled down and whistled, and put his ear to the snow. As he did so his black eyes twinkled up.

"Ha! Ha!" she laughed, warmed by the whimsical way in which he mocked at her verbal extravagances. He was always teasing her, mocking her ways. But as he in his mockery was even more absurd than she in her extravaganzas,* what could one do but laugh and feel liberated.

She could feel their voices, hers and his, ringing silvery like bells in the frozen, motionless air of the first twilight. How perfect it was, how *very* perfect it was, this silvery isolation and interplay.

She sipped the hot coffee, whose fragrance flew around them like bees murmuring around flowers, in the snowy air, she drank tiny sips of the Heidelbeerwasser,* she ate the cold, sweet, creamy wafers. How good everything was! How perfect everything tasted and smelled and sounded, here in this utter stillness of snow and falling twilight.

"You are going away tomorrow?" his voice came at last.

"Yes."

There was a pause, when the evening seemed to rise in its silent, ringing pallor infinitely high, to the infinite which was near at hand.

"*Wohin?*"

That was the question—*wohin?* where to?* *wohin?* What a lovely word! She *never* wanted it answered. Let it chime for ever.

"I don't know," she said, smiling at him.

He caught the smile from her.

"One never does," he said.

"One never does," she repeated.

There was a silence, wherein he ate biscuits rapidly, as a rabbit
5　eats leaves.

"But," he laughed, "where will you take a ticket to?"

"Oh heaven!" she cried. "One must take a ticket!"

Here was a blow. She saw herself at the wicket,* at the railway
station. Then a relieving thought came to her. She breathed freely.
10　"But one needn't go," she said.

"Certainly not," he said.

"I mean one needn't go where one's ticket says."

That struck him. One might take a ticket, so as not to travel to the
destination it indicated. One might break off, and avoid the desti-
15　nation. A point located. That was an idea!

"Then take a ticket to London," he said. "One should never go
there."

"Right," she answered.

He poured a little coffee into a tin can.
20　"You won't tell me where you will go?" he asked.

"Really and truly," she said, "I don't know. It depends which way
the wind blows."

He looked at her quizzically, then he pursed up his lips, like
Zephyrus,* blowing across the snow.
25　"It goes towards Germany," he said.

"I believe so," she laughed.

Suddenly, they were aware of a vague white figure near them. It
was Gerald. Gudrun's heart leapt in sudden terror, profound terror.
She rose to her feet.
30　"They told me where you were," came Gerald's voice, like a
judgment in the whitish air of twilight.

"*Maria!*"—you come like a ghost," exclaimed Loerke.

Gerald did not answer. His presence was unnatural and ghostly to
them.
35　Loerke shook the flask—then he held it inverted over the snow.
Only a few brown drops trickled out.

"All gone!" he said.

To Gerald, the smallish, odd figure of the German was distinct
and objective, as if seen through field glasses. And he disliked the
40　small figure exceedingly, he wanted it removed.

Then Loerke rattled the box which held the biscuits.

"Biscuits there are still," he said.

And reaching from his seated posture in the sledge, he handed them to Gudrun. She fumbled, and took one. He would have held them to Gerald, but Gerald so definitely did not want to be offered a biscuit, that Loerke, rather vaguely, put the box aside. Then he took up the small bottle, and held it to the light.

"Also there is some Schnapps," he said to himself.

Then suddenly, he elevated the bottle gallantly in the air, a strange grotesque figure leaning towards Gudrun, and said:

"Gnädiges Fräulein," he said, "wohl—."*

There was a crack, the bottle was flying, Loerke had started back, the three stood quivering in violent emotion.

Loerke turned to Gerald, a devilish leer on his bright-skinned face.

"Well done!" he said, in a satirical, demoniac frenzy. "C'est le sport, sans doute."*

The next instant he was sitting ludicrously in the snow, Gerald's fist having rung against the side of his head. But Loerke pulled himself together, rose, quivering, looking full at Gerald, his body weak and furtive, but his eyes demoniacal with satire.

"Vive le héros, vive—"*

But he flinched, as, in a black flash Gerald's fist came upon him, banged into the other side of his head, and sent him aside like a broken straw.

But Gudrun had moved forward. She raised her clenched hand high, and brought it down, with a great downward stroke, over* the face and on to the breast of Gerald.

A great astonishment burst upon him, as if the air had broken. Wide, wide his soul opened, in wonder, feeling the pain. Then it laughed, turning, with strong hands outstretched, at last to take the apple of his desire. At last he could finish his desire.

He took the throat of Gudrun between his hands, that were hard and indomitably powerful. And her throat was beautifully, so beautifully soft. Save that, within, he could feel the slippery chords of her life. And this he crushed, this he could crush. What bliss! Oh what bliss, at last, what satisfaction, at last! The pure zest of satisfaction filled his soul. He was watching the unconsciousness come into her swollen face, watching her eyes roll back. How ugly she was! What a fulfilment, what a satisfaction! How good this was,

oh how good it was, what a god-given gratification, at last! He was unconscious of her fighting and struggling. That struggling was her reciprocal lustful passion in this embrace, the more violent it became, the greater the frenzy of delight, till the zenith was reached,
5 the crisis, the struggle was overborne, her movement became softer, appeased.

Loerke roused himself on the snow, too dazed and hurt to get up. Only his eyes were conscious.

"Monsieur!" he said, in his thin, roused voice: "Quand vous aurez
10 fini—"*

A revulsion of contempt and disgust came over Gerald's soul. The disgust went to the very bottom of him, a nausea. Ah, what was he doing, to what depths was he letting himself go! As if he cared about her enough to kill her, to have her life on his hands!
15 A weakness ran over his body, a terrible relaxing, a thaw, a decay of strength. Without knowing, he had let go his grip, and Gudrun had fallen to her knees. Must he see, must he know?

A fearful weakness possessed him, his joints were turned to water. He drifted, as on a wind, veered, and went drifting away.
20 "I didn't want it,* really," was the last confession of disgust in his soul, as he drifted up the slope, weak, finished, only sheering off unconsciously from any further contact. "I've had enough—I want to go to sleep. I've had enough." He was sunk under a sense of nausea.
25 He was weak, but he did not want to rest, he wanted to go on and on, to the end. Never again to stay, till he came to the end, that was all the desire that remained to him. So he drifted on and on, unconscious and weak, not thinking of anything, so long as he could keep in action.
30 The twilight spread a weird, unearthly light overhead, bluish-rose in colour, the cold blue night sank on the snow. In the valley below, behind, in the great bed of snow, were two small figures, Gudrun dropped on her knees, like one executed, and Loerke sitting propped up near her. That was all.
35 Gerald stumbled on up the slope of snow, in the bluish darkness, always climbing, always unconsciously climbing, weary though he was. On his left was a steep slope with black rocks and fallen masses of rock and veins of snow slashing in and about the blackness of rock, veins of snow slashing vaguely in and about the blackness of rock.
40 Yet there was no sound, all this made no noise.

To add to his difficulty, a small bright moon shone brilliantly just ahead, on the right, a painful brilliant thing that was always there, unremitting, from which there was no escape. He wanted so to come to the end—he had had enough. Yet he did not sleep.

He surged painfully up, sometimes having to cross a slope of black rock, that was blown bare of snow. Here he was afraid of falling, very much afraid of falling. And high up here, on the crest, moved a wind that almost overpowered him with a sleep-heavy iciness. Only it was not here, the end, he must still go on. His indefinite nausea would not let him stay.

Having gained one ridge, he saw the vague shadow of something higher, in front. Always higher, always higher. He knew he was following the track towards the summit of the slopes, where was the Marienhütte, and the descent on the other side. But he was not really conscious. He only wanted to go on, to go on whilst he could, to move, to keep going, that was all, to keep going, until it was finished. He had lost all his sense of place. And yet, in the remaining instinct of life, his feet sought the track where the skis had gone.

He slithered down a sheer snow-slope. That frightened him. He had no alpenstock, nothing. But having come safely to rest, he began to walk on, in the illuminated darkness. It was as cold as sleep. He was between two ridges, in a hollow. So he swerved. Should he climb the other ridge, or wander along the hollow. How frail the thread of his being was stretched!

He would perhaps climb the ridge. The snow was firm and simple. He went along. There was something standing out of the snow. He approached, with dimmest curiosity.

It was a half-buried crucifix, a little Christ under a little sloping hood,* at the top of a pole. He sheered away. Somebody was going to murder him. He had a great dread of being murdered. But it was a dread which stood outside him, like his own ghost.

Yet why be afraid. It was bound to happen. To be murdered! He looked round in terror at the snow, the rocking, pale-shadowy slopes of the upper world. He was bound to be murdered, he could see it. This was the moment when the death was uplifted, and there was no escape.

Lord Jesus, was it then bound to be—Lord Jesus? He could feel the blow descending, he knew he was murdered. Vaguely wandering forward, his hands lifted as if to feel what would happen, he was waiting for the moment when he would stop, when it would cease. It was not over yet.

He had come to the hollow basin of snow, surrounded by sheer slopes and precipices, out of which rose a track that brought one to the top of the mountain. But he wandered on unconsciously, till he slipped and fell down, and as he fell something broke in his soul, and immediately he went to sleep.

Chapter XXXII

Exeunt

When they brought the body home, the next morning, Gudrun was
shut up in her room. From her window she saw men coming along
with a burden, over the snow. She sat still and let the minutes go
by.

There came a tap at her door. She opened. There stood a
woman, saying softly, oh, far too reverently:

"They have found him, madame?"

"Il est mort?"*

"Yes—hours ago."

Gudrun did not know what to say. What should she say? What
should she feel? What should she do? What did they expect of her?
She was coldly at a loss.

"Thank you," she said, and she shut the door of her room. The
woman went away mortified. Not a word, not a tear—ha, Gudrun
was cold, a cold woman.

Gudrun sat on in her room, her face pale and impassive. What
was she to do? She could not weep and make a scene. She could
not alter herself. She sat motionless, hiding from people. Her one
motive was to avoid actual contact with events. She only wrote out a
long telegram to Ursula and Birkin.

In the afternoon, however, she rose suddenly, to look for Loerke.
She glanced with apprehension at the door of the room that had
been Gerald's. Not for worlds would she enter there.

She found Loerke sitting alone in the lounge. She went straight
up to him.

"It isn't true, is it?" she said.

He looked up at her. A small smile of misery twisted his face. He
shrugged his shoulders.

"True?" he echoed.

"We haven't killed him?" she asked. He disliked her coming to
him in such a manner. He raised his shoulders wearily.

"It has happened," he said.

She looked at him. He sat crushed and frustrated for the time

475

being, quite as emotionless and barren as herself. My God, this was a barren tragedy, barren, barren.

She returned to her room to wait for Ursula and Birkin. She wanted to get away, only to get away. She could not think or feel until she had got away, till she was loosed from this position.

The day passed, the next day came. She heard the sledge, saw Ursula and Birkin alight. And she shrank from these also.

Ursula came straight up to her.

"Gudrun!" she cried, the tears running down her cheeks. And she took her sister in her arms. Gudrun hid her face on Ursula's shoulder, but still she could not escape the cold devil of irony that froze her soul.

"Ha—ha!" she thought, "this is the right behaviour."

But she could not weep, and the sight of her cold, pale, impassive face soon stopped the fountain of Ursula's tears. In a few moments, the sisters had nothing to say to each other.

"Was it very vile to be dragged back here again?" Gudrun asked at length.

Ursula looked up in some bewilderment.

"I never thought of it," she said.

"I felt a beast, fetching you," said Gudrun. "But I simply couldn't see people. That is too much for me."

"Yes," said Ursula, chilled.

Birkin tapped and entered. His face was white and expressionless. She knew he knew. He gave her his hand, saying:

"The end of *this* trip, at any rate." Gudrun glanced at him, afraid.

There was silence between the three of them, nothing to be said. At length Ursula asked, in a small voice:

"Have you seen him?"

He looked back at Ursula with a hard, cold look, and did not trouble to answer.

"Have you seen him?" she repeated.

"I have," he said, coldly.

Then he looked at Gudrun.

"Have you done anything?" he said.

"Nothing," she replied, "nothing."

She shrank in cold disgust from making any statement.

"Loerke says that Gerald came to you when you were sitting on the sledge at the bottom of the Rudelbahn,* that you had words, and Gerald walked away.—What were the words about?—I had better know so that I can satisfy the authorities, if necessary."

Gudrun looked up at him, white, child-like, mute with trouble.

"There weren't even any words," she said. "He knocked Loerke down and stunned him, he half strangled me, then he went away." 5

To herself she was saying: "A pretty little sample of the eternal triangle!" And she turned ironically away, because she knew that the fight had been between Gerald and herself, and that the presence of the third party was a mere contingency—an inevitable contingency perhaps, but a contingency none the less. But let them 10 have it as an example of the eternal triangle, the trinity of hate. It would be simpler for them.

Birkin went away, his manner cold and abstracted. But she knew he would do things for her, nevertheless, he would see her through. She smiled slightly to herself, with contempt. Let him do the work, 15 since he was so extremely *good* at looking after other people.

Birkin went again to Gerald. He had loved him. And yet he felt chiefly disgust at the inert body lying there. It was so inert, so coldly dead, a carcase, Birkin's bowels seemed to turn to ice. He had to stand and look at the frozen dead body that had been Gerald. 20

It was the frozen carcase of a dead male. Birkin remembered a rabbit which he had once found frozen like a board on the snow. It had been rigid like a dried board when he picked it up. And now this was Gerald, stiff as a board, curled up as if for sleep, yet with the horrible hardness somehow evident. It filled him with horror. 25 The room must be made warm, the body must be thawed. The limbs would break like glass or like wood if they had to be straightened.

He reached and touched the dead face. And the sharp, heavy bruise of ice bruised his living bowels. He wondered if he himself 30 were freezing too, freezing from the inside.—In the short blond moustache the life-breath was frozen into a block of ice, beneath the silent nostrils. And this was Gerald!

Again he touched the sharp, almost glittering fair hair of the frozen body. It was icy-cold, hair icy-cold, almost venomous. 35 Birkin's heart began to freeze. He had loved Gerald. Now he looked at the shapely, strange-coloured face, with the small, fine, pinched nose and the manly cheeks, saw it frozen like an ice-pebble—yet he had loved it. What was one to think or feel?—His brain was beginning to freeze, his blood was turning to ice-water. So cold, so cold, a 40 heavy, bruising cold pressing on his arms from outside, and a heavier cold congealing within him, in his heart and in his bowels.

He went over the snow-slopes, to see where the death had been. At last he came to the great shallow among the precipices and
5 slopes, near the summit of the pass. It was a grey day, the third day of greyness and stillness. All was white, icy, pallid, save for the scoring of black rocks that jutted like roots sometimes, and sometimes were in naked faces. In the distance a slope sheered down from a peak, with many black rock-slides.
10 It was like a shallow pot* lying among the stone and snow of the upper world. In this pot Gerald had gone to sleep. At the far end, the guides had driven iron stakes deep into the snow-wall, so that, by means of the great rope attached, they could haul themselves up the massive snow-front out on to the jagged summit of the pass,
15 naked to heaven, where the Marienhütte hid among the naked rocks. Round about, spiked, slashed snow-peaks pricked the heaven.

Gerald might have found this rope. He might have hauled himself up to the crest. He might have heard the dogs in the Marien-
20 hütte, and found shelter. He might have gone on, down the steep, steep fall of the south side, down into the dark valley with its pines, on to the great Imperial road leading south to Italy.

He might! And what then? The Imperial road! The south? Italy? What then? Was it a way out?—It was only a way in again. Birkin
25 stood high in the painful air, looking at the peaks, and the way south. Was it any good going south, to Italy? Down the old, old Imperial road?

He turned away. Either the heart would break, or cease to care. Best cease to care. Whatever the mystery which has brought forth
30 man and the universe, it is a non-human mystery, it has its own great ends, man is not the criterion. Best leave it all to the vast, creative, non-human mystery. Best strive with oneself only, not with the universe.

"God cannot do without man." It was a saying of some great
35 French religious teacher.*—But surely this is false. God can do without man. God could do without the ichthyosauri and the masto-don. These monsters failed creatively to develop, so God, the creative mystery, dispensed with them. In the same way the mystery could dispense with man, should he too fail creatively to change and
40 develop. The eternal creative mystery could dispose of man, and

replace him with a finer created being: just as the horse has taken the place of the mastodon.

It was very consoling to Birkin, to think this. If humanity ran into a cul de sac, and expended itself, the timeless creative mystery would bring forth some other being, finer, more wonderful, some new, more lovely race, to carry on the embodiment of creation. The game was never up. The mystery of creation was fathomless, infallible, inexhaustible forever. Races came and went, species passed away, but ever new species arose, more lovely, or equally lovely, always surpassing wonder. The fountain-head was incorruptible and unsearchable. It had no limits. It could bring forth miracles, create utter new races and new species, in its own hour, new forms of consciousness, new forms of body, new units of being. To be man was as nothing compared to the possibilities of the creative mystery. To have one's pulse beating direct from the mystery, this was perfection, unutterable satisfaction. Human or inhuman mattered nothing. The perfect pulse throbbed with indescribable being, miraculous unborn species.

Birkin went home again to Gerald. He went into the room, and sat down on the bed. Dead, dead and cold!

"Imperial Ceasar dead, and turned to clay
Would stop a hole to keep the wind away."*

There was no response from that which had been Gerald. Strange, congealed, icy substance—no more. No more!

Terribly weary, Birkin went away, about the day's business. He did it all quietly, without bother. To rant, to rave, to be tragic, to make situations—it was all too late. Best be quiet, and bear one's soul in patience and in fulness.

But when he went in again, at evening, to look at Gerald between the candles, because of his heart's hunger, suddenly his heart contracted, his own candle all but fell from his hand, as, with a strange whimpering cry, the tears broke out. He sat down in a chair, shaken by a sudden access. Ursula, who had followed him, recoiled aghast from him, as he sat with sunken head and body convulsively shaken, making a strange, horrible sound of tears.

"I didn't want it to be like this—I didn't want it to be like this," he cried to himself.

Ursula could but think of the Kaiser's: "Ich habe es nicht gewollt."* She looked almost with horror on Birkin.

Suddenly he was silent. But he sat with his head dropped, to hide his face. Then furtively he wiped his face with his fingers. Then suddenly he lifted his head, and looked straight at Ursula, with dark, almost vengeful eyes.

5 "He should have loved me," he said. "I offered him."

She, afraid, white, with mute lips answered:

"What difference would it have made!"

"It would!" he said. "It would."

He forgot her, and turned to look at Gerald. With head oddly
10 lifted, like a man who draws his head back from an insult, half haughtily, he watched the cold, mute, material face. It had a bluish cast. It sent a shaft like ice through the heart of the living man. Cold, mute, material! Birkin remembered how once Gerald had clutched his hand, with a warm, momentaneous grip of final love. For one
15 second—then let go again, let go for ever. If he had kept true to that clasp, death would not have mattered. Those who die, and dying still can love, still believe, do not die. They live still in the beloved. Gerald might still have been living in the spirit with Birkin, even after death. He might have lived with his friend, a further life.

20 But now he was dead, like clay, like bluish, corruptible ice. Birkin looked at the pale fingers, the inert mass. He remembered a dead stallion he had seen: a dead mass of maleness, repugnant. He remembered also the beautiful face of one whom he had loved, and who had died still having the faith to yield to the mystery. That dead
25 face was beautiful, no one could call it cold, mute, material. No one could remember it without gaining faith in the mystery, without the soul's warming with new, deep life-trust.

And Gerald! The denier! He left the heart cold, frozen, hardly able to beat. Gerald's father had looked wistful, to break the heart:
30 but not this last terrible look of cold, mute Matter. Birkin watched and watched.

Ursula stood aside watching the living man stare at the frozen face of the dead man. Both faces were unmoved and unmoving. The candle-flames flickered in the frozen air, in the intense silence.

35 "Haven't you seen enough?" she said.

He got up.

"It's a bitter thing to me," he said.

"What—that he's dead?" she said.

His eyes just met hers. He did not answer.

40 "You've got me," she said.

He smiled, and kissed her.

"If I die," he said, "you'll know I haven't left you."

"And me?" she cried.

"And you won't have left me," he said. "We shan't have any need to despair, in death." 5

She took hold of his hand.

"But need you despair over Gerald?" she said.

"Yes," he answered.

They went away. Gerald was taken to England, to be buried. Birkin and Ursula accompanied the body, along with one of Gerald's 10 brothers. It was the Crich brothers and sisters who insisted on the burial in England. Birkin wanted to leave the dead man in the Alps, near the snow. But the family was strident, loudly insistent.

Gudrun went to Dresden. She wrote no particulars of herself. Ursula stayed at the Mill with Birkin for a week or two. They were 15 both very quiet.

"Did you need Gerald?" she asked one evening.

"Yes," he said.

"Aren't I enough for you?" she asked.

"No," he said. "You are enough for me, as far as woman is 20 concerned. You are all women to me. But I wanted a man friend, as eternal as you and I are eternal."

"Why aren't I enough?" she said. "You are enough for me. I don't want anybody else but you. Why isn't it the same with you?"

"Having you, I can live all my life without anybody else, any other 25 sheer intimacy. But to make it complete, really happy, I wanted eternal union with a man too: another kind of love," he said.

"I don't believe it," she said. "It's an obstinacy, a theory, a perversity."*

"Well—" he said. 30

"You can't have two kinds of love. Why should you!"

"It seems as if I can't," he said. "Yet I wanted it."

"You can't have it, because it's false, impossible," she said.

"I don't believe that," he answered.

APPENDIX I

Foreword to *Women in Love*

Note on the text

Written following a suggestion made to Thomas Seltzer on 7 September 1919 – 'would you like me to write a short Fore-word?' (*Letters*, iii. 391) – the autograph manuscript (Roberts E442a) was first printed in an advertising leaflet distributed by Seltzer in the autumn of 1920 (Roberts A14.5). This exists in the forms of a first printing, with title and Lawrence's name in green (hereafter A1), and a corrected printing, with title and name in black (hereafter A1a); see Roberts 39. The Foreword was republished in March 1936 by Nathan Van Patten (hereafter A2; Roberts A74), probably from the autograph manuscript. The latter, together with page and final proofs of A2 (Roberts E442b and c), are all now missing from the Library of the University of Stanford.

Base-text here is A1; the Textual apparatus records the variants of A1a and A2. Because the latter probably also derived from Roberts E442a, it has been used to emend A1, but the concern of its publisher to produce an elegant and beautiful pamphlet suggests that certain details of its styling are probably not authorial.

Foreword to *Women in Love*

This novel was written in its first form in the Tyrol, in 1913. It was altogether re-written and finished in Cornwall in 1917.* So that it is a novel which took its final shape in the midst of the period of war, though it does not concern the war itself. I should wish the time to remain unfixed, so that the bitterness of the war may be taken for granted in the characters.

The book has been offered to various London publishers.* Their almost inevitable reply has been "We should like very much to publish, but feel we cannot risk a prosecution." They remember the fate of "The Rainbow,"* and are cautious. This book is a potential sequel to "The Rainbow."

In England, I would never try to justify myself against any accusation. But to the Americans, perhaps I may speak for myself. I am accused, in England, of uncleanness and pornography. I deny the charge, and take no further notice. In America the chief accusation seems to be one of "Eroticism." This is odd, rather puzzling to my mind. Which Eros? Eros of the jaunty "amours," or Eros of the sacred mysteries? And if the latter, why accuse, why not respect, even venerate?

Let us hesitate no longer to announce that the sensual passions and mysteries are equally sacred with the spiritual mysteries and passions. Who would deny it any more? The only thing unbearable is the degradation, the prostitution of the living mysteries in us. Let man only approach his own self with a deep respect, even reverence for all that the creative soul, the God-mystery within us, puts forth. Then we shall all be sound and free. Lewdness is hateful because it impairs our integrity and our proud being.

The creative, spontaneous soul sends forth its promptings of desire and aspiration in us. These promptings are our true fate, which it is our business to fulfil. A fate dictated from outside, from theory or from circumstances, is a false fate.

This novel pretends only to be a record of the writer's own desire, aspirations, struggles: in a word, a record of the profoundest experiences in the self. Nothing that comes from the deep, passional soul is bad, or can be bad. So there is no apology to tender, unless to the soul itself, if it should have been belied.

Man struggles with his unborn needs and fulfilment. New unfoldings struggle up in torment in him, as buds struggle forth the midst of a plant. Any man of real individuality tries to know and to understand what is happening, even in himself, as he goes along. This struggle for verbal consciousness should not be left out in art.

5 It is a very great part of life. It is not superimposition of a theory. *It is the passionate struggle into conscious being.*

We are now in a period of crisis. Every man who is acutely alive is acutely wrestling with his own soul. The people that can bring forth the new passion, the new idea, this people will endure. Those

10 others, that fix themselves in the old idea, will perish with the new life strangled unborn within them. Men must speak out to one another.

In point of style, fault is often found with the continual, slightly modified repetition. The only answer is that it is natural to the

15 author: and that every natural crisis in emotion or passion or understanding comes from this pulsing, frictional to-and-fro, which works up to culmination.

D. H. Lawrence

*Hermitage, 12 September 1919.**

APPENDIX II

The 'Prologue' and 'Wedding' Chapters

Note on the text

This extended manuscript fragment (Roberts E441b), located at UT, is written in pencil on fifty-five pages of ruled paper measuring 25.2 × 20 cm ($9^{15}/_{16}$ × $7^{27}/_{32}$ inches). The Textual apparatus records variants in the first publications and editorial emendations.

Chapter I.

Prologue.

The acquaintance between the two men was slight and insignificant. Yet there was a subtle bond that connected them.

They had met four years ago, brought together by a common friend, Hosken, a naval man. The three, Rupert Birkin, William Hosken, and Gerald Crich had then spent a week in the Tyrol together, mountain-climbing.*

Birkin and Gerald Crich felt take place between them, the moment they saw each other, that sudden connection which sometimes springs up between men who are very different in temper. There had been a subterranean kindling in each man. Each looked towards the other, and knew the trembling nearness.

Yet they had maintained complete reserve, their relations had been, to all knowledge, entirely casual and trivial. Because of the inward kindled connection, they were even more distant and slight than men usually are, one towards the other.

There was, however, a certain tenderness in their politeness, an almost uncomfortable understanding lurked under their formal, reserved behaviour. They were vividly aware of each other's presence, and each was just as vividly aware of himself, in presence of the other.

The week of mountain-climbing passed like an intense brief life-time. The three men were very close together, and lifted into an abstract isolation, among the upper rocks and the snow. The world that lay below, the whole field of human activity, was sunk and subordinated, they had trespassed into the upper silence and loneliness. The three of them had reached another state of being, they were enkindled in the upper silences into a rare, unspoken intimacy, an intimacy that took no expression, but which was between them like a transfiguration. As if thrown into the strange fire of abstraction, up in the mountains, they knew and were known to each other. It was another world, another life, transfigured, and yet most vividly corporeal, the senses all raised, till each felt his own body, and the presence of his companions, like an essential flame, they radiated to one enkindled, transcendent fire, in the upper world.

Then had come the sudden falling down to earth, the sudden extinction. At Innsbruck they had parted, Birkin to go to Munich,
5 Gerald Crich and Hosken to take the train for Paris and London. On the station they shook hands, and went asunder, having spoken no word and given no sign of the transcendent intimacy which had roused them beyond the everyday life. They shook hands and took leave casually, as mere acquaintances going their separate ways. Yet
10 there remained always, for Birkin and for Gerald Crich, the absolute recognition that had passed between them then, the knowledge that was in their eyes as they met at the moment of parting. They knew they loved each other, that each would die for the other.

Yet all this knowledge was kept submerged in the soul of the two
15 men. Outwardly they would have none of it. Outwardly they only stiffened themselves away from it. They took leave from each other even more coldly and casually than is usual.

And for a year they had seen nothing of each other, neither had they exchanged any word. They passed away from each other, and,
20 superficially, forgot.

But when they met again, in a country house in Derbyshire, the enkindled sensitiveness sprang up again like a strange, embarrassing fire. They scarcely knew each other, yet here was this strange, unacknowledged, inflammable intimacy between them. It made
25 them uneasy.

Rupert Birkin, however, strongly centred in himself, never gave way in his soul, to anyone. He remained in the last issue detached, self-responsible, having no communion with any other soul. Therefore Gerald Crich remained intact in his own form.

30 The two men were very different. Gerald Crich was the fair, keen-eyed Englishman of medium stature, hard in his muscles and full of energy as a machine. He was a hunter, a traveller, a soldier, always active, always moving vigorously, and giving orders to some subordinate.

35 Birkin on the other hand was quiet and unobtrusive. In stature he was long and very thin, and yet not bony, close-knit, flexible, and full of repose, like a steel wire. His energy was not evident, he seemed almost weak, passive, insignificant. He was delicate in health. His face was pale and rather ugly, his hair dun-coloured, his eyes were of
40 a yellowish-grey, full of life and warmth. They were the only

noticeable thing about him, to the ordinary observer, being very warm and sudden and attractive, alive like fires. But this chief attraction of Birkin's was a false one. Those that knew him best knew that his lovable eyes were, in the last issue, estranged and unsoftening like the eyes of a wolf. In the last issue he was callous, and without feeling, confident, just as Gerald Crich in the last issue was wavering and lost.

The two men were staying in the house of Sir Charles Roddice, Gerald Crich as friend of the host, Rupert Birkin as friend of his host's daughter, Hermione Roddice. Sir Charles would have been glad for Gerald Crich to marry the daughter of the house, because this young man was a well-set young Englishman of strong conservative temperament, and heir to considerable wealth. But Gerald Crich did not care for Hermione Roddice, and Hermione Roddice disliked Gerald Crich.

She was a rather beautiful woman of twenty-five, fair, tall, slender, graceful, and of some learning. She had known Rupert Birkin in Oxford. He was a year her senior. He was a Fellow of Magdalen College, and had been, at twenty-one, one of the young lights of the place, a coming somebody. His essays on Education had been very well received,* and he became an inspector of schools.

Hermione Roddice loved him. When she had listened to his passionate declamations, in his rooms in the Blackhorse Road,* and when she had heard the respect with which he was spoken of, five years ago, she being a girl of twenty, reading political economy, and he a youth of twenty-one, holding forth against Nietzsche, then she devoted herself to his name and fame, she added herself to his mental and spiritual flame.

Sir Charles thought they would marry. He considered that Birkin, hanging on year after year, was spoiling all his daughter's chances, and without pledging himself in the least. It irked the soldierly knight considerably. But he was somewhat afraid of the quiet, always-civil Birkin. And Hermione, when Sir Charles mentioned that he thought of speaking to the young man, in order to know his intentions, fell into such a white and overweening, contemptuous passion, that her father was non-plussed and reduced to irritated silence.

"How vulgar you are!" cried the young woman. "You are not to dare to say a word to him. It is a friendship, and it isn't to be broken-in upon in this fashion. Why should you want to rush me into marriage? I am more than happy as I am."

Her liquid grey eyes swam dark with fury and pain and resentment, her beautiful face was convulsed. She seemed like a prophetess violated. Her father withdrew, cold and huffed.

So the relationship between the young woman and Birkin continued. He was an inspector of schools, she studied Education. He wrote also harsh, jarring poetry, very real and painful, under which she suffered; and sometimes, shallower, gentle lyrics, which she treasured as drops of manna. Like a priestess she kept his records and his oracles, he was like a God who would be nothing if his worship were neglected.

Hermione could not understand the affection between the two men. They would sit together in the hall, at evening, and talk without any depth. What did Rupert find to take him up, in Gerald Crich's conversation? She, Hermione, was only rather bored, and puzzled. Yet the two men seemed happy, holding their commonplace discussion. Hermione was impatient. She knew that Birkin was, as usual, belittling his own mind and talent, for the sake of something that she felt unworthy, some common correspondence which she knew demeaned and belied him. Why would he always come down so eagerly to the level of common people, why was he always so anxious to vulgarise and betray himself? She bit her lip in torment. It was as if he were anxious to deny all that was fine and rare in himself.

Birkin knew what she was feeling and thinking. Yet he continued almost spitefully against her. He *did* want to betray the heights and depths of nearly religious intercourse which he had with her. He, the God, turned round upon his priestess, and became the common, vulgar man who turned her to scorn. He performed some strange metamorphosis of soul, and from being a pure, incandescent spirit burning intense with the presence of God, he became a lustful, shallow, insignificant fellow running in all the common ruts. Even there was some vindictiveness in him now, something jeering and spiteful and low, unendurable. It drove her mad. She had given him all her trembling, naked soul, and now, he turned mongrel, and triumphed in his own degeneration. It was his deep desire, to be common, vulgar, a little gross. She could not bear the look of almost sordid jeering with which he turned on her, when she reached out her hand, imploring. It was as if some rat bit her, she felt she was going insane. And he jeered at her, at the spiritual woman who waited at the tomb, in her sandals and her mourning robes. He jeered at her horribly, knowing her secrets. And she was insane, she knew she was going mad.

But he plunged on triumphant into intimacy with Gerald Crich, excluding the woman, tormenting her. He knew how to pitch himself into tune with another person. He could adjust his mind, his consciousness, almost perfectly to that of Gerald Crich, lighting up the edge of the other man's limitation with a glimmering light that was the essence of exquisite adventure and liberation to the confined intelligence. The two men talked together for hours, Birkin watching the hard limbs and the rather stiff face of the traveller in unknown countries, Gerald Crich catching the pale, luminous face opposite him, lit up over the edge of the unknown regions of the soul, trembling into new being, quivering with new intelligence.

To Hermione, it was insupportable degradation that Rupert Birkin should maintain this correspondence, prostituting his mind and his understanding to the coarser stupidity of the other man. She felt confusion gathering upon her, she was unanchored on the edge of madness. Why did he do it? Why was he, whom she knew as her leader, starlike and pure, why was he the lowest betrayer and the ugliest of blasphemers? She held her temples, feeling herself reel towards the bottomless pit.

For Birkin did get a greater satisfaction, at least for the time being, from his intercourse with the other man, than from his spiritual relation with her. It satisfied him to have to do with Gerald Crich, it fulfilled him to have this other man, this hard-limbed traveller and sportsman, following implicitly, held as it were consummated within the spell of a more powerful understanding. Birkin felt a passion of desire for Gerald Crich, for the clumsier, cruder intelligence and the limited soul, and for the striving, unlightened body of his friend. And Gerald Crich, not understanding, was transfused with pleasure. He did not even know he loved Birkin. He thought him marvellous in understanding, almost unnatural, and on the other hand pitiful and delicate in body. He felt a great tenderness towards him, of superior physical strength, and at the same time some reverence for his delicacy and fineness of being.

All the same, there was no profession of friendship, no open mark of intimacy. They remained to all intents and purposes distant, mere acquaintances. It was in the other world of the subconsciousness that the interplay took place, the interchange of spiritual and physical richness, the relieving of physical and spiritual poverty, without any intrinsic change of state in either man.

Hermione could not understand it at all. She was mortified and in despair. In his lapses, she despised and revolted from Birkin. Her mistrust of him pierced to the quick of her soul. If his intense and pure flame of spirituality only sank to this guttering prostration, a low, degraded heat, servile to a clumsy Gerald Crich, fawning on a coarse, unsusceptible being, such as was Gerald Crich, and all the multitudes of Gerald Criches of this world, then nothing was anything. The transcendent star of one evening was the putrescent phosphorescence of the next, and glory and corruptibility were interchangeable. Her soul was convulsed with cynicism. She despised her God and her angel. Yet she could not do without him. She believed in herself as a priestess, and that was all. Though there were no god to serve, still she was a priestess. Yet having no altar to kindle, no sacrifice to burn, she would be barren and useless. So she adhered to her god in him, which she claimed almost violently, whilst her soul turned in bitter cynicism from the prostitute man in him. She did not believe in him, she only believed in that which she could gather from him, as one gathers silk from the corrupt worm. She was the maker of gods.

So, after a few days, Gerald Crich went away and Birkin was left to Hermione Roddice. It is true, Crich said to Birkin: "Come and see us, if ever you are near enough, will you?", and Birkin had said yes. But for some reason, it was concluded beforehand that this visit would never be made, deliberately.

Sick, helpless, Birkin swung back to Hermione. In the garden, at evening, looking over the silvery hills, he sat near to her, or lay with his head on her bosom, while the moonlight came gently upon the trees, and they talked, quietly, gently as dew distilling, their two disembodied voices distilled in the silvery air, two voices moving and ceasing like ghosts, like spirits. And they talked of life, and of death, but chiefly of death, his words turning strange and phosphorescent, like dark water suddenly shaken alight, whilst she held his head against her breast, infinitely satisfied and completed by its weight upon her, and her hand travelled gently, finely, oh, with such exquisite quivering adjustment, over his hair. The pain of tenderness he felt for her was almost unendurable, as her hand fluttered and came near, scarcely touching him, so light and sensitive it was, as it passed over his hair, rhythmically. And still his voice moved and thrilled through her like the keenest pangs of embrace, she remained possessed by him, possessed by the spirit. And the sense of beauty and perfect, blade-keen ecstasy was balanced to perfection, she passed away, was transported.

After these nights of superfine ecstasy of beauty, after all was consumed in the silver fire of moonlight, all the soul caught up in the universal chill-blazing bonfire of the moonlit night, there came the morning, and the ash, when his body was grey and consumed, and his soul ill. Why should the sun shine, and hot gay flowers come out, when the kingdom of reality was the silver-cold night of death, lovely and perfect.

She, like a priestess, was fulfilled and rich. But he became more hollow and ghastly to look at. There was no escape, they penetrated further and further into the regions of death, and soon the connection with life would be broken.

Then came his revulsion against her. After he loved her with a tenderness that was anguish, a love that was all pain, or else transcendent white ecstasy, he turned upon her savagely, like a maddened dog. And like a priestess who is rended for sacrifice, she submitted and endured. She would serve the God she possessed, even though he should turn periodically into a fierce dog, to rend her.

So he went away, to his duties, and his work. He had made a passionate study of education, only to come, gradually, to the knowledge that education is nothing but the process of building up, gradually, a complete unit of consciousness. And each unit of consciousness is the living unit of that great social, religious, philosophic idea towards which mankind, like an organism seeking its final form, is laboriously growing. But if there *be* no great philosophic idea, if, for the time being, mankind, instead of going through a period of growth, is going through a corresponding process of decay and decomposition from some old, fulfilled, obsolete idea, then what is the good of educating? Decay and decomposition will take their own way. It is impossible to educate for this end, impossible to teach the world how to die away from its achieved, nullified form. The autumn must take place in every individual soul, as well as in all the people, all must die, individually and socially. But education is a process of striving to a new, unanimous being, a whole organic form. But when winter has set in, when the frosts are strangling the leaves off the trees and the birds are silent knots of darkness, how can there be a unanimous movement towards a whole summer of florescence? There can be none of this, only submission to the death of this nature, in the winter that has come upon mankind, and a cherishing of the unknown that is unknown for many a day yet, buds that may not open till a far off season comes, when the season of death has passed away.

And Birkin was just coming to a knowledge of the essential futility of all attempt at social unanimity in constructiveness. In the winter,
5 there can only be unanimity of disintegration, the leaves fall unanimously, the plants die down, each creature is a soft-slumbering grave, as the adder and the dormouse in winter are the soft tombs of the adder and the dormouse which slip about like rays of brindled darkness, in summer.

10 How to get away from this process of reduction, how escape this phosphorescent passage into the tomb, which was universal, though unacknowledged, this was the unconscious problem which tortured Birkin day and night. He came to Hermione, and found with her the pure, translucent regions of death itself, of ecstasy. In the world the
15 autumn was setting in. What should a man add himself on to?—to science, to social reform, to aestheticism, to sensationalism? The whole world's constructive activity was a fiction, a lie, to hide the great process of decomposition, which had set in. What then to adhere to?

20 He ran about from death to death. Work was terrible, horrible, because he did not believe in it. It was almost a horror to him, to think of going from school to school, making reports and giving suggestions, when the whole process to his soul was pure futility, a process of mechanical activity entirely purposeless, sham growth
25 which was entirely rootless. Nowhere more than in education did a man feel the horror of false, rootless spasmodic activity more acutely. The whole business was like dementia. It created in him a feeling of nausea and horror. He recoiled from it. And yet, where should a man repair, what should he do?

30 In his private life the same horror of futility and wrongness dogged him. Leaving alone all ideas, religious or philosophic, all of which are mere sounds, old repetitions, or else novel, dexterous, sham permutations and combinations of old repetitions, leaving alone all the things of the mind and the consciousness, what remained in a man's
35 life? There is his emotional and his sensuous activity, is not this enough?

Birkin started with madness from this question, for it touched the quick of torture. There was his love for Hermione, a love based entirely on ecstasy and on pain, and ultimate death. He *knew* he did
40 not love her with any living, creative love. He did not even desire her:

he had no passion for her, there was no hot impulse of growth between them, only this terrible reducing activity of phosphorescent consciousness, the consciousness ever liberated more and more into the void, at the expense of the flesh, which was burnt down like dead grey ash.

He did not call this love. Yet he was bound to her, and it was agony to leave her. And he did not love anyone else. He did not love any woman. He *wanted* to love. But between wanting to love, and loving, is the whole difference between life and death.

The incapacity to love, the incapacity to desire any woman, positively, with body and soul, this was a real torture, a deep torture indeed. Never to be able to love spontaneously, never to be moved by a power greater than oneself, but always to be within one's own control, deliberate, having the choice, this was horrifying, more deadly than death. Yet how was one to escape. How could a man escape from being deliberate and unloving, except a greater power, an impersonal, imperative love should take hold of him? And if the greater power should not take hold of him, what could he do but continue in his deliberateness, without any fundamental spontaneity?

He did not love Hermione, he did not desire her. But he wanted to force himself to love her and to desire her. He was consumed by sexual desire, and he wanted to be fulfilled. Yet he did not desire Hermione. She repelled him rather. Yet he *would* have this physical fulfilment, he would have the sexual activity. So he forced himself towards her.

She was hopeless from the start. Yet she resigned herself to him. In her soul, she knew this was not the way. And yet even she was ashamed, as of some physical deficiency. She did not want him either. But with all her soul, she *wanted* to want him. She would do anything to give him what he wanted, that which he was raging for, this physical fulfilment he insisted on. She was wise, she thought for the best. She prepared herself like a perfect sacrifice to him. She offered herself gladly to him, gave herself into his will.

And oh, it was all such a cruel failure, just a failure. This last act of love which he had demanded of her was the keenest grief of all, it was so insignificant, so null. He had no pleasure of her, only some mortification. And her heart almost broke with grief.

She wanted him to take her. She wanted him to take her, to break her with his passion, to destroy her with his desire, so long as he got satisfaction. She looked forward, tremulous, to a kind of death at his hands, she gave herself up. She would be broken and dying, destroyed, if only he would rise fulfilled.

But he was not capable of it, he failed. He could not take her and destroy her. He could not forget her. They had had too rare a spiritual intimacy, he could not now tear himself away from all this, and come like a brute to take its satisfaction. He was too much aware of her, and of her fear, and of her writhing torment, as she lay in sacrifice. He had too much deference for her feeling. He could not, as she madly wanted, destroy her, trample her, and crush a satisfaction from her. He was not experienced enough, not hardened enough. He was always aware of *her* feelings, so that he had none of his own. Which made this last love-making between them an ignominious failure, very, very cruel to bear.

And it was this failure which broke the love between them. He hated her, for her incapacity in love, for her lack of desire for him, her complete and almost perfect lack of any physical desire towards him. Her desire was all spiritual, all in the consciousness. She wanted him all, all through the consciousness, never through the senses.

And she hated him, and despised him, for his incapacity to wreak his desire upon her, his lack of strength to crush his satisfaction from her. If only he could have taken her, destroyed her, used her all up, and been satisfied, she would be at last free. She might be killed, but it would be the death which gave her consummation.

It was a failure, a bitter, final failure. He could not take from her what he wanted, because he could not, bare-handed, destroy her. And she despised him that he could not destroy her.

Still, though they had failed, finally, they did not go apart. Their relation was too deep-established. He was by this time twenty-eight years old, and she twenty-seven. Still, for his spiritual delight, for a companion in his conscious life, for someone to share and heighten his joy in thinking, or in reading, or in feeling beautiful things, or in knowing landscape intimately and poignantly, he turned to her. For all these things, she was still with him, she made up the greater part of his life. And he, she knew to her anguish and mortification, he was still the master-key to almost all life, for her. She wanted it not to be so, she wanted to be free of him, of the strange, terrible bondage of his domination. But as yet, she could not free herself from him.

He went to other women, to women of purely sensual, sensational attraction, he prostituted his spirit with them. And he got *some* satisfaction. She watched him go, sadly, and yet not without a measure of relief. For he would torment her less, now.

She knew he would come back to her. She knew, inevitably as the dawn would rise, he would come back to her, half exultant and triumphant over her, half bitter against her for letting him go, and wanting her now, wanting the communion with her. It was as if he went to the other, the dark, sensual, almost bestial woman thoroughly and fully to degrade himself. He despised himself, essentially, in his attempts at sensuality, she knew that. So she let him be. It was only his rather vulgar arrogance of a sinner that she found hard to bear. For before her, he wore his sins with braggadaccio,* flaunted them a little in front of her. And this alone drove her to exasperation, to the point of uttering her contempt for his childishness and his instability.

But as yet, she forebore, because of the deference he still felt towards her. Intrinsically, in his spirit, he still served her. And this service she cherished.

But he was becoming gnawed and bitter, a little mad. His whole system was inflamed to a pitch of mad irritability, he became blind, unconscious to the greater half of life, only a few things he saw with feverish acuteness. And she, she kept the key to him, all the while.

The only thing she dreaded was his making up his mind. She dreaded his way of seeing some particular things vividly and feverishly, and of his acting upon this special sight. For once he decided a thing, it became a reigning universal truth to him, and he was completely inhuman.

He was, in his own way, quite honest with himself. But every man has his own truths, and is honest with himself according to them. The terrible thing about Birkin, for Hermione, was that when once he decided upon a truth, he acted upon it, cost what it might. If he decided that his eye did really offend him, he would in truth pluck it out. And this seemed to her so inhuman, so abstract, that it chilled her to the depths of her soul, and made him seem to her inhuman, something between a monster and a complete fool. For might not she herself easily be found to be this eye which must needs be plucked out?

He had stuck fast over this question of love and of physical fulfilment in love, till it had become like a monomania. All his thought turned upon it. For he wanted to keep his integrity of being,

he would not consent to sacrifice one half of himself to the other. He would not sacrifice the sensual to the spiritual half of himself, and he could not sacrifice the spiritual to the sensual half. Neither could he obtain fulfilment in both, the two halves always reacted from each
5   other. To be spiritual, he must have a Hermione, completely without desire: to be sensual, he must have a slightly bestial woman, the very scent of whose skin soon disgusted him, whose manners nauseated him beyond bearing, so that Hermione, always chaste and always stretching out her hands for beauty, seemed to him the purest and
10   most desirable thing on earth.

He knew he obtained no real fulfilment in sensuality, he became disgusted and despised the whole process as if it were dirty. And he knew that he had no real fulfilment in his spiritual and aesthetic intercourse with Hermione. That process he also despised, with
15   considerable cynicism.

And he recognised that he was on the point either of breaking, becoming a thing, losing his integral being, or else of becoming insane. He was now nothing but a series of reactions from dark to light, from light to dark, almost mechanical, without unity or
20   meaning.

This was the most insufferable bondage, the most tormenting affliction, that he could not save himself from these extreme reactions, the vibration between two poles, one of which was Hermione, the centre of social virtue, the other of which was a
25   prostitute, anti-social, almost criminal. He knew that in the end, subject to this extreme vibration, he would be shattered, would die, or else, worse still, would become a mere disordered set of processes, without purpose or integral being. He knew this, and dreaded it. Yet he could not save himself.

30   To save himself, he must unite the two halves of himself, spiritual and sensual. And this is what no man can do at once, deliberately. It must happen to him. Birkin willed to be sensual, as well as spiritual, with Hermione. He might will it, he might act according to his will, but he did not bring to pass that which he willed. A man cannot
35   create desire in himself, nor cease at will from desiring. Desire, in any shape or form, is primal, whereas the will is secondary, derived. The will can destroy, but it cannot create.

So the more he tried with his will, to force his senses towards Hermione, the greater misery he produced. On the other hand his
40   pride never ceased to contemn his profligate intercourse elsewhere.

After all, it was *not* that which he wanted. He did not want libertine pleasures, not fundamentally. His fundamental desire was, to be able to love completely, in one and the same act: both body and soul at once, struck into a complete oneness in contact with a complete woman.

And he failed in this desire. It was always a case of one or the other, of spirit or of senses, and each, alone, was deadly. All history, almost all art, seemed the story of this deadly half-love: either passion, like Cleopatra, or else spirit, like Mary of Bethany or Vittoria Colonna.*

He pondered on the subject endlessly, and knew himself in his reactions. But self-knowledge is not everything. No man, by taking thought, can add one cubit to his stature.* He can but know his own height and limitation.

He knew that he loved no woman, that in nothing was he really complete, really himself. In his most passionate moments of spiritual enlightenment, when like a saviour of mankind he would pour out his soul for the world, there was in him a capacity to jeer at all his own righteousness and spirituality, justly and sincerely to make a mock of it all. And the mockery was so true, it bit to the very core of his righteousness, and showed it rotten, shining with phosphorescence. But at the same time, whilst quivering in the climax-thrill of sensual pangs, some cold voice could say in him: "you are not really moved; you could rise up and go away from this pleasure quite coldly and calmly; it is not radical, your enjoyment."

He knew he had not loved, could not love. The only thing then was to make the best of it, have the two things separate, and over them all, a calm, detached mind. But to this he would not acquiesce. "I should be like a Neckar,"* he said to himself, "like a sea-water being, I should have no soul." And he pondered the stories of the wistful, limpid creatures who watched ceaselessly, hoping to gain a soul.

So the trouble went on, he became more hollow and deathly, more like a spectre with hollow bones. He knew that he was not very far from dissolution.

All the time, he recognised that, although he was always drawn to women, feeling more at home with a woman than with a man, yet it was for men that he felt the hot, flushing, roused attraction which a man is supposed to feel for the other sex. Although nearly all his living interchange went on with one woman or another, although he was always terribly intimate with at least one woman, and practically never intimate with a man, yet the male physique had a fascination for him, and for the female physique he felt only a fondness, a sort of sacred love, as for a sister.

In the street, it was the men who roused him by their flesh and their manly, vigorous movement, quite apart from all individual character, whilst he studied the women as sisters, knowing their meaning and their intents. It was the men's physique which held the passion and the mystery to him. The women he seemed to be kin to, he looked for the soul in them. The soul of a woman and the physique of a man, these were the two things he watched for, in the street.

And this was a new torture to him. Why did not the face of a woman move him in the same manner, with the same sense of handsome desirability, as the face of a man? Why was a man's beauty, the beauté mâle, so vivid and intoxicating a thing to him, whilst female beauty was something quite unsubstantial, consisting all of look and gesture and revelation of intuitive intelligence? He thought women beautiful purely because of their expression. But it was plastic form that fascinated him in men, the contour and movement of the flesh itself.

He wanted all the time to love women. He wanted all the while to feel this kindled, loving attraction towards a beautiful woman, that he would often feel towards a handsome man. But he could not. Whenever it was a case of a woman, there entered in too much spiritual, sisterly love; or else, in reaction, there was only a brutal, callous sort of lust.

This was an entanglement from which there seemed no escape. How can a man *create* his own feelings? He cannot. It is only in his power to suppress them, to bind them in the chain of the will. And what is suppression but a mere negation of life, and of living.

He had several friendships wherein this passion entered, friendships with men of no very great intelligence, but of pleasant appearance: ruddy, well-nourished fellows, good-natured and easy, who protected him in his delicate health more gently than a woman would protect him. He loved his friend, the beauty of whose manly limbs made him tremble with pleasure. He wanted to caress him.

But reserve, which was as strong as a chain of iron in him, kept him from any demonstration. And if he were away for any length of time from the man he loved so hotly, then he forgot him, the flame which invested the beloved like a transfiguration passed away, and Birkin remembered his friend as tedious. He could not go back to him, to talk as tediously as he would have to talk, to take such a level of intelligence as he would have to take. He forgot his men friends completely, as one forgets the candle one has blown out. They remained as quite extraneous and uninteresting persons living their life in their own sphere, and having not the slightest relation to himself, even though they themselves maintained a real warmth of affection, almost of love for him. He paid not the slightest heed to this love which was constant to him, he felt it sincerely to be just nothing, valueless.

So he left his old friends completely, even those to whom he had been attached passionately, like David to Jonathan.* Men whose presence he had waited for cravingly, the touch of whose shoulder suffused him with a vibration of physical love, became to him mere figures, as non-existent as is the waiter who sets the table in a restaurant.

He wondered very slightly at this, but dismissed it with hardly a thought. Yet, every now and again, would come over him the same passionate desire to have near him some man he saw, to exchange intimacy, to unburden himself of love to this new beloved.

It might be any man, a policeman who suddenly looked up at him, as he enquired the way, or a soldier who sat next to him in a railway carriage. How vividly, months afterwards, he would recall the soldier who had sat pressed up close to him on a journey from Charing Cross to Westerham;* the shapely, motionless body, the large, dumb, coarsely-beautiful hands that rested helpless upon the strong knees, the dark brown eyes, vulnerable in the erect body. Or a young man in flannels on the sands at Margate,* flaxen and ruddy, like a Viking of twenty three, with clean, rounded contours, pure as the contours of snow, playing with some young children, building a castle in sand, intent and abstract, like a seagull or a keen, white bear.

In his mind was a small gallery of such men, men whom he had never spoken to, but who had flashed themselves upon his senses unforgettably, men whom he apprehended intoxicatingly in his blood. They divided themselves, roughly, into two classes: these white-skinned, keen-limbed men with eyes like blue-flashing ice and hair like crystals of winter sunshine, the northmen, inhuman as sharp-crying gulls, distinct like splinters of ice, like crystals, isolated, individual; and then the men with dark eyes that one can enter and plunge into, bathe in, as in a liquid darkness, dark-skinned, supple, night-smelling men, who are the living substance of the viscous, universal, heavy darkness.

His senses surged towards these men, towards the perfect and beautiful representatives of these two halves. And he knew them, by
5 seeing them and by apprehending them sensuously, he knew their very blood, its weight and savour; the blood of the northmen sharp and red and light, tending to be keenly acrid, like cranberries, the blood of the dark-limbed men heavy and luscious, and in the end nauseating, revolting.

10 He asked himself, often, as he grew older, and more unearthly, when he was twenty-eight and twenty-nine years old, would he ever be appeased, would he ever cease to desire these two sorts of men. And a wan kind of hopelessness would come over him, as if he would never escape from this attraction, which was a bondage.

15 For he would never acquiesce to it. He could never acquiesce to his own feelings, to his own passion. He could never grant that it should be so, that it was well for him to feel this keen desire to have and to possess the bodies of such men, the passion to bathe in the very substance of such men, the substance of living, eternal light, like
20 eternal snow, and the flux of heavy, rank-smelling darkness.

He wanted to cast out these desires, he wanted not to know them. Yet a man can no more slay a living desire in him, than he can prevent his body from feeling heat and cold. He can put himself into bondage, to prevent the fulfilment of the desire, that is all. But the
25 desire is there, as the travelling of the blood itself is there, until it is fulfilled or until the body is dead.

So he went on, month after month, year after year, divided against himself, striving for the day when the beauty of men should not be so acutely attractive to him, when the beauty of woman should move
30 him instead.

But that day came no nearer, rather it went further away. His deep dread was that it would always be so, that he would never be free. His life would have been one long torture of struggle against his own innate desire, his own innate being. But to be so divided against
35 oneself, this is terrible, a nullification of all being.

He went into violent excess with a mistress whom, in a rather anti-social, ashamed spirit, he loved. And so for a long time he forgot about this attraction that men had for him. He forgot about it entirely. And then he grew stronger, surer.

40 But then, inevitably, it would recur again. There would come into

a restaurant a strange Cornish type of man,* with dark eyes like holes in his head, or like the eyes of a rat, and with dark, fine, rather stiff hair, and full, heavy, softly-strong limbs. Then again Birkin would feel the desire spring up in him, the desire to know this man, to have him, as it were to eat him, to take the very substance of him. And watching the strange, rather furtive, rabbit-like way in which the strong, softly-built man ate, Birkin would feel the rousedness burning in his own breast, as if this were what he wanted, as if the satisfaction of his desire lay in the body of the young, strong man opposite.

And then in his soul would succeed a sort of despair, because this passion for a man had recurred in him. It was a deep misery to him. And it would seem as if he had always loved men, always and only loved men. And this was the greatest suffering to him.

But it was not so, that he always loved men. For weeks it would be all gone from him, this passionate admiration of the rich body of a man. For weeks he was free, active, and living. But he had such a dread of his own feelings and desires, that when they recurred again, the interval vanished, and it seemed the bondage and the torment had been continuous.

This was the one and only secret he kept to himself, this secret of his passionate and sudden, spasmodic affinity for men he saw. He kept this secret even from himself. He knew what he felt, but he always kept the knowledge at bay. His a priori were: "I *should not* feel like this," and "It is the ultimate mark of my own deficiency, that I feel like this." Therefore, though he admitted everything, he never really faced the question. He never accepted the desire, and received it as part of himself. He always tried to keep it expelled from him.*

Gerald Crich was the one towards whom Birkin felt most strongly that immediate, roused attraction which transfigured the person of the attracter with such a glow and such a desirable beauty. The two men had met once or twice, and then Gerald Crich went abroad, to South America. Birkin forgot him, all connection died down. But it was not finally dead. In both men were the seeds of a strong, inflammable affinity.

Therefore, when Birkin found himself pledged to act as best man at the wedding of Hosken, the friend of the mountain-climbing holiday, and of Laura Crich, sister of Gerald, the old affection sprang awake in a moment. He wondered what Gerald would be like now.

Hermione, knowing of Hosken's request to Birkin, at once secured for herself the position of bridesmaid to Laura Crich. It was inevitable. She and Rupert Birkin were running to the end of their friendship. He was now thirty years of age, and she twenty nine. His feeling of hostility towards Hermione had grown now to an almost constant dislike. Still she held him in her power. But the hold became weaker and weaker. "If he breaks loose," she said, "he will fall into the abyss."

Nevertheless he was bound to break loose, because his reaction against Hermione was the strongest movement in his life, now. He was thrusting her off, fighting her off all the while, thrusting himself clear, although he had no other foothold, although he was breaking away from her, his one rock, to fall into a bottomless sea.

Chapter II.

The Wedding.

The Criches lived at Willey Green, a hamlet near to the large mining village of Beldover, where the Brangwens had gone to live. In Willey Green was the grammar school in which Will Brangwen was handicraft instructor, and Ursula had become a class mistress. About a mile away from the Grammar School stood Shortlands, the home of the Criches, a low old house that had once been a sort of manor-farm.

William Crich, Gerald's father, was the principal owner of the mines that went down the valley of Beldover. All round the east, south, and west was a colliery district, a land of desolation now. Only to the north was fair country. The Criches were the only considerable people in the whole neighbourhood.

Yet, as a family, they figured very little in the local interest. William Crich was loved by the miners, so kind and gentle and human he was. But Mrs Crich was haughty, and the children took after her. They looked down upon the working-people of the neighbourhood, as dirt, and the working-people were hostile or indifferent, chiefly the latter.

Still it was an event of some importance for Beldover when Laura Crich was going to be married from Longmeadow, to Henry Hosken, a naval commander.

On the morning of the wedding, Ursula and Gudrun sat in the large window-bay of their father's house in Beldover, talking desultorily. They were a good deal changed. Ursula was twenty seven years old now, and Gudrun twenty-six.

On the face of the elder girl was a little of that look of blighted expectation which disfigures the young, eager women who have settled down to earning their own living, and who begin to feel the meaninglessness of their own activity. Ursula was strained, over-open, over-excitable, and as if a little bit ashamed. She was sewing a piece of embroidery, with brilliant silks.

Gudrun too was changed, but in a different way. She sat crouched in a loose, luxurious fashion over a drawing board which she held on her knee. Her whole bearing was slack, easy, rather voluptuous. She was a very beautiful girl, with large soft limbs and a silken, soft white skin that looked warm and lovely to touch. All her body was soft and full and rich, languorous with a languor that [was] born of strength and deep, unplumbed reserves of life. Her warm-dark hair fell carelessly in loose twinings in her neck and on her soft cheeks. Desultorily, she drew on the sheet of pinned paper, and leisurely, with a few loose strokes, she progressed with her design.

She wore a dress of dark blue colour, a soft, silky poplin, having ruches of blue silk lace in the neck. And her stockings were cherry-coloured. It was evident at a glance that she did not take her stand with ordinary mortals, particularly in Beldover. She had spent the last two years or more in London, studying at an art school. She had won a scholarship in Nottingham, and in London she had lived freely. Her work had attracted considerable notice, particularly her little models in clay, of animals and birds and people. She was a success, both as an artist and in the social life.

Now she had a certain aplomb, and a loose, graceful indifference that made her rare and remarkable in Beldover. Ursula, wearing an ordinary blouse and skirt, admired her sister intensely.

Gudrun had been home only a couple of days. There was talk of her taking up a post as art-mistress in Willey Green Grammar School.

"Ursula," she said, putting the question nearest her heart, "don't you want to get married?"

Ursula's face closed a little. She hesitated before she gathered speech. A deep shadow was on her.

"Not for the sake of getting married—no," she answered, troubled.

"Don't you—not even to have a better time?" said Gudrun.

The frank mundanity of the question gave a set to Ursula's wavering feelings. She was inclined to be too meaningful with her sister, too deep and near. Now she answered, more recklessly:

"I often think of myself arranging a house and having soul to soul talks with a man. But it's never real. When it actually comes to 'the man', the vision collapses like a balloon."

"Don't you really love anybody?" asked Gudrun calmly, as she put her head on one side to look at her drawing.

"No I don't—do you?" asked Ursula.

She had not sufficient calm to be able to continue stitching, through this conversation.

"No—but I'm not very much interested in marriage," replied Gudrun. "There's more of the loving wife in you than in me."

Ursula suffered in spite of herself.

"I suppose there isn't anybody at all, here, for you to have," said Gudrun.

"Not really," said Ursula, apologetic.

"I suppose they are all too blind to see you, really. I think you ought to go away."

"Yes, but why did you come back?" asked Ursula.

"I wanted to," said Gudrun.

"Why?"

"I can't say. I felt I was going into a whirlpool, and I wanted to feel safe."

"You came home to be safe?" said Ursula.

"I think so. I felt after all this *was* my home."

"And do you think so now?"

"I suppose I do. It's rather hard to be sure what a home *is*, really—whether it is the place where one is *never* oneself, and never can be oneself, or whether one is most natural there. I thought I'd come home and try."

"And do you think you're natural or false?"

"False, I think," said Gudrun, calmly rubbing out a piece of her drawing, and sweeping away the crumbs with a slow, heavy motion.

"I think Father is the greatest stranger I ever set eyes on—the greatest outsider, too," she added.

Ursula watched with grave, troubled eyes. She knew her father had become an outsider and a stranger to her also, whilst it seemed her mother had scarcely been anything else. Yet she had never *admitted* it.

"We ought both to be away from home, Prune," she said, troubled; "as far away as possible.—Do you think we are cowards?"

Gudrun frowned slightly. Then, lifting her head, she glanced swiftly, almost furtively at her sister, then looked out of the window.

"Cowards for being here?" she answered.

They neither of them replied to the question. Gudrun remained staring out of the window, Ursula continued to draw the emerald silk carefully through her canvas. They were aware of the room in which they sat, the familiar furniture, the burdensome, familiar atmosphere, more insistent and obtrusive than violent change.

A sudden spasm, like lightning, ran across Ursula's veins. "How I hate it!" she said, involuntarily, to herself. It startled her, frightened

her, and rather pleased her to have declared her antagonism. She meant her home, her whole surroundings, her entire familiar form of life. Under Gudrun's influence, the hatred had flashed across her consciousness like a spark struck from a flint. She had never before
5 admitted this violent, radical loathing of all her condition, of all the old, close, familiar things that had formed her. But now she knew.

"I believe I *am* a coward!" said Gudrun, turning from the window. Her face was quite surprised and wondering, like that of a child that suddenly sees and dislikes itself.

10 Again there was a silence, slow and heavy, like a challenge, or a judgment.

"Let us go out," Gudrun exclaimed.

Ursula put down her work.

"Yes, let us," she said.

15 The two girls were soon walking swiftly down the main road of Beldover. It was a wide, irregular, ugly street, broken and formless.

"It's terribly sordid," said Gudrun, looking at a black patch of earth with cabbage stumps, intervening between grimy brick houses.

"It is amazingly and astoundingly sordid," said Ursula. "It is
20 unbelievable, the strong, universal sordidness the whole place has."

"It is like a country in another world," said Gudrun; "the people all ghosts, and everything a ghostly, degraded replica of what it should be. Ursula, it's marvellous, it is like being mad."

The two sisters were crossing a black path across a soiled, worn
25 field. Before them was a large landscape, a valley with collieries whose white steam and black smoke waved and rose in strong columns, hill-sides where rows of grimy dwellings with slate roofs climbed in a naked contour, fields with iron fences, fields with deep clayey holes dug in them, then more brittle rows of houses. The
30 paths on which the girls walked were of black, trodden earth, the grass of the fields was worn and padded. They passed through a stile of two posts, rubbed shiny by the transit of many colliers in moleskins, then along the end of some alleys. Children called loudly after the two sisters, women folded their bare arms over their
35 coarse-aprons, and stared, making loud gossip.

Gudrun, coming back after more than two years of London, felt the place react upon her like madness. She hardly knew where she was. The strong familiar feeling of the old life—for Beldover was just the same, in kind, as Ilkeston—jarring back into the new form of life
40 which she had taken, was too strong for her. What was she, where

was she? Her whole being seemed a chaos, for the old and the new clanged together with a noise like insanity.

"Ursula," she said, "it gives me the horrors."

They crossed away towards Willey Green, towards the more unspoiled country.

"We will go to Laura Crich's wedding, shall we," said Ursula brightly, playing the home sister.

"I should love to," Gudrun replied.

But she was uncomfortable, as if all her defences were gone. Ursula plodded on, more at home. But she was more at ease only because her sensitiveness was blunted by custom, by ugly habit. She walked this road every day. But although she felt it less, yet the road was just as destructive of her as of Gudrun.

They passed into the purer country. But still, everywhere was bitten with a kind of sordidness, the atmosphere seemed black, the fields seemed grimed, the roads were trodden to a kind of deadness, the paths were black, the stiles polished by dirty moleskins of the colliers.

Coming to Willey Green, they saw the old church standing proud on its little eminence, grey and erect like a stag, whilst beyond, through the etched poplar-trees, was the Grammar School, a big red building with an iron fence round its yard.

It was a spring day of white clouds and blue sky, when the sunshine was warm and the shadows were chilly. Celandines were many and yellow under the hedges, there was a little purple of ground-ivy, and some fruit-trees in the cottage gardens were in blossom, white and feathery. But this all seemed like survival, or reminiscence, the actuality was Beldover, with its hundreds of rows of cottage-dwellings, all degraded and sordid.

The road to Willey Green Church ran between high banks, through a little cutting. Drawing near the lowest dip, Ursula and Gudrun saw a small crowd of people round the church-yard gate.

"There are all those people—let us go back," said Gudrun, swerving away. They were so alien and hostile to her.

"Never mind them," said Ursula. "They're all right."

And together the two sisters approached the watchful, rather mean group of common folk at the church yard gate, chiefly inquisitive women with watchful, underworld faces.

The two sisters held their heads high, their mouths closed rather tight in embarrassment.

"What price the stockings," someone said loudly, against Gudrun.

A fierce anger flamed in the girl's blood. She could have turned and rended the watchful, cackling, degraded little group of human-
5   ity. She longed to be able to kill people, like a witch, by wishing their destruction. They were all so unproud, so degraded.

But she was walking up the steps of the churchyard, to the sunniness above. A red carpet was laid down the old stone path, a policeman was guarding the steps.
10   "I won't go into church," said Gudrun.

She knew her father would be playing the organ, and she was filled with ridiculous shame and resentment.

Ursula faltered on the path beside the red carpet.

"What will you do then?" she asked, confused.
15   "I'm going home through the other gate," said Gudrun, her colour brilliant in her cheeks. She was very beautiful, but the people had eyes only for her cherry-coloured stockings and her big, soft, wine-coloured beaver hat. They thought she looked a freak.

"No, don't let us go away, now," said Ursula. "Let us stand by the
20   school gate."

There was a small gate opening from the shrubbery of the Grammar school on to the church yard. There the two girls stood, screened by some laurel bushes.

They could not see the road, which passed low under the
25   church-yard wall, under the overhanging beeches, but they could see the whole length of the red carpet along the stone path; and behind them, they could see the hill to Whatmore, with the grey road winding up it.

"Do you wish you hadn't come?" asked Ursula.
30   "I don't like the people," said Gudrun.

"You used not to mind them," said the elder sister, nettled.

"I know that. They used to seem quite natural. Now I think they are rather horrible, sinister. They're worse than Goya."*

The sunshine fell in the church yard, serene and vivid, little red
35   daisies were shut up in shadow, many wide daisies were sprinkled over the grass and over the graves.

Punctually, the carriages began to arrive. There was a stir in the crowd at the gate. People, wedding guests, were coming up the steps and down the red carpet. Ursula looked at their faces, Gudrun more
40   at their clothes, their bearing, the whole figure they made. People

had a knack, to her, of looking like dressed artificial figures, marionettes. She was not interested in character; only in plastic form.

Several carriages had arrived, the guests had passed along the red carpet to the church, and still the bridegroom had not come. Now the bridesmaids appeared.

Two were dressed in pale yellow, and carried bunches of pink flowers, cyclamens and pink anemones. Ursula admired Hermione Roddice extremely. She saw the conscious effect of her appearance, the touch of deliberate study which slanted the large hat of yellow velvet on which flat, natural ostrich feathers lay closely, and which had chosen the fine shoes and stockings of brownish grey. In spite of the extreme fashionableness of the dress, there was something trailing and poetic in the slim, fair woman's appearance, a touch of the deliberate Aspasia.*

Hermione was proud, but very wincing. She was afraid of criticism, keeping herself on the defence against it. She walked leaning slightly forward, graceful, but like a patroness, and as if consciously, rather heavily restraining her vision. She was too much aware of her own exposure, and, though perfectly dressed, still not confident, supplicating rather, and on the defensive.

"I know her—she is one of the clever ones," said Gudrun, as the bridesmaids went along the path.

"She looks lovely, though," said Ursula, upon whose heart Hermione made an impression.

"I like the yellow and pink and grey," said Gudrun. "But she doesn't look as if her clothes were part of her, like leaves. They're put on from the outside. I don't care for her herself, like paper flowers."

"Oh yes," said Ursula. "She's beautiful."

"But quite unliving," said Gudrun.

"I think she's lovely," said Ursula, in whose heart some deeper, troubled note was struck by the formed, yet rather pathetic, yearning beauty of Hermione.

Hermione knew she was well dressed, and she was on the brink of the elation of triumph. But all the while, something prevented her. She was not sure. She could only be quite sure when everybody, everybody bowed before her completeness. She needed the last confirmation of her own perfection to come from outside.

Always, within her soul, gnawed this deep uncertainty. She was

overweeningly proud, she held her own mind, her own judgment infallible. But all her pride was built over a chasm, down which at any moment she might be precipitated, to a bottomless depth. Any common maid-servant of robust, positive temper could fling Her-
5 mione down this bottomless pit of insufficiency, by a slight movement of jeering or contempt. And all the while, the pensive, tortured woman piled up her own culture, her own knowledge, as evidence of richness. And it was all like a wonderful elaboration built over a terrible void of insufficiency.
10 Only Birkin, by forming a close and complete alliance with her, could fill up this void, could make her sound and invulnerable, triumphant over all the people of the earth, even over the angels of heaven. *How* she wanted to be beautiful, oh, so beautiful that he would be enchanted once and for all. He was always trying to fight
15 her off, to withdraw and leave her without defences against the world, without fulfilment in this insistent life. He was almost on the point of leaving her.

Yet surely, with all her beauty and her deep knowledge, she could compel him. He was not blind, he *could* see. Ah, if only he would be
20 true to the deep things he shared with her, if only he would establish and maintain with her the foundations of eternal reality!

But she dreaded, she dreaded his slipping away to the mundane things, the common, frivolous activities of vulgar life. And she tried so hard to make herself mistress of these common things. She
25 wanted to outdo the fashionable women in dress, she wanted to surpass the frivolous women in light, sportive attractiveness.

He had not seen her yet. Perhaps, when he saw her in this beautiful dress, he would acknowledge her once and for all, he would take his stand with her finally, against the outer, vulgar world. She
30 needed his conjunction so much: she needed him alone. If he were true to her, she would be mistress of all, she would be unshakeable, infallible, complete. But oh, if he would not be with her, she was like a fragment, incomplete, she was like a torn fragment whose raw edge of insufficiency could never be saved from exposure.
35 The bridesmaids entered the church. Hermione was looking for Birkin. Nothing would exist till he was there, he, her fulfilment in life. She was like an unlighted candle, save he was present.

But he had not come yet, neither he nor the bridegroom. Hermione's heart was gnawed hollow by his absence, she was
40 tormented as by a neuralgia, she could hardly bear to stay there

exposed in the church. If only he had been there, he would have been like a cloak thrown round her exposed soul. In a faint, unexpected delirium of nervous torture, she awaited him, bearing herself pensively, beautiful, the distract* look making her beauty, rather formal and unexpressive, really poignant.

Outside the people waited anxiously. The bridegroom had not come. The bride's carriage, adorned with ribbons and white cockades, drove up. Mr Crich, the father, was out on the pavement, a tall, thin, pale man with a black beard touched with grey. He waited at the carriage door, simply, sadly, rather tenderly. One could see he thought only of his daughter and of her going away from home, nothing of the ceremony and the publicity.

In the doorway of the carriage was a shower of green foliage and white flowers, then the bride's stooping young head, with its flower-buds, then a delicate white foot reaching down to the step, a white foot, a slim, young white ankle, then a sudden foaming rush, and the bride was beside her father, laughing, shaking her veil, putting her hand on his arm. He looked sad and yellowish, his black beard making his face more careworn. Rather stiff, rather formal, with the laughing mist of the bride beside him, he moved towards the steps.

The bridegroom had not come. All the people's hearts were in consternation, they could scarcely watch the bride. Only Ursula and Gudrun, anxious, were watching the carriage bowling down the foot of Whatmore hill.

As the bride and her father came to the top of the steps there was a shout and a rattling among the carriages below, and a louder shout. The bride looked round. The bridegroom and his man were seen to drop out of their cab and go dodging among the horses' heads, holding their hats in their hands. There was a hoarse shouting of excitement among the crowd. The bride lifted her bouquet and waved it, shouting gaily,

"Harry! Harry!!"

He came to the footpath, not having heard. She and her father waited suspended. Then the bridegroom, looking up unawares, saw the bride and her father standing. A queer, startled look went over his face. He hesitated one moment.

"I'm first," she cried, with a little of her family arrogance.

Again his face hardened, and he drew himself instinctively together, to run. Instantly, as if startled by magic, she snatched up

her skirts and was flying up the path, helter-skelter, her white
flowers scattering like spray, her veil streaming out, but her young,
intense, reckless body speeding on, running hard, as if seized with
some mad determination not to be overtaken. Quick as a pulse, her
5 young, persistent feet beat the ground in flight, she seemed to be
carried along almost magically in the swift, deadly aim of her will.

The bridegroom hung in suspense for a moment. Then

"After her!"

said one of the grooms, as at a chase, and as if released from a
10 spring, the young naval commander leapt up the steps and, bending
forward like some hound, was bounding up the path after her.

She, her flowers shaken from her like petals, was steadying herself
to turn the corner. With a wild, roused, laughing cry she veered and
was gone behind the grey buttress. In another instant his supple,
15 relentless loins swung round after. They were both gone.

For a moment, there was complete silence everywhere. Ursula
glanced from the dark, rather stooping figure of Mr Crich, who
stood at the top of the steps watching this flight with a rather queer,
almost cynical look on his face, to the figure of Birkin, who moved at
20 once forward, mounting the steps, saying, with a certain courtly
affability to the older man:

"That's one way of going to church."

"Aye—rackapelt!"* said Mr Crich, slowly. "No heed for anything,
they're all the same."

25 "A real Atalanta," said Birkin.

The two men went side by side, hats in hand, along the path.
Birkin had a slight limp in his walk, a slight trailing of one foot, which
betrayed his self-consciousness. To a stranger, he looked amazingly
pleasant and at his ease. Only Hermione Roddice would have
30 recognised his complicated shyness, that made him feel as if tangled
up in ropes.

He appeared quite easy and gallant, laughing, leaning rather loose
and nonchalant as he walked, very courteous to the elder man.

"It is a disgrace that we are so late," he said, and Ursula could
35 hear his calm, pleasant voice. "But you are even a little before time, I
believe."

"We're usually punctual," said Mr Crich.

"Yes, I'm sorry we are late. But it's very gay and sunny," said
Birkin, "a proper wedding-day."

40 Mr Crich looked up at the sky, as if he had not known the sun was
shining, and must see to make sure.

The two men were gone round the corner. Ursula remained thinking about Birkin. With him another world seemed to take place. He was different from all the rest, from everything.

She had seen him for one moment forget himself, watching the bride running up the path. Then she had seen his sombre, powerful soul watching as from another world. All his rather ridiculous tricks of sociability were gone, he stood a moment undisguised, plain and stark and rather terrible, inhuman like a pure force.

Instantly he had changed into his rather versatile, superficial manner from which he scarcely ever escaped. He was always being somebody else, not himself all his life.* Always he must adjust himself to other people. And therefore he was never real, he was always three-quarters somebody else.

Because he was different from other people, and his world was a different world, he denied both himself and his own world, assuming that the majority were right. He had about him the shadow of some other world, like a darkness and a strangeness, but it was ignored as much as possible. He must be one with the rest, when his nature was, to be apart, different.

Ursula had seen Rupert Birkin once before. He had lately come as inspector of schools, to this district. When she first saw him, she felt there was a strangeness about him, that made her uneasy. His eyes had a dark, inhuman glow, that half repelled her, in spite of his attractive, almost deferential manner. He was *so* amiable. She was troubled in spirit by him. She stood vaguely thinking. Some atmosphere of her old life and her old trouble with Skrebensky came back. She fell away from the present, as if the present were unreal.

At length they heard the organ booming, and soon the wedding party was coming out of church. The bride was laughing and talking excitedly to the bridegroom, who kept shutting his eyes and opening them, involuntarily, to shut out all external presence, to draw near the female, and immediately, perforce, opening them again to become a social, public being.

Then came Birkin with Hermione leaning on his arm. She was very beautiful, with a sort of confident demureness, as if to say 'now I've won.' And he was smiling slightly, maliciously. He was thin and narrow, but tight-woven, essential in vigour.

"That's Rupert Birkin," said Gudrun, surprised.

"Do you know him?" cried Ursula.

"I've met him at Lady Bridget's," said Gudrun. "She thinks he is wonderful."

The Brangwen sisters went home to Beldover, the wedding party gathered at Shortlands. The Criches were a large family. Gerald, the eldest son, was newly home from the wilds of South America; next to him came two married sisters with their husbands, then Wilfrid

5 Crich, who had come up from London, where he was working at the bar. Richard, who was in the Royal Engineers,* was absent. Then there was Laura, and then Diana, and lastly, the child, Winifred, fourteen years of age.

Including the guests, therefore, some thirty people were gathered

10 at Shortlands. The house was not very large, and every room seemed crowded. There was considerable confusion.

[end of manuscript]

APPENDIX III

'Beldover' and the Eastwood Region

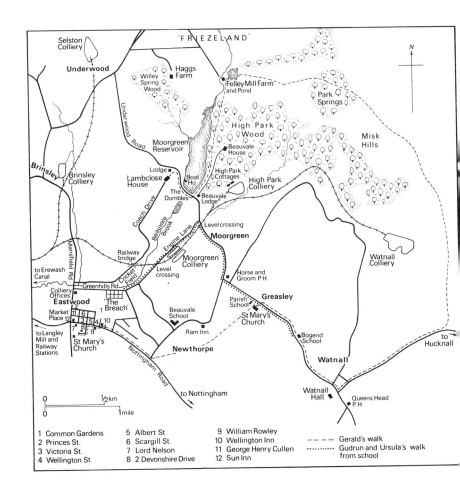

1 Common Gardens
2 Princes St.
3 Victoria St.
4 Wellington St.
5 Albert St.
6 Scargill St.
7 Lord Nelson
8 2 Devonshire Drive
9 William Rowley
10 Wellington Inn
11 George Henry Cullen
12 Sun Inn

– – – – – Gerald's walk
·············· Gudrun and Ursula's walk from school

'Beldover' and the Eastwood region

Lawrence drew extensively on his home town of Eastwood and its surroundings for details of places he described and re-created in *Women in Love*. Many of these real-life originals can readily be identified; others were listed by Steve Bircumshaw (d. 1968) in a document entitled 'Women in Love' now in NCL (hereafter: Bircumshaw).

Beldover (see note on 7:4) corresponds in many details to Eastwood. The 'main road. . .a wide street, part shops, part dwelling houses' (11:11) is Nottingham Road, Eastwood. The colliery 'offices at Beldover' (463:37) correspond to the Barber Walker & Co. offices in Mansfield Road, at the corner of Greenhills Road. The Friday night market (117:29) took place outside the Sun Inn at the junction of Nottingham Road, Mansfield Road and the road to Langley Mill. It was 'a hectic time for us youngsters, Auction sales, quacks, herbalists, occasionally a quack dentist, a tooth taken out for sixpence, fish and chip stalls. To liven things up the Salvation Army band. Sometimes a good fight when some of the miners came out of the pubs to settle their disputes. Then to Teddy Rayner's travelling theatre, *The Blood Tub*. Then home tired but happy' (Bircumshaw 2–3). The cinema visited by Gudrun (118:1) is either the Empire Picture House built in 1913 at the corner of King Street and Nottingham Road, or Parker's Picture Pavilion in the Sun Inn Croft, also operating *c.* 1913. The Brangwens' house in 'Somerset Drive' (339:24: see note on 7:4 and 117:25) is based on the house of Lawrence's Eastwood friends Sarah Annie ('Sallie') and William ('Willie') Hopkin (see *Letters*, i. 176 n. 2) in Devonshire Drive; now no. 2, and the second house on the right, not 'th' last o' th' three' (340:13). Lawrence stayed in the house on his August 1913 visit to Eastwood (*Letters*, ii. 54–5, 58). It is accurately described, with its front door up a side-path, a mosaic of coloured tiles (now removed) in the hall, the dining room with large bay window and 'big oak chimney piece' (340:39) at the foot of the stairs, and a landing below first-floor level. In the novel, however, Lawrence gave the house an extra storey where Gudrun's room is situated, up a 'second flight of stairs' (341:34). Eastwood Parish Church, St Mary's, is only a short distance from Devonshire Drive, and Gudrun can hear the 'church clock' (346:15) from her room.

In chap. 1, Ursula and Gudrun walk from their parents' house to the church in 'Willey Green' (12:25) – Greasley Church, Moorgreen. They turn off Nottingham Road into the 'common-garden' (11:24), 'situated where the extension of Wood Street has been built. The old name Gabes

Lane. In my early days there were only five cottages in the lane' (Bircumshaw 1). See too *The Lost Girl*, ed. John Worthen (Cambridge, 1981), note on 67:36. From the common-garden they see 'the long rows of dwellings, approaching curved up the hill-slope' (11:37), 'locally known as the Buildings. . .Princess Street, Wellington Street, Albert Street, Scargill Street and Victoria Street' (Bircumshaw 1). There is a stile at the bottom of the field, and 'some rows of dwellings, of the poorer sort' (12:3); Bircumshaw describes 'The path at the bottom, where the gardens used to be, with the stile, at the end of the path leading to the Breach' (Bircumshaw 1). The Lawrence family lived here 1887–91: 'six blocks of miners' dwellings, two rows of three, like the dots on a blank-six domino, and twelve houses in a block' (*Sons and Lovers*, chap. 1). Gudrun and Ursula proceed 'over the curve of the hill' (12:24) behind Moorgreen colliery to 'the cottage gardens of Willey Green' and 'the high-road' (12:33): 'Church Road, leading from the Horse and Groom, to Greasley Church' (Bircumshaw 1). The Church of St Mary, Greasley, with Barber family memorials in the churchyard (see below), is described in *Griseleia in Snotinghscire* (1901), by Rodolph, Baron von Hube, pp. 110–51. In the 1881 Census, several professional men and women appear as boarders in Moorgreen and High Park; Gudrun herself eventually lodges here (376:17), as does her electrician boy-friend in chap. IX (117:18), at 'High Park Cottages' (Bircumshaw 1).

She and Ursula watch the wedding from 'Willey Green Grammar School' (9:6, 13:23), a combination of two real-life schools: Beauvale Board School (erected 1878, able to accommodate 850 children, attended by Lawrence 1892–8), and the 'old private school at Bog End' (Bircumshaw 5) on the road to Watnall. Roberts E441b locates the school on the e. side of the churchyard (see Appendix II, 512:20–8).

In chap. IX, Gudrun and Ursula walk home from school down 'the hill between the picturesque cottages of Willey Green. . .to the railway crossing' (110:5): 'the hill leading from the Horse and Groom down to the railway crossing' (Bircumshaw 1). 'The one legged man [110:8] in the signal hut was Thomas Wakefield. My grand parents lived at the big house at the crossing. As a boy when I visited my grand parents sometimes my grandmother would say take this to Tom. It would be some food and tea' (Bircumshaw 2). Miners disabled at work were frequently employed on the colliery railway; according to Mabel Collishaw, her father – Mr Thurlby – who had lost an arm in a colliery accident, and who had been given the job of crossing-keeper at Moorgreen crossing, on one occasion refused to open the gates for Thomas Philip Barber, saying 'Are you going to make that horse's mouth bleed'. Lawrence was present at the time. Gudrun and Ursula proceed 'down the lane' (113:29), 'the old pit lane, an ordinary narrow cart road, with high thorn hedges on each side of the road. The coal mine on the left [113:37] is Moorgreen' (Bircumshaw 2). They go over a second level-crossing with 'many bright rails', near a farm and 'a disused boiler' (114:3); the exceptionally wide railway tracks from Moorgreen Colliery cross Engine Lane at 'Beggarlee crossing. Where the present workshops are one part used to be workshops, and the other part farm buildings, chiefly stables. The huge boiler was a water storage boiler which supplied the loco engines with water' (Bircumshaw 2). They pass on down a dusty road with 'dwellings on one side, and dusty young corn on the other' (114:25): 'The dusty road with. . .workmens houses, the dusty corn fields and the cricket field on the other side is Engine Lane. Council houses have been built on the corn fields and the cricket field' (Bircumshaw 2). The 'blocks of miners' dwellings' which they come to are, again, the Breach.

Outside Beldover itself, the station Ursula goes to in chap. XXVII for her train to see Birkin in Nottingham is Eastwood and Langley Mill Station, on the Great Northern Railway (366:21); she has to go on to 'the junction' (366:22), Langley Mill Junction on the Midland Railway. The 'big mill-house' (123:9) where Birkin lives when he is not in Nottingham is Lawrence's recreation of Felley Mill Farm (now demolished): see note on 134:14, and *The White Peacock*, ed. Andrew Robertson (Cambridge, 1983), pp. 1–4. The mill-pond (123:9) where Birkin punts (chap. XI) and throws stones (chap. XIX) is Felley Mill pond. Ursula finds her way to the Mill past 'bright hill-sides' with 'a subdued smoulder of gorse' (123:5); the area is that known as 'the Friezeland' (also described in 'Second-Best', *The Prussian Officer*, ed. Worthen, note on 114:36). She follows a 'bright little stream' which runs from Felley Mill pond to Moorgreen Reservoir (the 'Willey Water' of 46:5). Moorgreen Reservoir is also the setting of chap. XIV ('Water-Party'); see notes on 155:5, 160:30, 180:27, 190:9. The 'stream-mouth' near which Gudrun and Ursula bathe in the same chapter (164:32) is on the w. side of the reservoir, where a small and sheltered inlet marks the entrance of a stream from Willey Spring Wood; there is a 'knoll' (164:32) on its n. side. Lawrence's friend Jessie Chambers (1887–1944) remembered how 'Lawrence and I went to the little creek one holiday afternoon, and saw the lake and the woods from quite a new viewpoint' (Delavenay, *L'Homme et la Genèse*, ii. 684).

There is still a sluice at the s. end of the reservoir (184:27): 'A good description of the lock, the stone basin, the sluice gate, and the steps. The water was occasionally run off from the reservoir into the brook course [Beauvale Brook] down to the Erewash Canal' (Bircumshaw 3). Lawrence's assumption, however, that the sluice and lock were 'to supply with water the distant mines' (184:29) is incorrect; the reservoir was not the property of the mining companies, but originally of the Nottingham and Grantham Railway and Canal Company, and later that of British Waterways. The 'water-keeper's cottage' (184:32) – for which Lawrence uses Beauvale Lodge – was inhabited by 'Mr Bates' (Bircumshaw 3). The 'mossy boat-house' (46:20) at the s.w. corner of the reservoir, with the landing stage from which Gerald dives in chap. IV, belonged to the Barber family of Lambclose House, just 'across the high-road' (184:16) – the Underwood Road. DHL uses the house as the Crich family home 'Shortlands' (23:2) ('Longmeadow' in Roberts E441b: see Appendix II); its lodge appears at 287:33. See notes on 48:21, 212:17, 287:40. The 'colliery valley beyond' (23:10) the house and reservoir contains both Moorgreen and High Park collieries, pits owned by Barber Walker & Co., with High Park here recreated as 'Denley' (333:19). The leakage of water into 'Denley' recalls the leakage of water into High Park Colliery in 1856–60, when the pit was being sunk; Barber Walker & Co. took legal action against the reservoir owners (Whitelock 28–9). The other Barber Walker & Co. Eastwood pits at Selston (Underwood), Watnall and Brinsley are recreated as 'Selby. . .Whatmore. . .Lethley Bank' (222:30); and like '"C. B. & Co."' (222:22), Barber Walker & Co. *c.* 1913, with collieries in the Eastwood region, and at Bentley Colliery in Yorkshire, 48 miles n. of Eastwood, had wagons 'running all over the country' (222:27).

Coach Drive, 'the long, lonely mile of drive' (328:22), runs s.w. from Lambclose House; Gerald and Gudrun can see 'the little yellow lights of Beldover' (329:28) from it. The 'square arch. . .under the colliery railway' (330:17) where they kiss 'is the arch near Beggarlee Works' (Bircumshaw 5).

Gerald's walk in chap. XXIV takes him from Lambclose House through High Park Wood (338:1), alongside Moorgreen Reservoir to Felley Mill (338:2); then up the hillslopes through Park Springs (identified by Bircumshaw as 'Watnall Wood') towards the Misk Hills, and finally out on the Hucknall–Watnall Road (the 'high-road' of 338:11). He then goes towards Watnall (the 'Whatmore' of 338:23), where he sees 'the Kings Head' and 'the hall gates' (338:31): Lawrence's version of the Queen's Head Public House and the gates to Watnall Hall (now demolished); an illustration of the wrought-iron gates appears in von Hube, *Griseleia in Snotinghscire*, p. 64. He then turns w. down 'the steep hill' (338:31) – 'Watnall hill' (Bircumshaw 5) – and follows the road 'through the hollow'

(338:32) – Bogend – to Greasley Church. A marble tomb now covers the brick vault grave of Thomas Barber in the churchyard, next to the tombs of the two Barber children who died in infancy (see notes on 26:10 and 180:27). Gerald then turns s. towards 'Winthorpe hamlet' (339:16) – Newthorpe, on the outskirts of Eastwood – and thence into Nottingham Road, Eastwood, 'the long street of Beldover' (339:18). Lawrence here recreates the Wellington Inn as the '"Lord Nelson"'; the real-life Lord Nelson Public House is much further up Nottingham Road towards the Market Place, opposite George Henry Cullen's drapery shop, the 'Coulsons' of 375:24 (see *The Lost Girl*, ed. Worthen, note on 2:20). Gerald asks his way to the Brangwen House in 'Somerset Drive' (see above), and is directed to take 'th' first turnin' on your left. . .past Withamses tuffy shop. . .past wheer th' water-man lives' (340:9): 'William Rowley's sweet shop, the first turning to the left Alexander Street, and past the waterman's house, *Mr Smith*' (Bircumshaw 5). MS (p. 87) describes the route as past 'Withamses pot shop' and past 'wheer th' Wesleyan parson lives'; i.e. past the Nottingham Road house of the Rev. William Arthur Lenton.

In chap. xxv Lawrence describes 'the old market-place in town' (354:4), and adopts many of the features of Sneinton market in Nottingham: the 'poor quarter of the town', 'granite setts' (squared stones used for paving), the fruit stalls, the street of little shops (perhaps Bath Street), and the public Victoria Baths (rebuilt 1895), then at 43 Gedling Street, 'of new red brick, with a clock-tower' (354:14). The 'hosiery factory' nearby (354:11) could be one of a number, and cannot now be identified. The 'great chocolate-and-yellow tram-car' (354:17) is a Nottingham Corporation tram; the tramway line was extended to Sneinton 1907–10.

Still further afield, for the country house Breadalby (82:2) Lawrence adopted many of the features of 'a Georgian house in Derbyshire I knew very well' (*Letters*, iii. 95); Kedleston Hall has 'Corinthian pillars' (82:3), golden stone (not the stucco of 82:11), a 'string' (82:5) of three small lakes below the house (see 100:38), and is 'some miles from the high-road, back from the Derwent valley' (82:10); it is $3\frac{1}{2}$ miles n.w. of Derby. It is not, however, 'not far from Cromford' (82:5) (10 miles n.), nor is it 'small' (82:25). Lawrence's name for it is probably influenced by the village of Breadsall, 5 miles e. (see Bridget Pugh, 'Locations in Lawrence's Writings', *A D. H. Lawrence Handbook*, ed. K. Sagar, 1982, p. 263). Some details, like the 'great tree' (an ilex in real life, but changed from 'ilex' to 'cedar' by DHL in TSII, p. 125) and the small front of the house (82:25 and 28) are taken from Garsington Manor, the home of Lady Ottoline and Philip Morrell (see note on 15:22), as is the use of the old 'fish-ponds' (82:6) for swimming (see *Garsington* 49, 53).

EXPLANATORY NOTES

EXPLANATORY NOTES

Note Information about the locations of those parts of the book set in the English Midlands will be found in Appendix III.

7:2 Sisters Cf. the title ('The Sisters') DHL gave to the first several writings of the novel; see Introduction. DHL added the chapter titles in his proof correction for E1.

7:3 Ursula ... Gudrun Brangwen Characters first appearing in *The Rainbow*. Ursula was a British saint, martyred with 11,000 virgins by the Huns near Cologne; the name has links with the Swabian moon-goddess Horsel ... Gudrun was, in Teutonic legend, the 'white-armed' daughter of the Nibelung king and rival of Brynhild for the affection of Sigurd; she finally murdered her husband Atli and tried to drown herself, but was carried away by the sea to another country. William Morris (1834–96) adapted the legend in *The Story of the Volsungs and Niblungs* (1870) and *The Story of Sigurd the Volsung* (1876); DHL also knew the version of the story dramatised by Wagner in the operas of his *Ring* cycle (see notes on 47:26, 206:34 and 405:21). Experiences of Frieda Lawrence and Katherine Mansfield (see *Letters*, i. 507 n. 3) contributed to the characters of Ursula and Gudrun; see e.g. notes on 161:28, 264:38, 302:2, 384:34 and 393:22. The characters' outward setting, however, owes a good deal to the lives of Louie and Ethel Burrows (see *Letters*, i. 29 n. 3, 34 n. 5), as does the rest of the family to the Burrows family: see notes on 156:15 and 194:28.

7:4 their father's house in Beldover, DHL describes William Brangwen in *The Rainbow* (chaps. IV–XV) (and see note on 156:15). Beldover is a recreation of DHL's home town Eastwood: DHL referred to it as 'Bellingdon' in TSI (pp. 136–7), the name of the Buckinghamshire hamlet where he began the last version of *The Rainbow*. Subsequent commentary on the English locations of the novel will be found in Appendix III.

8:17 sisters of Artemis ... Hebe. Daughter of Zeus; virgin goddess of chastity, Greek equivalent of the Roman Diana ... daughter of Zeus; goddess of youth, who does housework, harnesses horses and (as cup-bearer of the gods) pours wine at table.

8:20 emerald-green stockings. Cf. Frieda's habit, *c.*1916, of wearing coloured – including 'grass-green' – stockings; see her *Memoirs and Correspondence*, 1962, p. 213 and Nehls, i. 367. The novel's reviewers paid particular attention to the descriptions of stockings and clothes; e.g. the *Nation and Athenæum* and *Saturday Westminster Gazette* (Draper 165–7, 170), *New Statesman* (9 July 1921), xvii, 388–90, and the *London Mercury* (August 1921), iv, 433.

9:1   **general." *P* There** Frequently, when typing in TSI (as here, p. 3), writing MS and revising TSII, DHL started lines flush left after ending the preceding dialogue some distance from the right-hand margin. The typists of the last two-fifths of TSI and TSII either ran on these lines, or typed them as new paragraphs. When the preceding lines do not go all the way to the right-hand margin, or where there are any signs of indentation, this edition starts a new paragraph.

10:7   **Prune?"** Early twentieth-century upper or upper-middle-class slang; a slightly disparaging, affectionate endearment for either sex. Cf. P. G. Woodhouse (1881–1975), *The Inimitable Jeeves* (1924), chap. IV: 'my heart warmed to the poor prune'.

10:14   *reculer pour mieux sauter.*" 'Draw back to jump better', from 'Il faut reculer pour mieux sauter' ('One must...'), Michel Eyquem de Montaigne (1533–92), *Essays* (1571), Book I. chap. XXXVIII.

11:22   **beetle toiling** DHL's references to beetles 1915–19 are numerous; cf. 'The Reality of Peace': 'Humanity is like a mass of beetles: it is one monstrosity of multiple identical units' (*Phoenix* 687–8: to be published in *Reflections on the Death of a Porcupine and Other Essays*, ed. Michael Herbert, Cambridge University Press). See also *Letters*, ii. 321. Cf. 69:35, 253:6–8 and 466:35. In TSII (p. 8) DHL revised to 'butterfly encumbered' before reverting to the original reading.

12:2   **moleskins** Working trousers, made of a strong cotton fustian.

12:31   **little flowers were coming white on the grey alyssum** Sweet alyssum (*Koniga maritima*) has white flowers. May Chambers described DHL remembering his garden at home, *c.* 1905: '"the white flower all over the grotto here is *alyssum*. I like it, don't you?" And he spelled the word out' (Nehls, iii. 605).

12:34   **banks,** DHL frequently double-typed letters at the right-hand margins of TSI; here he overtyped the 's' of banks with a comma (p. 8), but probably wanted both. Similar typing errors led to errors of transmission at 48:38, 53:17 and 276:4 which have been corrected in this edition.

12:38   **The daughter of ... Thomas Crich,** I.e. Laura. The Crich family (the 'i' pronounced as in 'crime') consists of Thomas (William in Appendix II), his wife Christiana (14:19, 214:40), and their children Gerald (14:19), an unnamed son killed as a child (see note on 26:10), Basil (334:12), Laura (here marrying Theobald Lupton, 25:19, 31:15; see note on 19:15), Lottie (married to Marshall, 31:9, 32:8), two daughters (one of whom may be Lottie) married to 'John' and 'James' (25:20), Diana (27:31) a little older than the last child, Winifred, 'a girl of thirteen or fourteen' (27:5). There are some differences in the family as described in Appendix II. DHL modelled some of them on the Barbers of Lambclose House, near Eastwood; Thomas Crich corresponds to Thomas Barber (1843–93 – see also note on 215:13) and Gerald in some respects resembles Thomas Philip Barber (1876–1961 – see also note on 64:20). Other details of family history are also paralleled by events in the novel; see notes on 26:10, 180:27.
  The name Crich was common in the Eastwood region; Samuel Crich was landlord at the Ram Inn, Newthorpe, in 1894, and Crich is a village 9 miles n.w. of Eastwood.

John Middleton Murry (1889–1957), husband of Katherine Mansfield (see note on 7:3), writer and close friend of DHL in 1915–16, wrote how 'one day, Frieda told me I was Gerald Crich ... it probably is true that Lawrence found the germ of Gerald in me' (*Between Two Worlds*, 1935, p. 411). See note on 352:26.

13:14 "What price 'What about', 'What do you think of'; from *c.* 1890, sometimes admiring but generally sarcastic or contemptuous; originally from racing ('what odds – ?').

14:25 sac coat The sac, sack, sacque or sack-back coat was not shaped to the figure but hung, loosely fitting, straight from the shoulders.

14:33 northern For DHL's symbolic and figurative distinctions between 'northern' and 'southern' *c.* 1916, see 'The Crucifix across the Mountains' and 'The Return Journey', *Twilight*.

14:35 cold DHL crossed out 'pale gold' and replaced with 'cold' in TSII (p. 14), but Seltzer's typist missed the addition squeezed between the deleted line above and the original adjectival phrase below.

15:1 totem ... repeated See note on 77:2 ... DHL deleted in TSII (p. 14) a previous occasion where Gudrun said the same.

15:22 Hermione Roddice, 'Roddis' was a common Eastwood name; Ethel Roddis was baptised the same day as DHL in Eastwood parish church (29 November 1885). In Appendix II the character's original name was 'Ethel' and (on one occasion) 'Hilda'; in TSI (p. 192) DHL typed 'Hilda Rolleston' (surname of another well-known Eastwood family). He used 'Ethel' and 'Hilda' elsewhere for fictional recreations of the intimate friend of his early years, Jessie Chambers (1887–1944); chap. I in Appendix II suggests some of her characteristics.

The fictional character also owes a good deal to Lady Ottoline Violet Anne Morrell (1873–1938); see *Letters*, ii. 253 n. 3, and notes on 15:40, 50:33, 90:29 and 279:24. DHL at first gave her Lady Ottoline's 'reddish-brown hair' (TSI, p. 11); Frieda included 'Ott' in an account of the novel's contents, but then deleted the name (letter to S. S. Koteliansky, 6 February 1917: BL). Lady Ottoline herself saw the character as a malicious and potentially libellous portrait; see *Garsington* 128–9 and *Letters*, iii. 41. But see DHL's letter to his agent J. B. Pinker of 20 February 1917: 'Hermione is not much more like Ottoline Morrell than Queen Victoria ... Ottoline flatters herself. – There *is* a hint of her in the character of Hermione: but so there is a hint of a million women' (*Letters*, iii. 95).

15:35 the Rossetti fashion, I.e. in the style of paintings by Dante Gabriel Rossetti (1828–82), one of the pre-Raphaelite Brotherhood: e.g. 'Beata Beatrix' (1864).

15:40 Her father ... the old school, Lady Ottoline was the daughter of Lieutenant-General Arthur Cavendish-Bentinck (1819–77); her half-brother William John Arthur Charles James (1857–1943), 6th Duke of Portland from 1879, became a baronet (Baron Bolsover) in 1880.

16:6 Rupert Birkin, Some of the character's experiences and many of his ideas recreate DHL's own: see notes below. The surname was a local name; in 1881, William Birkin (b. 1855) was landlord of the Coach and Horses public house at Hill Top, Eastwood, as was Joseph Birkin in 1908.

16:20 *Kulturträger,* 'Vehicle for culture' (German).

17:3 **established on the sand,** Cf. Matthew vii. 26–7. (Unless stated otherwise, subsequent biblical annotation refers to the Authorised Version.)

17:24 **Her ... higher ... first** The typist of TSII mistyped 'higher' as 'high', and DHL attempted to repair the text by changing 'Her' to 'His' and 'first' to 'central' (p. 19); his original readings have been restored.

19:15 **"Tibs!** I.e. Theobald (from the old pronunciation 'Tibbald').

21:14 **a marvellous personality.** Cf. DHL's anger with Lady Ottoline and Bertrand Russell (see note on 83:39) in August 1915, because they 'say, I – D.H.L. am wonderful, I am an exceedingly valuable personality, but that the things I say are extravaganzas, illusions ... they say to me, "You are wonderful, you are dynamic", then they filch my life for a sensation unto themselves...' (*Letters*, ii. 380–1).

22:7 **their father's playing on the organ.** William Brangwen's organ practice is described in *The Rainbow*, chap. XIII.

25:1 **"Not many people are anything at all,"** Cf. 'The Crown', as written 1915, chap. III: 'Very few men have being at all. They perish utterly, as individuals' (*Phoenix II* 384; to be published in *Reflections on the Death of a Porcupine and Other Essays*, ed. Herbert).

25:20 **John ... James** These names were added in pencil to TSIa and TSIb (p. 25) for 'one ... the other'; the hand is probably DHL's.

26:10 **Cain's cry ... slain his brother.** Thomas Philip Barber accidentally killed his brother Kenneth Forbes Barber (b. 1877) on 23 April 1890; the boys 'were amusing themselves in the boathouse, at the Moorgreen reservoir ... when the elder brother picked up a gun that he found lying there, which was loaded. The younger brother's head was nearly blown off, death being instantaneous ... it appeared that his brother was looking into the muzzle, but he did not see him when the gun went off ... there being a quantity of smoke ... the jury returned a verdict of accidentally killed, and expressed deep sympathy with the parents of the deceased' (*Ilkeston Advertiser*, 26 April 1890). Cain (son of Adam and Eve) 'rose up against Abel his brother, and slew him. And the Lord said unto Cain, Where is Abel thy brother? And he said, I know not: Am I my brother's keeper?' (Genesis iv. 8–9).

26:32 **the elderly man-servant, Crowther,** According to a document prepared *c.* 1935 by Steve Bircumshaw (d. 1968) listing the real-life correspondences of the novel (now in NCL: hereafter Bircumshaw), in real-life a 'Mr Cliff'. He is referred to as 'the butler' at 216:9; see note on 216:13. In Cornwall during the summer of 1916 DHL knew a couple, 'Crowther and his wife', who appear to have been servants (*Letters*, ii. 632).

28:13 **There was** From here to the end of chap. II, DHL retyped most of TSII (pp. 37–40, 43–5), with the original p. 40 following the retyped p. 40; thus leaving two pages numbered 40. He discarded and did not replace the original p. 42. He must have done the work at some stage between March 1917 and September 1919, but apparently not on the same typewriter as he used for TSI. He then revised the new pages by hand. Cf. note on 124:34 below.

28:20 **race is the ... Europe at least,"** Cf. the 'Epilogue', written 1924, to *Movements in European History* (Oxford, 1971): 'the races of mankind have grown in their different directions ... the Mediterranean peoples that include Greece and Rome and Carthage, then the Germanic and Slavic races, and the modern Europeans: all huge branches on the one tree of mankind' (p. 308).

29:30 **my liberty as a free and indifferent man.** Cf. DHL to Catherine Carswell, 9 July 1916: 'I know, that if the Germans wanted my little house, I would rather give it them than fight for it: because my little house is not important enough to me' (*Letters*, ii. 626; see also p. 635).

30:13 **an old hat,** Literally and figuratively; 'old hat' is something old-fashioned, or trite.

30:34 **"accidentally on purpose."** Catch-phrase, frequently in inverted commas, first recorded 1862: 'both deliberately and accidentally' (*OED*).

31:15 **Lupton?"** The bridegroom is 'William [or 'Harry'] Hosken' in Appendix II. There are similarities with DHL's friend Harold Hobson (1891–1974): see *Letters*, i. 443 n. 3.

31:38 **in your road."** In your way.

32:2 **Christ** [31:39] **... bloody** One of the readers of TSIa substituted 'Strewth!' and 'damn' respectively (p. 32), but DHL did not alter TSIb.

33:37 **inconcern,** An obsolete form of 'unconcern'.

35:6 **over dark,** EP (p. 36) printed 'after dark'; DHL deleted the first word and marked 'over' for insertion as in TSII (p. 45a). E1 printed as one word; DHL's reading in his duplicate proof set has been given priority.

36:20 **corporate** Apparently *OED* (3), recorded as 'obsolete', last use 1865: 'embodied, material'.

36:24 **gynaecious ... androgynous** A slightly inaccurate distinction between the flowers of the gynoecium (the female organs) and the androecium (the male organs): 'androgynous' would here mean 'with both stamens and pistils in the same flower'.

36:40 **with teeth—so—** ." DHL drew the 'face' on three different occasions; the drawings in TSIb and TSII are reproduced in the Textual apparatus; that in TSIa (scored through by an unknown hand) is as follows:

37:37 **some new, bizarre picture.** Perhaps a reference to the portrait of Lady Ottoline by Duncan Grant (1885–1978); DHL saw it on 22 January 1915 (Nehls, i. 266).

38:7 **"Little red flames,** Cf. Lady Ottoline's memory of a walk with DHL in Sussex, *c.* 23 February 1915: 'he showed me the little flame-red buds of the trees not yet in leaf and said, "See, here is the little red flame in Nature"' (*Ottoline* 273).

40:22 **"The eternal apple,"** The fruit of the Tree of Knowledge of Good and Evil (Genesis ii. 9 and iii. 1–6).

42:4 **that Lady of Shalott business,"** 'The Lady of Shalott' (1832), poem by Alfred, Lord Tennyson.

42:14 **a stricken pythoness of the Greek oracle.** Apollo's priestess at Delphi, possessed of an oracular spirit.

43:7 **one self** EP printed as 'oneself': DHL corrected that to his original reading, but E1 reads 'one's self' – a variant for which the printer has been judged responsible.

43:16 **"*Woman wailing ... demon lover—*"** Line 16 of 'Kubla Khan' (1798), by Samuel Taylor Coleridge (1772–1834) ['By woman ... demon-lover!'].

44:15 **You've got to learn ... come into being.** Cf. 'He has still to let go, to know what not-being is, before he can *be*' ('The Theatre', *Twilight*).

44:30 **life itself.** See Textual apparatus for an additional passage cut by DHL in EP. Similar language is used in chap. XXIII, so the cut here does not appear to be self-censorship.

46:16 **electric ... the dumbles** *OED* (3), 'chiefly with reference to the swiftness of electricity, or to the thrilling effect of the electric shock' ... local name for a valley with a stream in it, commonly given to the valley immediately below Moorgreen reservoir (see Appendix III).

46:20 **a mossy boat-house** See Appendix III and note on 26:10. In 'The Wedding Ring' (the 1914 version of *The Rainbow* and *Women in Love*), it was the scene of the first sexual encounter between Gerald and Gudrun: see Introduction.

47:26 **a Nibelung,"** A mythical king of the underworld race of dwarfs, the Nibelungs; at the start of Wagner's *Rheingold*, the Nibelung king Alberich is seen at the bottom of the Rhine. Cf. DHL's description of swimmers on Lake Constance: 'One man with a round, fair head lifted his face and one arm from the water and shouted a greeting to us, as if he were a Nibelung, saluting with bright arm lifted from the water, his face laughing, the fair moustache hanging over his mouth' ('Italians in Exile', *Twilight*).

48:21 **"What period ... Jane Austen,** Lambclose House was a farmhouse until 1753, then a shooting box; the present house was built 1797–1829, and enlarged by Thomas Barber ... Dorothy Wordsworth: 1771–1855 ... Jane Austen: 1775–1817 (see also 355:28–9).

50:33 **these free women ... from the aristocracy."** Lady Ottoline went to the University of St Andrews in 1897, and as an out-student to Somerville College, Oxford, in 1899. She married Philip Morrell (1870–1943) in 1902: 'both Philip and I were what is called radicals' (*Ottoline* 121). He became Liberal MP for S. Oxfordshire (1906–10) and Burnley (1910–18).

50:35 **pour moi, elle n'existe pas.** 'For me, she doesn't exist' (French).

51:34 **à terre,** 'Down to earth' (French).

51:40 **speeches like Corneille,** Pierre Corneille (1606–84), French verse dramatist of the classical period. Cf. DHL's ironical description in 1910 of the plans of a 'devotee of Corneille ... to expound to me the passages "plus nobles, plus élevés". Oh Lordy!' (*Letters*, i. 217).

52:10 **Je m'en fiche."** 'I don't give a damn' (French).

52:21 **life was** DHL typed over 'was' in TSI (p. 58), so that it appeared to the typist of TSII to have been crossed out.

53:4 **his work** A description of how Birkin became a School-Inspector appears in Appendix II.

53:32 **third'll be all right.** Third-class travel on railways in Britain before and after World War I was crowded but respectable; compartments would commonly seat four or five passengers to a side, whereas first-class would have only three or four, with armrests, etc.

54:3 **Daily Telegraph,** The newspaper usually printed either one or two leaders, but no such 'essay' as Gerald describes was published between January and August 1916; given its political stance, it is unlikely that the newspaper would have printed such an essay.

54:25 **we s'll** The reading of EP (EI reads 'we sh'll'); it is most likely that DHL corrected both sets of proofs to 's'll' (his normal dialect abbreviation of 'shall'), but that the printer of EI ignored or misunderstood the correction.

55:15 **the Ritz, or the Empire, Gaby Deslys** Luxury hotel in Piccadilly ... music hall in Leicester Square ... actress, dancer, review and music hall artiste (1884–1920), who worked in London 1906–15 (Obituary in *The Times*, 13 February 1920, p. 14).

55:31 **a Brocken mist,** The 'Spectre of the Brocken' is the magnified image of an observer projected on to cloud or mist; common on the Brocken mountain in East Germany.

55:40 **to help my neighbour** Cf. Luke x. 25–37.

57:17 **the be-all and the end-all** *Macbeth* I. vii. 5.

59:14 **versatility** AI and EI printed as 'venality' (p. 60); the new typescript Seltzer had had made from TSII was the source of both texts, and of the error. One reviewer of EI specified 'venality' as one of 'the many words of which Mr. Lawrence simply does not know the meaning' (Rose Macaulay, *Time and Tide*, ii, 1 July 1921, 628–9).

59:24 **destroyed like Sodom,** Genesis xix. 24–5. DHL told Lady Cynthia on 26 April 1917 that 'there will fall a big fire on the city before long, as on Sodom and Gomorrah' (*Letters*, iii. 118).

59:39 **Soho.** Area of London s. of Oxford Street, traditionally of small shops, restaurants and immigrant housing; 'Chelsea' in TSI (p. 65): see note on 73:11.

60:15 **young fellows down from the University,** Replacing 'mostly Oxford fellows' in TSI (p. 66). Of the Heseltine circle (see next note), Heseltine himself, Robert Nichols (1893–1944) – whom he met there – and Hasan Shahid Suhrawardy (1893–1963) were (or had been) at Oxford.

60:30 **Halliday** DHL admitted to Donald Carswell that Julius (originally 'Sidney') Halliday 'is Heseltine ... taken from life' (see Introduction). The composer Philip Heseltine ('Peter Warlock') (1894–1930) met DHL in the winter of 1915, and stayed with the Lawrences in Cornwall 1 January–*c.* 21 February 1916; see *Letters*, ii. 569, 580, 598 and Paul Delany, *D. H. Lawrence's Nightmare* (New York, 1978), pp. 198–205. For an opposing view of DHL's use of Heseltine, see the latter's friend and biographer Cecil Gray (1895–1951): 'the unpleasant person [Heseltine] is represented to be in the pages of Lawrence is a malignant caricature, bearing only the remotest and most deceptive resemblance to actuality' (Nehls, ii. 96).

60:33 **the Pompadour.** DHL's recreation of the Café Royal (opened 1865) at 68 Regent Street, London. Madame de Pompadour (1721–64) was a mistress of Louis XV (1710–74). DHL called it the Café Imperial in TSI, but Donald Carswell advised him to change the name; there already was an 'Imperial Restaurant' in London. See DHL's comments on the Café Royal, *Letters*, ii. 498–9 (where he associates it with 'a sordid brawl') and 649–50; he himself knew it as early as August 1914 (*Letters*, ii. 207).

61:13 **"Where the ... Half asleep—"'** 'Love Among the Ruins (1855), ll. 1–4, by Robert Browning (1812–89) ['... quiet-coloured ... miles / On the solitary pastures where our sheep / Half-asleep...']. Ll. 7 and 9 continue: 'was the site once ... Of our country's very capital'.

62:10 **the bubble of pleasure.** The painting of the Domino Room, Café Royal, by Sir William Orpen (1878–1931), now in the Musée d'Art Moderne in Paris, conveys vividly the gilded walls, the romanticised French ornamentation, the red plush, the 'great mirrors in the walls' and the world of artists and intellectuals who frequented it.

62:20 **Egyptian princes's.** See note on 98:37.

62:22 **a girl ... all her form,** DHL's September–October 1921 revisions for Secker of this and other descriptions of the Pussum, Halliday and their milieu are recorded in the Textual apparatus: see Introduction, footnote 81. It is possible that some of the changes were Secker's own alterations. The girl, later named as 'Miss Darrington' and 'the Pussum' (altered, apparently at Heseltine's suggestion, to 'Minette' in E1a and E2), was 'a model called the Puma ... taken from life' (*Letters*, iii. 36): Minnie Lucy Channing (b. 1894), the daughter of a hotel waiter, m. Heseltine 22 December 1916 (see note on 68:13). She stayed with the Lawrences 26 January to *c.* 21 February 1916: 'a quiet, quite nice little thing really, unobtrusive and affectionate', and according to Frieda '*very* pretty' (*Letters*, ii. 517, 546). See DHL's letter of 13 January 1916 to Lady Ottoline: 'I think Heseltine will go ... back to his Puma (the girl, the model). He says he despises her and can't stand her, that she's vicious and a prostitute, but he [will] be running back to her in a little while, I know. She's not so bad, really. I'm not sure whether her touch of licentious profligacy in sex isn't better than his deep-seated conscious, mental licentiousness' (*Letters*, ii. 504). For 'Puma', cf. 71:40. See also *Letters*, ii. 481 n. 2, 598. A photograph of her appears in Harry T. Moore and Warren Roberts, *D. H. Lawrence and his world* (New York, 1966), p. 55. There appears (in spite of the similarity of surname) to be no connection with Dora Carrington (1893–1932), the painter (see *Letters*, iii. 112 n. 2).

63:6 Lady Snellgrove's ... Warens The name of a famous London outfitters (Marshall and Snelgrove) which DHL misspelled elsewhere: see *The Lost Girl*, ed. John Worthen (Cambridge, 1981), note on 3:23 ... Mistyped 'Wraons' by DHL in TSI (p. 69), and then corrected to 'Warens': perhaps a recreation of the Dutch musician Bernard van Dieren (1884–1936), close friend of Heseltine. Gray described DHL's meeting with him in 1917 (Nehls, i. 438–9): see too *Letters*, iii. 176 and n. 2, 181.

63:14 Bentley's Perhaps DHL's recreation of Gerald Leslie Brockhurst (b. 1890), for whom Minnie Channing 'often sat' (G. Deghy and K. Waterhouse, *Café Royal*, 1955, p. 157).

63:20 "Lord Carmarthen TSI (p. 70) read 'Lord Cardigan', but Donald Carswell wrote in TS1b: 'Change this name. The Cardigan peerage is extinct I think, but the Balaklava hero's relatives would have a grievance. Enough trouble has been brought on the name by her late, scurrilous ladyship. D.C.' The Cardigan peerage was not, as Carswell thought, extinct; George William James Chandos (1873–1961) was 6th Marquis of Ailesbury and Earl of Cardigan. There was, however, also a Marquis of Carmarthen – John Francis (1901–64), son of George Godolphin Osborne, Duke of Leeds (1862–1927). The typist of TSII (p. 89) left blanks for the name which DHL filled in. Secker altered the name to 'Frederick Carmarthen' in E1a and E2.

63:35 The wind still sits in that quarter, From *Much Ado About Nothing* II. ii. 108 ('Sits the wind in that corner?').

64:20 a soldier, and an explorer, Thomas Philip Barber had joined the South Nottinghamshire Hussars Yeomanry in 1895, served in the South African War in 1900 and throughout the First World War: he was mentioned in despatches and awarded the DSO in 1917. In Appendix II, Gerald is 'newly home from the wilds of South America' (cf. 78:4).

64:24 the last war," Altered in TSI (p. 71) from 'South African' to 'last': see note above.

64:27 ruling over coal-mines." Thomas Philip Barber was twenty-one on 28 January 1897, and became chairman of Barber Walker & Co.

65:3 her loose, simple jumper A loose garment, frequently of knitted cotton, and not tucked into the waist-band: here of crêpe-de-chine with a draw-string at the neck.

65:25 a pale, full-built ... his black hat, Cf. Gray's description of Heseltine in the Café Royal, spring 1916: 'tall, slender, pale, with bright blue eyes and longish fair hair, dressed in a neat black suit, soft black hat, and orange-coloured shirt' (*Peter Warlock*, 1938, p. 125).

65:26 a smile at once naive and warm, and vapid. To the painter Augustus John (1878–1961), Heseltine's 'pale handsome face ... always wore a smile, but not a reassuring smile: it was more of a derisive smile and made one feel rather uncomfortable' (*Chiaroscuro*, 1952, p. 56).

68:13 And now I'm going to have a baby, Minnie Channing's son Nigel Heseltine was born 3 July 1916.

69:9 another man, Named below as 'Maxim Libidnikov': the name clearly derived from David [known as Maxim] Litvinov (1876–1951), in 1916 'a poor Russian revolutionary of forty – quite nice-looking, I believe, but of no account' (*Letters*, ii. 629); married that year to the Lawrences' friend Ivy Low (1889–1977); Russian Commissar of Foreign Affairs, 1930–9, Russian Ambassador to the USA, 1941–3. Libidnikov, in the novel a contemporary of Halliday, may be a recreation of Heseltine's friend Nichols (with a pun on 'Nik'); see note on 60:15. The word 'Libido' – one of the key words of contemporary psychoanalysis – had first appeared in England in 1909, in a translation of Freud.

70:27 a young man Later described as 'a Jew, really'; probably DHL's recreation of Dikran Kouyoumdjian (1895–1956), born in Bulgaria of Armenian parents, friend of Heseltine; later the successful writer 'Michael Arlen'. He stayed with the Lawrences in Cornwall, 10–22 January 1916: see *Letters*, ii. 504–5, 508. To Lady Ottoline he was 'a fat dark-blooded tight-skinned Armenian Jew' (*Garsington* 77).

71:1 Curse you," DHL originally typed '"Curse you, you ugly bitch,"' in TSI (p. 80); Frieda revised the last word to 'rat' in both copies, but DHL deleted the last three words in TSII (p. 103).

71:14 Garn [71:10] . . . to cat, 'Go on' . . . to vomit, especially from too much drink.

73:11 a large block of buildings, Heseltine lived at 13, Rossetti Mansions, Chelsea, 1915–16.

73:16 Hasan," A Muslim name, as is the 'Shahid' of TSI (p. 83), in spite of the character being 'a Hindu'. But cf. the names of DHL's Muslim acquaintance Hasan Shahid Suhrawardy.

74:10 several negro statues, wood-carvings from West Africa, According to Gray, Heseltine surrounded himself with 'African fetishes' (*Peter Warlock*, p. 144): he himself referred to his 'West African carving' in a letter to Frederick Delius of 22 April 1916 (Nehls, i. 351). DHL's artist friend Mark Gertler (1892–1939) had also acquired an African carving by 1915 (*Mark Gertler: Selected Letters*, ed. Noel Carrington, 1965, p. 85). See next note and note on 253:11.

74:13 sitting in childbirth, African carvings of single figures in childbirth are apparently unknown, though a few small carvings (or parts of larger figures) show it. DHL may be confusing the 'bands' he describes with the unnaturally elongated breasts, held in both hands, common on Yoruba figures; some Yoruba carvings also show women holding a band or strip draped over the shoulders. Figures of kneeling women are common, as are those with protruding bellies. DHL was still thinking of this kind of figure in 1925 when in 'Him with his Tail in his Mouth' he referred to 'an African fetish-idol of a woman pregnant' (*Phoenix II* 434; to be published in *Reflections on the Death of a Porcupine*, ed. Herbert).

74:24 the Futurist manner; DHL became interested in the Futurists (so called because they repudiated the past and glorified youth, mechanism and the future) in 1914; see *Letters*, ii. 180 and nn. 3–5.

74:35 **a bottle of Kümmel.** A cumin and caraway-flavoured liqueur of which DHL was particularly fond; see *Letters*, ii. 488.

75:34 **friends since Eton.** Heseltine went to Eton (1908–11).

77:2 **Fetish** The reading of E1. EP reads 'Fetishes', while 'TOTEM' was substituted in E2. In January 1916, DHL asked Lady Ottoline – about to visit him in Cornwall – to bring with her 'one or two books ... anything really African, Fetish Worship or the customs of primitive tribes' (*Letters*, ii. 510–11); a book he first read in the spring of 1916, Sir E. B. Tylor's *Primitive Culture*, 2 vols (1871) – 'a very good sound substantial book' (*Letters*, ii. 593) – has a great deal about fetishism; e.g. ii. 143–67. DHL discussed the 'origin of totem' in a letter of December 1915 (*Letters*, ii. 470–1). See too note on 74:10.

77:11 **in, knowing ... and shirt.** On eight occasions in chap. VII, the text of E1 is altered where there are no corresponding revisions by DHL in EP. At least some (and perhaps all) of these revisions are authorial (see Introduction and *Letters*, iii. 628), but as they were made in response to Secker's desire to tone the chapter down, they have not been accepted. The revisions are recorded in the Textual apparatus at 77:10, 77:34, 78:26, 78:36, 79:2, 79:4, 79:5, 79:31. See also notes on 108:2, 108:21 and 352:39.

80:32 **an ash of corruption,** DHL's TSII revision (p. 120) was a consequence of the typed 'f' in 'of' appearing to be an 'r'. He revised the phrase twice; first to 'as an ash or a corruption,' then by adding 'in' after 'corruption,'. His original reading is restored.

81:9 **gloating triumph,** Cf. Heseltine's letter to DHL after breaking with him in April 1916 (Nehls, i. 351), and his triumphant reaction to Secker's withdrawal of the novel's first English edition (ibid., ii. 92–4).

82:18 **her brother ... a Liberal member of Parliament.** Alexander Roddice is a fictional recreation of Philip Morrell (see note on 50:33).

82:25 **an English ... old school,** DHL typed 'a water-colour drawing of the old school' in TSI (p. 94), and replaced it in TSIa with 'an old English aquatint'. Frieda failed to cross out 'of the old school' in TSIb, but DHL revised the phrase again in TSII (p. 123).

83:39 **a young Italian woman ... Miss Bradley ... Baronet of fifty ... a Fräulein März,** Fictional versions of people DHL associated with Garsington Manor. The young Italian 'contessa' in some respects resembles the young Belgian woman Maria Nys (1898–1955), who married Aldous Huxley ... 'Miss Bradley' may be drawn from Bertrand Russell's friend Helen Dudley, who stayed with the Lawrences in 1914 (see *Letters*, ii. 229 and n. 1, 230); Lady Ottoline noted her habit 'of repeating after one what one has said' (*Garsington* 98): see 100:1 ... the sociologist Baronet (named as 'Sir Joshua Malleson' below) resembles the philosopher Bertrand Russell (1872–1970), Earl Russell; between the summer of 1916 and 1920 Russell had an affair with Constance ('Colette') O'Neill, wife of Bernard Malleson, actor and playwright. TSI (p. 97), created no later than August 1916, shows DHL first typing the name 'Bernard Malleson', then 'Mattheson' (p. 99), the name adopted in the English editions of the novel: finally 'Joshua

Malleson' (p. 104) ... 'Fräulein März' – 'Miss March' – resembles Juliette Baillot (b. 1896), employed as a governess at Garsington and known as 'Mademoiselle' (the original reading of TSI, p. 96, corrected to 'Fräulein').

84:32 **Salsie!"** Morrell was known as 'Pipsie' in the family circle (*Carrington: Letters and Extracts from her Diaries*, ed. David Garnett, 1970, p. 39).

85:3 **a Meredith hero who remembers Disraeli.** Probably Alvan in Meredith's *The Tragic Comedians* (1892), distinguished by his 'political leadership' (chap. II), his 'gifts of speech' and 'robustness of body and soul' (chap. III), and his Jewishness (chap. II); cf. the rhetorical power, striking appearance and Jewish origins of Benjamin Disraeli (1804–81), Tory Statesman and Prime Minister.

85:16 **the minister for Education ... adverse criticism.** Walter Runciman was President of the Board of Education 1908–11, J. A. Pease 1911–15, Arthur Henderson 1915–17: the latter resigned from the war cabinet in August 1917. There was, however, a spectacular cabinet resignation 'owing to adverse criticism' on 3 May 1916, when the Chief Secretary for Ireland, Augustine Birrell (1850–1933), resigned following the Easter Rising in Dublin.

86:6 **"Silent upon a peak in Dariayn,"** Last line of Keats's sonnet 'On First Looking into Chapman's Homer' (1817) ['Silent, upon ... Darien'].

86:23 **things concluded, in the past.** DHL wrote 'things past' in TSIa (p. 99); Frieda copied 'things in the past' into TSIb, but DHL's addition of 'concluded,' to TSII (p. 129) precludes any return to his original reading.

86:26 **laws of gravitation,** DHL revised TSIa to read 'laws gravitation,' (p. 100); some emendation is required, and Frieda's correction to 'laws of gravitation' in TSIb has been accepted, together with DHL's comma.

86:36 **"Bazarov came ... the street,"** The sentence does not appear in any extant edition of *Fathers and Sons* (1862), by Ivan Sergeyevich Turgenev (1818–83); the American edition of 1867 was translated directly from the Russian, and had no connection with the first French edition of 1863. DHL's spelling 'Bazarov' suggests that he knew Constance Garnett's 1895 English translation. He may have found the comic elements of the translation in another Russian novel.

88:16 **my lady."** Frieda's revision 'madam' in both copies of TSI (p. 102) has been rejected in favour of DHL's 'my lady' on the grounds that her knowledge of English idiom is less trustworthy than his. See too Explanatory note and Textual apparatus at 136:31.

88:40 **copying it ... and vividness.** Lady Ottoline records DHL at Garsington in November 1915 'absorbed in copying most beautifully a Persian miniature' (*Garsington* 70); in April 1916 he copied 'a 15th century indian picture' (*Letters*, ii. 601). There are many pictures of geese in the volume of reproductions *The Ajanta Frescoes* (Oxford, 1915) which DHL liked and gave to Lady Ottoline at Christmas 1915 (see *Letters*, ii. 483, 488 and n. 3); he still remembered the Ajanta geese in 1925 ('Him With His Tail in His Mouth', *Phoenix II* 434).

89:18 **the flux** A highly significant word for DHL, 1915–16. It is used extensively in John Burnet's *Early Greek Philosophy* (1908 edn.), which DHL read in July 1915 and wished to refer to again in September 1916 (*Letters*, ii. 364–5,

652); see Burnet, pp. 161, 163, 167. DHL entitled chap. III of 'The Crown' (1915) 'The Flux of Corruption' (*Phoenix II* 382) – a phrase which appears below (383:4). The word was used frequently in the 'Water Party' section of TSI (pp. 209–11), and often appears in his writing and correspondence (see 'The Crown', *Phoenix II* 382–5, 388, 394; 'The Return Journey', *Twilight*; *Letters*, ii. 448). In TSI, Birkin remarks that his own being 'is a flux, ever-changing' (p. 35).

90:12   **net-work of grey, Ursula ... was crimson** DHL revised all the details of the dresses in TSII (p. 135), and the location of 'of grey' appeared to Seltzer's typist to make it belong to Miss Bradley's dress, whereas it actually refers to Gudrun's.

90:19   **like a *revenant*.** Something – especially a ghost – which returns. Cf. Syson in the proofs version (Roberts E326.6) of 'The Shades of Spring': 'Like a *revenant* he had returned on a visit to the country of his past' (p. 193). See also 390:12.

90:23   **long warden pipes** I.e. 'churchwarden', long-stemmed pipes.

90:29   **Cassandra,** Daughter of Priam and Hecuba, given the spirit of prophecy by Apollo, but doomed not to be believed; ravished by Ajax at the capture of Troy, given to Agamemnon as spoil, and murdered with him. DHL told Lady Ottoline in March 1915 that 'you belong to a special type, a special race of women: like Cassandra in Greece ... the great *media* of truth, of the deepest truth: through them, as through Cassandra, the truth came as through a fissure from the depths and the burning darkness that lies out of the depth of time' (*Letters*, ii. 297). Russell wrote to her on 21 June 1915 that DHL 'keeps saying you are a priestess, a Cassandra' (*Garsington* 59).

91:6   **Anche tu, Palestra ... per piacere.** 'You too, Palestra, will you dance? – yes, please' (Italian). 'Palestra' means 'Gymnasium': unlikely as a surname, and practically impossible as a first name (which it appears to be here); either an obscure play on words, or an error by DHL.

91:14   **had collected gradually.** After staying a few days at Garsington in the winter of 1915, DHL wrote: 'The Ottoline has hundreds of exquisite rags, heaps of coloured cloths and things, like an Eastern bazaar. One can dress up splendidly' (*Letters*, ii. 465). She frequently offered her guests 'gay Persian, Turkish, and other Oriental clothes, of which I had a store' (*Ottoline* 277).

91:17   **"Vergini Delle Rocchette,"** 'Virgins of the little rocks' (Italian). *Le Vergini delle rocche* (1895), by Gabriele D'Annunzio (1863–1938), Italian poet, novelist and dramatist, contains three princesses. DHL had read it before 1 December 1916 (*Letters*, iii. 43).

91:20   **Naomi and Ruth and Orpah.** Ruth and Orpah are the widowed Naomi's widowed daughters-in-law in the Book of Ruth. There is a particular connection with Lady Ottoline, who wrote about her girlhood: 'All I desired was never to leave my mother. The words of Ruth and Naomi were our mutual chant' (*Ottoline* 83).

91:23   **the Russian Ballet of Pavlova and Nijinsky.** David Garnett (1892–1981) told DHL and Frieda about the Russian Ballet in the summer of 1912; at that time, according to the version in *Mr Noon*, ed. Lindeth Vasey (Cambridge,

1984), p. 255, neither of them had any personal knowledge of it, but they may have seen it in the summer of 1913. Anna Pavlova (1882–1931) and Vaslav Nijinsky (1890–1950) were the leading dancers in the Compagnie des Ballets Russes founded by Sergei Diaghilev (1872–1929) in Paris in 1909.

91:33 **All her men were dead ... the former life,** See Ruth i. 5, 14–15.

92:1 **cleaving** Ruth 'clave unto' Orpah in Ruth i. 15.

92:6 **Malbrouk.** Arrangement of the French folksong 'Malbrouck s'en va-t'en guerre' ('Marlborough is off to the wars'), said to date from *c.* 1709; quoted at length in *Trilby* (1894), Part Sixth, by George Du Maurier (1834–96).

92:16 **some Hungarian music,** Lady Ottoline records her husband Philip playing, in 1914, 'tunes of all kinds on the pianola, which was a new toy – Brahms's Hungarian Dances, Russian ballet music...' and remembered her guests being inspired 'to dance gaily, wildly and often very beautifully' (*Ottoline* 277).

92:21 **rag-time sort of dancing,** Dancing influenced by rag-time piano music, developed *c.* 1893 by Scott Joplin (1868–1917).

92:30 **"Cosa vuol dire,** Either 'what does that mean?' or 'what do you mean?' (Italian).

93:29 **are?" said** The reading of TSI (p. 108); the typist of TSII changed the question mark to an exclamation mark, and DHL's revision of 'exclaimed' for 'said' in TSII (p. 141) has been judged a response to that error.

93:40 **"Handicraft instructor in the schools."** See *The Rainbow,* chap. XIV, for Will Brangwen's work as Art and Handicraft Instructor for the County of Nottingham.

94:19 **the Algernon Strange set.** DHL probably recreates the circle of Augustus John; they did not meet until November 1917, but had many friends in common. John was an habitué of the Café Royal – appearing, for example, in the Orpen painting (see note on 62:10). TSI (p. 109) reads 'the painting set'.

95:8 **really mad.** DHL's correction to TSIa (p. 110). Frieda (apparently responsible for the copying at this point) failed to transfer any of his corrections on that page into TSIb; almost certainly, she had turned over two pages of TSIa at once. Other parallel cases on that page appear in the Textual apparatus at 95:12–21.

95:15 **a pure lily ... defile himself with her."** Reflecting DHL's analysis of Heseltine, 15 February 1916: 'It is queer. He declares he does not like this one, the Puma, but he does really. He declares he wants her to go. But he is really attached to her in the senses, in the unconsciousness, in the blood. He is always fighting away from this. But in so doing he is a fool. She is very nice and very real and simple, we like her. His affection for Mlle. [Juliette Baillot: see note on 83:39] is a desire for the light because he is in the dark. If he were in the light he would want the dark. He wants Mlle. for *companionship,* not for the blood connection, the dark, sensuous relation. With Puma he has this second, dark relation, but not the first' (*Letters,* ii. 539). Cf. a letter from Heseltine to Phyllis Crocker of 19 April 1917 about the Puma, 'with whom I had never had and could never have any but a purely bestial relation...' (BL).

96:18 **"Render unto ... are Caesarina's,"** Cf. Matthew xxii. 21 ['Render therefore unto Caesar ... Caesar's,' R.V.].

96:39 **Integer vitae scelerisque purus—"** 'Of unblemished life and spotless reputation—', Horace, *Odes* I. xxii. 1. Cf. *Letters*, ii. 36, 352; iii. 65. DHL wrote the first four lines of the Ode, in Latin, on the last page of one of his college notebooks (Roberts E320.1).

97:2 **"And I don't ... I am."** DHL deleted '"And I don't care whether you see it or not – that's your affair."' in TSIa (p. 112). Frieda failed to delete the line in TSIb, which meant that – following Birkin's '"Nasty, I wish I felt nasty about it. It only bores me."' – it became Gerald's. DHL revised both lines in TSII (p. 146), however, which precludes any return to the reading of TSIa.

97:4 **brought the water,** The hot water, brought to bedrooms in old houses which had no piped water.

97:8 **the lovely accomplished past** Cf. DHL's letter about Garsington Manor to Lady Cynthia, 5 December 1915: 'it is in its way so beautiful, one is tempted to give in, and to stay there, to lapse back into its peaceful beauty of bygone things, to live in pure recollection, looking at the accomplished past, which is so lovely. But one's soul rebels' (*Letters*, ii. 465).

98:7 **"Salvator femininus,"** 'A female saviour' (Latin).

98:37 **a figure ... some Egyptian tomb,** DHL's interest in Ancient Egypt is first recorded in September 1914, when he 'went to the British Museum – and I know, from the Egyptian and Assyrian sculpture – what we are after. We want to realise the tremendous *non-human* quality of life ... coming unseen and unperceived as out of the desert to the Egyptians' (*Letters*, ii. 218). In the British Museum DHL could have seen, for example, the two black granite seated figures of Amenophis III (18th Dynasty) from his Mortuary Temple in Thebes (see 318:10–12 and note on 318:34). See also *Letters*, ii. 293, 521 n. 3, 556.

101:22 **Dionysos, because his hair was really yellow,** The Greek god of wine, fruitfulness and vegetation. In Gilbert Murray's translation of Euripides' *The Bacchae* (1904), Dionysos's hair is 'all gold': DHL knew the version from 1909 (see *Letters*, i. 160, 261 and n. 1). He made a drawing of Dionysos early in 1916, and sent it to Lady Ottoline for her to embroider (see *Letters*, ii. 517 and n. 2, 598 and n. 2).

102:23 **the *social* equality of man.** DHL's objections to this idea are expressed particularly in 'Democracy' (*Phoenix* 699–718) and in his annotations to the manuscript of Russell's 1915 lecture programme (see *D. H. Lawrence's Letters to Bertrand Russell*, ed. Harry T. Moore, New York, 1948, pp. 79–96). Russell's own point of view was not that of Malleson: see his *Principles of Social Reconstruction* (1916), chap. II.

102:31 **Herr Obermeister and Herr Untermeister.** 'Mr Over-foreman and Mr Under-foreman'.

103:28 **Every man ... two legs.** 'Democracy' (written in 1919) parallels and clarifies this passage: 'The average human being: put him on the table, the little divinity, and let us see what his works are like ... He has two legs, two eyes, one nose – all exact. He has a stomach and a penis. He is a little organism. He is one very complicated organ, a unit, an identity' (*Phoenix* 699; text from that established for *Reflections on the Death of a Porcupine*, ed. Herbert).

104:28 **a large volume,** In March 1916, following his request for it, Lady Ottoline sent DHL a copy of the *History of the Peloponnesian War* by the Greek historian Thucydides (471–*c.* 401 B.C.); see *Letters*, ii. 572 and n. 7, 592, 614. The 'thick' volume Birkin reads (105:37) suggests the 1874 Longmans, Green & Co. edition, tr. Richard Crawley.

105:14 **ball of lapis lazuli** Lady Ottoline apparently gave DHL a piece of lapis lazuli which he in turn gave to the poetess H.D. [Hilda Doolittle] (1886–1961); her novel *Bid Me To Live* (New York, 1960) is in most respects a fictionalised version of real events, with 'Elsa' the equivalent of Frieda and 'Julia' of H.D. herself: 'The lump of lapis-lazuli that someone had given him, that he had given her one day, "Take this, do you want it?" "Isn't that what Lady Ottobourne gave you?" said Elsa. "Yes – I'm sick of the Ott, she bores me," he said, leaving the lump of lapis there on the table, where Julia had been sitting, writing' (p. 139).

105:35 **she was left-handed.** A traditional antagonism and fear attaches to the left-handed and to the left. Lady Ottoline's copy of *Women in Love* is recorded as having 'at this point in the story a marginal annotation, "Frida [sic] was left-handed!"' (Harry T. Moore, *The Priest of Love*, New York, 1974, p. 271).

107:34 **What had he to do with her?** Cf. John ii. 4: 'Woman, what have I to do with thee?'

108:2 **He knew ... growing leaves.** Although Secker asked DHL for changes on this page (see note on 108:21), he does not appear to have told DHL that he was expurgating this sentence, which was omitted from E1.

108:18 **without hats,** As late as 1939, it was still relatively unusual for a professional man in Britain to go out without a hat.

108:21 **lying with** EP (p. 111) reads 'lying with'; E1 reads 'lying against'. Martin Secker asked DHL on 28 January 1921 for revisions at this and four other places, and DHL supplied emendations on 4 February (*Letters*, iii. 660 and n. 1); the other three changes accepted by Secker on that occasion are recorded (under *EP*) in the Textual apparatus at 353:16, 422:24 and 449:1. See also notes on 108:2, 352:39 and 353:20. In TSI, DHL had typed 'lying against', then revised to 'lying with' (p. 127a).

108:24 **Alexander Selkirk,** Original name Alexander Selcraig; Scottish sailor (1676–1721) marooned on one of the islets of Juan Fernandez, and the main prototype of Daniel Defoe's Robinson Crusoe.

110:2 **Coal-Dust** DHL first entitled this chapter 'Collieries' on contents page and opening page of chapter in EP (p. 113); he later revised the latter (though without E1's hyphen) but failed to alter the contents page. See also notes on 77:2,

244:2, 266:2, 302:2, 387:2 and Textual apparatus entries for 119:2, 123:2, 155:2, and 441:2.

110:29 **came into Gerald's** DHL typed 'came Gerald's' in TSI (p. 129); TSII's typist added 'into' (p. 168). As something is required, and DHL tacitly accepted this reading, it has been incorporated into the text.

111:4 **sat glistening and** DHL deleted 'bright' in both copies of TSI (p. 130), leaving 'sat and tense and'; the typist of TSII typed 'sat   tense and' (p. 168), which DHL revised to the final reading.

113:4 **jockey,** Half-contemptuous, half-affectionate dialect term, often for young or mischievous things.

113:14 **welly** 'Almost', 'nearly': a dialect contraction of 'well-nigh'.

113:31 **sense of indomitable ... strong, indomitable** An ink blot in TSII (p. 173) makes it impossible to read the words between 'of' and 'indomitable', and between 'strong,' and 'indomitable', although they are probably deleted. They are now irrecoverable.

116:5 **a new Daphne,** Nymph beloved by the sun-god Apollo; pursued by him, she changed into a laurel tree.

116:26 **kerosene flares,** I.e. paraffin, used for lamps from the 1860s; 'flares' signifies lamps with unprotected flames.

117:4 **these** DHL revised 'their' to 'these' in TSII (p. 179); Seltzer's typist picked up the dot from the 'i' and restored 'their' (p. 126).

117:15 **an electrician,** Named as 'Palmer' in the next paragraph ('Constantine' deleted in TSI, p. 139); identified by Bircumshaw as 'Mr George Routledge, Barber and Walker's chief electrical engineer ... One of the most respected officials of the firm. The men who came under his direct supervision idolised him'. Bircumshaw also noted that his landlady was 'Mrs H. Saxton ... in the first cottage of High Park cottages'. L. G. F. Routledge was appointed Electrical Engineer at Morgreen Power Station in August 1907 (Whitelock 44).

119:2 **Sketch-Book** In *Kangaroo*, chap. XII, a sketch-book belonging to 'Lady Hermione Rogers' (cf. Hermione Roddice) is in the possession of Richard Lovat Somers.

119:5 **seated like a Buddhist,** Either cross-legged, or the lotus position: the posture for meditation.

119:8 **the water-plants ... its festering chill,** Cf. 'The Reality of Peace', chap. II: 'how shall it be a shame that in my consciousness appear the heavy marsh-flowers of the flux of putrescence, which have their natural roots in the slow stream of decomposition that flows for ever down my bowels?' (*Phoenix* 679) ... I.e. putrefying or corrupting: cf. 'The Crown', chap. V: 'The snake is the spirit of the great corruptive principle, the festering cold of the marsh' (*Phoenix II* 407).

120:31 **the marsh-fire,** A flitting phosphorescent light seen at night over marshy ground, supposedly caused by methane gas, the product of the decomposition of organic matter: the *ignis fatuus*. Cf. 'The Crown', chap. IV: 'the *ignis fatuus* of a poisonous marsh of corruption' (*Phoenix II* 396).

124:23 *Paul et Virginie* ... **Watteau picnics** Romance (1787) by Bernardin de St Pierre (1737–1814); DHL knew it by December 1910 (see *Letters*, i. 205). An extract describing the death of Virginie appears in the *International Library of Famous Literature*, ed. Richard Garnett (1899), x. 4488–95, which the Lawrence family owned ... the French artist Jean Antoine Watteau (1684–1721) painted and drew many pieces showing gatherings and groups in the open air (not strictly 'picnics'; people talk, flirt, sing, play, dance, sit and drink, but do not eat).

124:34 **small islands** [124:7] ... **replied coldly.** DHL retyped TSII p. 190 on the same typewriter he had used for TSI (compare note on 28:13). The typed variants from TSIb are thus his, and there are handwritten revisions as well.

126:1 **the smother-fly,** Either 'black-bug', or another small black insect appearing in great numbers in hot weather.

126:14 **apples of Sodom ... Dead Sea Fruit, gall-apples.** Apples of Sodom (or Dead Sea fruit) are, traditionally, of external beauty but disappointing and hollow, when touched turning to dust and ashes. Gall-apples are excrescences produced on trees (especially the oak) by the action of insects.

126:40 **love is the greatest, and charity is the greatest** Cf. 1 Corinthians xiii, 13.

127:1 **By their works ye shall know them,** Cf. Matthew vii. 20 ['Wherefore by their fruits ye ...'].

127:7 **"Completely. If** The typist of TSII (p. 194) mistyped as 'Completely, if', and DHL responded to the error by inserting 'because' before 'if'; his original reading has been restored.

127:27 **clean thought ... sitting up?"** Cf. DHL to Waldo Frank, 15 September 1917: 'To me, the thought of the earth all *grass* and trees – grass, and no works-of-man *at all* – just a hare listening to the inaudible – that is Paradise' (*Letters*, iii. 160). The revision was inserted in TSII (p. 195); TSI (p. 149) read simply '"What a really beautiful thought."'

128:17 **the mistakes ... the ichthyosauri.** Extinct Mesozoic reptiles, in early twentieth-century science believed to combine the characters of saurian reptiles (cf. 101:11) and of fishes, with some features of whales (*OED*).

128:30 **monkeys and baboons."** Clarified by 'The Crown', chap. v, where baboons are 'highly developed life-forms, now arrested, petrified' (*Phoenix II* 407).

128:39 **Salvator Mundi** 'Saviour of the world' (Latin).

130:4 **Sunday-school ... stiffest type.** The reading of TSII (p. 199) and E1. In EP alone, DHL revised to 'righteous corrector of mankind' (p. 134).

130:25 **the Ark of the Covenant at the right moment,"** The Ark of the Covenant, made according to instructions given by God to Moses (Exodus xxv. 10–22), contained the tablets of stone on which were inscribed the Ten Commandments (1 Kings viii. 9); God punished the Philistines of Beth-shemesh for merely looking into it (1 Samuel vi. 19).

131:19 **a company of florets ... become individual.** 'What is popularly called the flower consists really of many small flowers ("florets")' (*OED*). Instead of 'become individual', TSI (p. 154) reads 'not an individual'.

132:8 **anything but trumpery,** DHL revised the reading of TSII ('anything but a lie', p. 203) by deleting the last three words and inserting 'trumpery'; an unidentified hand supplied 'but' in pencil.

132:12 **four hundred a year.** TSI (p. 158), TSII (p. 203) and A1 (p. 143) read 'two hundred': the alteration in EP and E1 makes a great difference to Birkin's independence. As a school-teacher in London in 1908, DHL earned £95 a year (*Letters*, i. 79); in June 1916, in Cornwall, he remarked that he and Frieda could manage 'on about £150 a year, here' (*Letters*, ii. 619).

134:2 **Carpeting** DHL's spelling in EP and E1, 'Carpetting', has no precedent and has been judged an error. Cf. Lady Ottoline's account of helping friends such as Bertrand Russell furnish their houses: in 1911 'I helped Bertie [then her lover] furnish a flat ... I enjoyed making it pretty and nice for him' (*Garsington* 279).

134:14 **Mrs Salmon** From at least 1881, Felley Mill Farm had been run by a labourer in charge of its 90 acres; cf. 'Limb' and 'Miss Limb', tenants of 'Strelley Mill Farm' in *Sons and Lovers*, chap. IX.

135:2 **the story of Fabre ... went to sleep?** Jean-Henri Casimir Fabre (1823–1915), French naturalist, recalled in his *Souvenirs Entymologiques* (1879–1907) how as boys he and his friends would hypnotise turkeys by catching them, putting their heads under their wings, and rocking them to and fro: 'the bird would not budge'. The experience assisted him, many years later, in explaining the common insect habit of 'playing dead'.

136:31 **Where you ... my lady!** Frieda substituted 'madam' in TSIb (p. 163) for DHL's 'my lady' (see note on 88:16). He disapproved of her change because he deleted 'Madam' in TSII (p. 214). In addition, TSII reproduced the phrase as 'Where would like it, Madam.', which DHL revised to 'Where would you like it?'. His original reading, before the transmission errors which provoked his revision, has been restored.

137:27 **Bergamos:** Hermione is wrong: 'Bergamot' is a tapestry or carpet made of a mixture of cotton and ox or goat hair, originally from Bergamo, in Lombardy, n. Italy, and not from Persia.

140:10 **an obscenity."** An important word for DHL, 1915–19: 'obscenity is the truth of our passion today' (*Letters*, ii. 660). At the 'quick of the disintegration' he discerned in Lugano, DHL noted that 'it was curiously and painfully sinister, almost obscene' ('The Return Journey', *Twilight*).

142:9 **there always is and always will be."** Added (with the comma preceding it) to both copies of TSI (p. 170) by Frieda.

142:33 **stickles for** Persists in, stands up for.

143:2 **lord of the beast and the fowl,** Cf. Genesis ix. 2: 'And the fear of you and the dread of you shall be upon every beast of the earth, and upon every fowl of the air ... into your hand are they delivered.'

144:2 **Mino** The abbreviation of an Italian diminutive: 'Giacomo' (James), for example, can be changed to 'Giacomino' and thus to 'Mino'. The Lawrences referred to their Italian cat in January 1914 as the 'Mino' (*Letters*, ii. 141).

144:29 **on to the real unknown.** The paragraph parallels Ursula's experiences at the end of *The Rainbow*, chap. XVI.

147:17 **faithlessness.** DHL apparently first typed 'faithful' and then overtyped 'ful' with 'lessness' in TSI (p. 176). Frieda clarified the alteration as she understood it by writing 'less' over the word in both copies.

148:5 **meretricious persiflage."** 'Meretricious' may mean 'showily attractive', or it may have the more serious overtone of 'prostitute-like'; DHL substituted it in revision of TSI (p. 177) for 'drivelling feminine'. 'Persiflage' is 'raillery'.

148:20 **"Isn't this rather sudden?"** An ironical use of the conventional maidenly reply to a proposal.

150:8 **Miciotto,"** 'Pussy' (Italian); cf. 'Micio' (Puss) at 299:26.

150:14 **the belle sauvage** The beautiful savage woman (French); inn-sign or business-sign in England, alluding to the American Indian princess Pocahontas.

150:23 **tell it to the Horse Marines."** From *c.* 1892, a response to something unbelievable: marines live on shipboard, and do not require horses.

150:26 **Wille zur Macht** Cf. *Der Wille zur Macht* (1887) by Friedrich Nietzsche (1844–1900), trans. as *The Will to Power* (1906). DHL commented in December 1915: 'That which we call passion is a very one-sided thing, based chiefly on hatred and Wille zur Macht. There is no Will to Power here – it is so lovely – in these [Ajanta] frescoes' (*Letters*, ii. 489); see note to 88:40. Cf. also 'Study of Thomas Hardy', written autumn 1914, chap. IX: 'The Wille zur Macht is a spurious feeling' (*Study of Thomas Hardy and Other Essays*, ed. Bruce Steele, Cambridge 1985, p. 104).

150:31 **a volonté de pouvoir,** A 'will to be able' (French): a 'will to ability'. Cf. the title of the French trans. of *Der Wille zur Macht* by Henri Albert, *La Volonté de Puissance* (1903).

150:33 **the old Adam."** See Romans vi. 6 and the service of Publick Baptism of Infants (*Book of Common Prayer*): 'O Merciful God, grant that the old Adam in this child may be so buried . . .' A favourite phrase of DHL for unregenerate man; by 1910 he knew the German novel *Der alte Adam und die neue Eva* (1895) by Rudolf Golm (pseud. of Rudolf Goldscheid, 1870–1931): cf. DHL's stories 'The Old Adam' and 'New Eve and Old Adam'.

150:37 **a star in its orbit . . . a satellite of Mars** 'Orbit' was developed in 'The Reality of Peace', chap. IV (*Phoenix* 692–3); and cf. *Letters*, ii. 288 . . . two satellites of Mars – Deimos and Phobos – were discovered in August 1877, the first in a series of discoveries of satellites of the outer planets.

151:16 **Mrs Daykin."** Birkin's landlady 'in town' is 'Mrs Varley' at 368:23; both were common names in Nottingham.

153:26 **her first love,** See Anton Skrebensky in *The Rainbow*, chap. XI, 'First Love'.

155:5 **water-party ... pleasure-launch ... rowing boats,** 'These parties were given on Whit. Mondays and August Bank holiday Mondays on Willey Water, Moorgreen reservoir, and the adjoining grounds. Lamb Close House guests, and other V.I.P.s used the grounds near the boat house ... Other people were allowed on the grounds through the lodge gates so far as the entrance of the drive leading to Beauvale House. Various stalls, and ice cream carts were allowed on these grounds. A few years after Mr Thomas Barber died [1893] these parties were discontinued ... *The people were cleared off the grounds before sunset*' (Bircumshaw). DHL amalgamates such a party with the events of 12 August 1892; see notes below ... 'The late Mr Thomas Barber has placed a steam houseboat and smaller craft on the reservoir' (Rodolph Baron von Hube, *Griseleia in Snotinghscire*, Nottingham, 1901, p. 96). Bircumshaw confirms the existence of 'the steam launch, and the little boats plying on the reservoir'.

155:28 **cotton** Typed by DHL in TSI; Frieda substituted 'silky' in both copies (p. 186). DHL demonstrated his disapproval of the change by deleting 'silky' in TSII (p. 247); his original reading has been restored.

155:34 **the Salon.** The annual exhibition in Paris of painting, sculpture, etc. by living artists (originally held in one of the 'salons' of the Louvre).

156:1 **get yourself up for** 'Dress yourself up as'.

156:7 **"Regarde, regarde ... hiboux incroyables?"** 'Look, look at these people! Aren't they incredible owls?' (French).

156:15 **her father** [155:34] **... and mother** Recreations of Alfred and Louisa Ann Burrows (see *Letters*, i. 35 n. 2), the parents of Louie and Ethel Burrows (see notes on 7:3 and 194:28).

157:11 **gabies,"** Idiots, often staring.

157:35 **And in this wise** Obsolete (and biblical); jocular for 'and in this manner': a common affectation, nineteenth–twentieth centuries.

159:9 **heard speak of** Although Frieda inserted 'them' after 'heard' in both copies of TSI (p. 192), her alteration has been judged to be a misunderstanding of the dialect construction, and DHL's original reading has been restored.

160:30 **the captain** Named as 'Rockley' at 180:23; according to Bircumshaw, 'Jesse Wheedon. An old sailor ... After the tragedy he was dismissed'. Lorenzo Weedon said at the inquest (see below) that he 'was a seaman by trade ... in the employ of Mr. Thomas Barber, and was captain in charge of the steam launch ...' (*Ilkeston Advertiser*, 20 August 1892).

161:2 **"Un peu trop de monde,"** 'Rather too many people' (French).

161:12 **'Rocked in the Cradle of the Deep'** (1832), words by Emma Hart Willard (1787–1870), music by Joseph P. Knight (1812–87): 'Rocked in the cradle of the deep, / I lay me down in peace to sleep.'

161:28 **a pleasure boat again—never."** Frieda wrote in *"Not I, But the Wind..."* (Sante Fe, 1934) of a Thames trip in late June or early July 1914: 'We went on one of the Thames boats to Richmond – Campbell, Murry, Katherine, Lawrence and I – there were a few seedy people on the boat – a sad object of a man was playing "Lead Kindly Light" on a harmonium – we got more and more silent with the dreariness of that enjoyment. And then, further along, people threw sixpences from the boat into that centuries-old, awful looking Thames mud and small boys dived for them – the Thames mud seemed to soak into our very souls …' (p. 94).

165:6 **as through a window.** Cf. 'The Shades of Spring': 'Syson … came again upon the open land, this time looking north as through a great window in the wood' (*The Prussian Officer and Other Stories*, ed. John Worthen, Cambridge, 1983, p. 98); and see Appendix III.

165:25 **"Ännchen von Tharau."** German folk song, words by Simon Dach (1605–59), music by Friedrich Silcher (1789–1860); no. 31 in the *Oxford Book of German Verse*, ed. H. G. Fielder (Oxford, 1911), which DHL reviewed in December 1911 (*Letters*, i. 331; reprinted in *Phoenix II* 269–70). Richard Lovat Somers sings it in *Kangaroo*, chap. XII. The umlaut over the 'A' was printed extremely high above the letter in EP and E1, and dropped out completely in E1a.

165:35 **Dalcroze** Émile Jacques-Dalcroze (1865–1950), Swiss composer and teacher, worked out a system of musical training through physical movement, 'eurythmics': a means of self-expression, and a method of teaching music through movement. Eurythmic Institutes were established throughout Europe; in 1910, one opened at Hellerau-Rähnitz, near Dresden (see 464:5).

166:11 **"My love——is a high-born lady—"** Chorus to 'My Gal is a High Born Lady' (1896), words and music by the American song-writer Barney Fagan (fl. 1892–9), advertised as 'The best high-class Coon song of the day': 'My gal is a high born lady, / She's black, but not to[o] shady, / Feathered like a peacock, just as gay, / She is not colored, she was born that way'.

167:31 **"Way down in Tennessee———"** 'Way down dar in Tennessee' (1893), words and music by Alfred Scott-Gatty (1847–1918). In *Kangaroo*, the colliers in war-time 'tried to keep up their spirits with this rag-time Tennessee' (chap. XII). TSIa (p. 203), TSII (p. 268) and A1 have 'It's a long way to Tipperary' (1912), words by Harry J. Williams (1874–1924) and music by Jack Judge (1878–1938), one of the most famous of the First World War songs. Deleted in TSIa: 'Down our street, there's been a blooming riot—'; music hall song 'Down Our Street' (1894) by Felix McGlennon and Albert Hall.

167:40 **figure carried** TSII (p. 269) reads 'figure, towards them, carried': the typist's eye was distracted by a phrase in the previous line.

169:24 **"Cordelia after all,"** Like the youngest daughter of Shakespeare's *King Lear*, one who will not declare her love. TSI reads 'You're the sweet Cordelia after all' (p. 206).

171:21 **the lake.** Martin Secker asked for chapter titles when he sent DHL the proofs of *Women in Love* on 14 October 1920 (see Introduction). DHL commented: 'When you broke up my loaves and fishes into a thousand little chapters, why didn't you break up Chapter XIV on p. 178, at the word "lake", line 17: and call the next bit *Under Water*' (*Letters*, iii. 617). Secker (who was not in fact responsible for DHL's division of the novel into chapters) never made the change, nor did DHL introduce it when he added titles (and one new chapter division) in EP: see note on 398:2.

172:25 **"It seethes [172:18] ... our real reality—"** See note on 120:31, and for the whole passage, cf. 'The Reality of Peace', chap. II: 'We must know that we, ourselves, are the living stream of seething corruption, this also, all the while, as well as the bright river of life' (*Phoenix* 676).

172:30 **our sea-born Aphrodite,** In the Hesiodic account of her birth, Aphrodite (Venus) is represented as having sprung from the foam (*aphros*) which gathered round the mutilated genitals of Uranus. See also *Letters*, iii. 39 and n. 3.

173:3 **fleurs du mal?** DHL brought a copy of *Les Fleurs du Mal* (1857) by Charles Baudelaire (1821–67), in September 1910 (*Letters*, i. 179). In 1913 he wrote how Baudelaire (and others) had 'got about them, the feeling that their own flesh is unclean – corrupt. And their art is the art of self hate and self-murder' (*Letters*, ii. 101).

173:8 **some roses, warm and flamy.** Cf. 'The Reality of Peace', chap. IV: 'We are roses of pure and lovely being ... I am a rose of lovely peace' (*Phoenix* 690, 694).

173:9 **Herakleitos says 'a dry soul is best.'** In Burnet's *Early Greek Philosophy*, Herakleitos says 'The dry soul is the wisest and best' (p. 152); see note on 89:18. This quotation and that in the next note were introduced into TSII (pp. 278–9) after March 1917.

173:26 **"The beginning comes out of the end."** Cf. Herakleitos as translated by Burnet: 'In the circumference of a circle the beginning and end are common' (p. 152).

175:14 **the heavens above, and the waters under the earth,"** Cf. Exodus xx. 4 ['... heaven above, or that is in the earth beneath, or that is in the water ...'].

180:27 **Miss Diana's ... Young Doctor Brindell,** Cecily ('Sissie') Frances Barber, 'aged 6 years and 4 months', youngest child of Thomas Barber, was one of a party of seven children on the Barber steam launch on Friday 12 August 1892 'celebrating a birthday ... enjoying themselves by having a trip upon the lake'. At about 2.15 p.m. she fell into the water, and Tom Herring Bingham (b. 1877), third son of Dr John Joseph Bingham (1844–1910) of Alfreton, Derbyshire, attempted to rescue her. He was 'a very good swimmer, and was well able to take care of himself in the water': he 'had thrown his "blazer" off before going into the water, otherwise he was dressed: and getting hold of the girl, who was also very wet and heavy, the weight was too much for him', though he 'held her up for some time'. The launch 'carried no life-belts'; an attempt to reach the children in the water with a boat-hook failed, and both drowned. The bodies were 'found near each other' and recovered, by dragging, later in the afternoon. The inquest jury returned a verdict of 'Accidental Death' on both children, 'and added expressions of condolence and sympathy with the parents of the children, and of admiration at the noble courage displayed by the lad Bingham' (*Ilkeston Advertiser*, 20 August 1892). A stained-glass window in the n. aisle of Alfreton parish church commemorates him.

181:5   **So** The reading of TSII and A1. DHL altered the erroneous 'She' in EP to 'She knew', the reading of E1. A2 was influenced by E1, but adopted the wholly unauthorised reading 'She felt'.

184:23   **overhead, an almost** The typist of TSII mistyped 'an' as 'and', and DHL altered this to 'with' (p. 298); his original reading has been restored.

184:31   **home** DHL typed 'along' in TSI (p. 224); Frieda revised to 'home' in both copies.

186:37   **break a way ... the prison,** DHL wrote to Catherine Carswell on 11 October 1916 how, with *Women in Love*, 'I have knocked the first loop-hole in the prison where we are all shut up' (*Letters*, ii. 663).

187:4   **One Hamletises,** Cf. DHL's account of 'Hamlet's melancholy self-absorption' in 'The Theatre' (*Twilight*).

187:39   **Then,** DHL typed 'Afterwards' in TSI (p. 228); Frieda revised to 'Then' in both copies.

188:6   **a word-bag,"** Not extant elsewhere; but cf. 'a wind-bag' – 'a voluble and senseless talker' (*OED*).

189:4   **of having ... putting things.** Added to both copies of TSI (p. 231) by Frieda. DHL had typed in TSI: 'He wished he had not got a telling way of putting things...', and then revised to 'He was irritated and weary beyond expression.' in TSIa; Frieda deleted the last two words and added 'of having a telling way of putting things.' She then copied the whole sentence into TSIb.

190:9   **dancing on the cabin roof of the launch,** Cicely Barber was 'climbing down the side of the boat from the top of the cabin, instead of going down the steps in front; her foot slipped, and she fell backwards overboard' (*Ilkeston Advertiser*, 20 August 1892).

191:13   **to leap like Sappho into the unknown.** Sappho, Greek poetess from Lesbos (fl. 7th century BC), threw herself into the sea in despair at her unrequited love for Phaon, who had been made young and beautiful by Venus. See also 'Study of Thomas Hardy', chap. VI (*Study of Thomas Hardy*, ed. Steele, p. 53), 'The Reality of Peace', chap. I (*Phoenix* 673), and 'The Crown', chap. II (*Phoenix II* 374). Ursula's meditation on death has many parallels with 'The Reality of Peace', chaps. I and II.

192:34   **rhythm** Originally in TSI 'motion' and revised in TSIa only to 'flux' (p. 236).

193:30   **they trespassed in the air to fight for it.** Cf. DHL's feeling 'the universal sickness ... when I see the inflated sausage of an airship edging through the blue heavens' (*Letters*, iii. 61). The aerial warfare of the First World War acted on DHL with particular force; cf. the Zeppelin 'which had assumed the heavens as its own' (*Letters*, ii. 394); see also *Kangaroo*, chap. XII.

193:40   **unabased.** DHL's hand-written revision in TSIa (p. 237) of 'inlimited'; he recreates a word obsolete since the seventeenth century, when it meant 'undaunted' (*OED*).

194:28 **Billy and Dora,"** In *The Rainbow*, chap. x, Ursula has a brother 'William, always called Billy, so that he should not be confused with his father': he is three when she is eleven. Ursula is here in her twenties; DHL recreates Billy as a much younger child, introduces Dora ('Doysie') for the first time, and later Rosalind (255:5). The other Brangwen children in *The Rainbow* are Gudrun, Theresa (deleted for 'Rosalind' in TSI, p. 310), Catherine, Cassandra and Tom. In the real-life Burrows family, the second son (b. 1905) was William ('Billy'), and the youngest girl Nora (b. 1907).

197:15 **who hadn't much restraint,"** DHL first typed 'who hadn't much reserve' in TSI (p. 242), and then revised the last word to 'restraint' in TSIa. On another occasion, in slightly different ink, he altered the first two words to 'without'. Frieda only copied his initial change into TSIb, suggesting that he may have made the second alteration in TSIa after she had assisted him by copying its revisions. The reading of TSIb as typed into TSII (p. 317) has therefore been accepted.

198:6 **her hate was quite abstract.** DHL typed 'she had no reason for hating him.' in TSI (p. 243); Frieda revised to the final reading in both copies.

199:12 **a sort of conscription.** The compulsory enlistment of men for military and naval service, never used on a large scale in Britain before the Second Military Service Act (Royal Assent 25 May 1916), conscripted all able-bodied men between 18 and 41. See *Letters*, ii. 597, 622. The passage was written by hand into TSII (p. 320) some time after the spring of 1917.

200:16 **Woman, the Great Mother** [200:12] ... **A Mater Dolorosa,** The 'Magna Mater' of the next paragraph: the old feminine principle, as worshipped in the ancient world. See note on 246:30 and Erich Neumann, *The Great Mother* (1955) ... A suffering mother; particularly the artistic representation of the Virgin Mary's agony over the suffering of her son Jesus Christ.

200:28 **a queen bee** Cf. DHL's name, 'the queen bee' or 'the q-b', for Frieda in *Sea and Sardinia* (1921).

200:37 **the broken-off fragment of a woman ... the laceration.** Cf. the speech of Aristophanes in Plato's *Symposium*; human beings are the divided halves of their original (bi-sexual) selves, and the sexual instinct is 'the desire of one another which is implanted in us, re-uniting our original nature, making one of two, and healing the state of man' (*The Dialogues of Plato*, tr. B. Jowett, 2nd edn, 1875, ii. 42).

203:10 **I'm sure;** DHL's revision in TSIa (p. 249) of 'I should think;' Frieda failed to transcribe the revision (from a heavily revised page) into TSIb.

204:8 **"'Timor mortis conturbat me',"** 'The fear of death disturbs me' (Latin); most famous as the refrain in 'Lament for the Makaris' by William Dunbar (?1460–?1520), though John Lydgate (?1370–?1451) has the same refrain in 'So I lay the other night'. Their common source was the *Responsorium* to the seventh lesson in the Roman Catholic office for the dead.

204:27 **devolution."** Perhaps in the sense of *OED* (1. 2) 'the rolling or passing on of time', but there seems a deliberate reversal of the idea of 'evolution' as developed by Sir Charles Lyell (1797–1875) and Charles Darwin (1809–82).

206:34 the old German knights used to swear a Blutbrüderschaft," 'Blood-brotherhood' (German); a pact between those not kin, created by the sharing of blood. Siegfried and Gunther swear such a pact in Wagner's *Götterdämmerung* (1876), I, though not in the way Gerald suggests, which is more reminiscent of Icelandic saga – cf. 'The Blood-Brothers' Saga'. A favourite word of DHL's at the period: see *Letters*, ii. 363, 570, 645. Middleton Murry recorded how, in the late spring of 1916, DHL 'talked of the blood-brotherhood between us, and hinted at the need of some inviolable sacrament between us – some pre-Christian blood-rite in keeping with the primeval rocks about us [in Cornwall]' (*Between Two Worlds*, p. 409).

209:2 "She's a ... said Gerald. Erroneously deleted by Frieda in TSIb (p. 254); the sentence came at the end of a series of revisions she was copying. DHL added 'said Gerald' to TSIb at the end of the next sentence to compensate; his original readings are here restored.

209:26 *want to* ... *would* not DHL originally revised TSIa (p. 255) to read 'want to *claim* social superiority: and he *would* not'; Frieda omitted both underlinings and the colon when she copied into TSIb. DHL however underlined 'want' and 'would' in TSII (p. 333), added a comma after 'superiority', and changed 'and' to 'yet'. These changes preclude any return to the reading of TSIa.

211:2 The Industrial Magnate One of the first readers of TSIb, Catherine Carswell, apparently criticised the placing of this chapter. DHL wrote to her on 20 December 1916: 'About the Gerald-Work part: I want it to come where it does: you meet a man, you get an impression of him, you find out *afterwards* what he has done. If you have, in your arrogance, writ him down a nobody, then there is a slap in the eye for you when you find he has done more than you have done. Voilà. (I don't mean *you*, Catherine Carswell, of course.)' (*Letters*, iii. 57).

211:26 quite the "go," Quite the attraction of the moment: nineteenth- and early twentieth-century slang.

212:17 Shortlands 'Highclose' in TSII, A1 and all subsequent texts: DHL appears to have mistakenly reverted to the name used in *The White Peacock* for his recreation of Lambclose House.

212:30 dry, sly face. DHL wrote 'wry, satiric face' in TSIa (p. 259); Frieda copied this as 'dry satiric face' into TSIb, which TSII typed with a comma after 'dry'. However, DHL's revision in TSII to 'dry, sly face' (p. 338) precludes any return to his original reading.

212:32 I nursed three of her children. Jessie Chambers told Emile Delavenay in 1934: 'All that he [DHL] says about the Crich family, the shooting of the younger brother, the water party, the turbulent self-willed children, he *must* have heard from us. My father's youngest sister was nursery governess to those children, and it was from her that we knew of these incidents. Lawrence's own people wouldn't know' (Emile Delavenay, *D. H. Lawrence: L'Homme et la Genèse de son Oeuvre 1885–1919*, Paris, 1969, ii. 684).

212:34 little fiends ... ay, at DHL originally typed in TSI (p. 259): 'little fiends—Master Gerald, a little devil if ever there was one, a fair devil, at'. He then revised TSIa to read 'proper ones! ... little demon ... a proper demon, at'. Frieda copied inaccurately, and left TSIb reading: 'little fiends ... little devil ... a proper demon, at'; DHL, however revised TSII (p. 328) to read 'little fiends—that Gerald was a demon ... a proper demon, ay, at', which precludes any return to his TSIa revision.

213:17 **a shine** A disturbance, row, fuss: colloquial from *c.* 1830.

215:13 **love for his neighbour ... than himself** Cf. Matthew xxii. 39. The local newspaper's obituary notice for Thomas Barber noted how he 'loved his home and his family, and the people among whom he lived, he spent his whole time with them trying successfully to make those about him happy and comfortable ... disposing of his surplus cash in graceful acts of charity close at home; and no worthy applicant ever besought him in vain either for private needs or public projects' (*Ilkeston Advertiser*, 16 December 1893).

216:13 **Crowther,** In TSI, DHL varied between 'Crowther' and 'Simpson' (first name 'Thomas' in both cases) as the name of the Crich butler and manservant. In TSII (p. 344) he twice altered 'Thomas' to 'Crowther', but failed to correct 'Simpson': this edition has done so.

222:1 **at Bonn, at Berlin, and at Frankfurt.** Three cities with universities of particularly high reputation; Clifford Chatterley lived at Bonn 'where he was studying the technicalities of coal-mining (*Lady Chatterley's Lover*, chap. 1).

222:22 **"C. B. & Co."** Perhaps 'Crich Barber & Co.' DHL knew the coal-wagons marked 'B. W. & Co.' (Barber Walker & Co.) very well; he put seven of them into his drawing of 'The Rainbow' of 2 March 1915 (*Letters*, ii. facing p. 293), and drew four wagons marked 'CW & Co' in his sketch for the wrapper of *Sons and Lovers* in 1913 (UT; *Letters*, i. 529).

223:14 **What mattered ... less perfectly.** Cf. the discussion of 'function' (with reference to 'the pruning knife') in Plato's *Republic*, I, 353 A–B.

223:21 **talk of closing down two of them.** By 1906, there was a worrying 'drop in output from the Top Hard Seam from High Park and Watnall' – two of the Barber Walker & Co. Eastwood region pits (Whitelock 93).

224:13 **Gerald's father, following in the second generation,** Thomas Barber was the fifth generation of his family in the colliery business.

224:27 **soon** The typist of TSII (p. 357) typed as 'so on', and DHL deleted 'on'; the original reading is here restored.

224:33 **the Masters' Federation ... accept a reduction.** In July 1893, the Midland Counties members of the Coal-Owners' Federation (or Federated Coal-Owners) 'endeavoured to obtain a reduction in wages' (Whitelock 40). This led, from 28 July, to a sixteen-week stoppage; the Coal-Owners did not obtain the reduction they wanted.

224:38 **the rich man ... his possessions,** Matthew xix. 23 ['a rich man shall hardly enter into the kingdom of heaven']; see also note on 226:35.

225:2 **"Ye shall ... eat bread."** Not a direct biblical quotation, but cf. Leviticus xxiii. 14 ['Ye shall eat neither bread, nor parched corn...'].

225:17 "**All men are** [225:13] ... **disquality?**" DHL discusses equality in 'The Lemon Gardens' (*Twilight*), 'Democracy' (*Phoenix* 699–718), and 'Education of the People' (*Phoenix* 587–665); see also note on 102:23. Someone underlined 'disquality' in pencil the three occasions it occurred in TSIb (p. 276), presumably querying it; the first underlining survived in TSII (p. 359), where DHL deleted the other two.

226:2 **Riots broke out** [225:34] ... **put out.** At New Watnall colliery occurred the 'one serious riot in the county' (Whitelock 92–3). On 6 September 1893, wagons standing in the railway sidings and various buildings were set on fire; seven ringleaders were arrested. Large military and police detachments were then brought into the district and remained until 20 September; '115 officers and men of the Staffordshire Regiment are quartered at the Sun Hotel' (*Ilkeston Advertiser*, 16 September 1893). At Featherstone colliery in Yorkshire, on 7 September, troops fired on a demonstrating crowd; two men were killed and sixteen wounded. DHL's account amalgamates the two events. Bircumshaw confirms some details: 'the soldiers were the 17th Lancers, they went up to the pit in the morning, Paddy Train [i.e. the colliery railway]. Watnall pit was better known locally as *Hell Hole*. The soldiers were billeted at the Sun Inn, and Mechanics Hall [Mechanics Institute]. There was not any fire, no shooting, no one killed. A lot of damage was done to the surface buildings, and underground waggons thrown down the shaft.'

226:9 **three ha'porth o' coppers,** Three half-pennies (see Note on pounds, shillings and pence). A contemptuous local way of referring to something insignificant; a variant of "you 'a'porth".

226:18 **great basketfuls of buns ... into the schools,** George Holderness, headmaster of the British Schools, Eastwood, recorded in the School Log of 15 September 1893: 'To-day in consequence of some person making a report to the Relief Committee that several children were attending school without having proper meals, five shillings worth of buns were sent to these schools to be distributed among the children. On making enquiries, found that not a single child was short of a meal. The buns, however, were not refused. This bun distribution is to continue as long as the strike lasts' (p. 214). Soup and other meals were also distributed; see the *Ilkeston Advertiser* of 14 October 1893.

226:35 **to give away all he had, to the poor.** Cf. Matthew xix. 21: '... If thou wilt be perfect, go and sell that thou hast, and give to the poor . . .'. See also 'The Crown', chap. III: 'Rich and poor alike are only, each one, a pit-head surrounding the bottomless pit. But the rich man, by pouring vast quantities of matter down his void, gives himself a more pleasant illusion of fulfilment than the poor man can get: that is all' (*Phoenix II* 385).

228:19 **the God of the Machine, Deus ex Machina.** The Latin means 'the God from the machine', the stage 'machina' by which the gods were suspended in Greek and Roman theatre; hence, something that comes as a providential interposition.

229:13 **The old grey managers ... clerks ... removed them** The modernisation of Eastwood collieries 1906–7 involved 'the appointment of a young up-to-date management staff ... Messrs. Alfred Chambers, Isaac Chambers, and

George Harrison, all managers of the old school, with long service, were retired with lump sums ... Mr Leonard Hodges, aged twenty-seven, was appointed Manager of Brinsley and Selston Collieries, and Mr Herbert Greener became Manager of High Park and Watnall Collieries. Both the new managers were young ambitious men' (Whitelock 44). Bircumshaw 'knew the old grey managers who were dismissed' and the 'old grey clerks' and names them, nine in all.

230:10   **at** DHL typed 'to' in TSI (p. 282); Frieda revised to 'at' in both copies.

230:12   **the sati in India?** Sati – often 'Suttee' – is Sanscrit for 'a virtuous wife', and refers to the Hindu custom (declared illegal in British India in 1829) of burning the widow on the husband's funeral pyre.

230:28   **An enormous electric plant** [230:23] ... **cutting machines ... thoroughly changed,** John William Fryar, General Manager of Barber Walker & Co. from 1905 (cf. 231:39–40), carried through the electrification of the Eastwood pits, 'not only with the object of superseding hand holing, by the introduction of coal-cutting machines, but also to replace the obsolete steam driven haulages and to reduce the large number of ponies underground and their drivers, by replacing all those on main roads with electrically driven haulages' (Whitelock 44). Moorgreen Power Station, costing £20,000, was installed by Barber Walker & Co. 1906–7 to supply electricity to all its Eastwood collieries; see note on 117:15.

230:29   **the butty system was abolished.** The 'little butty' system – in which DHL's father John Arthur Lawrence worked as a butty – depended upon individuals taking responsibility for working sections of the coal face, and receiving and passing on payment to those who worked with them. The introduction of coal-cutting machines led to considerable changes in working conditions and pay (see next note); not, however, until 1919 was 'an agreement signed in Nottinghamshire and Derbyshire that all experienced men at the face must share equally' (A. R. Griffin, *The Miners of Nottinghamshire, 1818–1914*, Nottingham, 1956, p. 138).

230:35   **they submitted to it all.** In fact a strike in the Eastwood collieries 'arose from the introduction of coal-cutting machines' between January and March–April 1907. Changes in working had involved a reduction of the working height at the coal face at High Park colliery from 4 ft 9 in to 2 ft 9 in; 'in consequence the workmen soon appreciated the advantages of machine-holing'. Two other strikes caused by 'the question of the coal-cutting price-list' took place between June–November 1910 and November–February 1911–12 (Whitelock 47).

231:33   **a greater output of coal than ever,** 'The output of Eastwood Collieries in 1907 was the record one of 1,166,508 tons' (Whitelock 47); in 1890 it had been 995,990 tons, and 1894–8 had been on average 750,000 tons.

234:15   **Mademoiselle.** Bircumshaw recalled 'A french lady' at Lambclose House; Lawrie Cliff (b. 1853 in Switzerland) was married to the butler.

236:5   **And** It is just possible that a page (288) is missing from both copies of TSI; p. 287 ends with 'beautiful!"' and p. 289 begins at the left margin with 'and again chuckling, and rushing to embrace...' The typist of TSII typed the latter as a new paragraph, and DHL revised 'and rushing' to 'she rushed' (p. 373).

237:10   **the Blue coat boys.** The boys of the Christ's Hospital Schools still wear an Elizabethan uniform of long blue cassock and yellow stockings. Middleton Murry attended the London school 1901–8; DHL would himself have seen boys from the Nottingham school (founded 1706).

237:27   **"Winifred veut tant faire** DHL typed '"Combien Winifred veut faire' in TSI (p. 291); Frieda revised to the final reading in both copies.

237:28   **toute la matinée c'est** TSI read 'tout le matin c'est' (p. 291); TSII (p. 376) was revised in ink, in an unidentified hand, over what appears to be the same wording in pencil. It is impossible to identify the pencil writing as DHL's. In TSII, 'c'est' appeared to be deleted by the revision, and was omitted from subsequent states of the text.

238:8   **"Bonjour mademoiselle [237:24] ... qu'un chancelier?"**
"Good-day miss," ...
"Winifred does so want to do Bismarck's portrait—! Oh, but all morning it's ... Bismarck, Bismarck, always Bismarck! It's a rabbit, isn't it, miss?"
"Yes, it's a big black and white rabbit. Haven't you seen him?" ...
"No, miss, Winifred has never wanted to show it to me. Many's the time I've asked her, 'What is this Bismarck, Winifred?' But she wouldn't tell me. Her Bismarck, it was a mystery."
"Yes, it's a mystery, really a mystery! ..."
"Bismarck ... it's a mystery, Bismarck, he is a marvel," ...
"Yes, he is a marvel," ...
"Is he really a marvel?" ...
"Certainly!" ...
"However he isn't a king ... he was only chancellor."
"What's a chancellor?" (French and German)
Otto von Bismarck (1815–98), Prussian prime minister and German Chancellor.

238:11   **a chancellor is ... a sort of judge,"** The word has moved away from its original connection with the legal profession and law courts. In the German Empire, it was the title of the President of the Federal Council, who had the general conduct of the imperial administration; Bismarck was the first Chancellor of the German nation as a whole, 1871–90.

238:22   **"Draw him and quarter him** Pun on two senses of 'draw': criminals were once 'hung, drawn [disembowelled] and quartered'.

239:7   **calculative.** DHL's hand-written revision in TSIa (p. 292). Frieda revised to 'calculating', which she also inserted in TSIb. On the grounds that she probably did not recognise an unusual but still perfectly acceptable word, which has the additional meaning of 'given to calculating' (*OED*), DHL's original reading has been restored.

239:11   **An access of worship** DHL typed 'An access of worship' in TSI (p. 292); TSII was typed as 'An excess of worship' (p. 379), and DHL revised 'worship' to 'appreciation'. On the grounds that the typist's error provoked the revision, the original reading has been restored.

242:32 knowledge of her Cf. the common biblical meaning of 'sexual intercourse'.

242:36 red ether Ether is the medium supposed to fill the upper regions of space, as air fills the lower regions; cf. 'The Proper Study': 'chemistry winds wearily to sea in the ether, or some such universal...' (*Phoenix* 723; to be published in *Reflections on the Death of a Porcupine and Other Essays*, ed. Herbert). The word is, however, used frequently in Burnet's discussion of Anaxagoras and others in *Early Greek Philosophy* – i.e. pp. 299, 308, 310–11; for Anaxagoras, 'a rotary motion produces two great masses, the one consisting of the rare, hot, light and dry, called the "Aether"; the other, in which the opposite qualities predominate, called "Air" ... Of these Aether or Fire took the outside while the Air occupied the centre' (pp. 311–12). The 'red' colour of DHL's 'ether' may thus relate to fire as well as to blood.

244:2 Moony There are four relevant meanings of the word: 'of or belonging to the moon', 'moon-shaped', 'illuminated by the moon', 'inclined to act in a listless, aimless manner'. DHL first entitled this chapter 'Moonshine' on contents page and the opening page of the chapter (p. 256) in EP; he revised only the latter to the reading of E1.

245:37 floating the moon upon it. This passage, and its central images, are clarified in 'The Spinner and the Monks' (*Twilight*): 'Only the moon, white and shining, was in the sky, like a woman glorying in her own loveliness as she loiters superbly to the gaze of all the world ... sometimes looking at her own superb, quivering body, wholly naked in the water of the lake.'

246:30 "Cybele ... The accursed Syria Dea! Cybele is the Phrygian goddess of fruitfulness, worshipped as the Great Mother (*Magna Mater*) by the Romans from 204 BC (see Sir James George Frazer, *The Golden Bough*, 1890–1915, Part IV, Vol. I, p. 263) ... The 'Syria Dea' is Astarte (see *The Symbolic Meaning*, ed. Armin Arnold, 1962, p. 144), 'a goddess latterly of lunar nature' (Sir E. B. Tylor, *Primitive Culture*, 1871, p. 301, which DHL read in April 1916 – *Letters*, ii. 593), a semitic goddess, everywhere the great female principle. See, e.g., the painting 'Astarte Syriaca' (1877) by D. G. Rossetti (see note on 15:35). Cf. DHL's letter to David Eder in 1917: 'I should like to talk to you also about the lunar myth – the lunar trinity – father – mother – son, with the son as consort of the mother, the *magna* Mater. It seems to me your whole psycho-analysis rests on this myth...' (*Letters*, iii. 150).

247:3 flakes of white and dangerous fire. Cf. the 'flakes' of elfish light in Coleridge's 'The Ancient Mariner' (1798), ll. 275–60; also l. 42 of 'Tithonus' (1860) by Tennyson: 'And beat the twilight into flakes of fire'.

248:41 "No." The previous sentence read, after revision in TSIa, 'One can't manage those things.' (p. 305); DHL revised to the final reading in TSII (p. 395).

251:10 the Dionysic ecstatic way," See note on 101:22, and *St. Mawr and Other Stories*, ed. Brian Finney (Cambridge, 1983), note on 15:37.

253:11 a statuette [253:1] ... slim long loins. The 'collars' suggest that the piece comes from the Temne or Mende of Sierra Leone, the Asante or Fante of Ghana, or the Baulé of the Ivory Coast: a Mende figure in the British Museum, *c.* 1900, with collars and 'melon-shaped' head, 1.181 m high, is characteristic. There were many such pieces on the English market by 1916. The 'glossy ... suave' surface would almost certainly have been produced by its European dealer or owner; African wood sculpture was not given such a surface by its makers.

253:25 **the Egyptians worshipped the ball-rolling scarab:** Images of the sacred dung-beetle, *Scarabeus* or *Ateuchus sacer*, were venerated in Ancient Egypt as types of the sun god, probably because the ball of dung rolled by the beetle to provide a place for its eggs was regarded as an image of the sun in its course across the heavens (see note on 98:37).

255:3 **like Jerusalem to his fancy.** Cf. '[Autobiographical Fragment]', written 1927: 'as a child, coming home from Moorgreen, I had looked up and seen the squares of miners' dwellings, built by the Company, rising from the hill-top in the afternoon light like the walls of Jerusalem...' (*Phoenix* 829).

255:9 **reproductions from Picasso,** Though drawings by Pablo Picasso (1881–1973) had been shown in London in the First Post-Impressionist Exhibition of November 1910, Middleton Murry was responsible for the first reproduction of a Picasso in England, in *Rhythm*, no. i (Summer 1911), and also wrote an article on 'The Art of Pablo Picasso', *New Age* (30 November 1911). TSIb shows 'Picasso' to be a handwritten correction of 'Pisarro' (p. 310): either Camille Pissarro (1830–1903), Impressionist and Pointillist, or his son Lucien (1863–1944), who had 'sworn adhesion' to Murry's *Blue Review* in March 1913 (see Anthony Alpers, *The Life of Katherine Mansfield*, 1980, p. 157).

256:17 **on foot—."** Afoot. In TSI (p. 312) Brangwen says 'intending', and Birkin wonders if he means '*impending*'.

256:37 **Certainly."** DHL revised TSIa's 'Yes' (p. 313) to 'Certainly'; Frieda failed to copy the alteration (from an extensively revised page) into TSIb.

257:4 **" 'She' ... is the cat's mother."** I.e. it is impolite to refer to someone by a pronoun; no-one knows who the cat's mother is. Cf. TSI (p. 313) as first typed: '" 'She'," thought Birkin to himself, repeating the words of his nurse, " 'Is the cat's mother.'" He wondered why it was so improper to say just "she"?'

257:20 **in and out like a frog in a gallipot.** An unrecorded dialect saying. A gallipot is a small earthen-glazed pot, used by apothecaries for ointments and medicines; also used as fly-traps, containing a mixture of vinegar and sugar (cf. *The White Peacock*, ed. Andrew Robertson, Cambridge 1983, 6:16). It seems possible that frogs would get into gallipots on window ledges in pursuit of the insects they contained, but could also escape as quickly as they got in. In TSI, the equivalent phrase is 'off and on as if it were a penny ride on a tram' (p. 313).

259:16 **'Girl's Own'?"** The *Girl's Own Paper* (founded 1880), then called *Girl's Own Paper and Woman's Magazine* (1908–27).

261:11 **bargust."** An abusive term (in Nottinghamshire dialect) for someone, often a child, who behaves badly or noisily. DHL typed 'creature' and then revised to 'bargust' in TSIa (p. 318); Frieda altered the word back to 'creature' in TSIa, and left TSIb unchanged. DHL wrote, then deleted, the word in the final MS of *Sons and Lovers* (Roberts E373e, p. 187).

264:2 **Lloyd George** David Lloyd George (1863–1945); Liberal MP; became Minister of Munitions in July 1915, Secretary of State for War in July 1916, and Prime Minister, December 1916–October 1922. Cf. DHL's remarks about him to Lady Cynthia Asquith in *Letters*, iii. 39.

264:9 **yellow-ammers** Common dialect word for yellow wagtails. TSIb was revised to 'yellowhammers' (p. 322), apparently not by DHL or Frieda.

264:38 **warm his foot-soles ... nauseous Meredith poem.** 'A Preaching from a Spanish Ballad' by Meredith, lines 33–6: 'At my breasts I cool thy footsoles; / Wine I pour, I dress thy meats; / Humbly, when my lord it pleaseth, / Lie with him on perfumed sheets...' The same error of 'warm' for 'cool' occurs in DHL's 1913 story 'New Eve and Old Adam', where a character drawn from Frieda quotes the poem 'as one she loved' (*Love Among the Haystacks and Other Stories*, ed. John Worthen, Cambridge 1987, p. 181).

266:2 **Gladiatorial** DHL first wrote the title as 'The Conquering' on contents page of EP.

266:15 **the Thirlbys.** A common Eastwood name; Mabel Thurlby (b. 1885) was a childhood friend of DHL (see Nehls, i. 28–32), and 'the Thurlby family had been very close to the Lawrences at one time' (Keith Sagar, 'Lawrence and Frieda', *D. H. Lawrence Review*, ix, Spring 1976, 120).

267:18 **each man** The reading of TSIa (p. 325). Frieda omitted it when copying into TSIb; DHL inserted 'each' in revision of TSII (p. 421): his original reading is here restored.

267:23 **"Some old Johnny ... sleep, drink, and travel,"** Reference unidentified (though cf. 'Red Trousers' in *Assorted Articles*, 1930: 'In the ancient recipe, the three antidotes for dullness or boredom are sleep, drink, and travel ... From sleep you wake up, from drink you become sober, and from travel you come home again.') In *The Anatomy of Melancholy* (1621), by Robert Burton (1577–1640), all three cures are suggested for melancholy.

267:24 **"All cold eggs,"** Cf. *St. Mawr*: 'Abandoned by the mother bird, incapable of hatching', ed. Finney, p. 152.

268:16 **silly," he said ... Birkin coldly.** After DHL's revision, TSIa read 'silly. I do, it's no joke." "No," said Birkin, "it's no joke."' (p. 327). Frieda omitted 'I do, it's no joke."' in TSIb, but DHL's revision to the final reading in TSII (p. 423) precludes any return to his original version.

269:9 **full electric fluid—like eels."** The *Gymnotus*, a fresh-water eel-like fish of South America, is capable of giving an electric shock, but contains no 'fluid'.

269:32 **tall and** Added by Frieda to both copies of TSI (p. 330). It is possible that she was also responsible for the deletion, in both copies, of the phrases following 'thin and fine' (269:33): 'his arms thin and small, his head a little too large for his frame' (p. 330).

269:33 **plastic.** I.e. moulded, or modelled, as in sculpture.

270:36 **clinched** Clasped, interlocked (dialect); cf. 'Study of Thomas Hardy', chap. VI: 'an absolute interlocking of the two in one ... a long, clinched, timeless embrace' (*Study of Thomas Hardy*, ed. Steele, pp. 74–5). TSI shows DHL first typing 'hammered like malleable metal into oneness' (p. 332), and then altering 'hammered' to 'clinched'.

272:30   Gerald, "it's life for me—" The reading of TSIa (p. 334). Frieda deleted 'for me' when copying into TSIb; the typist of TSII replaced the dash with a period; DHL revised TSII to 'Gerald.' (p. 430). His original reading is here restored.

273:29   a caftan in Bokhara," Or Bukhara (now in Uzbek Republic, USSR); the terminus of an ancient caravan route from China. Gerald's attention to his clothes was commented on by Catherine Carswell, and DHL accepted her criticism: '*I* can't understand his persistence in "dressing". But good to cross him out' (*Letters*, iii. 44). TSI shows DHL, for example, altering 'exceedingly carefully dressed' to 'noticeably well-dressed' (p. 10), though he altered it again to 'exaggeratedly well-dressed' (14:29) in TSII (p. 14).

275:3   to wrestle with your good angel, Cf. Genesis xxxii. 24–30, where Jacob wrestles with a being popularly supposed to be an angel; but the 'good angel' (added in TSI, p. 337) suggests, too, Shakespeare's Sonnet 144, with its 'better angel' 'a man right fair' opposed to the 'worser spirit' of the 'woman coloured ill': 'Till my bad angel fire your good one out' (l. 14).

275:29   draw something out. Words and action are both strongly reminiscent of a letter of 11 October 1916 from DHL to Dollie Radford: the Lawrences' Cornish neighbour William Henry Hocking—'most marvellously understanding' – says '"Yes, there's something one wants, that isn't money or anything like that – But shall I ever get it? – I want it –" he puts his hand to his chest with a queer, grasping movement – "I can feel the want of it here – but shall I ever get it? – That's what I begin to doubt. Lately, I begin to doubt it"' (*Letters*, ii. 664).

277:11   Dresden ware ... Copenhagen ware. A fine, hard, glazed porcelain made at Meissen (16 km from Dresden) from 1709 ... from the end of the nineteenth century, a style excelling in the production of porcelain animal figures in delicate tints. The 'girl ... with a lamb' below is probably a 'Dresden Shepherdess', the most famous product of the Meissen works.

**278:15   *mauvaise honte* 'Bashfulness' (French).

279:6   Wilson Bircumshaw noted that 'Mr Daniels' was head gardener at Lambclose House; the 1881 census lists George Daniels (b. 1850) as 'Gardener Domestic Servant'.

279:24   the Duchess of Portland?" Lady Ottoline's half-brother was Duke of Portland (see note on 15:40). The Portland family was the most prestigious of the area; Lady Ottoline found in 1914 that DHL 'also liked to talk of my family in Nottinghamshire, for he had a romantic feeling for them... "Bentincks were always looked up to as being disinterested"' (*Ottoline* 272).

279:26   a rare poppy-show I.e. a puppet-show, a peep-show, a display.

280:14   flush DHL typed 'flame' in TSI (p. 344); Frieda revised to 'flush' in both copies.

284:39   like the Romans, one should be master of one's fate I.e. in committing suicide; and see 'Invictus', iv. (1875), ll. 15–16, by W. E. Henley (1849–1903): 'I am the master of my fate: / I am the captain of my soul.'

285:1 **the great serpent of Laocoön.** The classical Greek statue (rediscovered 1506; located in the Vatican at Rome) shows the priest Laocoon, with his two sons, wrestling with sea serpents. Cf. DHL's feelings about 1916 in a letter to Catherine Carswell: 'It is worse than any *Laocoon* with the snake round him: such a weight on one's arms and limbs and heart: an utter imprisonment in the tightening folds of this heavy serpent, and oneself impotent' (*Letters*, iii. 64).

285:34 **Sure** 'Of course'.

287:13 **Best to dance while Rome burns,** To be engaged in trifles in the face of a crisis. Cf. DHL's description of the Roman Emperor Nero (37–68) 'Watching the sea of flames ... he is said to have danced and sung with extravagant pleasure' (*Movements in European History*, chap. I). DHL's source for both was probably the translation of *The Annals of Tacitus* by A. J. Church and W. J. Brodribb (1869, reprinted 1906), where 'the emperor appeared on a private stage and sang of the destruction of Troy' (p. 302): the development from 'stage' to 'dance' being DHL's own.

287:23 **abandonments of Roman licence,** DHL knew the descriptions of 'abandonments' in the Roman historian Tacitus (*Movements in European History*, chap. III); cf. too 'After the year 180 ... Rome itself became a centre of shame and degradation' (chap. I).

287:40 **Marshall** The lodge-keeper is given the name of the Crich family brother-in-law (31:9); TSI (p. 353) reads 'Holliday' (a name used in *The Trespasser*, ed. Elizabeth Mansfield, Cambridge, 1982, pp. 218–23), but DHL probably decided it was too similar to 'Halliday'.

289:2 **called Gudrun ... "Why?"** DHL typed 'called Gerald' in TSI (p. 354), but the typist of TSII produced 'called Gudrun' (p. 458). However, DHL altered Birkin's reply from '"It's beyond me,"' to '"Why?"' in TSII, making it impossible to restore his original reading.

289:5 **she's a bird that prefers the bush."** Referring to the deleted exchange about relationship and marriage at the beginning of the novel in TSI, where Ursula says 'I'm sure a bird in the bush is worth two in the hand ... And while I am by myself ... I am more or less a bird in the bush' (p. 1).

289:32 **the ticket,** The correct thing: what is wanted, expected, or fashionable.

289:37 **"As you please ... she echoed.** Gerald's previous speech in TSII (p. 459), before revision, read: '"And marriage is just thrown in, or not thrown in, as you please?"'

290:15 **to tie himself to the mast."** Like Ulysses resisting the song of the Sirens, who tempted sailors to their death.

290:26 **"Not being a Mohammedan,"** A reference to the Muslim paradise, which includes sensual delights.

291:2 *et puis?"* **"Le paradis!"** 'And what then?' 'Paradise!' (French).

292:11   **away at Aix—"** Lady Ottoline visited Aix-en-Provence in the summer of 1910, staying at the *Hotel des Thermes* (*Ottoline* 198–200).

293:9   **Mammon, the flesh, and the devil** Cf. the 'Litany' (*Book of Common Prayer*): '... from all the deceits of the world, the flesh, and the devil, *Good Lord, deliver us*'. TSI shows DHL revising 'the world' to 'Mammon' (p. 358): a personification of riches and greed, a false god.

293:11   **suckled in a creed outworn,** From 'The World is too much with us' (pub. 1807) by William Wordsworth: 'I'd rather be / A Pagan suckled in a creed outworn' (ll. 9–10).

294:14   **I *can* do it."** DHL revised to 'I *can* give myself up to him—why should I? Why should I give up my independence, and only subserve him?"' in TSIb (p. 359), but then deleted everything after '*can*', without inserting closing punctuation or inverted commas. Frieda added 'do it.' in both copies of TSI.

296:37   *si jeunesse savait* 'If youth knew' (French); first half of the traditional saying which ends 'si vieillesse pouvait' ('if age was able').

298:16   *fat* 'One believing himself irresistible to women'; 'affected' (French).

298:19   **Florence for the winter,"** Lady Ottoline visited Florence in the winter of 1892 and again in 1898 (*Ottoline* 86–7, 108–10); she also honeymooned there in the winter of 1902 and met 'the Berensons' (p. 122; see next note).

298:27   **Barnes ... Olandese ... Italian national policy—"** Probably a recreation of Bernhard Berenson (1865–1959), art historian, who lived near Florence for many years ... 'Olandese' is Italian for 'Dutch'; a most unusual name, apparently invented ... the most famous exponents of 'Italian national policy' *c.* 1913 would have been Enrico Corradini (1865–1931) and Alfredo Rocco (1875–1935).

299:6   **"il Sandro ... imparare tutto———"** "Sandro [Alexander, Hermione's brother] writes to me that he has been greeted with the greatest enthusiasm, all the young people, both girls and boys, are passionate, passionate for Italy, and they absolutely want to learn everything———" (Italian). TSII (p. 473) failed to type 'appassionati ... imparare', and probably as a result DHL altered 'tutto' ('everything') to 'tutti' ('all'); with the restoration of the full sentence from TSI (p. 365), 'tutto' has also been restored.

299:17   **My mother died in Florence."** Lady Ottoline's mother died in England, shortly after spending the winter of 1892 in Florence (*Ottoline* 87–8).

299:32   **"Vieni—vieni** [299:29] **... vero?"** "Come—come here" ... "Come and say Good Morning to auntie. He remembers me, he remembers me well— isn't it true, little one? Is it true that you remember me? Is it true?" (Italian).

300:25   **"Siccuro che** [300:17] **... superbo, questo!"** "Of course he understands Italian ... he won't have forgotten it, Mummy's language" ... "Look, the nice boy, how proud he is, this one!" (Italian). 'Siccuro' should be 'Sicuro', 'italiano' should be 'l'italiano' and 'come è' should properly be 'com' è'. Here and elsewhere, Hermione's errors in Italian words have not been corrected, but accents have been emended.

300:40 **"Ti imparano [300:35] ... Bel giovanotto—"** "They are [teaching] you to do bad things, bad things——" ... "Nice boy—" (Italian). 'Imparano' [learning] should be 'insegnano' [teaching]: 'fare' should be 'a fare'.

301:6 **"No! Non ... così selvatico—!"** "No! One is not allowed to put one's little paw in the saucer. Daddy doesn't like it. Such an uncivilised gentleman cat—!" (Italian). 'Il zampino' should be 'lo zampino'. TSI (p. 368) completed the sentence "... dispiace molto a lui": "is most displeasing to him".

302:2 **Excurse** EP (the proof set not returned to Secker) reads 'Excursion' on contents page and p. 318. DHL may be using the verb 'to excurse' ('to wander'), which he was to use in *Kangaroo* (1923): 'he was to excurse ahead...' (chap. v); he is as likely to be re-inventing a rare and obsolete noun, last used 1587, meaning 'an ambush, a raid, a mad sally' (*OED*). An 'excursus' is a discussion of a special point in a book. 'Excurse' parallels DHL's creation of 'discursing' in *The Lost Girl*, ed. Worthen, note on 17:17. Frieda wrote to Harry T. Moore on 1 October 1952: 'the outer setting of *Women in Love* is Louise Burrows, but the inner relationship is L's and mine, like the ring scene, where I throw the ring at him; that happened' (*Memoirs and Correspondence*, p. 316). The typing of TSI in Pinker's office began at this point (p. 369); at that time there was no chapter division.

303:3 **a round opal, red and fiery,** The so-called 'fire-opal'.

303:39 **Worksop."** On the edge of Sherwood Forest, 24 miles n. of Nottingham and 17 miles n.w. of Southwell (see note on 312:6).

304:10 **she was superstitious.** Opals have long been associated with ill-luck.

307:11 **a fishwife,** Women in fish-markets were traditionally loud-mouthed.

311:24 **mounted the car** DHL originally wrote 'went to the car' in MS (p. 21), and then revised to 'mounted the car'; the typist of TSI produced 'mounted to the car' (p. 384).

312:6 **Southwell Minster.** The Minister at Southwell, 12 miles n.e. of Nottingham, has 50-foot-high pyramidal lead spires ('like quartz crystals'), designed by Ewan Christian, erected on its western towers during the 1879–80 restoration; the rest of the building is Norman to Decorated.

312:14 **the Saracen's Head."** Fourteenth-century inn near the Minster; cars still park in the extensive 'old yard of the inn'.

312:18 **the Minster bells ... the light——"** DHL quotes the first two lines ['... to Thee, ... God, ... light;'] of a hymn by Bishop Thomas Ken (1637–1711); the tune traditionally linked with these words is the Canon by Thomas Tallis (?1520–85). A set of chimes at Southwell, worked by the clock at midday and 6.00 p.m., from 1897 played three tunes; 'Bedford' ('Oh help us Lord, each hour of need'), by W. Wheall (d. 1727), has resemblances to Tallis's Canon.

312:27 **it true ... said, wondering.** Ela (p. 329) replaced these words with a phrase from four lines further down the page; the error was introduced during page re-setting.

312:37   **Book of Genesis ... they were fair.** Genesis vi. 2: '... the sons of God saw the daughters of men that they were fair; and they took them wives of all which they chose'. Cf. *The Rainbow*, chap. x.

313:15   **mysterious life-flow** DHL is influenced throughout this passage (which he revised heavily in TSII) by J. M. Pryse's *The Apocalypse Unsealed* (New York, 1910), a book he knew by 25 August 1917 (*Letters*, iii. 150 and n. 3). Pryse argues that cosmic energy, 'kundalini', 'lies at the base of the spinal chord and is the starting point of the central current' (p. 128). See Delavenay, *L'Homme et la Genèse*, i. 493.

313:26   **It was ... in the beginning.** Cf. Genesis vi. 4 and i. 1: 'There were giants in the earth in those days; and also after that, when the sons of God came in unto the daughters of men, and they bare children to them, the same became mighty men which were of old, men of renown' and 'In the beginning God created the heaven and the earth.'

314:32   **the smitten rock** Exodus xvii. 6: '... thou shalt smite the rock, and there shall come water out of it, that the people may drink'.

317:31   **elvin** DHL's coinage, also at 426:24; he would have known 'elfin' from his reading of Spenser's *Faerie Queene* (see *Letters*, i. 73).

317:33   **a crew-yard** A bedded fold: a straw-covered yard, with sheds, in which cattle are wintered.

318:34   **the Greek ... the Egyptian,** DHL's differentiation depends on qualities he began to distinguish 1914–16: see notes above for details of the books he read about the two cultures. In 1913 he associated the Greek with 'the eternal stillness that lies under all movement' (*Letters*, ii. 137); over the next few years, he started to associate the Greek with a capacity for 'consciousness' (*Study of Thomas Hardy*, ed. Steele, p. 103), while he linked the Egyptians with the 'unknown forces of life' (*Letters*, ii. 218; see note on 98:37). In 1925, he made the distinction in a characteristic way: 'In the Egyptians, the spark between man and the living universe remains alight for ever in those early, silent, motionless statues of Pharaohs. They say, it is the statue of the soul of the man ... The Greeks began the cutting apart business' ('Him With His Tail in His Mouth', *Phoenix II* 434, text corrected from *Reflections on the Death of a Porcupine*, ed. Herbert).

320:5   **Sherwood Forest."** Surviving remnants include Clipstone Forest, e. of Mansfield, and Birklands, n. of Edwinstowe (where the 'Major Oak' is situated).

321:33   **a sword of Damocles** In classical myth, Damocles was forced by Dionysius, tyrant of Syracuse, to sit under a sword suspended by a hair, to demonstrate that kingship was not a happy state. DHL referred to the myth several times in 1916; see *Letters*, ii. 502 and iii. 47.

322:8   **Like a Red Indian undergoing torture,** DHL read the novels of James Fenimore Cooper as a child, and made many references to Red Indians and torture 1915–17: see 'The Reality of Peace', chap. 1 (*Phoenix* 671–2), 'The Crown', chap. v (*Phoenix II* 405) and 'The Return Journey', *Twilight*; he also read widely for *Studies in Classic American Literature* (1923) early in 1916.

322:34   **a bubble filled with darkness,** Cf. 'Elegy', a poem associated with the death of DHL's mother in 1910, ll. 7–9: 'Still, you left me the nights, / The great dark glittery window, / The bubble hemming this empty existence with lights' (*The Complete Poems of D. H. Lawrence*, ed. Vivian de S. Pinto and Warren Roberts, 1964, i. 193).

324:22   **rapt,** In TSII (p. 517), DHL altered 'so absorbed' to 'rapt' in such a way as to leave Seltzer's typist with the impression that 'so' had not been deleted. A1 printed it; this edition has deleted it.

327:13   **What have you ... seeing it through?** DHL originally wrote in MS 'What have *you* to do, going along with it?' (p. 57). TSI inserted 'got' after 'you' (p. 411), and DHL revised the last three words to 'through it all?'. TSII (p. 521) typed 'through it all.'; DHL revised to 'taking it upon yourself?' and finally to 'seeing it through?'.

327:16   **nuts** 'A source of pleasure or delight ... now *slang*' (*OED*).

327:29   **"Let the dead bury their dead** Matthew viii. 22, frequently quoted by DHL: see *Letters*, ii. 638, 'The Reality of Peace', chap. III (*Phoenix* 683) and Nehls, i. 440. Cf. too his letter to Catherine Carswell of 9 July 1916: 'Let the dead bury their dead. Let the past smoulder out. One shouldn't look back...' (*Letters*, ii. 627).

329:28   **hill-side. Across,** DHL wrote this in MS (p. 62), but the typist of TSI typed 'hill-side, across', and DHL revised to 'hill-side. Far across' (p. 416). His original reading has been restored.

332:15   **come down ... upon her.** The last word was typed as 'him' in TSII (p. 530), and DHL revised 'come' to 'she came'. His original reading has been restored.

332:24   **radio-active** First recorded 1898, the word originally meant 'undergoing spontaneous nuclear decay, involving the emission of radiation'. DHL used it as a type of spontaneous psychic out-going; cf. 'The Two Principles' (1919); 'Our plasmic psyche is radio-active, connecting with all things, and having first-knowledge of all things' (*The Symbolic Meaning*, ed. Arnold, p. 176).

333:17   **eau-de-cologne in the room.** The traditional scent of middle- and upper-class sick rooms; the spirit would either be sprinkled or vaporised, to hide other odours.

333:37   **His brain seemed to re-echo,** In TSII (p. 533) Gerald originally said 'Ah God—Ah God!' after 'horror.' and after 'limbs.'

334:34   **to the unseen witnesses of the air.** Cf. DHL to Barbara Low, 1 May 1916: 'one goes on writing, to the unseen witnesses' (*Letters*, ii. 602). MS reads 'to herself' (p. 73), revised in TSI to 'as if to the presence of all her children' (p. 425).

336:31   *en ménage,***"** I.e. a couple at home (French).

336:40   **the man below ... the dog-cart** A small horse-drawn cart with two transverse seats back to back: those at the rear originally forming a box for transporting sportsmen's dogs. Bircumshaw identified a 'Mr Rooth' as coachman to the Barber family; Benjamin Ruth (b. 1845) appears as 'Coachman/Domestic Servant' in the 1881 Census.

340:2 lasses as teaches, aside hisself [339:36] **... back your life ... Yi ... ca' it ... the lercality o'** 'Girls who teach, apart from himself ... of course ... Yes ... call it ... the locality of'.

340:11 tuffy ... nowt but 'Toffee ... only'.

343:32 the young Hermes. In Greek myth the messenger and herald of the gods, represented as a youth wearing winged sandals.

345:15 And his seared ... with new life. Expurgated in A1 by Seltzer: see Introduction.

350:5 in town ... a marriage licence, To judge by other references, Nottingham; 'town' is 'Nottingham' in TSI (p. [128]) ... if a marriage is not preceded by the calling of banns in church, or by the acquisition of a registrar's certificate, a common or special licence has to be obtained: both remain valid for three months.

351:26 like Lord Bacon, The essay 'Of Marriage and Single Life' by Francis Bacon, Baron Verulam, Viscount St. Albans (1561–1626) might well be said to be argued by 'a lawyer', as Bacon was. An article on Bacon and justice appeared in the *International Library of Famous Literature*, ed. Garnett, vi. 2629–38.

352:5 *Egoïsme à deux* 'Egoism for two'; Madame de Staël (1766–1817) may be responsible for the original remark, 'L'amour est un égoïsme à deux', but the attribution to her is uncertain (*Larousse des Citations*, Paris, p. 678).

352:26 "You've got ... to marriage." Middleton Murry noted in *Between Two Worlds* that this exchange was 'taken from conversations between Lawrence and me' in Cornwall, April–June 1916; 'That is more or less what Lawrence said to me' (p. 412).

352:39 Gerald moved [352:30] **... and women."** Although Secker asked for changes from DHL on this page (see note on 108:21), he does not appear to have told DHL that he was expurgating this passage, which was omitted from E1.

353:20 in absolute, mystic marriage. In January 1921, Secker asked DHL for 'verbal alterations' at this point (see note on 108:21, and *Letters*, iii. 660 n. 1); DHL offered 'in *a new, vital ⟨happy cooperation⟩ activity*' but Secker did not adopt it. (⟨ ⟩ indicates a deleted reading in the *Letters* quotation.)

355:21 It was bought. In August 1915, DHL recorded a similar occasion in a letter to Dollie Radford: 'I went to the Caledonian Market [off the Caledonian Road in North London] this morning ... I bought one chair. 10/-' (*Letters*, ii. 377).

356:36 Poiret, Paul Poiret (1879–1943), originally a clothes designer (see 'Education of the People', *Phoenix* 651), became a designer of decoration and furnishing.

356:39 Rodin, Michael Angelo ... raw rock unfinished E.g. 'Pan and Nymph' (1898) and 'Puvis de Chavannes' (1910), unfinished marble sculptures by Auguste Rodin (1840–1917), and the unfinished sculptures of slaves for the tomb of Pope Julius II by Michelangelo.

358:11 **contributed.** I.e. 'given over' or 'given up to'; this meaning is DHL's coinage.

358:28 **"What she warnt?'** 'What does she want?' As is clear from later remarks (e.g. 'Cawsts [costs] something to chynge [change] your mind"), DHL here reproduces a London accent (see note on 355:21).

359:24 **'arf a quid,** Ten shillings: see Note on pounds, shillings and pence.

360:2 **"'Slike when ... time married."** 'It's like when' ... cf. the saying 'you're a long time dead'.

360:6 **niver whip a dead donkey.** Cf. 'never flog a dead horse' (don't try to stir up things already dead), but n.b. 'to work for a dead horse' (to work without hope of future reward).

360:18 **Mike** Make.

361:13 **"Children of men ... inherit the earth.'"** Not the sons of God ... from the 'Sermon on the Mount' (Matthew v. 5): 'Blessed are the meek: for they shall inherit the earth'.

362:16 **the whole** DHL originally revised TSII (p. 577) to read 'a whole other'; a hand which is probably his then revised to 'the whole' in pencil (there are other pencil corrections by him on that page).

364:32 **Why when** Because of the error (p. 580) in TSII ('Why then' for 'Why when' in MS and TSI, pp. 139, 472), the correction ('Why,') in EP (p. 385) has been ignored, and DHL's original phrase reinstated.

369:2 **like a grain of mustard seed.** Cf. Matthew xvii. 20 and xiii. 31–2.

369:18 **his resurrection and his life.** Cf. John xi. 25.

369:35 **How** DHL adjusted the typist's mistake 'Now' to 'Nor' in TSII (p. 589); his original reading is restored.

371:38 *amant en titre.* 'Recognised lover' (French), i.e. with both job and title.

371:39 **somebody says ... wives or mistresses,** Unidentified; but cf. a remark DHL is reported to have made in 1910: 'You are not the wife and mother type – you must be *femme de plaisir*' (Helen Corke, *D. H. Lawrence: The Croydon Years*, Austin, 1965, p. 14). He also knew Bacon's 'Of Marriage and Single Life': 'Wives are young men's mistresses, companions for middle age, and old men's nurses'.

372:35 **if** DHL originally wrote 'What must human beings be like, if this is the outward shape of their daily life!' In TSII (p. 594) he altered 'human beings' to 'we', and attempted to make the end of the sentence read 'if we are the contents of *this*!'. He omitted, however, to delete 'this' following 'if'; Seltzer's typist deleted it.

372:37 **covers of "Vogue"** *Vogue* (1/- fortnightly) published drawings of women in fantastic and extravagant costumes on its (coloured) covers. The reference in MS (p. 159) is to *Fashions for All* (3d monthly), primarily a dress-making journal. The alteration to *Vogue* stresses the style – and cost – of the magazine.

374:8   **7 Pinchbeck Street** Not an identifiable street name.

374:11   **a Glücksritter.** 'An adventurer', 'a soldier of fortune' (German).

374:21   **"The little grey home in the west,"** 'Little Grey Home in the West' (1911), words by D. Eardley-Wilmot (b. 1883), music by Hermann Löhr (1871– 1943): 'It's a corner of heaven itself, / Though it's only a tumble-down nest, / But with love brooding there, / Why, no place can compare, / With my little grey home in the west.'

375:19   **"Il faut [375:14] ... des voisins,"** 'One must respect one's own follies,' ... 'one must respect daddy's follies.' ... 'And mummy's,' ... 'And those of the neighbours,' (French). TSI replaced DHL's colon before 'il faut' with a comma and omitted the single inverted commas, turning that after 'papa' into a question mark (p. 491). DHL responded to the cumulative effect of the punctuation change by deleting 'il faut avoir le respect' in TSII (p. 599). It has here been restored.

375:24   **Coulsons.** DHL's recreation of 'Cullens', the Eastwood drapers run by George Henry Cullen (1845–1915); see *The Lost Girl*, ed. Worthen, note on 2:20.

377:7   **too much soda** Sodium bicarbonate, to make the cake rise.

377:35   **insult at the liberty** DHL wrote 'insult / liberty' in MS (pp. 171–2); the typist of TSI (p. 495) added 'at the'.

378:5   *type* Commonly male, 'mate' or 'bloke' (French); 'typesse' is possible for the female. But Gudrun means 'girl'.

378:37   **forty kilometers from Innsbruck,** See note on 398:4.

380:2   **Gudrun in the Pompadour** The chapter draws on the events of 1 September 1916 (see note on 384:34), and occurs in MS in Notebook 5, written in October 1916; see Introduction.

380:30   **Carlyon** If drawn from a real-life original, now impossible to identify with absolute certainty. But MS (p. 178) reads 'Thomas', and a pun on 'John Thomas' (slang for the penis) is possible; the sexual prowess of Augustus John (see note on 94:19) was legendary. The distinctive broad-brimmed felt hat habitually worn by Augustus John – often called a 'Carlyle' (see *Ottoline* 215) – would confirm the play on words. It would be wrong, however, to ignore the possibility that 'the inimitable Evan Morgan [1893–1962], poet, painter, musician, aristocrat and millionaire' (Sybille Bedford, *Aldous Huxley*, 1973–4, i. 85), who frequented the Café Royal, contributed to the character.

381:5   **splashed and ... motley effect.** See note on 62:22.

382:26   **'Lord, *what* must I do to be saved'.''** Acts xvi. 30 ['Sirs, what ... saved?'].

382:29   **'Desire is holy—'''** Cf. DHL's letter to Catherine Carswell of 16 July 1916, which at several points compares to Birkin's letter here: e.g. 'God in me is my desire' (*Letters*, ii. 635).

383:10   **the sing-song ... the Scriptures,** Cf. 'the mock clerical voice ... frequently adopted by Philip [Heseltine] in satirical vein' (Nehls, ii. 95).

384:11   **"Surely goodness ... hath followed ... my life—"** Psalm xxiii. 6 ['...shall follow...'].

384:21   **reacting in** [384:15] **... utterly—"** Cf. 'The Crown', chaps. III and v (*Phoenix II* 388, 398). The readings of A1 (see Textual apparatus for 384:16 and 17) were taken from deletions in TSII (p. 614); TSII has a pencil '?' in the margin next to the censored passage and the deletions.

384:34   **And she turned ... with the letter,** On 1 September 1916, Katherine Mansfield was in the Café Royal with S. S. Koteliansky and the painter Mark Gertler. A letter from Gertler to Lady Ottoline of the following day describes how two 'coloured' men and 'a long Thin White Herring of a Woman' with 'a terrific High Bunch of Crimson Hair'

> began to talk "Intellectualy" – they were University Blacks – using "perfect" English very long words carefully chosen. They talked about Dostoevsky, Russia – the new Age, all in a very advanced manner. All this irritated us enough, But imagine our Hatred & Horror when the Red headed peice of dried Dung produced a Volume of Lawrence's poem's & commenced to discuss Lawrence with the other, in this perfect English & carefully picked, long words! We had been ragging them all the time, but now we knew something drastic must be done. We sat & thought. Suddenly, Katharine leant towards them & with a sweet smile said "*Will* you let me have that Book a moment?" "Certainly" they all beamed back – even more sweetly. Imagine then their horror & utter amazement, when Katharine without a word more, Rose from the table, Book and all, we two following most calmly – most calmly we walked out of the Café!!!
>
> We heard them hiss & make various sounds to try & stop us or have us stopped, but every body only stared & no one made the slightest attempt to stop us. So we got away with their book of Lawrence's Poems! What revenge! Outside we simply trembled with excitement. It was indeed a good end. (UT)

The book was DHL's recently published *Amores*. One of the 'University Blacks' was Hasan Shahid Suhrawardy (see note on 60:15): the other is unidentifiable, but was certainly not Philip Heseltine and probably not Dikran Kouyoumdjian (see notes on 60:30 and 70:27). The woman was possibly Minnie Lucy Channing (see note on 62:22). Gertler, Koteliansky and Katherine Mansfield first argued with Suhrawardy and companions, before Katherine Mansfield took the book and the three of them left together in a taxi, according to a letter from Aldous Huxley to Lady Ottoline dated 'Thursday' (UT), which reports the incident as having happened 'last night' (Huxley's informant was Suhrawardy). As DHL knew from Koteliansky about the incident by Monday 4 September 1916 (see *Letters*, ii. 649–50), Huxley's letter would apparently date it to Wednesday 30 August; but Huxley probably misunderstood or misreported his informant. Gertler's letter to Lady Ottoline, also reporting the incident as having happened the previous night, shows him correcting the date on his letter from '2 August' to '2 September': the correction is characteristic of a person forgetting, then remembering, a change in the month. It is also unlikely that Koteliansky would have waited until Saturday 2nd to write to DHL, if the incident had really happened on Wednesday. Katherine

Mansfield gave the copy of *Amores* to Dora Carrington (see note on 62:22) within a week of the incident: see Alpers, *The Life of Katherine Mansfield*, p. 218.

See too Delany, *D. H. Lawrence's Nightmare*, pp. 247–8.

385:3   **her coat was dark green,** In MS and TSI, 'an emerald velvet coat' (p. 189, p. 506). Presumably after a query from Catherine Carswell, DHL wrote to her on 2 December 1916: 'Gudrun's coat was supposed to be that pale and lovely bluish green which is a painter's emerald green – really a beautiful shade. Is that still common?' (*Letters*, iii. 44). He rewrote the description during revision of TSII (p. 615), perhaps after October 1917; the recreation of Dorothy Yorke (see *Letters*, iii. 173 n. 3) in *Bid Me To Live* by H.D., located in the period October–November 1917 (when DHL and Frieda were living in the same house as Dorothy Yorke and H.D.), is strikingly similar to DHL's revision: 'She was beetle with a hard shell, her green silk might have been plate metal, she seemed metallic . . .' (p. 96).

385:20   **Wagstaff's—Barton Street."** Neither of London's two Barton Streets contained a hotel, 1910–16, nor is there any record of a London hotel called Wagstaff's (an Eastwood surname). MS reads 'Wallenhof—Kingsway' (p. 190), a recreation of the Waldorf Hotel, Aldwych.

385:21   **put down the flag.** Lowered the small metal plate bearing the words 'FOR HIRE' fixed to the meter of a taxi, and thus started the meter.

385:35   *Dogs!*—**they** *are* **dogs!** Gerald had originally referred to 'dirty dogs', revised to 'jackasses' by DHL in TSII (p. 617).

387:2   **Continental** This chapter was first entitled 'Snow' on the contents page and the opening page of chap. XXIX in EP (p. 409); DHL revised the contents page when he decided to make a new chapter at 398:2 (see note below).

388:24   **of bliss in foreknowledge,** The typist of TSI (p. 511) at first omitted 'of bliss', and when retyping to include the words, typed 'foreknowledge' in TSIb with a slight extra space between 'e' and 'k'; the typist of TSII (p. 621) typed as two words, and DHL added the hyphen. His original reading (including punctuation) is restored.

389:22   **doorway and** Typed in TSI (p. 513) as 'doorway. And', which DHL revised to 'doorway, and'; his original reading is restored.

389:29   **ELSASS—LOTHRINGEN ... BASEL."** The German name for Alsace-Lorraine (n.e. province of France, under German occupation 1871–1918) ... the German name for Basle (English) and Bâle (French).

389:32   **"A Bâle—deuxième classe?—Voilà."** 'To Basle—second class?—Here you are' (French).

389:38   **"Nous avons ... demi-heure."** 'We still have—?' . . . 'Half an hour left' (French).

390:20   **Cossethay.** Ursula's childhood village in *The Rainbow*, its name drawn from the village of Cossall (4 miles s. of Eastwood) and the village of Cotmanhay nearby.

390:24 **the Marsh Farm ... Tilly,** The home of Ursula's grandparents in *The Rainbow* ... Tilly appears in the early chapters, and is seen with Ursula in chap. IX.

392:1 **porter** DHL revised TSII's 'waiter' (p. 626) to 'porter' in EP and E1 (p. 414), but left the three subsequent references unchanged (at 392:33, 392:35 and 392:38): this edition has adjusted them to 'porter'.

392:5 **"Yu-hu!"** Mistyped as "Zu-hu!" in TSI (p. 517) and altered by DHL to "Shu-hu!"; his original reading is restored.

393:22 **Fanny Rath's studio."** According to Frieda, a reference to 'just a bit of a party where Campbell was in Paris at Ann Estelle Rice' (Letter to S. S. Koteliansky, 6 February 1917; BL). Gordon Campbell (1885–1963), barrister and friend of the Lawrences since 1913; Anne Estelle Rice (1879–1959), American painter and friend of the Scottish painter F. D. Fergusson. The party was at Christmas 1912; Middleton Murry and Katherine Mansfield were also there (see Beatrice, Lady Glenavy, *'Today we will only Gossip'*, 1964, p. 58). In his copy of *Women in Love*, Murry marked this passage 'This is Katherine's experience'; he wrote 'This is *like* Katherine' against the sentence at 403:15–16. DHL also appears to be drawing on memories of the drunken party at the studio of Dorothy Brett (1883–1977) in Earl's Court Road, London, on 5 November 1915 (see *Letters*, ii. 428 and Nehls, i. 340–2).

393:26 **Billy Macfarlane.** See note above on Fergusson. DHL may also be influenced by William ('Willy') MacQueen (b. 1891?), whom he met in 1915 (*Letters*, ii. 319 and n. 2); Catherine Carswell's maiden name was MacFarlane.

393:31 **a Roumanian,** Reminiscent of Middleton Murry's stories of a circle of émigré Russian artists from the Baltic provinces he knew in Paris in 1910 (*Between Two Worlds*, pp. 146–8). During 1915–16, DHL was also in contact with the Roumanian diplomat Prince Antoine Bibesco (1878–1951); see *Letters*, ii. 453 and n. 3.

393:34 **La vie ... d'âmes impériales** 'Life, it's a matter of imperial souls' (French).

393:37 **Donald Gilchrist** A recreation of Gordon Campbell (see note on 393:22). In MS, 'Sholto Bannerman' (p. 209), a character in Catherine Carswell's novel *Open the Door!* (1920), which DHL read in manuscript in June 1914; he corresponded with her about it April–August 1916 (*Letters*, ii. 187–8, 595, 639–40, 643), and discussed it with her during her visit to Cornwall September–October 1916 (*The Savage Pilgrimage*, first edn., 1932, p. 62). On 2 December 1916 he wrote about her comments on TSIb, which she still retained: 'You might just put Thomas Bannerman instead of Sholto – or Balfour – any ordinary Scotch name' (*Letters*, iii. 44). She wrote 'Donald Gilchrist' into TSIb (p. 520); her husband's name was Donald.

394:8 **a whole-hogger."** One who goes 'all the way', often with a direct sexual meaning: cf. *The Prussian Officer*, ed. Worthen, note on 132:11.

394:11 **Chanticleer** Traditional name for a cock: the sexual vigour of Chaucer's 'Chaunticleer' in 'The Nun's Priest's Tale' makes the reference clear; see also note on 413:20.

394:16　**caught a Sultan** Version of the more common 'caught a Tartar': 'got hold of one who can neither be controlled nor got rid of': in this case, 'one who has a harem'.

394:31　**übermenschlich** 'Superhuman' (German); a sixteenth-century word now often associated with Freidrich Wilhelm Nietzsche (1844–1900), e.g. 'ich lehre euch den Übermenschen' – 'I teach you the Superman' (*Also sprach Zarathustra*, 1883–91).

396:10　**And leave her,"** Cf. MS (p. 216), where Birkin had remarked: 'I do think it is one's business to leave the dying England, and to discover in one's heart the world to come.' TSI (pp. 524–5) had revised the same sentence: 'I only want to get out now, and leave the dying England to her death, since it must be so.—I want the Hesperides, myself.'

396:16　**"*Tant pis pour moi,*"** 'So much the worse for me' (French).

396:25　**radium ... this fatal, living metal.** Discovered 1898; a rare, metallic, radioactive element, 'originally a scientific curiosity' (*OED*). See also note on 332:24.

398:2　**Chapter XXX / Snow** DHL inserted this chapter division and title in the text (p. 419) and on the contents page of EP. E1 did not print it; it has been assumed that it appeared on the proofs returned to Secker, but that the latter preferred not to make the extensive changes to layout and pagination which its adoption in E1 would have entailed. Subsequent chapter numbers in this edition consequently vary from A1 and E1.

398:4　**Hohenhausen, at ... valley railway.** DHL's recreation of Mayrhofen, in the Austrian Tyrol, where he and Frieda stayed in August 1912; about 36 kilometres from Innsbruck, 'a village with 1300 inhab[itants]., the terminus of the Zillertal railway' (Baedeker, *Eastern Alps*, Leipzig, 1911, p. 237).

398:19　**changeless** The MS (p. 218) is damaged, but appears to read 'changele': it is unlikely to read 'changed'.

399:34　**a gulley,** Reminiscent of the Klamm gorge, just south of Mayrhofen, as DHL described it in 'The Crucifix Among the Mountains', *Twilight*.

400:8　**a lonely building** DHL's recreation of the Dominicus-Hütte, where he, Frieda, David Garnett and Harold Hobson spent the night on their journey to Italy in August 1912; a photograph of the Dominicus-Hütte (now rebuilt) appears on the postcard to Ada Lawrence, *Letters*, i. 443. See also *Mr Noon*, ed. Vasey, pp. 262–5.

400:26　**overbolster,** Not a long pillow, but a thick quilt for the bed.

402:34　**Kuchen?"** 'Cake' (German).

403:19　**Kaffee mit Kranzkuchen?"** 'Coffee with cake', the latter in the form of a ring (German).

403:24　**prachtvoll ... wunderbar ... wunderschön ... unbeschreiblich** 'Splendid ... wonderful ... very beautiful ... indescribable' (German).

403:29　**a Gasthaus.** 'An inn' (German).

403:35 **the great green stove,** A wood-burning stove to heat the room, very commonly covered with green tiles; the Lawrences had 'a warm old stove of green tiles' in Irschenhausen in 1913 (*Letters*, i. 541).

404:4 **coign of vantage** *Macbeth* I. vi. 7.

404:8 **the Reunionsaal.** Austrian word later translated by DHL as 'play-room' (404:33); one of the inn's public rooms, used as a ballroom, for meetings and games; a 'recreation room'.

404:30 **the Wirt's** 'The landlord's' (German).

404:36 **Then the host** DHL failed to delete the comma after 'Then' in MS (p. 237) when he revised the original reading 'Then Franz, the waiter,'; as throughout this section, he removed 'Franz' and 'waiter', adding 'host' over the last word, but neglected to remove either comma.

404:38 **"Herr Professor, darf ich Sie vorstellen—"** "Professor, may I introduce you—" (German). The typist of TSI reproduced 'Sie' as 'zu', which DHL deleted (p. 538); his original reading has been restored.

405:1 **"Nehmen die ... unserer Unterhaltung?"** DHL meant to write 'Will the ladies and gentlemen take part in our entertainment?' (Gerald translates 'Unterhaltung' as such a few lines later), but the word he used means 'conversation'; he needed 'Vergnügungen' (German).

405:12 **loden** Tightly woven, usually green, woollen material, traditionally used for hiking and mountaineering clothes in Germany and Austria.

405:16 **small,** Frieda substituted 'thin' in TSIb (p. 539) only.

405:21 **Herr Loerke** Reminiscent of 'Loki' (in Wagner's *Ring*, Loge), disruptive Scandinavian god of jokes and destruction, responsible for the death of the young god Balder, and associated with death by fire: William Morris described him as 'the World's Begrudger, who maketh all labour vain' (*Sigurd the Volsung*, 1877, 2nd edn, p. 98.) The name has been linked with DHL's friend Mark Gertler, but appears in Roberts E441a (p. 294), dating from 1913, before DHL knew Gertler. The name Loerke is, anyway, well-known in Germany: Oskar Loerke (1884–1941) was a young German poet of whom DHL might well have heard.

406:37 **"Ja, das war [406:31] ... Wissen Sie———"** 'Yes, that was remarkable, that was great—' 'Really great!' ... 'Oh what a pity, what a pity,' ... ...'Yes, that's really a shame, that's a shame, gracious lady. You see———" (German). DHL's 'merkwürdig' (MS, p. 242, umlaut added editorially) is old-fashioned but (for a Professor before the war) perfectly acceptable. Frieda corrected the phrase to 'Das war ausgezeichnet' in TSIb (p. 541), presumably assuming that 'excellent' was the required meaning. 'Gnädige Frau' is formal, polite, the proper address to a married (or superior) lady; DHL's own equivalent is 'gracious lady' in *Mr Noon*, ed. Vasey, p. 240. 'Wissen Sie' is literally 'You know', but with the sense 'You see' or 'Listen'.

407:3 **"Annie Lowrie,"** 'Annie Laurie', Scottish poem by William Douglas (1672–1748), altered and set to music by Lady John Douglas Scott (1810–1900).

407:26 **"Wie schön ... aber wirklich!"** 'How beautiful, how touching! Ah, Scottish songs, they have such feeling! But the gracious lady has a *wonderful* voice; the gracious lady really is an artist, really!' (German).

408:3 **Orion sloping up.** Brilliant constellation, low in the sky (hence 'sloping up'), with many bright stars; of special significance to DHL – see 'Hymn to Priapus', *The Collected Poems*, ed. Pinto and Roberts, i. 198, and *The Rainbow*, chap. v: 'Orion, stately and magnificent, was sloping along'. There are further references in *The White Peacock*, pt. III, chap. III, ii, 'A Modern Lover' and 'The Old Adam'.

409:7 **glouring** Derbyshire spelling of 'glowering': gleaming, shining clear and bright.

409:25 **Ilkeston,** Town 1 mile w. of Cossall, and 3½ miles s.w. of Eastwood.

409:38 **no father, no mother,** Cf. Ursula in *The Rainbow*, chap. XVI: 'I have no father nor mother nor lover...'

410:26 **the Schuhplatteln,** The dance is as DHL describes it, but (as the name suggests) it also involves rhythmic shoe stamping.

410:32 **zest, when ... came. Birkin** The typist of TSI typed this as 'zest. When ... came Birkin' (p. 549), and DHL responded to the error by adding 'even' before 'Birkin' in TSII (p. 660); his original reading is restored.

411:2 **"Prosit—Prosit!"** 'Your health—your health!' (German).

411:14 **Leitner,** The name of DHL's and Frieda's landlady at Icking in 1912; see *"Not I, But the Wind..."*, p. 54. In MS he is Loerke's 'associate' (p. 258); in TSI, 'travelling companion' is deleted for 'love-companion' (p. 551), the reading of 411:36. Cf. note on 422:25.

413:20 **"He should ... his nature."** Cf. DHL's remarks to Lady Ottoline about Heseltine, February 1916: 'I don't see why there should be monogamy for people who can't have full satisfaction in one person, because they themselves are too split, because they act in themselves separately. Monogamy is for those who are whole and clear, all in one stroke' (*Letters*, ii. 539).

413:22 **Mene! Mene! upon the wall.** King Belshazzar of Babylon saw a hand writing on the wall during a feast ('MENE, MENE, TEKEL, UPHARSIN', Daniel v. 25): the words foretold his downfall (17–31).

413:39 **"Ein schönes Frauenzimmer ... Ja!"** 'A beautiful lady' ... 'Yes!' (German: in 1916 the word 'Frauenzimmer' did not have the derogatory associations it has since acquired.)

414:37 **nonchalant,** DHL wrote 'nonchantly' in MS (p. 266), and then revised to 'nonchalant'; TSI's typist combined the revision with the original (p. 555).

416:2 **strap. She ... stooping down, servile.** TSI's typist reproduced as 'strap, servile.' (p. 557); DHL revised 'servile' to 'inattentive' in TSII (p. 669). With the omission restored, the TSII revision has had to be discarded.

416:5 **a cormorant plucking her breast—"** In an ancient fable, the pelican was supposed to pluck its breast and feed its young with the blood, as a model of self-sacrifice; the cormorant is a type of devouring, greedy rapacity.

418:1 **the woman behind him ... Bismarck's letters,** Either *Prince Bismarck's Letters to his Wife, his Sister, and others* (1878), or *The Love-Letters of Prince Bismarck*, 2 vols. (1901) or (most likely) *Bismarck's Letters to his Wife from the seat of war, 1870–71* (1915).

419:6 **Parnell and Katherine O'Shea.** Charles Stewart Parnell (1846–91), Irish politician and leader of the Nationalist movement, had had an adulterous relationship with the woman he later married, Katharine O'Shea, and was forced to resign from Parliament. DHL read her book *Charles Stewart Parnell: his love story and political life* (1914) early in May 1916: 'It is *very* poignant, now, when the political life, and Ireland, are so torn' (*Letters*, ii. 604).

419:7 **the nationalisation of Ireland** *OED* (2): 'the act of forming into a nation'. A topical subject after the Nationalists' abortive rising (for separate nationality) in Dublin against the English administration, 26 April–2 May 1916; see *Letters*, ii. 603–4, 611–12, and note on 85:16.

419:38 **"Mach mir ... ich nass—"** 'Let me in, let me in, you proud woman, / Make me a fire of wood, / I am wet from the rain, / I am wet from the rain—' (German). A verse of a common European folk-song, usually called 'Die Müllerin' ('The Miller's Wife'), first recorded before 1430. The song recounts the miller's wife's rebellion. The miller returns to the mill and demands admittance (verse quoted): his wife refuses. In MS (p. 280) the verse originally quoted showed the miller's wife flaunting her independence: 'Ich hab' ⟨heut⟩ die Nacht gemahlen / Mit zwei so wunderschönen Knaben / Vom Abend bis zum Tag / Dass ich nicht aufsteh'n mag.': 'I've spent ⟨last⟩ the night on the grind / With two such beautiful boys / From evening till morning / That I don't want to get up.' In revision of MS, DHL quoted instead the miller's response: 'Die Mühl will ich verkaufen / Mein Geld will ich versaufen / Schaffhausen an dem Rhein / Schaffhausen an dem Rhein': 'I'll sell the mill, / I'll drink up the money / Schauffhausen on the Rhine'. The reference to Schaffhausen (in Switzerland, visited by DHL 19 September 1913) is common in one derivation of the song. In TSI (p. 564) DHL reverted to the original quotation; he adopted the final reading in TSII (p. 676). The version of the song he quotes is close to that printed in Georg Heydemarck, *Soldatenlieder* (Berlin, post 1916), IV, 966; he probably learned it from Frieda, who had a large repertoire of soldiers' songs dating from her youth in the garrison town of Metz.

421:19 **could direct the sledge** The typist of TSII (p. 679) altered 'could' to 'would'; it is just possible that this provoked DHL to delete 'as if it were a pencil', which originally followed 'sledge'.

422:25 **together in the last degree of intimacy,** EP and E1 (p. 445) read 'together, sharing the same bedroom': see note on 108:21.

422:32 **a Westphalian cap ... over his ears,** A Westphalian cap, strictly part of peasant costume, is a close fitting dark cap, often embroidered, worn only by women.

423:14 **a great frieze for a factory in Cologne,** DHL told Mark Gertler on 5 December 1916 that 'In my novel there is a man – not you, I reassure you – who does a great granite frieze for the top of a factory, and the frieze is a fair, of which your whirligig, for example, is part. – (We knew a man, a german, who did these big reliefs for great, fine factories in Cologne)' (*Letters*, iii. 46). DHL refers to Gertler's painting 'The Merry-Go-Round' (1916): see *Letters*, ii. 660–1. He had seen a photograph of it on 9 October, and in mid-November altered the description of the frieze in TSI. MS (p. 289) had read: 'It was a village attacked by wolves, great naked men, ten feet high, fighting with ⟨h⟩ ⌐a⌐ horde of wolves, and women running, falling, and a rush of wolves sweeping all ⟨round the building like⟩ ⌐like a storm driving in⌐ a shaggy whirl ⟨of leaves⟩ across the whole frieze.' (⌐ ⌐ indicates an addition.) In MS (p. 288) he had first written 'Dresden' but immediately substituted 'Cologne'. The real-life German remains unidentified, but see note on 424:6. 'Roundabouts' (423:30) are merry-go-rounds.

423:20 **"Aus was ... Granit,"** 'What in?' ... 'Granite' (German).

423:24 **"Alto rilievo."** 'High relief' (Italian).

424:3 **"Sculpture and architecture ... an architectural conception.** Cf. DHL to Gertler, 5 December 1916: 'Sculpture, it seems to me, is truly a part of architecture ... Painting is so much subtler than sculpture, that I am sure it is a finer medium. But one wants the unsubtle, the obvious, like sculpture, as well as the subtle' (*Letters*, iii. 46).

424:6 **our art ... ecco!"** DHL refers to the movement in Germany during the decade before the First World War to link art and industry; cf. the history of the Deutscher Werkbund, and the work of men like Richard Riemerschmid (1868–1957) ... 'You see!' (Italian).

424:18 **machinery ... maddeningly beautiful.** Reminiscent of Futurist ideas: see note on 74:24.

424:37 **He enjoys ... own body."** One of the tenets of Futurism (see note on 74:24); but Sigmund Freud (1856–1939) had described in 'Infantile Sexuality' 'those pleasurable sensations, caused by forms of mechanical agitation of the body' (*Essays on the Theory of Sexuality*, 1905).

425:9 **"Travaillé—lavorato ... avez fait?"** 'Worked—worked?' ... 'And what work—what work? What work is it you've done?' (French and Italian).

425:15 **my daily bread."** Cf. Matthew vi. 11 ['our daily ...'].

425:29 **Austria, Polish Austria.** Gertler's family returned to their home village of Przemysl (in Galicia: 1814–97, part of Poland within the Austrian Empire) for a time in his childhood. His own memoir recalls the soldiers, his father's fights and the family's poverty (*Mark Gertler: Selected Letters*, ed. Carrington, pp. 15–19).

426:4 **"Dunque—"** 'So—' (French).

426:16 **adesso—maintenant** 'Now—now' (Italian and French).

426:25 **"Wie alt?"** 'How old?' (German).

426:31 **"Und Ihr Herr Gemahl ... ist er?"** 'And your husband, how old is he?' (German). 'Herr Gemahl', old-fashioned and formal, means 'consort'.

427:2 **a brown seal ... talk to her.** DHL inserted the reference to the seal in TSII (p. 688); by the end of September 1917 (but not, probably, much earlier), Cecil Gray had introduced him to the 'Seal Woman's Song' and other Hebridean folk songs, which, though 'marvellous' were also 'songs of the damned: that is, songs of those who inhabit an underworld which is forever an underworld, never to be made open and whole' (*Letters*, iii. 164, 180): see 427:23. The seal is also the central symbol of Loki (see note on 405:21), apparently the only mythological deity to assume that form.

428:18   **the river of corruption,** Cf. 'The Reality of Peace', chap. ii, *passim*: e.g. 'we, ourselves, are the living stream of seething corruption' (*Phoenix* 676).

428:21   **a Jew—or part Jewish."** Cf. DHL's response to Gertler's 'The Merry-Go-Round', 9 October 1916: 'It would take a Jew to paint this picture. It would need your national history to get you here, without disintegrating you first. You are of an older race than I, and in these ultimate processes, you are beyond me, older than I am … it will be left for the Jews to utter the final and great death-cry of this epoch: the Christians are not reduced sufficiently' (*Letters*, ii. 660–1).

430:14   **a certain *form* [430:11] … work of art."** Cf. *Art* (1914) by Clive Bell (1881–1964): 'Art transports us from the world of man's activities to a world of aesthetic exaltation … In this world the emotions of life find no place' (pp. 25, 27). Bell was also responsible for the popularisation in England of the notion of art as 'Significant Form'.

430:15   *de haut en bas,* 'Condescendingly' (French).

431:7   **My art stands in another world,** Cf. Bell on great art: 'its kingdom is not of this world' (*Art*, p. 37).

431:11   **"Ja—so ist es, so ist es."** 'Yes—so it is, so it is' (German).

431:22   **rushing in … not gladly.** 'An Essay on Criticism' (1711), l. 625, by Alexander Pope: 'For fools rush in where angels fear to tread' … cf. ii Corinthians xi. 19: 'For ye suffer fools gladly.'

432:2   **"Nein, sie war … eine kleine Malschülerin."** 'No, she wasn't a model. She was a little art-student' (German).

432:21   **Lady Godiva … wife of some Earl or other,** Lady Godiva (11th century) is supposed to have been the wife of Earl Leofric.

432:23   **"A la Maud Allan,"** Like Maud Allan (1883–1956), Canadian dancer and teacher; her 'Dance of Salomé' (1908) was celebrated.

432:37   **"The little** MS read 'Of this little' (p. 308), following 'fond of' three lines earlier. TSI typed as 'Of the little' (p. 587); in TSII (p. 698), DHL altered the construction three lines earlier to '*understood*', and also revised to 'The little'.

433:13   **"Ja, sie war hübsch.** 'Yes, she was pretty' (German).

434:2   **The Venus of Milo** Broad-hipped classical Greek statue in the Louvre; cf. DHL's comment of January 1914 (*Letters*, ii. 137).

434:10   **and stupid form."** DHL inadvertently left MS reading (after revision) 'and and form' (p. 311); TSI typed 'and—and form' (p. 590); DHL revised TSII to 'and—and stupid form' (p. 701). He intended neither repetition nor dash; this edition has removed both.

435:6　**Verona ... Romeo and Juliet ... the amphitheatre** Verona (city in n. Italy) is the home of Romeo and Juliet in Shakespeare's play; 7 Via Cappello has a memorial tablet linking it with the Capulet family ... DHL visited the Roman amphitheatre ('really a wonderful arena') in April 1913 (*Letters*, i. 540; see also ibid., ii. 120).

436:23　**agonistes.** In the grip of inner conflict: an 'agon' is a conflict between two protagonists (Greek). MS (p. 318) and TSI (p. 594) read 'like a young victor.'

437:7　**"that 'you ... to return—'** DHL adjusted the punctuation of this sentence at least once and perhaps twice in MS (p. 320); the comma remaining after 'return' in MS (see Textual apparatus) was probably meant to be superseded by the dash which is the reading adopted.

438:41　**Blessed Isles."** The Hesperides, where the daughters of Hesperus keep watch with a dragon over the garden of golden apples; a favourite reference of DHL's. See *Letters*, ii. 434, 641, 645 and 651.

439:26　**I don't look ... what is not,"** Cf. ll. 86–7 of 'The Skylark' (1820), by Shelley; 'We look before and after / And pine for what is not'.

442:25　**she repeated,** In MS (p. 332) and TSI (p. 604), Gudrun repeated that Gerald 'can't love', not that 'it was never love' (TSII, p. 714).

444:30　**destruction, ultimate.** In MS (p. 338), DHL wrote 'destructive tension'. TSI (p. 608) typed as 'destruction, tension'; DHL's revision to the final reading in TSII (p. 718), however, prevents any return to MS.

445:2　**'thou shalt', 'thou shalt not'.** Opening words of eight of the ten Commandments (Exodus xx. 1–17).

446:10　**like a seed ... in being,** Cf. Ursula's vision of 'the new germination' in *The Rainbow*, chap. XVI, and DHL to E. M. Forster, 30 May 1916: 'We have to come out like seeds from a shell, pushing the future out of our uncreated selves, into existence' (*Letters*, ii. 612).

448:10　**Mestrovic ... Aztec art, Mexican and Central American.** Ivan Městrović; Yugoslavian sculptor (1883–1962): DHL may have seen an exhibition of his work in London, summer 1915; in 1916 he owned a photograph of a piece of his sculpture (*Letters*, ii. 578 and n. 2; see too *Letters*, iii. 137 and 261)... DHL could have seen examples of Aztec, Mexican and Central American (perhaps Mayan) art in the British museum.

448:19　**Their whole ... the Mexicans.** TSI (p. 614), after revision, read: 'They might have been sharers in some religious mystery, some black and symbolic knowledge belonging to ⟨Baal⟩ ⌜Bel⌝, or an obscene African deity, or the Syria Dea.' See note on 246:30.

448:30　***peu de rapport,*** 'Little relationship' (French), but DHL almost certainly meant to give the French for what Gudrun goes on to say, 'it doesn't signify much': '*peu d'importance*' would convey that.

449:1　**Mary Stuart ... Eleonora Duse ... her lovers** Mary Stuart (Mary Queen of Scots, 1542–87) was married three times: to Francis II of France (1558–60), her cousin Lord Darnley (1565–67) and the Earl of Bothwell

(1567–71) – commonly regarded as his predecessor's murderer . . . Eleonora Duse (1858–1924), famous Italian actress: DHL noted on 16 April 1916 that 'I often think of the Duse with her lovers, how they were keen and devouring excitements to her, but only destructive incidents, really, even D'Annunzio' (*Letters*, ii. 595 and n. 3). In December 1916, Donald Carswell marked the reference in TSIb (p. 615) as 'a grave libel', but DHL did not alter it. However, Martin Secker wrote to DHL in January 1921 that the reference 'is, I think, actionable' (*Letters*, iii. 660 n. 1: see note on 108:21). DHL altered it to 'the great Rachel' for the English edition (Elisa Rachel, 1821–58, Alsatian Jewess and tragic actress, was famous for her performances as Phêdre).

449:7 Italy and Tripoli. Tripoli, in n. Africa, occupied by Italy 1911–12, had been ceded to the King of Italy in October 1912 by the treaty of Ouchy. DHL had seen and heard the rejoicings of returning soldiers (with their friends and families) in Italy, 1912–13; see *Letters*, i. 474, 478, 515–16.

449:21 "Sehen Sie . . . gnädige Frau," 'You see, Gracious lady—' . . . 'Please don't keep saying gracious lady' (German).

449:22 Medusa. In Greek myth, a mortal woman transformed into one of the three Gorgons (with brazen claws and live snakes for their hair); those who looked directly at her were turned to stone.

449:32 "Sagen Sie nur nicht das," 'Don't say that, at any rate' (German).

449:36 "Soll ich Fräulein sagen?" 'Shall I say Miss?' (German).

451:16 the central serpent . . . at the core of life. See note on 313:15; in Pryse's *Apocalypse Unsealed*, the 'kundalini' 'is poetically said to lie coiled-up like a slumbering serpent' (p. 16).

452:4 the Alexander seeking new worlds. An anonymous epitaph on the conqueror Alexander the Great runs 'A tomb now suffices him for whom the whole world was not sufficient'.

452:28 attachment to . . . the whole. An important concept for DHL, 1915–17; cf. an annotation on Russell's manuscript: 'We want to create a new *Whole*: that is our fundamental desire' (*Letters to Bertrand Russell*, ed. Moore, p. 81). The revision was written into TSI (p. 621): MS reads 'desire for good, for right' (p. 361).

452:29 borné, 'Limited' (French).

453:5 the period of Goethe . . . Shelley . . . Mozart. 1749–1832 . . . 1792–1822 . . . 1756–91.

453:27 Goethe at Weimar . . . his own poetry. Goethe first lived in Weimar in 1775 . . . Friedrich von Schiller (1759–1805) lived in great poverty throughout the 1780s: his love for Charlotte von Kalb was famous, though he married Charlotte von Lengefeld in 1790 . . . Jean-Jacques Rousseau wrote in his *Confessions*: 'My passions are extremely violent . . . everything alarms and terrifies me: the very buzzing of a fly will make me shudder' (*International Library of Famous Literature*, ed. Garnett, ix. 4052) . . . Voltaire lived at Ferney (near Geneva) for the last 18 years of his life; on several occasions he visited Friedrich II – 'the Great' – (1712–86),

King of Prussia, and they discussed the King's poetry. MS reads 'Goethe ... faithful love, or to see again Hazlitt receiving Coleridge, or Shelley's first glance at Mary Godwin' (p. 363).

453:30 **Flaxman ... Böcklin.** John Flaxman (1755–1826), sculptor and draughtsman ... William Blake (1757–1827), poet and visionary artist ... Henry Fuseli (1741–1825), Swiss painter who lived in England ... Anselm Feuerbach (1829–80), German painter ... Arnold Böcklin (1827–1901), Swiss painter.

453:31 **in petto,** 'In their minds' (Italian).

455:7 **a power** The reading of TSII (p. 735); 'force' in A2 was an unauthorised alteration probably provoked by the repetition of 'power' immediately before.

455:13 **remember. I** TSI typed the words very close together (p. 626), and TSII typed with no punctuation (p. 735); DHL's original punctuation has been restored.

455:21 **stupid, that's** DHL accidentally crossed out the comma while revising MS (p. 369).

455:27 **Blake's representation ... of a flea.** Either the drawing (1819) 'The Head of the Ghost of a Flea', or his painting (post 1819) 'The Ghost of a Flea' (both now in the Tate Gallery).

456:31 *laisser-aller* 'Free and easy quality' (French).

457:27 **eine seltsame Frau.** DHL almost certainly wishes to translate what he has just written, 'a remarkable woman', but his German actually means 'a strange woman'.

457:39 **common standards.** Cf. 'Democracy': 'Society means people living together. People *must* live together. And to live together, they must have some Standard, some *Material* Standard. This is where the Average comes in' (*Phoenix* 701); also 32:28–32 above.

458:22 **new turning to Jesus,** A reference to the revival of religious writing and belief in France before the First World War; e.g. the work of Paul Claudel (1868–1955), André Gide (1869–1951), Romain Rolland (1866–1944), and the famous conversion to Catholicism in 1908 of the writer Charles Péguy (1873–1914).

458:33 **L'amour, l'amore, die Liebe** 'Love' (French, Italian, German).

458:38 **he repeated.** In MS (p. 378) Gudrun had remarked in the previous speech: "Love is an accidental.", and Loerke had echoed "An accidental,". DHL deleted her remark, and revised Loerke's comment to "A bore" in TSI (p. 632), but did not alter 'repeated'.

459:17 **chétif,** 'Puny' (French).

459:20 **the *me* ... the *thee*** I.e. 'das *Ich* ... das *Du*': 'Du' is the familiar form in German.

459:28 **this amour, this *baiser* ... soit ou soit pas,** 'This love, this *kiss* ... whether it is or whether it isn't' (French). The verb 'baiser' means 'to fuck', but 'baiser' here must be a noun, and the noun only ever means 'kiss'.

460:10 **the Marienhütte ... on the crest of the pass,** On the crest of the Pfitscher Joch there was, in 1911–13, the Pfitscher-Joch-Haus ('Rainer's Inn', with 36 beds). DHL's name, 'Mary's Hut', appears to be invented.

460:14 **the old Imperial road, below the pass.** 'The imperial road to Italy goes from Munich across the Tyrol, through Innsbruck and Bozen to Verona, over the mountains' ('The Crucifix Across the Mountains', *Twilight*); it goes over the Brenner pass, just to the w. of the Pfitscher Joch.

463:20 **boring as the phallus,** The reading of TSII and A1. E1 bowdlerised to 'boring'; A2 was influenced by E1 and A1, and printed the unauthorised 'boring as his sort of love'.

463:29 **grind on at the old mills** Cf. l. 1 of 'Retribution', trans. by Henry Wadsworth Longfellow (1807–82) of *Sinngedichte* (1653), III. ii. 24, by F. von Logau (1604–55): 'Though the mills of God grind slowly, yet they grind exceeding small'. Gudrun quotes more directly from the poem at 464:1.

465:12 **illusions,** The typist of TSII typed 'no illusions' for MS and TSI's 'illusions' (p. 752), and DHL altered 'no' to 'her'; his original reading is restored.

465:23 **Dignity and Impudence,** Painting (by 1839) of two dogs in a kennel, by Sir Edwin Landseer (1803–73).

466:10 **An infant crying in the night,** Tennyson, *In Memoriam* (pub. 1850), LIV, ll. 17–20: '...what am I? / An infant crying in the night: / An infant crying for the light: / And with no language but a cry.' DHL quoted the line many times in the period: see *Letters*, ii. 266, 'Italians in Exile', *Twilight*, and 'The Crown', chap. 1.

466:11 **Yes,** Typed as 'Zeu' in TSI (p. 645) and revised by DHL to 'Ooh' in TSIb; his original reading is restored.

466:12 **like** In TSIb only (p. 645) an unidentified person revised 'like' to 'as'.

466:14 **Hetty Sorrell ... Arthur Donnithorne's infant** In *Adam Bede* (1859), by George Eliot, Arthur Donnithorne abandons Hetty Sorrell, and she is responsible for the death of their illegitimate child. DHL asked to be sent a copy of the novel in November 1913 'to read again' (*Letters*, ii. 101).

466:26 **the donkey-engine,** A small steam-engine, for subsidiary or auxiliary operations at a colliery.

466:33 **a chronometer-watch.** A chronometer watch was originally distinguished from an ordinary watch by the quality of its escapement and its compensation balance.

468:3 **to Munich,** DHL chooses what Martin Green refers to as 'a symbolic city' for Gudrun's independence; its suburb of Schwabing, in particular, was a centre of artists, revolutionaries and independent women; see *The von Richthofen Sisters* (1974), pp. 88–100.

469:7 **Kekse ... Schnapps.** Biscuits ... clear spirits (the correct German spelling is 'Schnaps').

469:9 **What a comble de joie** 'What absolute bliss' (French).

469:22 **extravaganzas,** This was mistyped in TSI as 'extravagences' (p. 650) which was set as 'extravagencies' in EP (p. 496); DHL's original reading is restored.

469:29 **Heidelbeerwasser,** Bilberry brandy; the 'wasser' is a common German suffix for perfectly clear fruit Schnaps. Frieda remembered DHL drinking 'heidelbeerschnapps' in 1912 (*"Not I, But the Wind..."*, p. 54).

469:38 **where to?** Altered to 'Whither?', possibly by Frieda, in TSIb (p. 651) only.

470:8 **the wicket,** The small opening at the ticket office where tickets are bought.

470:24 **Zephyrus,** The god of the west wind in Greek myth.

470:32 *Maria!* 'Mary', i.e. Holy Mary (German or Italian).

471:11 **"wohl—."** Untranslatable without the rest of the sentence: it could mean 'I suppose', 'perhaps', 'well', etc.

471:17 **"C'est le sport, sans doute."** 'It's sport, doubtless' (French), i.e. 'I suppose you think that's fun.'

471:22 **"Vive le héros, vive—"** 'Long live the hero, long live—' (French).

471:27 **stroke, over** The reading of MS (p. 417); TSI omitted the comma (p. 654); DHL revised to 'stroke on to' in TSII (p. 763). The MS reading is restored on the grounds that DHL's revision was provoked by TSI's error.

472:10 **"Monsieur ... aurez fini—"** 'Sir!' ... 'When you've quite finished—' (French).

472:20 **I didn't want it,** See note on 479:39.

473:30 **a little Christ under a little sloping hood,** Cf. 'Christs in the Tirol': 'As one goes higher the crucifixes get smaller and smaller. The wind blows the snow under the tiny shed of a tiny Christ...' (*Phoenix* 85), and cf. *Mr Noon*, ed. Vasey, p. 265.

475:10 **"Il est mort?"** 'He is dead?' (French).

476:40 **the Rudelbahn,** The toboggan-run (Tyrol dialect). 'Rodelbahn' would be a more common spelling, and DHL spells it thus earlier in MS (p. 284).

478:10 **a shallow pot** See *Mr Noon*, ed. Vasey, pp. 265–6, and cf. DHL's description of the plateau near the summit of the Gotthard Pass (which he saw in September 1913): 'this shallow pot among the peaks' ('The Return Journey', *Twilight*).

478:35 **"God cannot ... French religious teacher.** Cf. ll. 7–8 and n., 'Masses and classes', *The Complete Poems*, ed. Pinto and Roberts, ii. 641, 1019: 'An old Frenchman uttered the truism: / God cannot do without me!' They refer to *The*

Essence of Christianity (1854), by Ludwig Feuerbach, tr. M. Evans [George Eliot], p. 225: 'God is nothing without man'; Feuerbach's footnote refers to his *Pierre Bayle* (1838). Bayle, the French sceptic and encyclopaedist (1647–1706), may well be the 'old Frenchman' of the poem and the 'religious teacher' of the novel. In the 1915 version of 'The Crown', DHL noted: '"God cannot move without me," some one said. That is foolish...' (Roberts E80a); and cf. the original reading of TSI (p. 150); 'Who was the impudent dirty skunk of a Frenchman who said that God couldn't get on without *him*? God would get on a great deal better without him, and without all the lot of Frenchmen.'

479:22 **"Imperial Caesar ... wind away."** *Hamlet* v. i. 206–7 ['...Might stop...'].

479:39 **the Kaiser's: "Ich habe es nicht gewollt."** 'I didn't want it.' On 31 July 1915 (the first anniversary of the war's outbreak) the Kaiser issued a manifesto from Main Headquarters in Berlin, which began:
> Ein Jahr ist verflossen, seitdem ich das Deutsche Volk zu den Waffen rufen musste. Eine unerhört blutige Zeit kam über Europa und die Welt. Vor Gott und der Geschichte ist mein Gewissen rein. Ich habe den Krieg nicht gewollt...

The Times's report on 2 August 1915 translated as follows:
> One year has elapsed since I was obliged to call to arms the German people. An unprecedented time of bloodshed has befallen Europe and the world. Before God and history my conscience is clear. I did not will the war... (p. 5)

DHL knew the remark, in a German version, by October 1916; it appears (without attribution to the Kaiser) in MS (p. 42). It seems likely that his source was German; Frieda had relatives in Court circles in Berlin, and she could have heard reports from them in letters from her mother. She also received German newspapers occasionally (e.g. in May 1916 'several copies of the *Berliner Tageblatt*' – *Letters*, ii. 609) and might have seen newspaper reports in 1915.

481:29 **a perversity."** Something misapplied, led astray, corrupted; it is possible that Ursula uses the word in its particular modern sense (from *c.* 1892) of a *sexual* perversity.

Foreword to *Women in Love*

485:3 **the Tyrol, in 1913 ... Cornwall in 1917.** The novel's first draft, 'The Sisters' (see Introduction), was begun at Gargnano, on the Lago di Garda, in the southern Tyrol, in March 1913. DHL and Frieda lived at Zennor, Cornwall, from January 1916 until October 1917; the 1917 date DHL gives is a reference either to January, when he sent his revised TSIb for retyping, or to some date later in the year, when he revised TSII extensively.

485:8 **various London publishers.** The novel was certainly rejected by Methuen (*Letters*, iii. 58), Duckworth (ibid. 80), Constable (Introduction, p. xxxviii), Cecil Palmer (ibid., iii. 149) and Fisher Unwin (ibid. 191, 206); but, as Catherine Carswell noted, 'I think it must have lain on the table at one time or another of every leading publisher in London' (*The Savage Pilgrimage*, p. 80).

485:11   **the fate of "The Rainbow,"** At Bow Street Court, on Saturday 13 November 1915, Lawrence's publisher Methuen was summoned to show cause why 1,011 copies of *The Rainbow* seized by the police should not be destroyed. The magistrate Sir John Dickinson said that the novel 'was utter filth; nothing else would describe it', and made an order for the copies of the book in the hands of the police to be destroyed (*Daily Telegraph*, 15 November 1915, p. 12).

486:19   *Hermitage, 12 September 1919.* DHL lived at Chapel Farm Cottage (belonging to Dollie Radford: see *Letters*, ii. 316 n.2) in Hermitage, Berkshire, intermittently 1917–19; after an absence of almost two months he returned there on the evening of 12 September 1919 (ibid. iii. 393) and would appear to have written (or have finished) the Foreword at once.

The 'Prologue' and 'Wedding' Chapters

Note   Annotation has not been supplied where the notes on *Women in Love* or Appendix III provide the requisite equivalent information.

489:8   **a week in the Tyrol together, mountain-climbing.** A reminiscence, perhaps, of the week DHL spent with David Garnett and Harold Hobson in Mayrhofen and on the journey to Sterzing, August 1912; DHL also walked in Switzerland with A. P. Lewis (see *Letters*, ii. 184 n. 3) in June 1914.

491:21   **had been very well received,** DHL's phrase was deleted in MS (p. 5) in favour of 'was thought brilliant' by Frieda, then adjusted to 'were brilliant'. DHL's own reading has been restored.

491:23   **Magdalen College ... inspector of schools ... the Blackhorse Road,** Cf. the career of Matthew Arnold (1822–88), fellow of Oriel College Oxford (1845) and subsequently inspector of schools (1851). There is no Blackhorse road in Oxford; but cf. Blackhall Road, where Hasan Shahid Suhrawardy (see note on 60:15) lived when DHL met him in 1915.

499:13   **braggadaccio,** DHL's version of 'braggadocio', empty boasting.

501:10   **Mary of Bethany or Vittoria Colonna.** Mary, sister of Lazarus (see John xi. 1–46, xii. 1–9) ... Marchioness of Pescara and poetess (1492–1547) to whom Michaelangelo wrote sonnets and letters: DHL was reading about her in April 1916 (see *Letters*, ii. 592 and n. 2).

501:13   **No man ... his stature.** Matthew vi. 27 ['Which of you by ... unto his stature?'].

501:29   **Neckar,"** DHL wrote 'Neckar' in MS (p. 23), as he did in the poem 'Tarantella' (E320.2) published in *New Poems* (1918). The Neckar is a river in s.w. Germany; he probably meant 'Neckan', a water spirit in German and Scandinavian folklore, his source almost certainly is the poem 'The Neckan' (1852) by Matthew Arnold. For a discussion of the legend, see *The Poems of Matthew Arnold*, ed. K. and M. Allott, 2nd edn (1979), pp. 297–300.

503:11   **David to Jonathan.** See 1 Samuel xix-xx and 2 Samuel i.

503:24   **Westerham;** Village in Kent; DHL was there in 1911 (*Letters*, i. 265).

503:27   **on the sands at Margate,** DHL and Frieda lived near Margate in July 1913, and had 'a tent in a little bay on the foreshore' (*Letters*, ii. 45–6).

505:1   **a strange Cornish type of man,** DHL and Frieda lived in Cornwall (where he wrote this chapter) between December 1915 and October 1917; for his relationship with William Henry Hocking, see Moore, *The Priest of Love*, pp. 278–9, and note on 275:29.

505:28   **from him.** DHL originally ended chap. 1 here, and headed the next page of MS 'Chapter 11/The Wedding' (p. 31). After writing pp. 31–2, he then deleted the title, twice inserted the instruction 'run on', and added 'Chapter 11' on p. 33 in a slightly different pencil.

512:33   **Goya."** The work of the Spanish painter Francisco José de Goya y Lucientes (1746–1828) includes two series of etchings, 'Caprices' (1793–6) and 'Disasters of War' (1808–12), as well as the so-called 'Black Paintings' of the period 1820–3; any of these might provoke Gudrun's comment.

513:15   **Aspasia.** 5th century BC Greek courtesan and mistress of Pericles.

515:4   **distract** Distracted: archaic adjective last used 1854 (*OED*).

516:23   **rackapelt!"** Noisy, boisterous (Nottinghamshire dialect).

517:11   **himself all his life.** A1 deleted the last three words; it is possible that there is a full stop after 'himself', in which case DHL may have intended to delete the following words. He did not, however, do so, and the 'full stop' may be the dot on an 'i'.

518:6   **Wilfrid ... Richard, who was in the Royal Engineers,** Not listed in the family as described in *Women in Love*; see note on 12:38. The Royal Engineers is Anton Skrebensky's regiment in *The Rainbow*, chap. xi (see 517:26).

TEXTUAL APPARATUS

TEXTUAL APPARATUS

The following symbols are used to distinguish states of the text:

MS = Autograph manuscript of chapters XXIII–XXXII
TSIa = Corrected ribbon and carbon typescript, chapters I–XXII typed by DHL, and XXIII–XXXII in Pinker's office
TSIb = Corrected ribbon and carbon typescript, companion copy of *TSIa*; used in preparation of *TSII*
TSII = Corrected ribbon and carbon typescript; prepared from *TSIb*
A1 = First American edition
EP = Duplicate page proofs for first English edition
E1 = First English edition
E1a = First English edition, second state
E2 = First English edition, second impression
E3 = First English edition, third impression

Whenever the *TSII* reading is adopted, it appears within the square bracket with no symbol. Other variants appear in chronological order as given above. In the absence of information to the contrary, the reader should assume that a variant recurs in all subsequent states.

When a reading from a source other than *TSII* has been preferred or coincides with the adopted reading, it appears with its source-symbol within the square bracket; the *TSII* reading follows the bracket along with further variants from later states.

When Frieda Lawrence introduced an error or her own alteration in *TSIb*, DHL's revision in *TSIa* is preferred; the reader should assume this is the case when a *TSIa* reading is preferred over *TSIb*. Explanatory notes alert the reader when it has not been possible to circumvent Frieda's influence.

The following symbols are used editorially:

Ed. = Editor
Om. = Omitted
~ = Substitution for a word in recording a punctuation or capitalisation error
/ = Line or page break resulting in an error
P = New paragraph

7:5	brightly-coloured *TSII, EP*] brightly coloured *A1*	7:15	be—" *TSII, EP*] ~"—*A1*
		7:16	now?] ~. *EP*
7:8	married?" *P* Ursula] ~?" Ursula *A1*	7:30	consider." *P* This *TSIb*] ~." This *TSII*
7:15	think, *TSIa*] ~ *TSII*	8:1	dark.—] ~— *EP*

8:6   abstract— *TSIb*] ~ *TSII*
8:7   tempted.—Oh *TSIb*] ~—oh
       TSII
8:11   to!" *P* They *Ed.*] marry!" *P*
       They *TSIb* to!" They *TSII*
8:15   women, *TSIa*, *E1*] ~. *TSII*
8:15   twenty-six *TSIa*] ~, *TSII*
8:23   sang froid *Ed.*] sang-froid *TSII*
8:29   anguish. *P* Ursula *Ed.*] dis-
       appointment. *P* Ursula *TSIa*
       anguish. Ursula *TSII*
8:34   well——] ~—*A1* ~—— *EP*
8:40   general." *P* There *TSIa*] ~."
       There *TSII see note on* 9:1
9:4   Gudrun. *P* Ursula *TSIa*] ~.
       Ursula *TSII*
9:15   Ursula,] ~ *A1*
9:17   coldly. *P* A] ~. A *A1*
9:25   superficially." *P* A *Ed.*]
       already?" *P* A *TSIa* superfi-
       cially." A *TSII*
9:32   is *EP*] was *TSII*
9:38   to put *TSIa*] and put *TSII*
10:4   of] or *A1*
10:9   finely-curved *TSII*, *EP*] finely
       curved *A1*
10:11 myself,] ~ *A1*
10:17 to *TSIa*] to *TSII*
10:21 slow, *TSIa*] ~ *TSII*
10:22 said,] ~ *A1*
10:22 words!" *P* And *TSIa*] ~!" And
       TSII
10:28 cold, *TSIa*] ~ *TSII*
10:37 time. *TSIa*] ~, *TSII*
11:3   situation, *TSIa*] ~ *TSII*
11:11 dwelling houses]
       dwelling-houses *EP*
11:14 midlands *Ed.*] Midlands *TSII*
11:15 long,] ~ *A1*
11:39 roofs. *P* The] ~. The *A1*
12:4   end *EP*] ends *TSII*
12:10 large,] ~ *A1*
12:10 full, *TSIa*] ~ *TSII*
12:34 banks, *TSIa*] ~ *TSII see notes*
12:35 trees and … churchyard …
       their heads, *Ed.*] trees and …
       church-yard … heads, *TSII*
       trees, *A1*

13:5   forward. *P* And *TSIa*] ~. And
       TSII
13:14 stockings! *TSII*, *EP*] ~? *A1*
13:15 violent *TSII*, *EP*] ~ *A1*
13:16 to be] *Om. A1*
14:16 were *TSIa*] was *TSII*
14:32 him. *P* Gudrun] ~. Gudrun *A1*
14:35 cold] *Om. A1 see notes*
14:38 wolf] ~, *A1*
15:25 a *EP*] *Om. TSII*
15:25 long,] ~ *A1*
15:25 blenched] blanched *A1*
15:39 midlands] Midlands *A1*
16:5   soul, *TSIa*] ~ *TSII*
16:7   for *TSIa*] of *TSII*
16:12 midlands] Midlands *A1*
16:40 someone *TSII*, *EP*] some one
       A1
17:7   aesthetic] æsthetic *EP*
17:23 Her *TSIa*] His *TSII see notes*
17:24 higher *TSIa*] high *TSII*
17:24 first *TSIa*] central *TSII*
17:33 church door *Ed.*] church-door
       TSII
17:35 surely he would understand,]
       Om. A1
18:20 careworn *TSII*, *EP*] care-worn
       A1
18:24 voice *TSII*, *EP*] ~, *A1*
18:29 flower buds *TSII*, *EP*]
       flowerbuds *A1*
18:35 careworn *Ed.*] care-worn *TSII*
18:38 careworn *TSII*, *EP*] care-worn
       A1
19:22 the] a *EP*
19:24 turned, *TSIa*] ~ *TSII*
19:25 a *TSIa*] *Om. TSII*
19:29 her!",] ~!" *A1*
19:29 women *TSII*, *EP*] woman *A1*
20:5   laconically. *P* And *TSIa*] ~.
       And *TSII*
20:22 tight-rope: *TSII*, *EP*] ~; *A1*
21:19 wedding-party *Ed.*] wedding
       party *TSII*
21:39 he too *TSII*, *EP*] ~, ~, *A1*
22:14 emotionally *TSII*, *EP*] ~, *A1*
22:21 good-looking *Ed.*] goodlooking
       TSII, *EP* good looking *A1*

23:16 smiled, *TSII*, *EP*] ~ *A1*
23:21 calling,] ~ *EP*
23:22 here! *TSIa*] ~. *TSII*
23:22 Oh] ~, *A1*
23:22 Witham—." *TSII*, *EP*] ~—". *A1*
24:2 vaguely. *P* And *TSIa*] ~. And *TSII*
24:8 Oh *TSII*, *EP*] ~, *A1*
24:14 one. Why] ~: why *A1*
24:30 well washed *TSII*, *EP*] well-washed *A1*
25:15 repeated. *P* And *TSIa*] ~. And *TSII*
25:17 said. *P* "There] ~. "There *A1*
25:20 me,] ~ *A1*
25:31 him,] ~ *A1*
25:34 wanting *EP*] missing *TSII*
26:23 this, *TSII*, *EP*] ~ *A1*
26:28 with] to *A1*
26:36 strange, *TSIa*] ~ *TSII*
27:12 table *TSII*, *EP*] ~, *A1*
27:19 say,] ~ *A1*
27:19 voice,] ~ *A1*
27:23 replied. *P* And *TSIa*] ~. And *TSII*
27:25 little, *TSIa*] ~ *TSII*
27:38 right *TSIa*] ~, *TSII*
27:38 amiably. *P* And *TSIa*] ~. And *TSII*
27:39 glanced challenge at *EP*] was afraid of *TSII*
28:16 musingly, *TSII*, *EP*] ~ *A1*
28:18 up. *TSII*, *EP*] ~: *A1*
28:19 nationality, *TSII*, *EP*] ~ *A1*
28:22 said,] ~ *A1*
28:24 proprietory *TSII*, *EP*] proprietary *A1*
28:36 altogether,] ~? *EP*
29:1 emulation." *P* Hermione] ~." Hermione *A1*
29:11 long *TSII*, *EP*] ~, *A1*
29:19 nonplussed *EP*] non-plussed *TSII*
29:24 Ninety-nine *A1*] Ninety nine *TSII*
29:28 why, *TSII*, *EP*] ~ *A1*
30:14 thieving *A1*] theiving *TSII*

30:25 glasses,—] ~— *EP*
30:35 servantlike *TSII*, *EP*] servant-like *A1*
31:1 pleasant:] ~; *A1*
31:2 high-road *Ed.*] highroad *TSII*
31:24 Hm] H'm *EP*
31:26 we *TSIa*] he *TSII*
31:27 Oh *TSII*, *EP*] ~, *A1*
31:32 The] *The A1*
31:37 soul, *TSIa*] ~ *TSII*
31:39 Christ!,] ~! *A1*
32:2 soul, *TSIa*] ~ *TSII*
32:4 stoutly-built *TSII*, *EP*] stoutly built *A1*
32:7 into *TSII*, *EP*] in to *A1*
32:12 churchyard *TSII*, *EP*] church-yard *A1*
32:16 does] ~, *A1*
32:24 No,] ~. *EP*
32:26 humorism *TSII*, *EP*] humourism *A1*
32:34 cliché *TSII*, *EP*] cliche *A1*
33:1 Yes] ~, *A1*
33:4 like?] ~. *A1*
33:16 cutting *TSII*, *EP*] cut *A1*
33:19 profound *TSII*, *EP*] ~, *A1*
33:19 lust *TSII*, *EP*] ~, *A1*
33:28 seem to *EP*] no doubt *TSII*
33:29 imagine *EP*] *Om. TSII*
33:37 inconcern] unconcern *A1*
33:41 free-and-easy *EP*] free and easy *TSII*
34:3 man and man] men and men *A1*
35:6 over dark] overdark *E1 see notes*
35:7 approached,] ~: *EP*
35:32 speak. *P* He *TSIa*] ~. He *TSII*
36:13 ones *TSII*, *EP*] ~, *A1*
36:15 scholars' *TSII*, *EP*] scholar's *A1*
36:27 emphasise *TSIa*] emphasize *TSII*
36:35 emphasise *TSIa*] emphasize *TSII*
36:35 a] the *A1*
36:36 red *TSII*, *EP*] ~, *A1*
36:39 so— ." *Ed.*] so—

(☻). TSIb so— (☻) ".
TSII so—." A1 so—" EP
37:10 Brangwen, TSII, EP] ~? A1
37:10 slow] low A1
37:16 sang froid TSII, EP] sang froid A1
37:27 they] you A1
37:27 them?" She TSIa] ~?" She TSII
37:28 half teasing TSII, EP] half-teasing A1
37:29 twig EP] piece TSII
38:4 they! TSII, EP] ~? A1
38:26 brilliantly-lighted TSII, EP] brilliantly lighted A1
38:34 No. TSIa] ~, TSII
38:37 do TSII, EP] Do A1
39:7 things?—she TSII, EP] ~? She A1
39:8 birds, TSIa] ~ TSII
39:10 way.—Why TSIb] ~.—why TSII ~—why A1
39:11 detached,] ~ A1
39:21 her. P He TSIa] ~. He TSII
39:29 you, TSIa] ~? TSII
40:15 it, TSIa] ~? TSII
40:20 there, TSIa] ~? TSII
40:24 Yes," A1] ~" TSII
40:28 do TSIa] do TSII
40:29 knowledge, TSIa] ~; TSII
40:31 animals TSIa] animals TSII
40:35 resumed, TSII, EP] ~. A1
40:37 themselves—— TSIa] ~—— A1
41:4 themselves.—— TSIa] ~—— A1 ~. EP
41:5 nothingness—.] ~. A1 ~—— EP
41:11 said, TSII, EP] ~ A1
41:12 mind— TSII, EP] ~, A1
41:28 quantity] quality EP
41:30 said; "knowledge TSII, EP] ~. "Knowledge A1
42:4 strong,] ~ EP
42:11 passion.' TSII, EP] ~'. A1
43:5 that,] ~ A1
43:7 involuntary TSII, EP] unvoluntary A1

43:7 one] one's E1 see notes
43:12 darkness.—Everything] ~—everything A1
43:15 demon—? TSII, EP] ~? A1
43:16 "Woman] "'~ A1
43:16 lover—"] ~'—" A1
43:16 quoted—"Why] ~. "Why A1 ~—"why EP
43:18 death-annihilation] death—annihilation A1
43:22 shrill EP] sneering, shrill TSII
43:28 clear TSII, EP] ~, A1
43:28 steel. P A] ~. A A1
43:37 fortnight?] ~. A1
43:39 Goodbye!] Good-bye. A1 Good-bye! EP
43:39 Goo-oodbye—.] Goo-oodbye.— A1 Good-bye! EP
44:10 night-time TSII, EP] night time A1
44:14 got to do TSII, E3] go to do E2
44:30 itself. EP] itself, something like laughter, invisible and satisfying. Also the magic of his thighs had fascinated her: the inner slopes of his thighs. TSII see notes
44:31 liberty EP] strong, free liberty TSII
45:6 they'd—.] ~—— EP
45:7 you, TSII, EP] ~? A1
45:15 weeping: TSII, EP] ~; A1
46:2 Diver Ed.] Om. TSII A Diver EP DIVER E1
46:3 soft,] ~ A1
46:4 rain TSII, EP] ~, A1
46:34 there!" P The TSIa] ~!" The TSII
47:4 "—But TSIb] "~ TSII
47:4 so] so A1
47:5 reluctantly. P She TSIa] ~. She TSII
47:15 them, TSIa] ~ TSII
47:19 a way EP] away TSII
47:23 Gudrun. P They TSIa] ~. They TSII
47:26 Ursula. P Gudrun TSIa] ~. Gudrun TSII

47:33 in *EP*] of *TSII*
47:36 desirable, *TSIa*] ~ *TSII*
47:39 Ursula,] ~ *A1*
48:10 living! *TSII, EP*] ~? *A1*
48:14 tree] trees *A1*
48:17 Ursula. *A1*] ~, *TSII*
48:20 Wordsworth,] ~ *A1*
48:34 Certainly *TSIa*] ~, *TSII*
48:34 fact *TSII, EP*] ~, *A1*
48:38 appliances. *TSIa*] ~! *TSII*
49:1 brother!] ~? *A1*
49:8 boys,] ~? *EP*
49:10 he *TSII, EP*] ~, *A1*
49:10 course *TSII, EP*] ~, *A1*
49:11 see *TSII, EP*] ~, *A1*
49:13 no-one] no one *A1*
49:15 too *TSII, EP*] ~, *A1*
49:20 a *TSII, EP*] *Om. A1*
49:25 Desire! *TSII, EP*] ~? *A1*
49:28 happens. *TSII, EP*] ~? *A1*
49:30 someone *Ed.*] some-one *TSII, EP* some one *A1*
49:33 coldly, "if] ~. "If *A1*
49:37 Ursula. *P* At *TSIa*] ~. At *TSII*
49:40 thing!" *P* They *TSIa*] ~!" They *TSII*
50:5 amazon-like *TSII, EP*] Amazon-like *A1*
50:9 do, *TSII, EP*] ~? *A1*
50:11 Yes. *TSII, EP*] ~? *A1*
50:13 —thank *TSII, EP*] Thank *A1* thank *E1a*
50:14 go-o-o-dby-y-e *TSIa*] g-o-o-d b-y-e *TSII, EP* g-o-o-d-b-y-e *A1, E1a*
50:17 tall,] ~ *EP*
50:17 frightening *TSII, EP*] frightened *A1*
50:21 burning, *TSII, EP*] ~: *A1*
50:25 Why *TSIa*] ~, *TSII*
50:26 Gudrun, *TSIa, A1*] ~ *TSII, EP*
50:27 manner—Oh] ~ —oh *A1* ~. Oh *EP*
51:1 slow] low *A1*
51:8 Really,] ~ *A1*
51:9 school-teachers] school teachers *A1*
51:14 Ursula, "no] ~. "No *A1*

51:19 Ursula *TSII, EP*] ~, *A1*
51:25 Undoubtedly! *TSII, EP*] ~, *A1*
51:33 Yes] ~, *A1*
51:35 ordinariness *TSII, EP*] ordinaryness *A1*
51:38 Really *TSII, EP*] ~, *A1*
52:3 Ursula, "one] ~. "One *A1*
52:17 school-week *Ed.*] school week *TSII*
52:21 life was *TSIa*] life *TSII see notes*
53:13 round *TSII, EP*] around *A1*
53:17 surface *TSIa, A1*] surfaces *TSII, EP*
53:19 this] his *A1*
53:19 noticed, *TSIa*] ~ *TSII*
53:25 Hallo *TSIb*] ~, *TSII*
53:26 you] ~, *A1*
54:2 in] in the *A1*
54:3 *Daily Telegraph A1*] Daily Telegraph *TSII*
54:13 it] it to *A1*
54:25 ourselves, that we s'll *EP*] themselves, that they'll *TSII* ourselves, that we sh'll *E1 see notes*
54:31 life—] ~. *A1*
54:31 yes] Yes, *A1* Yes *EP*
54:37 He too *TSII, EP*] ~, ~, *A1*
55:11 foulness,] ~; *EP*
55:17 readjust *TSIa, A1*] re-adjust *TSII, EP*
55:28 Higher! *TSII, EP*] ~? *A1*
55:29 colliers'] collier's *EP*
56:1 myself. *TSII, EP*] ~? *A1*
56:3 person singular *TSII, EP*] ~, ~, *A1*
56:4 Gerald. *P* Which *TSIa*] ~. Which *TSII*
56:8 for?" *P* Gerald's *TSIa, EP*] ~?" Gerald's *TSII*
56:13 *more TSIa*] more *TSII*
57:17 love] live *E1a*
57:27 pure *TSII, EP*] ~, *A1*
57:28 single *TSII, EP*] ~, *A1*
58:4 woman? *EP*] ~, *TSII*
58:19 together] *together A1*
58:33 it's] its *EP*
59:14 versatility] venality *A1*

59:16 considered: *TSII, EP*] ~; *A1*
59:36 asking, *TSII, EP*] ~: *A1*
60:11 —painters *TSII, EP*] Painters *A1*
60:18 was *TSIa*] *Om. TSII*
60:22 too *TSII, EP*] ~, *A1*
60:28 Birkin. *TSIa, A1*] ~, *TSII, EP*
60:29 to the flat,] *Om. E1a*
60:29 you] you can *A1*
61:7 asked, *TSIa*] ~ *TSII*
61:8 saying?" *P* Birkin] ~?" Birkin *A1*
61:13 asleep—'" *P* Gerald *EP*] ~—'"/Gerald *TSIa*
61:32 the little] a little *EP*
61:32 swiftly-running *TSII, EP*] swiftly running *A1*
62:2 Crême *EP*] *Om. TSII* CRÊME *E1* [p. 63] CREME *E1* [contents page], *E1a*
62:6 dimly, *TSII, EP*] ~ *A1*
62:6 ad infinitum *TSII, EP*] *ad infinitum A1*
62:8 drinkers *TSII, EP*] ~, *A1*
62:18 dark, soft, fluffy] bobbed, blond *E1a see note on* 62:22
62:19 level and ... Egyptian princes's *TSIa*] level ... princess's *TSII* straight and curving slightly inwards to her ears *E1a*
62:20 warm colouring and large, dark, hostile *TSIa*] warm ... dark hostile *TSII* fair colouring and large, innocent, blue *E1a*
62:21 beauty] floweriness *E1a*
63:4 he *TSII, EP*] ~, *A1*
63:8 Well *TSIa*] ~, *TSII*
63:19 Carmarthen—?] ~? *A1*
63:20 Lord] Frederick *E1a*
63:22 decent." *P* There *TSIa*] ~." There *TSII*
63:26 altogether?" *P* But *TSIa*] ~?"—But *TSII* ~?" But *A1*
63:30 *Hallo*] Hallo *A1*
63:30 *Pussum*] Minette *E1a*
64:6 flat] house *E2*
64:8 Bertha's." *P* There *TSIa*] ~." There *TSII*

64:12 an *TSIb*] *Om. TSII*
64:12 camaraderie *A1*] camaradèrie *TSII*
64:16 before. *A1*] ~? *TSII*
64:22 cold, *TSIa*] ~ *TSII*
64:29 proud *TSII, EP*] ~, *A1*
64:30 face *TSIa*] ~, *TSII*
64:31 hair *TSIa*] ~, *TSII*
64:39 dark, hot-looking] blue, exposed-looking *E2*
64:39 dark, fully-opened, hot, *TSII, EP*] dark, fully opened, hot, *A1* flower-like, fully-opened, *E2*
65:1 film of ... of misery] curious iridescence, a sort of film of disintegration, *E2*
65:2 on *TSII, EP*] and *A1*
65:2 hat,] ~ *A1*
65:4 peach-coloured] yellow *E2*
65:4 crêpe-de-chine *A1*] crèpe-de-chine *TSIa* crepe-de-chine *TSII*
65:7 soft dark *TSII, EP*] soft, dark *A1* shiny yellow *E2*
65:7 full] curved *E2*
65:8 Egyptian] provoking *E2*
65:9 fulness *TSII, EP*] fullness *A1*
65:9 neck,] ~ *A1*
65:16 of the] of his *A1*
65:20 new-comer *Ed.*] newcomer *TSII*
65:22 dark, soft] fair, close *E2*
65:23 pale, full-built] swarthy, slender *E2*
65:24 fair] black *E2*
65:27 straight *TSIa*] *Om. TSII*
65:29 pale] green *E2*
65:29 high, *TSIa, A1*] ~ *TSII, EP*
65:32 palely *EP*] ~, *TSII*
65:33 a black] an ice-cold *E2*
65:38 viscous] ice-blank *E2*
66:3 No *TSII, EP*] ~, *A1*
66:10 No] ~, *A1*
66:11 afwaid] afraid *A1*
66:23 dull,] ~ *A1*
66:27 very *TSII, EP*] vewy *A1*
66:39 *ever*] ever *A1*
66:39 afraid *TSII, EP*] afwaid *A1*

67:3   dark] naive *E2*
67:7   dark] *Om. E2*
67:13   said; *TSII, EP*] ~: *A1*
67:22   said *EP*] ~, *TSII*
67:26   black] *Om. E2*
68:5   corrupt] *Om. E2*
68:20   dark] blue *E2*
68:25   replied,] ~ *A1*
68:28   dark, inchoate] *Om. E2*
68:33   said. *TSIa*] ~, *TSII*
68:34   oysters." *P* And *TSIa*] ~." And *TSII*
69:9   But *TSII, EP*] ~, *A1*
69:9   quick,] ~ *A1*
69:19   Yes *TSII, EP*] ~, *A1*
69:19   lisped,] ~ *A1*
69:26   hair, *A1*] ~ *TSII, EP*
69:30   handsome *TSIa*] ~, *TSII*
69:30   red lotus] fair ice-flower *E2*
69:34   naïveté *A1*] naïvetè *TSIa* naiveté *TSII, EP*
69:35   essept] except *EP*
69:36   black] round *E2*
70:1   afraid *TSII, EP*] afwaid *A1*
70:2   ugh!—" *TSIa*] ~!" *TSII*
70:20   way,] ~ *A1*
71:10   nothing *TSIa*] ~, *TSII*
71:12   man,— *TSIa*] ~— *TSII*
71:14   warningly. *P* The *TSIa*] ~. The *TSII*
71:19   really *TSII, EP*] weally *A1*
71:22   really *TSII, EP*] weally *A1*
71:25   *tewwified TSIa*] tewwified *TSII, EP* terwified *A1*
71:26   Hm] H'm *EP*
71:29   really *TSII, EP*] weally *A1*
71:40   rather;— *TSII, EP*] ~; *A1*
72:1   Oh god] ~, God *A1* ~ God *EP*
72:6   things— *TSII, EP*] ~. *A1*
72:7   he *TSIa*] He *TSII*
72:9   along. *TSII, EP*] ~? *A1*
72:14   idiot, *TSIa*] ~? *TSII*
72:15   *not TSIa*] not *TSII*
72:16   Oh *TSII, EP*] ~, *A1*
72:18   Hc!-er *TSIa*] Ho!—er *TSII*
72:21   *do TSIa*] do *TSII*
72:26   his *TSII, EP*] this *A1*

73:11   large block of buildings] street of quiet houses *E2*
73:11   in a lift] a garden path *E2*
73:12   Hindu] dark-skinned servant *E2*
73:14   Hindus] Orientals *E2*
73:27   Russian *TSII, EP*] ~, *A1*
73:30   Hindu] man *E2*
73:32   good-looking *A1*] good looking *TSII*
73:38   Hindu's] Arab's *E2*
74:8   flat] house *E2*
74:8   common and ugly] haphazard but pleasant *E2*
74:9   negro] *Om. E2*
74:9   West Africa] the West Pacific *E2*
74:10   negroes] natives *E2*
74:11   foetus] fœtus *A1*
74:11   was of *TSIa*] was *TSII*
74:13   childbirth] child-birth *EP*
74:14   of the *TSII, EP*] of a *A1*
74:17   foetus] fœtus *A1*
74:33   balked *TSIa*] baulked *TSII*
75:21   oh *TSII, EP*] ~, *A1*
75:23   Oh *TSII, EP*] ~, *A1*
75:24   you. *TSII, EP*] ~? *A1*
75:27   cold, *TSIa, A1*] ~ *TSII*
75:28   Rupert's *TSII, EP*] Wupert's *A1*
75:30   matter?"] matter? There is the studio—" *E2*
75:34   since *TSII, EP*] from *A1*
75:39   black and] fierce and *E2*
76:1   Goodnight *Ed.*] Good-night *TSII*
76:3   interval, *TSII, EP*] ~; *A1*
76:6   slight] silent *A1*
76:13   then, *TSII, EP*] ~? *A1*
76:22   black] *Om. E2*
76:23   some *EP*] some dreadful, *TSII*
77:2   Fetish *Ed.*] *Om. TSII* Fetishes *EP* FETISH *E1* TOTEM *E2*
77:6   devouring,] ~ *A1*
77:10   in, knowing ... and shirt.] in. He had on a silk wrap of a beautiful bluish colour, with an amethyst hem. *E1 see notes*

77:14   towels?" *P* And *TSIa*] ~?" And
         TSII
77:15   naked,] ~ *A1*
77:28   white] dark *E2*
77:31   blue] hazel-yellow *E2*
77:32   fireglow *TSII, EP*] fire-glow *A1*
77:34   degenerate] weak *E1*
78:3   Oh *TSII, EP*] ~, *A1*
78:5   Oh *TSII, EP*] ~, *A1*
78:19   golden coloured   *TSII,   EP*]
         golden-coloured *A1*
78:22   repelled.] ~? *A1*
78:24   dignity. *TSII, EP*] ~? *A1*
78:26   also in ... somehow apart.] in
         white pyjamas and wet hair,
         and a towel over his arm. He
         was aloof and white, and
         somehow evanescent. *E1*
78:36   present] ghostly *E1*
78:37   negro] savage *E2*
79:2   naked] *Om. E1*
79:4   immediate] indefinite *E1*
79:5   defined] assigned *E1*
79:8   vividly, *TSIa*] ~ *TSII*
79:8   spirit, *TSIa*] ~ *TSII*
79:9   negro] savage *E2*
79:9   African] dark *E2*
79:17   High *TSIb, A1*] *High TSII*
79:21   African] barbaric *E2*
79:23   *ultimate* physical *TSIa*] ultimate
         physical TSII
79:31   It seemed   ...   deliberately
         nude.] He was so conventional
         at home, that when he was
         really away, and on the loose, as
         now, he enjoyed nothing so
         much as full outrageousness.
         So he strode with his blue silk
         wrap over his arm and felt
         defiant. *E1*
79:34   dark] blue *E2*
79:34   eyes *TSII, E1*] ~, *A1*
79:35   black ... black] stagnant ...
         dead *E2*
80:13   Hindu] Arab *E2*
80:25   flat] house *E2*
80:26   man-servant] Arab *E2*
80:32   an ash of corruption, *TSIa*] as

         an ash or a corruption, in *TSII*
         see notes
81:5   animosity *EP*] ~, *TSII*
81:6   Café] café *EP*
81:10   absent, *TSII, EP*] ~; *A1*
81:13   she did ... she would] he did
         not know whether she wanted
         money or not. But she might *E2*
81:17   short clipped *TSII, EP*]
         short-clipped *A1*
81:18   Halliday, *TSIa, A1*] ~ *TSII, EP*
81:22   difficulty. Because *TSIa*] ~;
         because *TSII*
82:10   valley *TSIa*] Valley *TSII*
83:4   Gudrun—"so *TSIa*]
         ~.—"so *TSII* ~.—"So *A1*
         ~—"so *EP*
83:10   No— *TSII, EP*] ~—, *A1*
83:25   coral coloured *TSII, EP*]
         coral-coloured *A1*
83:27   you! *TSII, EP*] ~? *A1*
84:18   surprising *EP*] ~, *TSII*
84:23   to] *Om. A1*
84:24   lounge   chairs   *TSII,   EP*]
         lounge-chairs *A1*
84:26   contessa] countess *A1* Con-
         tessa *EP*
84:28   lawn, *TSIa*] ~ *TSII*
84:38   contessa] Contessa *EP*
85:1   then,] ~ *A1*
85:3   everybody, *TSII, EP*] ~; *A1*
85:7   lawn: *TSII, EP*] ~; *A1*
85:9   P. M. *TSIa, A1*] P.M. *TSII, EP*
85:23   a] *Om. A1*
85:27   vigorous *TSII, EP*] vigourous
         A1
85:31   Well— *TSII, EP*] ~—, *A1*
85:37   m- m- m- *TSIa*] m—m—m—
         TSII M—m—m— *A1*
85:37   know.———] ~ *A1*
85:39   *unbounded*———————] ~
         ... *A1* ~ ...... *EP*
86:14   Malleson *A1*] Mattheson *TSII,*
         EP
86:15   tabloids, *A1*] ~ *TSII*
86:25   Can *TSIa*] Can *TSIb*
86:25   baronet] Baronet *A1*
86:26   gravitation, *TSIa*] ~ *TSIb*

86:33 contessa] Contessa *EP*
86:34 contessa] Contessa *EP*
86:40 *Fathers and Sons, Ed.*] Fathers and Sons, *TSII, EP* 'Fathers and Sons,' *A1*
87:4 Ha! *TSIa*] ~!— *TSII*
87:19 sure." *P* There *TSIa*] ~." There *TSII*
87:32 goodbye] good-bye *A1* good-bye, *EP*
87:33 Goodbye *TSIa*] ~, *TSII* Good-bye, *A1*
88:13 mild, *TSIa, A1*] ~ *TSII, EP*
88:16 my lady *Ed.*] madam *TSIa see notes*
88:17 he.] ~? *A1*
88:21 crying: *A1*] ~; *TSII*
88:31 you,] ~? *A1*
88:33 safe *TSII, EP*] safely *A1*
88:38 unconsciously, *TSIa*] ~. *TSII* ~ *A1*
89:1 table *TSIa*] ~, *TSII*
89:2 Yes—] ~. *A1*
89:23 dropping] drooping *EP*
89:31 Yes. *TSIa*] ~, *TSII*
90:1 stiff *TSII, EP*] ~, *A1*
90:8 Malleson] Mattheson *E1*
90:9 contessa] Contessa *EP*
90:11 of grey *Om. A1 see notes*
90:12 crimson] of grey, crimson *A1*
90:25 Wiill you smooke] Will you smoke *A1*
90:25 prettily. *P* There *TSIa*] ~. There *TSII*
90:36 melting pot *TSII, EP*] melting-pot *A1*
90:40 Birkin, *TSIa*] ~ *TSIb*
91:3 all-powerful *TSIa, EP*] all powerful *TSIb*
91:11 half-trance. A] ~. *P A A1*
91:17 Vergini Delle Rocchette *EP*] Vergine Delle Roche *TSIa* Vergini Delle Rocche *TSII* Virgins of the Rocks *A1*
91:17 contessa] Contessa *EP*
91:19 usefully. *P* It *Ed.*] ~./ It *TSIa* ~. It *TSII*
91:21 contessa] Contessa *EP*

91:24 contessa] Contessa *EP*
91:24 first. *TSIa*] ~, *TSII*
91:25 cleared, *TSIa*] ~. *TSII*
91:34 interplay] inter-play *A1*
91:40 contessa's] Contessa's *EP*
92:6 contessa] Contessa *EP*
92:26 contessa] Contessa *EP*
92:30 vuol dire *Ed.*] vuol'dire *TSII, EP* voul'dire *A1*
92:31 contessa] Contessa *EP*
92:33 sang *TSIa*] said *TSII*
92:38 dissolution, *TSIa*] ~ *TSII*
93:6 Ursula, *TSIa*] ~ *TSII*
93:11 moment, *TSIa*] ~ *TSII*
93:17 together——"] ~—?" *A1* ~—" *EP*
93:18 silently, *TSIa*] ~ *TSII*
93:26 Beldover! *TSII, EP*] ~? *A1*
93:26 they, *TSIa*] ~ *TSIb*
93:29 are?" said *TSIa*] are!" exclaimed *TSII see notes*
93:32 me? *TSIa, A1*] ~! *TSIb, EP*
93:32 No.—But *TSIa*] ~—~ *TSII* ~—but *EP*
94:5 school? *TSIa*] ~! *TSII*
94:8 indifferent, *TSIa*] ~ *TSII*
94:27 guinea— *TSIa*] ~, *TSIb*
94:27 guineas—." *Ed.*] ~—". *TSIa* ~." *TSIb*
94:40 gives *TSIa*] might give *TSIb*
95:8 really mad *TSIa*] somewhat insane *TSIb see notes*
95:9 a religious maniac *TSIa*] had religious mania *TSIb*
95:12 split mad *TSIa*] insane *TSIb*
95:13 baby] Botticelli *E1a*
95:13 —the good . . . same time *TSIa*] on the one hand, and on the other, *TSIb*
95:19 away with *TSIa*] into the filth of *TSIb*
95:20 turns towards *TSIa*] calls on the name of *TSIb*
95:21 gets another thrill *TSIa*] enjoys himself all round *TSIb*
95:21 game *TSIa*] story *TSIb*
95:25 her!] ~, *A1*
95:35 minutes *TSII, EP*] moments *A1*

95:36   again; "we *TSIa*] again. "We
         TSII
96:1   dues, *TSIa*] ~ *TSII*
96:13   matter,] ~ *AI*
96:17   really. *AI*] ~.— *TSII* ~— *EP*
96:18   Caesarina ... Caesarina's]
         Cæsarina ... Cæsarina's *AI*
96:20   talking. *P* "Go] ~. "Go *AI*
96:27   morning, *TSIa*] ~ *TSII*
96:28   out: *P* "I *TSIa*] ~: "I *TSII*
96:29   ten pounds] some money *EIa*
96:30   God," *TSIa*] ~" *TSIb* ~!"
         TSII
96:33   you." *EP*] you," came the
         laconic answer. *TSII*
96:38   vitae] vitæ *AI*
96:39   scelerisque *TSIa, EP*] scleres-
         que *TSIb*
96:39   purus— *TSII, EP*] ~! *AI*
97:28   queer] ~, *AI*
97:33   you— *TSII, EP*] ~.— *AI*
98:24   sideboard,] ~? *AI*
98:26   Oh *TSII, EP*] ~, *AI*
98:29   her, *EP*] ~ *TSII*
98:38   Malleson] Matheson *EI*
99:3   countess] Countess *EP*
99:3   no *TSIa*] Om. *TSII*
99:3   anybody] everybody *EP*
99:20   himself, *TSIa*] ~ *TSII*
99:24   mechanical, *TSII, EP*] ~; *AI*
99:24   at] at the *AI*
99:26   her *TSII, EP*] ~, *AI*
99:32   Oh *TSIa*] ~, *TSII*
99:32   the Fräulein *TSIa*] Mademo-
         iselle *TSIb* Fräulein *TSII*
99:37   countess] Countess *EP*
99:41   the Fräulein *TSIa*] Fräulein
         TSIb
100:1   Oh *TSIa*] ~, *TSII*
100:14   No, *TSIa*] ~. *TSII*
101:5   countess] Countess *EP*
101:12   ever you *TSIa*] you ever *TSII*
101:26   countess] Countess *EP*
101:35   slow,] ~ *AI*
102:1   in, *TSIa*] ~ *TSII*
102:5   properly-dressed,]   properly
         dressed *AI* properly-dressed
         EP

102:5   correct] Om. *AI*
102:32   Roddice, *TSIa*] ~. *TSII*
103:22   from] from the *AI*
103:36   equality—] ~ *AI*
104:3   imagine,] ~ *EI*
104:3   nature. *P* "I *Ed.*] ~. *P I TSII* ~.
         I *AI*
104:15   megalomania] megelomania *EP*
104:28   took] took up *EP*
104:28   volume, *TSIa*] ~ *TSII*
104:40   wall—she *TSII, EP*] ~. She *AI*
105:3   Terrible *TSIa*] Terribly *TSII*
105:12   last. *TSII, EP*] ~! *AI*
105:21   lightning, *TSIa*] ~ *TSII*
105:23   way, *TSIa*] ~ *TSIb*
105:24   Nevertheless *TSIa*] ~, *TSII*
105:35   hand, *TSII, EP*] ~; *AI*
105:40   her, *TSIa*] ~ *TSII*
106:2   bits. Yet *AI*] ~, Yet *TSII*
106:4   No *TSII, EP*] ~, *AI*
106:26   motion, *TSII, EP*] ~ *AI*
107:1   then] Om. *AI*
107:16   birch-trunk *TSII, EP*] birch
         trunk *AI*
107:32   immeasurably   *TSIa,   AI*]
         immeasureably *TSII, EP*
107:39   He knew ... seed:—along ...
         fresh growing leaves. *TSII, EP*]
         He ... seed;—along ... fresh-
         growing leaves. *AI* Om. *EI see
         note on* 108:2
108:10   human-being *TSIa*] human
         beings *TSII*
108:21   with] against *EI see notes*
108:24   island, *TSII, EP*] ~ *AI*
108:29   wrote *TSII, EP*] ~, *AI*
109:1   sulking, *TSIa*] ~; *TSII*
110:2   Coal-Dust *Ed.*] Om. *TSII* Col-
         lieries *EP* [contents page] Coal
         Dust *EP* [p. 113] COAL-
         DUST *EI see notes*
110:9   obscurity *TSIa*] security *TSII*
         security, *AI*
110:20   light,] ~ *EP*
110:31   high-road *TSIa, AI*] high-
         /road *TSII* highroad *EP*
110:35   back,] ~ *EP*
111:1   fool,] ~! *EP*

111:1 Ursula,] ~ *EP*
111:2 by.] ~? *A1*
111:3 spell-bound] spell-/bound *A1* spellbound *EP*
111:25 *fool——!*] ~——! *A1*
111:37 threading] treading *A1*
112:12 by,] by, and *A1*
112:19 unstained. *P* The *TSIa*] ~. The *TSII*
112:26 is *TSII, EP*] was *A1*
112:30 one half] one-half *EP*
112:31 half, *TSII, EP*] ~ *A1*
112:39 crossing, *EP*] ~ *TSII*
113:4 that;—] ~; *EP*
113:10 gate-keeper *A1*] gate keeper *TSII*
113:13 wouldn't] couldn't *A1*
113:16 There] Then there *A1*
113:20 the cautious] a cautious *A1*
113:31 horse: *TSII, EP*] ~; *A1*
113:33 soft *TSII, EP*] ~, *A1*
114:5 drinking trough *TSII, EP*] drinking-trough *A1*
114:21 hard-faced,] ~ *A1*
114:22 laborer *Ed.*] labourer *TSII*
114:22 twenty-three *A1*] twenty three *TSII*
114:31 minutes;—] ~; *EP*
114:32 younger *TSIa*] young *TSII*
114:33 Missis *TSIa*] missis *TSII*
114:36 pale grey *TSII, EP*] pale-grey *A1*
115:12 heavily; *TSIa*] ~, *TSII*
115:13 squalor *TSII, EP*] squalour *A1*
115:15 the *TSIa*] *Om. TSII*
115:15 feel,] ~ *A1*
115:16 *I TSIa*] I *TSII*
115:16 stupefies *A1*] stupifies *TSII, EP*
115:25 laborer's *TSII, EP*] labourer's *A1*
115:26 glamorous *TSII, EP*] glamour-ous *A1*
115:27 maleness] ~, *A1*
116:13 an] and *A1*
116:14 half-resignation] half resignation *A1*
116:30 pavements *TSII, EP*] pavement *A1*

116:36 district] districts *EP*
116:38 public-houses *TSII, EP*] public/ houses *A1*
116:39 stream, *TSII, EP*] ~; *A1*
117:4 these] their *A1 see notes*
117:12 cinema: *TSII, EP*] ~; *A1*
117:14 boy'.] ~.' *A1*
117:19 him: *TSII*] ~; *TSII*
117:21 bath] bathe *A1*
117:22 underclothing *TSIa*] under-/clothing *TSII* under-clothing *A1*
117:25 Brangwens' *Ed.*] Brangwen's *TSII*
117:33 fellow mind *TSIa*] fellow-mind *TSII*
118:4 elegants,] ~ *A1*
118:4 sense: *TSII, EP*] ~; *A1*
118:5 people, *TSII, EP*] ~ *A1*
118:15 glamorous *TSII, EP*] glamour-ous *A1*
119:2 Sketch-Book *Ed.*] *Om. TSII* The Sketch-Book *EP* SKETCH-BOOK *E1*
119:10 dark lurid *TSII, EP*] ~, ~ *A1*
119:11 turgid *TSII, EP*] ~, *A1*
119:16 nothingness *TSII, EP*] nothing *A1*
119:23 stupor *TSII, EP*] stupour *A1*
120:1 colliers—he] ~. He *A1*
120:17 you. *TSIa*] ~? *TSII*
120:20 Well— *TSII, EP*] ~, *A1*
120:23 there. *TSIa*] ~? *TSII*
121:2 Hermione, *TSIa*] ~ *TSII*
121:16 into *TSII, EP*] in to *A1*
121:22 sorry—so] sorry— *EP*
122:13 course *TSIa*] ~, *TSII*
122:20 Gooood-byyye!" Hermione *TSIa*] Gooood-bye!" Her-mione *TSII* Goo-ood-/bye!" *P* Hermione *A1* Gooood-bye!" *P* Hermione *EP*
122:23 subtly-smiling *TSII, EP*] subtly smiling *A1*
122:33 obliviousness, *TSII, EP*] ~; *A1*
123:2 An *Ed.*] *Om. TSII* The *EP* AN *E1*
123:10 laborer *TSII, EP*] labourer *A1*

123:10 wife, *TSIa*] ~ *TSII*
123:18 animal] ~, *A1*
123:24 do! *TSIa*] ~? *TSII*
124:3 it, *TSIa*] ~ *TSII*
124:4 carries *TSIa*] ~, *TSII*
124:10 in] it *EP*
124:16 manoeuvred] manœuvred *A1*
124:22 *Paul et Virginie TSIa*] Paul et Virginie *TSII*
124:34 Yes.] ~, *A1*
125:9 Maybe *TSIa*] May-be *TSII*
125:15 Why *TSII, EP*] ~, *A1*
125:40 into] to *EP*
126:10 dry-rotten] ~, *A1*
126:13 Fruit *TSII, EP*] fruit *A1*
126:21 asked,] ~ *A1*
126:23 Why? Why *TSIa*] ~, why *TSII*
126:30 *you EP*] you *TSII*
126:30 cried. "Where *TSIa*] ~, "where *TSII*
126:37 lies.——] ~.—*A1* ~. *EP*
127:7 Completely. If *TSIa*] Completely, because if *TSII see notes*
127:12 into] with *A1*
127:13 nitro-glycerine *TSII, EP*] nitroglycerine *A1*
127:19 ghastly *TSIa*] ~, *TSII*
127:20 Fruit *TSII, EP*] fruit *A1*
127:24 people.] ~? *A1*
127:25 Yes *TSII, EP*] ~, *A1*
127:35 *all* TSIa] all *TSII*
128:2 *man!*] ~? *A1* ~! *EP*
128:18 days;] ~;—*A1*
128:23 Ah *TSII, EP*] ~, *A1*
128:25 proud: *TSII, EP*] ~; *A1*
128:33 final *EP*] great *TSII*
129:12 distinct] distant *A1*
129:24 asked,] ~ *A1*
129:24 mocking *TSII, EP*] mockingly *A1*
129:30 aloof *EP*] priggish *TSII*
130:2 man: *TSII, EP*] ~; *A1*
130:3 Salvator *TSII, EP*] Salvador *A1*
130:3 Sunday-school teacher . . . stiffest type *TSII, E1*] righteous corrector of mankind *EP see notes*
130:13 proscribed] prescribed *EP*

130:13 tabooed *EP*] tabood *TSII*
130:17 Ah *TSII, EP*] ~, *A1*
130:27 He too *TSII, EP*] ~, ~, *A1*
130:28 crouching] ~, *A1*
130:32 dervish] Dervish *EP*
131:7 her *TSII, EP*] Om. *A1*
131:11 shy *TSII, EP*] ~, *A1*
131:14 lovely?] ~, *EP*
131:21 compositae] compositæ *A1*
131:31 said: "if *TSII, EP*] ~. "If *A1*
132:9 tomorrow] to-morrow, *A1* to-morrow *EP*
132:12 four *EP*] two *TSII*
132:23 minutes] ~' *A1*
132:27 asked,] ~ *A1*
132:29 'love.' *TSII, EP*] "~." *A1*
132:31 thought] though *E1*
133:2 out: *TSIa, A1*] ~; *TSII*
133:7 I?——] ~?—*A1* ~? *EP*
133:10 Yes *TSII, EP*] ~, *A1*
134:2 Carpeting *Ed.*] Om. *TSII* Carpetting *EP* CARPETTING *E1 see notes*
134:7 large,] ~ *A1*
134:34 deceived? *TSIa, A1, E1*] ~, *TSII, EP*
134:35 Oh *TSIa*] ~, *TSII*
135:9 in! *TSII, EP*] ~? *A1*
135:15 Gudrun *TSII, EP*] ~, *A1*
135:18 you.——] ~?—*A1* ~? *EP*
135:20 lake *TSIa*] ~, *TSII*
135:21 you! *TSII, EP*] ~? *A1*
135:21 earth!] ~. *A1*
136:12 you] Om. *EP*
136:30 glad. *A1*] ~? *TSII*
136:31 you would like it, my lady! *TSIa*] you would like it, madam! *TSIb* would you like it? *TSII see notes*
137:3 you, *TSII, EP*] ~? *A1*
137:5 No] ~, *A1*
137:18 you? *TSIa*] to you? *TSII*
137:27 Bergamos:—] ~—— *EP*
137:27 seven—. *TSII, EP*] ~.—*A1*
137:27 would] will *A1*
137:30 it *TSIa*] it to *TSII*
138:18 to *TSII, EP*] of *A1*
138:23 Gerald *TSII, EP*] ~, *A1*

138:29 railway crossing *Ed.*]
     railway-crossing *TSII*
138:34 me,] ~ *A1*
138:35 whistles. *TSII, EP*] ~? *A1*
138:39 was *EP*] is *TSII*
138:39 horrible—! *TSII, EP*] ~! *A1*
139:11 fulfil *TSII, EP*] fulfill *A1*
139:16 ourself *TSIa*] ourselves *TSII*
139:31 intelligently *TSIa*] intelligibly
     TSII
139:34 me, *TSIa, A1*] ~ *TSII, EP*
139:39 them—] ~, *A1*
140:17 maleström *EP*] maelstrom
     TSII, E1
140:25 maelström *EP*] maelstrom
     TSII, E1
140:27 And *TSII, EP*] ~, *A1*
140:30 completely,—] ~— *A1*
141:1 love-impulse: *TSII, EP*] ~; *A1*
141:11 thing *TSII, EP*] ~, *A1*
141:15 beautiful! *TSII, EP*] ~? *A1*
141:33 *not TSIa*] not *TSII*
141:40 stopping *TSII, EP*] ~, *A1*
142:4 the,— *TSIa*] ~— *TSII*
142:33 the *TSIa*] *Om. TSII*
143:21 unconsciously, *A1*] ~ *TSII*
144:6 that] and that *A1*
144:15 *want TSIa*] want *TSII*
144:18 on *EP*] in *TSII*
144:19 lodging *TSII, EP*] lodgings *A1*
144:31 He too *TSII, EP*] ~, ~, *A1*
145:1 couldn't *TSIa*] could not *TSII*
145:4 room *TSIa*] ~, *TSII*
145:8 they! *TSII, EP*] ~? *A1*
145:23 harder,— *TSII, EP*] ~— *A1*
146:2 no] not *EP*
146:7 say: *TSIa*] ~; *TSII*
146:10 *is TSIa*] is *TSII*
146:11 But *TSIa*] ~, *TSII*
146:15 here!] ~? *A1*
146:24 whilst *TSIa*] while *TSII*
146:40 that *TSIa*] what *TSII*
147:4 entirely *TSIa*] ~, *TSII*
147:16 his] this *A1*
147:25 least, *TSII, EP*] ~? *A1*
148:12 you— *TSII, EP*] ~, *A1*
148:13 right: *TSII, EP*] ~; *A1*
148:14 beings: *TSII, EP*] ~; *A1*

148:19 stars!] ~. *A1*
148:37 wonderful *TSIa*] ~, *TSII*
149:13 half way *TSII, EP*] half-way
     A1
149:13 round *TSII, EP*] around *A1*
149:24 Ursula *TSII, EP*] ~, *A1*
149:26 her!" cried Ursula. *TSIa*] her?"
     TSII
149:30 to *TSIa, EP*] *Om. TSII*
150:2 fate: *TSII, EP*] ~; *A1*
150:23 she! *TSII, EP*] ~? *A1*
150:26 Wille zur Macht *TSII, EP*]
     Wille zur Macht A1
150:27 Wille zur Macht *TSII, EP*]
     Wille zur Macht A1
150:31 volonté de pouvoir *TSII, EP*]
     volonté de pouvoir A1
150:32 pouvoir *TSII, EP*] *pouvoir A1*
150:33 Ah—! *TSII, EP*] ~! *A1*
150:34 kept *TSII, EP*] and *A1*
150:37 satellite!—] ~— *A1*
151:7 'a satellite,'] ~ ~, *A1*
151:9 *I*] I *A1*
151:12 *prevaricator*! *TSII, EP*] ~. *A1*
151:21 tea-table *TSIa*] tea table *TSII*
151:26 exposulations] expostulation
     A1
152:11 ever there *TSIa*] there ever
     TSII
152:13 asked *TSIa*] said *TSII*
152:34 forever] for ever *EP*
152:35 selfless *TSII, EP*] selfish *A1*
153:8 said: *Ed.*] ~. *TSII*
153:10 egotism] egoism *A1*
153:15 subserved] subservient *A1*
153:18 so] *Om. A1*
153:22 chagrin. *EP*] chagrin and
     weariness. *TSII*
153:38 we! *TSII, EP*] ~? *A1*
154:3 go] go to *A1*
155:2 Water-Party *EP* [p. 161]] *Om.*
     TSII Water Party *EP* [contents
     page] WATER-PARTY *E1*
155:3 more-or-less *TSIa*] more or
     less *TSII*
155:4 Water, *TSIa*] ~ *TSIb*
155:5 rowing boats *Ed.*] rowing-boats
     TSII

155:7 walnut tree *Ed.*] walnut-tree *TSII*

155:8 Grammar School *Ed.*] Grammar-School *TSII*

155:14 own] *Om. E1a*

155:16 awkwardness. Nevertheless *TSIa*] ~. *P* Nevertheless *TSII*

155:28 cotton crape *Ed.*] silky crape *TSIa* crape *TSII* crepe *A1* crêpe *EP see notes*

156:6 gens-là] gens-lá *A1*

156:9 distinctly. *P* And *TSIa*] ~. And *TSII*

156:31 look. *P* "Oh *TSIa*] ~. "Oh *TSII, EP* ~. "Oh, *A1*

157:3 Gudrun. *P* Now *TSIa*] ~. Now *TSII*

157:7 father *TSII, EP*] ~, *A1*

157:14 jackanapes— *TSII, EP*] ~, *A1*

157:18 Brangwen *TSII, EP*] ~, *A1*

157:34 angry. *P* And *TSIa*] ~. And *TSII*

158:3 sotto voce *TSII, EP*] *sotto voce A1*

158:7 Ursula. *P* "It *TSIa*] ~. "It *TSII*

158:16 Gudrun. *P* They *TSIa*] ~. They *TSII*

158:17 saw the *TSIa*] saw *TSII*

158:26 clothes *TSII, EP*] ~, *A1*

158:31 policemen *TSIa*] policeman *TSII*

158:31 abreast:] ~; *A1*

158:33 fresh-faced, *TSII, EP*] ~ *A1*

158:33 collected *TSII, EP*] ~, *A1*

159:8 cool *TSII, EP*] ~, *A1*

159:8 heard *Ed.*] heard them *TSIa see notes*

159:21 appearance. *TSII, EP*] ~? *A1*

159:34 do! *TSII, EP*] ~? *A1*

160:6 black-and-brown *Ed.*] black-and-orange *TSIa* black and orange *TSIb* black and brown *TSII*

160:7 He too *TSII, EP*] ~, ~, *A1*

160:17 Grammar-School *EP*] Grammar-school *TSII* Grammar School *A1*

160:18 landing-stage *A1*] landing stage *TSII*

160:28 Oh *TSII, EP*] ~, *A1*

160:28 lovely. *TSII, EP*] ~! *A1*

160:34 No *TSII, EP*] ~, *A1*

160:40 do." *P* Her *TSIa*] ~." Her *A1*

161:3 *Trop de monde TSII, EP*] Trop de monde *A1*

161:3 Yes, *TSIa, A1*] ~ *TSII, EP*

161:19 and *EP*] and down *TSII*

161:21 ''Ere *TSIa, A1*] 'Ere *TSII*

161:24 ha'penny *TSIa, A1*] ha-penny *TSII, E1a*

161:25 those] these *A1*

161:30 said: *TSIa*] ~; *TSII*

162:3 rebuke. There *TSIa*] ~. *P* There *TSII*

162:8 here *TSII*] ~, *A1*

162:13 outspoken *TSIa*] out-/spoken *TSII, EP* out-spoken *A1*

162:21 on a] on the *A1*

162:29 out." He *TSIa*] ~." *P* He *TSII*

163:17 hand? *TSII, EP*] ~! *A1*

163:17 hurt? *TSII, EP*] ~! *A1*

163:23 Oh,] ~ *EP*

163:26 it? *TSII, EP*] ~! *A1*

163:29 hurt it] hurt *A1*

164:10 child-like *Ed.*] childlike *TSII*

164:12 child-like *Ed.*] childlike *TSII*

164:13 good-looking *Ed.*] goodlooking *TSII*

164:32 a] the *A1*

165:25 Ännchen *EP*] Annchen *TSII, E1a see notes*

165:31 partaker *TSII, EP*] partner *A1*

166:2 do——?] ~——? *A1*

166:11 love——] ~——*A1*

166:14 slower *TSII, EP*] slow *A1*

166:37 Ursula! *TSII, EP*] ~? *A1*

167:16 back *TSII, EP*] *Om. A1*

167:30 false, *TSIa*] ~ *TSII*

167:31 Way down in Tennessee——— *Ed.*] It's a long long way to Tipperary——— *TSII* Way … Tennesee——— *EP* Way … Tenessee——— *E1*

167:32 Nevertheless] ~, *EP*

167:33 strange, *TSIa*] ~ *TSII*

167:40 figure *TSIa*] figure, towards them, *TSII see notes*
168:9 Ursula spell-bound *TSIa*] ~, ~, *TSII*
168:16 Hi—eee] Hi-eee *EP*
168:19 suspended, *TSIb*] ~ *TSII*
168:23 wondering, *TSIa*] ~ *TSII*
168:24 come—?] ~? *A1*
168:29 aloof *TSII, EP*] ~, *A1*
169:24 satirically. P She *TSIa*] ~. She *TSII*
169:28 full!] ~? *EP*
169:35 women *TSII, EP*] woman *A1*
170:5 mask-like,] ~ *A1*
170:16 Any way] Anyway *A1*
170:32 light *EP*] Om. *TSII*
170:33 said, mocking. *EP*] said. *TSII*
170:34 desire for deep violence *EP*] lust for deep brutality *TSII*
170:38 slight blow on his *EP*] heavy blow across the *TSII*
171:2 emotion ... emotion *EP*] rage ... anger *TSII*
171:11 automatically, "Why *TSIa*] ~: P "Why *TSII*
171:12 fashion?] ~. *EP*
171:25 landing-stage *TSIa*] landing stage *TSII*
172:27 said; *TSII, EP*] ~, *A1*
172:27 the] that *EP*
172:35 flood] blood *A1*
173:26 Yes *TSII, EP*] ~, *A1*
174:33 also,] ~ *E2*
175:19 vibrating *TSII, EP*] ~, *A1*
175:27 fearful! *TSII, EP*] ~? *A1*
175:36 Well— *TSIa*] ~ *TSIb, EP* ~, *A1*
175:40 cuttle-fish *TSII, EP*] cuttlefish *A1*
176:16 Ursula." By *TSIa*] ~." P By *TSII*
177:10 said. Again *Ed.*] asked naively. Again *TSIa* said. P Again *TSII*
178:4 him *TSIa*] ~, *TSIb*
178:18 landing-stage *A1*] landing stage *TSII*
178:19 Anywhere, *A1*] ~ *TSII*
178:39 shouting *TSIa*] ~, *TSIb*

179:8 forward. The *TSIa*] ~. P The *TSII*
179:11 heavy, *TSIa*] ~ *TSII*
179:12 irony. P But *TSIa*] ~. But *TSII*
179:23 sharp, *Ed.*] blank, *TSIa* sharp *TSII*
179:27 "Di—Di ... Oh Di! *TSIa*] "Di—Di—Di—Di—Oh Di—Oh Di—Oh Di! *TSIb*
179:34 answering. "Where *TSIa*] ~. P "Where *TSII*
179:34 Where?] where? *EP*
179:35 No-o-o *TSII, EP*] No—o—o *A1*
180:3 "Di—Oh...Di—! *TSIa*] "Di—Oh Di—Oh Di—Di—! *TSIb*
180:8 stooping *TSII, EP*] ~, *A1*
180:16 its *TSIa*] her *TSIb*
180:17 yellow *TSIa*] yellow light *TSIb*
180:19 "Oh get ... Oh Daddy! *TSIa*] "Oh get her out! Oh Di, *darling*! Oh get her out! Oh Daddy, Oh Daddy! *TSIb* "Oh ... *darling*! Oh ... Daddy! *A1*
180:21 life-belt *TSIa*] life belt *TSII*
180:36 Get her ... her out," *TSIa*] Get her out, Gerald, Oh get her out," *TSIb* Get ... oh ... out," *A1*
181:5 So] She knew *EP see notes*
181:9 her *TSII, EP*] ~, *A1*
181:34 She could scarcely believe it. *TSIa*] Om. *TSII*
181:37 gone, *TSIa*] ~ *TSII*
182:11 water! *TSIa*] ~. *TSIb*
182:17 Gerald! Gerald? *TSIa*] Gerald! Gerald? *TSIb* Gerald! Gerald! *TSII*
182:29 of the *TSIa*] of *TSII*
182:40 white, *TSIa*] ~ *TSII*
183:15 silent,] ~ *A1*
183:25 Yes *TSII, EP*] ~, *A1*
183:33 Well *TSII, EP*] ~, *A1*
184:6 said,] ~ *A1*
184:19 all *TSIa*] Om. *TSIb*
184:20 here.— *TSIa*] ~— *TSII* ~. *EP*
184:23 an *TSIa*] with *TSII see notes*

184:30 Ursula. "And *Ed.*] ~, "And *TSII* ~, "and *A1*

184:37 scattered, *TSIa*] ~ *TSIb*

185:3 become] became *EP*

185:13 high, *TSIa*] ~ *TSII*

185:16 up *TSIa*] *Om. TSII*

185:36 it! *Ed.*] they! *TSIa* they? *TSIb* it? *TSII*

186:1 living, *TSIa, A1*] ~ *TSII, EP*

186:4 *you TSIa*] you *TSII*

186:8 death-process] death process *A1*

186:20 yield, *TSIa*] ~ *TSII*

186:20 were,] ~ *E1*

186:25 defences] ~, *E1a*

186:26 a *TSIa*] and *TSII*

186:37 prison, *TSIa*] ~ *TSII*

187:4 show] show you *A1*

187:8 know." *P* Then *TSIa*] ~." Then *TSII*

187:33 sleep-loveliness *TSII, EP*] sleep-loveiness *A1*

187:34 up] up to *A1*

188:14 landing-stage *TSIa, EP*] landing stage *TSIb*

188:16 watched.] ~, *A1*

188:38 neck! *TSIa*] ~. *TSIb*

189:5 place—?" *TSIa*] ~"— *TSIb*

189:5 urged, *TSIa*] ~ *TSII*

189:7 Gerald *TSII, EP*] ~, *A1*

189:18 Gerald,] ~ *A1*

189:26 Birkin. *P* And] ~. And *A1*

189:32 last, the *TSIa*] ~. The *TSII*

189:37 with] with the *A1*

190:7 at] in *A1*

190:10 Everywhere, *TSIa*] ~ *TSII*

190:27 house— *TSIa*] ~,— *TSII*

190:29 all the] all *A1*

191:4 within *TSII, EP*] with *A1*

191:33 balk *TSIa*] baulk *TSII*

191:33 but *TSII, EP*] not *A1*

192:1 'I daren't.'? *TSIa*] '~ ~.' *TSIb, EP* "~ ~." *A1* '~ ~'? *E1*

192:10 balking ... balking *TSIa*] baulking ... baulking *TSII*

192:18 there———] ~ ——— *EP*

192:32 transmutation ... trans-

mutation *EP*] dissolution ... dissolution *TSII*

192:40 will, *TSII, EP*] ~ *A1*

193:33 great,] ~ *E1a*

194:3 death. Whatever] ~. *P* Whatever *EP*

194:22 Oh *TSII, EP*] ~, *A1*

194:33 her,] ~ *A1*

195:12 Why,] ~ *EP*

195:30 Goodnight *TSIa*] Good-night *TSII* good-night *A1*

195:39 *you TSIa*] you *TSII*

196:2 Well *TSII, EP*] ~, *A1*

196:5 Well *TSII, EP*] ~, *A1*

196:33 Ah! *TSIa*] ~!! *TSII* ~!! *EP*

196:33 Well *TSII, EP*] ~, *A1*

196:35 it *TSII, EP*] that *A1*

197:9 minute *TSIa*] ~, *TSII*

197:14 overexcited *TSII, EP*] over-excited *A1*

197:18 vindictively;] ~, *A1*

197:18 One] one *A1*

197:24 false! *TSII, EP*] ~? *A1*

197:29 Well— *TSII, EP*] ~, *A1*

198:11 assertion, *A1*] nonchalance, *TSIa* assertion *TSII*

199:21 admitted: *TSII, EP*] ~; *A1*

199:29 her self] herself *A1*

200:16 hers,] ~ *A1*

200:23 subservience claiming,] ~, ~ *A1*

200:27 too *TSII, EP*] ~, *A1*

200:40 whole.] ~? *E1*

201:7 beings,] ~ *A1*

201:10 in] into *A1*

201:12 then *TSII, E1a*] them *EP*

201:13 where] when *A1*

201:16 mingling,] ~ *A1*

201:40 asked, *TSIa*] ~ *TSII*

202:5 health. *A1*] ~? *TSII, EP*

202:6 me," said Birkin. *TSIa*] me." *TSIb*

202:10 eyes. "I *TSIa*] ~. *P* "I *TSII*

202:13 demands] demand *A1*

202:14 Gerald; "at *TSIa*] ~. "At *TSII*

202:18 are *EP*] is *TSII*

202:18 rest] best *E1a*

202:22 Yes *TSIa*] ~, *TSIb*

202:25 you, *TSIa*] ~ *TSIb*
202:25 me *TSII*, *E1a*] he *EP*
202:26 the *TSIa*] Om. *TSIb*
202:27 face! *TSIa*, *EP*] ~? *TSIb*
202:29 Really! *TSII*, *EP*] ~? *A1*
202:36 said— *TSII*, *EP*] ~: *A1*
202:37 'Why—?'—And *TSIa*] 'why,'?
and *TSIb* 'why', and *TSII* 'why,'
and *A1*
203:6 Hm] H'm *EP*
203:10 I'm sure *TSIa*] I should think
TSIb see notes
203:11 self-conscious] ~, *A1*
203:12 uncalled for *TSIa*] uncalled-for
TSII
203:15 hurt *TSIa*] harm *TSIb*
203:17 her *TSIa*] ~, *TSIb*
203:19 laughed *EP*] laughed lightly
TSII
203:23 *resent TSIa*] resent *TSII*
204:8 "'Timor mortis conturbat
me',"] *"Timor mortis conturbat
me," A1*
204:8 adding— *TSII*, *EP*] ~: *A1*
204:17 voice— *TSII*, *EP*] ~, *A1*
204:26 through: agelong *TSII*, *EP*]
through; age long *A1*
204:26 death, *TSII*, *EP*] ~ *A1*
204:27 aeons of] of *A1* in *EP*
204:29 this: *TSII*, *EP*] ~; *A1*
204:32 head:— *TSII*, *EP*] ~: *A1*
204:38 his *A1*] is *TSII*
205:3 school, *TSII*, *EP*] ~. *A1*
205:4 the] a *A1*
205:5 oughtn't? *TSIa*] ~. *TSII*
205:9 school,— *TSIa*] ~.— *TSIb*
~— *TSII*
205:11 away *TSII*, *EP*] way *A1*
205:19 *you TSIa*] you *TSII*
205:37 ordinary?] ~! *EP*
205:40 felt. He *TSII*, *EP*] ~; he *A1*
206:3 child-like: *TSII*, *EP*] ~; *A1*,
E1a
206:6 freak! *TSII*, *EP*] ~? *A1*
206:33 Blutbrüderschaft,] *Blutbruderschaft? A1* Blutbruderschaft, *EP*
207:1 implicitly] ~, *A1*
207:21 contempt *TSII*, *EP*] ~, *A1*

207:23 not] Not *A1*
208:5 Really! *TSII*, *EP*] ~? *A1*
208:5 Oh *TSII*, *EP*] ~, *A1*
208:14 cheap, *TSIa*] ~ *TSII*
208:27 wrong, *TSIa*, *A1*] ~ *TSII*, *EP*
208:36 not! *TSII*, *EP*] ~? *A1*
209:2 "She's a . . . said Gerald. *TSIa*]
Om. *TSIb see notes*
209:4 Win." *TSIa*] Win," said
Gerald. *TSIb*
209:14 ought—and *Ed.*] ought to
be—and *TSIa* ought to be. And
TSIb ought. And *TSII*
209:17 she! *TSIa*] ~? *TSII*
209:18 Yes. And *Ed.*] is. And *TSIa* is
and *TSIb* Yes, and *TSII*
209:24 —It bores me—. *TSIa*] It bores
me— *TSIb* Om. *TSII*
209:31 honor *TSIa*] honour *TSII*
209:32 said,] ~ *A1*
209:37 you!] ~? *A1*
210:5 bed, *TSIa*] ~ *TSII*
210:11 Birkin, "goodbye *TSIa*] ~.
"Goodbye *TSII* ~. "Good-bye
A1
210:17 warm *EP*] vivid *TSII*
210:21 Goodbye] Good-bye, *A1*
Good-bye *EP*
211:26 go," *TSIa*] ~" *TSII*
211:34 too tidy *TSII*, *EP*] too-tidy *A1*
212:2 place] ~, *EP*
212:5 find] found *A1*
212:15 then! *TSII*, *EP*] ~? *A1*
212:17 Shortlands *Ed.*] Highclose
TSII see notes
212:27 proud, *TSIa*, *A1*] ~ *TSII*, *EP*
212:29 her." *P* The *Ed.*] to." *P* The
TSIa her." The *TSII*
212:34 old." *P A TSIa*] ~." A *TSII*
212:35 curious *TSII*, *EP*] ~, *A1*
212:36 Really! *TSIa*] ~, *TSIb*
212:38 demon! *Ed.*] fiend! *TSIa*
demon. *TSII*
213:2 word!] ~. *A1*
213:8 coward. *TSII*, *EP*] ~? *A1*
213:9 her;— *TSIa*] ~; *TSII*
213:10 it! *TSII*, *EP*] ~? *A1*
213:18 asking— *TSII*, *EP*] ~: *A1*

213:24 master *TSIa*] Master *TSII*
213:27 him—] ~, *A1*
213:27 did—.] ~. *A1* ~— *EP*
213:28 'I ... him,' *TSII, EP*] "~ ... ~," *A1*
214:3 lying *TSIa*] being *TSIb*
214:12 life, *TSIa*] ~ *TSII*
214:16 slight, *TSIa*] ~ *TSIb*
214:17 It was superficial *TSIa*] But it was historical *TSIb*
215:1 his] this *A1*
215:5 thin *TSII, EP*] him *A1*
215:5 dread, *TSIa*] ~ *TSII*
215:18 they, *TSIa, A1*] ~ *TSII, EP*
215:19 labour, *TSIa, A1*] ~ *TSII, EP*
215:35 licence *TSII, EP*] license *A1*
216:8 off. *TSII, EP*] ~! *A1*
216:11 supplicants; *TSIa*] ~: *TSII*
216:13 Crowther *Ed.*] Simpson *TSII*
216:13 away, *TSIa*] ~ *TSII*
216:17 fowls *TSIa*] ~, *TSII*
216:30 dinner?—send *TSII, EP*] ~? Send *A1*
216:36 know *TSII, EP*] ~, *A1*
217:1 Christiana *A1*] Christian *TSII*
217:12 Gittins? *TSIa*] Gittins. *TSII* Gittens. *A1*
218:1 hemorrhage] hæmorrhage *EP*
218:4 arms,] ~ *A1*
218:10 chaste,] ~; *A1*
218:26 he too *TSII, EP*] ~, ~, *A1*
218:26 forgotten. *P* Whereas] ~. Whereas *A1*
218:40 the *TSIa*] *Om. TSII*
219:1 Charity, *TSIa*] Charity, and *TSIb* Charity; and *TSII*
219:1 it; *TSIa*] ~, *TSIb*
219:20 These too *TSII, EP*] ~, ~, *A1*
219:40 motor-car, *TSIa*] ~ *TSII*
220:24 who *TSII, EP*] ~, *A1*
220:26 relationship, *TSIa*] ~ *TSII*
221:1 lived, *TSIa*] ~ *TSII*
221:4 its] his *A1*
221:25 savage freedom *TSIa*] savagedom *TSII*
221:28 so *TSIa*] *Om. TSII*
221:29 blackened *TSII, EP*] blackening *A1*

221:32 coal-mines *Ed.*] coal mines *TSII*
222:20 heavily-laden *TSIa*] heavily laden *TSII*
222:22 Co."/These *TSIa*] ~." *P* These *TSII*
222:38 motor-car *A1*] motor car *TSII*
223:23 Pah! *TSIb, A1*] ~!, *TSII*
223:26 brain *TSII, EP*] brains *A1*
224:22 well-off *TSII, EP*] well off *A1*
224:27 soon *TSIa*] so *TSII see notes*
224:29 masters *TSIa*] master *TSII*
224:30 out-of-all-proportion *EP*] out of all proportion *TSII*
224:35 honor *Ed.*] honour *TSII*
224:36 patriarch] Patriarch *EP*
225:4 love, *TSIa*] ~. *TSII*
225:8 illusion— *TSIa*] ~, *TSIb* ~ *TSII*
225:17 disquality *TSIa*] *disquality TSIb see notes*
225:32 God *A1*] god *TSII*
225:33 earth—and] ~.—And *A1* ~. And *EP*
226:24 part: *TSII, EP*] ~; *A1*
226:25 abstraction *EP*] being *TSII*
226:32 father however *TSII, EP*] ~, ~, *A1*
227:1 loving-kindness] loving kindness *A1*
227:6 self-sacrifice *A1*] self sacrifice *TSII*
227:35 organisation *EP*] order *TSII*
228:8 resistant *TSIa*] resistent *TSII*
228:14 complex, *TSII, EP*] ~ *A1*
228:18 Machine] machine *A1*
228:28 in to *TSIa*] into *TSII*
228:36 fulfil *TSII, EP*] fulfill *A1*
229:18 Letherinton] Letherington *EP*
229:29 worst *TSII, EP*] worse *A1*
229:32 withdrew *TSIa*] drew *TSII*
230:15 cartage too *TSII, EP*] ~, ~ *A1*
230:16 many] the many *A1*
230:18 the week *TSII, EP*] a week *A1*
230:25 to *TSIa*] in *TSII* into *EP*
230:34 mechanicalness *EP*] mindlessness *TSII*

231:5   wanted, it] ~. It *A1*
231:38 day *TSIa*] days *TSII*
232:3   perfect, *TSIa*] ~ *TSII*
232:3   sometimes, *TSIa*] ~ *TSII*
232:13 healthy *TSII, EP*] ~, *A1*
232:16 sockets *EP*] look *TSII*
232:20 babble *TSII, EP*] bubble *A1*
232:31 small,] ~ *A1*
232:31 final,] ~ *A1*
232:39 church *TSIa,A1*] Church *TSII, EP*
234:7   After] after *A1*
234:20 face *TSII, EP*] her face *A1*
234:21 sang froid *Ed.*] *sang froid TSII*
234:24 do, *TSIa*] ~? *TSII*
235:1   Well *TSIa*] ~, *TSII*
235:6   Daddy *Ed.*] Daddie *TSII*
235:8   asked, *TSIa*] ~ *TSII*
235:17 mostly *TSII, EP*] most *A1*
235:22 Soon *TSIa*] ~, *TSII*
235:23 beings, *TSIa*] ~ *TSII*
235:29 pekinese *TSII, EP*] Pekinese *A1*
235:35 Oh *TSII, EP*] ~, *A1*
235:39 mummy *A1*] Mummy *TSII*
236:12 time *TSIa*] time with *TSII*
237:4   humorous *TSII, EP*] humour-ous *A1*
237:10 Blue coat] Bluecoat *A1*
237:12 rather heavy *TSIa*] heavy heavy *TSII, EP* heavy, heavy *A1*
237:20 Oh I *TSIa*] oh ~ *TSII*
237:24 Bonjour mademoiselle *TSIa*] Bon jour, Mademoiselle *TSII*
237:28 c'est] *Om. A1 see notes*
237:34 Qu'est-ce *Ed.*] Qu'est ce *TSII*
237:39 Bismarck *TSIa*] ~, *TSII*
238:8   Qu'est-ce *Ed.*] Qu'est ce *TSII*
238:10 is I *TSIa*] ~, ~ *TSII*
238:11 Gerald *TSII, EP*] ~, *A1*
238:17 Non monsieur *TSIa*] ~, Mon-sieur *TSII*
238:18 Ah] Ay *A1*
238:24 no! *TSIa*] no, *TSIb*
238:34 wonderful! *TSIa*] ~? *TSII*
239:7   calculative *Ed.*] calculating *TSIa see notes*

239:11 access of worship *TSIa*] excess of appreciation *TSII see notes*
239:34 beautiful! *TSII, EP*] ~? *A1*
239:35 silly! *TSII, EP*] ~? *A1*
239:35 added *TSII, EP*] ~, *A1*
239:39 *extremely*] extremely *A1*
240:2   *fearful*] fearful *A1*
240:5   Winifred *TSII, EP*] ~, *A1*
240:11 strange *TSII, EP*] ~, *A1*
240:15 now?"—She] ~?" she *A1* ~?—" she *EP*
240:25 *terribly*] terribly *A1*
240:26 Oh *TSIa*] ~, *TSII*
240:37 said, *TSIa*] ~ *TSII*
240:39 Oh *TSIa*] ~, *TSII*
241:13 unearthly, *TSIa*] ~ *TSII*
241:24 really—.] ~. *A1*
241:28 seagull's *A1*] sea-gull's *TSII* sea-/gull's *EP*
241:30 silly,] ~ *A1*
241:35 child] ~, *A1*
241:37 funny? *TSII, EP*] ~. *A1*
242:1   victor *EP*] equal *TSII*
242:10 walls, *TSIa,A1*] ~ *TSII, EP*
242:19 *fool*." *P* The *TSIa*] ~?" / The *TSII* ~?" *P* The *A1* ~?" The *EP*
243:6   walls, *TSIa*] ~ *TSII*
243:24 on *TSII, EP*] in *A1*
243:27 Ah *TSII, EP*] ~, *A1*
243:28 "—All *TSII, EP*] " ~ *A1*
243:34 mysterious——] ~——. *A1* ~—— *EP*
244:2   Moony *EP* [p. 256]] *Om. TSII* Moonshine *EP* [contents page] MOONY *E1*
244:15 animals: *TSII, EP*] ~; *A1*
244:33 repudiation, repudiation,] repudiation, *EP*
246:25 sing *TSII, EP*] sink *A1*
246:25 at] to *A1*
246:26 lies—then *TSIa*] ~.—then *TSIb* ~.—Then *TSII* ~. Then *EP*
246:27 anything— *TSII, EP*] ~. *A1*
246:31 —What] —what *A1* What *EP*
246:31 there—? *TSII, EP*] ~? *A1*

247:4 clamorous *TSII, EP*] clamour-
      ous *A1*
247:34 fragments, *TSII, EP*] ~ *A1*
247:34 an *TSIa*] in *TSII*
248:4 places, *TSIa*] ~; *TSII*
248:6 listened,] ~ *EP*
248:9 spent, *TSIa*] ~ *TSII*
248:12 stealthily *TSIa*] steadily *TSII*
248:14 together, *TSIa*] ~ *TSIb*
248:25 him, *TSII, EP*] ~ *A1*
248:27 he asked.] *Om. A1*
249:19 light? *TSIa, A1*] ~, *TSII, EP*
249:22 so *TSIa*] *Om. TSII*
249:24 would] could *A1*
249:35 one-sided. *TSIa*] ~! *TSII*
249:39 *yourself,—* *TSII, EP*] ~—*A1*
250:5 spark,] ~ *A1*
250:37 it] it to *A1*
251:4 She] she *A1*
251:7 school *TSII, EP*] School *A1*
251:7 teacher—*you*] ~. *You A1*
      ~—*You EP*
251:7 preacher. *TSII, EP*] ~! *A1*
251:16 me!] ~. *A1* ~! *EP*
251:17 a *TSII, EP*] *Om. A1*
251:30 Why! *TSII, EP*] ~? *A1*
251:31 insistence—your] ~. Your *A1*
      ~—Your *EP*
251:31 Brangwen,'] ~,'— *A1*
251:38 it. *TSII, EP*] ~? *A1*
252:13 his] this *A1*
252:22 you— *TSII, EP*] ~?— *A1*
252:25 said.] ~, *A1*
252:27 crooned *TSII, EP*] ~, *A1*
252:28 he too *TSII, EP*] ~, ~, *A1*
252:31 day, *TSIa, A1*] ~ *TSII, EP*
252:35 fulfilment.] ~? *A1*
252:38 did] did not *A1*
252:39 darker] ~, *A1*
253:4 vividly: *TSII, EP*] ~; *A1*
253:17 Africans: *TSII, EP*] ~; *A1*
253:20 mindless *TSII, EP*] ~, *A1*
253:24 beetle's: *TSII, EP*] ~; *A1*
253:25 scarab: *TSII, EP*] ~; *A1*
253:27 death-break: *TSII, EP*] ~; *A1*
253:28 where] when *A1*
253:39 curious,] ~ *A1*
254:13 in *TSII, EP*] of *A1*

254:15 north? *A1*] ~. *TSII*
254:18 frost-mystery] frost mystery *A1*
254:25 Paradisal] paradisal *A1*
254:28 free proud *TSII, EP*] free-
      proud *A1*
254:28 accepts] accepted *A1*
254:29 other *TSII, EP*] others *A1*
254:32 This] There *A1*
255:2 miners-dwellings]
      miners'-dwellings *A1* miners'
      dwellings *EP*
255:11 shirt-sleeves *Ed.*] shirt sleeves
      TSII
255:12 he too *TSII, EP*] ~, ~, *A1*
255:16 you. *TSII, EP*] ~? *A1*
255:23 inexplicable, *TSIa, EP*] ~ *TSII,
      A1*
255:26 fifty *TSII, EP*] fifty years *A1*
255:28 himself?] ~. *A1*
256:1 said:] ~. *EP*
256:6 dining-room *Ed.*] dining room
      TSII
256:15 you *TSII, EP*] ~, *A1*
256:17 —of] *Om. A1*
256:17 foot—.] ~. *A1* ~— *EP*
256:22 added— *TSII, EP*] ~, *A1*
256:25 "—not *TSII, EP*] "~ *A1*
256:27 herself— *TSII, EP*] ~. *A1*
256:37 Certainly *TSIa*] Yes *TSIb*
257:3 *She TSIa*] She *TSII*
257:5 *Do TSIa*] Do *TSIb*
257:5 asked simply *TSIa*] said aloud
      TSIb
257:9 as was *TSIa*] as as *TSIb* as *TSII*
257:10 Birkin. P Which *TSIa*] ~, /
      Which *TSIb* ~, which *TSII*
257:11 most *TSIa*] *Om. TSIb*
257:18 Why!" he repeated. "Why
      don't I? Because I *TSIa*]
      Why!—because I *TSIb*
      Why!—*I TSII* Why? *I A1* Why!
      I EP
257:19 and your *TSIa*] and *TSIb*
257:21 steady, *TSIa*] ~ *TSIb*
257:28 that *TSIa*] *that TSIb*
257:30 this—?] that? *A1* that—? *EP*
257:31 hesitated. He *TSIa*] ~, he *TSIb*
257:32 say,] ~ *A1*

257:33 daughter—"] ~"—*A1*
258:1 looking *TSIa, EP*] looked *TSII*
258:6 after *TSIa*] for *TSIb*
258:7 queer, *TSIa, A1*] *TSIb, EP*
258:9 am at] am *EP*
258:12 them— *TSIa*] ~, *TSIb*
258:15 well— *TSII, EP*] ~—. *A1*
258:26 my business] *my* ~ *A1*
258:30 you *TSIa*] your *TSIb*
258:31 again *TSIa*] *Om. TSIb*
258:31 wi' *TSIa*] with *TSIb*
258:31 me. She'll *TSIa*] ~, she'll *TSIb*
258:39 well *TSII, EP*] ~, *A1*
259:14 dining-room *Ed.*] dining room *TSII*
259:16 'Girl's Own' *Ed.*] ~ ~ *TSII*
259:18 right, *TSIa*] ~ *TSII*
259:26 Oh *TSII, EP*] ~, *A1*
259:26 do! *TSII, EP*] ~? *A1*
259:37 he! *TSII, EP*] ~? *A1*
260:1 "—To *TSII, EP*] "~ *A1*
260:8 'propose.'" *TSIa*] ~." *TSIb*
260:10 you! *TSIa*] ~? *TSII*
261:5 yellow *TSIa*] *Om. TSII*
261:7 me! *TSIa*] ~? *TSII*
261:8 you! ... you! ... you! *TSII, EP*] ~? ...~? ...~? *A1*
261:11 bargust *Ed.*] creature *TSIa see notes*
261:14 He too *TSII, EP*] ~, ~, *A1*
261:15 no-one *TSII, EP*] no one *A1*
261:15 soft, *TSIa, A1*] ~ *TSII, EP*
261:24 her father cried *TSII, EP*] cried her father *A1*
262:3 bright *TSII, EP*] ~, *A1*
262:5 Ah *TSII, EP*] ~, *A1*
262:16 blind *TSII, EP*] ~, *A1*
262:21 wanted, *TSII, EP*] ~ *A1*
263:8 And of course *TSII, EP*] ~, ~ ~, *A1*
263:9 impossible— *TSII, EP*] ~, *A1*
263:16 mind *EP*] ~, *TSII*
263:16 self-criticism—. *TSIa*] ~— *TSIb* ~. *A1*
263:25 deadly?" *P* This *TSIa*] ~?" This *TSII*
263:27 soul, *TSIa*] ~ *TSII*

263:27 distaste. She *TSIa*] ~. *P* She *TSII*
264:2 air! *TSII, EP*] ~? *A1*
264:3 Georges] George *EP*
264:8 yellow-ammers *TSIa*] yellowhammers *TSIb see notes*
265:3 by] *Om. A1*
265:7 her: he] ~. He *A1*
265:9 he] she *A1*
266:7 me?",] ~?" *EP*
266:26 woman] women *EP*
266:26 no one *A1*] no-one *TSII, EP*
266:31 smile:] ~. *A1*
267:10 you're *TSIa*] you are *TSIb*
267:11 Bored! *TSIa*] ~ *TSIb* ~, *TSII*
267:17 voice. *P* There *TSIa*] ~. There *TSII*
267:18 pause, *TSIa*] ~ *TSII*
267:18 man *TSIa*] *Om. TSIb see notes*
267:22 *ennui*:] ~, *A1*
267:24 sleep, *TSII, EP*] ~ *A1*
267:40 boxing—? *TSII, EP*] ~? *A1*
268:2 Ay— *TSII, EP*] ~. *A1*
268:11 terror, *TSIa*] ~ *TSII*
268:22 I've *TSII, EP*] I'd *A1*
268:23 even] ever *EP*
268:28 said, *TSII, EP*] ~: *A1*
268:31 Half *TSIa*] Hold *TSII*
268:31 minute— *TSII, EP*] ~. *A1*
269:2 polyp— *TSII, EP*] ~. *A1*
269:10 Well—, yes—, *TSII, EP*] ~—~— *A1*
269:13 was *TSIa*] *Om. TSII*
269:14 Well *TSII, EP*] ~, *A1*
269:14 Gerald; *TSII, EP*] ~. *A1*
269:14 shall *TSIa, EP*] Shall *TSII*
270:5 more *TSIa*] *Om. TSII*
270:27 ever *TSIa*] *Om. TSII*
270:27 tighter, *TSIa, A1*] ~ *TSII, EP*
270:32 thickly-carpeted *TSII, EP*] thickly carpeted *A1*
270:33 white, *TSIa*] ~ *TSII*
271:10 sliding] ~, *EP*
271:12 hammer-strokes *TSIa*] hammer-stroke *TSII*
271:19 was] had *A1*
271:23 Gerald however *TSII, EP*] ~, ~, *A1*

271:26 course— *TSII, EP*] ~, *A1*
271:34 violence— *TSII, EP*] ~, *A1*
272:2 Almost—] ~ *A1*
272:20 whisky *Ed.*] whiskey *TSII*
272:24 delicate *EP*] fine *TSII*
272:30 Gerald, "it's life for me—"
    TSIa] Gerald, "it's life—"
    TSIb Gerald. *TSII see notes*
272:36 me." *P* He] ~." He *A1*
272:39 "—I *TSIa*] "~ *TSII*
273:3 enjoyable *TSII, EP*] ~, *A1*
273:7 beautiful *TSIa*] ~, *TSII*
273:11 Brüderschaft] Bruderschaft
    EP
273:23 dressing-gown *TSII, EP*]
    dressing gown *A1*
273:26 thick *TSII, EP*] ~, *A1*
273:30 it *TSII, EP*] ~, *A1*
273:32 expensive *TSII, EP*] ~, *A1*
273:33 Curious! *TSII, EP*] ~. *A1*
274:7 me. *TSII, EP*] ~? *A1*
274:14 family *TSIa*] father *TSII*
274:16 before about it, *TSII, EP*] about
    it before, *A1*
274:28 Why] ~, *A1*
275:2 Well *TSIa*] ~, *TSII*
275:5 Well *TSIa*] ~, *TSII*
275:19 it, *TSIa*] ~ *TSII*
275:19 nowadays? *TSIa, A1*] ~! *TSII*
275:29 that——] ~— *A1* ~—— *EP*
275:33 change——] ~— *A1* ~——
    EP
276:4 it. *TSIa*] ~! *TSII*
276:6 *love*— *TSIa*] love— *TSII, EP*
    love. *A1*
276:12 that *TSII, EP*] ~, *A1*
276:14 he *TSII, EP*] He *A1*
276:18 fulfilled;— *TSIa*] ~; *TSII*
277:5 might, *TSIa*] ~ *TSII*
277:9 faïence] faïence *A1*
277:10 faïence] faïence *A1*
277:10 mice are] mice were *A1*
277:15 being *TSII, EP*] ~, *A1*
277:19 silly *TSII, EP*] ~, *A1*
277:20 "Dear *EP*] ~ *TSII*
277:20 Brangwen] ~, *A1*
277:26 "Father *EP*] ~ *TSII*
277:33 own.———" *TSIa*]

~,——— *TSII* ~,..." *A1*
~,———" *EP*
278:11 smiling *TSII, EP*] ~, *A1*
278:14 Oh, *TSII, EP*] ~ *A1*
278:31 Daddy—] Daddie, *A1*
    Daddie— *EP*
278:32 What] ~, *A1*
278:37 Daddy—!] Daddie! *A1*
    Daddie—! *EP*
278:37 laconically— *TSII, EP*] ~, *A1*
279:2 suspected *TSII, EP*] expected
    A1
279:17 her *TSIa*] *Om. TSII*
279:23 bouquet! *TSII, EP*] ~? *A1*
279:23 coming *TSII, EP*] ~, *A1*
279:23 the *TSII, EP*] The *A1*
279:26 Well *TSII, EP*] ~, *A1*
279:29 do! *TSII, EP*] ~? *A1*
279:39 man-servant *A1*] manservant
    TSII
280:11 flowers." *P* She *TSIa*] ~." She
    TSII
280:13 Mine! *TSII, EP*] ~? *A1*
280:31 Really! *TSII, EP*] ~? *A1*
281:1 Ah come] ~, ~, *A1*
281:2 paper *TSIa*] newspaper *TSII*
281:11 once— *TSII, EP*] ~. *A1*
281:18 make-belief *Ed.*] make belief
    TSIa make believe *TSII*
281:37 Thomas——] ~— *A1* ~——
    EP
281:38 No *TSII, EP*] ~, *A1*
282:4 there] ~, *A1*
282:6 curacao——] curacao— *A1*
    curaçao— *EP*
282:7 curaçao— *TSII, EP*] curacao,
    A1
282:9 would. *TSII, EP*] ~? *A1*
282:9 Well then *TSII, EP*] ~, ~, *A1*
282:9 curaçao *EP*] Curaçao *TSII*
    curacoa *A1*
282:16 said *TSII, EP*] ~, *A1*
282:19 letter?] ~! *A1*
282:21 idea— *TSII, EP*] ~. *A1*
282:21 indulgently. *P* The] ~. The *A1*
282:26 Gudrun] ~, *A1*
282:32 —Of course. *TSIa*] *Om. TSII*
282:39 liked— *TSII, EP*] ~. *A1*

283:17 softly, *TSIa*] ~/ *TSIb* ~ *TSII*
283:24 too *TSII, EP*] ~, *AI*
283:32 children *TSII, EP*] ~, *AI*
283:34 as] as if *AI*
284:6 sotto-voce *Ed.*] *sotto-voce TSII*
284:10 Daddy] Daddie *AI*
284:15 again *TSII, EP*] ~, *AI*
284:15 rule *TSII, EP*] ~, *AI*
284:15 lunchtime *TSIa*] lunch time *TSII*
284:18 house,] ~: *EP* ~; *EIa*
284:35 liked *TSII, EP*] like *AI*
285:22 slight *TSII, EP*] light *AI*
285:39 random— *TSII, EP*] ~. *AI*
285:40 time *TSII, EP*] ~, *AI*
286:3 this, *TSIa*] ~— *TSII*
286:27 father is] father's *AI*
287:2 asserted] ~, *AI*
287:5 absorbedly, *TSIa*] ~ *TSII*
287:6 cried *TSIa*] said *TSII*
287:9 met; *TSII, EP*] ~: *AI*
287:13 Best *TSII, EP*] But *AI*
287:17 Oh— *TSII, EP*] ~, *AI*
287:35 with *TSII, EP*] to *AI*
288:5 *don't TSIa*] don't *TSII*
288:7 they—and *TSII, EP*] ~? And *AI*
288:8 Marshall,—] ~, *AI*
288:9 Yes] ~, *AI*
288:10 Oh *TSII, EP*] ~, *AI*
288:11 Winifred. *TSII, EP*] ~? *AI*
288:14 Oh *TSII, EP*] ~, *AI*
288:29 anything *TSII, EP*] any thing *AI*
288:37 Gudrun] ~. *EP* ~, *EIa*
289:15 on *TSIa*] *Om. TSII*
289:20 repellant *TSII, EP*] repellent *AI*
289:31 "—You *TSIb*] "~ *TSII*
289:33 *permanency*] permanency *AI*
289:35 penultimate *TSII, EP*] ~, *AI*
290:8 it! *TSII, EP*] ~? *AI*
290:16 there *TSII, EP*] ~, *AI*
290:22 nowhere—] ~. *AI*
290:24 shoulders. P "*Je m'en fiche*] ~. "Je m'en fiche *AI* ~. "*Je m'en fiche EP*
290:40 trouble,] ~ *EP*

291:1 *et puis TSII, EP*] et puis *AI*
292:11 Hermione— *TSII, EP*] ~. *AI*
292:21 one half *TSII, EP*] one-half *AI*
292:23 was *EP*] ~, *TSII*
292:26 confidence *TSIa*] evidence *TSII*
293:17 knowledge, *TSIa*] ~/ *TSIb* ~ *TSII*
293:18 faithful, *TSIa, AI*] ~ *TSII, EP*
293:21 "—You *TSIa*] "~ *TSII*
293:26 vaunt: *TSII, EP*] ~; *AI*
293:27 he! *TSIa*] ~? *TSII*
293:33 *he TSIa, AI*] He *TSII, EP*
293:35 slow *TSII, EP*] ~, *AI*
293:37 even *TSII, EP*] Even *AI*
294:10 he,] ~? *AI*
294:21 Hermione, *TSII, EP*] ~ *AI*
294:25 finally——] ~— *AI*
294:28 himself— *TSII, EP*] ~. *AI*
294:30 Hermione *TSII, EP*] ~, *AI*
294:31 no-one *TSII, EP*] no one *AI*
294:40 her! *TSIa*] ~? *TSII*
295:1 in him *TSIa*] *Om. TSII*
295:2 own——] ~— *AI* ~—— *EP*
295:3 Hermione *TSII, EP*] ~, *AI*
295:6 Ursula *TSII, EP*] ~, *AI*
295:7 *not*] not *AI*
295:16 satisfactions *TSIb*] satisfaction *TSII*
295:27 Hermione slowly— *TSII, EP*] ~, ~. *AI*
295:28 strong-willed— *TSII, EP*] ~. *AI*
295:31 shout——] ~.... *AI* ~—— *EP*
295:32 *virile TSIb*] virile *TSII*
295:32 man——" there] ~."... There *AI* ~——" There *EP*
296:1 him.——] ~.— *AI* ~. *EP*
296:2 is.——] ~.— *AI* ~. *EP*
296:7 them.——] ~.— *AI* ~. *EP*
296:8 destruction.——] ~. *AI*
296:9 reaction.——] ~. *AI*
296:10 good— *Ed.*] ~.— *TSIa* ~—.— *TSIb* ~.— *TSII* ~. *AI*
296:11 nothing——] ~— *AI* ~—— *EP*
296:17 all——] ~. *AI* ~—— *EP*
296:22 you,] ~? *AI*

296:24 she too *TSII, EP*] ~, ~, *A1*
296:26 happy—.] ~. *A1* ~— *EP*
296:29 disastrous——] ~— *A1*
296:33 health——] ~—*A1* ~——*EP*
296:40 No *TSII, EP*] ~, *A1*
296:40 No indeed! *TSIb*] ~, ~! *TSII*
297:1 *young TSIa*] young *TSII*
297:5 I! *TSII, EP*] ~? *A1*
297:7 Nevertheless——] ~— *A1*
~—— *EP*
297:13 him *TSIa*] with him *TSII*
297:15 *don't TSIb*] don't *TSII*
297:20 love—you *TSIa, EP*] ~—You
TSII ~. You *A1*
297:24 in] in an *A1*
297:40 good——] ~ …*A1* ~— *EP*
297:40 he too *TSII, EP*] ~, ~, *A1*
298:7 well— *TSII, EP*] ~. *A1*
298:8 Oh?] ~! *A1*
298:25 aesthetics] æsthetics *A1*
299:3 il] Il *A1*
299:4 più *Ed.*] piu *TSII*
299:5 appassionati, appassionati …
imparare *TSIa*] *Om. TSII*
299:6 tutto———" *TSIa*]
tutti———" *TSII* tutti."…*A1*
tutti——" *EP see notes*
299:9 industrialism,—] ~— *EP*
299:10 that,] ~ *A1*
299:16 well.——] ~. *A1*
299:17 mother.——] ~. *A1*
299:18 Oh. *TSII, EP*] ~! *A1*
299:19 Hermione however *TSII, EP*]
~, ~, *A1*
299:20 eye *TSIa*] eyes *TSII*
299:21 overwrought *TSIa*] over-
/wrought *TSII* over-wrought
A1
299:24 would] could *A1*
299:29 qua] quá *A1*
299:29 caressive,] ~ *E1a*
299:31 Buon *Ed.*] Buon' *TSII*
299:32 è…È…È *A1*] è…Ē…Ē…
TSII è … E … E *EP*
299:37 basket, *TSIa*] ~ *TSII*
300:3 inhabited *TSIa*] had inhabited
TSII
300:9 withered, *TSIb*] ~ *TSII*

300:15 graceful *TSIa*] gracious *TSII*
300:25 ragazzo] regazzo *EP*
300:25 è *A1*] ĕ *TSII*
300:26 strange *TSII, EP*] ~, *A1*
300:33 in] *Om. A1*
300:34 humorous *TSII, EP*] humour-
ous *A1*
300:34 sing-song:] ~. *EP*
300:35 cose——] ~… *A1* ~——
EP
300:40 giovanotto— *TSII, EP*] ~, *A1*
301:5 è *EP*] ĕ *TSII* e *A1*
301:6 così *A1*] cosï *TSII* cosi *E1a*
301:8 humorous *TSII, EP*] humour-
ous *A1*
301:12 said *TSII, EP*] ~, *A1*
301:13 anger. *P* "But] ~. "But *EP*
301:17 said:] ~ *A1*
301:18 Goodbye—] Good-bye, *A1*
Good-bye— *EP*
301:22 will——] ~—*A1* ~—— *EP*
302:2 Excurse *Ed.*] *Om. TSII* Excursion *EP* EXCURSE *E1 see notes*
302:16 novel? *TSII, EP*] ~. *A1*
302:26 lovely! *MS*] ~. *TSIa* ~, *TSII*
303:2 wonderful— *TSII, EP*] ~. *A1*
303:9 *is MS*] is *TSII*
303:10 best— *TSII, EP*] ~. *A1*
303:12 wonderful— *TSII, EP*] ~. *A1*
303:24 three *MS*] these *TSII*
303:33 finger *MS*] fingers *TSIa*
304:21 desire *MS*] a desire *TSII*
304:34 where] when *A1*
305:1 motor-car *A1*] motor car *TSII*
305:2 dim, she] ~. She *A1*
305:5 all enclosed nowadays *E1*] all
enclosed *TSII* nowadays all
enclosed *EP*
305:7 remaining *EP*] *Om. TSII*
305:10 re-acted] reacted *A1*
305:20 idiosyncrasies *A1*] idiosyncra-
cies *TSII, EP*
305:24 —wouldn't *MS*] Wouldn't
TSIa
305:27 tomorrow—. *MS*]
to-morrow—. *TSIa* to-
morrow. *A1* to-morrow— *EP*
305:29 her—] ~. *A1*

305:34 care—why *MS*] ~—Why *TSIa*
~. Why *A1*

305:34 mind?" *P* Her *MS*] ~?" Her
TSIa

305:40 Ah *TSII, EP*] ~. *A1*

306:6 then *TSII, EP*] ~, *A1*

306:13 where *MS*] when *TSIa*

306:16 jealousy, *MS*] ~ *TSIa*

306:19 Hermione, *TSII, EP*] ~; *A1*

306:22 *hate, MS*] ~. *TSII*

306:22 it, it *MS*] ~. It *TSII*

306:24 living— *TSII, EP*] ~; *A1*

306:28 spindle berries] spindleberries
A1

306:32 clevernesses, *MS*] cleverness.
TSIa

306:33 sort. You've *MS*] ~—you've
TSII, EP ~; you've *A1*

306:36 aren't *MS*] are *TSII*

306:37 fleshly] fleshy *A1*

306:39 me, *MS*] ~ *TSIa*

306:40 brides, *MS*] ~ *TSII*

306:40 background.— *MS*] ~— *TSIa*
~. *TSII*

307:2 afraid *MS*] afraid that *TSIa*

307:7 *is* her *MS*] is ~ *TSIa*

307:10 sordid] ~, *E1a*

307:14 —show *TSII, EP*] Show *A1*

307:14 —where *TSII, EP*] Where *A1*

307:17 *pretence*] pretence *A1*

307:18 spirituality, *TSII, EP*] ~; *A1*

307:22 spindle berry *Ed.*] spindleberry
TSII

307:26 fingers: and at *Ed.*] ~: and ~,
TSII ~. And ~ *A1* ~: and ~
EP

307:28 said *TSII, EP*] ~, *A1*

307:32 you *MS*] You *TSII*

307:35 candour *TSII, EP*] candor *A1*

307:35 yes *MS*] ~, *TSII*

307:38 say *MS*] ~, *TSIa*

307:38 dirt,] ~ *E1a*

308:7 motor-car, *Ed.*] motor car, *MS*
motor-car *TSIa*

308:9 Birkin *TSII, EP*] ~, *A1*

308:12 main *TSII, EP*] ~, *A1*

308:19 breath.] ~! *A1*

308:21 I,] ~ *A1*

308:24 *you,*] ~ *A1*

308:31 me—.] ~—*A1*

309:6 share *EP*] share of *TSII*

309:23 woman,] ~ *A1*

309:26 come: and] ~; and *A1* ~: And
EP

309:32 *moment*] moments *A1*

310:9 wistfully, *TSIa*] ~ *TSII*

310:11 branch: *TSII, EP*] ~; *A1*

310:15 cry: *TSII, EP*] ~; *A1*

310:21 simply] simple *A1*

310:29 smiled *TSII, EP*] ~, *A1*

310:30 she *TSII, EP*] he *A1*

310:30 good." *P* He *MS*] ~." He *TSIa*

310:35 round *MS*] around *TSIa*

310:36 cried, *MS, A1*] ~ *TSIa, EP*

311:2 happiness *TSII, EP*] ~, *A1*

311:23 go,] ~? *A1*

311:24 mounted *MS*] mounted to *TSIa*
see notes

311:26 mild *MS*] wild *TSIa*

312:7 here! *TSII, EP*] ~? *A1*

312:10 shop-windows] shop/windows
A1 shop-/windows *EP*

312:12 minster *MS*] Minster *TSIa*

312:18 light——] ~—*A1*

312:27 it true?" ... wondering.] it?"
she replied, laughing, but
unassured. *E1a see notes*

312:33 soul, she] ~. She *A1*

312:36 Sons *Ed.*] sons *TSII*

313:8 hearth-rug *A1*] hearthrug *TSII*

313:9 Riches?] ~! *A1*

313:21 Sons] sons *A1*

313:25 the Sons] ~ sons *A1*

313:25 inhuman Sons *Ed.*] ~ sons
TSII

313:35 Sons] sons *A1*

314:16 Source] source *A1*

314:27 Sons] sons *A1*

314:41 Shall *MS, A1*] shall *TSIa, EP*

315:2 her *TSII, EP*] *Om. A1*

315:10 thinking. We'd] ~ we'd *A1*

315:32 asked, *MS*] ~ *TSIa*

316:3 even——] ~—*A1*

316:7 where—? *TSII, EP*] ~? *A1*

316:10 Yes— *TSII, EP*] ~, *A1*

316:19 it, *TSII, EP*] ~? *A1*

316:20　across,] ~ *A1*
316:31　quietly. *P* And] ~. And *A1*
316:34　woke *TSII, EP*] awoke *A1*
317:1　stands— *TSII, EP*] ~.— *A1*
317:2　month— *TSII, EP*] ~.— *A1*
317:2　Anyhow *TSII, EP*] ~, *A1*
317:6　Now *TSII, EP*] ~, *A1*
317:11　say *MS*] ~, *TSIa*
317:12　coincidence!', *MS*] ~!' *TSIa*
317:23　in to *MS*] into *TSII*
317:31　elvin] elfin *A1 see notes*
317:37　Shortlands.] ~! *A1*
318:6　them, *TSII, EP*] ~; *A1*
318:10　Pharaoh *E1a*] Pharoah *TSII*
318:40　spending *TSII, EP*] Spending *A1*
319:5　place *TSII, EP*] ~, *A1*
319:10　perfected] perfect *E1a*
319:10　She too *TSII, EP*] ~, ~, *A1*
319:28　darkness *TSII, EP*] ~, *A1*
319:29　suave *TSII, EP*] ~, *A1*
319:32　he too *TSII, EP*] ~, ~, *A1*
319:34　fulness *Ed.*] fullness *TSII*
319:35　he too *TSII, EP*] ~, ~, *A1*
320:3　motor-car *A1*] motor car *TSII*
320:18　supervened. *P* They] ~. They *A1*
320:25　living *EP*] mystic *TSII*
320:27　maximums] maximum *A1*
320:30　vital, *EP*] mystic *TSII* mystic, *A1*
320:32　fulfilled, he] ~. He *EP*
321:4　everybody, *MS*] ~ *TSIa*
321:10　nurses, *MS*] ~ *TSIa*
321:11　morning, *MS*] ~ *TSIa*
321:13　weary *MS*] dread *TSII*
321:19　make *MS*] making *TSII*
321:26　sang froid *TSII, EP*] *sang froid A1*
321:32　inflammation, *MS*] ~. *TSIa*
322:2　after] after a *A1*
322:17　business, *MS, EP*] ~ *TSIa*
322:18　death, *MS*] ~ *TSIa*
323:2　grotesque— *MS*] ~,— *TSII*
324:22　rapt] so rapt *A1*
324:24　asked *MS*] ~. *TSII* ~, *A1*
324:26　heart. *P* He] ~. He *A1*
324:33　"—I *MS*] "~ *TSIa*

324:39　Then,] ~ *A1*
325:8　Gudrun; *MS*] ~: *TSII*
325:11　teeth, *MS*] ~ *TSIa*
325:23　hearth-stone] hearth-stones *A1*
325:23　to] in *EP*
325:23　room *TSII, EP*] rim *A1*
325:31　for ever *TSII, EP*] forever *A1*
326:19　saying: *P* "You *MS*] ~ "You *TSIa, EP* ~: "You *A1*
327:5　*are* you *MS*] are you *TSIa* are *you* TSII
327:12　have *you*] ~ you *A1*
327:12　to *MS*] got to *TSIa see notes*
327:13　through?] ~. *A1*
327:18　away? *MS*] ~! *TSIa*
327:23　*yourself, Ed.*] yourself, *MS* yourself— *TSIa*
327:40　Ah. *MS*] ~! *TSIa*
328:8　farther *MS*] further *TSIa*
328:9　farther *Ed.*] further *TSII*
328:10　cross *MS*] across *TSII*
328:20　Gudrun, *MS*] ~. *TSIa*
328:25　would? *MS*] ~! *TSIa*
328:32　drive, *MS*] ~ *TSIa*
328:35　equilibrate] equilibriate *EP*
328:37　infinite] indefinite *A1*
329:12　him? *MS*] ~! *TSIa*
329:14　*was*] was *A1*
329:28　hill-side. Across, *MS*] hill-side. Far across *TSIa see notes*
329:31　me? *MS*] ~! *TSIa*
329:32　understand." *Ed.*] ~" *MS* ~!" *TSIa*
329:35　So, *MS*] ~ *TSIa*
330:9　true." *P* He *TSIa*] ~." He *TSII*
330:15　wanted. *P* They *MS*] ~. They *TSIa*
330:32　embrace, *MS*] ~ *TSIa*
330:33　theirs, *TSIa*] ~ *TSII*
330:36　unthinkable, *MS*] ~ *TSIa*
330:37　undulating, he] ~. He *EP*
330:39　So, *MS*] ~ *TSIa*
331:9　round *MS*] around *TSII*
331:18　in to *MS*] into *TSIa*
331:38　encroaching,] ~ *EP*
332:5　firm *MS*] ~, *TSIa*
332:6　strange *MS*] ~, *TSIa*

332:15 come *MS*] she came *TSII see notes*
332:15 her *MS*] him *TSII*
332:24 hands, *MS*] ~ *TSIa*
332:29 afterdays *MS*] after days *TSIa*
332:29 birds, *MS*, *A1*] ~ *TSIa*
332:30 form. Till *MS*] ~—till *TSIa*
332:38 You'd *TSII, EP*] You *A1*
333:1 goodnight *Ed.*] good-night *TSII*
333:3 Goodnight *Ed.*] Good-night *TSII*
333:6 note, *MS*] ~ *TSIa*
333:11 offices *MS*] office *TSII*
333:23 you—? *MS*] ~? *TSIa*
333:23 extinction. *P* There *MS*] ~. There *TSIa*
333:30 Wha—a—ah-h-h— *MS*] Wha-a-ah-h-h— *TSIa* Wha-a-ah-h-h- *A1, E2* Wha-a-ah-h-h *E1a, E3*
333:34 being, the] ~. The *EP*
333:40 soft, *MS*] ~ *TSIa*
334:1 Ah—h *MS*] Ah-h *TSIa*
334:27 Oh mother—! *MS*] ~, ~! *TSIa*
334:31 warm. *P* She] ~. She *A1*
335:1 are *A1*] *Om. TSII*
335:11 No] ~, *EP*
335:17 daughters *TSII, EP*] daughter *A1*
335:29 house— *MS*] ~. *TSIa*
335:34 coffee, *MS*] ~. *TSIa*
335:36 girls, *MS*] ~ *TSII*
335:40 fireplace *MS*] ~, *TSIa*
335:40 turkish *MS*] Turkish *TSIa*
336:5 have— *MS*] ~, *TSIa*
336:11 day, *MS*] ~ *TSIa*
336:17 invisible *MS*] invisibly *TSIa*
336:20 asked, *MS*] ~ *TSIa*
336:33 intruder. *MS*] ~? *TSIa*
336:37 stage, *TSII, EP*] ~ *A1*
336:39 back—back *MS*] back-back *TSIa*
337:5 else] ~— *A1*
337:14 London *MS*] ~, *TSII*
337:14 days, *MS*] ~ *TSIa*
337:31 chains *MS, A1*] chain *TSII, EP*
338:2 way, *MS*] ~ *TSIa*

338:11 a *MS*] *Om. TSII*
338:11 high-road *MS*] high road *TSIa*
338:17 sensation: *MS*] ~, *TSIa*
338:23 goos] goes *EP*
338:28 high-road *Ed.*] highroad *MS* high road *A1*
338:30 village *MS*] Village *TSIa*
338:30 Kings] King's *EP*
338:33 churchyard *MS, EP*] Church-/yard *A1*
338:37 clammy: there *MS*] ~: There *TSII* ~. There *A1*
339:9 Gudrun.—She *MS*] ~—she *TSIa*
339:10 *would MS*] would *TSIa*
339:28 heerd *MS*] heard *A1*
339:29 wheer *MS*] where *TSIa*
339:34 OO—O—O—Oh *MS*] O-o-o-oh *TSIa, EP* O—o—o—oh *A1*
339:35 Yes, Yes *MS*] ~, yes *TSIa*
339:35 teaches] teachers *A1*
339:36 him!—that's *MS*] ~—~ *TSIa*
339:36 certainly *TSII, EP*] ~, *A1*
340:10 right-hand *MS*] right hand *TSIa*
340:12 believe—] ~,— *A1*
340:30 dining-room *TSII, EP*] dining room *A1*
340:30 side, *MS*] ~ *TSIa*
340:35 half-opened *MS*] half opened *TSIa*
340:37 tiles *EP*] mosaic *TSII*
340:40 foreshortened] fore-shortened *A1*
341:7 ajar *MS*] again *TSIa*
341:11 Then *MS*] ~, *TSIa*
341:16 was *MS*] *Om. TSIa*
341:26 near] near to *EP*
342:18 Gerald! *TSII, EP*] ~? *A1*
342:18 amazement. *P* He *MS*] ~. He *TSIa*
342:20 breast, *MS*] ~ *TSIa*
342:23 Then *TSII, EP*] ~, *A1*
342:34 open." She *MS*] ~." *P* She *TSIa*
343:7 see, *MS*] ~ *TSIa*
343:15 his *MS*] this *TSII*

343:19 repeated, *MS*] ~ *TSIa*
343:31 naive *Ed.*] naïve *TSII*
344:7   no one *A1*] no-one *TSII*
345:8   lovely, *MS*] ~ *TSIa*
345:9   Ah *MS*] ~, *TSIa*
345:13 And his ... new life. *TSII, EP*]
        Om. A1 see notes
345:23 lie *MS*] be *TSIa*
345:24 waves *MS*] ~, *TSIa*
345:26 like] life *EP*
345:31 passed, *MS*] ~ *TSIa*
346:3   clear, *MS*] ~ *TSIa*
346:10 dark] ~, *A1*
346:11 an otherworld *TSII, EP*]
        another world *A1*
346:14 superconsciousness *TSII, EP*]
        super-consciousness *A1*
346:28 conscious *MS*] consciousness
        TSIa
347:1   last, *MS*] ~ *TSII*
347:4   reverberation—"Three——
        — *MS*] ~. "Three—— *TSIa*
        ~. "Three—— *EP*
347:4   four———] ~——— *EP*
347:4   *five MS*] five *TSII*
348:19 resented] ~, *EP*
348:20 straight, *MS*] ~ *TSIa*
348:21 well-shapen] well-shaped *A1*
348:22 to] could *A1*
348:29 cautious: one] ~. One *A1*
348:37 night *TSII, EP*] light *A1*
349:4   her,] ~ *A1*
349:4   away. She *MS*] ~. P She
        TSIa
349:11 And, *MS*] ~ *TSIa*
350:5   licence *TSII, EP*] license *A1*
350:23 laughing. "Oh] ~. P "Oh *A1*
351:9   —why] —Why *A1* Why *EP*
351:37 *that—.*] ~— *EP*
352:5   *Egoïsme TSII, EP*] *Egoïsm A1*
352:30 Gerald moved ... [352:39] and
        women."] *Om. E1 see note on*
        352:39
353:16 love] alliance *EP see note on*
        108:21
354:8   market square] market-square
        EP
354:9   usually, *MS*] ~ *TSIa*

354:9   fruit-stalls *MS, EP*] ~, *TSIa*
354:17 tram-car *MS*] tram-/ car *TSIa*
        tramcar *TSII*
354:23 aisles *MS*] aisle *TSII*
354:32 ashamed *MS*] ~, *TSIa*
354:33 self-conscious, he *Ed.*] self
        conscious, he *MS* self-
        conscious. He *TSIa*
354:34 young *MS*] *Om. TSII*
355:4   Oh *MS*] ~, *TSIa*
355:9   harp-strings *MS*] harp-/
        strings *TSIa* harpstrings *TSII*
355:14 attractive—look *MS*] ~. Look
        TSIa
355:39 materialism: *TSII, EP*] ~; *A1*
356:3   past— *MS*] ~. *TSIa*
356:4   *is TSII, EP*] is *A1*
356:6   at *MS*] to *TSII*
356:6   us— *MS*] ~. *TSIa*
356:9   Yes— *MS*] ~, *TSIa*
356:19 her,] ~ *A1*
356:28 do,] ~? *A1*
357:17 There, *MS*] ~— *TSII*
357:22 Look, *MS*] ~ *TSII*
357:27 else, *MS*] ~ *TSIa*
357:29 it] it to *A1*
357:29 them— *MS*] ~. *TSIa*
357:36 on] at *EP*
358:3   it] it to *A1*
358:9   brows,] ~ *A1*
358:23 smiling. P His] ~. His *A1*
358:25 mocking *EP*] low *TSII*
358:27 amiable *A1*] aimiable *TSII*
358:28 Eh!] eh— *A1* eh? *EP*
358:29 ironical *EP*] leering-drooping
        TSII
358:33 hostility *E1*] freemasonry *TSII*
358:33 male, *TSII, EP*] ~ *A1*
358:33 understanding *TSII, E1*] hosti-
        lity *EP*
358:36 it,] ~ *A1*
359:1   coolly *EP*] insolently *TSII*
359:2   eh? *EP*] I'll bet. *TSII*
359:3   resentment *EP*] contempt *TSII*
359:9   full built] full-built *A1*
360:15 altered?] ~. *A1*
360:21 cushion." P And] ~." And *A1*
360:32 arm-chairs] armchairs *EP*

360:38 good afternoon *A1*]
good-afternoon *TSII*
360:39 Goo'—luck] Goo'-luck *EP*
361:6 square,] ~ *A1*
361:12 Jesus'] ~': *A1* ~: *EP*
361:16 tram-car] tramcar *A1*
361:30 tram-car] tramcar *A1*
361:39 it,] ~? *A1*
361:40 tram-car] tramcar *A1*
362:13 —Again] ~ *A1*
362:29 said. "But *EP*] ~./ "But *TSII*
~. P "But *A1*
363:12 *force*] force *A1*
363:22 Gerald.] ~? *A1*
363:23 ultimates] ultimate *A1*
364:7 said, *MS*] ~ *TSIa*
364:7 voice: *P* "Rupert *MS*] ~,
"Rupert *TSIa*
364:15 about! *MS*] ~. *TSIa*
364:25 her] the *EP*
364:26 mean, *MS*] ~ *TSIa*
364:26 *you knew*'?" He *MS*] you
knew'?'" *P* He *TSIa* you
knew'?" *P* He *A1*
364:31 Why when *MS*] Why then *TSII*
Why, *EP* see notes
365:2 agree,] ~ *A1*
365:3 licence *TSII*, *EP*] license *A1*
365:18 mother. Ursula *MS*] ~. *P*
Ursula *TSIa*
365:19 No *MS*] ~, *TSIa*
365:27 you—? *MS*] ~? *TSIa*
365:30 to——] ~—— *EP*
365:33 What—? *MS*] ~? *TSIa*
365:37 voice—"It *MS*] ~, "It *TSIa* ~,
"it *TSII*
365:37 *impossible*] impossible *A1*
365:38 door handle *EP*] doorhandle
TSII
366:1 meant— *MS*] ~, *TSIa*
366:21 heedlessly, *MS*] ~ *TSII*
366:33 stepped *MS*] slipped *TSIa*
367:1 There, *MS*] ~—, *TSII* ~—— *A1*
367:29 wept. "And *MS*] ~, "and *TSIa*
367:31 can't—. *MS*] ~—— *TSIa*
367:35 wept, *MS*] ~. *TSIa*
367:36 has—. *MS*] ~—— *TSIa*
368:1 again——] ~—— *EP*

368:2 immediately—] ~. *EP*
368:13 again, *MS*] ~ *TSIa*
368:24 darkened, *MS*] ~ *TSII*
368:33 Now,] ~; *EP*
368:33 clear *MS*] clean *TSIa*
368:36 on] at *A1*
369:5 lovely *MS*] lively *TSII*
369:9 overstatement. For *MS*] ~, for
TSIa over-statement, for *EP*
369:16 her *MS*] ~, *TSIa*
369:21 form *MS*] ~, *TSIa*
369:22 weight *MS*] ~, *TSIa*
369:22 strange *MS*] ~, *TSIa*
369:28 'I', *MS*] '~' *TSIa*, *EP* "~"
A1
369:30 ego *MS*] age *TSII*
369:34 One *MS*] one *TSIa*
369:35 How *MS*] Nor *TSII* Now *E2* see
notes
369:35 you",] ~," *A1*
369:36 be,] ~: *EP*
370:7 afternoon, *MS*] ~ *TSIa*
370:12 Ursula, *MS*] ~ *TSIa*
370:19 Really? *MS*] ~! *TSIa*
371:5 that." *P* She *TSIa*] ~." She
TSII
371:19 Gerald, *MS*] ~. *TSIa*
371:33 you! *TSII*, *EP*] ~? *A1*
371:37 Gudrun! *TSII*, *EP*] ~? *A1*
371:40 husbands? *MS*] ~, *TSIa*
372:10 making *MS*] of making *TSII*
372:11 behind, *MS*] ~ *TSIa*
372:19 amazing? *MS*] ~! *TSIa*
372:21 conceive! *TSII*, *EP*] ~? *A1*
372:22 dining-room *EP*] dining room
TSII
372:23 now, *MS*] ~ *TSIa*
372:34 *must MS*] must *TSII*
372:35 if *A1*] if this *TSII* see notes
372:37 half-burnt covers *A1*] half
burnt ~ *TSII*
372:39 drawing-room *EP*] drawing
room *TSII*
372:39 air, *MS*] ~; *TSIa*
373:17 out-of-doors *TSIa*] out-of-
door *TSII*
373:29 mother's— *MS*] ~, *TSIa*
373:30 all *MS*] all of *TSII*

373:30 bringing-up *TSII, EP*] bringing up *A1*

373:33 *meaning*] meaning *A1*

373:34 *not* lived *MS*] not ~ *TSII*

374:8 7] ~, *EP*

374:15 it! *MS*] ~, *TSIa*

374:16 establishment— *MS*] ~. *TSIa* ~! *TSIb*

374:17 *think MS*] think *TSIa*

374:22 *Doesn't MS*] Doesn't *TSIa*

374:22 too! *MS*] ~, *TSIa*

374:24 Birkin— *MS*] ~. *TSIa*

374:29 downstairs. *P* And *MS*] ~. And *TSIa*

374:36 Gudrun *MS*] ~, *TSII*

374:38 gone— *MS*] ~, *TSIa*

375:5 Ursula, *MS*] ~ *TSIa*

375:13 asked *MS*] said *TSII*

375:15 bêtise] *bêtise A1*

375:17 then: 'il ... du papa'." *MS*] then, il faut avoir le respect des bêtises du papa?" *TSIa* then, des bêtises du papa?" *TSII see note on 375:19*

375:30 harshly, *MS*] ~ *TSIa*

375:35 reckless, *MS*] ~ *TSIa*

375:39 herself, she *Ed.*] ~ she *MS* ~. She *TSIa*

376:17 cottages] cottage *A1*

376:18 in— *TSII, EP*] ~, *A1*

376:22 really— *TSII, EP*] ~. *A1*

376:24 really! *TSII, EP*] ~? *A1*

376:24 came *MS, A1*] Came *TSII*

376:40 glad eye *Ed.*] glad-eye *TSII*

376:41 obtrusive *MS, A1*] obstrusive *TSII*

376:41 glad eye." *MS*] glad eye". *TSII* glad-eye." *A1*

377:2 herself, *MS*] ~ *TSII*

377:3 glad eye] glad-eye *A1*

377:10 intimate, *MS*] ~ *TSIa*

377:12 sister,] ~ *EP*

377:17 hard plaited *TSII, EP*] hard-plaited *A1*

377:26 *cool*!] ~? *A1* ~! *EP*

377:28 liked *MS*] like *TSIa*

377:33 Ursula. "So *MS*] ~, "so *TSIa*

377:33 lovable *MS, A1*] loveable *TSII, EP*

377:41 difficulty, *MS*] ~ *TSIa*

378:3 a thing] things *A1*

378:3 who *TSII, EP*] ~, *A1*

378:3 You *MS*] you *TSIa*

378:6 word, *TSIa*] ~ *TSII*

378:6 'type.' *Ed.*] 'type.' *TSIa* "*type*". *TSII* "*type*." *A1*

378:7 eye] eyes *A1*

378:10 out— *MS*] ~. *TSIa*

378:11 Oh ... Oh *TSII, EP*] ~, ... ~, *A1*

378:24 absolutest *MS*] absolute *TSIa*

378:27 lovable] loveable *EP*

378:29 closed *MS*] ~, *TSIa*

378:37 kilometers] kilometres *EP*

378:37 Innsbruck *TSII, EP*] Innesbruck *A1*

378:40 snow—? *TSII, EP*] ~? *A1*

379:4 *shouldn't*] shouldn't *A1*

379:4 a little] an *A1*

379:7 he! *TSII, EP*] ~? *A1*

379:7 Why *TSII, EP*] ~, *A1*

379:11 only] *Om. A1*

380:6 choose *EP*] choose on *TSII*

380:10 a] the *A1*

380:16 dissolution: *TSII, EP*] ~; *A1*

380:24 apish, *MS*] ~ *TSIa*

380:28 their *TSII, EP*] her *A1*

381:3 silk *TSII, EP*] ~, *A1*

381:4 splashed and ... curious motley] with long pale rays, a curious rayed *E2 see note on 62:22*

381:5 hotter] wider *E2*

381:7 across. *P* She *MS*] ~. She *TSIa*

381:8 brown] fair *E2*

381:11 blackly] coldly *E2*

381:14 you—? *MS*] ~? *TSIa*

381:16 well *MS*] ~, *TSII*

381:24 No. *TSII, EP*] ~? *A1*

381:26 known, *MS*] ~ *TSIa*

381:30 ugly *MS*] ~, *TSIa*

381:31 short-haired *MS*] depraved *TSII*

381:32 Gerald *EP*] Birkin *TSII*

382:5 to the flat] *Om. E2*

382:8 'Goodnight', *MS*] "Goodnight," *A1* 'Good-night,' *EP*

382:11 said. *P* There *MS*] ~. There *TSIa*

382:15 flat] *Om. E2*

382:26 saved'." *MS*] ~!" *TSIa* ~!'" *TSIb, EP* ~?'" *A1*

382:30 splendid!] ~, *A1*

382:32 pocket book *TSII, EP*] pocket-book *A1*

382:38 dark, soft] close fair *E2*

382:39 indecent, obscene,] indecent *E2*

382:40 dark] fair *E2*

382:41 *No—o MS*] *No-o TSIa*

382:41 you] to you *A1*

383:1 bits—*hic MS*] ~,—*hic TSIa* ~—hic *A1* ~,—hic *EP*

383:1 drank] drink *A1*

383:18 beautiful! *TSII, EP*] ~? *A1*

383:20 reduction process *MS*] reduction-/ process *TSII* reduction-process *A1*

383:20 origins *MS*] origin *TSIa*

383:22 being—' *MS*] ~—?' *TSIa* ~—!' *TSII*

383:22 *almost*] almost *A1*

383:24 Russian.] ~, *A1*

383:26 Corwuption *MS*] Corruption *TSIa*

383:27 corwupt *MS*] corrupt *TSIa*

383:33 those] these *EP*

383:33 Oh *TSII, EP*] ~, *A1*

383:34 '—and *MS*] 'And *TSIa*

383:39 —I *MS*] ~ *TSIa*

384:2 mud.— *MS*] ~— *TSIa*

384:2 Fleurs] *Fleurs A1*

384:2 —du mal] *du mal A1*

384:4 next. *MS*] ~? *TSII*

384:8 course— *MS*] ~, *TSIa*

384:8 saviour] Saviour *A1*

384:10 "Surely," *TSII, EP*] "'~,'" *A1*

384:10 "Surely goodness *MS*] "surely ~ *TSIa* "'surely ~ *A1*

384:11 life—"] ~—'" *A1*

384:11 off, *MS*] ~ *TSIa*

384:12 "Surely] "'~ *A1*

384:15 part,— *MS*] ~— *TSIa*

384:16 by friction between] reducing *A1 see note on* 384:21

384:17 obtaining a ... satisfaction] from their highly complex unity *A1*

384:19 sensations,] ~,— *EP*

384:21 utterly—'] ~—'" *A1*

384:32 foolishly *TSII, EP*] ~, *A1*

385:3 lustrous *E1*] brilliantly glossy *TSII*

385:12 her! *MS*] ~: *TSII* ~. *EP*

385:17 hôtel *MS*] hotel *TSIa*

385:17 out, *TSII, EP*] ~ *A1*

385:19 Then,] ~ *A1*

385:19 driver: *MS*] ~, *TSIa*

385:22 deliberate, *MS*] ~ *TSIa*

385:24 feeling *MS*] feelings *TSII*

385:34 *are*] are *A1*

385:36 *Why MS*] Why *TSIa*

385:37 *borne— MS*] ~. *TSIa*

386:3 *foul*] foul *A1*

386:3 again—. *MS*] ~— *TSIa*

387:2 Continental *EP* [contents page]] *Om. TSII* Snow *EP* [p. 409] CONTINENTAL *E1*

387:4 herself— *MS*] ~,— *TSII*

387:6 imminent *TSII, EP*] immanent *A1*

387:11 to, *MS*] ~ *TSIa*

387:20 anaesthetic] anæsthetic *A1*

387:30 in to *MS*] into *TSIa*

388:2 withdrew, *MS*] ~ *TSII*

388:6 fall, *MS*] ~ *TSIa*

388:20 infallibly. *P* In *MS*] ~. In *TSIa*

388:24 foreknowledge, *MS*] foreknowledge/ *TSIa* fore-knowledge *TSII see notes*

389:13 unEnglish *MS*] un-English *TSIa*

389:22 doorway *MS*] ~, *TSIa see notes*

389:25 trains *MS*] train *TSIa*

389:26 Berlin— *TSII, EP*] ~. *A1*

389:28 saw: *P* "ELSASS—LOTHRINGEN *MS*] ~: *P* "ELSASS-LOTHRINGEN *TSIa* ~: "ELSASS-LOTHRINGEN *A1* ~: "Elsass—Lothringen *EP*

389:29 BASEL] Basle *EP*
389:30 That . . . Basle!] "~ . . . ~!" *A1*
389:31 up: *MS*] ~. *TSIa*
389:32 Voilà." *P* And *MS*] ~." And *TSIa* ~!" And *E1*
389:36 encore—? *TSII, EP*] ~? *A1*
390:5 dirt-grey *MS*] dirt grey *TSIa*
390:9 continent *MS*] Continent *TSIa*
390:12 He, *MS*] ~ *TSIa*
390:12 immobile, *MS*] ~ *TSII*
390:17 darkness. *P* Ursula *MS*] ~. Ursula *TSII*
390:19 Marsh *TSII, EP*] marsh *A1*
390:21 go! *TSII, EP*] ~? *A1*
390:22 life-time *TSII, EP*] lifetime *A1*
390:22 aeons] æons *A1*
390:22 memory, *MS*] ~ *TSIa*
390:24 Tilly *A1*] Tilley *TSII*
390:27 now, *MS*] ~ *TSIa*
390:34 vast, *MS*] ~ *TSIa*
390:39 large, *MS*] ~ *TSII*
391:1 long *TSII, EP*] ~, *A1*
391:23 streets *MS*] street *TSII*
391:31 world, *MS*] ~ *TSIa*
391:33 snow: *TSII, EP*] ~; *A1*
392:1 porter *EP*] waiter *TSII*
392:5 staircase: *MS*] ~. *TSIa*
392:5 Yu-hu *MS*] Shu-hu *TSIa see notes*
392:8 cried. *P* and *MS*] ~. And *TSIa*
392:14 here! *TSII, EP*] ~? *A1*
392:19 *immensely!" P* She *MS*] ~!" She *TSIa* ~!" She *A1*
392:22 like! *TSII, EP*] ~? *A1*
392:26 Birkin. *P* For *MS*] ~. For *TSIa*
392:33 porter *Ed.*] waiter *TSII see note on* 392:1
392:35 Second *TSII, EP*] ~, *A1*
392:35 madam *MS*] Madam *TSIa*
392:35 lift—! *MS*] ~! *TSIa*
392:35 porter *Ed.*] waiter *TSII*
392:35 replied, and *MS*] ~. And *TSIa*
392:36 elevator, *MS*] ~ *TSIa*
392:38 porter *Ed.*] waiter *TSII*
393:9 café, *Ed.*] Café Imperial, *MS* Café Imperial. *TSIa* café. *TSII*
393:12 it *TSII, EP*] it to *A1*
393:12 said. But *MS*] ~. *P* But *TSIa*

393:22 Rath's] Bath's *EP*
393:22 studio *MS, EP*] Studio *TSIa*
393:27 *He MS*] He *TSIa*
393:30 is, *MS*] ~ *TSIa*
393:34 impériales *MS, A1*] imperiales *TSIa* impèriales *TSII*
394:3 Saturnalia *MS*] saturnalia *TSIa*
394:5 harvest: there] ~. There *EP*
394:8 said, *MS*] ~. *TSII*
394:11 him— *MS*] ~. *TSIa*
394:11 Chanticleer *EP*] Chanticler *TSII*
394:11 Rath] Bath *EP*
394:11 genuinely] *genuinely A1*
394:21 bodice,] ~ *A1*
394:23 beautiful, *MS*] ~ *TSIa*
394:30 wonderful! *TSII, EP*] ~? *A1*
394:31 übermenschlich] *übermenschlich A1*
395:12 ears, *MS*] ~ *TSIa*
395:22 may.] ~, *A1*
396:8 You] you *EP*
396:16 *Tant pis pour moi*] Tant pis pour moi *A1*
396:38 Birkin, *MS*] ~ *TSIa*
397:3 said] ~, *A1*
398:1 Chapter XXX *EP*] *Om. TSII, E1 see notes*
398:2 Snow *EP*] *Om. TSII, E1*
398:5 up up *MS*] up *TSIa*
398:5 on] an *EP*
398:6 crags *MS*] ~, *TSIa*
398:8 to] *Om. A1*
399:8 cottages *MS*] ~, *TSIa*
399:16 Good! *MS*] ~, *TSIa*
399:17 fierce,] ~ *A1*
399:32 Gerald, *MS*] ~ *TSIa*
399:34 rock, *MS*] ~ *TSIa*
399:39 *heu-heu!,*] hue-hue! *A1* hue-hue!, *EP*
400:1 gradually, *MS*] ~ *TSIa*
400:8 white-heavy *MS*] white heavy *TSIa*
400:11 half buried *TSIa*] half-buried *TSII*
400:21 warm-gold *MS*] warm gold *TSIa*
400:29 blue-checked] blue checked *EP*

401:7   white-folded *TSII, EP*]
           whitefolded *A1*
401:9   slopes, *MS*] ~ *TSIa*
401:23   cul de sac] cul-de-sac *A1*
401:40   bronze, *MS*] ~ *TSIa*
402:8   superhumanly] super-humanly
           EP
402:26   lay *MS*] ~, *TSIa*
402:29   should] could *A1*
402:37   everyday *MS*] every day *TSIa*
           every-day *A1*
402:38   click. P She *MS*] ~. She *TSIa*
403:11   strange, *MS*] ~ *TSIa*
403:18   *good* Kranzkuchen! *MS*] good
           ~! *TSIa, EP* good ~? *A1*
403:18   *good*!] good! *A1*
403:19   Kranzkuchen? *TSII, EP*] ~! *A1*
403:20   added, *MS*] ~ *TSIa*
403:21   bench, *MS*] ~ *TSIa*
404:3   daughters,— *MS*] ~— *TSIa*
404:4   new-comers *Ed.*] newcomers
           TSII
404:20   and] to *A1*
404:25   English, *MS*] ~ *TSIa*
404:26   Reunionsaal *MS*] ~, *TSIa*
404:30   black, *MS, E1*] ~ *TSIa*
404:35   new-comers *Ed.*] newcomers
           TSII
404:36   Then *Ed.*] ~, *MS see notes*
404:37   voice: *MS, EP*] ~. *TSIa*
404:38   Sie *MS*] Om. *TSIa see notes*
405:8   sans cérémonie, there *MS*]
           ~~. There *TSIa sans cérémo-*
           nie. There *A1*
405:16   small *MS*] thin *TSIb see notes*
405:17   detached:] ~; *A1*
405:29   big *MS*] ~, *TSIa*
405:30   cosy *TSII, EP*] cozy *A1*
405:35   Please,] ~ *A1*
405:40   Then *MS*] ~, *TSIa*
406:1   audience, *MS*] ~ *TSIa*
406:2   off, *MS*] ~; *TSIa*
406:6   mocking, *TSIa*] ~ *TSII*
406:7   spell-bound *MS*] ~, *TSIa*
406:8   artist: *MS*] ~, *TSIa*
406:10   strange, *MS*] ~ *TSIa*
406:13   Then the *MS*] The *TSIa*
406:14   laughter, the *MS*] ~. The *TSIa*

406:19   Gudrun, *MS*] ~. *TSII*
406:19   her: *MS*] ~, *TSIa*
406:21   involuntarily, *MS*] ~. *TSIa*
406:25   in] of *A1*
406:26   ultimate *MS*] ~, *TSIa*
406:26   laughter, the *MS*] ~. The *TSIa*
406:30   loudly: *MS*] ~. *TSIa*
406:31   Ja, das war merkwürdig *Ed.*] Ja,
           das war merkwurdig *MS* Das
           war ausgezeichnet *TSIb see note*
           on 406:37
406:32   famos! *MS*] ~, *TSIa*
406:34   leider," *Ed.*] ~" *TSIa* ~!" *TSII*
406:35   students *MS, A1*] Students
           TSIa, EP
406:36   new-comers *MS*] newcomers
           TSIa
406:37   Sie——— *MS*] ~——— *TSIa*
           ~— *TSII*
406:38   new-comers *MS*] newcomers
           TSIa
407:40   intense, *MS*] ~ *TSIa*
408:2   invisible *EP*] Invisible *TSII*
408:3   wonderful enough *TSII, EP*]
           wonder-/full enough *A1*
408:11   Suddenly, *MS*] ~ *TSIa*
408:19   answered, *MS*] ~ *TSII, EP*
           answerd *A1*
408:22   much— *Ed.*] ~—, *TSIb* ~,
           TSII
408:24   wistful. P He *MS*] ~. He *TSIa*
408:28   ignominious, *MS*] ~ *TSIa*
408:31   —why *MS*] why *TSIa* Why
           TSII
408:39   it, I *MS*] ~.~ *TSIa*
409:1   the snow,] *Om.* A1
409:7   glouring *MS*] glowing *TSIa*
409:19   enough *MS*] *Om. TSIa*
409:21   Oh *MS*] ~, *TSIa*
409:24   lantern: *MS*] ~; *TSIa*
409:24   the] The *EP*
409:25   shadowy, *MS*] ~ *TSIa*
409:26   shadow-play   *TSII,   EP*]
           shadowplay *A1*
409:27   magic-lantern *TSII, EP*] magic
           lantern *A1*
409:29   is] was *A1*
409:34   'remember' *MS, EP*] "~" *A1*

410:14 strange, *MS*] ~ *TSIa*
410:27 air *EP*] ~, *TSII*
410:31 clapping, *MS*, *EP*] ~ *TSIa*
410:32 zest, when *MS*] ~. When *TSIa*
410:32 came. *MS*] came *TSIa* came even *TSII see notes*
411:2 chinking *MS*] clinking *TSIa*
411:2 mug-lids *TSII*, *EP*] muglids *A1*
411:2 Prosit—Prosit *TSII*, *EP*] Prosit-Prosit *A1*
411:3 gnome— *MS*] ~, *TSIa*
411:11 schuhplattern *Ed.*] Schuhplattern *MS* Schuhplatteln *TSIa* schuhpletteln *TSII*
411:14 enough, *MS*] ~ *TSIa*
411:23 Loerke *TSII*, *EP*] ~, *A1*
411:35 sardonic, *MS*] ~ *TSII*
411:36 for his] for this *A1*
412:22 strange] ~, *A1*
412:24 this? *TSIa*] ~. *TSII*
412:31 sardonic *EP*] ~, *TSII*
412:33 him, *TSIa*] ~ *TSII*
413:22 Mene! Mene] *Mene! Mene A1*
413:37 landing, *MS*] ~ *TSIa*
413:37 railing, *MS*] ~ *TSIa*
413:39 assented *MS*] asserted *TSIa*
414:14 Whom] Who *A1*
414:16 Oh *MS*] ~, *TSIa*
414:18 pale. *P* The *MS*] ~. The *TSIa*
414:23 Well *MS*] ~, *TSII*
414:27 busy, *MS*] ~ *TSIa*
414:37 asked, *MS*] ~ *TSII*
414:37 nonchalant *MS*] nonchalantly *TSIa see notes*
415:3 replied; *MS*] ~, *TSIa*
415:7 saying: *P* "God *MS*] ~: "God *TSIa*
415:8 nervous,— *MS*] ~— *TSIa*
415:8 *nervous*, *MS*] nervous *TSIa* nervous, *A1*
415:9 for ever ... for ever *TSII*, *EP*] forever ... forever *A1*
415:30 said *MS*] ~, *TSIa*
415:33 Oh *MS*] ~, *TSIa*
415:34 my——— *MS*] ~—— *TSII* ~—— *EP*
416:1 strap. She ... down, servile.

MS] strap, servile. *TSIa* strap, inattentive. *TSII see notes*
416:21 Ah *MS*] ~, *TSIa*
416:25 smiling *MS*] *Om. TSII*
416:27 "'Shouldn't ... so!'" *MS*] "~...~!" *TSIa*
416:34 girl——] ~—— *EP*
417:8 vaguely-illumined] vaguely-illuminated *A1*
417:9 watch:] ~; *A1*
418:7 everything, *MS*] ~ *TSIb*
418:16 their *TSII*, *EP*] there *A1*
418:23 England, she *MS*] ~. She *TSIa*
418:23 ideals *MS*] ideas *TSII*
418:35 concern, *MS*] ~ *TSIa*
418:36 splendidly-organised *MS*] splendidly organised *TSIa*
418:36 alike indifferent ... were *MS*] *Om. TSII*
419:10 old, *MS*] ~ *TSIa*
419:11 ideals] ideas *EP*
419:12 old bowler hat? *MS*] ~ ~ ~! *TSII*
419:16 moments, oh *MS*] ~. Oh, *TSIa*
419:20 smiled *MS*] ~, *TSIa*
419:23 remembered, *MS*] ~ *TSIa*
419:31 heart, *MS*] ~ *TSIa*
419:33 reckless, *MS*] ~ *TSIa*
419:36 Holze] ~, *A1* ~. *EP*
419:37 nass *TSII*, *EP*] ~, *A1*
419:39 knew, *MS*] ~ *TSIa*
420:4 mountain-tops *MS*] mountain tops *TSIa*
420:7 both *MS*] but *TSII*
420:40 eyes, *MS*] ~ *TSIa*
421:11 hair's-breadth *MS*] hair-breadth *TSIa*
421:19 could *MS*] would *TSII*
421:31 otherwise, *MS*] ~ *TSIa*
421:36 humour *TSII*, *EP*] humor *A1*
421:36 usual. But *MS*] ~. *P* But *TSII*
422:8 mag-pie *MS*] magpie *TSIa*
422:10 not— *MS*] ~. *TSIa*
422:13 almost of *MS*] almost *TSII*
422:20 toboganing, *Ed.*] tobogganning, *MS* tobogganning *TSIa* tobaganing *EP*
422:21 or ski-ing, *MS*] *Om. TSIa*

422:24 men, *MS*] ~ *TSIa*

422:24 together in ... of intimacy] together, sharing the same bedroom *EP see note on* 108:21

422:32 brown-velvet *MS*] brown velvet *TSIa*

422:40 French, *MS*] ~ *TSIa*

423:7 temples, he *MS*] ~ He *TSIa* ~. He *TSII*

423:17 'griffes,' *MS, EP*] '~', *TSIa* "~", *AI*

423:18 in] *in EP*

423:24 rilievo *Ed.*] relievo *TSII*

423:26 Gudrun, *MS*] ~ *TSIa*

423:32 swing-boats *TSIb*] ~, *TSII*

424:6 Parthenon—] ~, *EP*

424:6 ecco] *ecco AI*

424:11 cried, "there *MS, EP*] ~. "there *TSII* ~. "There *AI*

424:17 machinery *TSIa*] the machinery *TSII*

424:40 needle-points *TSII, EP*] needle points *AI*

425:3 God *TSIa*] god *TSII*

425:6 replied. "But *MS*] ~, "But *TSIa* ~, "but *AI*

425:7 worked? *MS*] ~! *TSIa*

425:8 cried] asked *AI*

425:8 E *TSII, EP*] É *AI*

425:14 said, *MS*] ~. *TSIa*

425:31 W.C. *TSII, EP*] W. C. *AI*

425:35 too. *MS, EP*] ~.— *TSII*

426:6 Later, *MS*] ~ *TSIa*

426:7 —I imprinted *MS*] —imprinted *TSIa*

426:12 "The *EP*] ~ *TSII*

426:13 honorable *MS*] honourable *TSIa*

426:13 night, *MS*] ~ *TSIa*

426:16 "Dunque *AI*] ~ *TSII*

426:17 thousand—. *MS*] ~— *TSIa*

426:21 above *MS*] about *TSII*

426:24 elvin *MS*] elfin *TSIa see note on* 317:31

426:24 eyes, *MS*] ~ *TSIa*

426:25 alt?] ~! *AI* ~? *EP*

426:28 twenty-six *AI*] twenty six *TSII*

426:29 Twenty-six *AI*] Twenty six *TSII*

426:31 Und Ihr ... ist er *Ed.*] Und ... is er *TSII* Und Ihr Herr Gemahl, wie alt is er *AI*

426:32 Who? *TSII, EP*] ~! *AI*

426:35 answered. *MS*] ~, *TSIa*

426:39 who has *EP*] and has *TSII*

427:1 fascinated, *TSII, EP*] ~ *AI*

427:2 bat] ~, *AI*

427:2 seal, *TSII, EP*] ~ *AI*

427:7 herself.—He *Ed.*] ~.—he *MS* ~—he *TSIa*

427:14 himself, *MS*] ~ *TSIa*

427:18 too *MS*] ~, *TSIa*

427:23 underworld] under-/world *AI* under-world *EP*

427:31 above *MS*] alone *TSII*

427:31 Birkin; *MS*] ~, *TSIa*

428:30 we ... we *EP*] you ... you *TSII*

429:1 thing *MS*] things *TSIa*

429:19 pent up] pent-up *AI*

430:4 Stiff! *MS*] ~? *TSII*

430:17 replied *MS*] ~, *TSII*

430:17 face: *MS*] ~. *TSIa*

430:20 the *MS*] a *TSII*

430:24 horse'?" *MS*] ~?'" *TSII*

430:26 This *MS*] There *TSII*

430:31 horse? *TSII, EP*] ~! *AI*

430:34 Sie *MS*] sie *TSIa*

430:38 the *MS*] *Om. TSII*

431:2 relative world *MS*] relative work *TSII*

431:8 Loerke, *MS*] ~ *TSIa*

431:9 her *MS*] ~, *TSIa*

431:10 murmured: *MS*] ~. *TSIa*

431:15 stock *MS*] ~, *TSIa*

431:19 charge. Gudrun *MS*] ~. P Gudrun *TSII*

431:21 there *MS*] then *TSIa*

431:24 replied; *MS*] ~, *TSIa*

432:6 hanging *MS, EP*] ~, *TSII*

432:8 well-brought-up *MS*] ~, *TSIa*

432:18 called *MS, AI*] ~, *TSIa*

432:23 A *TSII, EP*] À *AI*

432:23 Gudrun,] ~ *AI*

432:32 again *TSII, EP*] *Om. AI*

432:37 figure. Gudrun *MS*] ~. P Gudrun *TSIa*

433:1 humourous] humorous *EP*

433:12 replied, *MS*] ~ *TSIa*
433:12 sie *MS*, *A1*] sir *TSII*
433:14 nuisance— *MS*] ~,— *TSII*
433:16 all-important *MS*] all important *TSIa*
433:18 coolly. He *MS*] ~. *P* He *TSIa*
433:21 to.—It *MS*] ~—It *TSIa* ~—it *A1* ~. It *EP*
433:30 said, *MS*] ~. *TSIa*
434:10 and stupid *Ed.*] and/and *MS* and—and *TSIa* and—and stupid *TSII see notes*
434:15 Suddenly, *MS*] ~ *TSIa*
434:18 miracle, *MS*] ~ *TSIa*
434:26 terrible *MS*] ~, *TSII*
434:26 static, *MS*] ~ *TSIa*
434:27 mountain-tops *Ed.*] mountain tops *TSII*
434:32 him, *MS*] ~. *TSIa*
434:37 *you?*] ~ ! *A1* ~? *EP*
434:37 asked, *MS*] ~ *TSII*
434:40 this *MS*] the *TSIa*
435:3 still, *MS*] ~ *TSIa*
435:4 *go MS*] go *TSIa*
435:5 find *EP*] be *TSII*
435:15 troubled. His *MS*] ~. *P* His *TSIa*
435:19 Why— *MS*] ~ *TSIa*
436:7 Ursula. *MS*] ~, *TSIa*
436:9 Gudrun *MS*] ~, *TSII*
436:10 quite believe *MS*] believe quite *TSII*
436:18 away. *P* There *MS*] ~. There *TSIa*
436:22 Gerald, *MS*] ~ *TSIa*
436:32 you *MS*] ~, *TSIa*
436:34 eying *MS*] eyeing *TSIa*
436:38 them—they're *MS*] ~. They're *TSIa*
436:38 there—. *MS*] ~— *TSIa*
437:7 'you are ... to return—' *Ed.*] 'you are ... to return—,' *MS* you are ... to return, *TSIa* you are going-away-for-ever, never-to-return, *TSIb see notes*
437:22 Father *MS*] father *TSIa*
438:5 illusion, *MS*] ~ *TSIa*
438:11 seen in] seen *A1*

438:16 *this*] this *EP*
438:18 said, "yes *TSIa*] ~. "Yes *TSII*
438:29 Unknown *MS*] unknown *TSIa*
438:32 both. *Ed.*] oh, so much. *MS* oh so much! *TSIa* both! *TSIb*
438:32 Then *MS*] ~, *TSIa*
439:2 cheek, *MS*] ~ *TSIa*
439:5 pillow *MS*] ~, *TSIa*
439:9 familiar, *MS*] ~ *TSIa*
439:14 Oh *MS*] ~, *TSIa*
439:15 Birkin. *P* Gerald *TSII*, *EP*] ~. Gerald *A1*
440:4 and"— *MS*] ~—" *TSIa*
440:7 electricity." *P* He *Ed.*] nothingness." *P* He *MS* nothingness." He *TSIa* electricity." He *TSII*
440:11 it: it's *MS*] ~! it's *TSII* ~! It's *A1*
440:25 farewells] farewell *EP*
441:1 XXXI *EP*] XXX *TSII*, *E1 see note on* 398:2
441:2 Up *EP* [p. 466]] *Om. TSII* up *EP* [contents page] UP *E1*
441:3 Ursula *TSII*, *EP*] Gudrun *A1*
441:8 will, *MS*] ~ *TSIa*
441:17 centred *TSII*, *EP*] centered *A1*
441:20 now *MS*] *Om. TSII*
441:23 the *MS*] this *TSIa*
441:32 beautiful? *MS*] ~! *TSIa*
442:8 flippant. His *Ed.*] coldly. His *MS* coldly. *P* His *TSIa* flippant. *P* His *TSII*
442:13 state,] ~ *A1*
442:14 stony *TSIa*] strong *TSII*
442:19 'It *TSII*, *EP*] "~ *A1*
442:19 love,' *MS*, *EP*] ~' *TSIa* ~," *A1*
442:25 repeated, *MS*] ~ *TSIa*
442:29 love',"] ~,'" *A1*
442:30 Yes *MS*] ~, *TSIa*
442:30 that you *A1*] that *TSII*
442:34 finally. "Will *MS*] ~, "will *TSIa*
442:40 free." It *MS*] ~." *P* It *TSIa*
443:9 for ever *TSII*, *EP*] forever *A1*
443:19 said, *MS*] ~ *TSIa*
443:32 now *TSII*, *EP*] now that *A1*

443:33 dressing-room *Ed.*] dressing room *TSII*
443:36 Yes *MS*] ~, *TSIa*
444:5 rigid *TSII, E1*] insentient *EP*
444:6 insentient *E1*] rigid *TSII*
444:11 sleeping-jacket *MS*] sleeping jacket *TSII*
444:12 bewildered *MS*] ~, *TSIa*
444:27 her, she *MS*] ~. She *TSIa*
444:27 crushed *MS*] ~, *TSIa*
444:29 ghastly *Ed.*] awful *MS* awful, *TSIa* ghastly, *TSII*
444:30 her, she *MS*] ~. She *TSIa*
444:32 God! *MS*] ~, *TSII*
444:32 cried *MS*] ~, *TSIa*
444:36 die? *TSII, EP*] ~! *A1*
445:2 'thou shalt',] "~ ~," *A1* '~ ~,' *EP*
445:2 'thou shalt not'. *TSIa*] '~ ~ ~. *MS* '~ ~ ~.' *TSII, EP* "~ ~ ~." *A1*
445:13 go? *TSII, EP*] ~! *A1*
445:16 Self-sufficient? *MS*] ~! *TSIa*
446:15 being. Though *MS*] ~ though *TSIa* ~, though *TSIb*
446:16 rebuffs *MS*] ~, *TSIa*
446:24 irreverent, *MS*] ~ *TSIa*
447:4 evening *MS*] the evening *TSIa*
447:11 sang, *MS*] ~ *TSIa*
447:12 and] to *A1*
447:24 at a] at the *A1*
447:26 chilled, *MS*] ~ *TSIa*
447:31 himself, *MS*] ~ *TSIa*
447:35 too-much *MS*] too much *TSII*
448:12 nature. *P* They *Ed.*] motion. *P* They *MS* motion. They *TSIa* nature. They *TSII*
448:18 lusts] lust *A1*
448:21 *nuances*] nuances *A1*
448:36 for ever *TSII, EP*] forever *A1*
448:37 *bagatelle—love Ed.*] bagatelle—love *MS* bagatelle. Love *TSIa bagatelle.* Love *EP*
449:1 Eleonora Duse] the great Rachel *EP see notes*
449:9 in spirit *MS*] of spirit *TSII*
449:10 arrogant, *MS*] ~ *TSIa*
449:18 child-like: *MS*] ~. *TSIa*

449:20 Sie] sie *EP*
449:20 Gnädige *MS*] gnädige *TSIa*
449:21 immer *MS*] ~, *TSIa*
449:35 So-o-o *MS*] So-o- *TSIa, EP* So-o— *A1*
449:37 She looked ... aversion. *MS*] *Om. TSIa*
450:2 Loerke, *MS*] ~ *TSIa*
450:9 again,] ~ *A1*
450:10 blow,] ~; *EP*
450:13 over, *MS*] ~ *TSIa*
450:13 leisurely, *MS*] ~ *TSIa*
450:28 innocent *MS*] ~, *TSIa*
451:9 not the *MS*] not *TSII*
451:10 Loerke, *TSII, EP*] *Om. A1*
451:12 knowledge, *MS*] ~. *TSIa*
451:13 he, *MS, A1*] ~ *TSIa, EP*
451:23 a *TSII, EP*] *Om. A1*
451:31 breaking-down] breaking down, *A1*
452:1 ne plus ultra] *ne plus ultra A1*
452:16 slow, *TSIa*] ~ *TSII*
452:18 subtleties *Ed.*] ecstasy *MS* ecstasy, *TSIa* subtleties, *TSII*
452:31 experiencing *MS*] experience *TSIa*
452:37 But, *MS*] ~ *TSIa*
453:3 past. Particularly *A1*] ~, particularly *MS* ~. particularly *TSII*
453:9 god] God *A1*
453:30 and with *EP*] and about *TSII*
453:31 felt, *MS*] ~ *TSIa*
453:31 in petto] *in petto A1*
453:34 groundwork *MS*] ground-/ work *TSIa* ground-work *EP*
454:6 indefinitely. She *MS*] ~, she *TSIa*
454:12 because——. *MS*] ~— *TSIa*
454:29 reiterated, *MS*] ~ *TSIa*
454:29 dangerous, *MS*] ~ *TSIa*
454:31 cold, *MS*] ~ *TSII*
454:32 Yes *MS*] ~, *TSIa*
455:9 It's *MS*] It is *TSIa*
455:10 body: she *MS*] ~. She *TSIa*
455:12 contempt. "It's *Ed.*] complete. "It's *MS* complete. *P* "It's *TSIa* contempt. *P* "It's *TSII*

455:13 remember. I *MS, EP*] ~.I *TSIa*
~.— *TSII see notes*
455:21 stupid, that's *Ed.*] ~ that's *MS*
~. That's *TSIa see notes*
455:30 fool—? *MS*] ~? *TSIa*
455:31 fool? *MS*] ~! *TSIa*
455:31 repeated— *MS*] ~. *TSIa*
456:12 sat, *MS*] ~ *TSIa*
456:20 apart? *MS*] ~! *TSIa*
456:38 way. P Loerke *MS*] ~. Loerke
TSIa
457:14 exclaimed *MS*] ~, *TSIa*
457:15 rich? *A1*] ~. *TSII*
457:16 coal-owner *MS*] coal owner
TSII
457:33 say, *MS*] ~ *TSIa*
458:6 The *EP*] Der *TSII*
458:17 and *MS, EP*] And *TSII*
458:21 *religion A1*] *réligion TSII, EP*
458:22 'ism', *MS*] 'ism, *TSIa*
458:22 Jesus *MS, EP*] Jesue *TSII*
458:24 work— *MS*] ~,— *TSII*
458:24 Oh *MS*] oh *TSIa*
458:33 l'amore *MS, EP*] l'amour *TSII*
458:38 matter, *MS*] ~ *TSIa*
459:39 love! *MS*] ~. *TSIa*
458:40 love, *MS*] ~ *TSIa*
459:3 gnädiges] gnädige *EP*
459:3 mind.— *MS*] ~— *TSIa*
459:6 was *MS*] were *TSII*
459:20 *thee TSII, EP*] thee *A1*
459:21 intelligence—You] ~—you *A1*
~. You *EP*
459:22 said. *MS*] ~, *TSIa*
459:36 slightest *MS*] lightest *TSII*
460:1 blenched] blanched *EP*
460:2 prognostications. But *MS*] ~,
but *TSIa*
460:5 night-fall *MS*] night-/ fall *TSIa*
nightfall *A1*
460:8 skis. He *MS*] ~, he *TSIa*
460:11 dark *MS*] dusk *TSIa*
460:11 pine-trees *Ed.*] pine trees *TSII*
460:12 home; *EP*] ~ *TSII*
460:14 Imperial *Ed.*] imperial *TSII*
460:14 road? *TSII, EP*] ~. *A1*
460:24 mountain-tops *Ed.*] mountain
tops *TSII*

460:29 Gudrun, *MS*] ~ *TSIa*
460:37 for ever *TSII, EP*] forever *A1*
460:38 for ever, *MS*] for ever; *TSIa,*
EP for-/ ever; *A1*
461:3 where *MS*] when *TSIa*
461:9 said. "Where *MS*] ~, "where
TSII
461:15 saying 'Over *MS, EP*] ~, 'Over
TSIa ~ "Over *A1*
461:17 finality.' *TSII, EP*] ~." *A1*
461:18 aloud, *MS*] ~ *TSIa*
461:19 been *MS*] ~, *TSIa*
461:26 paused, *MS*] ~ *TSIa*
461:36 himself, *MS*] ~ *TSIa*
461:36 saying: *MS*] ~, *TSIa*
461:36 'I ought . . . her.' *TSII, EP*] "~
~ ~." *A1*
461:37 overcharged   *MS*]   over-
/charged *TSIa, EP*
over-charged *A1*
461:37 desire, *MS*] ~ *TSIa*
461:38 death, *MS*] ~ *TSIa*
461:38 him. P She *MS*] ~. She *TSIa*
462:16 satisfaction, *MS*] ~ *TSIa*
463:2 for ever] forever *A1*
463:10 across, *MS*] ~ *TSIa*
463:15 game: he *MS*] ~. He *TSIa*
463:18 Doña] Dona *A1*
463:20 boring as the phallus] boring
E1 see notes
463:30 mill-stones] millstones *A1*
463:32 things—] ~. *EP*
463:32 Oh *MS*] ~, *TSIa*
463:40 men, *TSII, EP*] ~ *A1*
464:3 least, *MS*] ~ *TSII*
464:7 much— *MS*] ~, *TSIa*
464:8 thing— *MS*] ~, *TSIa*
464:14 *haven't MS*] haven't *TSIa*
464:14 back-ground *MS*] background
TSIa
464:16 people— *Ed.*] society— *MS*
society, *TSIa* people, *TSII*
464:21 *third——*] ~—— *EP*
464:22 much——] ~—— *EP*
464:23 more. The *MS*] ~. P The *TSIa*
464:25 ad infinitum] *ad infinitum A1*
464:28 days,—Oh *MS*] ~—oh *TSIa*
464:30 her, *MS*] ~ *TSIa*

464:38 horrible, *MS*] ~ *TSIa*
465:1 Ha— *MS, EP*] He— *TSIa*
465:6 *had MS*] had *TSIa*
465:7 thoughts *MS*] ~, *TSIa*
465:12 illusions *MS*] her illusions *TSII*
see notes
465:15 round, *MS*] ~ *TSIa*
465:16 spine *MS*] ~, *TSIa*
465:18 reading, she *MS*] ~. She *TSIa*
465:25 clock-dial *Ed.*] clock dial *TSII*
465:25 roundish, *MS*] ~ *TSIa*
465:31 Oh *MS*] ~, *TSII*
465:35 Oh *MS*] ~, *TSII*
465:37 *he MS*] he *TSIa*
465:37 sleep? *TSII, EP*] ~! *AI*
466:4 famished *MS*] ~, *TSIa*
466:11 Yes *MS*] Zeu *TSIa* Ooh *TSIb*
see notes
466:12 like *MS*] as *TSIb see notes*
466:17 wills *MS*] ~, *TSIa*
466:26 eight; *MS, AI*] ~, *TSIa, EP*
466:29 twenty thousand] twenty-thousand *AI*
466:29 manager, *MS*] ~ *TSIa*
466:40 stupefied] stupified *EP*
467:1 stupefied] stupified *EP*
467:6 bear, *MS*] ~ *TSIa*
467:20 coffee *MS*] coffee when *TSII*
467:22 appearances *MS*] appearances' *TSIa* appearance's *TSII*
467:25 'Perhaps' *TSII, EP*] "~" *AI*
467:27 quickly, *MS*] ~ *TSIa*
467:32 Gudrun, *MS*] ~ *TSIa*
467:38 figure *MS*] ~, *TSII*
468:5 snowy,] ~ *AI*
468:7 charm— *MS*] ~,— *TSII*
468:15 brown-velvet *Ed.*] brown velvet *TSII*
468:21 chétif] *chétif AI*
468:21 puny, though] puny *AI* puny, *EP*
468:32 tobogganing *MS*] toboganning *TSII*
468:35 wildly *MS*] ~, *TSIa*
469:5 slope, *TSII, EP*] ~; *AI*
469:7 Kekse *Ed.*] Keks *TSII*
469:8 cried, "what *MS*] ~. "What *TSII*

469:8 comble de joie *MS*] *comble de joie TSIb*
469:9 indeed] *indeed AI*
469:14 can *TSII, EP*] Can *AI*
469:14 Isn't] Isn't *AI*
469:14 wonderful! *MS, AI*] ~. *TSIa* ~? *TSII, EP*
469:22 extravaganzas *MS*] extravagences *TSIa* extravagencies *EP*
see notes
469:38 where to *MS*] Whither *TSIb see notes*
469:38 *wohin? Ed.*] wohin? *MS* Wohin? *TSII*
469:39 for ever *TSII, EP*] forever *AI*
470:7 ticket! *MS*] ~. *TSII*
470:10 said *MS*] cried *TSIa*
470:32 —you *MS*] You *TSIa*
470:36 brown *TSII, EP*] Om. *AI*
471:9 bottle] battle *EP*
471:9 strange *MS*] ~, *TSIa*
471:11 Fräulein *Ed.*] Fräulein *MS* Fraulein *TSIa*
471:11 wohl—. *MS*] ~— *TSIa*
471:16 satirical, *MS*] ~ *TSIa*
471:22 héros *TSII, EP*] heros *AI*
471:23 as, *TSII, EP*] ~ *AI*
471:26 had *MS*] Om. *TSII*
471:27 stroke, over *MS*] stroke over *TSIa* stroke on to *TSII see notes*
471:35 soft. Save *MS*] ~, save *TSIa*
471:39 her eyes *MS*] the eyes *TSIa*
472:1 god-given *MS*] God-given *TSIa*
472:2 That *MS*] The *TSII*
472:32 figures, *MS*] ~. *TSIa* ~: *TSIb*
473:9 end,] end, and *AI*
473:12 higher, in *MS*] ~ ~ *TSIa*
473:13 following *EP*] going *TSII*
473:17 yet, *MS*] ~ *TSIa*
473:20 snow-slope *MS*] snow slope *TSIa*
473:24 hollow. *MS*] ~? *TSIa*
473:25 stretched! *P* He *MS*] ~! He *TSII*
473:29 crucifix *MS*] Crucifix *TSIa*
473:33 afraid. *MS*] ~? *TSII*
473:34 pale-shadowy *MS*] pale, shadowy *TSIa*

473:38 Jesus? *MS*] ~! *TSIa*
474:5 mountain *EP*] mount *TSII*
474:5 on *MS*] *Om. TSIa*
475:1 XXXII *EP*] XXXI *TSII, E1 see note on* 398:2
475:9 madame? *MS*] madam! *TSIa*
475:16 ha, *MS*] ~! *TSIa*
475:23 suddenly, *MS*] ~ *TSIa*
475:32 asked. He *MS*] ~. P He *TSIa*
476:1 God, *MS*] ~! *TSIa*
476:7 alight. And *MS*] ~, and *TSIa*
476:13 Ha—ha *MS*] Ha, ha *TSIa*
476:26 rate." Gudrun *MS*] ~." P Gudrun *TSIa*
476:29 asked, *MS*] ~ *TSIa*
476:39 to you *MS*] ~ ~, *TSIa*
477:2 know *MS*] ~, *TSIa*
477:3 child-like *MS*] childlike *TSIa*
477:6 saying: "A *Ed.*] saying: "*Here's MS* saying: P "Here's *TSIa* saying: P "A *TSII*
477:8 herself, *MS*] ~ *TSIa*
478:3 snow-slopes *MS*] snow slopes *TSIa*

478:14 snow-front] ~, *A1*
478:21 south side] south-side *A1*
479:1 being; just] ~. Just *A1*
479:4 cul de sac *Ed.*] *cul de sac TSII*
479:4 expended *TSII, EP*] expanded *A1*
479:5 new, *EP*] ~ *TSII*
479:8 inexhaustible] ~, *A1*
479:22 away." *P* There] ~."/ There *A1*
479:29 to *EP*] taking *TSII*
479:33 Ursula,] ~ *A1*
479:37 himself. *P* Ursula] ~. Ursula *A1*
479:38 could *EP*] could not *TSII*
479:38 es] as *A1*
480:3 dark, *TSII, EP*] ~ *A1*
480:15 for ever *TSII, EP*] forever *A1*
480:21 pale *EP*] blue *TSII*
480:27 new, *TSII, EP*] ~ *A1*
480:37 thing *EP*] disappointment *TSII*
481:1 smiled,] ~ *A1*
481:20 woman] a woman *A1*
481:33 false *EP*] wrong *TSII*

Appendix I
Foreword to *Women in Love*

A1 = First American edition (Seltzer, 1920), first printing
A1a = First American edition (Seltzer, 1920)
A2 = Second American edition (Gelber, Lilienthal, San Francisco: 1936)

485:1 Foreword to *Women in Love Ed.*] FOREWORD *A1* FOREWORD TO "WOMEN IN LOVE" BY D. H. LAWRENCE *A2*
485:4 war *A2*] the war *A1*
485:16 notice. In] ~. *P* In *A2*
485:16 America *A1, A2*] ~, *A1a*
485:18 amours,"] ~", *A2*
485:22 spiritual mysteries *A1a*] spirit-/ ualmysteries *A1*
485:26 God-mystery *A1, A2*] God-/ mystery *A1a*
485:31 it] *Om. A2*
485:32 circumstances] circumstance *A2*

485:33 desire] desires *A1a*
485:34 struggles:] ~; *A2*
486:1 forth] forth in *A1a* forth from *A2*
486:5 superimposition *A2*] super-/ imposition *A1* super-imposition *A1a*
486:5 *It is ... conscious being*] It is the passionate struggle into conscious being *A2*
486:18 D. H. Lawrence *Ed.*] D. H. LAWRENCE *A1 Om. A2*
486:19 *Hermitage, 12*] *Hermitage./ 12 A2*

Appendix II
'Prologue'

MS = Autograph manuscript (Roberts E441b)
A1 = *Texas Quarterly*, vi (Spring 1963), 98–111.

489:1	Chapter I.] CHAPTER I *A1*
489:2	Prologue.] *Prologue A1*
489:34	raised,] ~ *A1*
490:22	embarrassing *A1*] embarassing *MS*
491:18	Fellow] fellow *A1*
491:20	had been very well received] were brilliant *A1* *see notes*
491:27	fame, she] ~. She *A1*
491:38	isn't *Ed.*] is n't *MS* is not *A1*
492:9	God] god *A1*
492:18	unworthy, some] ~. Some *A1*
492:26	common,] ~ *A1*
492:33	now,] ~ *A1*
493:1	Crich,] ~ *A1*
493:29	loved *A1*] loved the *MS*
494:11	god] God *A1*
494:13	god] God *A1*
496:8	dormouse] ~, *A1*
496:11	universal,] ~ *A1*
496:20	horrible,] ~ *A1*
496:31	philosophic,] ~ *A1*
497:32	wise,] ~; *A1*
498:5	had had] had *A1*
499:12	braggadaccio] braggadocio *A1*
499:30	Hermione,] ~ *A1*
500:16	recognised] recognized *A1*
501:23	"you] "You *A1*
501:28	calm,] ~ *A1*
501:29	Neckar] Neckan *A1* *see notes*
501:35	recognised] recognized *A1*
502:14	beauté *A1*] beaûté *MS*
502:21	towards] toward *A1*
503:14	non-existent] nonexistent *A1*
503:21	enquired] inquired *A1*
503:28	twenty three] twenty-three *A1*
503:30	keen,] ~ *A1*
503:32	men,] ~: *A1*
503:35	themselves, roughly,] ~ ~ *A1*
503:36	keen-limbed] keen limbed *A1*
504:2	universal,] ~ *A1*
506:4	twenty nine] twenty-nine *A1*

'The Wedding'

MS = Autograph manuscript (Roberts E441b)
A1 = *Texas Studies in Language and Literature*, vi (Summer 1964), 137–47.

507:1	II.] II *A1*
507:2	The Wedding.] *The Wedding A1*
507:5	grammar school] Grammar School *A1*
507:22	Longmeadow,] ~; *A1*
507:26	twenty seven] twenty-seven *A1*
508:4	[was] *Ed.*] *Om. MS* [is] *A1*
508:6	in her] on her *A1*
508:36	man',] ~,' *A1*
508:39	Ursula. *P* She] ~. She *A1*
510:16	wide, irregular,] ~ ~ *A1*
510:16	street,] ~ *A1*
510:23	marvellous] marvelous *A1*
511:6	Crich's *A1*] Criche's *MS*
511:35	They're *A1*] They re *MS*
511:37	church yard] churchyard *A1*
511:40	embarrassment *A1*] embarassment *MS*
512:22	school] School *A1*
512:22	church yard] churchyard *A1*
512:34	church yard] churchyard *A1*
513:2	character;] ~, *A1*
514:30	much:] ~; *A1*
515:33	Harry!!" *P* He] ~ !" / He *A1*
516:4	mad *A1*] ~, *MS*
516:7	Then *P* "After] ~ "After *A1*
516:8	her!" / said] ~!" said *A1*
516:30	recognised] recognized *A1*

517:11 himself all his life.] himself. *A1*
        see notes
517:18 was,] ~ *A1*
517:24 amiable *A1*] aimiable *MS*

517:32 the] his *A1*
517:35 'now ... won.'] "~ ... ~."
        A1
518:4   husbands,] ~; *A1*

Of the compound words which are hyphenated at the end of a line in this edition, only the following hyphenated forms should be retained in quotation:

11:23 common-garden	247:36 white-burning
15:27 rose-coloured	260:27 half-frightened
23:24 maid-servant	264:8 yellow-ammers
31:9 brothers-in-law	264:36 foot-soles
39:38 hollow-cheeked	271:12 hammer-strokes
50:5 amazon-like	278:20 self-conscious
51:9 school-teachers	279:33 hot-house
71:31 good-humouredly	307:39 death-eating
73:14 man-servant	308:16 emotional-jealous
73:32 good-looking	309:17 self-destruction
82:11 house-front	309:29 all-comprehensiveness
83:35 athletic-looking	313:17 life-motion
83:37 horse-laugh	317:30 grass-spaces
84:32 sing-song	319:37 star-equilibrium
90:15 pitter-patter	323:17 drawing-room
90:26 eighteenth-century	327:2 forget-me-nots
90:31 drawing-room	336:2 coffee-maker
95:5 old-fashioned	336:29 self-abasement
119:23 water-plants	342:22 match-box
125:22 self-deception	361:30 winter-grey
128:26 elder-flowers	391:8 winter-heavy
160:6 black-and-brown	404:30 beetle-like
162:38 water-spiders	405:11 plain-cut
164:31 stream-mouth	405:15 good-breeding
166:3 self-consciousness	416:40 re-echoes
168:31 spell-bound	417:6 half-revealed
171:13 self-conscious	445:27 self-complete
172:37 marsh-flowers	449:18 child-like
200:9 self-importance	459:9 good-looking
201:16 self-abnegation	465:21 twelve-hour
215:37 half-appealing	468:3 girl-friend
230:33 heart-breaking	507:31 over-open
235:14 good-humour	

Pounds, shillings and pence

Before decimalisation in 1971, the pound sterling (£) was the equivalent of 20 shillings (20/- or 20s). The shilling was the equivalent of 12 pence (12d).

A price could therefore have three elements: pounds, shillings and pence (£, s., d.). (The apparently anomalous d. is an abbreviation of the Latin *denarius*; but the other two terms were also originally Latin; the pound was *Libra*; the shilling *solidus*.) Such a price might be written as £1. 2s. 6d. or £1/2/6; which was spoken as 'one pound two-and-six', or 'twenty-two and six'.

Prices below a pound were written as (for instance) 19s. 6d. or 19/6, and spoken as 'nineteen and six'. Prices up to £5 were sometimes spoken in terms of shillings: so 'ninety-nine and six' was £4/19/6.

The penny was divided into two half-pence and further into four farthings, but the farthing had minimal value and was mainly a tradesman's device for indicating a price fractionally below a shilling or a pound. So 19/11¾ (nineteen and elevenpence three farthings) produced a farthing's change from a pound, this change often given as a tiny item of trade, such as a packet of pins.

The guinea was £1/1/- (one pound, one shilling) and was a professional man's unit for fees. A doctor would charge in guineas (so £5/5/- = 5 gns). Half a guinea was 10s. 6d. or 10/6 (ten and six).

The coins used were originally of silver (later cupro-nickel) and copper, though gold coins for £1 (sovereign) and 10s. (half-sovereign) were still in use in Lawrence's time. The largest silver coin in common use was the half-crown (two shillings and sixpence, or 2/6). A two-shilling piece was called a florin. Shillings, sixpences and (in Lawrence's time) threepences were the smaller sizes. The copper coins were pennies, half-pence (ha'penny) and farthings.

Common slang terms for money were 'quid' for pound, 'half a crown', 'two bob' for a florin, 'bob' for a shilling, 'tanner' for sixpence, 'threepenny-bit', 'copper' for a penny or half-penny.

The pound since 1971 has had 100 pence, distinguished from the old pennies by being abbreviated to p. instead of d.